THE END OF THE WORLD AS WE KNOW IT

THE END OF THE WORLD AS WE KNOW IT

NEW TALES OF STEPHEN KING'S *THE STAND*

Edited by
Christopher Golden and Brian Keene

GALLERY BOOKS
New York Amsterdam/Antwerp London
Toronto Sydney/Melbourne New Delhi

G
Gallery Books
An Imprint of Simon & Schuster, LLC
1230 Avenue of the Americas
New York, NY 10020

For more than 100 years, Simon & Schuster has championed authors and the stories they create. By respecting the copyright of an author's intellectual property, you enable Simon & Schuster and the author to continue publishing exceptional books for years to come. We thank you for supporting the author's copyright by purchasing an authorized edition of this book.

No amount of this book may be reproduced or stored in any format, nor may it be uploaded to any website, database, language-learning model, or other repository, retrieval, or artificial intelligence system without express permission. All rights reserved. Inquiries may be directed to Simon & Schuster, 1230 Avenue of the Americas, New York, NY 10020 or permissions@simonandschuster.com.

This book is a work of fiction. Any references to historical events, real people, or real places are used fictitiously. Other names, characters, places, and events are products of the author's imagination, and any resemblance to actual events or places or persons, living or dead, is entirely coincidental.

Introduction copyright © 2025 by Stephen King
Volume copyright © 2025 by Daring Greatly Corporation, Inc. and Brian Keene
Copyright credits continued on page 779

The Stand (both in its original published form and its Complete and Uncut edition) © 1978, 1990 by Stephen King, and originally published in hardcover in the United States by Doubleday, an imprint of The Knopf Doubleday Publishing Group, a division of Penguin Random House, LLC. Randall Flagg, Mother Abagail, and all other associated characters and original concepts and text included in *The Stand* are the property of Stephen King, and are used herein with permission from the author.

All rights reserved, including the right to reproduce this book or portions thereof in any form whatsoever. For information, address Gallery Books Subsidiary Rights Department, 1230 Avenue of the Americas, New York, NY 10020.

First Gallery Books hardcover edition August 2025

GALLERY BOOKS and colophon are registered trademarks of Simon & Schuster, LLC

Simon & Schuster strongly believes in freedom of expression and stands against censorship in all its forms. For more information, visit BooksBelong.com.

For information about special discounts for bulk purchases, please contact Simon & Schuster Special Sales at 1-866-506-1949 or business@simonandschuster.com.

The Simon & Schuster Speakers Bureau can bring authors to your live event. For more information or to book an event, contact the Simon & Schuster Speakers Bureau at 1-866-248-3049 or visit our website at www.simonspeakers.com.

Interior design by Hope Herr-Cardillo

Manufactured in the United States of America

10 9 8 7 6 5 4 3 2 1

Library of Congress Control Number: 2025934194

ISBN 978-1-6680-5755-1
ISBN 978-1-6680-5757-5 (ebook)

For Chuck Verrill, James A. Moore, and Weston Ochse

CONTENTS

Foreword • Christopher Golden xi

Introduction • Stephen King xv

PART ONE: DOWN WITH THE SICKNESS

Room 24 • Caroline Kepnes 3

The Tripps • Wrath James White 27

Bright Light City • Meg Gardiner 47

Every Dog Has Its Day • Bryan Smith 71

Lockdown • Bev Vincent 95

In a Pig's Eye • Joe R. Lansdale 115

Lenora • Jonathan Janz 151

The Hope Boat • Gabino Iglesias 181

Wrong Fucking Place, Wrong Fucking Time •
   C. Robert Cargill 197

Prey Instinct • Hailey Piper 219

Grace • Tim Lebbon 239

CONTENTS

Moving Day • Richard Chizmar 263

La Mala Hora • Alex Segura 287

The African Painted Dog • Catriona Ward 303

Till Human Voices Wake Us, and We Drown •
　Poppy Z. Brite 321

Kovach's Last Case • Michael Koryta 341

Make Your Own Way • Alma Katsu 359

PART TWO: THE LONG WALK

I Love the Dead • Josh Malerman 379

Milagros • Cynthia Pelayo 393

The Legion of Swine • S. A. Cosby 403

Keep the Devil Down • Rio Youers 417

Across the Pond • V. Castro 455

The Boat Man • Tananarive Due and Steven Barnes 473

The Story I Tell Is the Story of Some of Us •
　Paul Tremblay 501

The Mosque at the End of the World •
　Usman T. Malik 521

Abagail's Gethsemane •
　Wayne Brady and Maurice Broaddus 549

CONTENTS

PART THREE: LIFE WAS SUCH A WHEEL

He's a Righteous Man • Ronald Malfi 571

Awaiting Orders in Flaggston • Somer Canon 591

Grand Junction • Chuck Wendig 611

Hunted to Extinction • Premee Mohamed 633

Came the Last Night of Sadness •
  Catherynne M. Valente 657

The Devil's Children • Sarah Langan 693

PART FOUR: OTHER WORLDS THAN THESE

**The Unfortunate Convalescence of
  the SuperLawyer** • Nat Cassidy 715

Walk on Gilded Splinters • David J. Schow 745

Afterword • Brian Keene 759

Acknowledgments 763

About the Authors 765

FOREWORD
Christopher Golden

I suspect I was twelve, just about to turn thirteen, when I spotted the first Signet paperback edition of *The Stand* in an airport bookshop. My family was on the way to Florida to visit my grandparents, back in the days when people still smoked on airplanes. That would've been 1980. I don't recall anything else about the trip, but I remember everything about the literary trip that Frannie and Harold took, and Stu Redman's odyssey, and the loneliness of Nick Andros. I remember that the fourth time I read the novel, I cried at the end, when I realized the folks in Boulder had named a massive rock in memory of the stalwart Ralph Brentner. I remember beginning to understand redemption at that tender age thanks to Larry Underwood. And so much more.

People always talk about their favorite films and their favorite books, and many people change what gets the top spot on their list over the years. *The Stand* has been my favorite novel for forty-four years, as of this writing. It carved paths in my imagination that no amount of time's erosion can ever wear away. I've often said that Stephen King was the narrative voice of my youth, that when I think back on my childhood, the tone of those memories is colored by his storytelling style. That's certainly true, and so many of his stories and novels have stayed with me all my life, and are part of my personal story. But *The Stand* is my desert island book. Readers don't simply turn the pages—we *inhabit* the story, and I knew if I felt that way, a lot of other writers must as well.

I was contemplating my visceral connection to the novel one day, and I had one of those *Wouldn't it be cool if* moments. Author Brian Keene and I had recently put together an anthology of stories set in the world of Joe R. Lansdale's shocking, milestone horror novel, *The Drive-In*, and I'd insisted it would be the last anthology I would edit. (I'd said the same thing about the one I edited before that, so Brian didn't believe me anyway.) We started our careers in different corners of the horror world, but over the years, Brian and I have become brothers. We were born the same year, so most of the films, comics, television series and, most important, fiction that forged our imaginations hit us at the same time. We've played the role of sounding board in each other's lives for some years now (not to mention the role of SWAT-officer-talking-the-guy-off-the-ledge). So trust me when I say, I knew *The Stand* meant just as much to Brian as it does to me.

I called him. Told him the idea. Said I figured Stephen King would never go for it, but that it never hurts to ask. Brian was of the same opinion, so I sent that email. When Stephen gave us the thumbs-up, I stared at the response for a minute. Surprise and elation were the obvious reactions, and yeah, I had a massive grin on my face, as names of authors instantly started popping into my head . . . but I was also terrified. What if we fucked it up? What if we went through this whole process and the narrative voice of my youth was disappointed in us? Holy shit.

The only way to combat that fear was to stack the deck in our favor by recruiting a roster of contributors we knew shared our love for *The Stand* and deep respect for its author. I'm not going to name-check the three dozen authors in this volume, but I will say that they

FOREWORD

delivered everything we'd hoped for. Stories from around the world, and beyond it. Tales that expanded our understanding of the few weeks surrounding the devastating spread of the "Captain Trips" superflu, examined the influence of Mother Abagail and Randall Flagg, and postulated about the landscape that remained after readers turned the final page of Stephen King's masterpiece.

Brian will have his own words to share when you've reached the end of this book, but I know I speak for us both when I say we are profoundly honored to have been able to bring this collection to our fellow Constant Readers. We're forever grateful to Stephen King for his blessing this project and for his support. If readers feel themselves immersed in the world of *The Stand* once again, inhabiting that harrowing world the way my imagination still does, then we will consider our mission accomplished.

INTRODUCTION
Stephen King

Although the unabridged version of *The Stand* concludes with Randall Flagg—an epilogue meant to show that life is a wheel and evil always comes around again—the originally published version ends, as it began, with Stu Redman and Frannie Goldsmith.

"Frannie," he said, and turned her around so he could look into her eyes.

"What, Stuart?"

"Do you think . . . do you think people ever learn anything?"

She opened her mouth to speak, hesitated, fell silent. The kerosene lamp flickered. Her eyes seemed very blue.

"I don't know," she said at last. She seemed unpleased with her answer; she struggled to say something more; to illuminate her first response; and could only say it again:

I don't know.

It wasn't Frannie who was unpleased; it was me. It wasn't Frannie who struggled to say something more; it was me. I remember very clearly coming to the final pages of *The Stand*, and knowing I would have to say goodbye to my friends (there's an epilogue, true, but I never consider Randall Flagg a friend). Of course I remember it. I lived with Stu, Frannie, Nick, Tom, Kojak, Lloyd, Abagail, and all the others for over two years, and that only covers the first draft, which consisted of nine hundred single-spaced pages and five hundred thousand words, give or take a few.

I was in Bridgton, Maine, when I finished it. I had an office below the main house, opposite the furnace room (I got very used to that soft rumble), with a ground-level view along the back lawn running down to Long Lake. I typed Fran saying, "I don't know." I struggled to say something that would sum up all that had come before and found only empty platitudes. In the end (and *at* the end), I simply had Fran repeat it as a thought to herself: *I don't know*. Because *I* didn't know; that became the truest summation I could manage.

I have never been satisfied with that ending. It struck me then as limp-dick. It did when I revised the original Doubleday version of *The Stand* and added in all that had been left out, including my favorite psycho, The Kid. (*"Don't tell me, I'll motherfuckin tell YOU."*) After all that work revising and replacing, mostly in 1986 and 1987, I found myself brought up short by Frannie's *I don't know*, and as unsatisfied as ever. But because I *still* couldn't think of anything better, I (pardon the pun) let it stand.

I did know some of what was supposed to happen to Stu and Frannie on their way back to the East Coast. I knew that Frannie was going to fall down a well and encounter the Walkin Dude one more time; call it *The Last Temptation of Frannie Goldsmith*. I knew that whole story with great clarity, but it had no place in the final (at least so far) version of *The Stand*.

For one thing, I wanted to finish with my main characters in Boulder. For another, the book was already long enough, and I could imagine the critical reaction to what would be seen as authorial self-indulgence if I lingered even longer. I remembered a particularly vicious review of a lengthy James Michener novel. The critic said,

INTRODUCTION

more or less, "I have two pieces of advice about this book. The first is, don't read it. The second is, if you do, don't drop it on your foot."

So that Frannie story—appendage, by-blow, encore, call it what you want—went unwritten. Then Josh Boone, a talented young director, made a deal to remake *The Stand* as a CBS All Access streaming limited series (the original done for ABC, then called a "miniseries," was entirely directed by Mick Garris and scripted by me). I had talked about the well story at some point, probably on a panel or some promotional tour. Josh knew about it and asked me to write "Frannie in the Well" as a kind of coda to the CBS series. Which I was happy to do. Between "Frannie in the Well" and Flagg's final appearance, I even got a chance to address, if tangentially, that troubling *I don't know*.

A few years after that, Chris Golden and Brian Keene suggested—I think maybe without too much hope—that I might agree to them editing a collection of stories based on *The Stand*'s basic scenario: that a worldwide plague is released, and 99.8 percent of the world's population is wiped out.

My first impulse was to tell them no, because it reminded me of how the music world has an unfortunate habit of producing "tribute albums" for elderly artists or those who have passed on to that great bebop choir in the sky. Ella Fitzgerald sings Duke Ellington, Dinah Washington sings Bessie Smith, Nilsson sings Randy Newman, and the world-famous Various Artists sing everything from the Carpenters to Jimi Hendrix to Warren Zevon.

So my original feeling was negative. I thought, *I'm not old, not dead, and not doddering*. Then I had a hip replacement operation as a result of a long-ago accident and woke up in a hospital bed, feeling old. When I finally got out of that bed—first on a walker, then on a crutch—I discovered I was also doddering (although only on days ending in *y*). At present I can walk *sans* crutch, for the most part, but post-op I saw this book proposal in a different light.

Part of that was recalling "Frannie in the Well." Every now and then I'd wonder how many other stories there might be in a world either suffering the superflu or in its aftermath. I'll freely admit that these thoughts came more frequently at the height of the Covid pandemic, when all at once you couldn't get half-and-half and people were wiping their asses with ads addressed to "Occupant" because toilet paper had pretty much disappeared from the shelves. I also wondered what was happening in other parts of the world and even what was happening in the animal kingdom. (I should add that one of the stories in this collection, Catriona Ward's "The African Painted Dog," answers that question admirably.)

There was another element, rather vital: I admired the proposed editors of *The End of the World as We Know It*. Messrs. Golden and Keene are fine writers, and as such, I trusted them to put together a fine and eclectic collection. Which they have in fact done. My only disappointment is that, perhaps out of misplaced modesty, they have elected not to include their own stories.

That said, what a bounty is here! I got my wish concerning stories in other parts of the world. In addition to Catriona Ward's story, there are tales set in England, Puerto Rico, Canada, and Pakistan . . . even one harrowing visit, courtesy of Tim Lebbon, to a spacecraft in a decaying orbit. There are thirty-four stories in this book, by some of the finest authors in the field of horror, fantasy, and science fiction. Others, such as Caroline Kepnes, S. A. Cosby, and Meg Gardiner, ordinarily write in other fields, giving their appearances here a special kind of freshness. In the end, every single one of these writers brought their A game, and the result makes me extremely happy. I'm glad I gave this very special book the green light.

It's the end of the world as we know it . . . and I feel fine.

PART ONE

DOWN WITH THE SICKNESS

ROOM 24
Caroline Kepnes

Just one more stop and he could call it a day. Abel rang the bell.

"Coming!"

He knew what he was dealing with, another accommodating housewife who doesn't want to leave anyone hanging.

"Two seconds," she yelled. "Bit of a situation with a cake!"

"No problem, ma'am."

They were all the same, the women who won't press charges, the dutiful misguided ones who won't leave their dirtbag husbands. She opened the door.

"Can I help you?"

She wasn't lying about the cake. He could smell it on her, in the kitchen. Chocolate.

"Sorry," he said. "Are you Mrs. Blanchard?"

"Yes," she said.

He lost his voice. But that's not fair. She stole it. Women could do that. Kill you by pulling at their reddish hair. Wiping their hands on a peach sundress. Smiling like something out of a horror movie. Glossy lying eyes, so beautiful it hurt. Freckles on forearms. Bruises, too. Abel remembered the cover of that book his mother kept on her nightstand. *The Bridges of Madison County.* He never read it.

"Sorry," he said again, the way women often do. "We got a call about a disturbance."

She blinked. He eyeballed the baby in the high chair in the kitchen. Babies made him stiff. Gurgling, pooping reminders of what men do to women, jam their peckers in and squirt. This lovely, sad woman lacked mystery now. To look at that baby was to know that she'd spread her legs.

She ran her hands over her forearms. "Ah," she said. "Rona, Rona, Rona."

"Excuse me?"

"My neighbor, Rona. This isn't . . . You should see the other guy, if you catch my drift."

She left space for him to laugh, as if he didn't know his way around crummy men and the women who think they deserve them. He stayed solid. Hard. "Are you alone, ma'am?"

She was melting a bit. Shaking her head, mumbling that her husband was "at work." She pulled her hair over one shoulder. A statue made of stone. Impenetrable. "I am in here baking a *cake* for that woman, which is something I do from time to time as a good neighbor, and she's over there calling the cops. That's a lot . . . even for her."

"She said she heard you screaming."

Mrs. Blanchard bit her lip. "Can you come in?"

Abel followed her into the house.

"See," she said. "Rona's alone. Never married. And as you can see, I've got my hands full. I'm making her a cake."

He took in the mess. Dirty dishes. Milk on the floor. "You mentioned that."

She was peering at him now and he liked it, hated himself for the way he never did learn how to hide it. "Look," she said. "Can I be direct?"

"Of course."

"Rona's a loner and this is what she does with her time. She gets in other people's business because she doesn't have any business of her own."

On the main road, an ambulance was speeding by, sirens and all.

"Can you believe this nonsense?" she huffed. "As if nobody ever got the flu before."

Abel was disappointed. She was the type who played tough instead of facing her fear. But he was also relieved. It was nice, talking with her like this, same way everyone was talking about this nasty flu going around. Abel did love big, bad, flashy news. It leveled the playing field, made it easier to have a chat. Bad things were good and unifying, like the way his mom used to talk about the day JFK was shot, how everyone would never forget where they were when they found out, how JFK's death made you feel like the world was a terrible place, but a soft one, too, with strangers hugging.

Mrs. Blanchard was staring at him, with good reason. The hell did JFK have to do with things? He needed to get out more, he did.

"Sorry," he said. "So, you're okay?"

"Honestly . . . No."

Abel leaned in. "Is he here?"

"I mean about Rona."

"Oh."

Women do this. They tell you the truth and lie at the same time. "Look," she said. "She's the nuisance, okay? If she's not claiming that Kip is parking on her lawn, she's yammering about how our dog is eating her carrots."

"Do you have a dog?"

"No. And she doesn't grow any *carrots*."

They both laughed, and Abel wanted to stay here, live here.

She tilted her head. "Are you married?"

He wanted to have things in common with Mrs. Blanchard. He wished he, too, had bruises, a spouse, a baby. "No, ma'am."

She pulled back, just enough where he knew that he got that stink on, that loneliness. He was doing it again, building bridges to places that didn't exist, wanting it all too much, too openly. His father always called him a pussy. That might be the reason he became a cop.

"Sorry," she said. "It's none of my business. But maybe you could talk to her, you know? Ask her to lay off."

On she went, patting her baby on the head, painting Rona as the perp, as if the old woman was the one who belted her. She stuffed the pacifier into the baby's mouth and Abel could see her prick husband stuffing his pecker into her with the same kind of impatient force. The baby was gonna suffer if Abel didn't do something.

He forced a smile. "You got a cute one there."

She laughed, like there was something funny about Abel, and then she was talking again. It was hard to listen, hard to follow. This happened to Abel. His ears filled with cotton and the words couldn't get into his head. And then he'd start thinking about his father, all the things he used to say about women, how the good Lord put them on this planet to challenge the men, how they're all snakes. *God gave them titties and holes to tempt us, Abel.*

Listen good, he'd say. *You can't trust anyone whose hot parts are on the inside hiding. That's why you treat them like they're just as good as us.* And then he'd adjust his tie and sidle up to that pulpit and preach like everything he said in private was a lie. Abel never knew which one was real.

"So, you know what I mean, right?" she asked.

Abel was clueless, but he nodded, which seemed to please her. "Good," she said. "What Rona doesn't understand is that the best part about fighting is making up."

He looked at her arms, at her bruises. He was not the best cop, but he was not the worst. "Okay," she said. "Kip . . . my husband. Well, he just lost his brother."

"I'm sorry to hear that."

"And Kip, he decides his brother died of this 'superflu' going around..."

"Okay."

"He gets all worked up and he takes my keys. He wants me and Randy here at home because he's one of those people... He thinks it's, you know, 'dangerous' out there."

Abel didn't like this feeling, the sense that Kip had his upsides. Smart and protective. But then look at her arms. Look at the ring on her finger, the little nipper on her lap. Abel didn't know that he had that in him, the violence, and sometimes it felt like women only wanted men who did, like they couldn't help it.

"Anyway," she said. "I'm not the 'victim.' Kip and I run hot. And when you run hot... I only mentioned the thing about my brother-in-law because, to be frank, the making up this time around was loud, even for us."

She toyed with her baby's pacifier in a way that cut off Abel's circulation. Why was she being like that? So graphic, blunt? He felt his downsides spread. He was a jealous man. An inexperienced man. Rendered cynical by one-too-many domestic calls. A candy-ass once again thinking about his dead preacher father, that motel off I-90 where they went on Abel's fifteenth birthday. The hooker with big yellow hair and long tits. The smell in Room 24. The way she spit in her hands and touched his pecker and laughed with his dad about how he couldn't get it up. The way the sun beat on the back of Abel's head as he stood outside while his dad did what Abel couldn't do, what he didn't want to do, not with that mean, yellow-haired hooker.

Mrs. Blanchard offered him a slice of hard cake on a chipped plate. "Is this enough?"

"That's perfect," he said.

She laughed. "It's Entenmann's, Officer. Let's not go over the top now..."

The way she said *Officer* lifted him out of the muck, fueled his upsides. He wasn't a bad-looking guy. Wasn't entirely *off*. He ate his stale cake. If they were married, would it be like this? Could he love that baby? The key right now was to stay calm, to eat the cake slowly and let the sugar hit. Maybe this was the start of something. Abel was pure of heart and body. He didn't have a violent streak, or a dead chain-smoking brother, and he'd never forced himself on a woman, never knocked her up just to limit her options.

Mrs. Blanchard reached for a button on her sundress. "Do you mind?"

And then it was there. Her breast. Loaded with milk. Abel felt his body build a *Bridge* to her County and it was hard not to smile, not to whip it out as she covered herself. There was nothing wrong with his pecker. He was not *off*, and the quiet in this kitchen was special. Theirs.

Maybe her prick husband would wreck his car on the way home. Maybe that baby would back off, let Abel have a sip, too.

"So," she began. "You know that thing I said?"

"What thing?"

"I changed my mind. You don't need to talk to Rona."

"Are you sure? Because I can do that."

"Nah," she said. "I'm good. It's good."

After Abel dropped off his car at the station, he couldn't go home. Not right away.

He was *too* happy.

One of the rookies was in the parking lot crying—her aunt was dead—and a few of the others were with her, making plans to mourn, to drink. Abel wasn't invited, and for once in his damn life . . . he didn't care.

He got into his car. *Vroom.*

Everything made sense. Of course he would find the love of his life when most people were all doom and gloom. Lately it felt like everyone knew someone who was sick, and Abel was lucky, lucky that he didn't love anyone or care about anyone except her.

Mrs. Blanchard in her peach dress.

He stopped at a bookstore and bought *The Bridges of Madison County*. He picked up some more of that cake that she fed him, and he left the box open so the cake would dry out.

Life was good. He read two pages and he had to unzip. He imagined the call on the radio.

Domestic disturbance.

He imagined himself speeding legally, breaking down her door and killing her husband. Right in front of her. He imagined her worse than she'd been today, bloody and beaten.

He came harder than he had in years, but after he was done, when he went for tissues, he avoided his eyes in the mirror. There was something wrong about what just happened. The way he wanted her like that, bloody and beaten, hateful.

The next two days were empty.

No call from nosy neighbor Rona. Too much chaos at work with everyone keyed up about the superflu in a way that wasn't fun, not anymore. The calls came in, but they were never from Rona, which meant that Mrs. Blanchard was either safe or dead. How those things became one and the same. Safe. Dead. And the nights were no good, either. His pecker was getting nasty, vile. Sometimes Mrs. Blanchard was tied up, and not in the fun way. Sometimes she was full of bullet holes and Abel was kissing those holes, sucking the blood out of them, sticking his pecker in those holes.

It didn't feel good, knowing there might be an afterlife, knowing his father might be up there eating popcorn, shaking his head at his sick, perv son.

On the third day, Abel bought two boxes of tissues at the market.

The broad at the register sighed. "I should stock up," she said. "That superbug, it's something isn't it?"

Abel took the long way home. He drove by the body shop, where he saw Kip Blanchard in real life. A monster. Filthy as he seemed in the framed wedding portrait hanging in their foyer, the photograph that Abel had tried to avoid noticing. Smoking and laughing and holding court for the other guys. Mean guys. True grime. Hair growing out of Kip's white T-shirt, grease on his shirt, on his hands. Kip held a cigarette between his lips and mimed taking a woman from behind. Foul. Abel thought of the devil, the white bandanna on Kip's head like a satanic mark, a signal. Abel didn't do a drive-by at Mrs. Blanchard's. The street was too small. He tried to be a good boy. He tried one story in his head where Mrs. Blanchard was in her peach dress and the husband was dead on the floor. Bloodied. Stabbed fifty times, maybe sixty.

His pecker didn't like that, so back he went to the other way. His juices squirting all over her bloodied corpse, bringing her back to life, his pecker in there doing CPR on her heart.

On the fifth day, Rona called.

Mrs. Blanchard opened the door. Jeans and a sad ratty T-shirt. Probably *his*. Abel wasn't one of those guys who liked it when women dressed like men. And he was heartened to feel his muscles tense up when he spotted the blood on her forehead.

Abel was not a monster. His pecker didn't like that blood, either.

"Jesus Christ," he said, and Mrs. Blanchard crumpled like a tissue.

Abel entered the house. The baby was out of sight.

"Before you start . . . Don't. I can't do it, okay? I can't leave him and it's not his fault. My mother . . . If I leave him, who's gonna pay for her assisted living? And Randy, you know?"

Abel knew enough to say nothing. To nod.

"Oh fuck," she said, and she fell into him, through him. Nothing ever felt better than her tears and her trembling shoulders. She was honest now. She said she was a fuckup. She said she always chose the wrong men.

"Not possible," Abel said. "There's no such thing as the right man. They're all evil."

The pads of her little fingers went this way and that way. "You're sweet," she said. "It's like you're not . . . I'm sorry."

And nothing had ever felt worse than her regaining her equilibrium, patting his backside, pulling away to pour coffee. She lit a cigarette. She sat in the chair and kicked her feet up on the table. Abel didn't feel like a man, not anymore. He was a cop again. Nothing more.

"So," she said. "Is this what you do all day? You go from one shit marriage to another?"

"Sometimes. But I'm not one to judge."

She huffed. She was nothing like the Mrs. Blanchard in his fantasies. "Right," she said. "Sure."

"Would you like to press charges?"

"Yes," she said. "You know that cake I made for Rona? She brought it back, left in on our porch, and the raccoons got into it, which pissed off Kip. So, I go to Rona and ask her to please not do that kind of thing and she says she *hates* devil's food cake. She likes *angel* food cake. I mean, who in their right mind would take angel food over devil's food?"

Abel would do that. He preferred angel food. "I hear you."

"I mean, hello . . . We're talking about chocolate."

He wouldn't do it, wouldn't cackle for her stupid stand-up act or spar with her and admit that he was like Rona in more ways than one, that he, too, found devil's food to be excessively rich, heavy. He was here to protect, to serve.

"Would you like to press charges against your husband?"

She blew smoke at him. "Would you?"

"You'd be surprised at how many systems are in place to help women in this situation."

"Right," she said. "Well, in the meantime I have to go help my sister. She's sick."

"Can you and Randy stay with her for a while?"

She looked at him like he shouldn't know her baby's name. "Wow."

"I'm good with names."

"I'm terrible," she said, and she was back. Lovely and scared and soft. "But I guess that's no surprise . . . Do you want to know something sick?"

Her feet were on the ground now. He was quiet. Ghost-in-the-graveyard-level still.

"When he came after me today, after the whole *cake* fiasco, I ran into the bedroom. I wanted Rona to hear, so I made a dig about his dead brother. I wanted him to belt me because then you'd come back and . . . I'm repulsive. I'm a *mother* and I'm poking the bear trying to get myself killed so this cop I met once will come back and 'rescue' me."

Abel's insides were melting and hard. "Maybe he will," he said.

She lit another cigarette. "Right. And then we'll run away and live happily ever after and make a big happy family. Nope. I'm a fuckup, Officer. I'm a real true fuckity-fucking fuckup."

"You're an angel, Amelie."

Abel did it. He said her name. She was quiet now. Too quiet. Did he overstep? Did she realize that he'd done a little recon at the station? She gulped a little, and maybe this was good. Maybe she wanted him to say it again. *A-muh-lee.* But then she chuckled.

"Oh, I'm not an 'angel,' Officer. That's your department."

Abel's warm insides turned cold. He didn't know the first thing about women, and he scratched the back of his head like he hadn't been murmuring her name in the shower, practicing.

"Oh, I'm no angel, either, Mrs. B. Far from it, in fact."

It was terrible, the way she laughed, like she saw right through him and his *Mrs. B* nonsense. What if she loved the devil too much to love him?

"So," she said. "What about you? Girlfriend? Crazy ex? Or maybe *you're* the crazy ex . . . "

"No," he said. "Not at the moment."

He always added that second part to sound like a more complete person.

"Mmm," she said. "The night me and Kip met, I'm sitting at this bar and I'm six thousand sheets to the wind . . . "

He didn't like this, any of it, and he chuckled. "I've been there."

It was a lie, and she knew it. "Anyway," she said. "Kip swaggers up like, 'Where's your boyfriend?' I'm feeling myself, so I go off on him, right? I tell him I hate when guys ask if you have a boyfriend. As if I need an excuse in the form of a man. If I don't like a guy, I don't like him. I shouldn't have to invent a *boyfriend.* Sometimes I think if I wasn't so drunk, so flippant . . . I don't know where I was going with this, but it's that thing where someone meets you and that first impression sticks. I can't blame Kip for thinking that drunk me was the true me. And maybe it is, you know?"

Abel didn't like her talking about her husband as if he wasn't a man, too, and the way she covered her mouth to emit a tiny burp, the way she shifted, she knew she was making him uncomfortable. He could feel her trying to change. He could see it.

This was love. It had to be.

"Anyway," she said. "What's your story? Seriously."

He didn't know how to tell her there was no one else, so he borrowed from *Bridges* and said he wasn't so lucky, that he'd only been in love once, that it wasn't in the cards. It was terrifying, waiting for her to respond, the way she was looking at him like she couldn't decide what to do with him, like he was a sundress she might just return for a refund. He was failing. She wanted to know him, but he couldn't tell her about his pecker, about the way his heart raced every time he thought she might be bleeding, wounded. He couldn't tell her about the boxes of Kleenex he'd torn through in her honor, the way he'd entered her in his mind, imagined his pecker soaked in her blood.

"You're sweet," she said. "I guess there has to be *one* good one in the world..."

She laughed and he laughed, and this was *The Bridges of Madison County*. It had to be. And then she looked down at her dirty fingers in this way where he felt invited to join her. So he did, and they sat there like that for a minute or two, both of them staring at her hands. "Well," she said. "I hope I never see you again..."

Something changed. It was her, Amelie. She was watching him, waiting. It was scary to be so close. What if he was wrong? The same old Abel, drowning in delusions. Didn't matter. He had to do it, he had to jump. And thank God he went through with it because the malarkey was all true, wasn't it? Love was powerful. You really could say a lot without opening your mouth. He smiled. She smiled. Abel was inside of something as real and private as this little kitchen table. The first flush, like that tickle in your throat that hints at things to come. Her eyes told him what she wanted. "Abel," he said. "It's Abel."

―――――

There was radio silence for two days, but that's how it goes in love stories, in sex.

In, out, in, out. People were dying. It was like JFK being assassinated all day, every day, and in crazy times, people do crazy things. They were both making their plans, probably.

Abel dug up his father's pistol. No one knew about it. Only him.

He drove to the market for tissues, but there was a big sign out front.

NO TISSUES NO TOILET PAPER MOVE ON

ROOM 24

At home, he mopped up with a washcloth, and he could feel it in his bones, in his eyeballs. Tomorrow was it. Tomorrow Rona would call.

But then tomorrow came and he was wrong. Stupid and sick. Sick to want the call from Rona. His pecker was achy—he needed to get nicer washcloths—and he couldn't go on like this. Waiting. She couldn't, either.

What if she was dead? What if she thought he didn't love her?

He flipped it around like one of the detectives. She'd opened up to him. She told him the husband beat her. She told him she wanted out, but she couldn't get out.

And what did Abel do?

Nothing.

It was a tragedy, really.

Kip Blanchard got himself killed.

The poor bastard was in the Safeway parking lot and the colder guys on the job were right. *What kind of an idiot brings a gun to a knife fight and loses?*

Kip Blanchard, apparently.

Three days after the funeral, Abel put two suitcases in the trunk of his car, one for him, one for her, for Amelie. He stashed Kip's handkerchief in his back pocket. Not in a serial-killer-with-a-trophy kinda way. More like a cat who kills the mouse for its humans. And he wasn't dumb. He wasn't gonna *show* it to Amelie. He also didn't expect things would get physical right away. It was just there to remind him of what he did, what he was.

A man.

He picked up fresh flowers and he drove slowly. There was no rush, not today. When you find the one, you want to savor every step of the beautiful ladder, each one a *Bridge* leading to someplace better, higher. Closer.

He popped a breath mint after he parked in front of her house.

It was quiet here, which said a lot about Amelie's life, about her friends. A dead husband and no one's here to help?

"Excuse me! Officer!"

It was her. *Rona.* And it was him. Stupid.

She froze up on her front lawn. He looked down at the bandanna in his hand. White and blood-soaked. *Off.* Abel was not a man, not fully. He was a boy clinging to an unlucky rabbit's foot and Rona was backing up, looking this way and that way. A bird going cuckoo.

He slipped the handkerchief in his back pocket.

Abel needed a minute.

Rona was old. Elderly kind of old. And Amelie was right. She was paranoid, sickly. While the house looked pert and quaint on the outside, it was a different story inside. Sticky notes everywhere, pink and green and blue. *Tape* Murder, She Wrote! *Milk! Kool-Aid!* It broke Abel's heart to think of a woman living like this, shit-stained granny panties and no grandchildren. He'd been smart about things, taming her the way you do a snake, holding her tight, telling her it was okay, leading her to the bathroom and helping her out of her clothes, running the water like a home health aide, making sure it wasn't too hot or too cold.

Eventually Rona submitted, as if she wanted this samaritan to send her to a better place. Protect and serve. Or maybe she just passed out from the stress.

In any case, she died before he could kill her, and if the cops did investigate—they wouldn't—they'd conclude that a shut-in died in her own tub. People don't like that kind of thing. They don't like it when lonely old people die alone.

Abel drank the last of Rona's tea. It was safer this way, taking a piece of her that he couldn't carry around in his back pocket. The *bandanna.* Stupid, yes. But stupid only matters if you refuse to get

ROOM 24

smart. He was kind, a chip off the old block, visiting Rona one last time, kneeling by her side. He was starting to see that his father was wrong about a lot, but right, too. Turned out Abel really was *off*. Anyone who kills two people and keeps his tea down is missing a piece or two. A heart. A conscience. Abel heard a siren and remembered the virus. Maybe the bad in him was in him all along. His mother used to paint her eyelids blue to bring out the blue in her God-given eyes. Maybe the virus was like the eyelid paint, drawing the truth out of Abel. It was good to sit here, though. Proof that his goodness was also true, same as the bad.

The dead don't die all at once. A soul goes slowly, in stages. Steeping tea.

And Abel was really doing it, wasn't he? Getting away with two murders.

Okay, one and a half, but still. It was something.

Room 24 hadn't changed much over the past twenty years, not that Abel told Amelie.

She looked around. She sniffed. "It's bleach," she said. "I hate bleach."

"At least it's clean," he said, like a husband. Not yet. Soon, though.

Things hadn't gone *exactly* as planned. When he rang Amelie's bell, she slammed the door on him. She said she was fine. She was *mourning* and she said Abel had no idea what that was like because he wasn't married, he didn't know that love and hate are in lockstep, that passion is ugly, that she didn't want *the father of her child* to die, that it wasn't even about Randy, that love was love. It hurt, the way she didn't invite him in, the way she said he had no business being here, as if he was in uniform, as if he wasn't hers.

Eventually, she opened the door.

"Okay," she'd said. "Okay."

Abel went into the house. Again . . . not the stuff of dreams. Papers everywhere. She was in those jeans, jeans and a sweater that belonged to him. *Kip*. She was frustrated with liens and mortgages. All of it was so ugly, more proof that what Abel had done was noble. Kip had been a secretive prick, and the house was underwater. Her life was underwater.

Abel sat at the table.

"Any leads?"

"Any what?"

"Leads," he said.

"I don't know. I have to focus on this so I can go get my sister's kids."

Oh right. Abel was still getting used to this whole relationship thing where a person comes into your life with all these other people. Amelie had a sister. A dead sister, as of three days ago. He tried to say the right things—*I'm sorry . . . We're gonna be okay*—and he did his best to hide the bad stuff, like the fact that he was a bit *happy* about the situation. Amelie was taking in the kids, so they were gonna be a big family. It was a relief, the shameful kind you had to keep to yourself, but Abel felt safe knowing that Amelie would need him even more now. And then it was bad clockwork. His thoughts drifted back to the bandanna, to the blood.

"Did you know about the gun?" he'd said.

She looked at him like he was bad. *Off.*

"The report," Abel said. "Your husband had a gun on him, no?"

"Well, of course I knew about the gun."

She was lying again. "Oh."

"Look," she said. "I don't know what you're doing here, okay? I told you . . . I'm a fuckup. But I'm not an idiot. Do you want to know the truth? Do you want to know how I am? How we were? I loved that gun, okay? Kip fucked me with that gun, and sometimes he put it in my mouth *while* we were fucking. The night he died, before he went to the store, he said he would kill me and the baby and himself with that gun if this fucking 'superflu' ever came for us, and it turned me on so much to think of him killing us in one fell swoop that before he went to the store . . . I fucked him again."

—⁓—

"Abel."

Now was now. Room 24. Amelie held a pillow and scowled. "Smell this."

Abel loved that he still loved her despite her being a filthy whore, a disgusting liar, the kind of illogical woman who doesn't fear a deadly flu but questions a hotel pillow. Some lies were good. All her dirty talk was bogus. Kip didn't have a gun. That gun belonged to Abel's father, and then to Abel, not to Kip. Never. And Abel was more than happy to play along.

He lifted the pillow to his face, half expected her to come at him, smother him. No dice, and he declared the pillow "fresh as a daisy" and then jumped on the bed and smiled at her. One of these days, she would be her old self. She would smile back at him.

She glared at his torso, at his feet. Was he ugly? Fat?

"Sorry," he said. "I'll take my shoes off."

"We can't sleep in the same bed."

Where did it go? The love. It wasn't gone. It was just hiding. Afraid of good things like Abel's angelic ways, his gentle hands, his good-boy pecker.

"Look," she said. "I told you . . . I need a minute."

This again. The way she liked to list all the bad things. Losing her house, her husband, her sister. He obliged and moved to the other bed, fighting the big new fear. What if her love wasn't hiding? What if it was gone and he was only in this room because Amelie was afraid to drive to Boise on her own?

Afraid, and maybe lazy.

But then she pulled at her sundress. The one from the day they met.

Abel smiled. He liked their little world, the portable crib that he assembled, little Randy gurgling. They had everything they needed, and that sundress was an omen in the good way. "You take all the time in the world, Amelie."

"Can you just . . . Can we be quiet? Randy needs to sleep and my head is spinning and I don't want to take it out on you, but . . . "

He zipped his lip with his finger. She didn't get a kick out of him and he didn't appreciate her foul language, or the way she picked her fingernails.

"I'm going out for a smoke," she said.

He'd get her to quit when they were settled in Boise. "Take your time."

The baby was snoozing, so Abel followed her—there were bad people in the world, there was a killer flu—and he watched her enter a phone booth. Time stopped when she dropped in a quarter. Was there another man? Another cop? Another *Kip*?

"Joanie," she said, and he felt his stomach drop.

Most of it was small talk, and then she sighed. "So, the cop and I . . . I know, but beggars can't be choosers. I might just be allergic to decency or maybe it's impossible to imagine anything good beginning at this point in my life."

Abel went back to the room. Those words didn't matter because they weren't meant for him. Women do that for their friends. They lie and downplay what's good. Joan was divorced, and Amelie was sweet. She didn't want Joan to feel bad about being alone.

Night had fallen, and it was time to eat.

Nothing was easy, not anymore. They couldn't take the baby into the poisonous world, but they couldn't leave the baby alone. Abel offered to go on his own, but Amelie was aghast. *Why? So you can bring all the germs back with cold fries?* Beyond that, she was tired of Room 24. She needed to get *out*. Abel fell in line and helped get the baby in the car seat. He suggested they hit a drive-thru, but Amelie shook him off. She needed to be in a booth, with people. He treaded lightly, made a casual remark about germs, and again Amelie snapped. *Stop questioning my every move.* Eventually, he spotted a diner and again Amelie scoffed. *I, too, know how to read.* He used the directional as he turned into the parking lot, and Amelie huffed. *We're the only ones on the road, you're such a Ronald Rule follower.* Abel said he was sorry, and she said to stop being so . . . *Never mind.* When they walked into the diner, her face fell. There was only one other party, an older couple. Abel requested a booth and Amelie and the hostess laughed at him, but that didn't hurt as much. He *was* a little silly when you considered all the open seats. Dinner came and went. Meatloaf for him, a cheeseburger for her, and a bottle for baby Randy. Abel couldn't let their big night out end like this, he had to do better, make her smile. He caught her eye as he ordered his dessert. "A slice of angel food cake, if you please."

It was supposed to be sweet, a private sundress kind of moment, but again, Amelie balked. *If you're going to make us sit here, you should at least get something substantial.* Abel hung his head. He felt it coming. He wanted to hold it in, but for the first time in their life together, he lost his cool and snapped. "At least I'm not a monster."

The look on her face. Her eyes bulging. Abel spit out an apology, but Amelie raised her hands in the air like she was in church. "Finally," she said. "A little *truth*!" She clapped her hands like this was progress, like she wanted him to be vicious. Abel looked at baby Randy. Sleeping and innocent, pure. Okay, yes, Abel did bad things, but Amelie didn't know about all that. He didn't want to be vicious. He *wasn't* vicious. When she went to the bathroom, he changed his order, and when she returned and saw the devil's food cake she frowned.

"Are you really that much of a doormat?"

It was time for bed.

Sure, they were in separate beds, but there was hope. Come the wee hours, Amelie might have a nightmare and wake up scared and go to him.

She turned on the TV. He looked at her. Really?

"I need the white noise."

"All night?"

"You will, too," she said. "I snore like a freight train. It drove Kip nuts."

She flipped past all the nice old movies. Amelie wanted the news, and Abel'd had enough of the doom and gloom. She didn't love the silence they made together, not the way he did, and when they were settled in their separate beds, he turned out the lights.

"Sweet dreams, my love."

"Fat chance," she said. "Between the stench of bleach and this mattress . . . I'm pretty sure you call this a *cot*."

This was not pillow talk, but it was early. She'd been through things. She might never be sweet with him. Her former marriage might have killed something inside of her, same way he was when they met, rendered cynical by all those domestic calls. Life wore you down, no matter what you did, and soon, she was out cold. She wasn't a liar. Her snore was something out of a dragon. Abel couldn't sleep, not with Amelie's gargling and the shiny newspeople on the TV barely able to contain their excitement over the thing, the virus, Captain something or other. He longed to be with Amelie, to open up to her the way she had with him so many times. And he wanted to know things about her. Did she believe in God? In good and evil?

Sometime after three, he smelled something funny. He went to check on Randy. So, this is what a dead baby looks like. A first for Abel, and he allowed himself a few tears. How did he miss it? He should've known something was wrong in the diner when Randy fell asleep, when he didn't wake up in the car, even after napping most of the day. And his drooling. He'd been drooling more, hadn't he? His little body was fighting, and what did Abel do to chip in, to save him? Nothing. This is the worst it gets. A life that doesn't get to be lived. He covered the almost-boy's tiny body, and he climbed into Amelie's bed. Her body was hot, her skin slimy with sweat.

She shuddered. She was alive.

"I killed Kip," he said. "I killed Rona, too. Sort of."

He could feel the wheels turning inside her head, but he couldn't see where they were going. So, he went again.

"Amelie," he said. "The pistol was my dad's. It was never inside of you."

She was shivering, and was it the virus? Was it love? Hate?

He opened his mouth to hers. He felt her hand find his pecker. Second time that happened in this room. She was delirious. Murmuring. "Kip . . . Kippy." She pulled Abel closer, and then closer. And then that word again. "Kip." Abel looked the other way. She'd said it herself. *I'm terrible with names.* This was it, the beginning and the end, and this was beautiful, the three of them together. He wanted her to pass while he was inside of her, to die without knowing about her baby. He kissed her to be sure he would catch it. He willed her toxic breath to penetrate his airways, shut down his lungs, and prove that, despite what she said to Joanie, she was not a beggar. She was a chooser. She chose him.

"Abel," he said. "It's Abel."

Her body rattled as if she would go anywhere with him, be it Boise or heaven or hell.

In the morning, Abel smacked his lips.

So that was love. Sex. Abel had just lost his virginity in the same place where he kept it all those years ago. He rolled over and the breath got trapped in his chest, his heart. There she wasn't. Amelie. Her body was cold, and he was stranded. Alive. She ran off to heaven or hell or Boise to be with Kip and Rona and Randy and he wasn't even feverish. The flu didn't want him. Amelie didn't want him. No one wanted him.

He leapt out of the deathbed and dug his gun out of his duffel bag. He was dizzy and fuzzy. *Off.* But there was more to it. The room was off. The light.

He had to focus. Choose.

He could pull the trigger and chase Amelie down in heaven or hell or Boise. She was weak. She was always going to stumble, but he could bring her back, knock them out all over again, Kip and Rona, Randy. And then what? Would they go on like this forever? Would she do it again, sneak out while he was *sleeping* and run back to the bastard who nearly put her in her grave?

Something tingled in him. He remembered about souls. About purgatory. He didn't see the light so much as he felt it. As it turned out, Abel was dead. Gone. This was a challenge, the kind of thing his dad talked about. If Abel wanted to be with Amelie, he had to pull the trigger, do to himself what he'd done to the others. God was testing him, and Abel would rise to the occasion, same way he did last night. He brought the pistol to his lips. He imagined it in Amelie's mouth. Did she really want that kind of action? He closed his eyes and—

"Housekeeping!"

A voice. Impatience and disgust. Abel dropped his pistol on his foot. The pain was real. Physical and earthly. He was alive. He had feet, toes. A pecker.

"Housekeeping!"

The woman on the other side of the wall pounded on the door with knuckles that made the room rattle. She was life, loud and demanding. Her fist lifted bleach off the tiles and dragged the must from the pillows, from the bodies, the dead bodies.

Abel slapped his face the way you slap a baby's bottom. "Coming!"

He slid the gun in a drawer. He didn't want to upset the housekeeper. And he couldn't blame Amelie for leaving him. She was honest. She preferred devil's food cake, always. Maybe that's why he was immune to this thing. Maybe he was an angel. Or maybe it wasn't about good and evil. Maybe it was just something in the sweet, lame cake he preferred. He was on his feet now, smoothing his hair, looking into his eyes in the mirror, a task that was usually so painful, so scary. Love was transformative, it was true. Maybe the housekeeper was like him. Maybe she knew *The Bridges of Madison County*. Already, she had one thing going for her. She was alive, and unlike Amelie in the deathbed, the housekeeper knew what she wanted. She wanted to come into his room. She wanted Abel to open the door.

THE TRIPPS
Wrath James White

"Ay, yo! Don't touch that nigga! He got the Tripps!" Freddy called out before taking a long pull on a huge blunt and suppressing a cough. He exhaled slowly. A miasma of marijuana vapors surrounded him. His hardened visage emerged from the narcotic cloud like a magician appearing in a puff of dry-ice smoke.

Talik looked up at Freddy, squinting at the taller man, whose back was to the sun, creating a glow around him that added to the magician image. He looked back down at Fat Steve. The big kid's dark earthy-brown complexion was now a sickly gray. A sheen of perspiration gave his skin a moist unctuousness, like something that had crawled up from the bottom of a lake. His eyes were sallow and rheumy, weeping a yellow pus from the corners. A steady flow of mucus leaked from his nose over his chapped lips, yet he seemed oblivious to it. His eyes were cloudy and distant, half-lidded, as if he were about to either fall asleep or die right there on the spot. Even when he coughed—a harsh, wet, phlegm-choked bark—his eyes remained inanimate.

"Fuck that! He snatched my mom's purse yesterday! I want her money back!" Talik protested, battling between the desire to dig through Fat Steve's pockets for his wallet and the urge to flee the cloud of pestilence engulfing the bigger kid.

Talik was only ten years old and shockingly skinny, even for this neighborhood, where so many kids went hungry. He didn't know a single kid who ate three meals a day. Most were lucky if they got one. For many families, the money that didn't go to necessities like keeping the rent paid and the utilities on often went to alcohol and drugs, with food and clothing a distant second. Fat Steve was almost fourteen, half a foot taller, and at least fifty pounds heavier than Talik. If the big kid hadn't been near death, there was no way Talik would have dared approach him about his mom's purse. He was brave, but not stupid. Fat Steve would have beaten him to a pulp and might have even killed him just to increase his rep on the streets. This was Talik's only chance. Besides, his mom was sick, too, and so was his older brother. It was probably just a matter of time before he and his little sister caught whatever was going around.

"Your mom probably ain't have no money in that purse anyway," Freddy replied. "It ain't worth getting sick for."

Freddy was an OG. Tall, light-skinned, long, matted, reddish-brown dreadlocks, and lean, wiry muscles. He wore a Bob Marley T-shirt, but had more of a Super Cat attitude—more dancehall reggae than roots. Freddy was a crack dealer and hard-core killer, but Talik wasn't in that game, and he knew Freddy respected Talik's mom too much to cause him any problems. He was only a few years younger than Talik's momma and had gone to high school with her back in the day.

Talik knelt down and studied Fat Steve. He looked bad. It wasn't just all the phlegm and mucus leaking out of him or that wet tubercular cough. He was shaking and shivering, and his breathing sounded all gurgly, like when Talik blew bubbles in his soda with a straw.

"What's Tripps, yo?" Talik asked as he stood and turned back toward Freddy.

"Captain Trips? You ain't been watching the news, little homie?" Freddy replied. "That shit is spreading all across the country. Half the neighborhood done caught it. It's some kind of superflu or some shit. Folks is saying the government made that shit to clean out the ghettos. I guess all the drugs they pumpin' in here ain't killin' niggas fast enough."

Talik found Freddy's conspiracy theories ironic considering he was the main drug dealer in their neighborhood, but perhaps that meant he knew what he was talking about more than most. For all Talik knew, Freddy might have been getting his crack directly from the CIA.

A single gunshot rang out, followed by a volley of curses and threats and the booming staccato of a semi automatic rifle. Then more gunshots and the piercing scream of someone witnessing the death of a loved one. It was an all too familiar melody of anguish and loss, normal for G-town, but not at this time of day. Gunfights and drive-bys typically took place after sunset. The sounds of gun violence were as much a symphony of the night as the mating calls of crickets and cicadas.

"You'd better get yo ass home, little homie. Sounds like shit is poppin' off out here," Freddy said, looking quickly up and down the street while reaching into his waistband for the chrome-plated 9-millimeter he kept on him at all times.

Talik didn't have to be told twice. When the shooting started, no one was safe, not even kids his age, who were sometimes even the shooters. He took one last look down at Fat Steve. The big kid wasn't breathing anymore. His eyes had fixed in place, and the snot dripping from his nose was now tinged with blood.

"Yo, I think Steve is dea—" Talik never got to finish his sentence. If he had, Freddy wouldn't have heard him. The wannabe Rastafarian's head exploded like a blood-filled water balloon. A thick hail of gore, shattered skull fragments, and chunks of brain matter rained down onto Talik. Freddy's body collapsed at his feet, landing beside Fat Steve's corpse like they had mutually decided it was nap time. The top of Freddy's head was gone from the bridge of the nose up.

Talik's feet began to move, running in the opposite direction of the gunfire. When he made it back to his home, he was winded more from screaming than running. He slammed the door shut and locked it behind him. His entire body was trembling while he sucked in huge gulps of air, trying to catch his breath.

"Boy, don't you be slamming my damn door!" his mother yelled before succumbing to a fit of coughing.

"Sorry, Mom! They shootin' out there! Freddy's dead! He got shot in the head!" Talik was wild-eyed and had still not caught his breath. Just the effort of speaking nearly caused him to black out. He bent over with his hands on his knees, inhaling deeply.

"Freddy? Oh, Lord no! Freddy was such a good man."

Talik didn't want to tell his mom all the rumors about Freddy on the streets. It wasn't right to speak ill of the dead. "Fat Steve is dead, too. The guy who stole your purse. The Tripps killed him."

His momma nodded solemnly. "Yeah, I been watching the news. Lots of folks dyin' all over the place from that Captain Trips. My job is shut down because everybody at the office got it. They dyin' left and right."

Talik stared at his mother intently. "But you okay, right? You ain't gonna die, right Momma?"

His mother reached out and rubbed Talik's head before gathering him into a hug. His tiny head nestled between his mother's mammoth breasts. He could hear that same wheezing and bubbling sound in her lungs he'd heard Fat Steve making. "You know your momma's too damn stubborn to die."

Talik nodded, but remained worried. Another fit of coughing racked her body. She covered her mouth and nose in the crook of her arm, soaking it with mucus and phlegm. She looked at the gooey mess, scowled, then wiped it off onto her pajama pants.

"I saw her again, Momma. I saw Mother Abagail," Talik said.

His mother scrunched up her face in a sneer of disgust. She coughed once more, dragging the sleeve of her blue and pink polka-dot house robe across her lips to wipe away the phlegm before smiling at Talik. "You mean the old Black woman you said looks like Nana?"

"Well, she doesn't really look like Nana. She just sort of feels like Nana. You know? When I dream about her, it feels the same as I used to feel when I was with Nana; you know I'm sayin'?" Talik said.

"Okay, well, I ain't seen her. But you can have your imaginary friend."

"She ain't imaginary. My friend Martin says he dreams about her sometimes. And his neighbor Monique dreams about her all the time. She said Mother Abagail is the one who warned her that her brother was going crazy and was gonna try an' kill all of 'em. She hid all the bullets or else he would have got 'em. He tried to kill their momma with a hammer."

His mother sneered again. "Well, enough with all that foolishness. I ain't seen no old Black woman in my dreams."

Talik frowned and huffed. "What do you dream about, then?"

She shuddered and pulled her robe tight to her neck to ward off a chill, despite the August heat and lack of air-conditioning. "Never you mind. Go upstairs and check on your brother. He's been sick all day. Ain't been out the bed since yesterday mornin'."

"Yes, Momma." Talik knew better than to argue with his mother. Even sick, he was sure she wouldn't have hesitated to take off her slipper and apply it to his backside.

The stairs leading up to the second floor had been constructed sometime during the Civil War, and Talik doubted they'd been maintained much since. The treads were warped and splitting. The landing had two holes in it just big enough for a small foot to slip into and twist an ankle. The handrail was loose, held in place at the top by two long screws his daddy had drilled into it. He doubted it would hold up to even his waifish adolescent weight if he needed it to prevent a fall. Whenever he walked up or down the stairs, Talik liked to imagine he was Indiana Jones on an adventure through a booby-trapped temple.

The second floor had two bedrooms, each not much larger than the average prison cell, with one big room on the third floor that had once been an attic but was now their mother's bedroom. At the end of the hallway on the second floor, a small bathroom with a tub, toilet, and sink—but no shower—served the entire home. The second-floor hallway was dark. The sole light fixture, a brass dome with clear glass and three bulbs that hugged the ceiling, had not worked for several months. The bathroom door was shut, as was the room he shared with his brother and the room his younger sister occupied, so no sunlight could get in anywhere.

Talik and his sister were the only ones in the house who weren't sick. His sister, Lawanda, was eighteen months younger than Talik, and his brother, Malcolm, was two years older. They were all extremely close. When one of them was sick, they all pitched in to care for them. For the last twenty-four hours, he'd heard the juicy wet coughs of his brother whenever he walked up the stairs. His mother said he had the flu, but that was before the news spread about the Tripps. Before Talik had begun dreaming about Mother Abagail.

The silence that greeted him as he walked down the hallway toward his brother's room made Talik feel like he was tiptoeing through a crypt on his way to the burial chamber. He heard his sister's singsong voice coming from her room, imitating the voices of her dolls as she guided them through conversations. Talik was grateful for the sound. It made the house feel less funereal. Even the sound of his mother's loud coughs coming from the kitchen was better than the void he faced beyond his brother's door.

Talik had seen many people die in his ten years on earth. Kids his age, some younger. Teenagers, adults, his friends' fathers and mothers. Lives abbreviated by gun violence or drug overdoses. He was well acquainted with the deathly emptiness that followed the end of a life, an echo of silence where sound should have been. That's what it felt like outside his brother's room now, like a body waiting to drop.

THE TRIPPS

His soft knock on the old warped wooden door with the cracked paint and rusted brass doorknob was loud as a gunshot in the emptiness of the hallway.

"Malcolm?" Talik could smell his brother's sickness wafting from the room, an acrid, darkly humid musk of funky sweat, vomit, and Vicks VapoRub. He opened the door and peeked his head in. That sick stench became nearly overpowering. "Malcolm? You awake?"

His brother's head was turned toward the closed window, staring blankly at the trees beyond. One of their favorite pastimes had been watching the squirrels chase each other through the branches. They'd even given them all names. Malcolm's breathing was shallow, a wheezing rattling sound like an old lawn mower engine had joined the bubbling sound coming from his chest as he labored to draw air in through the mucus clogging his lungs. Talik crept closer. He didn't want to get sick, but he didn't like the idea of his brother suffering all alone. People were dying from the Tripps. As much as he wanted to believe this was just a regular flu, he couldn't escape the image of Fat Steve drowning in his own fluids.

"You doing okay, bruh? Can I get you something?" Talik asked.

Malcolm continued to stare out the window. He hadn't blinked in several seconds.

"You still seeing Mother Abagail?" Malcolm finally asked.

"Yeah. I still see her."

"I see her, too, now. I can see her right now. She told me not to be scared." Malcolm turned his head to look at Talik. "And she told me to tell you to watch out for the Walkin Dude. She—" Malcolm began to cough. Snot and phlegm sprayed from his nose and mouth and dotted the window.

Talik stepped closer, then stopped, wary of catching the Tripps. He didn't know the exact process by which disease spread, but he didn't think getting Malcolm's snot all over him would be a good idea. There was nothing he could do for his brother anyway. Whether it was the flu or the Tripps, it had to work its course.

The coughing stopped and Malcolm returned to staring out the window. "She says the Walkin Dude is here—in this house. She says you should get out of here. You should go to her. Go to her . . ." Malcolm let out a long, rattling wheeze that bubbled up through his snotty nose and his phlegm-choked throat. Then his breathing stopped. His head lolled to the side; eyes still fixed on the window.

"Malcolm? Malcolm!" Talik fell to his knees at the foot of Malcolm's bed. Tears flooded from his eyes as his body jerked and hitched with sobs. He looked up through blurry eyes at his brother's face, then followed his gaze to the window. For a brief moment, he thought he saw the outline of the old woman from his dreams, then it was gone, and he was just staring at the squirrels, watching them leap from branch to branch only a few feet away from the window.

"What is it? What happened?" His sister, Lawanda, rushed in behind him, and Talik grabbed her and pulled her into his arms.

"Malcolm's gone."

"Noooo! Noooo! Malcoooolm! No-ho-ho!" Lawanda cried.

When Talik looked up, his mother was standing in the doorway. There was not a single tear in her eyes.

"I just got a call from your grandma. Your daddy's dead. He died about thirty minutes ago. The Tripps got 'im. Your grandma's sick, too," she said with no more emotion than if she'd been announcing the death of a mosquito. She began to cough again. Her eyes were yellow where they should have been white, with livid red capillaries forming a road map all over them. She still hadn't uttered a word about her dead son.

Talik's mouth dropped. The tears he'd shed for his brother were now joined by a fresh volley of tears for his deceased father. "Dad's dead?"

"Yeah, he wasn't worth shit nohow," his momma said.

"Momma! Momma, Malcolm's dead!" Lawanda cried.

"Yeah, I can see that. Y'all come on out of there before y'all get sick, too."

That was all she said. No words of comfort or sympathy. When Talik walked past her out of the room, he could have sworn he saw a smirk on her face. She shut the door behind them, then started back down the stairs.

"Dad's dead?" Lawanda asked her momma.

"That's what I said, ain't it?"

"Ain't you gonna call the ambalance?" Talik asked.

"For your daddy? Ain't nobody worried about his ass."

"For Malcolm!"

His mother paused on the stairs and turned her yellow eyes on Talik. She still wore a slight smirk that was half scowl, but her eyes were far away, the way they sometimes looked when she smoked too much weed. "You hear what's going on outside?"

Talik listened. Screams and gunshots, breaking glass, and angry shouts drifted in through the thin walls. It sounded like a full-scale riot. Either that or a war.

"Folks is goin' crazy out there. They's lootin' and killin', prolly rapin' folks, too. Ain't no ambalance comin' in here. Just leave 'im where he at till all this blows over. And don't go in there. Y'all stay in your sister's room." She began coughing again, then staggered a bit as she turned around and started back down the stairs.

Talik turned to his sister and saw the worry in her eyes.

"Is Momma sick?" Lawanda asked.

Talik nodded. "I think she might be. She'll be all right, though."

"Is she gonna die like Malcolm?"

"I said she'll be okay."

"She actin' strange, though."

Talik nodded again. He looked down the stairs, where his mother had reached the bottom. She turned and looked up at him, smiled and winked. Talik couldn't think of a single thing anyone should be smiling about right now.

"Come on, Lawanda. Let's go in your room."

Talik didn't know what was going on, but something was definitely off with his momma. He locked the door behind them. He couldn't stop thinking about what Malcolm said about Mother Abagail's warning.

The Walkin Dude is here—in this house.

A shrill, agonized scream sang out, chasing chills up Talik's spine and raising goose bumps. He looked at his sister, whose eyes were wide.

"That's Tonya!" she cried out as she raced to the window.

Talik followed quickly behind her. They opened the window and peered down into the street. There were so many people out it looked like a block party. They were breaking windows, kicking in doors, dragging people out onto the sidewalk, running out of homes with TVs, game consoles, whatever cash they could find, and whatever women they could grab. The attacks seemed random. Some homes were left untouched, while the house just two doors down was ransacked. A few were now on fire. On the pavement just below them, their neighbor Tonya was being stripped naked and beaten. Moose and Diesel, two known killers who were members of the Junior Black Mafia, seemed to be leading the horde of looters and vandals, directing the carnage and mayhem. They were attacking Tonya like two hungry jackals.

Tonya was their sometimes babysitter, but was still a kid herself, just barely fourteen. Too young for what those two violent thugs were attempting to do to her. Moose had his massive hands on her blouse, ripping it open and tearing it in half in the process, exposing the teenage girl's budding breasts. She clawed his face and tried to kick him in the balls, receiving an uppercut to the gut in response. The girl dropped to her knees on the hard pavement and fell over onto her side, curling into a fetal position, dry heaving. Talik could hear Moose laugh. Diesel stepped forward and began kicking and stomping her. His size thirteen Nikes came down hard on Tonya's ribs and the side of her face, knocking out several teeth and smearing her nose across her face like brown Play-Doh. Blood began to leak from her ears and nose as Diesel stomped her skull into the sidewalk.

THE TRIPPS

"They're killing her!" Lawanda yelled.

Talik put his hand over her mouth and pulled her back inside, hoping Moose and Diesel hadn't seen or heard her and that theirs would be one of the homes overlooked.

"Shhhh! We don't want them comin' in here!" Talik whispered, still cupping his sister's mouth. Her eyes were wide and wet with tears. The two huddled together below the edge of the window, listening to their neighbors' screams and pleas for help.

They recognized several voices. One was Mrs. Sonya, the old lady who lived across the street and made homemade ice cream for all the kids on the block each summer, selling it for a nickel a scoop. It sounded like she was being murdered.

"No! Don't hurt me no mo'! Y'all stop hittin' me! I ain't done nothin'! I ain't done nothin' to nobody! Come on, man. Stop! Stop! NOOOOO!!!" That was Nate Pratt, the big slow kid who lived just a few doors down. He was twenty-five, but still couldn't count his change or tie his own shoes. Talik dared another peek out the window and saw Esther and Tamika kicking and punching poor Nate. Tamika had a big kitchen knife and was stabbing Nate in between kicks and punches as he begged for his life. Esther and Tamika were two hoodrats who were known to trade pussy for crack. It was not uncommon to see them walking around with busted lips and black eyes courtesy of some mean trick. It was also not uncommon to see people in the hood who'd been abused redirect their trauma onto someone weaker and more vulnerable than themselves. Talik watched in horror as Nate succumbed to their assault, collapsing in a puddle of his own blood and urine. Lawanda tried to look, but Talik pushed her back down.

"Don't look. It's bad. You don't wanna see what's goin' on out there. Fools are goin' crazy, killin' everybody." Talik watched for a little while longer, until he saw the Jamaican posse round the corner, opening up with a street sweeper and an Uzi, mowing down everyone in sight, rioters and innocent people alike. Even looking down from the second-floor window, Talik could tell they were all sick. Snotty noses, yellow eyes, coughing and sniffling, but still coming. Esther and Tamika, Moose and Diesel, Tonya, Nate, even the Jamaicans. They were all leaking streams of snot and coughing up big wads of yellow mucus. They looked as bad as Talik's momma, but instead of staying home, lying in bed, and acquiescing to their imminent mortality, they'd chosen to hit the streets to settle old grudges and steal whatever they'd been coveting from their neighbors.

Talik pulled Lawanda down onto the floor and covered her with his body as bullets suddenly pierced the brick facade on the front of their house, blasting holes in the sheetrock, buzzing like angry hornets whizzing over their heads. Lawanda held her hands over her ears to dampen the sounds of gunfire and her own screams. Talik was screaming, too.

There was a firefight going on between the JBM and the Jamaicans right outside their door. *The whole world is dying, and niggas is still tryin' to kill each other*, Talik thought. He wondered if the poor white and Puerto Rican neighborhoods were going through the same shit. He'd seen Kensington, Manayunk, and Fishtown on the news many times. From what he could tell, they were no better than G-Town when it came to poor folks killing poor folks. If people were murdering each other in his little neighborhood, they were probably doing it all over the city. The City of Brotherly Love had become the City of Bodily Harm.

The gunfire ended as abruptly as it had begun, and silence descended with the suddenness of a summer storm. The meaty metallic scent of blood and organs mixed with the burning sulfur of gun smoke and chalky sheetrock dust, irritating Talik's eyes and tickling the back of his throat. He crawled off of his sister and checked her for wounds.

"You okay, sis? You hurt anywhere?"

Lawanda continued to sob as she shook her head no. "I'm okay. I didn't get hit."

Talik looked her over from head to toe until he was satisfied she was uninjured, then he returned to the windowsill and risked another look down at the street. Bodies were everywhere. Some people had managed to hide behind cars or duck low enough to the ground to avoid getting hit, but they were few. Most folks had been mowed down right where they stood. Incredibly, Moose was still alive, though Diesel's chest had been hollowed out with shotgun blasts. Esther, Tamika, Tonya, and Nate were all dead.

"Momma!" Lawanda called. Talik felt a twinge of shame. He had forgotten all about his mother. "Momma, you okay?" There was no answer. Talik joined in the call.

"Mom!" His voice sounded like a trumpet blast in the stillness left in the wake of the mini-gang war. Still there was no reply. Talik walked over to the door and put his ear to it. He closed his eyes and listened. At first, he heard nothing, then a familiar voice filled his ears, one he'd only heard before in his dreams. It wasn't coming from the other side of the door but from his thoughts. Mother Abagail.

Run, child! Get out of there! The Walkin Dude is here. He's got yo momma. The Walkin Dude has yo momma!

Talik leapt back away from the door, startled. He'd heard Mother Abagail's voice as clearly as if she'd been standing beside him.

"Did you hear that?" he asked Lawanda.

She scowled and raised an eyebrow quizzically while wiping tears from her eyes.

"Hear what?" They both listened and all they could hear were the wails and moans of the injured on the street below, the screams and cries of their loved ones, and more gunfire and sirens in the distance. "They's still killin' people out there?"

Talik waived off her question. "Not that—that voice. It was Mother Abagail. Did you hear her?"

"Who's Mother Abagail?" Lawanda asked, scowling even harder now.

"The old Black lady that sits on the porch of, like, this old farmhouse in the middle of nowhere. I see her in my dreams sometimes.

She tells me to sit on the porch beside her in this old wooden rocking chair. She pours me a glass of sweet tea. It's sweet like Kool-Aid and cold as a slushie. I sit there beside her and she tells me things that's gonna happen. She told me it wasn't safe in this house. That we gotta leave. She wants us to go to Nebraska."

Lawanda wiped away the last of her tears and coughed sheetrock dust from her lungs. Her perplexed expression remained. "You buggin', bro. Why would I be seeing some old chick that you be dreamin' 'bout?"

Talik shrugged. "I don't know. Lots of people dream about her. Malcolm told me he saw her before he died."

"And she said we need to go to Nebraska? How we supposed to get to Nebraska? Momma ain't takin' us to no Nebraska." Lawanda was looking at him like he'd lost his fool mind.

"Never mind. Let's just go check on Momma."

Talik unlocked the bedroom door and crept out into the hallway. There were bullet holes in the walls. High-velocity rounds had not only penetrated the front exterior wall but had flown through the bedroom wall and into the hallway.

"Momma?" Lawanda said in a quiet voice, as if afraid to disturb the silence. Talik wondered if it was out of respect for the dead. They reached the top of the stairs and Talik heard his mother's voice.

"I can't. Don't ask me to do that, Mr. Flagg. Them's my babies. I can't kill my own flesh. No. I won't. I— Okay. Okay. No. I understand. I'll do what needs doin'. I promise."

Talik had started down the stairs, but froze midway down when he saw his mother pacing back and forth in the kitchen talking to no one. The phone was still on the hook. Her eyes had that weepy yellow look, pupils dilated like she'd just hit the crack pipe. She was bleeding. Her shirt was soaked red from below her left tit all the way down her pants leg. She'd been shot, but hardly seemed to notice. Her movements were herky-jerky as she paced the kitchen talking to herself. Talking about killing them. Finally, she stopped and turned her head toward her children. Her gaze landed on Talik, went straight through him, then turned to Lawanda.

"Come here, kids," she said, smiling while removing a big carving knife from the kitchen drawer. Talik began backing up the stairs, pushing his sister behind him. His mother walked toward the stairs, holding the knife out in front of her, smiling like a lunatic.

"Momma? What's wrong, Momma? You ain't gonna hurt us, is you?" She didn't respond, just continued to smile as she walked closer to the stairs, to her kids. Talik looked beyond her at the front door, but it was too late to make a run for it now. They would never get past her. Going back up the stairs had been a mistake. He'd trapped them both.

"What's wrong, Momma? What's wrong?" Lawanda yelled. Her voice cracked with fear.

Their mother's steps became more rapid. When she reached the stairs, she sprinted toward them, raising the big kitchen knife above her head as she closed the distance, taking the stairs two at a time.

"Run! Go! Go!" Talik yelled, pushing Lawanda up the stairs and into the hallway, careful to avoid the holes in the landing.

Their mother's foot fell through one of the holes, and they heard her curse, but it barely slowed her down. She yanked her foot free, scraping skin from her ankle, then continued the chase. Talik could hear his mother's footsteps and ragged, wheezing breaths right behind them. He heard her succumb to another coughing fit. This time, her footsteps paused. Talik and Lawanda kept running. They dashed down the hall and back into Lawanda's room, slamming the door and locking it. Seconds later, there was a loud *boom* as their mother crashed into the door, cracking it down the center.

"Y'all kids get out here! Get your asses out here, I said! Y'all listen to your momma! Get your little bad asses out here this minute!"

"No! You ain't right, Momma! I heard you talkin' to yourself—talkin' about killin' us!"

There was a moment of silence, and Talik could hear what sounded like weeping.

"I don't want to kill you both. Mr. Flagg said all I had to do was kill you, Talik. I kill you and he'll let Lawanda live. He'll let us all live. He just wants you."

"Who's Mr. Flagg? Why you listenin' to him? Why you lettin' somebody tell you to kill me?" Talik said.

The reply came as a whisper through the door.

"He knows about Mother Abagail. He knows you been talkin' to her."

Talik froze.

"He knows you been talkin' to Mother Abagail," she repeated.

"Help me push the dresser in front of the door! Talik! Help me!" Lawanda said. The tip of their mother's knife slid between the door and the doorjamb , jabbing and slicing, trying to stab anything she could reach. "Talik, come on! Help!"

Talik shook himself back to reality, a reality more surreal than his dreams and nightmares. He ran over to help his sister, and together they slid a large dresser across the room to barricade the door.

"What's wrong with her, Talik? Why is she doin' this?"

"I—I don't know," Talik said. "She said she been talkin' to some dude named Flagg. She said he wants me dead because I been talkin' to Mother Abagail."

"That old woman you tol' me about that wants us to go to Nebraska?"

"She only said me," Talik said quietly. "She said she wants me to go to Nebraska. She—she never mentioned you. That's why Momma only wants to kill me. She'd probably let you go."

"I ain't goin' out there with her crazy ass! What the fuck is goin' on, Talik?"

Talik shook his head. "It don't make no sense. None of it makes sense. People dyin' of the Tripps. Rest of 'em out there shootin' each other. Our own mother tryin' to kill us. It don't make no damn sense."

Their mother began chopping at the door with the knife. Talik had seen their father put his foot through a door the day their momma finally kicked him out, so he knew the doors were hollow and not worth a damn. Her knife sank through the wood like it was cardboard. She stabbed it again and again, weakening it to the point that she'd have no problem punching a fist through the fragile tapestry of splinters that remained.

Talik looked out the window. They could jump, the fall wasn't too great, and there were still bodies below they could land on. But Talik didn't know if that would be better or worse than hitting the concrete, and then where would they go? What if either one of them broke a leg or twisted an ankle in the fall? Then they would be helpless.

He looked around the room for something to fight his mother with; a thought that would have seemed insane just a few minutes ago and still boggled his mind. Their mother was trying to kill them. There was nothing. No weapons. In the room he shared with Malcolm, they had a baseball bat, nunchucks, ninja stars, and even a samurai sword. But his sister's room had only worn stuffed animals, busted thrift store Barbie dolls, and moth-eaten lace curtains. *The curtains!* Talik thought. Maybe they could use the curtain rods as weapons?

Hopping up onto his sister's bed, Talik tore down the curtain rods on both windows, hefting them in his hand to test the weight before tossing one to Lawanda and keeping one for himself. The rod was heavy, made of wrought iron. It would do.

The door was completely destroyed now. Their mother kicked the cracked wood, and it fell apart with little resistance.

"You badass kids shoulda listened when I tol' y'all to come out. We coulda done this quick," she said, reaching through the hole she'd made in the door and unlocking it before pushing the dresser out of the way. She coughed that strangled death rattle, not bothering to cover her mouth anymore. Flecks of bloody phlegm splattered Talik, and he winced in disgust.

"Stop, Momma. Please stop. You don't have to do this!" Tears streamed from Talik's eyes.

"I'm sorry, baby, but you have to die. The whole world's dyin'. If I kill you, Mr. Flagg says he'll save us. Me and your sister. Can't you understand that? We have to sacrifice you for the family."

She stepped forward, and Talik swung the curtain rod at her head, catching her right above the temple and opening up a huge gash. She staggered. Blood leaked from the wound into her eye, but she kept coming forward, knife still gripped firmly, jabbing at the air between them.

"I'm so sorry, Momma." Talik swung again and again. Lawanda was swinging her curtain rod now as well, beating their mother in the head until she finally fell to her knees, still gripping the big carving knife, eyes fixed on Talik. Her head began to come apart. Blood rained down her face, forming a mask of gore and turning her blue and white polka-dot robe red and purple. She collapsed onto the floor and began to convulse. Her body bucked and kicked, fighting to hold on to her spirit.

"Just die, Momma. Please, just die!" Talik said, choking on sobs.

Lawanda reached down and retrieved the knife from the floor. She wasn't crying anymore, wasn't screaming. She calmly walked over, straddling her dying mother. She reached down and seized a fistful of her mother's permed hair.

"Lawanda? What are you doing?" Talik asked, watching his eight-year-old baby sister jerk their mother's head back and slit her throat, unzipping the flesh and opening a yawning pink maw where smooth brown skin had been. More blood cascaded from the wound, raining down like a red waterfall.

Lawanda sat down on top of her mother. Her eyes were blank. She still held the knife in her hands.

"Come on, sis. Let's get outta here," Talik said quietly, reaching out for his sibling and taking her hand, helping her to her feet.

Talik guided his little sister out of the room, sparing one last look at his mother's battered corpse. Lawanda was in shock. Her eyes were still wide and glazed, and she was mumbling quietly to herself. Talik

THE TRIPPS

couldn't believe Lawanda slit her own mother's throat. It was as hard to believe as him beating her half to death with a curtain rod, or that she'd tried to kill them—him.

They walked down the stairs and out the front door. Talik stepped over Tonya's and Diesel's bullet-riddled carcasses. Moose was gone. Probably crawled into some hole to die. Screams, gunshots, and sirens continued to echo in the distance. Billowing black clouds of smoke and ash choked the air as the neighborhood burned. There was nothing for them here anymore.

Talik looked back at his sister, who had fallen behind, still staring off into space, mumbling and whispering. A trickle of snot dripped from her nose, and she began to cough, not bothering to cover her mouth. She had the Tripps. She began whispering again. Talik stopped in his tracks as he finally made out what she was saying.

Mother Abagail had warned him the Walkin Dude was in their house. He hadn't understood what she'd been trying to tell him, but now he put it all together. Mr. Flagg and the Walkin Dude were one and the same. He wiped a tear from his eye as he watched his little sister slowly raise the knife, aiming it at the center of his chest.

"Don't worry, Mr. Flagg," she whispered. "He'll never make it to Nebraska."

BRIGHT LIGHT CITY

Meg Gardiner

Las Vegas, *June 1990*

"Close the cabin door. Close it." The gate agent sprinted aboard the United 737. "Close it, *close it*."

Startled, Danielle Cooper scrambled alongside another flight attendant to pull the door shut. She swung the handle and locked it as a horde of people charged down the jetway toward the plane.

"Oh my God." Dani backed into the galley, beside the wild-eyed gate agent. Outside, faces crowded the window and hands pounded on the door.

The captain came over the PA. "*Cabin crew, be seated for departure.*"

The hell? Back in economy, passengers still packed the aisle, struggling toward their seats. The cockpit door was open, the captain coughing heavily, the first officer shaky and slick with sweat. Dani gaped at the gate agent.

The woman violently shook her head. "I'm not getting off this plane."

Dani raised her hands. They were already pushing back from

the gate. On the jetway, the throng undulated forward like a python. Shoved, people at the front plummeted to the tarmac.

Sweet mother. She hurried to close the cockpit door and saw a man in a suit leap from the jetway onto the nose of the plane.

The captain barked, "*Judas shitting Priest!*"

Suit Guy landed with a metallic thud and salamandered up the windshield to grab the wipers.

The pushback tractor swung the jet around. Suit Guy shouted, lost his grip, and slid off. Dani shut the cockpit door and strapped into a jump seat.

Why did I take this flight assignment?

Yeah. Scheduling had begged. *Bonus. Big one. We can't fill rosters. Everyone's out sick.* Plus, whiny boyfriend in Seattle. Time for *buh-bye*.

The engines spooled up. Their howl couldn't drown out the coughing that filled the cabin, the moans, the feverish craziness. The gate agent strapped into the seat beside Dani. Uniform torn, a slap mark reddening her cheek.

She muttered, "C'mon, let's go let's go let's go."

Dani was adept at soothing nervous passengers, but the agent's jitters leached into her. She peered out the window as they taxied to the runway, saw bronzed mountains, heat shimmer, a cobalt sky boiling with thunderheads.

And the pushback tractor, racing after them. Suit Guy at the wheel.

Holy God. The jet turned onto the runway and immediately accelerated. Dani stretched to scan outside, thinking, *We're clear, we're good*, hearing the gate agent chant, "Go go go," and saw the tractor cut across the taxiway, across the dirt, aiming to intercept them. Her mouth dropped. Suit Guy thought he could wrangle a 160,000-pound airliner, jump onto the wing or grab the landing gear like a cowboy wrestling a steer . . .

Come on, come on, take off. She urged the wheels to lift, but heard a shout from the cockpit and a monstrous *bang* as the tractor clipped the fuselage. It caromed into the left engine. The explosion shook the jet. Shrapnel shredded the cabin wall.

The airliner raked over the tractor at 150 mph, skidding, people screaming. Dani yelled, "Brace! Brace!" They slid off the runway, dust flying. *We're all dead.*

That was when she saw the little girl.

Chocolate-syrup pigtails, a pink backpack. Unaccompanied minor. Dani had handed her stick-on wings when she boarded. Mollie—eleven years old, going to see her dad in San Francisco.

Mollie with the huge brown eyes pinned on her.

"Brace!"

Mollie ducked.

Bam, they jolted to a stop. Silence. Then crackling. The left wing was burning. Dani unbuckled, adrenalized, heard a weak order from the cockpit: "*Evacuate.*"

Right main door open. Slide deployed. Yelling, "*Leave your carry-ons behind!*" Passengers staggered, shoving, some skittering over the seats like spiders, but many stayed seated, disbelieving. As though the plane could still take off, someone shouted, "Get back on the runway!"

The gate agent sat paralyzed. "No, no, no." A screaming man flailed up the aisle toward the cockpit, with—*Whoa, crap*—a machete raised overhead.

Behind him, Mollie fought to stay on her feet against stampeding adults.

Dani elbowed her way to the little girl, hauled her to the exit, and practically tossed her onto the slide. Then a man slammed into Dani like Mike Singletary sacking a passer and she flew out the door, plunged face-first down the slide, and hit the sandy dirt.

Flames towered and roared. Heat, smoke, insanity. The little girl climbed to her feet.

Mollie Tajima. That was her name. Dani grabbed her hand and ran.

Fifty yards clear, sixty, *seven Mississippi*. A fireball consumed the jet, booming across the desert afternoon, and knocked them flat.

She turned to the little girl. "You okay?"

"Yeah." Flames shivered in Mollie's eyes. "Are they all like this?"

"Honey?"

"Plane crashes. This is my first one."

No fire trucks were coming.

The terminal was anarchy. Podiums overturned; boarding doors locked. Superflu casualties. A Cinnabon cashier was stuffed in a trash can. Mid-concourse a grandmotherly woman on a mobility scooter sat at a slot machine, cigarette to her lips, shoving quarters in as if feeding a ravenous god.

The security checkpoint was unstaffed. That explained the machete. Check-in desks were abandoned. Dani tried a phone. United didn't answer.

She squeezed Mollie's shoulder. "We'll call your mom."

"She's on her way to Mexico. With her boyfriend. Until this is over?"

This. Over. Damn. "Then let's get hold of your dad."

"Please."

Dani phoned the girl's father. Nothing. "Who else is here? Who can we call?"

Mollie's voice quavered. "There's just me."

Outside the terminal, Dani hailed a cab. It was waiting there in the blistering sunshine because who the hell wanted to go *into* Vegas now? The driver had black stripes beneath his watery eyes, but could steer. At the corner of Las Vegas Boulevard, he squeezed past an overturned school bus. SANTA BARBARA SCHOOL DISTRICT inside the windshield, a Volkswagen Beetle smashed beneath it. He dropped them at Mollie's apartment building.

It was on fire.

"Like the plane," Mollie said. She jerked a breath. "My books."

Dani put an arm around the girl's shoulders. Calming-Dani was in charge, but Freaked-as-shit-Dani pulsed just beneath her skin. Airline, gone. Dad, MIA. Mom, fleeing to an unidentified beach in Baja.

Yeah, she herself had fled Seattle. But that was to ghost wheedling, needling Scott, an adult man, forty-eight hours ago when bonus pay for a SeaTac–Chicago–Las Vegas–San Francisco trip sounded infinitely easier than telling him, *Dude, we're over*. She wouldn't forsake this kid, with her heat-pink cheeks and coltish limbs and rock-solid misunderstanding that grown-ups were in charge.

No. She'd take her to a friend's house.

Bad idea.

Then: a teacher's house. Then Child Protective Services. The police. A church.

Snake eyes.

Near sunset, Dani found a motel three blocks off the Strip, its office unattended, room keys hanging on a pegboard. She scooped them up.

"Wait here," she told Mollie.

She unlocked Room 1 and froze. A couple lay entwined on the bed surrounded by empty bottles of Stoli and Jim Beam. They'd died with their boots on and nothing else.

Dani had once seen a billboard: ENSLAVED TO LUST? JESUS HAS THE ANSWER. It seemed this couple had gone to ask him for it, mid-thrust. Guns in their hands, blood on the walls.

Mollie walked up behind her. Dani slammed the door.

She took a room across the parking lot, empty and clean. They showered, got vending machine Cokes and snacks.

The TV lasted through six *Green Acres* reruns before collapsing into a test pattern. The phone system died an hour later. Mollie's dad had never answered.

Dani sat down beside the girl on the lumpy bed. This might sound brutal, but she had to ask. "Your mom—you think she'll come back? If she can?"

"She'll come. If. She'll . . ." Tears shimmered in Mollie's eyes. Then they spilled. Her shoulders heaved. She buried her face in her hands.

Dumbass. Dani pulled Mollie close and rocked her until the tears ebbed, then tucked her in. "Sleep, kid. We've had a day."

But at midnight Dani lay awake, listening to Mollie's exhausted breathing. The city outside was unnaturally silent. No laughter. No cars. No planes. No helicopters.

Somebody had to come, right? The National Guard. Wayne Newton. Siegfried and Roy. The Rat Pack would save her.

She pressed a hand over her mouth to stifle a sob.

What was she going to do with a sixth-grader at the end of the world?

Elvis Presley, pray for us.

The motel had no café. Restaurants were toast, the nearest grocery store a wasteland. Finally, the next evening, Mollie was the one who said, "We'll go to the kitchen at the Desert Inn."

Her mom worked there as a waitress. "Sometimes she brings dinner home. Leftover lasagna. Pie. Lobster once."

The walk was eerie in the evening sunshine. Cars were wrecked along the Strip, beneath lights that glittered and danced, harlequin bright, enticing an empty city to come play. Distantly Dani saw one other person—a stooped man shuffling along the gutter, stabbing litter with a steel-tipped stick. She waved, but he carried on, engrossed, as if performing a ritual.

The Desert Inn hotel kitchen was derelict, but the walk-in fridge fully stocked. Dani fried up fat burgers, and nearly cried with joy at the taste. She suppressed thoughts of the rooms stacked overhead, ripe with dead gamblers.

"Ice cream sundae?" she said.

Mollie beamed—and the lights went out.

The refrigerator hum, the air-conditioning, every mechanical background noise, died. Mollie squeaked.

"Emergency generator will kick on in a minute," said Calming-Dani.

The kitchen stayed dark. *Dark* dark.

"Sorry, kid. We'll have to skip the sundaes."

Hand out in front of her, Dani led Mollie through the kitchen's swinging doors into the hotel restaurant. Like any reputable casino, it had no windows. She gingered her way forward in the blue twilight filtering through the hotel's main doors.

From across the casino came a crashing sound. Something had fallen over. Dani spun and caught a glimpse of a shape—a man. Tall, swift. Big guy.

"Let's go." She grabbed Mollie's hand and pulled her through the restaurant.

"No—this way." Mollie zigzagged in a new direction. "You look scared."

"Nah." Petrified. Dani broke into a jog.

"You're cold. It's bad, right?"

"We're good. Faster."

They shoved through the hotel doors, onto the street. The Strip lay in darkness.

Dani nearly stumbled from shock. The absence. The silence. Her feet kept moving.

"Oh," Mollie said.

A shroud had fallen. Stillness, uselessness, a void. Dani felt a strange pressure in her chest. They needed to get back to the motel.

"You *are* scared."

"Just . . . surprised." She held tight to Mollie's hand and began to hum.

Mollie hurried along beside her, quick small steps, her hand hot. "I know that song. Everybody who comes here sings it."

"I bet."

Bright light city gonna—

Out of the dark, headlights rose. A car, cruising, slowly.

Mollie slowed. "Somebody's here!"

But Dani pulled her behind a hedge. The car neared—a BMW, its engine a silky rumble.

The driver was young, blond, with rock star hair kicking in the wind beneath a sequin-studded cowboy hat. Her hand was draped out the window, eyes scanning the street. Shadows filled the passenger seats. Static poured from the radio.

Dani swallowed. The static chewed the air.

"We don't want to talk to them," Mollie said. It wasn't a question.

"Come on." Dani pulled her away from the street.

―――

Around four a.m., multiple engines roared up the street past the motel. Brakes squealed. Dani stole to the window. Heard screams.

At sunrise, while Mollie slept, she slipped out and crept up the block. Broken headlight glass. Blood in the gutter. Looked like somebody had been hit by a car.

A late-afternoon thunderstorm washed it away.

―――

The day after, more people appeared. Healthy. Stunned. Blinking like baby birds. Numb. Or giddy and broken. A woman shambled past the motel in a red business suit and pearls, her Afro dusty.

"Wait here," Dani told Mollie. "Don't open the door unless it's me."

Her name was Sharon. She'd come to Vegas for a realtors' convention. Her vacant expression suggested that her psyche had taken repeated shots from a Taser.

"Incredible inventory available now," she said, and laughed, and began to weep.

Dani made comforting sounds, Calming-Dani sounds. The sun beat down. Then Sharon looked around. Weirdly. Expectantly.

She leaned in and lowered her voice. "It's coming."

"What is?" Rescue? A plague of frogs? Cher?

"It'll be soon. Can't you feel it?"

Dinnertime, Dani and Mollie found a mini-mart. The food in the fridge/freezer section was still chilled. Dani was grabbing cold cuts when, with an electric *whoosh*, a mobility scooter turned into the aisle.

It was the gambler—the woman from the slot machine at the airport. Cat-eye sunglasses, cigarette in her mouth. She stopped, and her glare convinced Dani she had a .22 in her purse.

Then, taking in Dani's airline uniform, she softened. "Not the layover you had planned, is it?" She looked at Mollie. "Summer vacation, either."

"I live here," Mollie said.

"Same." She stuck out her hand. "Eleanor."

She was a court clerk. She had planned to fly to Louisville to ride out the superflu at her sister's. But here she was.

Dani said, "You hear the cars last night?"

"Saw 'em." Eleanor grabbed beef jerky from a rack, tore open the package, and wrestled a strip loose with her teeth. "Nasty business."

"You're calm," Dani said.

"You too."

"Calm and perky. I've trained for it."

Eleanor shrugged. "Necessity's a mother. TV's fried, my soap's off the air. I'll never know which twin is carrying the archbishop's secret baby." Her shoulders dropped. "My poker group is dead."

She looked away, then rallied and grabbed a second pack of jerky. "I'm pacing myself."

"This store won't last too long."

Her face was in shadow. "Looters up and died, honey. It's just us now." She squinted out the door. "Us and *them*."

"You mean that young woman in the BMW? She listens to static. Like it's calling to her."

"Sounds about right."

"What does she want? Everything you could desire is suddenly, freely, available."

Eleanor's expression sharpened. "'He who dies with the most toys wins.' Well, keeping score with toys ain't fun anymore. Makes her angry." She pursed her lips. "The world burned, but she didn't light the match, and that makes her angry, too. She don't create—she *inflicts*. That's what she wants."

Dani stilled. "Sounds like you know who she is."

"I'm a juvenile court clerk. She made multiple appearances."

Dani urged Mollie to go find comic books and paperbacks. She edged closer to Eleanor. "Theft? Prostitution?"

"She's a rich girl, not a street kid. She pulled the claws out of a kitten with pliers. Threw muriatic acid on a girl in school. Expected never to face consequences. And didn't."

"That's . . . horrifying." And alarming. A red-alert threat.

"Daddy's lawyers got her community service. And then . . ." She waved her cig at the world. *This happened*. "Her name's Amber. Think of her as . . . Amber waves of pain."

She scanned the street, the maddened world that felt like a set of teeth coming at them.

"If you leave, don't let anyone see you go. This place will fire back up, but till it does, Amber and her crew can set the rules, and declare your existence a crime they get to punish."

Them—off-kilter, but finally finding their axis. One that spun toward night.

"Maybe it's safer to stay."

"It's not. And forget the notion that Miss Mollie could stay here with me while you split. I ain't up to it."

Dani felt a brush of shame. She tried to hide it.

"When I say watch out," Eleanor said, "I mean they're putting bounties on folks who try to leave. Be careful who you tell, who sees you."

"Bounties."

She gripped Dani's wrist. "Hear me, girl. Take care, 'cause people will snitch on you."

Hiking back to the motel, a cold stone seemed to lodge in Dani's throat. Amber was doing more than watching shit burn. She was prepping.

It's coming. Soon. Can't you feel it?

Something was inbound and Amber wanted to be ready for it. To have . . . *offerings*. Spoils that would prove her chops and buy her a place in a new power structure.

The next day Dani saw a spray-painted billboard. *EXIT FEE = $10,000.*

Her stomach knotted. Below that, on the wall of a building: *OR UNTOUCHD YOUNG BLOOD TENDER.*

Beneath that: *OR ELSE.*

On the dirt below lay the man who walked the Strip picking up litter. His trash-poking stick was stabbed into his neck like a whaling harpoon.

That night she and Mollie climbed to the roof of the Mirage. Distantly they saw a patrol on dirt bikes chasing down people in the desert. Headlights, circling, screams, gunfire.

Dani felt the impulse, visceral. *Take wing.*

Back in the oppressive heat of the motel room, she sat at the window eyeing the chittering night. She desperately missed Seattle. Mollie lay hard asleep in the moonlight.

Dani wasn't her mother, her teacher, her social worker. She half thought that the girl looked up to her because she wore a uniform. A now funky, grime-streaked airline uniform. She needed to get the girl help. Shelter. Something. Something other than herself.

Covers rustled. Mollie sat up and hugged her knees, eyes dark. "You're thinking about leaving, aren't you?"

"No!" That was exactly what she was thinking. "I would never leave—"

"Because we can't stay here. We have to go."

We. "This is your home. I could stay, a while. See if help arrives. The power comes back on, phones. Don't you want—"

"Staying isn't safe."

They stared at each other. Mollie seemed to vibrate with urgency.

"Then we leave," Dani said.

In the morning, the first of July, they hit Big 5 Sporting Goods. They needed clothing, camping gear, bikes.

Weapons.

The store was cavernous, shadowy, a cornucopia. Aisle by aisle, they loaded a shopping cart. Then, rounding a display, a rustling noise stopped Dani cold.

In the HUNTING ARMS section, a young man was foraging behind the counter. Dark hair, broad shoulders. His T-shirt sported a great white shark. He spun and shined a flashlight in her face.

He'd beaten her to the guns. So far she'd only picked up a USMC tactical knife. She set her hand on it.

He aimed the flashlight at Mollie, and back. *Kid and flight attendant.* Killing the light, he spread his hands. "Startled me. We cool?"

Not a grown man—a teenager. Dani kept her hand on the knife.

Mollie stared with X-ray focus, then relaxed. "You were at the Desert Inn when the power went out."

"That was you?" He lifted his chin, giving her an *All right*. "Those burgers smelled bitchin'."

He hopped over the counter. "And we're too late. The guns are cleaned out."

A voice in Dani's head said, *Really?* This kid was quick, agile, bright-eyed. His T-shirt said SANTA BARBARA SWIM CLUB. Dani kept her hand on the knife.

Mollie said, "Are you from California?"

"I was here with my team for a meet. I'm Jesse. Blackburn."

Mollie touched a hand to her heart. "Mollie. Tajima."

It clicked. Dani remembered. "The bus. 'Santa Barbara School District.' It was—"

"Somebody hit us," Jesse said. "The bus driver was sick, couldn't hold it. We flipped onto a VW, crushed it . . . " He looked pained.

"Hit you?"

"Deliberately." His expression darkened. "Some girl. In a BMW. Driving down the road sideswiping people."

A chill scissored down Dani's back. "Was she wearing a spangled cowboy hat?"

"Yeah. Huge hair. Like the singer from Poison."

Amber.

Mollie looked up at Jesse. "Are you going home?"

He paused. "That's my plan."

Snitch.

Snitch—don't let him out of here.

"Across the desert?" Dani said. "How?"

"Dirt bike, if I can get gas. Otherwise . . . " He jerked a thumb at the mountain bikes.

"How old are you?"

"Seventeen."

He said *seventeen* like it meant *bulletproof*. He was tall, strong, his blue eyes sharp, his hair shiny with that chlorine sheen that swimmers got. And oh my God too young.

"Did you win?" Mollie said. "At the meet?"

His voice turned somber. "Hugely. Doesn't matter now."

He was in this store solo, Dani thought—but that didn't mean he was alone. "Anybody else from the bus make it?"

He shook his head.

Did she believe him? The knife felt alive in her hand.

She'd had self-defense training. Mostly it was aimed at disabling unruly drunks. Neutralize them, with passenger backup if necessary. Zip-tie their wrists, restrain them until the plane landed. But she'd practiced more. Throw scalding coffee in an attacker's face. Jab an ice pick into his eye.

If it's you or them, make it them. Dani's palm, gripping the knife, was slick.

Mollie's X-ray gaze targeted Jesse. "You shouldn't go back to California."

"Why?" he said.

Mollie blinked and began kneading her fingers together. After a second he crouched down, getting to eye level with her.

"Going west means we'll die, doesn't it?" he said.

Mollie hupped a breath and whispered, "Yes."

"But if we stay . . . "

"Worse."

He parsed her demeanor. She was buzzing at a quantum frequency. "You dreamed it?"

Nodding hard, Mollie crouched down as well, her brown eyes pinned on his face.

"Me too." His voice quieted. "I'm at sea, swimming toward shore. I thought it meant I was supposed to come home to the coast. But I'm about to get pulled under by a riptide." He paused, forced his voice to stay even. "Because home is gone, isn't it?"

"All gone."

Anguish broke across his face. He squeezed his eyes shut. When he opened them again, they held acceptance. Mollie spoke truth. Dani was shocked at how quickly he absorbed it.

"The sea," he said. "Last night, it was bright. It's a sea of green. But—"

"It's corn," Mollie whispered. "The sea. Cornfields."

His intake of breath was like a slowly rising wave. "And I heard..."

"Her voice?" Mollie's chin quivered, with—relief? Connection?

He nodded. Mollie's eyes were deep and wide. She mouthed, *Mayhap.*

Jesse held her gaze, then turned to Dani. "We have to go."

He stood. Mollie followed suit. Their faces had the certainty of saints who'd been confronted by angels. Or devils.

Dani inhaled. "But not west."

Mollie slowly shook her head.

Dani deflated. San Francisco. Santa Barbara. Seattle. If not there, where?

Kill him.

Where the *fuck* did that voice come from? Hissing, inside her head.

Stab him in the ribs.

Dani gasped. Mollie stared at her in the half-light—confused, then frightened.

Her eyes widened. "No, no, Dani, no."

Dani scrutinized Jesse. She wanted to run from this city. To flee, to fly. But if he was a snitch...

Mollie started to cry. "Stop, Dani, no!"

He'll talk, you'll die.

She glared at him. "You know who that girl is, don't you? Amber. Did you talk to her? You know how to find her?"

Snitchhhhhh.

"Yeah. That's right. *Snitch*. That you?"

Jesse tensed. "What the hell?"

"Answer the question."

Mollie reached toward her. "He's good, he's okay, *who is talking to you?*"

The knife hung in Dani's hand, blade catching the light. Jesse coiled. The thoughts behind his eyes seemed to race. *Bolt. Get gone, stay gone.* Then he looked at Mollie. He held steady.

He was either an all-pro liar, or was genuinely more worried for Mollie than for his own safety.

Kill him and live? Believe him and die? Or—

A sea of green.

Dani backed against a shelf, tears stinging her eyes. She threw the knife to the floor.

Mollie rushed to her. Cheeks hot, eyes frightened. Dani hugged her.

"I'm okay. It's okay. We're cool."

But nothing was cool. Something—some*body*—wanted her to kill this boy, then to stay in Vegas with Mollie, terrorized and frozen.

She pressed the back of her hand to her mouth. Bugs seemed to scurry under her skin. "We have to go. Together. *Today.*" Before that voice returned, that silky hiss, and tried to feed on her again.

"Righteous," Jesse said. "Let's do it."

Dani straightened and wiped her eyes. "If not west, south? Mexico?"

Mollie turned to the windows, looking east. Jesse said, "Over the Rockies."

"Fuck me," Dani said.

⁓

They packed up. Food, water. Hiking boots. Bikes. Dani fitted Mollie's helmet. Jesse snagged gas station maps and plotted a route in red marker. It would avoid main roads, winding through residential neighborhoods and past silent warehouses to a state road that eventually intersected I-15. The kid was not just strong, but smart and organized. Solid. Older than his years.

Survival tempered you.

"I scoped out two gun stores," he said. "Both were stripped clean. One had 'Eat me, bitches,' spray-painted on the door."

"Poetry."

"I wrote, 'Not without a tetanus shot' underneath it."

Or maybe he was born sarcastic.

They waited until nightfall. Leaving the motel, Dani paused to gaze into the star-freckled darkness of the western sky. She had clung to the fiction that her family and friends were alive in Seattle. That the cavalry would come—the literal 1st Cavalry, helicopters thrumming.

Mollie changed that. And now Jesse. Two kids, anchoring her in reality.

"Let's go," she said.

They rode side by side under gaudy moonlight. After several miles, Dani murmured, "It's like being guided by Elvis's jumpsuit."

"The King is our copilot. Don't hate on him . . ."

Jesse trailed off. They were coasting down a rise toward the edge of the city. He held up a hand and they all braked. Dani's hair rose.

Ahead, visible under the chalky light, was a roadblock. Two pickups blockaded the blacktop. Mollie raised binoculars to her eyes. Her little mouth tightened.

Dani took the binocs. Trucks, men. Guns. And, half-hidden in the brush, more men, waiting to ambush anyone who tried to slip past off-road.

Behind them rose the guttering rumble of a diesel engine.

"Get out of sight," she said.

They hid in an abandoned filling station as a Land Rover rolled by. A man sat on the roof, feet propped against the luggage rack, cradling a shotgun. A cigarette dangled from his lips, glowing red. Inside the SUV, rifle barrels glinted under the dashboard lights. Flashlights searched the roadside.

They ducked as the beams swept the gas station windows.

Then, with a smooth German purr, the BMW arrived. They heard a door open. Footsteps scuffed on the asphalt.

From the SUV, a man called, "Nothing yet."

"They cleared out of the motel," Amber said. "They're running. Catch them."

Even her voice hissed and sizzled like radio static. Christ, did she sound aggrieved.

"The girl's smaller, weaker. Separate her from the woman like cutting a calf from the herd. Bring her to me."

Mollie curled into herself. Dani slipped an arm around her shoulders.

"And the stewardess?"

"Dealer's choice. Now get on the walkie-talkie to the other posts," she said. "They do not slither past. Sneaky fucks."

Jesse cut a glance at Dani, his blue eyes chilly in the moonlight.

They were trapped.

Car doors slammed. The vehicles peeled out.

Dani breathed. After ten minutes, she peeked her head up. Clear. They retreated.

They woke in a casino parking garage. They'd slept in cars left at valet parking. The sky outside blazed blue. While Mollie sat on the tailgate of a Bronco eating a granola bar, Dani pulled Jesse aside.

"I don't know why Amber wants Mollie so bad. Why she . . . *covets* her. But—"

"She doesn't get hold of her. Or you. Period," Jesse said. "And she's a psychopath."

Yeah. Maybe the radioactive static was actually Amber's internal monologue, broadcasting through the radio. Dani nodded crisply, grateful to Jesse. Terrified.

Pensive, he scanned the sun-sickened street outside. "She doesn't know about me. Thinks it's just you two. Keep that in mind."

The hum of a motorized scooter drew their attention.

Eleanor was cruising up the center of the Strip, hauling a shopping trolley stuffed with $100,000 chips from Circus Circus. Wearing a full-length mink, a leopard-print tube top, and four-inch purple platforms. A sun umbrella topped the scooter.

Dani waved from the shadows. Casually, almost discreetly—the umbrella was traffic-cone orange, with Christmas lights—Eleanor veered into the garage. She braked and lit a Winston.

Jesse crossed his arms. "You got ahead of the parade."

"I been ridin' in everybody's wake. My whole life. Now . . . " She shrugged as if a burr had lodged beneath her tube top, goading her. " . . . think I might get upwind."

Mollie hopped off the tailgate and walked over. Eleanor eagle-eyed the three of them.

"Y'all tried to leave?"

Jesse brusquely nodded. "You aren't scared to go?"

She squinted through curling smoke. "I ain't nobody to them. They'd take cash and let me pass. And I got enough to shower it like cupcake sprinkles. I'm off, and they won't stop me." She turned to Mollie. "You follow the local news, pumpkin?"

Mollie shrugged. "Kinda."

"You know about them tunnels?"

After a second, Mollie's face cleared.

"Push comes to shove, surface streets may not be the way out." Eleanor flicked her cigarette butt. "And no way the riffraff down there got by better than the rest of us. It'll likely be cleared out."

Her eyes cut to Dani. "Not what you wanted, but it's what you got. You understand that?"

Dani nodded, throat tight.

Eleanor put on her cat-eye shades. "Be good, babies. I'm off. Viva Las Vegas." Nudging the throttle, she buzzed forward and tenderly set a hand against Mollie's cheek. "Stay safe, angel."

She rode away.

"What did she mean, tunnels?" Jesse said.

⇒

He got maps from City Hall.

"Flood-control tunnels." He unrolled them on the hood of a turquoise Impala.

"Oh, yeah," Mollie said. "I *did* see the news. The mayor cut a ribbon with giant scissors."

Dani bit her thumbnail. "'Riffraff.'"

Jesse slid a glance at her. "Homeless. And people who don't want to be found."

He tapped the maps. "I think we can do it."

———

Mollie led them to the entrance, near sunset, as mirages shimmered and clouds boiled in the heat, riding up a concrete drainage channel behind Caesars Palace.

She stood on the pedals, excited. "I rode bikes up here once with my friends—"

Friends. Her face scrunched and her lip trembled.

Thunder rumbled, reverberating off dead hotels.

Jesse tented a hand over his eyes. "Jesus, those clouds are black." A shiver ran across his shoulders. "Like they're more than thunderheads."

Gut check. Graffiti splashed the tunnel entrance, green, violet, crimson, but past that, it was inky. Dani inhaled and got a nod from him. They couldn't wait. Dismounting, they walked the bikes inside.

Dani's breathing echoed off the walls. What was down here? "I'll take out the zombies."

"*I'll* take out the zombies," Jesse said. "You tackle the Zodiac."

She felt thankful for his presence. Even if he was a baby. He was cute. Hell, he was handsome. But so alone. As if he was—severed. From the life he'd planned. From a love, somebody meant for him, he hadn't even met yet. Maybe gone now. Who knew?

Daylight quickly weakened. When they reached the first branch in the tunnel Jesse pulled out a marker and drew an arrow on the wall.

"So we know we've been here, and which way we went."

They flicked on their flashlights. The sharpened glare turned their faces ghoulish. A hundred yards on they reached the first encampment.

A stench hit them. Mollie moaned. They pulled bandannas over their faces.

"Walk beside me, Mollie," Dani said.

Electric bulbs were strung overhead on a tangle of extension cords. Beds, camp stoves, old dressers, a broken guitar, rotting food. And the dead. A body. Then another.

Dani set her hand atop Mollie's, on her handlebars. "I'm here."

Above them, a grate let in stormy light. Perched atop it, pecking, was a crow.

Snap. Lightning bleached the view. Thunder cracked and the clouds ruptured.

Rain pelted through the grate, splashing, echoing. The crow clicked its head sideways, staring at Dani. A biting chill seeped into her.

Cawing, the bird flew away.

Jesse forged on to a branching tunnel. Immediately they hit another dead encampment. Mollie balked, whimpering. Dani hugged her tightly to her side and began to hum. Low, barely a sound. "Viva, Las Vegas." Don't hate on the King. They inched forward.

Jesse glanced back over his shoulder. Dani mouthed, *How much farther?*

He mouthed back, *Mile and a half.*

Then the space opened into a wide chamber. Tunnels branched off, black mouths. Aboveground, thunder boomed. Jesse paused to check the map.

And they heard scuffing sounds. Footsteps. Jesse straightened, alarmed. Mollie grabbed Dani's shirt. Dani frantically shook her head. *Not a word.*

But her heart plummeted. Had Amber's people spotted them? How? *Crowcrowcrow.* No. Crazy.

A new rumble echoed through the tunnel. Dirt bikes. They were coming.

She killed her flashlight. Jesse did the same. Then Mollie, her entire body chattering.

And then Dani heard a trickle. Water was running down the center of the tunnel floor.

A steel band seemed to tighten around her chest. She needed air. Sky. To soar above it all. Away. Away. *Away.*

The water grew from a trickle to a stream.

Jesse whipped out the map, flicked his flashlight on just long enough to check it, and pointed at one of the branching tunnels. "This way."

Dani hesitated. Water flowed around her boots. Mollie stared at her intensely.

Dani gazed up the tunnel they'd been following. She dropped her bike. Her pack.

She held out her hand to Mollie. "Give me your flashlight."

She was going to run. On her own. It was the only possibility for escape.

"What?" Mollie said. "No . . . "

Jesse understood. Gently he took the flashlight and passed it to Dani. "It's okay."

The water gushed, now ankle-deep. The voices in the dark, the rumblings, were louder.

Dropping his bike, too, Jesse pointed at the branching tunnel. Mere drips of water fell from it to the channel where they stood. "Different watershed. It runs uphill, and a mile along we'll reach an exit."

"Don't go," Mollie said.

Dani crouched in front of her. "Sometimes you brace. Sometimes you jump. Now you run. *Run.*"

"I don't want you to leave."

"I'll see you on the other side. We'll meet at . . . "

Jesse said, "I-15, exit 64."

"That's the place," Dani said emphatically. It was pure wish, but might get Mollie moving.

She clasped the girl's shoulders. "Remember the stick-on wings I gave you?"

Tears fell. "I lost them."

"You didn't." She tapped Mollie's chest. "They're here. You understand?"

Mollie blinked. Clamped her jaw to stop her chin from trembling. Inhaled. Pinned Dani with her gaze.

"*Fly*," Dani said.

They clambered into the branching tunnel and took off.

Dani stood in the channel for another moment, braced against the increasing rush of water, hearing engines. And chains. And voices.

A young woman's voice, like radio static.

Dani aimed both flashlights at an arrow Jesse had drawn on the wall. The arrow that would let her backtrack to the big junction, where floodwaters would fill the tunnel to the top with pitiless force.

The arrow that would let her draw the gang away from Mollie.

She inhaled and shouted, loud and raw, then swung both flashlights around the tunnel, as if two people were running.

"This way," she guttered, a sob in her voice. It wasn't playacting.

Her greatest fear had arrived: that one day she would face trouble she couldn't run from.

Fuck you, greatest fear. She spun and raced down the tunnel, splashing, the water now a foot deep. She crazily swung the flashlights. She heard bikes revving. Closer.

Dark, so dark, nothing but concrete, and she ran around a bend and knew the bikes were following her now—her, not Jesse and Mollie. Just her.

Amber didn't know Jesse was with them.

Adrenaline jacked into her veins. She shouted again, desperate, straining. Ahead, far, far ahead, where the water was going to fill the tunnel to the top, she saw a faint light. An exit. She ran.

Hope. That's what you need. That's what she'd given Amber. Hope, and a chance.

That's what she'd given Mollie. Hope. A chance. And time.

Fly away.

She heard the bikes, engines closer.

Gods of fortune, give me strength.

Headlights bounced off the curving tunnel walls behind her. *Frank Sinatra, bring me grace.*

She ran. *Someone guide me—I'm alone.*

Ahead, water roared. Beyond it, dimly, was daylight.

Elvis Presley, sing me home.

Daylight. Distant, but there. A voice rang, deep inside her.

Bright light city—

Gonna send her soaring.

She dug in, sprinting, water splashing over her knees.

On fire. Soul and spirit. Burning, roaring.

Heart blazing, she ran toward the light.

EVERY DOG HAS ITS DAY
Bryan Smith

A week and a half or so into the plague (he'd lost track of the days), having had enough of sitting alone in the silent urban mausoleum that the house he'd grown up in had become, Corey Adams decided to go for a walk. He was a seventeen-year-old kid who should have been enjoying a final carefree summer before beginning his senior year of high school, but now he wasn't going to have a senior year.

Captain Trips, the superflu, had seen to that.

Before leaving the house, he'd slouched for hours on the sofa in the dark living room, staring at the test pattern on the Zenith television with a glassy-eyed, slack-jawed expression. He felt numb and hollowed-out, an immobile, mannequin-like shell masquerading as a human being, rendered temporarily incapable of movement or coherent thought. He was a bit high from the weed he'd been smoking, but he was also in a state of emotional shell shock. The entire world was collapsing. His last friend in the world, his very *best* friend, was gone, and for that he had only himself to blame. Other significant losses had occurred, terrible losses, but those things were always beyond his control.

But the loss of Bluto, his German shepherd?

That was on him. *Only* on him.

Slowly, little by little, he began to emerge from this state of absolute disconnection, and as he began to come back to himself, his first thoughts coalesced around a single, surreal concept.

Am I real? Am I an actual person? Is any of this happening, or am I merely an actor on a shabby, cheap stage, waiting to enact his next scene in some overwrought drama?

It was a disorienting way to think. It was even more disorienting to realize he had no satisfactory answers to any of those questions. Even worse, he suspected his stage drama analogy was inapt, because in truth he wasn't anything as significant as an actor in a play. He was, at best, a background extra, an unnoticed, minor part of the scenery. The phone wasn't ringing, no one had come knocking on the door, and no one would, because there was no one left in this world who gave one shit about him.

He left the front door ajar as he left the house, an act of supreme apathy reflective of his despairing state of mind. Now that everything had gone so drastically awry and society itself was crumbling, all the usual security concerns struck him as irrelevant. Everyone had bigger worries now, even all the homeless alcoholics and two-bit criminals. He doubted anyone would bother looting the house at this point, but if they did, so fucking what?

He rambled about for a considerable period, with only the dimmest awareness of the actual amount of time passing. Not many people were out and about as he traipsed up and down the neighborhood's bright white sidewalks, baking in the heat of the relentless summer sun. Only an occasional car went whizzing by in the streets. This was a normally bustling neighborhood adjacent to Vanderbilt University, but a lot of the people he'd typically encounter walking around in the middle of the day were likely dead now. Or, like his sister, they'd fled the city.

A voice cried out from somewhere nearby shortly after Corey

veered away from the sidewalk to begin cutting through Mackey Park, but it didn't fully register. An unconscious impulse was steering him, spurring him to take a shortcut back toward home. The city was too quiet now, that constant urban background din too distressingly absent. In its own way, this absence of the normal drone felt as oppressive as the silence of the house.

Also, worst of all, he'd seen too many dead dogs. They were everywhere. On sidewalks and in a lot of the yards he'd passed, others reduced to pulpy smears of crimson roadkill. Every such glimpse triggered grim thoughts regarding Bluto's unknown fate. It hurt to think about it. Losing track of his dog was the kind of thing that simply would not have been possible prior to this unraveling of things, and the pain of having allowed it to happen was at least as great as the pain imparted by the other losses he'd endured in recent days.

That same voice cried out again, louder now, closer, but he was too lost in thought to take much note of it. He walked with his head down, his eyes focused on the park's bright green grass, a healthy shade that struck him as faintly obscene given the city's otherwise pervading atmosphere of grinding dread and slow-motion doom.

Things had changed so much so quickly, a whirlwind of upheaval so extreme he sometimes wondered if he'd slipped out of the world he'd inhabited all his life and into some alternate dimension or universe, a nightmarish dreamscape from which he could not escape. Deep down, though, he knew that wasn't true, because when he slept at night, the real nightmares came, repeatedly taunting him with unnerving visions of a dark man, a strange, evil sorcerer of some type with an all-seeing red eye. The feeling of foreboding the visions elicited was only marginally counterbalanced by the foggier dreams of the old woman in Nebraska.

Less than a week ago, his formerly hale and hearty father started sniffling and sneezing. A summer cold, he called it. Not the superflu. Three days later, he was in his death throes, moaning and squirming miserably on sweat-soaked sheets, muttering and hallucinating, saying things to people who weren't there, some of whom had been dead for years.

Then, shockingly fast, he was gone.

Corey's stepmother, Linda, succumbed to the same symptoms just two days later, less than twenty-four hours after transporting her husband over to Baptist Hospital, where he'd been treated like a disposable piece of meat, shunted aside with the rest of the sick and dying.

The family of four was reduced by half, leaving just Corey and his older sister, Angie. The siblings were distraught, reeling with grief and terrified by the lack of options available to them. There was nowhere to turn to for help, no one they could ask for guidance, because by then all the adults in their world were sick. Or already dead.

They sat and watched news reports on the Zenith. The government was trying hard to reassure people, but it was evident something really fucked up was going down, some heavy truth the powers that be desperately wanted to keep hidden. A vaccine was being promised, but Corey believed in that about as much as he believed in Santa Claus.

"They think we're blind," Angie had said two days ago while they sat in the living room and smoked weed. "Blind and stupid."

Then today his sister was gone. Not dead. Just gone.

She left a note, and that's all it said.

I'm gone.

She didn't even sign it.

He spent some miserable time wondering how she could do that, just walk away without a proper goodbye, without inviting him along, leaving him alone with the corpse of their stepmother moldering away in the master bedroom upstairs. An ungenerous person would describe what she'd done as a supremely selfish act, and for a time he was exactly that type of ungenerous. He was pissed at her, but he also understood. Their home was a tomb, a tainted repository of broken dreams and sullied memories.

The circumstances were almost unspeakably bleak, but even so, he thought he might have been able to bear up a while longer with Bluto at his side.

But the dog was gone, too, departed to points unknown.

Against his will, his thoughts again became laser-focused on his beloved missing pet, particularly in regard to how he hadn't even realized the animal had disappeared until probably hours after he was gone. A little while ago, he'd emerged from the mental fog engulfing him long enough to go into the bathroom and take a piss, and on his way back into the living room he happened to glance over at the sliding glass door that led out to the patio and the backyard. Instead of returning to the sofa and resuming his impersonation of a person in a vegetative coma, he stopped and stared out at the yard, feeling like something was wrong without quite being able to put his finger on what it was.

Then it came to him and he felt that twist in his guts.

No. Nonono.

Corey ran outside and glanced around. Seeing no sign of the dog, he dashed around to the side of the house, pulling up short at the gut-wrenching sight of the gate that went out to the front yard standing open.

Right away, he understood what must have happened. He'd let Bluto out in the morning, mere minutes before discovering Angie's earth-shattering note. Reeling from his sister's act of desertion, that loss of his final remaining anchor to normality and sanity, he'd become mired in self-pity, spending the whole damn day glued to that stupid fucking sofa, stunned into insensibility by all he'd lost. At some point during the day, while he smoked the last of his weed and wallowed in misery and depression, maybe nodding off now and then, someone had come along and let the dog out of the yard. Why? Who knew? It might have been a malicious act. Or some well-meaning animal lover might have spotted Bluto through the chain-link fence and set him free, perhaps on the assumption that his owners were as dead as practically everyone else in the city. What troubled him most was the lack of a knock at the door that surely would've come from anyone with good intentions.

Maybe they did, a voice from a traitorous part of his mind ventured, taunting him, twisting that metaphorical knife. *Maybe someone knocked and you were too out of it because you're too much of a stoner loser to cope with what's happening like a normal person.*

"Shut up," he muttered, digging his nails into his palms. "Just shut the fuck up."

Either way, his best buddy was gone, a fact confirmed by his subsequent dash out into the street to check for him. He walked up and down the street, calling for Bluto at the top of his lungs, until he was hoarse from screaming, until all he could think to do was return to the house and collapse into immobile self-pitying misery all over again.

Goddammit. I'm sorry, Bluto, he thought, tears welling in his eyes. *I'm an asshole. A worthless piece of shit. I might as well eat a goddamned bullet.*

That same voice cried out yet again, loud enough and close enough now to finally snag Corey's attention and snap him back to the present moment. Glimpsing a blur of rapid movement in his peripheral vision, he came to an abrupt halt, glancing to his left with an immediate jolt of apprehension.

A girl he recognized was running straight at him.

He knew her in the sense that he saw her around from time to time in the neighborhood, but he didn't actually *know* her. She was pretty, but that wasn't why she'd made enough of an impression for her face to stick in his memory. He thought he'd sometimes seen her in the company of a grade A piece of shit named Jared Montgomery, one of a group of older kids from the neighborhood who'd tormented him when he was younger. That was years ago, back before he even had hair on his balls, but the memory of those times was still a deep wound.

The girl was out of breath as she lurched to a stop a few feet away from him. "Damn, dude . . . " She inhaled and exhaled a few times, making quite the show of being winded. "Jesus . . . Are you deaf or something, Corey?"

He frowned. "Um . . . "

After a moment of befuddlement, it came to him that this girl was either a friend or former friend of his sister. That was the other reason she was familiar. She and Angie were classmates, and he used to see her at their house now and then, but that'd been a while ago. A few years, at least.

She smiled. "What's the matter? Cat got your tongue?"

He shrugged. "I fucking hope not. That would hurt."

She laughed. "You're funny. I'm Kristen."

"Yeah, I know."

He narrowed his eyes at her, an automatic sense of distrust coloring the way he perceived every aspect of their interaction. Much of this feeling had to do with her association with his childhood bully, but it was also because he was unaccustomed to girls as hot as her accosting him in what he supposed still marginally qualified as a public place, even if there were precious few other people around to bear witness to the event.

She said, "Dude, come on, relax. I promise I don't bite. I just thought maybe you'd like to hang with us."

Corey's frown deepened.

Who was this *us* she was talking about?

Then he looked past her and saw two other people, a boy and a girl, lounging nearby on the rusted-out merry-go-round that was part of the park's shabby playground area. The guy saw him looking and casually flipped a hand at him, a half-hearted gesture of greeting. The other girl sat at the edge of the merry-go-round, feet dangling a few inches above the ground as she leaned against one of the corroded rails and stared at the ground with a blank expression. They were both the approximate age of the girl who'd approached him, a few years his senior, early twenties, maybe. A torn-open suitcase carton of Budweiser cans sat between them on the rusted metal disk.

Corey looked at Kristen and sighed. "I don't know. I was just on my way home."

She snorted. "What for?"

He frowned again. "Because it's where I fucking live. Where else would I go?"

A strange look crossed her face, one he needed a moment to recognize as something akin to pity. "But nobody's there."

He became wary again, taken aback by her proclamation. "Yeah? And how would you know that?"

A crease formed in the middle of her brow, deepening his impression of being pitied. "I know because I talked to Angie early this morning, right before she . . . you know, took off."

Now she had his full attention.

"Yeah? She say anything about that?"

Her tone became more solemn as she said, "She told me about your folks dying, that she was leaving town. So, you know, condolences or whatever." She laughed again, but this time there was a ragged quality to it, like it was one small emotional nudge from becoming a sob. "We're all losing our people. I'm all alone, too, now." She hooked a thumb over her shoulder, indicating the pair lounging on the merry-go-round. "Except for them, I mean."

Corey grunted. "Where did you see Angie?"

"At J.J.'s Market. You know, over by the Great Escape. She was loading a bunch of shit into your stepmom's station wagon. Just going in and out of the store with armloads of shit. The place was open, but no one was around."

Corey's confusion intensified. "Are you saying she was robbing the place?"

"Way to assume the worst about your own flesh and blood." That crease in the middle of her brow became more pronounced. "And, no, it wasn't like that. I mean, not really. Angie was only doing what everyone else has been doing. The ones still alive, anyway. In case you hadn't noticed, a lot of the people who used to run things, like probably the owner of J.J.'s, are dead now. People have just been walking into places and taking whatever they need. Some places are locked up tight, but others are wide open. You can't rightly call it theft when the people you're quote-unquote 'stealing' from aren't still breathing."

Corey figured she had a point. "Yeah, okay. So . . . did Angie say anything about me?"

She shook her head. "No, not really, dude. I guess it's kinda shitty how she just took off and left you all alone, huh?"

He grunted. "I guess it kinda is, yeah."

Kristen reached out and touched his arm. "Seriously. Come hang a while. Have some beers. What else have you got to do?"

For the first time, Corey took full note of the sense of aching need in her voice. Need and desperation. Hearing this made him feel sorry for her, eroding some of his resistance. He nonetheless hesitated a beat longer, craning his head around and seeing no one else in the vicinity.

He met her gaze again. "Where's Jared?"

She grimaced. "He's dead. Fucking Captain Trips took him away."

A part of Corey rejoiced at this news, while another part was aghast at this gut reaction. It made him feel like a ghoul, but he couldn't help it.

So long, Jared, he thought. *Rest in pieces, you fucking asshole.*

Now Kristen really was crying, silently, her thin shoulders shaking as tears trickled down her cheeks.

Corey surrendered, feeling bad in light of his private thoughts on Jared's demise. "Okay. I'll hang out a while."

She brightened immediately, smiling as she took his hand and led him over to the merry-go-round.

As soon as they were within range, the lanky, long-haired male half of the lounging couple reached into the open carton and extracted a dripping-wet can of Bud. He tossed the can at Corey with another casual flip of his hand, sending it sailing through the air on a high, arcing trajectory that forced Corey to jog a few steps to his right and jump to snag it out of the air.

The lanky guy laughed. "He shoots, he scores. Wait, wrong fucking sport. Touchdown. That's it, right?" He glanced at Corey again, an eyebrow raised as if seeking confirmation that he had it right. "Or whatever the fuck."

He laughed again.

The guy sounded three sheets to the wind already, and it was only the middle of the afternoon. He shifted around on the edge of the big disk, leaning the back of his head against another of the rails. His eyes were red-rimmed and his hair was greasy, as if he hadn't showered in days. The other girl hadn't reacted to Corey's presence at all yet and was still doing that thousand-yard-stare thing. She wore faded ripped jeans with large holes at the knees, and her fingers kept pulling at the loose threads of one of them, a nervous habit that was steadily making the hole bigger, unraveling the garment strand by strand.

Corey popped open the beer and foam rushed through the opening. He shook the moisture from his fingers and took a sip. "Thanks."

The lanky guy smirked, his eyes at half-mast as his head lolled to one side. "No prob."

Kristen said, "Guys, this is Corey Adams. You probably know his sister, Angie."

A smile came to the lanky guy's face. "Oh, yeah. Yeah, yeah. Angie fucking Adams. She's one fine mama jama. You guys live over on Phillips Street, yeah?"

Corey nodded. "Yeah."

Kristen glanced at him, smirking as she said, "And these future members of Alcoholics Anonymous are Sean Hicks and Rebecca Robinson."

Corey acknowledged this information with a grunt before taking another, larger sip of beer. The names were unfamiliar to him, not that it mattered. He fully expected to never see any of these people again after today.

Sean Hicks laughed. "An alcoholic I may be, but there ain't no

AA anymore, I'm pretty fuckin' sure. All the drunks are dying off, just like everybody else. Just like us soon, maybe."

Rebecca's gaze came away from the ground for the first time. "Just like me, for sure," she said, sniffling. "My clock's already ticking."

Corey was unable to suppress a wince upon glimpsing the large dark smudges under her eyes, a hideously stark contrast to her milk-white skin. Her eyes were red and her face was shiny with perspiration. Mucus leaked steadily from her nostrils, like water trickling out of a slightly open spigot.

Captain Trips. No fucking doubt about it.

Corey felt a sharp tug of bitter sorrow. "I'm sorry."

She sneered. "Why the fuck are you sorry? It doesn't matter. I'm not mad about it. Why would I want to stick around? The world's gone to shit and this might be my last halfway okay day. So I'm gonna keep drinking and stay fuckin' wasted as long as I can, and when I bite it, you all can just toss my ass in a dumpster and have a drink in my honor."

Her brittle tone belied the toughness of her words. She was trying hard to make herself believe she didn't care, but she was clearly terrified.

Corey took a much larger gulp of beer.

He already wanted to be far away from these people. They weren't his friends. Their problems weren't his problems. He felt bad for this girl, but only in the way he'd feel reflexively for anyone on the cusp of enduring the worst stages of the superflu.

Kristen made a sound of profound annoyance. "Stop talking like that, bitch."

Rebecca looked at her. "Like what?"

Kristen tossed up her hands, a frustrated gesture. "Like you've already given up. You might still just have a regular-ass cold. You don't know. Not yet."

Rebecca snorted and shook her head, but said nothing.

Corey had the sense they'd already had this same argument many times.

A silence of more than a minute elapsed.

Sean crushed his latest empty and belched as he tossed the can to the ground. "Guess I'm never gonna hear that new Guns N' fuckin' Roses album now. Man, I was so looking forward to that."

He sang a few off-key lines from "Civil War," a song the band had debuted on a televised live performance at Farm Aid a few months earlier.

Corey said nothing, but that was something he'd been hotly anticipating prior to the plague as well. He'd watched his VHS recording of the Farm Aid performance times beyond counting. What Rebecca had said was the truest thing he'd heard anybody say in a while. The world had gone to shit. They weren't just losing people. They were losing all the things that had enriched everyone's lives and made existence less tedious. There'd never be any new books, movies, video games, or metal albums. All of which were things some might view as trivial compared to the massive loss of life, but Corey didn't think they were trivial at all. Even if he never contracted the superflu, the world would be a gray, dismal place. Would it even be worth surviving in a place like that?

Another awkward silence stretched out.

Kristen grabbed him by the arm and started tugging him away from the merry-go-round. "Come with me."

He frowned as he stumbled along with her. "Where are we going?"

She indicated a nearby line of trees with a tilt of her chin. "Right there. In the woods. I thought maybe we could fool around a little, and . . . maybe . . . who knows . . . "

She shrugged, seeming a little shy for the first time.

Corey laughed. "Already? You don't want to get to know me first? Maybe see a movie, go on a date?"

She snorted. "Is that a joke? Look, fuck all that getting-to-know-you shit. Waste of time. Rebecca was right about one thing. The clock is ticking, probably for all of us. I think you're cute and I want to feel something good while I still can. Wait. Have you ever been with a girl before?"

"Sure."

This wasn't a lie, but his experience in that area was limited. He hoped he wouldn't be asked to elaborate, because the true details of his one and only sexual experience were embarrassing and he didn't want to spin a false story just to seem cool. Fortunately, she didn't press him on the matter.

They were almost to the trees when Corey heard something that made him come to a sudden stop. He turned away from Kristen and stared off into the distance, his gaze oriented in a direction that would eventually take him to his house if he started walking and continued in a straight line for about a mile.

Kristen gripped him by a shoulder and tried turning him toward her, but he resisted, shrugging her hand off and moving a few steps away from her. The entirety of his attention was still focused in the same direction, ears straining as he listened intently for even the faintest repetition of what he'd heard. Only, now he was wondering if he'd truly heard it at all. It might only have been a sadistic trick of his subconscious mind, an auditory hallucination conjured from gray, unknowable depths by the sheer magnitude of his grief and regret, because all he could hear now were Rebecca's sniffles and the muted rustling of the breeze.

"Did you hear that?"

"Hear what?" Kristen's voice evoked exasperation. The previously soft and pleasing contours of her face took on a hard, chiseled look, betraying a capacity for severe anger. "What's wrong with you? Don't you like me?"

Corey didn't know if he liked her, but he was attracted to her. He nonetheless would not allow base desire to sway his attention until he was certain he'd been wrong about what he thought he'd heard. He remained immobile and unresponsive a little longer, his attention still fixed on the same open expanse of the park's grounds. From his current vantage point, he saw only a wide swath of green grass ringed by more trees. He'd need to walk a significant distance and go over a couple of hills before catching a glimpse of the street and houses beyond the other side of the park.

Kristen grabbed hold of his arm again, turning him toward her more forcefully this time. "Hey, look at me. You're real close to missing out on something pretty great, you know that?"

Corey sighed.

"I'm sorry. I thought I heard—"

The sound came again, still from far away, but slightly more distinct now.

Corey again turned away from Kristen. "That's barking. There's a dog out there somewhere."

A silent beat passed.

Then Kristen said, "Yeah. Okay. I hear it, too. So what?"

He pulled free of her and started moving in the direction of the sound, his heart thudding so heavily behind his ribs he could feel his flesh vibrating. The beer can slipped unnoticed from his fingers, splashing his feet with foam as it hit the ground. A quivering smile pulled at the edges of his mouth as hope bloomed inside him. There was a dog out there somewhere, perhaps not that far away, unfelled by the plague, a thing that felt miraculous after all the dead ones he'd seen today. The odds against it being Bluto were astronomical, an inner voice warned him, and he knew it was right. This was almost certainly a different dog, but the possibility of locating any living canine after all the relentlessly bleak shit he'd endured was something to celebrate.

He heard a voice somewhere behind him, someone yelling.

Multiple voices, actually.

He ignored them all and walked faster still. The voices fell silent, but soon he heard someone running, racing to catch up with him.

Kristen slowed her pace as she fell into step next to him, panting now, trying to catch her breath. "Serious question. Have you lost your goddamn mind?"

Corey kept his gaze straight ahead and picked up the pace A small pond came into view as they crested the hill. The water's still surface shimmered brightly, reflecting the light of the blazing sun. Around the pond were a few benches, all of which were empty save for one, upon which sat a portly older man in a rumpled suit. The man's posture was awkward, his body listing sideways, head lolling in precarious fashion. He'd either fallen asleep on the bench or he was dead. The way things were now, Corey was inclined to believe the bleaker possibility was the likeliest one.

He moved quickly down the slope to the flatter ground surrounding the pond, and once again Kristen hurried to keep up with him.

"Could you please slow down?"

Corey didn't answer, nor did he slow down even an iota, but he did glance toward the big man on the bench once they were within range.

Yep, definitely dead.

He kept up the brisk pace as they moved past the pond and again emerged onto a wider expanse of open ground.

"You're starting to piss me off."

Corey finally glanced at Kristen. "I don't care."

"You're an asshole."

He nodded. "You might be right about that."

Kristen groaned. "Why are you so dead fucking set on finding some damn dog?"

He looked at her "I just am."

She rolled her eyes. "Great answer. That's some quality fucking insight right there."

Corey didn't respond.

They went up and over another hill, a significantly smaller rise than the previous one, but once they were on the downward slope Corey caught a glimpse of a residential street through a scattering of trees. He saw cars parked at the curb on both sides of the street, including a silver compact that was missing a door. The dog had been silent the last few minutes, a development that stirred anxiety in Corey.

Then the barking started back up, an agitated eruption.

Corey started running.

"Goddammit!" Kristen shouted after him.

He reached the edge of the park and weaved his way through the narrow band of scattered trees, emerging seconds later on a strip of white sidewalk. He stopped there, breathing heavily as he craned his head around, looking up and down the street for signs of the animal, which had once again fallen silent. The intermittent nature of its outbursts was maddening, impeding his ability to home in on the sound.

The car missing a door was about fifteen feet up the street to his right. Once Corey stepped off the sidewalk and onto the strip of faded asphalt, he discovered that the door wasn't missing at all, at which point it became easy to surmise what had happened. Someone had left the door on the street-facing side of the vehicle standing open, and another car had come careening heedlessly down the street, smashing into the parked car with enough force to knock it clean off its hinges. The door had gone skidding along the asphalt, coming to rest just a few feet from where Corey now stood. He saw more evidence of vehicular damage to other cars parked on both sides of the street. Huge dents and ripped-asunder side panels. There were many more strewn bits of twisted metal littering the asphalt, along with more than one sheared-away side mirror, with cracked fragments of glass glittering in the sun.

"Holy shit. What a mess."

Kristen had caught up to him.

"Yeah."

The dog barked

The sound was coming from somewhere to his right, much nearer than before, yet still too far away to precisely gauge the animal's location. It might be in a yard a couple blocks up on this same street, or maybe one street over, but either way, he was getting closer. He turned away from Kristen and started moving up the street in the direction of the sound, which had ceased yet again.

Kristen followed, but now she stayed a few feet behind him instead of tagging along at his side. Like the dog he was seeking, she stayed silent for the entire length of the first block he explored. He felt her sullenness like a physical thing, like an alien death ray boring into his back. They crossed an intersection and started up another block. So far they had the entire street to themselves, with nary a sign of living residents out and about.

Kristen said, "You're stupid."

Corey didn't say anything.

She said, "You're *really* fucking stupid. And ugly. You know that?"

This was in direct contradiction to what she'd previously said, but he didn't bother pointing that out. All he said was "But not too ugly to fool around with, apparently."

She made a noise of disdain. "You can consider that offer off the goddamn table."

He glanced over his shoulder at her. "Then why are you still following me? Leave me alone. Go back to the park."

She said nothing, nor did she heed his suggestion to depart. Her breathing changed, coming in shorter, harsher gasps, and he sensed she was hovering on the precipice of an even more scathing outburst.

They walked another dozen feet before he tried again. "Seriously, Kristen, please just go back. I'm sorry I've upset you. Sorry I disappointed you."

He wasn't sorry at all, but figured appeasement might be his best bet.

Turned out he was wrong about that.

She slammed the heel of a hand between his shoulder blades, causing him to stumble forward a few feet. He resumed moving up the street after regaining his balance, but half turned toward her long enough to say, "Knock it off."

She sneered, but didn't say anything until he'd turned away from her again.

Then she said, "I hate you."

"You don't even know me."

She thumped him between the shoulder blades again. "I hope you get Captain Trips. Angie hates you, too. That's why she left. She couldn't stand to be around you anymore. Your stupid ugly face gave her nightmares."

"You're lying."

She laughed. "Am not. She said her nightmares about you were worse than her nightmares about the dark man."

What happened next was unthinking impulse, a result of her finally pulling at the loose strands of his frayed nerves a little too hard. She was so close he could feel her beer-stinking breath on his neck. He felt crowded, uncomfortable. All he knew was he wanted her away from him, and he wanted it *now*.

He whirled about and slammed the heels of both hands into her chest. Her eyes went wide with alarm as she stumbled away from him. The heel of one of her shoes bumped against the ridged edge of a sloppily patched pothole, eliminating any chance she had of regaining her balance or breaking her fall. She fell straight backward, the crown of her skull smacking hard against the asphalt. For Corey, the impact sound immediately conjured memories of his stepmom cracking an egg open for breakfast.

He felt sick.

A pool of blood was already spreading around her head. Her body had gone terribly still. Her mouth was open and her eyelids were motionless. He couldn't hear her breathing. A pitiful, shrill whine rose up from somewhere, and it took him a moment to realize the sound was issuing from his own mouth.

She looked dead.

Only seconds had passed, and she looked fucking dead.

How was that possible?

It had happened with such shocking suddenness, with no true malicious intent on his part. He hadn't wanted to hurt her. *All* he'd wanted was for her to stop harassing him and go away, but now she was dead.

I'm a killer, he thought. *A fucking killer. Oh, Jesus.*

Tears filled his eyes and his whole body trembled as he approached her unmoving form. As he drew close to her body, he came perilously close to stumbling over the same ridge of dark and gooey asphalt patch. Then he was on his knees at her side, lifting a limp arm to check her wrist for a pulse, but there was none to detect.

He sat down on his butt, folding his arms tight over his belly as he rocked back and forth and sobbed. "I'm sorry," he wailed, his vision blurring. "So fucking sorry. I didn't mean to. I really didn't. You have to believe me, God." He looked toward the sky as tears rolled sideways down his cheeks. "You have to take it back. This is a mistake. A terrible mistake. You have to fucking take it back!"

Corey was close to screaming by the time his voice hoarsened too severely to continue. Even after the wailing subsided, he stayed where he was, still clinging tight to Kristen's arm. He felt bereft and adrift, shaken to his core. Too late, he felt a greater level of empathy for her. She'd only been seeking companionship and comfort, had been desperate for it, and he'd rejected her on a whim.

What a fool I am.

He wept and vocally reiterated his sorrow countless times. A part of him expected someone to eventually come along and take care of things in an adult way. Surely the police would be called soon. He'd be arrested and hauled away to spend the first of many nights in jail.

Only, those were the ways of the old world, the world that was ending.

This new world was no place of order and decorum.

All that was left was chaos and death. So much death.

He might have stayed right where he was for hours to come, until long after nightfall. That was how broken he felt. The dog had stopped barking a while ago, at least several minutes prior to the moment when he'd turned toward Kristen and given her that fateful shove. Even the hope the dog's barking had bestowed had drained away. He wished he had a gun.

Wished he had the guts to stick that gun in his mouth.

This is what he was thinking when he heard the sound that finally roused him from the worst depths of misery and self-pity. Not the resumption of barking he might have hoped for, but another sound, one that stirred instant unease and prickled the hairs at the back of his neck. Boot heels clocking on asphalt. Not too close yet, but not far away, either. And there was another sound, that of someone—a man—humming a vaguely recognizable tune, a pop song that had been popular in recent weeks, prior to the onset of the plague. Corey didn't like the song and he didn't like the steady, inexorable clocking sound of those boot heels. A sound like the heels of a prison guard walking a condemned man to the electric chair.

He'd heard that sound before, in his dreams each of the last two nights.

Corey was on his feet at once, terror dispersing the last of his grief. He felt alert and on edge, anxious to get far away without being seen. Spinning about in the middle of the street, he saw no signs of the oncoming stranger, but the clocking of those heels was louder now.

And close. So close.

There wasn't time to run.

Not knowing what else to do, he started moving down the street, trying the door handles of cars parked at the curb. The humming was growing in volume, the tune becoming even more recognizable. Now and then, the humming paused, and the stranger chuckled before picking up the tune again.

The first several cars Corey tried were locked, but, at last, the back door of an old Cutlass Supreme yielded to his yanking. He scrambled inside, eased the door shut as quietly as he could manage, and hunkered down as low as possible beneath the level of the seat, trembling uncontrollably as his gut pressed against the hump in the middle. He screwed his eyes shut and pressed his face against the coarse floor carpet, willing himself to stay quiet until the stranger went away. A part of him, a faint part, suggested he was being unreasonable, illogical even. There was no reason to fear this stranger, who had not threatened him, who was someone he didn't know.

Only, that wasn't true, and that was another thing he felt on a gut level. He didn't know how he knew it, but he did.

This might even be the man with the crimson gaze from his dreams.

The dark man.

He didn't know it with absolute certainty, but what else could explain how instinctively powerless he felt, how consumed with crippling dread?

The clocking of those heels was louder than ever. The stranger sounded like he was humming the odious tune right against Corey's ear. He was in the street right outside the Oldsmobile now, with only the door standing between them.

A door that wasn't even locked.

Fuck.

The man in the street had come to a stop. He exuded an aura of awesome power even through the barrier of glass and steel. This stranger wasn't *just* a man. He was something beyond that, something beyond nature itself. Whether this presence was truly the dark man of his dreams, he did not know, but if not, it must be closely associated with him.

He might be looking inside the car even now, grinning down at his cowering form. Corey whimpered softly, a sound that was nearly like a mewl, and pressed his face harder against the carpet, wishing he could push all the way through to the pavement below. A rapping of knuckles against the glass above his head made him yelp in fright, but his eyes stayed closed.

The man outside chuckled, a sound with a distinct note of mockery.

A brief silence followed, one that felt heavy and ominous, suffocating.

Corey whimpered and clawed at the carpet.

Go away. Please just go away.

The dark, malefic presence, the thing that was somehow a man and more than that at the same time, chuckled again, as if it'd looked into Corey's mind and heard this silent prayer, and felt only a mild amusement. He lingered outside the car a while longer, softly clicking a fingernail against the window, a sound that elicited tears from Corey, who fully expected to next hear a sound even more ominous and doom-laden, a squeaking of door hinges. An eternity elapsed, but in reality it was barely more than another full minute.

Then the man started humming and the clocking of his heels resumed as he began walking away.

Corey stayed where he was until after both sounds receded, unable to believe he'd been passed over by the dark stranger, who he imagined was not ordinarily inclined toward mercy. He thought he might stay in this spot forever. That changed when he heard another sound from right outside the vehicle. The same sound that had brought him to this part of the neighborhood in the first place. His eyes fluttered open when the sound repeated, and he raised up high enough to peer over the edge of the door.

A grinning dog was sitting in the middle of the street, staring at the car with a look of eager anticipation. The dog wasn't Bluto. Of course not. He'd been right about his luck. Fate would never smile on him so favorably. This dog was a mutt. A cute one of about medium size, with a predominantly white coat colored here and there with speckles and splotches of black, including a black ring around one eye.

Corey couldn't help smiling.

He raised up higher and reached for the door handle, hesitating for only a moment as he looked up and down the street. There was still no sign of the dark stranger, but he didn't need visual evidence. He felt the man's absence on a physical level, like the lifting of a black, smothering fog. The day was bright and sunny again instead of dark and cold.

He opened the door and shakily emerged from the car.

The dog wiggled its butt while still sitting, looking up at him now. On the pavement in front of the dog was a pistol that hadn't been there before Corey took refuge in the Cutlass. It looked like an army-issue .45. Old, but clean and functional, still entirely capable of doing what it'd been designed to do with great efficiency. The sight of it instilled a chill that resonated in every atom of his body. That it'd been left where it was on purpose could not be doubted. He'd wished for a gun and here was a gun. Somehow the stranger had sensed his suicidal thoughts and had left behind this dark gift. It didn't matter that this notion defied all logic and everything he'd thought he understood about the rational world.

It was the truth.

Corey closed the Oldsmobile's door and sat down, leaning his back against the warm metal. He met the dog's gaze, prompting the animal to thump its tail against the pavement. Leaning forward a little, he scratched the back of its neck. The dog turned its head sideways, panting as its tongue lolled out the side of its mouth. Its expression now was one of perfect canine ecstasy.

Corey smiled and scratched the dog's neck some more. "You're a good boy, aren't you? A real good boy. Yes, you are. I can tell. Thanks for letting me scritch you, buddy." There were tears in his eyes again. "Good boy. Good, good boy. I bet you and Bluto would have been great friends."

His hand came away from the animal.

He picked up the gun and jammed the barrel in his mouth. He'd been presented with a choice to make, granted an opportunity to take himself out of the equation. A game was being played by elemental forces that were bigger than him, too big for him to even begin to comprehend. He was a piece on a vast, invisible board, a pawn, and it was within his power now to remove himself from it.

To opt out.

He wouldn't mind not being a part of that game, not at all.

He closed his eyes and increased the pressure of his finger against the trigger, his hand shaking as he willed himself to find the strength necessary to finish the job and end his pain. In his mind, he visualized how it would happen, the big boom as the weapon discharged, the back of his head blowing apart in glorious Technicolor, a splash of bright red against black chrome, an instant, irrevocable obliteration of everything he'd ever been.

Corey's moment of self-annihilation was perhaps just one more second away when he felt the dog's tongue lap against the back of his hand, conveying an insistent urgency tinged with desperation. When he opened his eyes, the dog lifted a paw and placed it lightly against his arm.

Corey eased the gun out of his mouth and stared at the ugly lump of metal.

He looked at the dog again and said, "You know what, buddy? Fuck this. Fuck all of it, actually. The fucked-up mind games. The dreams. Even the guilt. Every goddamn bit of it."

Corey got to his feet and so did the dog, the animal turning in rapid, tight circles, wagging its tail in a frenzy of joy.

Corey laughed.

He reared his hand back and heaved the gun away, sending it clattering down the street.

Then he looked at the dog and said, "Let's let all the gods and demons and whatever else play their big game of good against evil. It'll all take care of itself without us, for better or worse, somewhere down the line." The dog tilted its head, ears perking as Corey talked. "What do you say you and me go for a walk? You like that idea, boy?"

The dog pointed its snout upward and snapped off three quick, enthusiastic barks.

He liked the idea a lot, it seemed.

Corey and the dog started walking.

They walked together for a long, long time.

LOCKDOWN

Bev Vincent

The meeting took place at the community hall on June 30. In the past, the building had been used as a schoolhouse, when there were children on the island, but the last teenager had moved to the mainland five years ago to attend community college in Portland, and there weren't many prospects for more youngsters to join the Maine island's aging population.

The hall also saw occasional use as a church, but only for major religious holidays and no preacher had made the six-mile journey by boat for years. There had been a few wakes and an affirmation ceremony when Nancy and Dottie solemnized their relationship. These days, it was mostly used for parties and for the occasional town meeting. It wasn't often Seacliff Island's thirteen residents needed to assemble to discuss something. Life here normally proceeded at a leisurely pace, with few disagreements other than the usual squabbles among neighbors who lived in close proximity.

On this Friday afternoon, the meeting hall held fifteen people. The honeymooners from Kentucky staying with the Bouchards, who rented their spare room to the occasional tourist, had been invited to attend, since the matter under discussion impacted them as well. Dick Collins, the retired historian, author of three books that did not appear on the shelves of anyone else on the island, had requested the gathering. He felt the situation was too urgent to let another day pass.

The stacking chairs had been assembled into a sweeping arc by Margaret Gagnon, who tended to appoint herself to such tasks. There was another chair at the focus of the curve. Dick occupied it now, but that did not imply he was the leader of the community. He had called the meeting, so he would speak first.

Once everyone was seated and the last breath mint had been unwrapped, Dick stood. He swiveled slightly in each direction to take everyone in. The fourteen faces before him were, without exception, grim. He knew these people well—except for the honeymooners, who looked more frightened than everyone else. The others had all lived here for years—decades, even. Several of the residents had been born here.

He drew in a breath and released it. "We've all seen the news from the mainland, and I'm sure you've heard from friends and relatives as well. It's a lot to take in, and I think it's safe to assume that we don't know everything. Politicians never tell the whole story and sometimes they out-and-out lie."

Several members of his audience murmured their assent. People who chose to live in such a remote location generally had less trust in the government than the average citizen.

"No one here is old enough to remember the pandemic of 1918—although Mildred would have been alive back then."

"Barely," Mildred Turner said with a shy smile. "You too, maybe?"

Dick pursed his lips. "Well over half a million people died, and it took two years for it to clear up. Based on what I'm hearing, this is far worse. Anyone who comes into contact with an infected person gets this so-called superflu. If you get it, you die. No exceptions." He took another deep breath. "Things are falling apart over there.

LOCKDOWN

Looting and rioting. I know the president said the disease isn't lethal and everything's under control, but I don't believe him."

There were grumbles in the audience. The few people on the island who'd bothered to vote in the last election had likely supported the man in the White House, but he wasn't rising to the occasion during this time of national crisis.

"My proposal is simple, but imperative. Seacliff Island is well provisioned. The supply boat arrived a week ago, and our pantries and cellars are well stocked. Our gardens are planted. There are plenty of fish and lobster in the gulf and there probably won't be any game wardens to enforce the daily bag limit. In a way, this is the sort of crisis we've always been preparing for." He paused before delivering his conclusion. "We have to lock the island down. No one gets on. That's the only way to keep us free of the virus."

"A lockdown?" Charles Bouchard asked. "For how long?"

Dick shrugged. "Until it's safe. We have fuel for our generators and the wind turbine is cranking out more electricity than we need."

"What about my sister?" Evelyn Martin asked. "She's over in Ellsworth, and when I talked to her last night she seemed fine. A few sniffles, that's all. Can she come here? We have room."

Dick shook his head. "We are disease-free today. Even if Jocelyn—that's her name, right? Even if Jocelyn is healthy, she could be a carrier. Or whoever she hires to bring her over." He sighed. "I'm sorry, but that's my proposal. I don't want to sound overly dramatic, but it's do or die, literally." He stepped aside and took a seat at the end of the semicircle. The floor was now open for discussion.

For a while, no one said anything. Finally, the young man from Kentucky stood. Dick wondered what the folks back home thought of him. He looked like a rock musician—long, stringy hair, shaggy beard, and tattoos covering his legs and arms. "What about us?" he asked. "We both have jobs, and our families are expecting us back home next week."

Bob Williams walked slowly to the speaker chair. He was in his late fifties, but moved like a much older man. "I can't speak for everyone, but I like to think we'd all welcome you to stay on the island. We look after our own, even if you're from away. It would be up to Helen, of course. And Charles. We aren't a Christian community, for the most part, but I think we're a charitable one."

"Stay?" the young man, James, said. He had a confused look on his face. His new bride took his hand, but remained seated. "On the island with all of you?"

"You are free to leave, of course. Someone would probably let you have a boat. We have no shortage of those." There were nods from several people in the room. "But if what Dick is saying is true—and I have no reason to doubt him—it seems likely Seacliff Island is the safest place for you. If you got to the mainland and didn't like what you saw . . ."

"You couldn't come back," Wally Martin said.

It was a breach of protocol, but Bob was happy someone else had delivered the verdict instead of him. "So, think long and hard before you decide. You may not have a job or a family to go back to anyway, to be honest. I know that's hard to hear, but that's how it sounds to me."

"Might as well stay until the end of your honeymoon, at least," Helen Bouchard said. "See if the situation changes."

Bob returned to his seat. The formality of the speaker chair now seemed needlessly foolish. This wasn't a town hall where they had to decide what to do about the increased cost of having provisions delivered from the mainland or an argument over installing the wind turbine. They were discussing their future—their very survival—and it seemed pointless to keep shuffling back and forth to the chair.

"I have a question," Dottie Phillips said after raising her hand. She taught school on the mainland before meeting Nancy and moving to Seacliff seven years ago. "How do we *keep* people from coming here? If it's so terrible over there, they're going to be looking for somewhere safe. We're not the easiest place to get to, but we're not completely off the grid, either."

LOCKDOWN

Dick stood. "There's only one way onto the island—the jetty. The cliffs are too steep for anyone who hasn't climbed Mount Everest, assuming their boat didn't get swept onto the rocks first. I propose we keep someone stationed at the dock—armed, of course—to fend off anyone approaching. We can take shifts. I suspect, though, that before too many days pass, we won't have to worry about intruders." He paused as if considering what to say next. "I think this is it, everybody. The big one. We'll be lucky if a few percent of the population is still alive by the end of the week. It's spreading that fast."

"On the East Coast?" Alice Williams asked.

Dick scrunched his lips.

"You mean . . . everywhere?"

"That's right."

"The whole country?"

"Yes. The whole country."

"What about . . . ?" Alice paused as if unsure how to formulate the question. "What about everywhere else? The rest of the world?"

"The president said the virus has been reported in both Russia and China. I'm not surprised." He pointed at the hall's tall windows and the sky beyond. "Back in 1918, people hardly traveled, so the spread was slow. We have tens of thousands of flights, both national and international, every day. They've probably closed the airways by now, but I doubt it was in time. All it would take is a few infected people getting on overseas flights. Now, I'm not saying the disease started here and we're spreading it across the globe. At this point, it doesn't much matter where it came from. It's here and it's deadly." Dick inhaled and exhaled before continuing. "Even if the president says otherwise."

More grumbles. The president was the man who, only two years ago, had loudly proclaimed, *Read my lips—no new taxes!* Look how that had turned out. It was ironic when Dick thought about it. Less than a month ago, the president and his Russian counterpart had signed a treaty to ban chemical weapons. Fat lot of good that did.

"Where's Governor McKernan?" Bob asked. "Why aren't we hearing from him?"

Dick straightened up. "I don't know. Maybe he's sick, too. Anyhow, like I said, my feeling is that we won't have to keep watch for long. We don't have anything the folks over there need. Our only asset is isolation, but that won't matter for long. Any survivors on the mainland will soon have all the living space and supplies they need."

The residents of Seacliff Island sat with that notion for a while. Then Wally stood. "I agree with everything Dick said, although we need to keep tabs on the news. Things could change in a heartbeat. The president said the CDC's vaccine might be available next week. He said the disease will eventually run its course." He cleared his throat. "My question is—how long do you think we can survive without supplies from the mainland?"

"Worried the beer's gonna run out?" Harry Gagnon asked, which generated a few half-hearted chuckles from the residents.

"Or toilet paper?" Charles added, which inspired more laughter.

"Both," Wally said with a good-natured smile.

"A valid concern," Dick said. "We'll run out of certain perishables before long, no doubt. If we're stuck here through the winter, we might have to start rationing some other things next spring, until the crops come in. We're lucky the supply boat came when it did. We all have well-stocked pantries and freezers." That got another laugh. It wasn't a condition of residency to have a survivalist mindset, but pretty much everyone on Seacliff had those tendencies. During the blustery winter months, they could be—and often had been—cut off from the mainland for weeks at a time. "As long as we don't get hit by a drought or any other biblical plague, we should be able to get by." He chuckled. "We could even cook up some sour mash for booze if push comes to shove."

"What about my arthritis medicine?" Mildred asked. "I have enough for three months. What then?"

LOCKDOWN

Dick frowned. "Not saying it's going to be easy. We just have to look out for each other as best we can."

There was another lull in the conversation. Finally, Charles asked, "Are we decided, then? No one comes on the island?"

For the next several minutes, Seacliff's residents discussed the issue among themselves. Ultimately, no one spoke out against the proposal, so it was accepted by acclamation.

The honeymooners emerged from their huddled conversation. "We've decided to stay," James said.

"For now," Sarah added, squeezing her husband's hand for emphasis.

"For now," James added.

Dick retrieved a clipboard and a sheet of paper from a cabinet. He made several strokes with a pen to divide the page into a grid, which he annotated with days of the week and hour ranges. "Here's a sign-up sheet for jetty watch. Eight-hour shifts. If you're comfortable with a gun, pick a slot. We shouldn't need to work more than two or three times a week each."

"Jesus H. Christ," Harry said. "I finally get to retire and now I'm back on the bleedin' clock agin." Despite his grumbling, he took the clipboard from Dick and filled in three late-night shifts. "Not like I sleep much these days, anyhoo."

Before long, the grid was full. Even the newlyweds signed up, opting to work together. Only Mildred abstained.

"Would anyone object if I bring over one of my TVs?" Bob asked. "I have a feeling we're going to be spending a lot of time in here."

"Good idea," Dick said. "And I'll let everyone know what I hear through my back channels. I still have access to my electronic mail account at the university," he said. "For now."

The meeting broke up and people slowly migrated homeward. It was still early in the day. The sun wouldn't go down for several hours, the summer solstice having only just passed. It was too soon for dinner. Islanders tended to eat late. There were, of course, chores to be attended to—laundry, cleaning, baking. Lawns needed to be mowed and the gardens needed to be watered and inspected for bugs, a task made all the more urgent by their current circumstances, but no one had any enthusiasm for these duties. There was a lot of silent contemplation in the homes on Seacliff Island that afternoon.

The Mitchells, however, had much to discuss. James had attempted to contact the mainland to get a message to their families in Kentucky, but no one answered the phone, and a scan of the entire band on Charles's shortwave radio produced little more than static and a couple of recorded messages that contained no useful information. They revisited their decision to stay and, while it didn't devolve into a full-fledged argument, emotions ran high, and tears were shed.

The only house that remained unoccupied that afternoon belonged to Dick Collins, who had taken the first shift at the jetty. After gathering a few provisions, he walked down the narrow gravel road to the wharf, a rifle slung over his shoulder and a pistol tucked into his waistband.

There was a small shed at the near end of the pier, where the harbormaster once sat, back in the days when there was on-demand ferry service to the mainland. Back then, over a hundred people lived on Seacliff. Now most of the houses were unoccupied and many were in an advanced state of disrepair. In a way, they were lucky—no ferry meant people didn't often travel off-island, so the virus hadn't spread here. Dick was determined to keep it that way.

He dropped his supplies off in the shack and stood at the edge of the wharf. The previous wooden structure had been swept away by a late-summer storm ten years ago, taking several boats with it. The replacement was built on a foundation of stones chiseled from the cliffs that gave the island its name. At considerable expense, Dick recalled, but the loss of all those boats had been a costly lesson.

He stared into the open waters. With a telescope or a pair of binoculars—the latter of which he had left in the shack—he would have been able to see faint shapes representing the nearest islands. In one direction was the coast of Maine. In the other, the southwestern tip of Nova Scotia. He tried to imagine the scenes playing out on the mainland based on what he'd heard. Chaos and calamity the likes of which no one had ever seen on this continent, barely six miles away. Someone claimed a radio talk show host from the Midwest had been killed by the army during a call-in program, and a former university colleague said there'd been executions broadcast live on WCSH a few nights ago. He wasn't sure he believed that—the man was getting on in years and tended to confabulate—but what if it was true? And what about the numerous reports of bodies being buried in mass graves or dumped into the ocean?

Nearly fifty years ago, Dick had been on one of the LSTs that delivered thousands of men—boys actually—onto Omaha Beach. He never thought he'd see anything like that again in his lifetime. Not just the devastation that day but the things he'd experienced on the continent afterward. Frightened people were capable of terrible things. If the reports and rumors were true, his fellow Americans had already started to turn their weapons on each other. Would he be able to point his rifle at a total stranger? He had before. But, he wondered, what about the others, especially the honeymooners? He hoped they wouldn't be put to the test.

He did the math. A scientist had disseminated a supposedly confidential government document that said fewer than one in a thousand had natural immunity to the disease—maybe only one in ten thousand. Worst-case scenario, that meant 25,000 survivors in the whole country. Best case, as many as 250,000, the population of a small city. The chance anyone on Seacliff was immune was virtually zero. And who knew if the virus would die out with everyone else or if it would lie in wait to infect anyone who showed up months, maybe even years, later? It felt like the end of the world had all but arrived. Not yet, but soon enough.

After meals were prepared and eaten in near silence, the residents of Seacliff headed back to the meeting hall. No one wanted to be alone. They brought desserts and drinks—mostly alcoholic. Bob Williams had already lugged his TV set into the hall and was wiring it up to the antenna on the roof that could pick up several stations from the mainland. He had a satellite dish in his backyard that could bring in over a hundred channels—the envy of his neighbors, he believed—but there was no way to run the cable from the dish down to the hall.

As a rule, islanders had little interest in national or global affairs, but now everyone was glued to the television news, which seemed to be the only thing broadcasting. There were no sports scores, only a very rudimentary weather forecast, and no clips from reporters on location. The normally jocular anchors looked exhausted and grim. And sick. Every one of them was coughing and sneezing. One man kept glancing to his left, as if something off camera troubled him.

Bob believed they were trying to put a positive spin on the situation—maybe they were being forced to—but he knew better. Dick liked to refer to the dial-up account that gave him access to an electronic messaging system on the university computer network, but Bob had his own network of people he kept in touch with across the country via ham radio, and he had been hearing things, too. Until communications went totally dark, like someone had flipped an off switch, that is. That told him everything he needed to know.

Eventually, Mary Pinette asked if they could listen to music instead. At forty-eight, she was the youngest Seacliff resident. She had brought a large combo radio/CD player with her. She tuned it to a Portland station and found the top twenty countdown. The newest entry was a soulful tune called "Baby, Can You Dig Your Man?" that had entered the chart at number eighteen, but Mary preferred the new songs by Sinéad O'Connor and Heart. She didn't think of herself as a feminist, but she favored female singers to male.

There was no DJ patter between songs, leading Dick to believe this was a preprogrammed broadcast. The countdown was in the middle of

LOCKDOWN

"U Can't Touch This" when the radio emitted an earsplitting shriek. After that, it produced nothing but static, no matter which way Mary turned the dial.

Bob, who thought the static was an improvement over MC Hammer, clicked the TV back on and found the same situation there. One station showed a handwritten placard reading *Sorry, we are having a problem*. The only station with actual programming was playing a rerun of *The Andy Griffith Show*. Mary wondered if little Ronnie Howard was still alive. Last fall, she'd taken the boat to the mainland to see his latest movie, *Parenthood*, with a gaggle of her university friends. They'd asked her why she wanted to live in such a remote place and whether it was just a phase she was going through. She'd inherited the house on Seacliff—and a sizable legacy—from her mother and found she didn't mind living away from the hustle and bustle. Look at how things had turned out. No tube neck for her.

The gathering broke up around midnight. Harry headed down to the pier to relieve Dick on watch duty, carrying a large cup of strong coffee in his hand and a flask in his rear pocket. Everyone else returned home and went to bed. Thus ended the first day of lockdown on Seacliff Island.

Early-morning sun streaming through the bedroom window awakened Nancy Landry on Saturday. Her partner, Dottie, was already awake, sitting up with a pillow behind her back, staring into the distance.

"What's up, hon?" Nancy asked.

"I had the strangest dream. It was so vivid."

"Tell me about it."

"There was this old woman. Really old, like a hundred, with a wrinkled face."

"More wrinkles than me? "Nancy asked.

That earned a smile. "Way more. She was Black and walked with a cane. She reminded me of my grandmother. She was on a farm surrounded by a cornfield. People were singing old-time hymns."

"Such detail!"

"I know. It felt real."

"What did you talk about with her?" Nancy asked, sure it would have something to do with the epidemic.

"She told me I should come see her. If I left now, I should go to Nebraska. If I was delayed, I should go to Boulder."

"That's really specific."

"I know. The thing is—I woke up wanting to go."

Nancy sniffed. "It was just a dream."

"I know. But still . . ." She paused, as if reluctant to continue. "There was something else. Something watching us. A man with no face, who turned into a crow with red eyes. He terrified me, but the old woman made me feel safe." Dottie didn't mention the vision she'd had of rows of people who'd been crucified.

After they got dressed, they made breakfast and carried it down to the community hall, certain they would find some of the others there. In fact, everyone was, even Harry.

"Them youngsters are on duty now," he said. "They was late, but they showed up."

"I made a lot of noise outside their room this morning," Helen said with a smug smile. "Made sure they were up."

Harry doffed a pretend hat at her. "Thank ya kindly, ma'am."

Helen blushed.

"I'm thinking about going to Vegas," Wally Martin said as he filled his coffee cup from the thirty-cup urn Margaret had started an hour earlier. His voice had an airy, dreamlike quality.

"Vegas?" Mildred said with obvious disdain. "Sin City?"

"Yup. I got a personal invitation from a guy named Randy in my dreams last night. Funniest damn thing. He told me to come on down, just like Bob Barker. It was the happening place and all the cool folks were headed there. Anyone want to come with me?"

LOCKDOWN

Nancy glanced at Dottie, who gave her a meaningful stare. Nancy got the message and remained silent.

"Might just do it. Go out with a bang. Throw snake eyes one last time."

Evelyn, his wife, swatted him on the shoulder. "You're not going anywhere."

"I don't like those odds," Dick said with a forced laugh.

Nancy wondered if anyone else had had vivid dreams, but no one volunteered to describe them if they had.

The TV stations were still broadcasting static except for the one where Barney Fife was contemplating the use of his one bullet. Helen gave her husband a couple cups of coffee and a tray of pastries to take down to the Mitchells. "Tell me what you think of them," Dick said. "Let me know if they've got what it takes."

"To do what?"

"Point a gun at someone. Pull the trigger if necessary."

"Gotcha."

Charles was back five minutes later, panting. "They're gone," he announced.

"Gone?"

"Vamoosed. Scrammed."

"They're not up at the house?" Helen asked.

Charles shook his head. "I checked, just to be sure, but they took one of the boats." He looked at Bob. "Yours."

"Son of a bitch," Bob said. "I just had that new navigation system installed." He looked at Dick. "Do you think they know how to use it?"

Dick grunted. "If not, they may be headed for Yarmouth. Or Africa." He threw his hands in the air.

"Son of a bitch," Bob repeated.

Wally was still going on about his Las Vegas dream. "I tell you," he said to his wife, "it was real. Like a message. Do you think those young people got that invitation, too? And that's why they left?"

"Wally Martin, don't be so foolish. No one is inviting you anywhere," Evelyn said, delivering another wallop to his shoulder. "Except me—I'm inviting you to come on home and take care of that tractor you've been meaning to fix for a while."

With that, the gathering broke up. End of the world or not, there were outside chores and housework to be done.

On Sunday morning, when Nancy awoke, Dottie wasn't by her side. She found her partner on the bench outside the front door, smoking a cigarette.

"I thought you quit," Nancy said.

"I found an old pack in the back of the kitchen drawer," Dottie said. "They're stale, but it doesn't look like we'll be getting more anytime soon, so what the hell?"

"I don't like it. And you're up early again."

"I had another dream. Mother Abagail, that's her name. She told me I should come right away. There are others already headed her way. But . . ."

"But?"

"She said *you* shouldn't come with me."

"Why the hell not?" Nancy said. Then she took a step back. "Sorry. It's just a dream."

"That's just it—I'm not sure it was."

Nancy remained silent.

"She said you shouldn't come because you're not immune. You'd die."

"And you are?"

Dottie opened her mouth but no words came out.

"Is this your way of saying you want to break up with me?"

Dottie looked aghast. "No. No way. Not at all. I love you."

"But . . ."

"But what if it's true?"

"Why would it be? Was there a talking crow with no face in this one, too?"

Dottie frowned. "You heard Wally. He had a dream, too."

"Not about some old woman in Kansas."

"Nebraska."

"Whatever. I had a dream, too."

"What about?"

"I was in school getting ready to take an exam, but I'd never gone to class. Not once."

Dottie said nothing.

"It was just a silly stress dream. But let's suppose yours isn't, for the sake of argument. Suppose it's some kind of message, although I'm not saying it is."

"Okay," Dottie said. She recognized Nancy's tone. She had to be on the lookout for land mines.

"Suppose the old woman is real and suppose you're immune like she says, and everyone who's immune is supposed to head for Kansas. No, excuse me, Nebraska."

Dottie waited.

"You're here. As long as you stay here, you're as good as immune. We all are. Doesn't matter one way or the other."

"Yes, but—"

"What I'm saying is . . . what I'm *asking*: Why go? Why take the risk? What does the old lady have that we don't have here on the island?"

Dottie took a deep breath, then remembered her cigarette and took a puff. "I think she's the voice of God."

"God?" Nancy said, taking another step back. "You don't believe in God."

"I didn't," Dottie said. "But I think God believes in me. I think she's calling me."

"I don't fucking believe this." Nancy swiveled and headed toward the community hall, but changed her mind and kept going all the way to the pier.

Wally Martin was on duty, but he was reading a magazine in the shed instead of watching for approaching boats. Nancy might have been sixty-two, but there was nothing wrong with her eyesight. There was something in the water maybe half a mile from the wharf, and it appeared to be coming this way.

She poked Wally in the shoulder, startling him, then reached past him to get the binoculars.

"What?" Wally asked.

"Someone's coming," Nancy said. It took her a few seconds to home in on the shape she'd seen, and a few more to twiddle the dial to bring the object into focus. Definitely a boat.

She handed the binoculars to Wally. As he scanned the rough water, Nancy asked, "Do you think it's them? The newlyweds coming back? Or someone else?"

"Whoever it is, they're rowing," Wally said.

"What should we do?"

Wally picked up the rifle and checked to make sure there was a round in the chamber. "Whatever we have to do to keep them away. Like we agreed."

Nancy stared at him for a long moment. "I'm going to get the others."

"Good idea. Might need the help."

She found Dick and Bob having breakfast in the hall. Bob went to fetch Charles and Harry, while Dick followed Nancy back to the jetty.

The boat was a little closer than when she'd first spotted it, but it was still too far away for their shouts to be heard. They waited anxiously as the craft drew nearer. By the time it was close enough that they could see the lone figure without binoculars, the island's entire population was gathered at the end of the wharf. Wally, Dick, Bob, and Harry all had rifles. There were enough pistols to arm everyone else.

"That's *my* boat," Bob said.

"Too bad we don't have no megaphone," Harry said.

Dick sighted through his rifle's scope. "Hold your fire. No point wasting ammunition until they're within range."

From the stranger's point of view, it might have looked like a welcoming party had assembled to greet him, but that was the furthest thing from reality, as he was about to find out.

"It's a woman," Nancy said, handing the binoculars to Dottie. "I think it's Sarah Mitchell."

"Don't matter who it is," Harry said. "Man, woman, or child. They ain't welcome here." He ratcheted a round into the chamber, shouldered his rifle, took aim, and fired. The sound was loud and jarring. No one could tell where his bullet went, but the woman in the boat didn't miss a stroke.

"What are you doing?" Alice Williams shrieked.

"What needs to be done," Harry said.

Dick fired next. Through the binoculars, Dottie saw a splash a few feet to one side of the approaching vessel. This time, the woman wielding the oars paused, allowing the boat to glide forward of its own momentum. She waved and appeared to yell something, but the sound didn't reach the shore. Her dark hair blew about her head in mad disarray, reminding Dottie of a painting of one of the Furies. If she remembered her mythology correctly, they were all about retribution. Wasn't there a goddess of pestilence, too?

The men with the rifles fired a few more times, while Alice and Margaret yelled at them to stop. Their protests were ignored. As the boat drew closer to shore, a kind of madness overtook them. Bloodlust. Even Mildred Turner got off a couple of shots. They were fighting for their lives. Dottie had never fired a gun before, but she felt compelled to protect Seacliff. According to her dream, she was supposedly immune, but no one else on the island was.

Most shots missed their target—the boat was being cast about by the rough waves—but a few found their mark. A hole materialized in the prow, well above the waterline. Another bullet took out the windshield. Dottie thought that one might have also grazed Sarah, who was crouched as low as possible, but still exposed.

Later, no one would claim responsibility for the kill shot, but Dottie was reasonably sure which rifle delivered the fatal bullet. A second after a cloud of red blossomed around the woman's head, Dottie heard Dick grunt with satisfaction. Sarah was thrown backward, no longer visible except for one arm that dangled over the starboard gunwale.

Still, the boat drew closer, carried by the waves.

"We gotta burn 'er," Harry said. "We can't let her reach the island." He went up the gravel road to his house, moving as quickly as his sixty-five-year-old legs would take him. A couple of minutes later, he was back with several glass bottles and a wad of rags. Charles took two bottles to the supply tank and filled them with gasoline. Then he handed one to Harry, who stuffed a rag into the openings to make a wick. By then, the boat was only a dozen or so yards away and they could all see Sarah Mitchell's body reclining in it, arms splayed, head disfigured. There was no sign of her husband.

Harry held up his improvised gasoline bomb. Wally lit the fuse. The flames reflected in his eyes, reminding Dottie of the crow from her dream. Harry reached back, then lobbed the bomb high into the air. It tumbled as it flew, but his aim was true. The bottle landed in the middle of Bob's boat and exploded.

Sarah's clothes caught fire. A moment later, the boat was engulfed in flames. They watched in dumbstruck awe as a black cloud formed over the boat and it started to fall apart. The engine tumbled from the back, and the craft began to take on water. The seawater extinguished most of the flames, but by then the boat was half submerged and it came no closer to shore. Sarah's smouldering body lingered on the surface for a while before it, too, sank into the depths of the Gulf of Maine.

LOCKDOWN

No one said anything for a long time. They stared at the remains of the boat and the vast body of water beyond. Each person contemplated his or her part in the scene that had just transpired. Some were proud they had defended the island. Others were ashamed they'd killed a defenseless young woman.

Except for Wally, who said he'd finish out his shift, everyone migrated back to the hall, where they picked over the remaining food with little interest and drank coffee. The television stations had all gone completely dark, and the radio still produced nothing but static.

"They musta made it to the mainland," Harry said. "She was probably full of that there virus."

"Probably couldn't start the motor," Bob said. "It was always tough to get going."

"We did what we had to do," Helen said. "Didn't we?"

There were nods of agreement, but no one said anything more, and a few people looked like they weren't sure they agreed. After a while, the residents of Seacliff Island returned home and tried to push all thoughts of this horrible Sunday morning from their minds, concentrating on making sure their crops were tended to and their pantries were free of pests.

That night, Wally was visited again in his dreams by the cool dude who called himself Randy. *"Come on down to Las Vegas, Walter, my pal,"* he said. *"You'll fit in here just fine and the house never wins. Not anymore."* Wally rolled over, but in his dreaming mind he was making plans to stock up on provisions and head over to the mainland, maybe as soon as the next day. If Evelyn didn't want to go with him, that was okay. He'd have more fun in Vegas without her.

Dottie Phillips didn't dream at all.

IN A PIG'S EYE
Joe R. Lansdale

The night air smelled of excited hog. But the sounds were human. Ricky knew they were in the trees below him. The pines and sweet gums ran along the bottom of the hill for miles and there were pines and oaks on the top of the hill, which was where he was. He threaded between the trees, watching his step, thinking maybe that Boy Scout merit badge he earned so many years back in Wilderness Survival might now be taken from him. He had lost a lot of his stealth since then, but compared to those below who were trying to be quiet, he was Chingachgook.

And as for taking his merit badge from him, who was left to do it and who was left to care?

The hunters below were stepping on sticks and dried pine needles and sweet gum leaves, crackly and stiff as un-milked cornflakes. They might as well be beating drums and farting the national anthem.

But they were dangerous, none the less. They were hunters, and there were quite a few of them, and they were desperate.

The bad stuff, the cough and snort and the world gone wild, started some time back when Ricky was at work in the video store, slipping movies out of their boxes and putting the boxes behind the counter so they could be checked out. If left in the boxes, there was always some light-fingered Louie ready to pluck and stash and quickly dash.

This way, they looked at a video cover, thought the movie looked interesting, and they wanted to rent it, they had to come to the desk and ask for it. The movie was in one of the rows of racks under the desk, which was a large round counter in the middle of the store.

Ricky was thinking what he had wanted to do was make movies, not rent them, not own a store, but it was as close to showbiz as he had gotten so far, and at thirty-two, it was beginning to look as if he had made a career choice when he wasn't thinking about it. It was like he had licked one of those psychedelic toads for a druggie experience, and all he had gotten was frog pee in his mouth.

It was 11:00 p.m., and one more hour and he was out. He had worked the entire shift, from 2:00 p.m. on, and he was thinking he had to hire some help. That schedule, seven days a week, was killing him. Thing was, though, those were the hours folks rented movies. During the two-to-five-p.m. shift, not so much, but enough, and after people got off work it was furious and went on hot until midnight. Weekends, all hours were busy enough.

Except tonight. Just one family in the store. It was probably due to the intense flu that was going around. Everyone was home filling garbage cans and commodes with snot-coated Kleenex.

Him, he hadn't so much as had a sore throat or a muscle ache.

As for rentals tonight, he had been doing better on the bags of popcorn he sold, hot-popped right in the store. It was a great smell at first, but now, after months of it, the stink made him woozy. He was at the point where he would have preferred the odor of a dead body.

Worse, there were predictions that the VHS tape was on its way out. But what the hell could replace that kind of technology, some little spinning disc of some sort?

IN A PIG'S EYE

Doubtful.

The couple in the back had a kid, a boy, about eight, with them, and they spent most of their time trying to keep him from climbing on video racks. Finally, they came to the desk with *Starman*.

The man, a fellow who looked as if parenthood or most anything else didn't agree with him, put the video cover on the counter. His eyes were red and he had the sniffles. He kept sucking up the contents of his nose like a four-year-old.

The mother, who made Ricky think of a former hot cheerleader who had run out of hair dye and lost the spring in her step, said, "Is this appropriate for children?"

Ricky glanced at the kid. A boy with longish blond hair in a bowl cut. He had a string of snot running out of his nose and older runs had dried on his cheeks, giving him a glazed-doughnut sheen.

"That depends," Ricky said. "I say yes, but you might say no."

"That's not much of an endorsement," said the father.

"Not a negative, either," Ricky said. "I can't say what will bother someone or won't. I rent out videos. I'm not in the endorsement business."

"Fair enough," the father said. "This will do."

He paid for the video and some popcorn. Ricky located the tape and slipped it inside the case. "Enjoy your movie."

"Rock and roll," the father said, though Ricky wasn't sure how that applied to anything.

The family went out coughing. Ricky was certain they had grown sicker within the thirty minutes they had been in the store. Through the store glass, Ricky saw the father lean against the hood of his Chevy and toss dark vomit on the left front tire.

The mother started around toward him, but he held up his hand in an *I'm okay* gesture. He didn't look okay to Ricky. He looked worse in the overhead lights that shone in the parking lot than he had in the store. He did not have the "Rockin' Pneumonia and the Boogie Woogie Flu." He had something less festive.

Ricky went to the bathroom and carefully washed his hands. He had handled the money the guy gave him. Money was nasty enough, but with that guy being sickly, he wanted to make sure his hands were clean.

When he came out of the restroom, his heart sank a little. Shelly the Shit was walking into the store.

"Hey, man, how's you?" Shelly the Shit said.

"Okay," Ricky said, flicking the panel door back and stepping inside the ringed counter.

Shelly the Shit came every night to hang out. Never rented movies, just hung out. He liked to come in earlier than tonight, and Ricky thought maybe he had missed out on his visit, but such a delightful hope had fizzled out.

Well, he had less than an hour to deal with Shelly. So that was something positive. They called him Shelly the Shit in high school because he was willing to do most anything to anybody for little to no purpose. He had, for reasons unknown, latched onto Ricky in recent years, coming into the store to hang out under the illusion that, because they knew one another, they were friends. Still, Ricky kept an eye on him. Shelly the Shit wasn't really anyone's friend. He didn't even like himself.

"Man, I got a Betamax," Shelly the Shit said. "You had some Betamax tapes, I would rent them."

"Like I been telling you," Ricky said, "every time you bring that up. They don't make them anymore. They lost out to VHS."

"Everyone said Beta machines would be better, and I bought one."

"Well, you fucked up. Lots of people did. There's not going to be a Betamax renaissance, Shelly. How many years you had that thing? See any movement toward Beta?"

"I don't know. I'm thinking people get a real comparison, they'll go Beta."

"They got a real comparison. They went VHS."

"Yeah. I guess. Hey, you been keeping up on current events?"

"What'd you mean?"

IN A PIG'S EYE

"There's been rioting on the far side of town," Shelly the Shit said. "Some serious business, amigo."

"Why would that be? You sure?"

"I'm sure. There's them getting so sick that people say there could be an epidemic. People are so scared they're tearing stuff up and stealing. Epidemic? Shit. I don't believe it. I mean, I feel fine. You?"

"Yeah. I'm all right."

It was as if on cue, Shelly the Shit cleared his throat. "That's nothing," Shelly said. "A tickle."

At home, Ricky warmed up some soup and had a bit of that with crackers while he watched the news. He switched around channels. This time of night, ought to have been movies and late shows about this and that, info-commercials, but the news was all that was on.

There was a panicked feel to all of it. A lot of people were sick, and rumor was an epidemic was about to be declared. The newsrooms all made a point of mentioning that most of their staff was out. One newscaster, a young blond lady, had a red sheen to her nose and her eyes looked watery.

The red-nosed lady showed a clip of army trucks moving into the East Texas town of Nacogdoches, not far from Mud Creek, where Ricky lived, and that gave him a feeling of unsteadiness. Martial law was being declared, or at least that was what was being said, but solid confirmation was yet to happen.

Ricky'd had enough. He turned off the TV. Maybe tomorrow things would be sorted, and it would turn out to be a series of isolated incidents.

While brushing his teeth, he checked to see if his tongue was coated with sickness. Nada. Eyes looked clear. No muscle aches, coughs, or leaky nose. He was fine. Just fine.

He went to his second-floor-apartment window and looked out at the street. Empty as an orphan's stocking on Christmas morning.

Well, it was late and Mud Creek was small, but it was an odd sort of emptiness. It was almost as if that emptiness had weight.

It was the kind of emptiness one could imagine if lost in a night sea without a boat, only one's legs and arms to paddle. Full dark around you, rolling seas and something underwater brushing against your feet.

A feeling of falling from an airplane during a storm without a parachute. All your life and accomplishments of no more importance than shit flushed down a toilet.

Slight variations on a theme. But in the end, all the same. Life didn't give awards or medals in the end. It was just the end.

Ricky pulled his curtains and went to bed.

In the late morning there came the sound of metal impacting metal, a clatter of what might have been an escaping hubcap rolling down the street.

Ricky, dressed only in his underwear, got up and went to the window, looked out at the street. Lights, a gathering of people around a mashed-up Buick stuck into a mashed-up Chevy. There were cop car lights.

Ricky pulled on some clothes and his shoes and went out to join the lookie-loo crowd. People, mostly in nightclothes, were gathered around the wreck.

What he saw wasn't so much about the wreck as it was about the man in the car. He was dark with a pus-filled infection. His throat looked like a tire that had been over-aired and was ready to pop. His eyes bulged like boiled eggs. The car smelled of vomit, blood, and shit.

With no less effort than pushing an elephant up a waterslide, the man in the car opened his eyes and turned his head. He was looking right at Ricky, who stood on the side of the driver's window. He couldn't tell if the man was actually looking at him or at nothing at all.

The man opened his mouth and a thick gob of yellow pasty stuff rolled out of it, dripped over his chin, and dropped off. His eyes were sticky with what looked like Elmer's Glue.

"There's a woman in the back seat," someone said.

Sure enough, there was. Ricky eased up closer and saw her lying there. She looked like a scarecrow that had been used for a piñata.

"It's the disease," someone else said.

Ricky turned as he heard sniffling and coughing, and even a clinging-sounding fart. The crowd, in the streetlight, looked like a fucking leper colony; faces swollen, lips swollen, most of them dripping from their noses. A few had turned to vomit in the street. A few had swollen necks.

From under the hood of the Buick, the one that had collided with the sick mobile, steam hissed into the morning air. A door opened. A young woman climbed out, clung to the door to stay afoot. In a surprising coincidence it was the blond, red-nosed woman from the newscast. She looked worse than before, not as bad as those in the collided car, but bad enough to expect a similar fate.

She said, "It's killing everyone. It's killing me." She wandered out into the street as if walking on ankle stubs. "Stay apart. It spreads so goddamn fast."

And with that she fell down in the street. People gathered around her. "Go away," she said. "It spreads. I can hardly see."

The woman on the asphalt rolled her eyes, showing only the bloody-stained whites. She said, "The poor elephants, and all those bears without ice."

She turned her head slightly, made a choking sound, like she was seriously trying to swallow an anaconda, then puked up a blackness that contained what looked like intestines, and that was it for the Red-Nosed Reporter.

Ricky stepped away from the crowd, and as he did, he saw military trucks, the National Guard, rolling into sight, and he saw another cop car, too. The cop car parked near him, and Gene West got out of it. He was a big cop. Ricky had gone to high school with him. They hated one another. Ricky had been better as quarterback, and Gene, who was a sometime quarterback, spent a lot of time on the bench. He had lost his girl to Ricky. Not that Ricky had done anything to take her. It just happened, and was long over now, but Gene was not a forgiver. They had three or four fistfights back in the day, real piss-and-vinegar stuff, and Ricky had won them all. This anger and disappointment had nested inside Gene West like a poisonous bird.

Gene was the kind of guy who threw gasoline on cats and lit them up. He had done it more than a few times in high school. He was proud of it and found the screeching horror of the running, finally smoky, charred, collapsing cat a real hoot.

Gene was a fucking bully. A rotten bastard who never forgot a slight. And as is often the case, shit floats to the top. Gene West was chief of police.

You could see his face change when he saw Ricky. They stared at one another for a long moment, then Gene turned away from him, pulled a bullhorn from the cop car, and yelled into it. "Everyone go back to your homes. Martial law has been declared. Medical help is being organized. If you're on the street in the next few minutes, you are subject to arrest. Or worse."

"What?" said someone from the crowd.

There was mumbled protest.

Ricky knew Gene, what he was capable of, the power he wanted, so he stepped back to his apartment. If he were arrested by Gene today things might become most uncomfortable. He felt that things were about to go wonky.

Ricky didn't go back to bed. He watched from his curtain-parted window and saw more National Guard trucks and soldiers roll in.

They came out of the back of the trucks in waves of tan uniforms, carrying rifles of some sort. They came out less than efficient. Some of them staggered and went down. They were sick, too.

Men and women dressed in white coats dragged them to the side of the road and ministered to them. He saw Gene waving his arms as if he were needed to guide the trucks in.

He wasn't.

A little later, while Ricky was having a cup of coffee in the kitchen, he heard shots. He went back to the window and looked out. People were running. Shots were snapping. My God, everyone had lost it.

He saw Shelly the Shit staggering about. The light wasn't good, but Ricky could tell Shelly's neck was swollen, had an accordion look to it.

Gene West was twelve feet away. He had his pistol drawn. Shelly said something. Ricky saw his mouth move, and then Gene shot him. A solid chest shot. Shelly dropped to his knees, blasted out a pond of vomit, then fell on his face.

This shit was real.

Ricky grabbed a backpack out of the closet, strapped on his sleeping bag. He put a clasp knife in his pocket, stuffed the backpack with some food that would keep. He had a first-aid kit, his old Boy Scout camp axe and mess kit that clamped on the outside of his pack, along with a flashlight that fit in a canvas holster. He had a spare flashlight in the pack. There was a flint and steel kit, and a box of matches.

He filled his Boy Scout canteen with water, placed it in its canvas pouch, on the pack. He even crammed his old Boy Scout manual with information for surviving in the woods into his scout pack. He put a couple of books inside, binoculars, a folder of Kleenex, and a roll of toilet paper.

Finally, just for the hell of it, he picked up his old forked slingshot and a bag of roundish rocks he'd gathered when he was a kid. Once upon a time, not that long ago, he had been a hell of a shot. The sling was a modern version. Made of metal with a thick rubber band that was taut to pull and strong to shoot.

Ricky put the pack on a chair and prepared a quick breakfast of a granola bar and a glass of water. He ate like a starved hound. He strapped on the pack and went out the back way, down the stairs and through the trash-canned alley of the apartment complex. There was a back fence, but he used a garbage can to climb on and slipped over it. Now there was an un-mowed strip of grass that led to a small patch of woods, and beyond that was the highway.

He went along snappy-like and into the woods. He found a thick wooded spot. There was a hickory tree there with a natural fork in it. He climbed into the fork, which was reasonably comfortable. There were enough limbs and leaves about so he could see the apartment complex, but unless someone were actually looking for him in that tree, he was unlikely to be spotted.

He sat there for a long time, finally climbed down, took a wee, dropped his pants and leaned against a tree, squatted a bit, and took a shit. He wiped his ass on the toilet paper he had brought, covered his pile with leaves and dirt that he raked over it with the side of his shoe.

He climbed back onto his perch. Hours fled by. He slept in the fork of the tree, feeling mildly safe and exhausted from stress. Light came. He climbed down and walked around the woods to put some feeling back into his legs and ass. Being in the tree had numbed them. He took out one of his books and sat beneath an elm and read a bit, but it was hard to concentrate.

When it was solid dark again, using his flashlight he made his way through the wooded patch and came out along the highway. There were a few houses there, spaced comfortably apart.

Ricky went past an open garage and saw a bicycle in there. The front door of the house was open, and a woman in a mumu lay face-down in the yard. The night wind picked at her hair. Not for a moment did he think she might be alive, but to make sure, he put the light on her. She was bloated and had a phone with an antenna on it clutched in her hand. Her face was pressed against vomit-coated grass. She smelled like the ass end of a diarrheic camel.

Ricky went into the garage and looked at the bike. Probably belonged to one of her kids, maybe long gone to college. He considered going into the house to check and see if anyone was alive, then decided against it. He didn't want to expose himself unnecessarily to the disease. Or surprise someone inside, who might decide to ventilate him with a few well-placed shots. This was Texas, after all.

The bike had a headlight. He clicked its switch and the light came on. It was risky to have the light on, but he felt it was a chance he had to take. He mounted the bike and rode across the highway and down a narrow blacktop road he knew that led toward the Sabine River. There were some old fishing and hunting trails he had used a few times, and he might find a place to hide for a while. Until he could figure out what to do. He was reasonably handy in the woods and along the river. It seemed like the right choice.

Along the road he went, pedaling steadily. He didn't so much as see one car. Not that he expected to see many out here, but not even one struck him as odd.

It was the disease. It was sweeping through East Texas like a pack of hungry weasels through a henhouse. If Gene West felt comfortable shooting people, fulfilling a lifelong dream, most likely everything had gone to hell.

As the night cracked open with a bloody explosion of sunlight, Ricky stopped pedaling and got off the bike, pushed it along the side of the road until he found a narrow trail on the other side of a poorly maintained barbed-wire fence. He lifted the bike over the fence, then carefully parted the wire and climbed through.

He went into the woods and found a place where he couldn't be seen from the blacktop road, rolled out his bedroll, and lay down. His legs vibrated, felt as if he were still pedaling, but finally the nerves settled and so did he.

When he awoke late morning, he had a breakfast of one of his packed items. A small can of beanie-weenies. He hardly remembered eating them.

He sat with his back against a tree where the light came through solidly from above, pulled out his book, trying to pass the time until night.

The book helped, but it didn't completely remove his mind from all that happened; how could it?

From time to time, a car did pass by. He could hear it out on the blacktop. Once or twice, he thought he heard heavy trucks. Military, maybe. Were they picking people up, doctoring them? He had a feeling that might not be their mission. He had heard the shots after they arrived.

When night came, Ricky packed up and got back on the road. He kept his bike light off, as the moon was bright enough to show him the blacktop, which looked like a large, well-licked strand of licorice.

He passed houses. None of them had lights on. He saw cars in driveways, and once he saw two people staggering beside the road, coated in shadows. They stuck out their arms, imploring him to do something he couldn't do. He pedaled faster.

By the time he came to an old fishing trail, planning to sleep out on one of the docks hanging over the river, he was tired, sad, and nearly defeated.

He wondered why he, too, didn't have the disease. He had certainly been exposed enough times. The dock he chose for a resting spot was occupied by half a dozen water moccasins, so that was out. He pushed the bike along the water's edge. He was using the headlight beam now, hoping he was deep enough in the country not to be seen.

Now and again, he would pause, pull out his flashlight, and shine it into the woods. He could hear deer moving through the trees, and once he saw a lone hog standing on a wooded hill, staring out at him.

You left them alone, they pretty much left you alone. But not always. And when they did decide to be nasty, they were a load. A few hundred pounds of stinky pork that could run at enormous speed with tusks as sharp as a samurai sword.

The hog grunted at him. Perhaps a note of courtesy, or a warning.

IN A PIG'S EYE

Finally, in the beam of his flashlight, purely by accident, he saw a large deer stand positioned high on the hill between two trees. It stood fifteen feet off the ground. There were cables on either side of it and they were fastened to the trees for support, secured that way against wind and rain. Had he not been standing at a certain angle, flicking the light in just the right place, he doubted he would have seen it.

It was hard to get himself and the bike through the undergrowth, but he managed. Besides the cables, the stand had thick wooden supports and there was a metal ladder that led up to it.

He turned off the light and leaned the bicycle against one of the deer stand's support trees, on the side away from the river below. He repositioned his backpack and climbed the ladder. There was a closed door, just wide enough for a person. He pushed it open. It was surprisingly large and clean inside, and there were some shelves and some canned goods. A sleeping bag, not too unlike his own, was rolled up and on a shelf. There were three boxes of ammunition for a rifle, but no rifle. There was food and big plastic jugs of water, as well as a wilted Robert B. Parker novel and a box of unopened crackers. Opened, they proved stale inside their wax paper.

The interior was tall enough he could stand up. There were sliding slots that served as windows on all four sides. He slid one of them open and looked out toward the river. A deer below, possibly pausing for a drink, would never know what hit it. And from the other windows he could look into the woods.

For now, Ricky had found a home.

And so, the days passed.

Ricky wondered what was going on out there in the real world, but not enough to investigate. He figured the disease had claimed most, but there had to be others like himself, unharmed, naturally immune; or so he assumed, considering he hadn't even experienced a telltale sniffle.

Chief West would be an example. He hadn't looked sick at all. Of all the people to be immune, why that asshole?

He ate canned goods cold, and those awful crackers. He used his Boy Scout mess kit to boil water from a little spring he discovered higher on the hill. Its water trickled not a hundred feet from the deer stand. There was also a deer feeder without anything in it. Ricky always hated the idea of feeding deer as if making a pet, then shooting them as if you were a mighty hunter. Bullshit.

Ricky found a place in the woods where he could pile some loose rocks into a fire circle and use his flint and steel to make a spark in dry leaves, then feed the fire natural tinder and finally larger sticks as the fire swelled.

He would now and again use this spot to heat up his food, cooking with his mess kit, which contained a frying pan with a fold-out handle and a boiling pot. He feared the smoke might attract a rover of some sort, but he cooked low and the smoke was mostly under the trees and thin due to his limiting the size of the fire.

Ricky's slingshot brought down more than a few squirrels, which he tried to dry fry with poor success, and finally decided on boiling the meat. It wasn't great, but he became accustomed to it. His family had been squirrel hunters from way back, and he enjoyed a good tree rat now and again.

As time passed, he practiced shooting with his slingshot, finding more rocks in a break by a creek on the hill that dipped down and into the Sabine. He got good again quick.

He boiled water in one of his mess kit pots and, once cooled, poured it in the plastic water jugs to keep them topped up. He read his two books, *Moby-Dick* and *Don Quixote*. He had never taken the time to read them before, but now with little to do during the day and only his dick to play with at night, he had learned to appreciate the languid prose of the two old novels. When they were finished, he started on the Robert B. Parker paperback that had been left in the deer stand. It was so good he read it in short time.

IN A PIG'S EYE

As time rolled on, he would occasionally hear gunfire in the distance. He had also noted more wild hogs roaming, not only at night, but during the day. Maybe that was what some of the shooting was about. Hog hunting. They might well be a prime food source now. Once, they were rarely eaten because, as garbage eaters, dead animal consumers, their meat smelled rancid unless you knew how to cut out the fat that held the odors, knew how to treat the meat and grill it right, but at this point, for many out there, a turd might start to look like an appetizer.

Once, in the deeper woods, hunting for squirrel, he had encountered a boar hog of enormous size. He had no idea they could get that big. It looked like a miniature hippopotamus.

It studied him for a moment, and seeing him as food, made a wild charge, scrambling up leaves and dark dirt.

A low-limbed tree was nearby, and Ricky clambered up it like the squirrels he was hunting. The hog actually rammed the tree and shook it a little. That was some pig. Ricky looked down at it, and it looked up. Its eyes were deep and dark like the pit to hell. That hog would eat his ass like a fine soufflé.

Ricky loaded a smooth round rock in the sling and aimed it down. He let it go. It hit the hog square on the head. It squealed and leaped a little and backed off. He let another rock fly, hitting it in the side of the head. He was damn accurate.

The boar didn't like it, seemed to take note of him, as if to store his memory in its mental piggy bank, and trotted away. In case of a sneaky hog tactic, Ricky waited a while before he climbed down.

That night, lying on his sleeping bag, the deer stand windows open, the night wind cool, he thought about his video store. Looted most likely, though he assumed the odds of people wanting movies right now was at an all-time low.

That life was gone. This life was his life, and lying there, a belly full of boiled squirrel and a can of tomato soup, pinching his recently grown beard for something to do, he felt pretty content. Like

Robinson Crusoe on a good day. Like the Swiss Family Robinson, though those self-righteous assholes could always find what they needed on their wrecked boat. It was like a general store.

Maybe, if he started catching fish from the river, gathering berries and nuts, he could make a go of this life down here in the woods tucked up in a deer stand. A few new books wouldn't hurt, but all in all, not so bad.

Never count your blessings. It only reminds you of what will be subtracted.

Late morning, near light, Ricky awoke to the sound of rain and sat up to close the windows in his little space. He could hear the river roaring, and not long after he shut the windows and tried to go back to sleep, he heard a sound like a giant bumblebee.

He sat up and slid open a window. Morning light had eaten the dark and made the inside of his deer stand home the color of a lemon wedge. The river was rolling, but the rain had stopped.

The giant bee sound was an outboard motor.

And then, looking through his binoculars, down and out at the river, he saw the boat.

It was running fast along the water, coming closer to shore. A woman with her hair tied back into a ponytail was sitting at the rear of the little boat, her hand on the throttle, running the motor.

The boat jumped out of the river as it hit a rise of sand along the bank. The front end of it went up and then slammed down and the woman was thrown from the boat and she rolled onto the shore. She scuttled about for a moment before gaining her footing. She was thin and her clothes were worn and her hair was matted. Her face and arms were so dirty she looked like she was painted in camouflage. Still, he could determine she was in his age range and scared.

Another boat was running behind hers, much bigger, more powerful. It had a cabin and it had men on the deck, three of them.

IN A PIG'S EYE

Ricky could tell right away, without fully seeing him, just from the way he stood, one of the men was Gene West.

The woman had taken to the woods. The other boat beached professionally, and the three men got out. West now had a thick black beard and his cop clothes had worn so much they looked less like a uniform and more like a couch cover. Gene had a pistol on his hip. The other two men had baseball bats. A fourth man came out of the cabin. Undoubtedly, he had been the one at the controls.

Gene was yelling orders, which were simply "Get her!" He might not be police chief anymore, but he still liked being in control. He and the other two men went into the woods, leaving the fourth man on the boat. They ran after the woman at a sprint. One of her pursuers ran low, as if he might prefer to go on all fours.

Ricky sat back. They hadn't seen the deer stand blended in with the trees, so they didn't know he was here. But that poor woman. They weren't meeting her for a beach party.

Sighing, Ricky took hold of his slingshot and his pouch of loads, his hunting knife, and scuttled down the ladder. As he ran through the trails he now knew well, the bag of stones bounced in the bag against his thigh. The slingshot hung from his belt.

He moved swiftly and quietly. The air smelled of pine and wet earth. He had not gone far when he could hear the woman coming up the trail toward him. She was about as quiet as a china cabinet falling over.

She almost ran into him. Her face twisted, her eyes popped, and she put up her hands in a stopping motion. Her face was filthy with dirt.

Ricky touched a finger to his lips.

"I'm on your side," he said.

The woman looked skeptical. She was breathing heavily.

Whispering, Ricky said, "It's me or them, and I'm all right."

The woman, panting, decided to be convinced, and nodded.

"Take a deep breath, slow your breathing, then come with me."

Ricky held out his hand. She looked at it, and then took it. He led her higher up the hill, where the woods were rich with pines and oaks and tangled with vines.

It took some time to climb to the higher reaches of the hill, and a lot of effort on the woman's part. She had probably been hiding out, not using her muscles a lot, and of course, she was frightened. So was Ricky, but he had learned to be much calmer from living in the woods with only his wits and deadeye with the slingshot to survive.

As they climbed, Ricky looked back. Gene and the other two were looking up. They saw him and the woman.

"You bastard!" Gene yelled out.

Ricky and the woman reached a temporary ledge of greenery and went to the left, and then up a zigzag trail, and then through trees and around an unusual pile of large rocks that had once been a chimney when someone had inhabited the spot in the old days. Now trees grew tight to it.

They kept climbing. For the moment, they had lost their pursuers.

On the hilltop Ricky located a roll of vines he had found before. They had made a kind of tunnel. Push aside a brush, and you could see there was a mouth you could slide into. The tunnel was thick all over, almost enough to keep rain out. It was not tall enough to stand inside, but you could get around easily on your hands and knees.

Ricky put his finger to his mouth again. The woman nodded. He slipped the slingshot off his hip, opened the ammunition bag, found a smooth rock, and slipped it into the pouch of the slingshot. He pinched the pouch and held it in place.

Gene hurried up the hill, holding his pistol, followed by his bat-wielding partners. Through the brush at the fore of the greenery tunnel, Ricky could see them pause and look at the ground. That gave Ricky worries. The ground was damp, and most likely Ricky and the woman had left their footprints, and that would lead right to them.

He turned to the woman, put his mouth against her ear. "Go to the far end of the tunnel and wait. I'll be right there. If not, go out the other side and down the hill. There's a trail down there and you can make good time. But don't stay on it. Get off of it after a while and hide."

She nodded, and on all fours crawled away from him.

Gene and the men were coming nearer. Ricky took a slow breath, raised the slingshot into the launch position.

And then the great boar that had treed Ricky charged out of the woods and went right at Gene and his thugs.

The man that slouched as he ran was hit by the hog and it was like being run over by a Mack truck. Slouchy was knocked to the ground in an explosion of mud and pine needles. The hog, nimble as an acrobat, wheeled and used its sharp tusks to catch him under the head. A stream of blood leapt from the man on the ground, widened and sprayed.

Gene shot the hog twice. The boar squealed, but it was as if he had shot into a bag of rocks. It was squealing with delight, not pain, as it mauled the man on the ground. Gene and the other man panicked, ran for it down the hill.

The man they left, still alive, tried to get up, but the hog had him again. Tore at his legs with its tusks, bit like a lion. The man was screaming and yelling for help.

Ricky decided this was his cue. He put his weapon and slingshot back in place and crawled through the vine tunnel after the woman. The man was still screaming and the hog was still grunting and squealing as Ricky made his getaway.

Ricky recognized the woman after she cleaned her face at the little spring he used for fresh water. He had been so involved with survival, he hadn't taken great note of her features. He realized now he had gone to school with her. She was two years younger than he was. Jett Marsh. She looked a lot better with the dirt gone, though she appeared near-starved. Her cheekbones looked sharp enough to be listed as lethal weapons.

Ricky and Jett hung in the woods, quiet, listening. They heard the distant sound of a boat, and braved creeping through the woods to where they could see the river. The big boat was moving away from the shore and the one Jett had come in had been smashed.

Waiting to make sure the big boat didn't come back, they crept down to the deer stand, but didn't climb up into it. Ricky left Jett waiting, went down and through the trees and brush, out to the water, and what was left of her boat.

It looked as if Gene or his partners had taken an axe to Jett's ride, and they had pushed the outboard motor into the river.

Ricky listened a moment for the sound of the boat returning, heard nothing, and went back to join Jett.

Jett took to the tomato soup Ricky had left, cold as it was. She drank it right out of the can as soon as he cut the top off with the can opener on his utility knife.

"Sorry," she said when she lowered the empty can, tomato-red coating her top lip like a scarlet mustache.

"Not at all. That's all the canned goods left, but I do a bit of hunting. *We* can do a bit of hunting."

She studied him, wiping her ragged sleeve across her mouth. "I can stay?"

"Yes."

"And you get what out of the deal?"

"Your sterling company. No obligations beyond that."

They talked for a while, Ricky with one ear cocked to the water, waiting to hear that damn boat and Gene coming back, but the day fled and there was nothing.

"The dogs all died," she said. "The people died. Damn cats lived on. Ones that didn't get eaten, that is."

"But you survived?"

"I did."

IN A PIG'S EYE

Turned out nearly the whole town died, and when it was obvious someone had caught the bug, the National Guard, what was left of it, put down the Sickies, as they called them. Gene, the police chief, helped them.

Pretty soon members of the Guard were dying. Most everyone was dying.

"I hid in the clock," she said.

The town center had a tall tower with a clock in it. It had been built in the thirties and still ticked with little metal animal figures that rode in a circle around the tower. Her father had been the man to take care of it and did so for many years. She knew the tower well and knew there was a hiding place there. Her father kept a room full of stored food, water, and tools. The room was hidden behind a sliding door that looked like part of the wall.

"Dad read a lot of Hardy Boys as a kid," she said. "He had that room built into the tower in the fifties. He showed it to me as a kid. When he died, I never thought about it much. I just took over his job."

She hid in there, came out at night and slipped from behind the clock tower, crept down to the creek, where she washed her face and drank water, not worried about germs because she had no choice but to drink. She would then creep into the woods to take care of bathroom matters. She spent time among the trees looking at the moon. Then, well before morning, she would sneak back to the tower.

"I should have shit in a can, but can you imagine the smell in that little room? And I should have stayed in there all the time, but I didn't. Foolishly, I felt I needed to know what was going on. At night, I would sometimes climb up in the tower and grease the clock and look out the little windows or the clock face at the town.

"It was coming apart out there. People killing one another. People like you and I, immune, gathering together and deciding anyone not immune had to go."

She explained how they had cookouts in the middle of the street. It got so even those immune to the disease fell to hunger after the stores had been looted of food. The survivors began to form gangs. Gene was head of one of them. When they ran out of dogs and cats, rats and mice, they killed one another for a food source. They had barbecues down there.

"The smell of meat cooking. It made me hungry. I'm ashamed, but it made me hungry."

The population fought and dwindled. In time, there were only a few visible out there in the street.

Jett did all right until the voluminous food supply in the secret room became less so. Rats had been in the crackers. The canned goods went faster than she expected.

"I thought someone would come, you know? A government agency. But they never did. I got very hungry pretty quick. I slipped out at night and started looking around the town for food, but the place was well plundered. I found a little something now and then. Hunger is what got me in trouble."

She explained how she had been spotted one night by a roving band led by Gene, who had finally found his spot in the world; ruling over a group of people dumber than he was, but equally cruel.

They wanted her, and not just to rape, but to eat. They caught her and told her how it would work, the way she would first service them, and then would serve as a delectable meal after they fattened her up with whatever they had.

They took her to a room in the courthouse. The place was filled with trash, and the group lived there and ruled over themselves, because the inhabitants of the town, due primarily to the disease, murder, and the cannibalism, were down to just them and her.

The room they put her in was warm and without circulating air. It had one chair and nothing else. They brought a mattress in, and she knew that wasn't for her comfort. It would have a onetime long-extended use, and then dinner, with her as the main course. They joked about it. They discussed who got what piece when she was well cooked and the meat ready to drop off the bone. Greg wanted a thigh.

But they messed up. They left her alone for a few minutes. She looked out the window. The room was three stories high, as any building went in Mud Creek, except for the clock tower, which would have measured about four stories.

She could see the street and what one of them had called the barbecue station. It was a big smoker barrel and the fire inside of it had already been started, working its way down to coals. The black smoke chugged out of the smoker pipe. She thought maybe she could break out of the window and jump. They might not have their mattress fun, just dinner if she did that.

Jett had a penny. She discovered it while idly sticking her hand in her pocket. A nervous gesture.

"I remembered that old rhyme about find a penny, pick it up, and all the day you'll have good luck."

Jett used the chair to stand on and used the penny as a kind of screwdriver to unscrew an air vent. She pulled herself into it.

It was dead dark in there, but she kept crawling, and after a while, the air vent warped beneath her, then gave way. She crashed through the ceiling and landed on the floor of a large empty room that had once been the DMV.

Chairs, tables, for some reason, they were all gone. She got up as soon as her stunned body let her.

"I limped out of there, and I hadn't gone far when one of Gene's men saw me. They came after me. I got down to the creek and ran along that, my leg having lost its limp by then. I managed across the little creek, up a hill, and through some trees. A trail led down to the Sabine, and I found the boat there. The outboard had gas. I got it cranked, and away I went. I had driven a boat a few times, but I was hardly an expert.

"I saw the men, Gene included, onshore. He fired his pistol at me.

Fortunately, I was moving fast. I went down the river, found a little cover of sorts, lots of willows hanging off the riverbank. I motored up there among the trees, tied off the boat to a cypress root, and slept on the boat bottom. I had to. I was about to fall over.

"I began to think I had it made. I decided I would try and find a place along the river where I might find food. An abandoned cabin. Anything.

"I was out on the water next morning, and I hadn't gone along far when I heard the growl of a motor, and there was the boat you saw. Gene on the deck. They had found their own ride, and they were trying to find me, or hoping to. I couldn't believe that idiot Gene, who couldn't find his ass with both hands, was within an ass hair of having me again.

"I knew he would catch up with me, so I ran the boat aground and made a run for it. From there, you know the rest."

"I think Gene hasn't given up," Ricky said. "I know him well enough to know how petty he can be. Now with power, he's got nothing else to do. As for his few followers, he has to keep them busy so they don't have time to figure out how truly stupid he is. They're just looking for a daddy to tell them what to do. So, they'll be back."

But they weren't right back. Things went fine for a while, and it started to look like they might be okay, surviving in the woods, eating squirrels, and in season nuts and papaws, muscadines, digging certain roots to be cleaned and boiled. Being a Boy Scout gave Ricky a leg up on that, as he had taken his scout learning seriously. He was rusty, but it was all coming back to him. He had his scout book as a backup. If necessary, he could also fold a flag, but that seemed like an unnecessary skill now and forever.

Ricky hadn't started out to seduce Jett, nor she him, but it happened. And it was a good thing, up there in the deer stand, a cool

IN A PIG'S EYE

night wind blowing through the open windows, their sleeping bags zipped together, finding the moment and the after moments, happy as children discovering Easter eggs.

Contemplating on it afterward, Jett sleeping beside him, his arm thrown over her, he knew it couldn't last. But where was there to go? What was there to do? A town could be worse. If Gene and his crew came looking for them, they would find them reasonably quick. The deer stand was somewhat hidden, but Ricky had found it easily enough, and so would they over time.

What to do was more than a mild conundrum.

Over the following days, Ricky showed Jett where they could find edible wild plants. The basics. He showed her trails he knew, the spring where he got his water. It was clean and clear and the water wouldn't need boiling. He showed her, too, that in the cool of the evening, it was a good idea to be in the deer stand to avoid the hogs.

The beasts ran in packs, and sometimes the Big Boy, as he had now decided to call the hog that had killed Greg's accomplice, roamed free of hoggish alliance. In short time, the hogs, already a menace, would grow fast and become even more comfortable with taking over not only the woods, but entire towns.

Ricky showed Jett certain trees that could be climbed quicky, and suggested they try and stay within a short run of them. He knew that wasn't an absolute, always being near those trees, but it was a wishful comfort.

They found and piled small rocks near the climbing trees so ammunition for his slingshot would be available.

And then on an afternoon when he was building a fish trap with rocks at the edge of the river, designed so fish could swim in easily, but not quite in the opposite direction, he heard a boat motor grinding over the water.

Jett had left her clothes at the edge of the river and was bathing in the water, trying to rinse off some of the worst of the day's survival dirt. When she heard the sound of the motor, she came out of the water and began to hastily dress in what were now little more than rags.

So as not to leave footprints that led directly to the deer stand, they ran across the small patch of shore and into the woods. Then they made their way toward the stand by a roundabout method, walking on piles of pine needles and rotten leaves. A good tracker could still follow them, but Ricky doubted Gene could have tracked his own feet. When it came to the former police chief, smart was a distant cousin twice removed.

Ricky and Jett came to the deer stand, stood at the bottom of the ladder, reluctant to climb up and put themselves into what would serve as an inescapable trap. Even below the stand, the view of the beach was good, so they squatted low, observed, and listened.

It was indeed the same boat as before, and when it beached, Gene got off first, followed by two others. Ricky recognized one of them who'd been with Gene before. The one that had run away from the hog. The second one was a stranger. Gene had found a new acolyte, a fat guy with a nearly bald head. And there was still the same guy who remained on the boat the last time. He was moving slowly, as if injured. He was holding the same rifle and didn't get off the boat.

Gene was carrying a large club and had a pistol in his belt. The recognizable one from Gene's band of brothers was armed with a crowbar, and the fat one had a tire tool. At least they weren't carrying a lot of artillery.

As Gene and his assholes moved into the woods, Ricky and Jett went silently away from the ladder, higher up the hill, taking a small trail that led off of the main one, still climbing. He was hoping Gene and his crew would search and decide it wasn't worth it, go back home, and end up eating each other.

That was as likely as a helicopter dropping a rope to pull him and Jett up to safety, whisking them away to Shangri-la. They climbed. Jett was in front of him, going fast. She was moving like a rocket-propelled mountain goat.

IN A PIG'S EYE

They were sighted quickly. It had to be partly because the little climbing trail they were on wasn't entirely sheltered by thick trees and fat leaves. Maybe Gene was a better tracker than Ricky assumed. Whatever the case, they had been spotted because he heard Gene yell, "*There they are!*"

Jett made a whimpering sound and climbed even faster. Ricky worked to keep up with her, making his own whimpers as he went.

Gene and his mugs weren't right on top of them, but they were close. Ricky could see them down the hill, now at the base of the trail, all sweat-grimed and limb-scratched, working their way up.

"*I'm going to eat your balls, Ricky!*" Gene yelled. "*Your balls!*"

"You'll choke on 'em!" Ricky yelled back.

This seemed to inflame Gene and his comrades, and they really dug in, coming up the hill, the fat one in the lead, which, considering how much meat he was carrying, was surprising.

Ricky wheeled about, slipped a stone from his ammunition bag into the pouch on the slingshot, drew it back, and let it go. The rock sailed smoothy and quickly and hit the fat guy between the eyes. And like Goliath falling from David's slingshot, back the man tumbled. Rolling, he knocked the skinny guy's feet out from under him. Gene barely dodged the rolling bodies, leaping up and over the barrel like a dog in a circus act.

The fat man didn't get up. He lay still and was now sliding slowly down the hill on his back. He finally came to a stop.

The skinny guy leaned over the fat one, said, "He's done killed him with a fucking rock!"

Ricky knew the shot had been true. Shit, he was good.

When Ricky got to the top of the hill just behind Jett, the trees broke open and the hill sloped down and there was a marshy stretch below them. A dozen hogs moved through the marsh, four of them piglets. Ricky saw a frog jump in the marsh grass. A blue crane sloped downward and skimmed over the back of one incredibly large hog.

It was Big Boy.

Big Boy looked up the hill at them. His nose twitched.

Hogs in front, assholes to the rear, all looking for a meal.

Ricky grabbed Jett's elbow and they ran along the ridge, through the trees that were sparser here. They went along quick, and twice a pistol shot rang out but missed them. One was so close it clipped a small limb near Ricky's head.

"Go, Jett—I'll catch up."

Ricky turned and saw Gene and his skinny pal were close. Ricky dropped to one knee and picked his target. Gene was in the lead, pointing his pistol. Ricky let the rock fly. It tumbled, slightly off the mark. It missed Gene by less than an inch, hit a tree, bounced off, and clipped the skinny dude in the side of the jaw.

Skinny went to his knees, said, "Motherfucker!" His voice sounded as if it came through a mouthful of cotton.

Gene fired a shot that hit Ricky in his lower left side, clipping off a piece of his shirt and sizzling into his flesh. The burning feeling made Ricky yelp.

Ricky was up and running again. He could feel blood running down his side, along his leg and into his boot. He didn't feel too bad, though, and concluded he had only been grazed by the bullet.

Glancing back, Ricky saw Gene running along the ridge, and now Skinny, who had recovered from the ricochet, was running behind Gene, but not briskly.

Ahead of him, Ricky saw Jett dodge downward on the side where the river would be, and scuttle out of sight. He knew she was going for one of the climbing trees, and though that would do all right to save her from a wild pig, it wouldn't protect her from the men if she were found. If they didn't look up, it just might. But if they did, Gene would shoot her out of the tree as if she were a squirrel.

For now, they hadn't seen her.

Ricky kept running along the ridge of the hill until it broadened and the trees gathered tighter. He could lead them away from Jett this way, and the tree area he knew well, and could get through with relative ease. Gene and his partner, unfamiliar with the terrain, would have their work cut out for them.

But Ricky was growing tired, and they were gaining. As soon as he was in the thickness of trees, he loaded another rock into his slingshot. Turned about and saw them. He took a deep breath. He lifted the sling. Gene fired a shot. It smacked into the pine tree he was partially behind. Bark and resin jumped into the air.

Ricky let the rock fly. Gene ducked. The rock caught Skinny, who was close behind him, and this time teeth and blood flew. That motherfucker was cursed.

Skinny went tumbling partly down the hill. Coming up the hill from the marsh was Big Boy and the other hogs. They caught Skinny and went at him with snorts and grunts. Teeth chomped and blood flew. Big Boy stripped a piece of flesh off Skinny's face like he was tearing a rotten cotton shirt. He stood there patiently munching it while the other hogs, including the piglets, took their turn.

Skinny screamed. The hogs were all over him. Slinging him about, ripping his clothes. Skinny struck out with the crowbar once, but it was useless.

Gene paused and took a shot at Big Boy. The bullet hit, made a smacking sound like a child kissing its mother with a mouthful of jelly. Big Boy, finishing up his strip of Skinny's face, stopped in mid-munch, flesh hanging from his mouth, and glared at Gene. The shot had merely annoyed him.

Ricky ran away then, leaving them to it. He heard one more shot.

Threading his way through the trees, he paused and pulled aside his rotting shirt, pushed his pants down enough that he could see his bullet wound. It was bleeding a lot, but the grazing didn't really look too bad.

Dropping to one knee, Ricky pulled in some deep, slow breaths.

The air had turned cooler and smelled of rain. The day was starting to fade. Shadows crept through the trees like ninja assassins.

Ricky thought that even if Gene escaped the hogs while they were chowing down on Skinny, went down to the boat and cruised away, he would come back. It was Gene's nature. He had been humiliated by a man with a slingshot.

No matter the situation, Ricky had to get to him. He had to kill him before he motored away, leaving him and Jett (if Jett was okay) to fret for his return on another day.

As Ricky was regrouping, he heard a crashing sound, and Gene broke through the underbrush, staggered between two trees, grabbed at one for support.

Gene saw Ricky, too. They were only about twenty feet apart, but in that moment, it was obvious Gene had more pressing matters. It was every man for himself. Behind Gene came Big Boy, looking in that moment more like a rhinoceros than a hog.

Gene ran right toward Ricky because Ricky, still kneeling, was on the only passable trail, narrow and uneven as it was. Ricky stood up, clutching his slingshot. He didn't have time to reload.

Ricky tried to turn and run, but Gene in his haste to get away from Big Boy smashed up against him and they both went rolling downhill, banging into trees, until there was just the grassy hill and finally, below them, the marsh.

They both rolled to the edge of the marsh, colliding. They tried to get up, but the swampy ground made it hard, and it couldn't be managed before Big Boy came squealing and grunting down the hill.

Gene was closest, so the hog picked him. It used its tusks to hook him. Gene flipped up in the air, the empty revolver flying from his hand and into the grass. The hog hooked him again, tossing him.

IN A PIG'S EYE

Big Boy nosed and bit at Gene. Gene screamed. The hog grunted. The hog's snout was coated with Gene's blood. Ricky could see the hog was bleeding, too. Had to be from gunshot wounds.

Ricky got up and was pleased to discover he still had the slingshot in his hand. He had clung to it all the way down the hill.

Ricky loaded a rock into the pouch and pulled it back. Big Boy had tired of Gene and was now coming after him; a new toy had been discovered.

In that moment, in the dying light, it was as if the hog were lit up internally. The recent wafer-like moon was in its eye.

In that eye Ricky felt as if he could see all the way back to the Stone Age. That he could see the bottom of the world.

He let the projectile go. The sling snapped loudly and the stone was propelled.

It was a perfect shot. It hit Big Boy in his right eye, went deep. The hog did what Ricky would have thought was an impossible leap for its size. It hit the ground, kangaroo-bounced, then its legs collapsed under it and the great beast rolled on its side, ending up right next to Ricky's feet. It squirted shit, and lay still.

And then Ricky saw Gene, weakened and bloodied, rise to his feet. He had pulled a hunting knife out of the scabbard on his belt, and he was mummy-walking toward Ricky. His face was covered with blood, and there was a cut on his neck where the hog had hooked him. A lot of blood was coming out of that wound.

Still, Gene was advancing. Ricky fumbled for another load, but Gene was too close; the bastard had him.

There was a sound like a beaver tail slapping water. Gene's expression changed. He made a prune face and went to his knees.

Standing behind him, holding a large branch, was Jett. She was wearing moon shadow, for it was full dark now. She had a limb about as long as her arms and as big around as a large man's wrists. She was swinging it savagely, striking Gene in the head again and again with a sickening, smacking noise. She hit him as he fell over. She hit him while he lay face down on the ground. At first, the sound of the branch against Gene's skull was solid, then it turned wet and a lot less solid. Gene's face began to blend into the marsh.

Ricky did nothing to stop her. She continued to hit Gene over and over until her arm was too tired to continue. She dropped the stick, hung her head, gulped in deep breaths, then coughed them out. Jett put her hands on her knees. She was breathing a bit more softly now. She lifted her head and looked at Ricky. She smiled slightly.

"I killed him," she said. "I killed the son of a bitch."

Ricky nodded. "He's the deadest person I've ever seen."

Ricky and Jett made their way in the dark, up the hill, along the major trail they both knew well. They passed the fat man's body. Hogs had been at it.

They ended up at the deer stand, but did not climb up. They stood at the base of it and looked out through the limbs and brush at the boat. The idiot on the boat had turned on a deck light, and they could see him sitting in a deck chair with the rifle across his lap. He was facing the woods. In the light, they could see bugs swarming around his head.

They watched for a while. Ricky checked his wound. He had stopped bleeding for the most part. It wasn't as good as he hoped or as bad as he feared.

Ricky and Jett whispered to each other. They left the stand and worked their way around and to the side of the boat on the shoreline, then edged quietly along the bank next to the water.

When they reached a spot close to the boat, Jett squatted on her haunches in the dark and watched Ricky slip off his boots, then glide into the water, go out into the deeper part. He swam around behind the boat.

Now she couldn't see him. Water lapped close to her feet. If she went forward, she would soon be in the pool of light the deck lights gave off, and that would be unwise. At least she had Gene's pistol.

She waited.

Ricky climbed up the back of the boat with some effort. When he was on the rear deck, he crouched, and crept toward the bow.

The man in the deck chair hadn't moved.

Ricky came up behind him and pulled his knife. He leaped forward, grabbed the man's chin, dropped his weight, pulling the man's head back so as to stab him in the throat. But the man didn't resist.

Now Ricky could see there were flies swarming around his head. He was dead.

Ricky pulled the rifle from the corpse and went into the wheelhouse, and after a brief moment, he came out. There was no one else.

Ricky took a breath and tried to ignore the pain in his side. He waved Jett forward. She came cautiously, carrying his boots, and climbed the hanging stairs to the front of the boat and looked at the man. His mouth was open and flies were going in and out of it as if it were a busy subway tunnel.

"Did he kill himself?" Jett said.

Ricky came around in front of the man and saw blood on his shirt. He pushed the shirt open with his knife. There was a bandaged wound and blood had seeped through it and hardened like old bread crust.

"He was wounded somehow," Ricky said. "That's why he didn't come ashore. He couldn't."

It seemed clear now. The man had been hurt in some fight away from them, and had stayed on board as a guard, but also nursing a wound that eventually got the better of him.

They picked him up, Ricky grabbing him under the arms while Jett took his legs. He wasn't heavy. He was almost like a husk. They tossed him over the side. He landed on the riverbank, but his feet were in the water and his legs were close together. The water was just deep enough to pick his legs up and move them, wash them back and forth like a mermaid's tail.

They looked through the boat. There was canned food and some jars of cashews and mixed nuts and one of those was open and about half full. There was a large cookstove that worked off a battery. It hadn't come with the boat. It had been rigged that way. There was a first-aid kit. There wasn't much in it, but there was enough for Jett to dress Ricky's wound.

They talked briefly. A decision was made.

Ricky went back to the deer stand to collect their goods, while Jett cranked up the anchor.

Ricky put their stuff in the wheelhouse, then started the boat by turning the key. The air was filled with a rumble and at first it was disconcerting. Ricky turned on the lights. He decided he could handle things. He had gone fishing on his uncle's boat once and his uncle let him drive it. That had been a long time ago. He motored backward into the river. It wasn't a smooth exit, but it did move the front of the boat away from the shore.

Jett stood on the foredeck and shined the flashlight Ricky had given her toward the woods and the deer stand that had been their cramped home. She couldn't decide if they were leaving relative safety for certain doom, or if they were doing the right thing. There had to be survivors that would want to work together, not just make lunch of them.

Had to be.

Hogs were coming out of the woods, trotting toward the body at the edge of the water. And then the boat was turned around and they were too far out for the beam of the flashlight to show much. There was only the deck and forward lights of the boat and the aft lights resting on the water. She snapped off the flashlight.

The boat was moving along the river slowly. Then it was moving more briskly.

The motor hit a sweet spot and began to hum like an enormous

IN A PIG'S EYE

bumblebee along the river. She went into the cabin and stood by Ricky and looked out at the water through the windshield, illuminated by forward lights. The water parted before the bow of the boat and then they were cruising along nicely, heading nowhere in particular.

LENORA

Jonathan Janz

Baker Ludlow was watching *Creepshow* when the preacher started wailing on his front lawn. He wasn't really watching the movie, just letting the VCR grind as he dozed in his La-Z-Boy. And the preacher wasn't actually in the yard, more like the crumbly edge of the driveway. But there was no question Pastor Wiggins was in dire straits. His voice was strident enough to rouse Baker from a bourbon-assisted stupor.

He retrieved his twelve-gauge and stepped onto the porch, where the sun glare was so intense he had to squint down the hill to see the preacher.

"Oh, thank God!" Wiggins cried, hands on knees.

What got Baker's attention wasn't the preacher's chalk-white hair, which was no longer teased into its accustomed pompadour but sprouted instead like the alabaster fronds of some blighted palm tree; nor was it the way the preacher's nipples peeked through his sweat-soaked polo shirt like the eyes of some grotesque beluga whale. Baker scarcely registered the little red wagon the preacher towed.

What got Baker's attention was the swelling beneath the preacher's jaw.

He'd heard it labeled all sorts of things: tube neck, superflu, choking sickness, Captain Trips. They could call it whatever they liked, but it all amounted to the same thing.

The end.

Seeing it in person was a far sight worse than hearing it described on TV. Living out here in the boonies, his only neighbor Sookie, owner of that shit show of an exotic animal farm a couple miles over, Baker relied on the evening news for information, and in the beginning, coverage of the disaster had been restrained:

At first: "Rumors of a New Virus."

Soon after: "Mysterious Illness Cause for Concern?"

Then: "Authorities Ease Flu Hysteria."

About the time the sniffling news anchor had announced, "The CDC is warning citizens to take precautions," pandemonium had been unleashed on the country. Baker stomached as much as he could, but when a band of radicals hijacked a TV station and commenced with public executions, he tapped out, preferring his modest library of movies to the real-time doom of humankind.

Yet when he journeyed to town for groceries, he'd been forced to confront the reality. Dead bodies everywhere. Purplish half circles under their eyes and twin contrails of mucus oozing from their nostrils. A utility worker starfished along the roadside with a throat so black and swollen you felt you could float down the river on it with a cooler of beer and some George Strait on the boom box.

Baker shivered and regarded the preacher.

"I only need a moment," Wiggins told him.

Baker raised the twelve-gauge.

"Please," Wiggins said. "I don't think it's airborne."

Baker nodded. "Take another step and your guts'll be airborne."

The preacher jackknifed in a coughing fit and produced a lime-green glob that resembled Jell-O left to sit too long at a church potluck. Baker watched impassively. His front yard was a good half-acre, and not only was Wiggins downhill but downwind as well. Nevertheless, if this shit was as contagious as advertised, the next state over was still too close.

He motioned with the barrel. "Get on back to your flock, Reverend."

Wiggins dragged a wrist over his mouth. "I need your help, Baker."

"There's nothing I can do for you."

"Not me," Wiggins answered. "It's for her." The preacher moved aside and Baker beheld what was in the little red wagon.

"Why're you hauling a baby deer?" he asked.

"She's a dik-dik."

Baker scowled at him. "What the fuck's a dik-dik?"

"Mini-antelope from Sookie's farm," Wiggins explained. "I've been going property to property, checking on folks."

"Spreading the plague, you mean. Jesus Christ, Wiggins, don't you have any sense?"

"You don't—" Wiggins barked out another croupy cough, and when he wiped his mouth, there were scarlet streaks in the saliva. The preacher inspected this gruel a moment before smearing it on his trousers. "Everyone's dying, Baker. Everyone. The fact that you're alive means you might be immune."

Baker said nothing.

Wiggins gestured feebly. "You wouldn't believe what I saw at the pet farm. Some of the creatures had perished from the flu. Others had been"—his face pinched—"strung up. There were zebras, a tiger. They were flayed open like deer some hunter had bagged. Sookie's dead, too."

"Flu doesn't spare you because you've got a hundred acres and a Porsche."

"It wasn't the sickness. Someone had . . ." Wiggins licked his lips. "Someone had *impaled* Sookie. Same with his wife and young son."

Baker's grip on the twelve-gauge tightened. "Any sign of Dead Ed?"

"Just his handiwork."

Fucking ghoul, Baker thought. "Dead Ed" Dedaker's rap sheet was so long the justice system had ceased trying to rehabilitate him. Whenever someone went missing, folks suspected Dedaker, and Baker suspected they were right. Some claimed he only worked at the pet farm so he could abuse the animals. Baker suspected they were right about that, too.

"These were *atrocities*," Wiggins said. He indicated the dik-dik. "This poor animal . . . she was the only one left. I found her hiding under a squirrel cage. She's dehydrated . . . on the verge of starvation. If you could—"

"Get your ass off my property," Baker said.

Wiggins blinked at him. "But—"

Baker racked the shotgun.

"*Please*," Wiggins moaned, and to Baker's horror the preacher actually sank to his knees and raised his arms in supplication. "I can't care for the animal. I'm dying."

"No shit."

"You've endured tragedy, Brother Baker. I know how you've suffered."

"Shut your piehole," Baker replied. "And if you call me 'Brother' again, I'll expedite the dying thing for you."

"That would be a mercy," Wiggins said. "I can't tell you how much it—" But he was off on another coughing jag, this one so severe it ended with him thrashing in the grass and clawing at his throat. Baker glanced at the dik-dik, who was so captivated by a white moth flittering through the wildflowers that she didn't notice Wiggins choking to death on his own snot.

The preacher gasped, wheezed, and flumped onto his back. His face had gone a bruisy mauve color. His eyes rolled sightlessly up to the midday sun. Dead.

"Gross," Baker muttered. He lowered the twelve-gauge.

The dik-dik studied him from the wagon.

"And you can fuck right off," Baker said, and went inside.

LENORA

A short time later, Baker was besieged by a whanging headache. He schlepped into the kitchen to swallow some painkillers, but paused at the sink, the glass to his mouth, his gaze fixed on something in the backyard. His upper lip rose in a snarl. "You little . . . "

He burst out the back door and stalked toward the dik-dik, who was nosing through the charred remains of the old house. "The hell's wrong with you? I told you to scat."

The dik-dik recoiled, but didn't flee. Around them, cicadas churred as though enjoying the show.

"*Move!*" he bellowed. "If you want food, it's not here." He indicated the woods. "See? All the roughage you need."

The dik-dik peered up at him, commas of milky foam in the corners of her mouth.

He settled his hands on his hips. "If you're thirsty, there's a stream just over the ridge."

The dik-dik lowered her muzzle and nudged the neck of a Jim Beam bottle. She was a tad over a foot tall, a tuft of snowy hair tacking on a couple inches. He put her at maybe ten pounds.

"Get out of here!" he shouted. Jesus, his head throbbed. It was ninety-five degrees, the humidity so thick it was like breathing chicken broth.

The dik-dik started toward him. Baker flung out his hands. "Don't you dare."

She stopped, her large brown eyes profound.

"Think that'll work on me?" He grunted. "Lemme tell you what I saw on my way to town. Half a dozen dogs along Highway 24, all of them goners. That shithole where my wife used to take riding lessons? You guessed it: every horse in the paddock."

The dik-dik watched him.

"You're toast, little lady. Everyone is."

That wasn't entirely true, but he didn't care to dwell on the exceptions. On his tour of the residential district, he'd heard more than one person weeping. From a navy-blue saltbox house near the bank had drifted anguished wails and what might have been a child's cry for help. The worst by far was the banana-yellow Dodge pickup truck burring down Main Street, its unmuffled engine boisterous enough to draw Baker from the crypt-like general store. He'd stumbled onto the sidewalk as the pickup whipped past, and he counted it a mercy its occupants hadn't spotted him. Because chained to the back bumper was Sheriff George Cromwell. Perhaps the sheriff had galloped behind the truck for a spell. If so, his galloping days were over. The front of his body had been chewed away by the asphalt, his legs stringy horrors, like cherry-red seaweed. The sheriff left a glistening blood trail as the Dodge thundered up Main Street, and though Baker hoped it was his imagination, he could've sworn he'd heard Cromwell begging the driver to stop.

The driver had been Dead Ed, the passenger his brother, Frankie. The truck wasn't theirs, but trifling matters like legal ownership had never fazed the Dedakers, and the end of the world had done nothing to reform their habits. Baker heard the fiends cackling as the Dodge swerved onto Poplar Street, and in the four nights since, he'd heard the same cackling as he lay unsleeping in his bed.

Baker didn't notice the dik-dik advancing until it was right under him.

"*Jesus,*" he gasped. He wheeled around to flee, but his legs got tangled and he performed a graceless header in the grass. He threw a frenzied glance at the animal, who kept on coming, then he blundered to his feet and beat the hastiest retreat he could manage.

To hell with that mangy creature. He was sixty-six and had no friends or family, but that didn't mean he was ready to strangle to death on phlegm. He slammed the back door and locked it just to be sure.

LENORA

He was dozing in his recliner, dreaming about his son's first birthday, when he heard a whispery sound. Baker palmed drool from his chin and swiveled his head to discover the dik-dik loitering in the kitchen, the rubber flap in the doggy door just coming to rest.

"Out," he said, rising. He strode down the hallway. "You can take your ass right—"

The dik-dik padded toward him. Baker went rigid, palms out to ward her off, while a nightmare reel of his town visit unspooled: a German shepherd decomposing under a haze of bluebottle flies; the stench from the looted pharmacy so putrid he had to forego the liquor aisle; Milt Markovich drooped in a rocking chair outside his barbershop, his puffy throat slit from earlobe to earlobe in a gleaming black grin.

The dik-dik ventured closer.

Baker backpedaled, overturned a coatrack to barricade the doorway, and for one ghastly moment he was certain the animal would vault it. Instead, she embarked on a leisurely ramble around the kitchen, her tiny hooves clittering on the linoleum. Baker grimaced. Of all the rooms for her to stage an occupation.

The dik-dik paused and lowered her head, her hind legs bracing wider.

"Now hold on," he said.

She appeared to concentrate.

"Don't you even—"

Her eyes never leaving his, the animal pissed on the floor.

―――

Three hours later, the furry little asshole was still in his kitchen. It wasn't the inconvenience that bothered him so much; it was her germs. Accordingly, he'd cut the air-conditioning to prevent the contagion from circulating, and the living room now hovered at a ball-sweating eighty-eight degrees. He fed the VCR a worn-out copy of *The Thing*, hoping the wintry setting would soothe him, but halfway into the movie it was still sweltering and he was obsessing about how swiftly the characters got infected.

Baker clicked off the TV. He craved a drink, but that required a trip to the kitchen. He'd kill for a bag of Orville Redenbacher. Goddammit, this was *his* house. He needed that animal gone. He shoved out of his chair and stormed down the hall.

But halted at the coatrack. The dik-dik was curled in a brown ball in the center of the kitchen, asleep.

He took a moment to examine her auburn pelt. Where there was fur, it was glossy with black and white pinstripes, but there were bare patches, too, valleys of pink skin. Like scourge marks.

Baker heaved a sigh. Scratched his ass and contemplated. If the animal wouldn't leave willingly, he'd have to flush her out.

He trooped up to his bedroom and raided his stash of Nutter Butter cookies. Returning, he opened the front door, scattered some on the porch, and sprinkled a trail all the way to the kitchen. Then, his eyes never leaving the dik-dik, he righted the coatrack and flicked some cookie crumbs at her.

The animal jarred and clambered up, but she paid no mind to the crumbs.

"Eat," he commanded.

She didn't move.

"You're probably thirsty," he muttered. "Well, hold on."

He snatched up his bourbon glass and hustled to the back bathroom. He filled the glass, stepped into the hallway, and yelped.

The dik-dik gazed up at him.

Hands trembling, he bent and deposited the glass on the floor.

"Drink," he said.

The animal crept forward as if to comply. Then she tensed, threw a glance over her shoulder, and bounded toward him. Baker plastered himself to the wall as she scampered past. If he had a goddamn brain cell left, he'd have strapped on a dust mask before allowing her out of the kitchen.

But what had her so spooked?

He trailed after her, but faltered at the threshold of the first bedroom. His son's.

Not really. All his son's stuff had gone up in the fire, but Baker had reproduced it as well as he could. A quilt embroidered with the MLB team logos. A pair of trophies, one a Little League runner-up, the other a Most Improved Player award. A poster of Chubby Checker because his son had loved "The Twist." Baker remembered the boy doing the dance in his diaper, remembered how they'd twisted together while his wife looked on and laughed.

No sound from his son's room. The dik-dik wasn't in there.

Baker moved on to the reproduction of his daughter's room. An empty hamster cage. A paint-by-numbers horse Baker had fucked up royally, the eyes smudged and the mane sticking straight out like the animal had stepped on a power line. A gymnastics plaque with a blank brass plate. His daughter had loved to tumble on the mat, but she'd been too young for competitions.

The chuff of anxious breathing. He waded into the gloom and tried to ignore the dust-dank scent that haunted this shrine.

A stirring under the bed. The rasp of hooves on oak?

He crouched and screwed up his eyes, but the space was too murky. "You under there, Bambi?"

An answering scrape. Careful not to startle the little girl, he hunkered down and raised the bedspread and found a pair of chestnut eyes peering out at him. Baker was forcibly reminded of how his daughter used to select this exact spot each time they played hide-and-seek, and he couldn't help but smile. "You don't have to be scared of me. Why don't you come out and—"

A creak behind him. Baker's flesh bunched into nodes, and his bowels performed a slow roll. He pushed to his feet and spun, but the stock of his twelve-gauge was already whistling toward him. The last thing he saw before impact was the vicious sneer on Dead Ed Dedaker's face and a flash of tombstone-white teeth.

Not for the first time, Baker dreamed of a cornfield. Of heading west. The images were fuzzy, insubstantial, but for some reason they comforted him. When he became aware of the tack-sharp pain in his temple, he wished he could remain unconscious a mite longer. He cracked his eyes to slits and was greeted with a formless blur. He made to sit up, but his limbs wouldn't cooperate. After a moment's toil, he realized his hands and feet were bound.

That got Baker's eyes open.

"There he is," Dedaker said.

Dedaker idled in the La-Z-Boy with the dik-dik in his lap. Even from a dozen feet, Baker could see the animal quivering.

"Look, darlin'," Dedaker said to her. "Sleeping Beauty decided to join us."

Dedaker looked like death. His pale blue eyes were bloodshot and wreathed with crepey skin, and what flesh showed through his salt-and-pepper stubble had a sickly green undertone. His denim jacket was ill-chosen for the heat, but for all that he was still perspiring too freely. Below the rucked-up cuff of one blue-jeaned ankle, Baker spied a holster and the nose of a pistol.

"You've got the flu," Baker murmured.

Dedaker snorted. "*Shit*. This is just allergies. I get 'em every—" He exploded in a messy sneeze, his saliva stippling the dik-dik's fur.

Something in Baker ached.

Dedaker dragged a hand over his nose. "Even if I do have it, I ain't gonna be like Frankie and the others. They haven't invented a bug yet whose ass I can't kick." A sly wink. "Don't you fret about me, Bake. I'm right as rain."

Uh-huh, Baker thought.

He took stock of himself. The news wasn't good. Ankles trussed with nylon rope. Wrists, too, the latter so fucking taut he had no feeling in his hands. But at least they rested in his lap rather than behind his back. That was something.

The dik-dik almost slipped through Dedaker's grasp before he hauled her down and cinched her in a body lock. "Easy there, darling. *Easy.* You leave now, you'll miss the fun."

Baker opened his mouth to speak, but the unhinging of his jaw drove a railroad spike through his temple.

"Je-*sus*, Bake," Dedaker muttered. "You look like dog shit." He put his lips next to the dik-dik's ear. "Wanna hear about Baker Ludlow? Everything he touches dies."

"Let her go," Baker said.

Dedaker grinned, his whiskery face satanic in the waning daylight. "Care about her, do you?" He stroked the animal without finesse, the poor girl quivering harder and harder. A nod at Baker. "This loser had himself a good woman, name of Annie. I tried to court her, but by the time ol' Ed came on the scene, she was already in love with this sad sack." He reached over and patted a picture frame, the one photograph Baker still had of his wife. It was age-spotted and curled from being in his wallet, but it displayed him and Annie at a cookout, her in his lap, him looking like he'd always felt—bemused that such a remarkable woman should choose him, but grateful for his good fortune all the same.

Baker tightened. "Don't touch that."

Dedaker chuckled, but it dissolved into a ragged coughing fit. Baker bucked until his back was propped against the sofa.

"Dude used to have it all," Dedaker said in a musing voice. "Wife, couple of urchins, pretty new house. But you know what he didn't have?" He leaned toward the dik-dik. "A working smoke detector!"

It went through Baker like a spear.

"Near as anyone can tell," Dedaker went on, "when he woke up, the house was already full of smoke. Fire started downstairs, where his kids were. One of them probably set it."

Baker's throat tingled. The dik-dik whimpered and writhed in Dedaker's grip.

"Stairs were an inferno, so Bake and Annie tried a window. They got out, all right. Bake landed in the bushes, but poor Annie smacked the porch." Dedaker made a clicking sound. "Broken neck."

"Enough," Baker said.

Dedaker scratched the animal between the ears. She flinched at his touch. "According to the papers, Bake tried the front door—no go, too hot—then attempted to climb through his daughter's window. That's why his hands look like Freddy fucking Krueger's."

A tear leaked down Baker's face. He drew up his knees, and as he did he noticed something he hadn't before: the rope around his ankles wasn't completely snug.

"When the fire trucks arrived, he was half-dead. Kept askin' where Annie was." Dedaker brayed laughter, but that set off a fusillade of sneezes.

Baker began to work his feet back and forth.

"Jesus," Dedaker muttered, and wiped his nose. "Isn't that hilarious, darlin'? Dumbshit thought he'd saved her, but she was lyin' on the porch, dead as a hammer." The dik-dik strove to wriggle away, but Dedaker vised her tiny body to his chest. "Know what this freak did then? He took the insurance money and rebuilt the same exact house."

"Please stop," Baker said.

"Rumor has it he furnished it with all the same shit his family had before." Dedaker looked around. "Spookier than a wax museum."

The dik-dik began to squeak, the sound shrill and birdlike: "*Zee*wuh! *Zee*wuh!"

"Still don't fancy me, darlin'?" Dedaker asked. "After all this time?"

Her cries became frantic: "*Zee*wuh! *Zee*wuh!"

"Now *stop* that," Dedaker snapped. "You know how that noise pisses me off."

LENORA

Baker thought of the scars latticing the dik-dik's hide. Dedaker gave her a rough shake, but the sounds persisted.

"Goddamn you," Dedaker said and unhooked something from the belt of his jeans. Blond wood haft, blade like a miniature scythe. A linoleum knife, though the thing was so caked with gore you could barely identify it. He recalled what Wiggins said about the pet farm, the animals strung up and gutted.

"I saw you dragging the sheriff," Baker said.

Dedaker eyed him with renewed interest. "You were in town? Hell, you should've let me know. I would've offered you a ride, too."

At the memory of the sheriff's glistening seaweed feet, Baker's stomach lurched.

Dedaker showed his teeth. "Four." At Baker's look, he explained. "How many I've killed. At least, before Captain Trips. Now the total's probably three times that. But before the outbreak, only four." He stroked the animal. "Everyone liked to speculate, so I let 'em. Sookie, he'd jump a mile every time I appeared. Maybe that's why he kept me around . . . because I scared the bejesus out of him." He fixed Baker with a shrewd look. "And because he knew I'd do whatever was necessary to procure his precious animals."

Dedaker tottered to his feet and stood swaying. The dik-dik continued to squeak and twist in his arms.

"You need medicine," Baker said.

"What I need is to shut this bitch up," Dedaker replied. He took a step toward the kitchen, but halted as a coughing fit seized him.

Baker strained against his ankle bindings.

The dik-dik squeaked: "*Zeewuh! Zeewuh!*"

"*I said shut the fuck up!*" Dedaker shouted into the animal's face. She scrambled against him, hooves digging at his neck. Dedaker grappled with her. "Now hold—"

The dik-dik sprang into the air and crashed down on a kerosene lamp, the antique glass shattering and flooding the room with an acrid stench. The animal flailed amid the strew of shards. Dedaker snatched at her, but she bounded toward the kitchen. Coughing, Dedaker lurched after her.

Baker dug his elbows into the sofa and got his legs under him. Beneath Dedaker's hacking, he could hear the dik-dik's alarmed cries. He rose up, damn near toppled backward, and stood there a second, his equilibrium wonky.

"Get back here!" Dedaker growled. "You little"—*cough*—"fucking"—*cough*—"cunt!"

There was maybe an inch of give in the ankle binding, but it permitted Baker to rotate clumsily around. As Dedaker shambled toward the kitchen, Baker hopped over and grabbed the linoleum knife. The keen blade sheared through the ankle rope in three swipes.

Dedaker lumbered into the kitchen, where the dik-dik cowered, her cries pitiful and wheezy. As Baker started forward, his hamstrings cramping, Dedaker bent down, fumbled with his pant leg, and came up with a pistol. He leveled it at the animal.

"Squeak at this, you little—"

Baker slashed hard at Dedaker's back. The knife ripped a diagonal swath through the jacket from shoulder to hip. The gun went off, and Dedaker roared, his arms splayed like a parishioner in the throes of holy ecstasy. Blood splurted from his back. Baker raised the blade again, but Dedaker's flailing arm whacked him in the jaw. Baker tried to catch himself, but his bound wrists failed him, and he face-planted, half in, half out of the kitchen.

Dedaker's mad eyes blazed down at him. "*You stupid cockknocker!*" He pointed the gun at Baker's head.

The dik-dik launched herself at Dedaker. She rebounded off his knee, but it was enough to distract him. Dedaker pivoted and took aim at the animal.

Baker swiped the knife at Dedaker's shin. The blade sliced through skin and bone with a meaty *schlink*. Dedaker howled and the gun cracked and searing pain sizzled through Baker's left shoulder. Wincing, he craned his head around in time to see the dik-dik's hind legs vanish through the doggy door.

Good, he thought.

Still squalling, Dedaker banged into the refrigerator and crumpled to the floor. Baker flopped over and army-crawled toward him. One of Dedaker's veiny hands was clamped over his shin, the blood burbling between his fingers. His other hand still clutched the pistol.

Baker closed the distance. He pushed up between Dedaker's spraddled work boots and raised the knife.

Dedaker's eyes shot wide. "Don't—" he started, but Baker whipped the blade sideways, cleaving the man's stretched cheeks. Scarlet sprayed everywhere, but Baker blinked it away and plunged the knife into Dedaker's larynx. Blood geysered over them both, and Dedaker slouched, fingers scrabbling at the embedded blade. Baker shoved away from the man's scissoring legs and went to work on his wrist binding. Dedaker's blood had lubed the fabric, so after some struggle he was able to slip his hands free. A wave of lightheadedness billowed through him. He rolled onto his belly. Dedaker's death gurgles had ceased, but the slaughterhouse smells of blood and feces clogged Baker's nostrils.

Jesus, he thought. *Jesus*.

The house was utterly silent. Evidently, the animal had run away for good. *Smart girl*, he decided. The farther she got from here, the better. He lay there a long time, so long he scarcely heard the doggy door bow inward. When he opened his eyes, the dik-dik stood before him. He watched, amazed, as her long snout dipped, hesitated, then brushed against his bloody fingers.

He dragged Dedaker's carcass through the yard and made it a few feet past the tree line before dizziness overtook him. He staggered back to the house, took one look at the grisly bloodbath in his kitchen, and vomited into the sink.

The dik-dik attending his steps, he hobbled to the bathroom and showered. An inspection of his shoulder disclosed an inch-long trough where the bullet had grazed him, so he dumped half a bottle of peroxide on it and hissed as it bubbled white. That done, he drew a bath, wrestled the dik-dik into the tub, and with a considerable amount of fuss managed to scrub away the kerosene stink. The lamp glass had harrowed her hide, so after tweezing out several slivers, he drizzled the rest of the peroxide on her wounds, and this time she sprang right out of his grasp and clattered about the bathroom squeaking in pain. After she got it out of her system, he wrapped her in a towel and situated her in the kitchen doorway. It took him the better part of an hour to collect the broken glass and mop up Dedaker's blood. The animal watched the whole process with interest.

He ventured into the attic, and after a great deal of rummaging and cursing, located the baby things he'd repurchased. The stuffed animals tore at his heart, but he soldiered through until he unearthed the bottles. He filled one with water, sprinkled in a pinch of sugar, and gathered the dik-dik into his lap. The laceration on her flank made him uneasy, but if she didn't get some liquids soon, infection wouldn't matter.

She refused to drink.

As he rocked the La-Z-Boy and stroked her fur, the lamplight revealed how wretched a state she was in. Old scars. Hairless grooves inflicted by a whip or a slender branch. He ran his fingers through her fur and detected welts too pronounced for bug bites. More likely from the brutal edges of work boots.

Baker compressed his lips.

"Come on, girl," he murmured, brushing the bottle's rubber nipple against her mouth.

The dik-dik turned away and nuzzled his thigh.

Baker sighed. "Every word that dickweed said is true. Look at this." He pinched the back of his hand, where the flesh was so runneled with scars you couldn't discern his knuckles. "See? Doesn't even hurt. What hurts," he said, drawing up a sleeve to expose unmarred flesh, "is this." He squeezed the skin. "I don't deserve this. Don't deserve any goddamn thing."

The dik-dik lolled her head and licked his scarred hand.

"Don't," he said, but he didn't stop her. He nodded toward the kitchen. "Know that door you've been using? I installed it for Petey, a Rottweiler who showed up ten years ago. At first I didn't let him in because he looked mean as hell. But at some point I started putting out a water dish for him and chopping up bologna. People are afraid of Rottweilers, but Petey was as gentle as a June breeze. I took him in. Bought him all kinds of toys. He used to watch *Happy Days* and *Three's Company* with me."

The dik-dik continued to lap at his scars.

"Petey started acting funny, and by the time I got him to the vet he was in bad shape. Cancer, Dr. Weizak said. It'd been growing in him a long time. Apparently, Petey was an old dog. Weizak said the poor boy was in a world of pain, so he put him down that night." Baker chewed his bottom lip. "I like to think the part of his life he spent with me was a good part. But I wonder. What if the cancer started because of his diet? I used to feed Petey whatever I was eating, since he didn't care for dog food, and that was probably a mistake. I still brood about it."

The dik-dik graduated from his left hand to his right, as though mothering a newborn.

Baker reclined his head. "Here's something: I dream damn near every night, but last night I dreamed of my grandma." He peered out the window, where a bat flittered against a yellow-blue dusk. "That generation was different. Some were shitbags. Big heaps of prejudice. But others . . . they had this glow. Grandma Lenora was one of them. She never made me feel bad. Never teased or judged. She'd wink at me sometimes, like we were in on the joke together. Then she'd fix me a sandwich or take me to her garden to pick vegetables." The thickness in his voice surprised him. "She's been gone thirty years, but I still miss her. She knew how to make you feel like you mattered. I tried to be that way with my kids, but—" He cut off and went quiet for a spell. He chuckled, passed a self-conscious hand over his mouth. "You know, you sort of remind me of her. How about we call you Lenora?"

Lenora licked him a couple more times, paused as if to deliberate, then took the bottle into her mouth and began to suck.

Evening of the next day, Baker sat cross-legged on the living room floor, *The Exorcist* showing on the television. He'd tried *Animal House* and *The Blues Brothers*, but Lenora didn't take to them. Only horror movies held her attention.

He scowled through his readers at the encyclopedia in his lap. "'Genus *Madoqua*, the dik-dik is an herbivorous dwarf antelope from the bushlands of Southern and Eastern Africa.'" He glanced at her. "Guess you came a long way." He found his place with an index finger. "'Family Bovidae.'"

He put a knuckle to his lips. *Bovidae* was only a hairsbreadth from *bovine*, and so far, cows seemed to be surviving this ordeal.

Lenora came over and nosed at the package of Nutter Butters, so he slid out the plastic sleeve and let her have at it. He set the encyclopedia aside and selected *The Complete Dog Owner Home Veterinary Guide*, which he'd mail-ordered after adopting Petey. He thumbed through it, came up with jack shit, then discovered an FAQ in the back.

Question: Can humans transfer infirmities to their dogs?

Answer: Though it is not impossible, it is exceedingly rare for a dog to contract a human illness.

He turned to Lenora. "That's promising. Animals catch sick from each other. Long as I keep you in the house, you should be good." He scratched her under the chin, where she seemed to prefer it. "Maybe I'll litter-train you. Should be plenty of pet supplies in town."

Baker frowned. Something about her breathing disquieted him. Was it faster than usual?

LENORA

He caressed her and surveyed her wounds. The one on her foreleg appeared to be healing nicely, but the livid gash on her flank concerned him. It glimmered with yellowish pus, like scummy pollution puddled in a ditch.

Baker fetched a pencil and a notepad. On it he scratched:

Kitty Litter
Band-Aids
Nutter Butters
Veggies
Dik-Dik Medicine

He paused, tapped the pencil against the pad, then added,

Soup

He rose. "I'm gonna fix you up, but in the meantime I'll put down some pee pads. Petey used them a lot when he . . . "

Baker clamped down on the memory. Best not to think of that.

"I should be back by midnight. It'll be dark, but you'll be locked in here, and safe. The Dedakers are dead, so that helps."

Lenora didn't look up from the movie.

Baker started toward the door, but hesitated. He recrossed the room and scratched Lenora under the chin. This time she did peer up at him. She had a cookie crumb on her snout. Baker reached out to brush it off, then reconsidered.

"Save it for later," he told her, and went out.

※

Though it'd only been a few days since he'd driven to town, things here had deteriorated. The sense of deadness remained, but now it was a baleful deadness, steeped in an aura of misery and decay.

His visit to the grocery was creepy as hell. The power had crapped out, so instead of entering via the automatic doors, he had to use the loading dock. Though some of the vegetables looked iffy, he procured everything on his list, then stocked up on items he judged Lenora might be partial to. Twinkies, graham crackers. He pegged her for a Pop-Tart gal, so he tossed a box of those into the wagon as well. By the time he'd loaded it all into his Ranger, it was ten thirty and full dark. He drove to Creekside Veterinary Clinic, disliking the way his pickup buzzed and grumbled down the wooded lane. All that noise in the charnel silence was unnerving, like he was picking a banjo during a funeral.

Deer all over the place. They observed him as he swept past, not spooking. *You assholes again?* their expressions seemed to ask. He rolled into Creekside and killed the engine. Overhead, the clouds had snuffed the moon. The clinic was locked, so Baker heaved a rock the size of a cantaloupe through the front window and winced at the crash. Worrying he'd drawn the attention of every creature within a five-mile radius, he wriggled over the splintered frame and managed to avoid disembowelment.

The clinic reeked like an open dumpster two days after a good rain. Baker pressed his T-shirt to his nose. The waiting area was barren, so whatever was broadcasting the unwholesome stench was in the back. In the treatment rooms.

"Ah fuck," he muttered.

He edged past the receptionist's desk, sure he'd find a flu victim, its neck bloated and its face pulpy with rot. He told himself not to look because if he did discover a corpse staring back at him, he might start shrieking and not be able to stop.

Baker looked.

The desk was vacant.

Exhaling, he opened the door to the treatment rooms and actually staggered back at the smell. Holy Christ. He didn't know if he could take it. A sewery, rancid meat-juice odor.

He was about to scrap the whole mission when he caught sight of

LENORA

a poster of a black Labrador retriever. Its size and color were nothing like Lenora, but the eyes were similar: large, trusting. *I'll never leave you*, those eyes declared. *You might not always be nice to me, but I'll never stop loving you.*

Baker drew in a shuddering breath and went in.

He shined the flashlight at a stainless steel exam table. Empty. He advanced, the odor intensifying. He reckoned he'd locate the culprit on the other side of the table, but there was nothing there. Baker proceeded through the next door, but faltered. For several seconds, he couldn't breathe.

The room was acrawl with cats.

A few scattered at his approach, but most went about their business. Calicos, Maine coons, others of no particular breed. They populated the floor, the exam table, a hydraulic-lift surgery table. Some observed him with mild interest, while others merely went on grooming themselves.

Baker wasn't troubled by the cats. What troubled him was Dr. Weizak, who dangled from a ceiling joist, having hanged himself with an orange extension cord. Baker's flashlight revealed a bloated gullet and a mouth so agape it put him in mind of a choir teacher demonstrating proper vocal technique. He shifted the beam and cringed. Weizak's bald pate had gone a disconcerting indigo color, the eyes rolled up to whites.

Weizak began to undulate.

Baker floundered back. A cat brushed his ankle and he danced away. He swung the flashlight toward Weizak and saw the crotch of the dead man's trousers twitching and bulging, as though Baker's presence had occasioned a woody. A whiff of the corpse made him gag, but he kept the beam steady long enough to see a cat poke its head out of the dead man's collar, its whiskers glistening with blood.

"*Jesus!*" Baker cried, and plunged into the next room.

Where the smell was even ranker. He battled his gorge for several instants, then shined his beam on the back wall, which was crammed with racks of ivory boxes.

Medicine. Thank God.

He rushed forward and promptly rued his forgetfulness. The print on the boxes was so microscopic he'd have difficulty deciphering it even with his readers. Baker was squinting at a label when he froze, a breeze whispering over his skin. He shifted the flashlight beam to the far side of the room.

Fuck me with a wood chipper, he thought.

The picture window was shattered. Draped over the jagged sill was a woman with frizzy brown hair and an airbrushed T-shirt, though Baker could only see the back, where shoddy pink-and-purple artwork depicted a shooting star against a night sky. The cursive script beneath this masterwork read *JEFF LOVES DEBRA*. He wagered the shirtfront featured caricatures of the smiling lovebirds.

He crept toward the window and the erstwhile Debra. Beyond her reposed a Yamaha motorcycle with a sidecar, the former driverless, but the latter occupied by a mutilated horror that was almost certainly Debra's beloved. He figured Jeff had been dying from the superflu, and Debra had ventured here because the pharmacy had been plundered, but in her haste to get inside, she'd botched her mission and bled to death. Baker grasped her hair and lifted, and sure enough, a glass wedge the size of a pizza slice had implanted itself in the soft tissue under her chin. He was surveying the pool of congealed blood on the floor when something brushed his pant leg. He nearly kicked out before he realized it was a tiny black kitten. He sagged against a medicine rack and shut his eyes until a rhythmic slurping forced them open again.

The kitten was lapping at the blood spill.

"Ah, *man*," Baker groaned. He was about to turn away when he discovered an object glinting within the puddle.

Tortoiseshell spectacles.

Taking care not to disturb the kitty's feast, he suppressed his revulsion long enough to try the glasses on. Debra had been as blind as a mole rat, yet when he brought a medicine box close to his face

LENORA

he could read the label. He spotted the word *dewormer* and chucked it aside. CHERISTIN, the next box read. Some kind of flea treatment.

Cursing, Baker moved down the aisle, primarily to find an antibiotic, but also to put some distance between him and the slurping feline, who was purring so rapturously he felt he should offer it some privacy. He spotlighted the topmost shelf and distinguished the word AMOXICILLIN. He'd have whooped for joy if not for the corpses and an atavistic dread of being eaten alive by feral cats. The place was giving him the willies, so he gathered as many boxes as he could and, eyes aching from Debra's overzealous lenses, he returned the spectacles and got the hell out of there.

The amoxicillin didn't touch Lenora's fever. For much of the night, she tremored so violently he worried she'd combust in his arms. She wouldn't eat, wouldn't drink. She wasn't even interested in the horror movies he screened for her. In desperation, he toted out the record player and a dusty LP of Chubby Checker's *The Twist*. He could hardly look at the album cover because it reminded him of his son. And when he dropped the needle and the first notes sounded, he decided this was a terrible mistake.

But Lenora was watching him from the La-Z-Boy, her ears pricked up.

"You like it?" he asked.

Her eyes widened, the sickness fog perhaps clearing a smidge. Baker swayed his hips, and Lenora sat up straighter. He started to sing, but his voice came out croaky. He swallowed, tried again, and this time it was better. He was no Chubby Checker, but under the gruffness of disuse, the melody was there.

Lenora rose unsteadily.

He finished the first verse, gyrating as vigorously as his body would allow, and crooned the chorus. Lenora tilted her head, fascinated.

Baker bopped over to her and twisted for a few beats. Lenora seemed to vibrate, her hooves jittering in place. Baker executed a spin, and all of a sudden the room took on a paler hue. It wasn't until he was falling that he realized how woozy he was. He smacked the floor—butt, skull, and shoulder blades all at once—and for a time he lay there, delirious and achy. The song ended, but Baker scarcely noticed. *Superflu*, he thought. Or he was just a dumbass who hadn't eaten enough today.

Something brushed his cheek. He blinked until his eyes refocused.

Lenora stared down at him. He could've sworn she was smiling. Before he could get his hands up, she darted in and licked his nose. He laughed and spluttered, but Lenora didn't seem to mind. She was too busy licking him.

They spent the next day pigging out, watching horror flicks, and reading a novel called *I Am Legend*. He'd planned on getting to it for years and figured now was as good a time as any for a story about the last man on earth. Lenora munched the lettuce he hand-fed her, but she didn't go wild until he broke out a fresh pack of Nutter Butters.

At five thirty that afternoon, she sneezed for the first time.

Baker shot her a sharp glance, heart thudding, and waited for the next sneeze. It didn't come. Dust, he told himself. He really ought to tidy up the place, especially now that he was a father again. About ten minutes later, Lenora let loose with a double-sneeze, and this time there was shiny stuff ringing her nostrils.

Mouth dry, Baker hastened into the kitchen and rifled through the medicines with shaking hands. Aside from the amoxicillin, what could he give her? He microwaved some soup, tested it to make sure it wouldn't scald her, and positioned it on the La-Z-Boy. She glanced at it, turned away like the world's harshest food critic, and nested her chin on her foreleg.

She sneezed again.

LENORA

Cold terror washed over him.

Baker snatched up the dog book and hurried back to the kitchen. No use letting Lenora see how worked up he was. Just paranoia. Understandable in such dreadful times. He scanned the list of human medicines that dogs could ingest, but the only one he owned was aspirin. He crushed half a pill and mixed it with sugar water. By the time he'd put on a brave face and reentered the living room, Lenora was breathing hard and looking at him imploringly. It knocked Baker's wind out.

No, he thought.

He offered her the bottle, but she ignored it. Her labored respiration made his stomach clench, the phlegmy rattle of it too much like Pastor Wiggins's.

"Goddammit, *no*."

He stroked her fur, and that seemed to calm her for a time, but then she burst out with a flurry of sneezes. He choked back a sob.

"It's okay, girl," he murmured. "It's okay." He caressed her back, kissed the tuft of hair between her ears, whispered words of encouragement. She looked at him appealingly. He got her mucus on his fingers, and he didn't give a damn. If this was superflu, she could very well have gotten it from Dead Ed, and wouldn't that be the worst fucking joke in history? This wonderful girl cut down by a shit stain like Dedaker?

Lenora scrambled up, her breathing rapid. He worried she was hyperventilating and had no idea what to do for her. Should he find a paper bag for her to breathe into? Did he own any paper bags?

He placed his hands on her sides and pressed his forehead to hers. "Stay with me, girl. Stay with me."

Her breathing grew shallower. Within a couple hours she was whimpering and struggling to take in air. Shortly after that, she was gone.

Baker held Lenora in his arms all night. He didn't sleep, didn't doze. Just cradled her in his recliner and wept soundless tears. At six that morning, the dawn overbright and the heat already closing over the countryside like a fist, he carried her to the backyard, where he stood with her amid the scorched ruin of the old house.

It wasn't fair. He might not deserve better, but Lenora did. By God, if anyone deserved to survive this plague, it was her.

He bared his teeth. *Goddammit*, he thought. *GODDAMMIT!*

Baker sank down, settled Lenora's body on the grass, and rested his forehead on her silky fur.

"Bring her back," he said.

No answer. The clearing was breezeless, the heat oppressive despite the early hour. His perspiration soaked into Lenora's pelt. He rocked back on his heels, a hand on her little head.

"I said bring her *back*."

No response from the clearing.

Baker trudged to the garage, returned with a shovel, and buried Lenora deep enough that nothing would disturb her. He yearned to eulogize her, but didn't trust himself to do her justice. He flung the shovel aside and strode to the Ranger. He fired it up, clicked the garage door opener, and rolled inside. There, he shifted into park, thumbed the button to shut the garage door, but left the pickup running.

Darkness enshrouded him. The engine rumbled.

How long would it take? Five minutes? Ten? It didn't matter. Lenora was gone and so was the world, and this death was as good as any other.

He glanced at the glowing dashboard clock.

7:17.

The garage was stifling, the Ranger pumping heat as well as poison into the air. He grew drowsy. He distinguished the clock through bleary eyes.

7:23.

He recalled the book he'd read Lenora, the loneliness of the main character and the way he'd tackled the problem of a world-ending plague. But Baker's only skill was repairing small appliances. He doubted he could save the world by fixing toaster ovens.

He caught himself nodding off. His vision carouseled, and when his eyes refocused he was astonished to find it was already 7:30.

So it was happening. Baker was about to close his eyes for good, when something in the other garage stall caught his gaze.

The red wagon.

Baker's chest burned, but he didn't think it was the carbon monoxide. He began to weep, his tears raw, ungovernable. He sobbed against the steering wheel and groped for the ignition. He found the key at last, twisted it, and heard the engine go silent. He slumped there, his body shuddering, and let it all flood out. The fire. The beautiful years that preceded it. His wife, his children. Petey. Such a good dog.

Lenora.

Baker reached up and pressed the garage door opener.

When his vision normalized, he climbed out of the Ranger and shuffled back to the house. It took him twenty minutes to load the truck. That done, he backed out of the garage and drove away.

He encountered a menagerie of corpses on his cruise through town. An elderly lady's slippered feet jutted through a tangle of tomato vines, varicose veins threading her calves like plum-colored calligraphy. An affluently dressed couple sat putrefying inside a factory-new sterling silver Cadillac. A naked man sprawled face down in a flower bed, the phlox and bluebells seeming to sprout from the crack of his ass.

The sun pummeling the Ranger, Baker motored on. When he passed the veterinary clinic, he tried to suppress images of Dr. Weizak and the doomed lovers. There was an idea nibbling at him, but he couldn't quite grab hold of it. After a time, he found himself gravitating toward the bank. He parked the Ranger there, wondered briefly if the perspiration slicking his skin was from the heat or the superflu. It was entirely possible he'd contracted it from Dedaker or Lenora. Or perhaps he wasn't sick at all. It didn't really matter.

He loaded the wagon, trundled it down the sidewalk, then halted and closed his eyes. When he opened them, the vague idea that had been nagging at him crystallized.

He turned and beheld the navy-blue saltbox house.

He rolled the wagon up the sidewalk, hefted it onto the porch, and cupped his hands against a sidelight. A deceased woman lounged on the sofa, her throat bulging like an amorous bullfrog. Prostrate on the floor was a girl of no more than six. Baker assumed she'd expired, too, but when he tapped the glass, she stirred, her eyes finding his through a tangle of auburn hair.

For a long moment, they just stared at each other.

She drifted to the door, and after tussling with the lock, drew it open and regarded him through the dusty screen.

"Everyone's dead," she said. "Mom. My brothers. Dad lives somewhere else, but he hasn't called."

Baker didn't comment.

The girl wiped her nose. "You sick?"

He thought it over. The sweating, the weariness.

"I don't know," he answered.

She lowered her eyes. "Don't know if I am, either. I don't feel very good."

"Had any sleep?"

"Some. I keep dreaming of a cornfield."

Baker glanced at her sharply and again experienced that magnetic westward tug. He wondered if she'd be comfortable in the wagon, should the roads become impassable.

What he said was "Are you hungry?"

She shrugged. Nodded.

He moved aside so she could see the wagon. "I've got Nutter Butters."

LENORA

She frowned. "What are those?"

"Health food."

Her eyes seemed a bit livelier. "Wanna come in?"

Baker took in the shininess on her upper lip, the bruisy discoloration under her eyes. Maybe the girl had it. Maybe she didn't. In the end, it didn't really matter.

He mulled it over. Gazed up at the brilliant blue sky and remembered the one who'd saved him at the end of the world. "Okay, Lenora," he murmured.

He faced the little girl, who watched him with large brown eyes. "What's your name?" he asked her.

"Juliet. What's yours?"

"Baker. Want to help me with these cookies?"

Now she did give him a smile. Just a small one.

She held the door open for him, and he towed the wagon into the house.

THE HOPE BOAT
Gabino Iglesias

Sandra knows the way to the beach, but she has no clue how long it will take her to get there on foot. It's probably only ten or twelve miles from her house. Puerto Rico is only a hundred miles long by thirty-five miles wide, so everyone is somewhat close to the beach. But ten or twelve miles on foot is still a lot of miles. Sandra used to walk almost four miles in just under an hour, but that was before she got pregnant, back when her friend Margaret was all about power walking and salads. It might take her more than fifteen minutes to complete a mile now. Maybe twenty? A little longer? That would make it a three-hour walk, give or take. But that would be under normal circumstances, and circumstances haven't been normal for a while now.

Make it four hours, then, but go. Go now. You have time.

The thought scares her. Going anywhere now is like venturing out into a jungle full of predators. Psychos. Scavengers. Sick people who have lost their minds. They're all out there. Still, it could be worth a shot if the information she received is true. It's early now, but she must be at the beach by midday if she wants to hop on the rescue boat. Although *rescue* is too big a word. It feels like an impossible word, something that should be cut from the dictionary. *Rescue boat* sounds like someone is in control. *Tell them you have hope.* That's what Mercedes said. *Hope* is a good word here. *Hope boat* sounds more accurate than *rescue boat*. It could also be desperate boat. Last chance boat. Boat to freedom. Those are better.

The voice in Sandra's head sounds a lot like her mother. It's been there all her life, but it's been much more present lately. It's her only companion, and Sandra is glad for its presence, but she often wonders if she's losing her mind. The way things have gone, it wouldn't surprise her.

The trip from Sandra's house to the beach was always a joyful one, but thinking about it now hurts. Baby Angie usually wore her favorite bathing suit, a bright pink one that was the cutest thing Sandra had ever seen. It had a circle of tiny blue fish on the chest that always made Sandra think of her beautiful daughter as a minuscule superhero. Super Baby, devourer of cookies. Her superpower? A natural aversion to naps, a million-watt smile, and more energy than the Energizer Bunny. This trip won't have any of that, but the idea of staying in a house with two bodies, no food, no water, no electricity, and no chance of being rescued is even less appealing.

So, four hours. That's a long walk, but she can do it. A long walk is nothing if what Mercedes told her is true.

Mercedes, Sandra's neighbor from three doors down, had knocked on her door the night before. Sandra had panicked for a second before Mercedes identified herself.

Sandra had been convinced Mercedes was immune to the disease, just like her. Their entire neighborhood had succumbed in a matter of days, but they hadn't. The more people died, the more they talked, checked on each other, and shared news and food. Mercedes was a very positive person, and she had helped a lot when Miguel died. Mercedes's own husband, Roberto, died two days later. She had dragged him out and buried him in their yard. "I don't want his angry spirit haunting my dreams," she said to Sandra afterward while

THE HOPE BOAT

scraping dirt from under her nails. "Men are moody, and dead men are no different." She'd tried to smile through the tears then, a bit of gallows humor, but all she managed was a strange twitch of her lips that spoke more of devastation than mirth. Now it was just the two of them, Sandra and Mercedes, a few doors from each other, surviving alone, but together.

The moment Sandra opened the door, she knew she was wrong. Mercedes—in her early forties, short and stocky, with dark skin and a beautiful mane of black curls framing a pretty face—looked like the ghost of her former self. Her face was bloated and strangely pale. She had dark bags under her eyes that seemed ready to pop. Her face and neck were slick with that shiny, oily sweat that the sick were always covered in. Mercedes had knocked on the door in the early afternoon and called out her name, but by the time Sandra reached the door, her friend had stepped back almost ten feet. She was shivering from the fever and had a glistening line of snot covering her upper lip.

"I . . . I got it," said Mercedes. It was obvious, but the words still felt like a gut punch to Sandra.

"Oh, Mercedes . . . "

Mercedes looked at Sandra's arms and then at her legs. Sandra knew what she was looking for. It filled her eyes with tears again.

"Baby Angie?" Mercedes asked, her voice low, like she was afraid of waking her up.

Sandra couldn't answer. She shook her head, the tears now running down her face.

"I'm so sorry," said Mercedes. The last word had been buried under so much emotion that it sounded like something else, a small animal drowning instead of a word.

For a moment, both women stood there, looking at each other. All the things they wanted to say were left unsaid. And maybe that was for the better. Nothing reveals the uselessness of words quite like the presence of Death, riding its black horse silently down your street with its scythe at the ready. Mercedes was dying. Sandra was surrounded by death. The enormity of their pain silenced them. Looking at each other was enough.

"I came to tell you something," said Mercedes. She sniffled and wiped her face with her hands before continuing. "I got a call three days ago. From my mom back home. She said whole families survived in the Dominican Republic. She told me they all moved to Punta Cana and they've . . . built a place there. A refuge. There's a lot of food and stuff from all the hotels there. They've been sending fishing boats over to pick up survivors from the beaches in Rincón, Joyuda, and a few other places. For a price, obviously. My mom, she . . . she got me a ticket. For tomorrow at midday. You should go."

"No, I can't do that," said Sandra. "That's your . . . " She wanted to say that was Mercedes's ticket, her opportunity to get out, but the woman would probably be dead before she reached the coast, even if she found a car to get her there. They both knew it. Turning down the opportunity was an instinct from a time when the world still worked. There, standing in front of each other with tears running down their faces and a decomposing world around them, turning it down made no sense. The social contract was no longer in place.

"I won't make it," said Mercedes. "We both know it. Just . . . go. You can walk to there from here. Leave early tomorrow. When the boat comes, someone will come to the beach. Tell them you have hope. That's the password. They'll take your temperature. If you're still fine, they'll take you to Punta Cana."

Sandra nodded. More tears came, and she didn't know who they were for. They could be for Mercedes because she was dying, but they could also be for Baby Angie. Or for Miguel. Or for the countless dead neighbors in all the dark houses up and down the street that had turned into graves.

Or for herself.

"Thank you," said Sandra. She didn't believe it. Whole families? Food? It had to be a rumor. But she couldn't tell Mercedes that. You don't snatch a dying woman's last dream from her.

"I'm . . . I'm so sorry about Baby Angie," said Mercedes, her voice cracking again.

There could be no hug and saying goodbye would hurt too much, so Sandra was relieved when Mercedes turned and walked away, grabbing her head and grunting as she went.

Sandra closed the door and stood there a minute, thinking about what Mercedes had told her. It couldn't be, but what if it was?

Tell them you have hope.

The smell smacked her in the face a few moments after she closed the door. Decay. Rotting flesh. Bodily fluids soaking into her bed, through her mattress, dripping onto the floor. Like every other house out there, Sandra's house contained dead bodies.

In her bedroom was her husband, Miguel. He had gone out one morning a few days ago to see if he could find some food. He'd come back a few hours later, tired and complaining of a headache. The fever started soon after. That night, he started talking about his brother Tomás, who died ten years ago in a car crash. The sweating and the headaches were horrible, but they didn't last long. He died in the middle of the night, calling for his brother. Sandra had been sitting right outside their bedroom, listening to him through the door and praying Baby Angie wouldn't catch the sickness from her own father.

After Miguel went quiet, she checked in on him. He looked bloated and shiny. Liquid was coming from his mouth and nose. He wasn't breathing or complaining. He wasn't talking to his dead brother. He would never do any of those things—or anything else—ever again. Sandra's heart cracked in half and she fell to her knees a few feet from the bed she had shared with Miguel for nine years.

After a while, Baby Angie cried. Sandra got up and went to her. She held her daughter and caressed her head, wanting to apologize for the way things had turned out.

An hour later, Baby Angie finally fell asleep again, so Sandra returned to her room. She didn't want to touch Miguel, so she grabbed some clothes from the dresser and her toiletries from the bathroom and stuffed them in the traveling backpack she kept under her side of the bed. Then she grabbed Miguel's gun from the closet. A small revolver in a leather holster he'd inherited from his father. From her nightstand, she took her mother's old rosary and the two novels she was trying to read whenever Baby Angie took a nap and she wasn't too tired: Stephen King's *The Dark Half* and John Grisham's *A Time to Kill*. With her backpack full and her heart empty, Sandra walked out into the hallway and closed the door to her bedroom for the last time.

The following day felt like an agonizing performance. Sandra took care of Baby Angie and pretended her father wasn't rotting in their bedroom while her daughter played with her food, blissfully oblivious of the crumbling world around her.

The sun was going down when Baby Angie started crying. Her face started swelling soon after. Sandra touched her lips to her daughter's forehead. She was burning up.

No, no, no. Please, God, no.

Sandra cried and prayed and held her mother's rosary against her daughter's bloated face, but God was tending to the apocalypse and her prayers went unanswered.

Baby Angie's fever got worse. She cried desperately and then became strangely calm, as if accepting her fate. Sandra kept talking to her. "You're gonna be okay, baby," she said through more tears. "You're gonna sweat the fever out and feel much better in the morning."

Every lie tasted sour. Every minute was torture. Baby Angie looked at her mother imploringly for a while, but Sandra could do nothing except spit lies at her in a soothing voice. A few hours later, Sandra's beautiful baby daughter started looking around the room, as if searching for someone. As if searching for God.

She was dead the following morning.

When pain and grief pile on top of more pain and grief, sometimes the only coping mechanism left is to welcome a deep sense of numb-

THE HOPE BOAT

ness and concentrate on breathing, on surviving one more minute even if we're not sure why we want to stay alive. That was what Sandra did. She sat on the sofa and cried until she felt separated from her body. Then she cried some more. Then she fell asleep.

The next day went by in a blur. She drank some water and tried to eat some crackers at some point, but that was it. The rest was hours that went by in a flash and minutes that stretched out forever. Her pain was a wave that crested and crested, but never broke. Her eyes hurt from crying. So did her stomach. And her grief wouldn't stop growing, like a crescendo that builds until it's so loud and fast that human ears can no longer hear it.

A few times, the revolver popped into her head. It was in her backpack. One bullet was all it would take. Quick and easy. Mostly painless if she did it right. But she couldn't. She refused to give up.

At some point in the afternoon, Sandra went into her daughter's room. A few flies circled over Baby Angie's crib. Their buzzing was the most horrific sound Sandra had ever heard. She slammed the door shut and screamed until she felt the metallic taste of blood flooding into her mouth from her ruined throat.

In the middle of that second night, after losing her husband and her daughter in less than two days, Sandra realized she was still feeling fine. No fever. No pain other than her throat. No headache. No aches anywhere. Nothing. Her husband and daughter were dead, but she was still alive and, for the moment, healthy.

Back when the sickness started, the news had said everyone who got it died from it. Right before the TV and radio went off the air, they then said that was wrong. Some people never caught it. Less than one percent of the population could be exposed to it and not die. No one knew how immunity worked or for how long, but it seemed to be true. They were calling those on the island who didn't catch it *elegidos*. The chosen ones. Sandra felt like she had been chosen, but by some cruel god curious to see how much agony one person could stand.

That was the first night there were no screams or gunshots or the sound of cars trying to outrun the nightmare that had killed almost everyone. With the electricity gone, not even the hum of the refrigerator's motor filled the quiet inside the house. Outside, insects and the incessant song of the *coquíes* filled the night. At some point, something scratched the house's door, but Sandra stayed on the sofa and didn't even bother to take Miguel's revolver out of the backpack.

When the sun came out, Sandra stepped outside to make sure the world was still there. The street was quiet and empty. Dead. The dew on the grass felt like an insult. A few birds were making a racket on the neighbor's tree. There were some scratches on her door. Big ones.

Sandra had eaten something and then cried for a while. That was when Mercedes had shown up. Her neighbor, who was dying, had thrown a possibility at Sandra's feet, and now that she had nothing to lose and no reason to stay in a house that had become a tomb for what she had loved the most in this life, Sandra wondered what it would be like to go.

Tell them you have hope.

Now the moment has come. All that's left is for her to start walking. Sandra feels like she doesn't have any hope left, but something is pushing her to go. She's standing next to the door. Her backpack contains her clothes, two books, some food, two bottles of water, and the small revolver. It's nothing and everything she has. On her feet are the tennis shoes Miguel got her after Baby Angie came home and she started complaining that she wanted to start walking again to lose the small pouch the baby had left behind.

She didn't even think about packing. The backpack was more or less ready. All she did was add the food and water. With that done, there's nothing between Sandra and the dead world except the door with the large scratches on it.

Just go.

The voice is there again. It's strong. It feels right. It's the only thing she has left.

Sandra looks at her watch, a small Seiko Miguel got her for Christmas. It's 8:40 a.m. She has enough time, but not enough to waste. She opens the door and stands there for a moment. She wants to run back in and say goodbye to her husband, to kiss her baby daughter one last time. Then she thinks about flies crawling over Baby Angie's face and she shuts the door.

None of this is fair. She doesn't deserve this. None of them do.

Sandra wipes the tears off with her T-shirt and starts walking toward the beach, toward hope. She doesn't look at Mercedes's house as she walks by, but she mumbles a prayer for her friend's soul.

The first mile or so is good, comfortable. The sun is out. Sandra feels tired, but she knows it's from bad nutrition and lack of sleep, not from the sickness. She keeps her eyes on the road as she walks. She ignores the bodies on the sidewalk and gives a wide berth to the ones on the street. *Don't look. Don't look. Don't look.* Sandra takes quick glances at some of the bodies despite the voice. Every single one is a shock. Every single body on the ground or in a car is someone's son or daughter, someone's significant other or best friend or sibling. Someone's parent or caregiver. Every untimely death is devastating, and it's impossible not to feel sadness and anger about each of them.

The birds are having a feast. They sound angry when Sandra walks by. The vultures beat their large, dark wings and make sounds that let her know she's not welcome to share their banquet. One of them comes at her aggressively and then goes back to eating. It's enough to make Sandra take off her backpack, look for the revolver, take it out of its leather holster, and put it in her jeans so she can get to it faster.

The bodies are everywhere. Some of them are old, but some are fresh. Some are missing limbs or have strange wounds that resemble shark bites. The bite marks make Sandra think about the noises she heard last night and the weird scratches on her door. The strangely sweet stench of death permeates everything. She can't be out here at night. She must make it to the damn boat. The hope boat.

Sandra walks a little faster. The metal of the gun is strangely cool. It feels like a small reassurance against the soft flesh of her belly.

Baby Angie.

Sandra touches her empty stomach, right next to the gun, and the tears come again. She rubs the wetness out of her eyes and tries to think about the future, but the present is too big and loud to ignore and the recent past is a demon howling in her soul, an endless cacophony of wailing voices trapped inside her that beat against her skull at all times. Sandra looks up at the clouds. The sky is perfectly blue, like it doesn't care about what goes on underneath it. A gentle breeze blows. A nearby tree sways. Sandra looks at it, begging it to take away some of her pain. The tree sways again in response, but her pain remains untouched, slicing to her core as she walks.

Sandra looks at the road ahead. Maybe her future is at the end of that road, where the sand meets the ocean. But first she must get there.

Sandra walks and walks. The tennis shoes are good. Nothing hurts, nothing rubs her the wrong way. She walks past rotting bodies, and scorched or abandoned cars. She walks past broken and forgotten things—pieces of a radio, a brown shoe, a kitchen knife, an open briefcase with some papers still inside it, a bicycle tire, a toothbrush, a book for children with a small bear wearing a blue tutu on the cover. She walks past houses that are full of dead people. Some have their doors open. Scavengers were common the first few days. She wonders how many of those houses have little beds and cradles with—

No. Sandra shuts that thought down immediately. No good will come of it. But the things we try to silence inside ourselves are usually the ones that scream the loudest, and Sandra can't help but think of millions of cradles across the world, all of them with dead, bloated babies inside. All of them covered with flies and, soon after, full of squirming maggots feasting on the flesh of those who were supposed to be the future, those who were the apple of someone's eye, those who made the world better just by being in it, with their big smiles and little hands and pure hearts.

Baby Angie. Tired and broken, Sandra lets the memories flood in. Baby Angie playing. Baby Angie giggling. Baby Angie squeezing handfuls of mashed potatoes, her dirty little face full of glee. Baby Angie splashing in the tub. Each memory is a gem covered in thorns that fills her heart while ripping it apart.

Half an hour later, Sandra starts thinking about the possibility of finding the boat and being taken to a better place, to a new community. Maybe there she can find hope again.

A big mongoose interrupts her thoughts. It walks out from behind the burned metallic skeleton of an overturned van that sits in the middle of the road. It's as big as a small dog. It's the biggest Sandra has ever seen. It looks swollen. Clearly infected. Saliva and something thicker fall from its mouth. Sandra stops walking and keeps her eyes on the animal.

The mongoose makes that little growling thing they do. It's a deep, primal sound that sends a shiver down Sandra's spine despite the heat. Every instinct in her body tells her to turn and run. Then she remembers the gun.

Sandra slowly brings her right hand up and pulls the gun from her waist.

The mongoose hisses and walks away before Sandra has time to aim. She's glad. Infected or not, she didn't want to shoot it. She watches as the animal trots over a front yard and disappears around a house.

Two weeks ago, she wouldn't have thought she would ever touch Miguel's gun. She didn't even want it in the house. But then everything collapsed, and she watched as people turned into savages, stealing, breaking into homes, running around in absolute anarchy, and slaughtering each other in the streets. Now she is sure she will pull the trigger.

About half a mile later, the residential part of town ends and Sandra walks onto a much larger road. This one will take her to the beach. She's halfway there. The thought of reaching the beach injects a bit of energy into her system and Sandra speeds up a bit, happy to no longer be surrounded by houses full of dead people.

But the big avenue is no better. Cars are piled everywhere, and many of them contain bodies. The stench is even worse than it was before. Here, it's also mixed with the smell of gasoline and charred things.

A while later, the driver's door of a black Lincoln Town Car opens about twenty feet in front of Sandra and a man stumbles out. He's wearing dirty jeans and no shirt or shoes. He looks like a corpse that's been in the water for too long. He takes a few steps toward Sandra.

"Stop," Sandra says. Fear has made her voice weak, and the screaming from the previous night isn't doing her any favors.

The man snarls, shakes his head, and moves toward her.

The oily sweat and swollen face are clear signs that he's infected, but it still takes a moment for Sandra to make up her mind.

The shot is too loud. It feels like Sandra split the day in half. It pings against the car. He keeps walking. Sandra takes a breath and aims again. The second shot is just as loud, but there's no metallic ping. It hits the guy in the stomach. He falls to his knees and grunts. Sandra squeezes the trigger one more time. The left side of the man's face explodes in a puff of red and pink.

Sandra walks around the man, making sure he's not moving. Her hands are shaking.

You killed a man.

The voice doesn't sound panicky or judgmental. Sandra ignores it and keeps walking past more cars, more bodies, more destruction.

The big avenue bends left before you see the beach. There's a Blockbuster on the corner before you have to turn. Sandra can see the blue of its marquee from where she's standing. She's close to the beach. Sandra looks at her watch. 10:15 a.m. She's going to make it. She takes a moment to drink some water and eat a few crackers.

An uneventful hour later, Sandra is at the beach. There are no bodies on the sand. She's grateful for that. The ocean is a darker blue than the sky. A few white clouds hang over the ocean. The palm trees and the sand and the few white clouds paint a pretty picture. For a while, Sandra sits near the ocean and allows her surroundings to dim the horrors in her head.

The horizon is an unperturbed line. By noon, it remains the same. Untouched. Empty. Unbroken.

By 1:00 p.m., Sandra begins to wonder what midday might mean to other people.

At 2:30 p.m., she gets up and pees behind a palm tree, looking around before she does, even though she hasn't seen a soul since the sick man she shot on the road.

Time keeps on keeping on.

2:55 p.m.

Sandra gets up and walks the length of the beach, scouring the horizon for a boat.

3:17 p.m.

The waves are never quiet. Birds make noises from time to time. A small crab makes a mad dash to some unknown destination. The world is dead, but life goes on here and there. An insect. A bird. Palm trees. The rock keeps spinning without people. It makes Sandra think about what the world would look like with everyone gone, with not even a single survivor. It's easy to imagine it now. All she has to do is look around. All the emptiness fills her with a new kind of sadness.

We're nothing but cosmic dust floating in an infinite beam of light.

4:00 p.m.

Anxiety tickles Sandra's heart with a feather like a scalpel.

4:25 p.m.

Sandra walks the beach again. She remembers Baby Angie's pink bathing suit with its circle of tiny blue fish. She thinks about grabbing the gun, walking into water until it reaches her waist, and then blowing her brains out. She thinks about her body sinking, becoming one with the ocean, turning into sand, her particles living forever in this gorgeous place.

4:43 p.m.

Desperation sets in.

5:12 p.m.

You messed up. The voice doesn't sound like her mother now. It sounds like an angry demon. *You killed a man.*

6:02 p.m.

Sandra is sitting again. Midday, no matter how you think of it, is gone. The sun has started moving down. The beach is not so big that Sandra would have missed a boat, especially not one with a motor.

It all makes sense. There is no boat. Of course there is no boat. There never was.

Mercedes's mother didn't buy a ticket for her daughter; she bought a ticket to a dream.

There is no boat because people are dead everywhere. There is no boat because it was all a lie someone told Mercedes's mom. Because people can be good to each other when things go bad, like she and Mercedes had been to each other. But people can also be awful when things go bad. Like now.

The sunset is an explosion of neon orange splashed with purple at its edges. The ocean keeps singing its endless song, the waves worrying about nothing as their unceasing rhythm caresses the shore.

In the Caribbean, night comes at you fast, almost aggressively. Like a warning.

Sandra drinks the last of her water and eats the last stale cracker. She has two options now. She can turn around and try to walk back home. There's nothing waiting for her there except the rotting bodies of her daughter and her husband. But home is always home. Maybe she can wait and see where things go. Maybe enough people survive, and they start again. Maybe the government finds a cure soon. She can wait. She can scavenge. She still has a few bullets left. She can put duct tape around Baby Angie's door and her bedroom door to keep the smell under control.

The second option is to walk into the ocean. Maybe at the bottom of the ocean, away from people, she can find some hope.

Sandra stands up and starts walking.

WRONG FUCKING PLACE, WRONG FUCKING TIME
C. Robert Cargill

Derek Cerny and Alan Mahr had always joked that Roosevelt, Texas, would be a great town if it weren't for all the people, and as it turned out, they were pretty much right.

Gone was the busybody Baptist mother of four, whose children had all long since found their way to Fredericksburg or Austin—as far as they could reasonably get from her. Gone was the bully of a sheriff's deputy, Willy Boggs, who sat outside of McCready's Bar on Friday and Saturday nights, ready to write a citation if anyone so much as looked drunk—only for Sheriff Dean to let them out the next morning without a fuss or ticket. Gone was Sheriff Dean, who, while not a bad guy, was still the law in a place that didn't really need it and spent a little too much time trying to justify his position.

Gone was the local rancher, Spike McInroy, who, while giving Derek and Alan their longtime gainful employment, paid them as little as he could get away with while keeping them both from quitting and finding something better. Gone was pretty much everyone who thought little of two ranch hands who believed the best part of the week was sitting down with a twelve-pack of Budweiser to watch a double feature of horror movies rented from Old Gil's video store.

They were by no stretch two of life's winners, but they weren't without their charms.

Roosevelt was a certified ghost town long before Captain Trips paid it a visit. It was one of the places you would expect to see Trips last, if at all. Just shy of one hundred people lived on the swaths of land that flanked both sides of Interstate 10 on the long, flat stretch of road smack in the middle of an eight-hour drive from San Antonio to El Paso. What had started as a mining community had faltered, contracted, and become more of a glorified truck stop than a town. It was home to two sorts of people—those that owned or worked the handful of vast ranches, and those that served the highway and its myriad of travelers.

In a way, the highway was far more important to the town than the ranchers, and thus it was folks like Violet May, Terrence McCready, and Old Gil who were in the chief seats of power in the town. Violet owned the combination gas station/diner, the single most frequented business fifty miles either way—she served a mean Salisbury steak with the best cheddar grits anywhere in Texas. Terrence owned the bar, which arguably brought in more money than Violet, though much of that was from locals, which did less for the economy overall. And Gil owned both motels along the highway, the first being the one he inherited from his father, the other bought from Garrett Meyer upon his retirement.

The reception this far out for anything resembling a television station was pretty much terrible. On a clear night, you could get a good atmospheric bounce and pick up a handful of fuzzy Austin stations, but for the most part, it was a wasteland of mind-numbing UHF television from a variety of smaller towns. You know, lots of preacher talk and *Mayberry R.F.D.* reruns.

Tired of complaints from travelers just wanting to relax in front of the TV after a long drive, Old Gil made a deal with a trucker for a couple dozen VHS players to fall off the back of his truck. Gil installed each room with a player and combed stores all over Central Texas to amass a collection of tapes unrivaled anywhere outside of the big cities.

Truckers had taken to putting combination TV/VHS players in the back of their cabs and so Gil started a video-swap service, which not only kept a steady traffic coming through his shop, but also kept it full of strange and exotic films from all over. Soon after opening, the video store—Moonrise Video—was taking in more revenue than its sister businesses, the Moonrise Motel and the Friendly 8 Roadside Inn, combined.

And for two ranch hands like Alan and Derek, it meant despite living this far out in the middle of nowhere, they had access to all the movies they could ever want. And it took only one visit from Captain Trips to the video store to make it such that they were two of its last remaining customers.

It took less than a week for Trips to clear out the rest of town.

There was a lot that could be said about Alan and Derek, and even as small as the town had been, a lot had been. But when people stopped showing up for their shifts, when the diner failed to open and the Roosevelt Food Mart didn't flick its neon on, the boys went to work. They checked in on folks, cared for who they found still breathing, and one by one buried almost every single person in Roosevelt. There were no authorities to come and claim bodies, no ambulances willing to drive this far out in a pandemic. No, it was up to the last remaining people of Roosevelt to care for themselves and their kin.

"I reckon we should wear masks or something," said Derek as he shoveled a pile of vomit from beside the Widow Harper's bed.

"What for?" asked Alan. "Ain't no mask gonna stop us from doin' this ourselves. If we're gonna get it, we're gonna get it."

"I meant about the smell."

"You don't wear a goddamned mask when you're shoveling cattle shit. Why start now?"

"Well, I mean, I'm used to the cattle shit. This is a rotting body."

"It's all decomposition and undigested material, dumbass."

"That's a fair point," said Derek. "It just don't smell remotely the same."

"Widow Harper deserves better than to be treated like trash to be taken out."

"That woman hated you."

"Most women hate me."

"Hated."

"There are still some left, I suppose," said Alan.

"You suppose our odds have improved?" asked Derek genuinely.

"I reckon they have to. Unless . . . "

"Unless what?"

"Unless mostly men survive."

"Well, that would suck."

"No more than it sucked before."

"That's fair."

"Still think the woman deserves to be handled with care and not treated like a fuckin' biohazard."

"All right, all right, I'll lay off about the mask."

The two resigned men carried on like this, chatting away, trying to figure out the *What next?* of it all, while collecting, boxing up, and burying the residents of Roosevelt in a large field beside the highway. They set up a system to make sure they remembered exactly who was buried where, and at night, the two would craft and then hand-carve crosses for each of them. Not everyone in Roosevelt was Christian or practicing, but this being Texas, everyone at least pretended, and so Derek and Alan didn't really know better and gave them all crosses anyway. Even Mrs. Levenson.

It wouldn't be until toward the end of the first week that the pair would discover that they were not, in fact, alone.

Bill Pertwee was a few years older than the boys and had mostly grown up around them. He didn't think much of them, nor they of him, but they'd never had any beef between the three of them and had always been cordial when running into one another. So, it was a bit uncomfortable the moment the two pulled onto his property in Alan's El Camino and Bill met them on his porch aiming a shotgun at the pair.

"Ain't nothin' here worth gettin' shot over stealin', boys!" he called out as the two got out of their car.

"Whoa, whoa, whoa!" yelled Alan, throwing his hands in the air.

Derek, on the other hand, held his arms out, palms open wide, giving the universal sign for *Yo, chill the fuck out*. "We ain't here to steal shit, Bill. We's just here to check on you and the girls. Everyone okay?"

"We don't need no checking in on."

"That may be so, but if that's true, you, me, Alan, and the girls are the only ones left alive in town. We just wanted to see who's still alive and take care of those that don't have much time left."

Bill narrowed his eyes and lowered his gun. He motioned over toward an ancient magnolia tree to the side of his house. There beneath it, underneath the massive off-white spring blossoms, were three mounds and three crosses. One each for his wife and daughters. "Ain't none but just me left. And I don't reckon I'm much longer for this world."

"You sick?" asked Derek.

Bill looked down at the shotgun in his hands. "Nope."

Alan and Derek nodded, exchanging glances. Then Derek reached into the El Camino and pulled out a battered Coleman cooler, holding it up like a peace offering. "Nice thing about six-packs is they split up evenly both two and three ways."

Bill looked at the two idiots for a moment, then nodded. "Yeah, come on in."

The three sat quietly for the next hour, someone only occasionally breaking the silence to ask an easily answered question. Bill was curious how everyone had gone, and Derek tried to find a way to get him to open up about the girls. But Bill would not budge on that front. So they drank, made the smallest of small talk, and when the sixth beer was crumpled in Bill's hand, the three stood up with a "Welp, time to get back at it."

On their way out the door, Alan turned back in to face Bill. "Me and Derek have been hitting up Moonrise Video about six o' clock. We're usually back at our place by seven. If you got nothin' to do and feel like being around some folk, stop by and watch some movies with us."

"We got beer," said Derek.

"I reckon you do," said Bill. "We'll see."

Come six o' clock, the boys were walking the aisles of Moonrise—having gotten the keys off Old Gil's limp corpse that had, just as Gil would have wanted it, expired slumped over the front desk of his motel, never having missed a day of work due to illness in his life. Of course, how many people he may have given the Trips as a result was something he would have to stand judgment for on his own.

The electric grid was still holding up, but the boys were unsure how long that would last, so they had raided the truck stop for a power inverter and every 12V car battery they could find, making sure each was fully charged. Alan had even designed a windmill battery charger that he put a little time into building each day to make sure that when the time came, and the grid failed, they would have enough juice to run a TV and VCR for the foreseeable future. As ranch hands, they could handle the heat and they could handle warm beer; what they could not abide was living without movies.

Derek and Alan always loved walking the aisles of the store, even the ones they knew like the back of their hand. There was a bit of sadness in their hearts, knowing that there was unlikely to ever be another New Release Day there in the store (Tuesdays, when all the new movies came in). Not that there wouldn't be a Tuesday anymore, but rather that Tuesday, Wednesday, Sunday, none of it mattered. For Derek and Alan, every day was Friday. They got up, cared for Spike's cattle, did their daily tour through the town to clean up any remains, hit the video store, then crushed a twelve-pack of

WRONG FUCKING PLACE, WRONG FUCKING TIME

Bud watching a double feature before retiring to bed and doing it all over the next day.

But that night was different. After selecting a pair of carefully considered horror gems, the two went back to their place on Spike's ranch (they felt it would be disrespectful to move from the ranch hands' quarters into the main house so quickly), cracked open their beers, and sat on the couch just as there came a knock at the door.

"This is like that old story," said Derek.

"Which one?"

"The last man on earth hears a knock at the door."

"We ain't the last yet, dumbass," said Alan.

"I'm just sayin'."

Alan answered to see Bill standing there, six-pack of his own in hand. Stroh's. He held it up.

"I know it ain't Bud," he said. "But it was bought and paid for in my fridge."

"Beer down at the market is free these days," called Derek from the couch.

"Didn't seem right to steal a peace offering," said Bill. "Sorry about the whole shotgun thing. You know how it is."

"Forgotten," said Alan. "Have a seat."

"Thank you much."

That'd be the last thing Bill said all night. Not because of Captain Trips or anything, but just because it was his way. He took a seat in a ragged armchair to the side of the couch and made himself comfortable.

This was Catholic Horror Night. The boys had borrowed *The Seventh Sign* and *The Unholy*, both new releases they hadn't gotten to. Bill sat in silence, taking the whole thing in wordlessly, the only sound he made being the cracking open of another cold one every half an hour or so. At the end of the night, he stood up, nodded, and said, "Thanks for the evening, boys." And he left, driving carefully, slowly, half-drunk, through the dark, silent town.

Derek and Alan thought they might run into him around town here or there over the next few weeks and certainly did not anticipate seeing him once again, seven p.m. sharp the next day, on their doorstep, sixer of Stroh's in his hand.

"Bill," said Alan, holding the door open for him.

"Boys," said Bill before entering and sitting in the same chair he had the night before.

This was Slime Trail Night. The boys had discovered a movie titled *Slugs* and felt the proper way to chase it down would be with *Night of the Creeps*, one of Alan's recent favorites. Bill didn't think much of *Slugs*—the boys liked it just fine—but he really enjoyed *Creeps*. Thought it was pretty funny and started to really wrap his head around the "watching horror movies together" thing the boys had going on.

Bill went the whole night without a word, thanked the boys on his way out, and was there, six-pack in hand, seven p.m. sharp the following night for Italian Zombie Night. "The good news is your dates are here," he said with a smile.

"The bad news is they're dead," cackled Alan, welcoming Bill back into their home.

This went on for about a week, until the boys rolled up to Moonrise Video right at the stroke of six to find Bill sitting in the parking lot waiting for them.

"Can I ask you something?" asked Bill as he walked the stacks with the boys, eyeing the ten thousand or so videos Gil had accrued over the years.

"Sure," said Derek. "What do you wanna know?"

"Why movies?"

"Why movies, what?" asked Derek, confused.

"You boys could have been doing anything all this time. Playing video games, going to the bar, driving to Austin for concerts, hell, woodworking. Why movies?"

Derek and Alan exchanged baffled looks. They liked movies. Hell, they loved movies. The why of it hadn't really crossed Derek's mind. But it had crossed Alan's.

"You know," said Alan, "I read somewhere that humans invented beer about ten thousand years ago, give or take."

"Really?" asked Bill.

"Yeah. Wasn't exactly the same as it is now, but same concept. I learned about it when I started looking into home brewing."

"Brewing your own beer?"

"Yeah. It's a thing. There's a shop in Fredericksburg that sells everything you need. I thought it might be fun and, you know, cheaper, to make my own. Makes more sense now, what with there only being so much beer left in the local stores. Anyhow, for ten thousand years, man has made beer. And every day, after a long day of hunting or gathering or farming, man would sit down with his friends around a campfire and tell stories."

"Yeah, I get that," said Bill.

"Well. It ain't a campfire, but I reckon sitting around a glowing box with friends and letting it tell us stories is about the same. 'Cept of course, this way we don't hear the same story about that time Derek got drunk with Sissy Heiser from over in Flatsbury and she let him do butt stuff."

"She did," said Derek. "Ain't no lie."

"Didn't say there was. Just that I've heard that story about eighty times and I'd like something new every now and again."

"Can't all be butt stuff," said Bill, agreeing.

"Exactly," said Alan. "So, for us, videos is our campfire."

"And we're happy to have you join us around it," said Derek.

Bill walked in silence with them for a moment, before breaking it once again. "Can I be real honest with you guys?"

"Shoot," said Derek.

"I mean nothin' by this, but I used to think y'all were two weird little assholes. It turns out y'all are just good, decent folk."

Derek and Alan shared a strained look with one another before bursting into laughter. "Well, truth is," said Derek through both chuckles and guffaws, "we are weird little assholes."

Then Alan piped in, "But we reckon being that and good folk ain't exactly mutually exclusive."

Bill laughed. Then he nodded, asking, "So what are we watching tonight?"

The three returned to the boys' place shortly thereafter with *Friday the 13th 3D*, *A Nightmare on Elm Street*, and *The Texas Chain Saw Massacre*. The boys reckoned it was about time Bill got a proper education in horror and that meant starting with the heavyweights—the all-time best slasher killers ever to grace the screen. It was Friday after all and no one exactly had work in the morning, so a triple feature was in due order.

"Wait, wait, wait," said Bill, mid-discussion. "So the hockey mask guy—"

"Jason," the boys said together.

"Yeah, him. You mean he ain't even in the first movie?"

"No, his mom is the killer in that one," said Derek. "I mean he kinda shows up at the end, but that is like a dream or something."

"And he doesn't actually get his mask until this one," said Alan.

"Part Three?" asked Bill.

"Yeah," said Alan.

"So why does everyone call him the hockey mask guy?" asked Bill.

"They call him Jason," said Derek.

"But he's the hockey mask guy," said Bill.

"Yeah," the boys answered.

"And he's dead," said Bill.

"Not yet," said Alan. "He dies in Part Four. Then he's resurrected in Part Six."

"Shit," said Derek. "We're gonna have to explain Part Five, aren't we?"

"I think it's just best if we show him," said Alan.

"We should have just started with the first one."

"Yeah, but Jason isn't really in that one and we wanted to show him the best of the baddies."

"I still contend no list of slashers is complete without Pinhead," said Derek.

"And I still contend that *that* is a conversation for another time," said Alan.

The three sat in silence, watching the triptych of horror classics, Bill's eyes glued to the screen as body after body dropped in gruesome fashion. Not all the kills were bloody, but each one was brutal, in some cases much more brutal than the last. As the night wore on and the number of beers in the fridge grew thin, Bill looked more and more perplexed. And once the movies had run their course, Alan and Derek stood up to bid Bill adieu, only to find Bill still in his seat, watching the credits roll.

"I don't get it," said Bill.

"Get what?" asked Alan.

"Why do you like these guys?" asked Bill. "Like, I get why you guys like horror movies. I'm really liking a lot of them as well. But *these* guys. Freddy, Jason, Leatherface. Why them? They're not the good guys."

Derek nodded, smiling. "No, that's what's cool about them."

"That they're the bad guys," said Bill.

"Yeah," said Derek, as if that was self-evident.

Bill just stared at the rolling credits, puzzled. Then Alan put on the stone-faced demeanor of a college professor.

"There are two types of horror," he said. "I mean, there are a lot of subgenres—the slasher, the thriller, the alien invasion, body horror, creature feature, the monster within . . . it's an endless array."

Both Bill and Derek stared at Alan, wondering who the fuck just possessed Alan's body and began working him like a ventriloquist's dummy.

Alan continued. "But when you talk about the basics, the fundamentals of what makes horror *horror*, there are just two types. Scary horror, in which we feel terror through empathy, and catharsis, in which we watch people who really deserve it get their just desserts."

"The hell are you talking about?" asked Bill.

"Yeah," asked Derek. "The fuck did this all come from?"

"They write books about this stuff. I got curious, so I've bought some when I visited Austin last time."

"You read this in a book?" asked Bill.

"No. *Fangoria*," said Alan. Bill's stare became somehow blanker. "It's a magazine."

"You read this magazine?" asked Bill of Derek.

"I fall asleep like three pages into reading anything," joked Derek. "This is all new to me."

"Look," said Alan bluntly. "If you like someone, a character, you get scared for them. You get scared *with* them. What the Greeks called tragedy. When you don't like someone, like a character you fucking hate, like someone who reminds you of that dick from work or a jackass neighbor, you enjoy watching them die, getting their just desserts. What the Greeks would pair with comedy."

"What does any of this have to do with slasher killers?" asked Bill, becoming more confused by the minute.

"What all this means is that sometimes it's okay to like watching slasher killers kill the fuck out of some annoying prick in a wheelchair like Franklin, and at the same time be scared for Sally. These guys become not just the figures in our nightmares, but expressions of our frustration and rage at how unfair life is."

"Wait," said Bill, struck by a bolt of inspiration. "You're saying the slashers are us. And the guys chasing us."

"They can be, yeah," said Alan. "You know . . . metaphorically."

"*Fuuuuuck*," Bill said, sighing out the entire middle of the word.

"Shit, man," said Derek. "You got all that from a magazine?"

"Where the hell else am I gonna get it, doofus?" Alan smarted off.

"Fair enough."

Bill nodded. "Y'all mind if I just sit here for a spell?"

WRONG FUCKING PLACE, WRONG FUCKING TIME

"Mi casa, you casa," said Derek.

No one moved, and for ten minutes they all sat in silence, sipping their beers, Alan and Derek growing ever more nervous as each wordless minute ticked by. The tension grew so thick, it boiled over inside of Derek and words just burst out of his mouth. "So, what would you do differently?" he asked.

Bill and Alan looked up. Derek was looking right at Bill, so everyone knew who he meant.

"Do what differently?" he asked in return.

"You know. With all this Captain Trips nonsense. If you had things to do differently, what would you do?"

"Nothing," said Bill.

"Nothing at all?"

"Derek," said Alan pointedly.

"No, it's okay," said Bill. "I know what he's asking."

"Yeah, but it ain't any of our business," said Alan.

"The hell it ain't. Y'all invite me into your home, take me in as one of your own. Hell, I've spent more time with you two beautiful clowns than any other grown man I've known in my whole adult life. Least I can do is answer a real question like that. You mean Sophie and the girls. Knowing what I know now, what would I do to protect them?"

"Yeah," said Derek. "Yeah. That's about the size of it."

"Nothing I could do. You, me, Alan. The three of us are just immune or something. God's will, I guess. Whatever the fuck that is. I've never been the churchy type. But God, no God, that sickness was gonna take 'em one way or another. They was just born in the wrong fucking place at the wrong fucking time. But I reckon that was always gonna be the case."

"Does that make you mad?" asked Derek.

"Every goddamned day."

Derek nodded and the three sat in silence finishing their beers.

Before he left, Bill looked at the boys and cocked his head a little, like he was conflicted whether or not to even speak. Then the thought got the best of him, and he scratched his neck, squinting his eyes, trying to make his most intrusive thoughts sound casual. "Y'all . . ." he began, taking a long pause. "Y'all been having strange dreams or anything?"

Derek and Alan looked at each other nervously. They had, but neither had mentioned it to the other. "Yeah," they both said in unison.

"Like, I've been having this . . . weird dream. Night after night. A dark figure standing along the highway. Behind him, I see Las Vegas. He wants me to go with him. He says I don't have to be alone anymore. Y'all have something like that?"

Derek and Alan shook their heads. They hadn't.

"No," said Derek. "I've actually just been dreaming about this nice old lady." Alan looked at him, confused, as he'd had the same dream, but decided not to speak up. That sounded too weird to him.

"Yeah, yeah," said Bill. "It's the stress. Losing the girls and all. Just weird dreams." He stood up, nodded a polite goodbye, and went home.

The next morning, Derek and Alan went about their morning rounds, first hitting up their ranch chores, feeding the cattle, collecting eggs, and making sure all the water troughs were full and clean. Then they went about their afternoon rounds, seeing that all was quiet and well in town.

As they made their rounds, they gave a wave to Bill, who was cutting up a cord of wood at the front of his property with a chain saw in both hands. He revved the beast and raised it high before giving a small pirouette like Leatherface at the end of *Chain Saw*. The two laughed at the little joke and rode on, not giving it a second thought.

One might think it strange how comfortable the three seemed living in a town populated mostly by the dead, but in truth, they had done so for so long that it seemed mostly normal. Working on the ranch, the boys could go a few days seeing no one at all but each other, so they fell rapidly into a groove of normalcy, despite the whole world having gone silent so quickly. They were sure the power would go out any day now, so they'd long since had the generators on standby, and with the truck stop gassed up to the gills, they imagined there would be some semblance of governmental return to civility before they ever ran out of juice. But if there wasn't, they always had their batteries.

So, life was quaint, quiet, and uncomplicated.

Derek was the first to notice the shattered glass door of the Roosevelt Food Mart. They weren't large enough of a town to have a proper grocery store, so they relied upon a glorified general store generously named *Food Mart*. The boys had mostly left it alone at this point, relying upon their own sundries and what was a mostly self-sustaining ranch. But seeing the front door smashed in sent a chill down both of their spines as they worried that their backup plan might be a bust as a result of some highway thieves.

"Shit," Alan pointedly swore.

"What?" asked Derek.

"We left the shotguns at home."

"Folks are probably just hungry."

"Yeah, but I don't want to be too careful."

"We got a tire iron in the back of the truck."

Alan nodded. "I reckon that'll have to do."

He grabbed the iron from the bed of his old truck, and they crept carefully, quietly, toward the front door.

"Oh, thank God," came a soft, enthusiastic voice from inside. "Men!"

The boys stopped in their tracks. From the dark of the Food Mart emerged a shape. A shapely shape. The shapely shape of a rather attractive woman. It had been weeks now since the boys had seen a live woman, and significantly longer since they'd seen one this pretty. She had blond hair spilling down over her shoulders, bright blue eyes that looked like pools of water on a travel brochure you'd find in a motel lobby, and a sprinkle of freckles across the bridge of her nose. Around her neck hung a simple gold cross—no Jesus, just the cross. A good Protestant girl.

"What?" called another soft voice from the dark behind her. Another woman, slightly taller, but thinner, with dark brown hair cascading down her back, wearing a black Judas Priest T-shirt, slipped up behind the first, bag of groceries in her hands. "Oh!" she exclaimed, pleasantly surprised.

"Ladies," said Derek.

"Gentlemen," said the blonde.

"Y'all ain't from around here."

"Riiiight," said the brunette.

"Any reason y'all are busting up our Food Mart?"

"Oh shit," said the brunette. "You own this place?"

"Nah," said Alan. "We's just looking after it for the owner."

"Is he dead? You know, from the Trips?" asked the blonde.

"Presently," said Derek, drawing a contemptuous look from Alan. *Presently?* Alan mouthed silently.

"So, you aren't so much looking after it for him as claiming it," said the brunette.

"Mary!" exclaimed the blonde. "Be nice. This isn't our town."

"Okay, okay. I'm just saying," she said, not really apologizing.

"What're y'all doing around here?" asked Derek.

"Our car ran out of gas up on I-10," said the blonde.

"Yeah," said Mary. "Do you know how hard it is out there to find an open gas station?"

"How bad is it out there?" asked Alan.

"We've heard this is happening everywhere," said Derek.

"Oh, it is," said the blonde. "Everyone is dying out there. Almost nothing works anymore. And Mary's right. Finding gas stations with anyone working them is impossible."

"I'm Derek. This is Alan. Where are y'all headed?"

"Vegas," the two girls said together.

"No shit," said Alan. "Our buddy was just talking about Vegas last night."

"You thinking about going to Vegas?" asked the blonde.

"Is that an invitation?" asked Derek, cranking the charm to what he thought was a Roosevelt eleven, but was actually more of a dive bar three.

Alan punched him in the arm. "Knock it off. These ladies have bigger problems than dealing with you."

The blonde smiled. "Oh, I don't mind a little innocent flirting. Been a while since we met nice boys."

"Really?" asked Derek.

"It's a nightmare out there," said Mary. "I'm Mary. This is Sheila." The blonde waved in response. "Y'all wouldn't happen to know where to get some gas around here, would you?"

"Yeah," said Derek. "Truck stop."

"Tried that," said Mary coldly. "It's shut down."

"Yeah, but Alan used to work there when he was a teenager. He knows how to work the pump switches."

"Yeah," said Alan. "We could get you filled up and back on the road in no time."

Mary softened, eyes wide and flush with sudden affection. She smiled and put a hand on Alan's arm. "You'd do that for us?"

"Neighborly thing to do."

"Christian thing to do," said Derek, eyeing the cross dangling above her bosom.

"So, you're not going to need that iron there, then, are you?" She looked down at the tire iron Alan was absentmindedly holding in his left hand.

"Oh, oh! I'm so sorry," he said, apologizing. "We just didn't know who you were."

"It's cool," said Mary. "But, you know, being two girls alone on the road, a tire iron sends a particular message."

Alan hid the tire iron behind his back for a moment sheepishly, then turned and walked back to the truck to throw it in the truck bed.

"Y'all want a lift?" asked Derek.

"Nah," said Mary. "We've got one."

That's when the two figures emerged from the dark behind them. Large men. Crew cuts and muscle shirts.

A chain rapped against Alan's skull, splitting his forehead open. A lead pipe cracked against Derek's knee. They both dropped to the ground, splayed out screaming in the parking lot.

The beating was slow and laborious, both of the crew cuts taking their time, savoring every punch, every kick, as Sheila and Mary cheered them on. "Get 'em!" yelled Mary, clenching her fist and spitting as she yelled. "Rack that fucker!"

"You want this?" asked Sheila, motioning to her body as one of the crew cuts took a breather from whaling on Derek. Derek looked up, shaking his head, left eye already beginning to swell shut. "Yeah, you do, you liar. You wanted this real bad. Too bad you hicks are just some dumbshits too stupid to know your shit from Shinola."

"Yeah," said one of the crew cuts, kneeling down next to Derek. "They wasn't lying about breaking down. But a couple of hicks like you probably had no reason to help out some girls without a little trade."

"And we weren't about to let that happen," said Mary. "No hard feelings."

"Do we have to kill them?" asked Sheila.

The crew cut beating on Derek looked up, stopping for a moment, cocking his head in confusion. "Why wouldn't we?"

"Yeah," said the other crew cut. "Do you know what these guys wanted to do to you? Well, whatever it is you think it is, it's probably way worse than that."

"Yeah," said the first. "When they were done with you, you'd likely end up in their freezer, cut into pieces like a deer. You know how these *good old boys* are."

"We're not like that," begged Derek. "We ain't like that at all."

Derek's crew cut kicked him across the face, opening a wide gash. "Shut up, you lying shitkicker."

"Guys?" a voice offered meekly from around the side of the store. "Guys."

WRONG FUCKING PLACE, WRONG FUCKING TIME

The four interlopers looked up as a large, burly, tattooed biker stumbled from behind the store. He looked down at his gut, where there was a massive gash, exposing his innards, a fistful of entrails dangling from his hand. "They have a friend."

At that, the loud chugging scream of a chain saw cut through the quiet afternoon air.

The chain saw swung out from behind the building, cutting the biker in two at the waist. His torso toppled backward, spilling organs out as it did, while his legs crumpled forward to the ground.

Bill emerged, roaring chain saw in hand, machete and hand ax dangling from his tool belt, a sickening smile on his face. "Bet you thought you were pretty smart, having a lookout and all."

"Smarter than you, hillbilly!" yelled one of the crew cuts, reaching for a .38 Special tucked into his waist. He raised it at Bill, ready to plug him for having killed his friend, only to find he'd been a hair too slow.

The chain saw severed his forearm at the elbow, dropping it to the ground, gun still gripped tightly in hand, as a spray of blood began spurting out like a sprinkler at the speed of his racing heart. For a moment, everyone stared in shock as the crew cut gawked at his dismembered arm. "What the FUCK?!" he shouted as Sheila shrieked behind him.

Those were his last words. The chain saw swung down from overhead, slicing six inches into his chest, bisecting his sternum. He careened backward into Mary, who raised her hands, pushing his limp body from toppling onto her, while stepping back screaming.

The chain saw went into her next, slicing straight through her stomach and out her back, the teeth of it chewing her flesh as it rested in place, spitting a rain of blood that painted a Jackson Pollock across the cinder-block wall of the Food Mart behind her.

"Wrong fucking place, wrong fucking time," said Bill, before pulling the chain saw from out of Mary and letting her slump to the ground next to her boyfriend.

The remaining crew cut grabbed Sheila by the arm and pulled her back through the shattered front door of the store, both in shock and neither of them thinking straight. Together, they disappeared again into the dark of the mart, only realizing seconds later that there was likely no way out.

Bill cut the engine to the chain saw and called into the store. "You know that part in horror movies when you're sitting there and the dumb jock and his bitchy girlfriend run towards a house or a cabin and you yell, 'Don't go in there! There's no way out!' 'Cause I was friends with the guy that owned this place and a lot of kids driving through used to steal beer and run out the back, where their friends were waiting to drive off. So, he added a double lock on that back door, and it requires two keys to open from the inside."

"Do you always talk so fucking much, you fucking fuck?!" called the crew cut from inside.

Derek stood, then helped Alan to his feet. They were beat to shit, blood running down both their faces, but they had a renewed look of determination. "No," Derek called into the store. "In fact, I reckon that might be the most number of sentences I've ever heard him string together at once."

Bill smiled, pulling the machete from his belt, and handing it to Derek.

"I don't want to hurt anyone," said Derek, refusing the offering.

"Derek," Bill said plainly. "Right now, son, we don't have much of a choice."

"I don't want to be the killer."

"You *ain't* the killer," said Bill. "We're the final girls. Or guys. Or, you know. And this is our . . . " He let the sentence hang in the air for a moment, searching for the right word.

"Catharsis?" asked Alan.

"*Catharsis*," said Bill. "Yeah. This is our catharsis."

Derek took the machete from Bill's hand, nodding. Then Bill handed Alan the ax. Alan waved it away, instead reaching down and

WRONG FUCKING PLACE, WRONG FUCKING TIME

prying the .38 Special from the dismembered crew cut's cold, dead hand. He looked at the gun in his hand, tucked it into his belt, then walked back to the truck to retrieve his tire iron.

"A tire iron?" asked Bill.

"It sends a particular kind of message," said Derek, picking up what Alan was putting down.

"Let's go make a mess in aisle nine," said Bill with a smile, revving his chain saw and waltzing through the door.

Alan and Derek exchanged looks. "Who the fuck is he all of a sudden?"

"Our last friend on earth," said Derek, following Bill inside.

Alan shrugged and followed his friends into the dark store.

An hour later, the three sat on the stoop of the Food Mart, each covered head to toe in blood, some of it even their own, sipping cold beers they'd snagged from the cooler.

"I don't ever want to do anything like that again," said Derek.

"I thought you guys liked that shit," said Bill before taking a big swig from his Stroh's.

"Only when it isn't real," said Derek.

"Yeah," agreed Alan. "I've seen enough real death for one lifetime."

"Ain't nothin' in lifetime but death," said Bill. "Wives. Daughters. Dogs. Everything. Sometimes, just sometimes . . . the bad guys get it, too."

Alan and Derek sipped their beers in troubled silence.

After a few more moments, Alan spoke up. "You know, they said they were going to Vegas. Said something about dreams."

"Yeah," muttered Bill. "Fuck that guy. Fuck those dreams. And fuck Vegas."

"You don't want to go?"

"Why? My home is here. In Roosevelt. Only place I got kin left."

Bill looked at the boys with affection. They knew who he meant. "I was thinking," he said.

"Yeah?" asked Derek.

"Maybe *I* pick the movies tonight."

"What'd you have in mind?" asked Alan.

"Y'all ever seen *The Road Warrior*?"

"Yeah," the boys said in unison.

"Well, things being as they are, I thought we might get some good ideas from it. You know, like a documentary or something."

"You ever see the first one?" asked Derek.

"There's a first one?" asked Bill.

"Oh, tonight's gonna be *fun*."

PREY INSTINCT

Hailey Piper

The killing comes easier when you see what people really are. What threats they can become.

Since Helena. After her, the rest haven't mattered, rare as they are. Humans and bullets have that in common. Rare and deadly.

But only humans can pretend they're harmless, like the gaunt-faced woman dropping to the sand in her loose jeans and once-white tank top. It's a steady, unpanicked shot through her heart. She should be dead instantly, at least from the outside. What abyss she's experiencing within is anyone's guess.

"Should've stayed away," Silvia whispers, the wind brushing auburn locks into her scrutinizing eyes. "I warned you."

Crimson stains the sand, but Silvia's pale hands look clear of blood. The woman never touched her. Not the deadly captain, only another of his crew. If she'd left with everyone else, she could've found a softer way to die.

Silvia should've left, too, rather than hiding in that forgotten beach house these past two weeks. On the third night, she watched camo-clad soldiers dump bodies off the northern rocks, into the outgoing tide. One or two might have sounded like a flat palm smacking the waves. A spill of hundreds sounded like violent rain.

Gone now. The beach has been quiet, at least until this dead woman's appearance, and her carelessness is just the beginning of Silvia's troubles today. She watches another one mounting offshore, the kind she can't gun down.

There's no more weather service to predict storms, no definitive channel to explain if that sharp wind is a summer squall or a monstrous hurricane.

But Silvia knows a predator when she sees one. The dimming sky gives a tiger's throaty roar, and from the sooty horizon climbs a black and bulging tower of cloud, with lightning forking ivy-like up its outer walls.

A new vessel for Captain Trips. Eager to learn how Silvia tastes.

None of it seemed real when Helena was alive. Silvia was already struggling to keep her goony act booked for children's birthday parties—too many kids shrank in terror at clowns lately, her magic act was rusty, and she was aging out of playing a careful-of-copyright Barbie knockoff. When work dribbled away entirely, she'd taken it as a sign to seek a new career.

Not a sign of the world's end. The reports and subsequent denial on TV at first seemed less intense than hers and Helena's time with the hospice boys, keeping them entertained and accompanied, wondering if the *I* in AIDS should stand for *Inevitable*. Even if sometimes inevitability wasn't the case.

"Lost in another puzzle?" Helena asked, striding inside the house. She could tell the difference between Silvia watching TV and Silvia daydreaming at the screen.

Her stare turned to Helena, soaking in her tall figure and tan face and endless sprawl of golden curls as if she stood on an entirely different planet from the news.

"Thinking about names," Silvia said. "For diseases. Like AIDS. And Captain Trips."

"Oh?" Helena dropped her keys in the door-side bowl.

Silvia tucked her throat muscles down and deepened her voice into a Sam the Eagle impression. "A good name. An *American* name."

Helena turned, and the TV's reflection flickered in her pretty earthen eyes. "We're going to want jugs for water. And canned food. Nonperishables."

"It's that serious?" Silvia asked.

"Bush-league president says what he says, I say what I say." Helena spoke with such confidence, you could believe she knew the future. You could even believe she knew how to survive it. Silvia had understood since they met in the hospice halls, two hopeful angels lost in grim space, that Helena was the smarter one, the leader. Lucky Silvia to orbit that star—the doctor and the fool.

Helena made sense. Besides, it seemed almost silly to believe that tiny DNA fragments could crush the power of human civilization. Sensible under a microscope, even in a movie, but hard to believe when looking out the window and seeing no such doom in the air. As invisible as a deity, and almost as deniable.

At least until the coughing began. Until the virus cored Silvia's world.

Partway up the narrow, tree-guarded road, Silvia accepts that she can't outrun the storm. She clutches a lavender umbrella overhead, rain or shine, since no one's manufacturing more sunblock anytime soon, and both sun and storm are predators. Or it's all Captain Trips, sticking out vicious tongues from different mouths.

His storm-tongue licks at Silvia's heels. She's been walking for hours, and the patchy paved road has curled too far from the beach houses to turn back, zigzagging between coastal brush and a thicket of birch trees. This has always been a remote route, tucked away from the nearby town. Vacationers used to pretend the coast hid them from the world, and maybe it did once.

But that didn't save them.

Thunder groans as if the sky has only known aching. Silvia jogs, but the pack clinging to her shoulders hangs heavy with water jugs. A rolled-up sleeping bag mounts its top, while the insides hold bagged jerky, broken Pop-Tarts, bandages, the vacancy of spare ammunition, toothpaste, a toothbrush, tampons, and changes of clothing.

She swapped outfits right after gunning down the gaunt woman. Off with the jeans and T-shirt, on with a white blouse and blue checkerboard dress. That woman's soul can tell Captain Trips a jeans-wearing stranger killed her.

Meanwhile, Silvia has become Dorothy of Oz.

Not the most practical outfit for basic survival, but at least she'll fool Death himself for a time. A couple more costumes await in case she meets more of his crew.

When did she stop calling the virus an *it* and start calling the virus *he*? Probably after Helena. Around when the dreams began.

Lost in another puzzle?

Silvia shakes herself to full attention as another rumble jostles the sky. She can't afford to daydream, let alone catnap. The trees stand thinner ahead—

And then bleary darkness closes around her. The air turns soupy as if she's stepped inside a tremendous mouth and the road is one long tongue.

Someone haunts the throat behind her. She shouldn't look back at the sound of clacking footsteps, hates herself for it, but can't help glancing over one shoulder where smoke ripples beneath a burnt sky, vibrant as a tiger's pelt.

And against it strides *his* silhouette. He isn't subtle in dreams. No gaunt woman, no virus. Only a figure crystallizing into the world, calling again to her as if, through his touch, she can go home.

She bolts along the road-tongue, toward what she hopes are the gray teeth of—

Daylight. Or what passes for it as the coastal storm creeps onto land. Silvia has run all the way to waking up.

"Stop," she whispers, wishing she could suck tears back into her eyes. She can't keep letting the dreams catch up, especially not during the day.

But she also doesn't know how to stop them. Only to keep moving.

The road splits into a Y-shaped fork, one prong aiming at civilization, the other at the interstate.

Since two weeks ago, when Silvia last saw town, it has transformed into a hell of barbed-wire checkpoints, traffic-jammed roads, untended storefronts, and a violent stench that makes her lips peel back from her teeth in revulsion.

There aren't any National Guardsmen prowling the checkpoint. A closer look tells Silvia they took their guns and ammo with them.

But not before punching bullet holes across the hoods and windshields of the nearest vehicles lying dormant at the checkpoint. The cars and trucks coating Main Street must be full of families, all believing they could be the lucky escapees. Like there's anywhere safe to go. Some of them might have ducked into the woods on foot, but most would've wanted their vehicles for distance.

And they died in those vehicles. A black blanket drapes the chrome-clogged asphalt with TV static. Main Street has become a world for flies.

Eventually the sun will chew through car paint, and the flies and their maggoty children will chew through the bodies, and they will hunt more corpses for growing and feeding and fucking. Small birds will have their fill, and things that eat them will have theirs, too.

Silvia turns with her stomach; all she can do to keep from vomiting over her blue Dorothy dress. The storm clears its throat, urging her onward, but not this way. Its wind thrusts against her umbrella, bending its spokes until two of them snap. She tosses it to the roadside. Should've closed it before the storm broke it.

And she'd better find shelter before the storm breaks her as well.

On the path aiming for the interstate, the trees open their green-and-white fortress at a gravelly dip leading into a gas station. A small wooden sign reads FILL UP BEFORE YOU HEAD OUT! in sunshiny lettering. Black hoses dangle alongside four red-and-steel pumps, and behind them sits the flat-roofed station. Its broad windows face the road, but solid concrete protects its other three sides.

Silvia glances at the angry sky and then back to the station. "Okay then."

Nearby tree limbs stroke one another, first with a lover's gentleness, and then a lover's ferocity. One last glance down Main Street shows a windy ripple in the insect blanket like fingertips brushing a coat of black hair.

The captain is near.

Silvia jogs along the tree line toward the gas station. Her ears catch a thin wooden *crack-crack* from the woods, and then another, almost footsteps through the underbrush. This storm might be chewing the trees. Or there might be someone here.

She reaches the gas station pumps, where dark blue graffiti asks, *Who's afraid of the big bad bug?* and beneath that, *ME!* Unoccupied vehicles linger nearby. Doesn't look like anyone's inside the station, either, and the shelves have been ransacked. It should be safe so long as the storm is a one-night event.

Silvia takes another step as that *crack-crack* sound clatters among the trees. A chill runs through her—definitely footsteps.

She turns to the waving white limbs as a stocky man charges loose from the thicket. He's in his fifties, wearing a blue button-down shirt, a farmer's tan, and thin blond strands where he once grew a thicker head of hair. Wild eyes blaze above a gaping jaw.

His desperate face curls in confusion when he spots Silvia.

And her pistol, drawn from her blouse, aiming his way. "Stay back!"

The man skids to slowing, but he doesn't stop. Trees jitter behind him like an audience caught in silent laughter.

"Get away!" Silvia tries again, begging him not to carry the captain any closer. Not when she only has four shots left.

"Make way," the man says, picking up speed. "Somebody let her out—"

The pistol screams for the second time today, but Silvia's aim isn't as certain as before. Her shot dives into the man's left shoulder, jerking him to one side. He stumbles undeterred, toward the gun, toward her.

She fires again, screaming with the shot. It bores a hole through the man's breast pocket, and he falls in a twisted heap of bandy limbs.

"You bastard." Silvia backsteps between the pumps. "Made me waste it."

A dark flower blooms over the man's chest. His fearful gaze aims frozen at the sky, and Silvia glances into the dimming emptiness, sensing predatory eyes upon her. It has watched her enough today. She needs to get inside.

And she needs to change. Both Dorothy and ordinary Silvia have already blown their cover before nightfall.

Helena's decline started like a cold. That was fine—Helena had been sick with colds before, and Silvia knew how to handle her. Tea, soup, Tylenol, entertainment.

"You don't have to do that," Helena said.

Silvia was in the middle of a card trick, dressed in her top hat, white button-down, and long black coat. A two of hearts lay face up on the stool beside the couch where Helena lay, her curly hair bunched into a bob, a loose robe draping her body.

"I need practice," Silvia said. She had another two of hearts hidden somewhere up her sleeve. "You're helping me keep fresh for when everything goes back to normal."

"How thoughtful of me," Helena said, and then coughed into a fistful of tissues.

But unlike a cold, this sickness didn't ease up after a couple of days. It was a mole of a virus, digging deeper into Helena's lungs each night and filling them with cobwebs of mucus and madness.

Silvia kept up the entertainment bit. She even looted a new costume, tucked in the back of a department store with a bunch of goodies from Halloween '89, and tended to Helena in a white skirt and red-crossed nurse's cap. Part of her hoped for a laugh, even a smile.

And maybe part of her needed that smile. It would be a sign that, unlike those people on TV, Helena could recover, and then Silvia could quit thinking of Captain Trips as another disease with an *I* standing for *Inevitable*.

Inside the gas station, in her new costume, Silvia spreads her sleeping bag behind the counter with its empty cigarette pack display and pointless cash register. The shelves are foodless, the refrigerators without drink. Beach blankets, plastic souvenirs, postcards—these remain.

Rainfall patters lightly on the roof and dots the gloomy windows. True darkness will eventually swallow this place, but so long as the windows don't shatter, Silvia imagines she'll be safe.

Until the door swings open.

Maybe it's the wind? Or some harmless animal has learned to open outward-swinging doors? Silvia rummages for her gun and aims over the checkout counter.

The glass-paneled door clacks shut behind the silhouette of a sopping-wet stranger. By the thinning light, she wears a forest-green tank top and camo pants. Sunburn tinges her skin, and toned muscle coats her arms. A Red Sox ball cap shadows her face.

She stands there dripping a moment, and then her head cocks

sideways as she notices Silvia. "Why are you a clown?" the stranger asks.

Silvia now wears striped baggy pants and a dark shirt with oversized orange buttons. A plastic canary-yellow flower juts over her heart. Kids at birthday parties used to ask a version of that *why* question, and she'd say, *Because life's a circus*, or *Maybe clowns dress like me*, or for mean kids, *Thought there should be two of us here.*

Along with the costume, the stranger must notice the gun. She ducks behind the shelves with her green duffel bag.

"Get lost," Silvia says, gritting her teeth. "I was here first."

"Have a heart, huh?" The stranger's voice is a fine blade laid on velvet. "Can't send me into *that*. Look, it's just until the worst settles. Me over here, you over there. You'd have to come closer to shoot me anyway. How thirsty is that little popgun, my clown?"

Silvia's quiet is almost acknowledgment that she's near empty. Two bullets left, a don't-shoot-until-you-see-the-whites-of-their-eyes situation.

She slinks behind the counter, steadying her breath while lightning stripes the sky. There's nothing she can do but wait out this storm as it wraps its thundering mouth around the gas station.

Around Silvia and the stranger.

"They're all going to die," Helena whispered one day.

They had moved her from the couch to the bed, where she spent most of her time coughing or shivering no matter the blankets. But sometimes, at her most feverish moments, she rambled out the worst things Silvia had ever heard.

"He looks for us," Helena went on. "Wants us. I've seen him. He walks the hospitals, and he opens the doors, and he watches the patients sleep, waiting for his chance to taste them. And sometimes he opens my office door. Especially at night. He opens it, and he stares at me, those cold eyes. Waiting to taste me, too."

"Who?" Silvia asked.

Helena coughed again, the force of it raking blood from her throat. "He's watching me now. Right by the door."

It took every ounce of Silvia's control not to glance at the bedroom's open doorway. Not to give credit to Helena's delirium. Not to see a figure standing there.

She wondered if this was a panicky phase of the virus. Or did Captain Trips command a ship of premonition, with Helena's soul keeping one foot on the pier and another on the gangplank? Except that assumed she had a choice between life and death.

Her fingers tore at the sheets. "He's hunting," she rasped. "Does he have territory? A psychic frontier at death? Or is it a trick? I've seen it in my patients, like they're going to pull through, and then he pulls them away."

Silvia couldn't make sense of this. She licked her lips and adjusted her nurse's cap, and then she tried for distraction with a hissing impish voice.

"Oh, what's that vision of the future over there, everybody's okay—nope, fooled you, time to die!"

Helena's eyes caught Silvia's, and then she wheezed through a cracked smile.

It was enough.

The rain's drizzly pitter-patter swells to crashing drums as light shrinks from the gas station, the storm blotting out the sky. A woman could sneak across a linoleum floor under this racket.

Silvia glances around the counter's corner, but she only sees three aisles of shelving clearly. The far wall beyond is a vague black curtain, hiding the stranger.

She speaks again, maybe summoned by Silvia's gaze. "I wonder about those gas pumps."

She pauses like she's pointing at something and expects Silvia's gaze to follow. Can she see Silvia looking across the floor? Silvia ducks behind the counter again, just in case.

"How long until the gas seeps out?" the stranger asks. "It's funny how we've made parts of our world depend on us. Farmland. Oil rigs. Zoos. Without our attention, it all goes to shit. Maybe our species has killed itself, but we're not going down alone, that's for damn sure."

Silvia keeps her mouth shut. The stranger can't hold a one-sided conversation.

But she tries. "Know what really annoys me? I got a little cut on the webbing between my left hand's middle and pointer fingers. Hard to bandage. And the world's end makes it near impossible for anyone to invent an easy solution someday."

"We don't have to talk," Silvia says.

The stranger chuckles. "What are you so afraid of? You've already outlived the worst."

Silvia quakes, half-angry, half-bewildered. The stranger can't understand the truth, has never met Helena. Never watched her slip away.

The rain bangs little fists on the roof and windows, and the sky flashes and growls, a wild animal desperate to get in.

Somebody let her out.

That was the last thing the man outside said before Silvia gunned him down. And what came next? The stranger's arrival.

Silvia licks her lips. "Ever been in prison?"

The stranger gives another chuckle. "Is it that obvious?"

Silvia bites her tongue to stop from licking her lips again. She imagines there must be ChapStick on the outer portion of the counter, but no way will she reach for it. That man outside, his wild eyes—he'd been terrified enough to run at a gun.

Somebody let her out.

"They never liked freedom," the stranger goes on. "Real freedom. This country was a mean joke, made up by the true clowns. But me? I'm an Angel of Liberty. I believe in freedom."

"They locked you up for that?" Silvia asks. "Nothing worse?"

"Less the belief, more the action." The Angel of Liberty turns reverent. "You can do plenty of nasty business sticking to your guns. But what the hell's a belief in God-given freedom without action? That's why I'm headed away from here. Out west. What's out there won't be a joke. It'll be real."

Angel breaks into laughter. It's a full, hearty outburst, the first laugh Silvia's heard in a long time, and she hates that she kind of likes it.

"Been a while since you chatted with anyone, huh?" Angel asks. "Always chasing them off, I bet. So, clown—do you believe in God?"

Silvia lets her eyes close and soaks in the presence she knows to be there, but not by the name Angel has given. The truth behind it, having given up the notion of a loving Almighty. Silvia used to instead imagine a vengeful thumb squishing friends, family, that boy who mopped the deli floor, the bodies plummeting into the Atlantic Ocean. Helena. All of them seemingly pilfered by some great crook in the sky.

Nowadays she's given up the notion of God altogether and accepted the captain. His ships are legion, crawling across the planet Earth like enormous prodding spiders, devouring love and connection while society writhes dying in his web. Captain Trips has more vessels than God could have saints. He is everything, everywhere. That roaring storm. That hungry virus.

Sun, time, death—the universe forms in carnivores.

Shadows deepen throughout the gas station. When Silvia glances from behind the counter again, only the nearest two aisles of shelving stand out from the black depths. No sign of Angel.

Except her voice in Silvia's ears.

"Who'd you lose?" Angel asks, another likely carnivore. "I mean, everyone lost people, but who was your big one? Mine was my mother. Agony, but also a blessing. When the bug stole her mind, it also stole her out of time. She thought she was at my confirmation, then my wedding. Time eats us, but she snatched crumbs from its teeth, like those birds that clean gator mouths. My mother, a time traveler. Only the bug can do that."

Silvia's reply comes haltingly. "He's a. Deadly captain. Not a blessing. There was somebody I loved. Who I took care of. Who died for me. Let me cheat death, for a little while."

She's choosy about her words without meaning to be. It's been second nature for her to hide that Helena was another woman. Old habits die harder than the human race, and Silvia's language hasn't caught up yet with a decimated world too sparsely populated to give a damn.

Cloth slides against the floor somewhere beyond the counter. Angel might only be shifting in place, getting comfortable, but Silvia has to check.

There's little to see. Darkness has eaten most of the gas station, now leaving only one aisle of shelving visible. Something shuffles again, as if Angel has shed her tank top and camo pants to dress herself in relentless night, an approaching fiend pretending to be nothing but the absence of light.

"The sickness is a liberator, like me," Angel says. Is her voice louder? Closer? "Freeing the dead of this world. Freeing the living of doubt."

Lightning forks beyond the glass-paneled door, illuminating the shelves and casting their shadows across the floor in stretches of black teeth. An uncertain form moves between them, almost a pacing animal.

And then it disappears along with the lightning.

"You got it wrong," Silvia snaps. "He's hunting me."

"Who is?" Angel asks. "Somebody from your past? I swear, this bug has the sickest sense of humor in who to spare."

"Him." Silvia takes a harsh breath. "Captain Trips."

"That's just a name." Angel pauses, then scoffs. "Is that the problem? You think I'll get you sick? Do I look like the superflu?"

No, she looks like an engulfing shadow. Silvia watches the darkness seep nearer, black silk coating a tile floor.

"A captain has his crew," Silvia says. "I've seen him coming. Out here, and in my dreams."

"In your dreams?" Angel laughs again, sharper now, and Silvia likes the sound less this time. "Honey, that's not Captain Trips. That's just—well, he's the Man. And he's not *just* anything. Those dreams are a beacon."

Silvia could scream in aggravation. She knows what she's seen and felt. Captain Trips, taking human form. Taking any form.

"Guess that's why you're skittish," Angel says, gentler now. "Let me put your mind at ease. Anyone still alive right now is immune to the bug, dear clown. Captain Trips is yesterday's news. The Man? In your dreams? He's tomorrow."

"Maybe for you, and everybody else left, but not me," Silvia says. "I know better. Like how a gazelle knows something isn't right that day on the savanna, before the cats close in. Prey instinct."

She wonders if gazelles are among the captain's victims, or if they still roam African grasslands, hunted by cheetahs. Were they spared, too? He's likely given the carnivores a pardon, respect passing from predator to predator. Lions and tigers and bears, oh—

—*Captain, my Captain, our fearful trip is done.*

Silvia jolts at the memory of Helena's voice. She's been puzzling again, not paying attention to whatever Angel's in the middle of saying.

"—underestimating the power of the human mind. But you can't see the forest for the trees."

Silvia can't even see her hand in front of her face, let alone the trees outside. Certainly not Angel if she's moving in the dark. A black hole has swallowed their world.

Silvia slides against her sleeping bag like it can hide her from this waking nightmare. "I don't have to see death to know it's real. And I didn't imagine Captain Trips."

Garbage and branches swat the windows as the storm chews on

the gas station, drowning out whatever Angel says next. Shadows haunt the lightning. The debris hopefully won't smash through the windows or blow up the pumps and set fire to the place in the night.

Lost in another puzzle?

Silvia starts again. Drifting into her head used to make enduring children's birthday parties easier, but it's less helpful for surviving the night, let alone the apocalypse. Reminiscing about Helena might be disastrous.

Is that what Captain Trips really wants? Not enough for him to drag Helena into a vicious, shaking, drowning death, but he has to use her to catch Silvia, too.

Even the part locked in Silvia's head.

"I know real Death," Helena said, and the way she wheezed that last word gave it the authority of a person's name. "What everyone's forgotten. Way back, Death was just another animal. Everyone lived forever unless Death caught you. And they'd chant and light fires and bang drums to scare away that beast. But then Death got smart. He started scavenging from the old, and then he learned how to make everyone sick. We developed medicines and vaccines, but it's been a mortality arms race. Eventually, we had to lose."

Silvia sat on the bed's edge, holding Helena's hand, wiping mucus from around her lips. She couldn't remember the last time she'd eaten. She'd only kept bringing tea and soup to Helena, who could barely manage a spoonful before coughing her lungs out.

She laid her head back with a rough swallow. "'O Captain, my Captain, our fearful trip is done.' Walt Whitman."

"Is that where it comes from?" Silvia asked. "Captain Trips?"

"Walt Whitman didn't kill the world," Helena said, patronizing, as if speaking to a kindergartner. "Oh, the name? I don't know. I never really knew anything. But it felt good to pretend I did." Her voice cracked then. "And I'm never going to learn anything else. I'll never see them find a cure for AIDS. Or cancer. I'll never learn German. I'm never going to find out who fucking killed Laura Palmer."

Silvia forced a tearful smile. She didn't know what else to do.

Helena's fingers tensed, but they couldn't squeeze anymore. "And I won't find out how you're going to look when you get old."

Her words turned to mumbling, then fragmented syllables against coughing, and then she dropped into a ragged sleep. Silvia stayed holding her hand another moment, in case she woke up. Sometimes she came and went in fits and starts.

But Helena slept, and Silvia let go, easing off the bed to keep it from creaking. Would Helena remember this conversation when she woke up? Or would her mind drift to another time, another world? Silvia couldn't know, but she wanted to do one last thing for Helena.

For that smile.

She headed into the bathroom and plucked up her costume makeup. Cakey foundation paled her skin. Some blue for veins, gray to deepen the bags beneath her eyes. A finger dabbed at contouring powder and drew thick lines along her forehead, cheeks, jaw, and neck. She then patted the makeup into a mimicry of crevices and canyons for wrinkles, and she puffed powder across her hair, tracing gray strands through her auburn locks.

This was too much effort for an ordinary gag, but to get one last smile? She would be the world's finest clown. Even its final clown.

"Helena?" Silvia called in a cartoonish old lady voice. "You whippersnapper, lollygagging in bed all day. Young lady, you'd better pop those peepers and look at me, or I'll give you the business, you'll see!"

She paced the bed using the lavender umbrella for a cane, back and forth, spitting out any elderly-isms she could summon from the weekends she used to spend with her grandparents. Anything so that Helena would wake up in the middle of this little show.

It took six minutes of playing the clown before Silvia leaned over the bed and noticed the stillness in Helena's chest. The smell sliding off of her, beneath the odor of sickness.

And Silvia realized there would be no smile ever again. Death had finished his hunt.

She only realizes she's dreaming when memories of Helena fade into a grim silhouette. That figure, the one Angel calls the Man, reaches for her.

Captain Trips is hungry again. If only he would devour Silvia's recollection of Helena, then everything could become that much sadder, yet that much easier. Silvia would never know her life used to be better than this.

Something shifts beside her, fully waking her from the miserable dream. She opens her eyes.

The pitch-black world has her in its jaws, a sudden tightness squeezing her sleeping bag around her as if she's caught in the coils of a powerful snake.

"Oh, no you don't."

Angel's voice, guttural now. Her constriction traps Silvia's limbs against her sides. She bucks and kicks, but Angel's weight thrusts down on her lap, pinning her to the floor.

"Easy, girl," Angel says, and her tone is a blade on velvet again. "You might want my life, but I'm not after yours. Just need a little help crossing the country." Zipper teeth unlatch—Silvia's pack. "Go back to your dreams, my nameless clown."

"Get away from that!" Silvia snaps. She squirms against what must be a thin rope beneath Angel's powerful body.

"That cut between my fingers?" Angel says. "There's no one left to invent a solution for problems like that on the East Coast. But out west? Where people gather? Maybe there's a way. A future for mankind."

Sloshing sounds—Angel's hands feel over Silvia's belongings before finding one of the water jugs and setting it on the floor. She must not have slept, letting her eyes adjust to the dark while Silvia's can hardly see at all. Silvia rummages in her sleeping bag, along her striped pants.

Angel rolls over, a nothing shape in the dark, and something wet and flat strokes Silvia's cheek. "See? No harm done. That old bug's finished hunting. But you're one of those yesterday types, only seeing the past."

Silvia's fingertips touch metal—there.

"Poor scared thing," Angel says. "I'd take you west if you'd come. You'd under—"

A gunshot thrusts up from the sleeping bag, briefly lighting Angel's middle. She curls inward and hits the floor hard with a hiss of frantic breath.

Silvia kicks until the roped sleeping bag loosens from her body. She abandons it, grabbing her pack and dashing around the counter. Her gun-wielding hand bangs the corner, and she's lucky it doesn't waste her last shot before she feels her way toward the door.

"You'll kill yourself!" Angel snaps through clenched teeth. "You got me, but you got you, too. She's out there."

Silvia doesn't know what that means. Angel groans with earth-deep hurting, reminding Silvia of a lowing steer. And of Helena.

She could use her remaining bullet on a mercy killing, but Angel's next groan pushes her out the door, into the torrent of wind and rain. She can't stand that agonized sound, can't stand being inside the gas station, and she needs to change clothes. New encounter, new outfit. Let Angel's soul tell Captain Trips to hunt a clown.

Silvia will be a magician.

The gas station door clacks shut behind her at the next lightning flicker, brightening the world except where black stripes haunt the road's edge.

Silvia stiffens. Her eyes fix on that gravelly dip, but there's only darkness beneath a quaking roar. Is that the storm rumbling, or something else?

No, what else could there be? Silvia must've imagined whatever she thinks she almost saw. But she holds still anyway, waiting as the storm drenches her and the wind bats dampening hair across her nose and lips.

The next lightning flash catches bright yellow eyes, rushing toward her.

She sees them clearly in this blinking light, through the un-dream of Angel's beacon and the heartache of Helena, remembering the man Silvia gunned down near the trees.

Somebody let her out.

But he didn't mean Angel as *her*. He meant Angel as *somebody*. And who was Angel?

I'm an Angel of Liberty. I believe in freedom.

Parts of our world depend on us. Farmland. Oil rigs.

Zoos.

Large feline eyes loom in fascination. They know secrets, have faced down death, the universe, predator acknowledging predator.

Somebody let her out.

Silvia lets her pack slide away as she reaches one hand for the door. With her other hand, she aims the pistol into the thunderous darkness.

Several hundred pounds of apex predator slam her against the gas station door with all the gentleness of a truck as her gun goes off, its blast meek against the feral roar. Glass paneling cracks, and bones crack with it, and Silvia smacks the wet asphalt on her right side.

The world turns briefly quiet beneath the pounding rain. Everything hurts, from Silvia's back to her empty hands. Where's the gun? She's lost it, and it's useless anyway after that last shot.

Maybe she got lucky and wounded the tiger. Even killed her. If only another tongue of lightning would lick the night and reveal the gas station's lot again, filled by a striped corpse.

No lightning comes. Silvia glances to the dark sky and imagines stepping from this world, past the storm clouds, onto the blue-black carpet of a clear, starlit night. Maybe in her dreams. It would be easier than climbing to her feet.

A weight worse than guilt and time crushes her chest, squeezing out her breath. It should be the paw of an animal, coming to claim her kill.

But in the stirring darkness, beneath wafting hot breath, it might be the grasp of the deadly captain. This creature can't comprehend she's only his vessel, as smart or clueless as any human.

Or maybe the killing comes easier when you see what people really are. What treats they can become.

When you're eager to learn how Silvia tastes.

GRACE
Tim Lebbon

She smells rotting corn and hears a breeze shushing through dead crops, and somewhere far away an old woman plucks the strings of a guitar and sings an unknown song. The guitar is out of tune, and the song itches and stings like insects inside her skull. But Gemma knows this is only a dream.

Reality is closer and darker, and it knows her name.

Gemma, you disgrace me! Her father's words, though he is over a decade dead, and these are spoken in mocking tones by another. *The old fool was wrong, Gemma. You're no disgrace. It was only fucking, after all, where's the disgrace in that? And now you can make yourself free.*

The voice is deep with a hint of terrible humor.

The man's fingers scratch at the door . . . *scrit, scrit* . . . and though he is already there, Gemma hears the approach of worn boot heels, close, closer. As if he has always been coming for her.

"Gemma!" Matt shook her again, hard. Everyone on board the space shuttle *Discovery* was having nightmares, but they had to hold themselves together. They needed each other. "Gemma, wake—!"

Her eyes snapped open and for a moment she stared right through him, her pupils dilated, and glimmering red. Matt shifted position, and the red glow disappeared. *Reflected light*, he thought. *That's all.*

"Hey, Gemma," Lizzie said. She was beside him, holding on to one of the sleeping bags tethered against the bulkhead. Her voice was calm, and Matt was glad she was still with them. If Frank had taken her with him instead of Hans, Matt didn't know what the fuck he would have done.

"I'm okay," Gemma said, plainly not. She was shivering, and a bead of sweat lifted from the end of her nose and drifted between them. "Bad dreams, that's all."

"Bad dreams," Matt said. He'd had a nightmare when he last slept, a rabid dog chasing him through a field of fading crops. And Lizzie said she'd slept fitfully, too. It was hardly a surprise.

They helped Gemma unstrap and she shoved herself across to the toilet, grabbing the handle and spinning herself around.

"Anything new?" she asked as she started undoing her suit. She left the door open and reached for her urine hose.

Matt turned away, hanging on to the ladder to the flight deck. Even with everything that was happening, they all deserved privacy and dignity.

"Plenty of transmissions on our last two orbits," Matt said. "None of them good."

"Such as?"

"Gemma, why don't you have something to eat before—"

"You're trying to protect me, Lizzie?" Gemma said, voice raised. "Seriously?"

Matt turned around. "Let's keep it down. We can't lose it."

"I'm not *losing* it," Gemma said, her voice softer. "But there's no point hiding anything. Is there?"

Matt sighed. "No point." He looked at Lizzie. They'd been talking about Gemma while she slept, the things she mumbled in her sleep, disturbing whispers of two-headed snakes and rabid canines that struck a chilling chord with them both. The similarity of their dreams was troubling, but he didn't believe they were relevant to the current situation. They were simply a product of it.

"Most of the broadcasts from Europe suggest they're a few days behind the U.S.," Matt said. "There are widespread lockdowns, borders are closing, mass burials. There've been skirmishes in the English Channel."

"Skirmishes?" Gemma asked.

"Naval battles." He didn't elaborate. The phrase was enough to shock them into a brief silence.

Matt glanced at the door to the air lock. His two dead friends and crew members were beyond, wrapped up in their sleeping bags. They'd pushed them into the air lock and through to the depressurized payload bay after their deaths. Frank Mancini was from London. He'd slit his wrists, and in the tussle when they tried to stop him, Hans took a knife jab to the throat that pricked his carotid. Some of their blood was still circulating the flight deck.

"But what about Kennedy?" Gemma asked. "They've been working on something. They can bring us down, right? Frank was the pilot, but you can fly this thing, too."

"I've said before—not without help."

Gemma zipped her suit and sanitized her hands, shaking her head, every movement angry.

"We're not giving up hope," Lizzie said. She and Matt swapped a glance, and Gemma turned to face them both.

"Kennedy," she said.

"Last orbit, there was only one reply to our transmissions," Matt said. "Tech guy I don't know, name of Joslin. He could hardly breathe, could barely talk. He said a few people have died in Mission Control, but most have gone home to their families."

"Abandoned us?" Gemma asked.

"Doing what any of us would do," Matt said.

"Except Joslin, right?"

"He said he's stayed there because he has no family, and all his friends are dead."

"So, you asked him about us? About what we should do?"

Matt sighed. "He's just a tech guy, Gemma. An engineer. He had no answers. He just said . . . " He drifted off, remembering Joslin's clotted voice, his hopelessness.

"What?" Gemma asked.

"He said he wished he was up here with us, instead of down there in hell."

―――

Matt brushed aside floating blood as he pulled himself onto the flight deck. It spread across the back of his hand, sticking in the hairs there, and he wondered whether it belonged to Frank or Hans. Lowering into the commander's seat and strapping in, he tried to blink away the memory of their violent deaths.

Earth was visible to his left, breathtakingly beautiful and awe-inspiring as ever, only now he saw it through different eyes. In *Discovery*'s payload bay was a large component for the fifth SDI satellite to be built, a multibillion-dollar venture to ensure safety and security down on earth. Their mission was secret, and their cargo even more secretive than usual. This SDI satellite was built to be offensive, with missle capabilities providing a rapid response to any attack.

Within ten meters of him were two fully armed nuclear missiles.

"Still beautiful," Lizzie said. "You never tire of that view." She moved forward to float above the pilot's seat beside him, but did not strap herself in. That had been Frank's place.

"How is she?"

"On the edge. Like all of us."

"I'm not on the edge," Matt said.

"Really? Your wife, your daughter? Aren't they in New York?"

Matt stared at the Pacific Ocean passing beneath them, wondering if some of those islands might survive. Then he understood that *Discovery* was the remotest island of them all.

"I'm mission commander," Matt said. "I can't be on the edge."

Lizzie laughed without humor. When Matt looked at her, she was blurred from the tears in his eyes.

"Maybe Frank did the right thing," Lizzie said.

"Killing himself? Killing Hans?"

"Hans was a mistake."

"No," Matt said. "Not the right thing. Not at all."

"But we're . . ."

"We're waiting," Matt said.

"For what?"

"We have food and water for another twelve days. More, now that Hans and Frank . . ." He sighed. "By then, maybe something will have changed."

"All that's going to change in that time is more Captain Trips, more dead people, and less chance than ever of us bringing *Discovery* down."

"Captain who?"

"It's a name I heard for the flu. In France it's 'Gorge Noire.' In New Zealand it's 'Whiu Hou.' It's *everywhere*, Matt. We can't assume anyone gives a fuck about us, and we can't just wait for a miracle."

"You know what we've got on this boat."

Lizzie shrugged. Her hair had come loose, strands floating around her head like unruly snakes.

"If I try to land and we come apart in low atmosphere, we'll spread radioactive contamination over hundreds of miles."

"We won't come apart."

"The chance of me landing *Discovery* successfully with no copilot and precisely no help from Mission Control—"

"Don't say zero," Lizzie said.

"—is five percent. Probably less."

"And the chance of us dying up here is one hundred."

They watched the beautiful, dying planet passing them by.

"That's not chance," Matt said. "That's certainty."

"Pedant."

Gemma opens one of their food lockers and brings out the bags of freeze-dried rations. A spot of blood lands on her forearm and rolls across her skin like an excited bug. She blows on it. It lifts away, drifting. She is shaking.

. . . scritch . . . scritch . . .

She looks at the door to her left, leading into the air lock and payload bay beyond. Frank and Hans are through there, dead, wrapped in their sleeping bags, and something is scratching at the door.

. . . scritch . . .

"Go away," she says. Soft, so the others won't hear.

Why don't you want them to hear? a voice asks from beyond the door. It's impossible. But she has heard this voice before.

"Go away!"

They already hear you talking in your sleep, apologizing to your father when there is nothing to apologize for, you never meant to—

Gemma slams her hand on the locker, loud, and the voice ceases. She runs her fingers across the top of the food packages, counting. With Frank and Hans dead, there is more for them, and Matt has already said they can ration. Twelve days, maybe more. Their mission was only supposed to be four days long, so their return is already two days overdue. These extra packets were only ever in case of emergency.

Gemma laughs, and it comes out as a loud yelp. "Emergency!"

"Gemma, you okay?" Lizzie floats down from the flight deck.

. . . scritch . . . scritch . . .

GRACE

"You hear that?" Gemma asks.

"Hear what?" Lizzie rights herself so they stand face-to-face. "Hey, Gemma. I'm here for you."

"Who's here for you?" Gemma asks. "Thirty-six meals. Plenty of water."

"That's good."

"Why? A meal each per day. Twelve more days to look down and wonder what's going on." Gemma glances at her watch. "How long until we're over Florida again? I want to talk to Joslin."

She does, and she doesn't. What she wants most is to get away from that voice—

They don't trust you, they talk about you, you should never *feel guilt for something you didn't do.*

—and the terrible scratching at the door, like something eager to be let in.

. . . scritch . . . scritch . . .

But I'm already inside, he says.

She shoves past Lizzie and grabs the ladder, pulling herself up toward the flight deck. Matt turns to her as she arrives.

"Hey, Gemma."

She looks from the window, crouching to see past him. They are coming up on the West Coast.

"Joslin," she says.

"I was just about to start trying him."

For the first three times, the only response is static. Lizzie comes in behind Gemma, and the two of them stand close by Matt's chair. Gemma breathes through her mouth, listening for the slightest hint of response. She tries to imagine Mission Control empty, screen displays still flowing, lights flashing, computers humming, everything meant to keep them safe now playing to the dead.

As the landmass of the USA passes by beneath them at three hundred miles per minute, the static is replaced by a low, long rattle.

A breath, Gemma thinks. From behind her, down on mid-deck, she hears a loud laugh. She glances at Lizzie wide-eyed. *She must have heard that!*

"Is that someone breathing?" Lizzie asks.

No, she didn't hear the laugh. Am I mad? Gemma thinks.

No, they're mad, the muffled voice says from down through the hatch and beyond the air lock door. *Scritch... scriiitch* ... as he speaks, as if determined to scratch his way through to her.

She feels those scratches against the inside of her skull.

"Joslin?" Matt asks. "That you, friend?"

"*Yeah,*" a voice says from the radio. It sounds like Joslin is speaking through a throatful of soup. "*Not doing so good here,* Discovery."

"Has anyone come back?" Lizzie asks. "Anyone come up with a plan to help us—"

"*Wish I could go... to her,*" Joslin says, drawing in agonized breaths. "*Wish I could... see. But he's got his... hands on my throat. Squeezing. Feel hot. And cold. Got better—*"

"Who's squeezing your throat, Joslin?" Matt asks.

"*—better yesterday, pulling through, then slept and... smells like death now, in here, and I think... I think it's me.*"

"Is there anyone else left?" Lizzie asks. Desperate. Leaning forward, as if to feed herself down along the radio waves.

Gemma watches the landmass of home passing beneath them. "No one," she whispers.

"*Only you,*" Joslin says. "*Damn I feel so...*" He says no more. His breathing is low and fast, wet and cloggy. Gemma hears a soft thud and imagines Joslin resting his head on the desk.

"Joslin?" Lizzie asks. "Joslin, what do we do? What do we do?!"

"We go round and round," Gemma says. "Eight days, or twelve. A hundred orbits, or two. And we watch the world die."

"No!" Lizzie says. "We take her down, right, Matt? We take *Discovery* down!"

GRACE

Gemma drifts back down through the hatch, and this time she does not look away from the air lock.

There is no voice. The scratching has ceased, as if he's allowing her grief. *A graceful man*, she thinks, without knowing why, but his grace is horrifying, like the dance of fire in zero gravity.

The Graceful Man's silence is the worst thing she has ever heard.

Passing over the Atlantic Ocean they picked up a distress call from a cruise ship that was adrift with no crew left alive or able to work. The call was from a seven-year-old child whose mother was telling her how to use the radio. The girl was fine. She said her mommy was feeling poorly and a man had fallen over in the kids' play area.

Approaching Europe, Matt tuned into several big news agencies and listened to the reports. All of them were dreadful and tragic. None projected hope. A French channel broadcast what appeared to be a series of public executions of government officials. An English voice talked of skirmishes all along the south coast as boats from Europe attempted to land. One Spanish radio station played frantic guitar music with the presenter coughing and shouting over the top. Matt was pleased he didn't speak Spanish.

He understood enough, though. He felt like that kid on the ocean liner, adrift and asking for help from a world that no longer had the ability to care. *I'm mission commander*, he thought, but the fact that there was no longer a mission and the only thing left to command was a dying crew . . .

He hated to think of them and himself like that, but it was the truth.

"I feel like that kid on the ship," Lizzie said, and Matt laughed. There was no other way to react. "So, I've been thinking . . . " she said, but a noise from behind silenced her.

Gemma came up from mid-deck and gave them both a food

packet. They were half-empty, the leftovers from yesterday. They'd stopped tasting of anything, but Matt still ate, and drank from the water bottle by his seat.

"Thinking what?" Gemma asked. She was quieter than ever now, eyes wide, the skin around them dark from exhaustion. She didn't want to sleep, she said, because she wanted to grasp every minute left to them.

Matt heard the lie every time she spoke it, because she was grasping nothing. Gemma hung around on mid-deck most of the time, staring at the air lock entrance, sometimes with her head cocked. She watched them with those wide eyes, hardly saying anything.

"Nothing," Lizzie said. "Just thinking."

"Thinking about how we finish things," Gemma said.

Lizzie caught Matt's eye. He'd been thinking about that, too. There would soon come a day when the food ran out. It would be a long time before the water was gone, and he knew they could live for weeks without food, but they'd weaken, fade, and if they were going to do something . . .

"Yes," Matt said. It needed saying. "Thinking about how we do that, when the time comes."

"Time came days ago," Gemma said. "Everything's worse. Nothing's better down there. Joslin's rotting in Mission Control."

"We can't try to land," Matt said. He was worried they were about to have that discussion again. But Gemma surprised him by nodding, smiling, and he thought it was the first time she'd smiled in a while.

"How long would we stay in orbit?" Gemma asked.

"A good while," Lizzie said. "Years. Maybe a lot of years."

"And our payload?" Gemma asked.

"Eventually our orbit will decay, and we'll skim the atmosphere. Probably too shallow, and *Discovery* will come apart high up, and Matt says . . . " She looked at Matt, the truth that they'd already been discussing this now hanging between them.

"That high up, pollution from the warheads shouldn't cause too much trouble down on the surface," he said. "It'll just be added to the upper atmosphere."

"And so will we," Gemma said. Matt and Lizzie followed her gaze through the window. "Kinda beautiful."

"But that time's not yet," Matt said. "So how about you grab that illicit bottle of Jack I brought on board?"

Lizzie raised her eyebrows. "You've waited til *now?*"

"In the small locker behind my sleeping bag."

"I'll get it," Gemma said.

As she moves down to mid-deck, she feels them talking about her. She doesn't actually hear this, but senses it in her gut. They sit up there and whisper, snicker, calling her a disgrace, scheming about how to get rid of her so that they can share her rations. She sees it in their eyes. She hears it in their voices.

She opens the small locker and grabs the bottle of Jack Daniel's.

Of course they talk about you, the Graceful Man says, and beyond the air lock door she hears his boot heels clacking at his steady approach, and then . . . *scritch, scritch* . . . against the door. *They're jealous. Because of what you're going to do for me.*

She stares at the bourbon bottle in her hand, but what she really sees is the memory of her disgrace.

She was in her bedroom with Paul Nevill. They were both naked, hot, flustered, and it felt deliciously daring and vital, because she had never been this far with anyone before. Neither had Paul, she knew that from his wide-eyed delight, his fluttery breaths. He was hard in her hand. And as she tugged softly, urging him closer, their hottest parts meeting at last, the bedroom door slammed open.

Her father's furious shout shattered her senses and echoed painfully in her skull, like a bullet fired into a tank. That scream never ran out of energy, and it is as powerful now as it was fifteen years before.

Gemma, you disgrace me!

And then her father is someone else and she sees *him* for the first time, standing in her bedroom doorway like a shadow given life, smiling. But that smile is terrible.

Poor Gemma. What an evil father. You never did anything wrong.

"But I did . . . " Gemma says, and she burns with the deep guilt that sustains her self-hate. Her silence around the house, unable to meet his eye. The awful names she called herself.

The dreadful thing she did.

What a bad man he was.

"No, he wasn't bad, my dad was . . . "

Changing around medicine capsules in the cabinet by his bed, just to make him feel sick so that she could help him, show him that she wasn't as bad, as *disgraceful* as he believed.

His eyes when they found him later that night, rolled back in his head as if in his final moments he chose to deny everything he had ever seen.

But I am good, the man says, smile filled with too many teeth, eyes aglow with the red light of eternity. *And you know it, Gemma. A good man, a* graceful *man, and if you're good for me, you'll know that forever.*

She's squeezing the bourbon bottle too hard, afraid that it will shatter and cut her hands, splashing glass shards and booze and blood around the cabin. And the small part of Gemma that clasps on to sanity realizes that this might be her last chance to make a decision of her own. She grips tighter, squeezing—

. . . scritch scritch SCRIIIIIITCH! . . .

Gemma shakes her head, afraid that he's going to scratch and tear all the way inside. She can feel him looking right at her, through the solid door and its protective packing and across the impossible gulf between them, and there's a frantic, animal eagerness in those deep, red eyes.

At last, the Graceful Man tells her what he wants.

Matt hoped that time might have settled Gemma's dreams.

They took it in turns sleeping two or three hours at a time so that at least one of them monitored communication, in the vain hope that there might be some good news. His own dreams were of a deep kindness sitting in the unseen distance like a rising sun. He was sad, because however fast he ran, he knew he would never reach that place. The rabid dog was just a shadow now, something left behind. Lizzie had a similar dream. They must have talked about it enough for their minds to be working in sync, consciously or otherwise.

But Gemma's sleep had remained light and very troubled, and she was growing more and more distant. He guessed they were all handling this nightmarish situation in their own way. Perhaps more time together might help them all.

As Gemma came back onto the flight deck with the bottle of Jack, Lizzie drifted across from the pilot's seat and nodded for her to sit. Gemma seemed surprised at this act of kindness.

"Let's raise a toast," Matt said.

"To who?" Gemma asked as she lowered herself into the seat.

"Who, what, where, when," Matt said. "Maybe just to us." Gemma handed him the bottle and he popped the top, revealing the drinking nipple he'd already attached before smuggling it on board.

"You'd have been in so much trouble if Flight had caught you with that," Lizzie said.

"Uh-huh. Last thing I'd want to be right now is in trouble." He chuckled, Lizzie laughed, and Gemma turned away, looking through the window at their dying world. "So . . . I'll make this to my wife and girls," he said. His voice caught and he blinked quickly, focusing only on the bottle in his hand, watching how light danced and burned in its auburn depths. "Because I was always in trouble with them when I was chosen for one of these flights." He raised the bottle quickly, and though he didn't need to, he tipped his head back as if to hold in the tears. The swig scorched deep and fine, warm and intimate, and the taste and smell brought good memories he held close.

Lizzie grabbed the bottle from him and held it up before her. "July '69," she said. "Moon landing. That was the moment I knew what I wanted from life, and here I am. With you guys." She sucked from the bottle and swallowed, smacking her lips. Then she held it out to Gemma.

"It's weird," Gemma said, "it all still looks so beautiful. But there's a fight going on down there. A war."

"For survival," Matt said, and he winced inwardly, because this moment was about them not surviving. It was being together in their final days or hours. But Gemma took the bottle and lifted it, and for that moment Matt believed that it really was going to be all right. However they approached the end, whatever they decided their final moments might be, they would face that time together as a crew.

"To him," Gemma said.

Matt frowned. "Who?"

Gemma flung the bourbon bottle toward Lizzie's face, and at the same time thrust herself from the pilot's chair toward Matt. He brought his hands up to meet her, but she knocked his right arm aside with her left, then her other hand jabbed toward his face. It was only in that final unbelievable moment that he saw what she was holding. Then the blade that Frank had used to take his own life slit through Matt's left eyelid and continued onward, deeper, destroying his vision and turning his head slightly before the pain sang in.

After the pain, nothing.

Gemma grabs the commander's seat and pulls, kicking out against the control panel with her right foot, shoving the blade deeper into Matt's eye. His mouth is open and his other eye stares at her in shock, but already the life within is flickering and fading to nothing. Blood and a clear fluid spurt from his ruptured socket. She thinks of her father's eyes rolled back in his head, and at last he can see no more.

"*Noooo!*" Lizzie screams.

Still holding the knife, using it as an anchor, Gemma forces her legs around and kicks Lizzie in the face.

Lizzie bounces back, her head turning to the side, her own legs lifting as her body starts to spin before striking the bulkhead beside the ladder face-first.

Gemma pushes away from Matt and the commander's chair, the bloody blade in her hand trailing gobbets of gore, but her trajectory is off. She drifts to the left and hits the bulkhead, pushing off, spinning slowly as her hand comes around toward the other woman.

Lizzie is pulling herself down the ladder through the hatch leading to mid-deck. Gemma lashes out and the knife flicks across the back of her thigh, parting material and skin, leaving a growing trail of blood as Lizzie disappears down through the hole. The impact sets her into an uncontrolled spin, and Gemma hears a sickening thud as Lizzie cracks her head against one of the ladder's struts.

Gemma grabs on and goes to follow, but then the Graceful Man says, *All you need is here. Don't be a fucking disgrace.*

She pauses, breathing hard, blood hazing the air around her, and for a few seconds she tries to grab on to dregs of the old Gemma as they flit by. Her hands clasp tight, the knife slicing into the base of three fingers as she makes a fist.

The pain brings her senses alight and all they know is that man from her dreams. He smells of dust and sun-scorched highways and deep, deep age. He tastes of long-buried memories and newly opened graves. His fingertips are hot against her jaw as he turns her head toward *Discovery*'s front windows, and the skin there bubbles into four burn blisters. She hears his voice, deep and controlling. And as she realizes that she is his, everything he desires is laid out before her in graceful, unending glory.

Gemma slams the hatch leading down into mid-deck, then pushes herself across to close the second opening. She glances down before she does so and sees Lizzie floating, bouncing off of surfaces, blood leaking from a gash above her right eye.

Maybe she's dead already.

Gemma secures herself in the flight deck, and she hears a sigh of triumph from somewhere other than herself.

"I ain't never going to meet you, girl, and for that I'm sorry," the old woman said. Lizzie couldn't see her, but she knew the woman was *very* old, and frail, and her voice was weighted with responsibility. "Reckon if we did meet, we'd be friends. Ain't had too many friends of late, but that's lookin' to change quite soon. Yes, Lord, change is coming."

Lizzie felt herself adrift, as if floating in cool deep water, but she could breathe and move and listen.

"Thing is, there's something I'd ask of you, even though you can't come here to me."

Lizzie felt a sudden rush of regret. This woman was the kindness she'd dreamed of, but she didn't realize until hearing these words just how much she wanted to be with her.

Mother . . . she thought.

"Quiet now, girl," the old woman said. "Don't have long. And I'm tired, and ain't proper sure you can even hear me."

I hear you, Mother.

"That thing you're on, it's comin' down. Steered by hands you don't wanna comprehend, it's aiming to spread its poison all across this place around me, the farm and all of Nebraska beyond. And if that happens, well . . . it's done before it's begun."

It's over anyway. We know that. We've been watching . . .

"You've been watchin' the end of the beginning," the old woman said, and her voice broke a little, growing weaker and more distant.

Mother? Mother?

"I gotta live just a little while longer, so help me, girl. And help everyone."

Lizzie heard a soft breeze passing through endless crops, and then something closer and more tangible, shaking the ground beneath her, a horrible grumbling growl vibrating into her core. *Wake up!* she heard and thought at the same time, and for that moment before coming to, her voice and that of the old woman were the same.

She opened her eyes, and a droplet of blood made her vision grow red.

"Matt," she said, and she remembered his death, and Gemma coming for her. The pain from the cut in her leg was tactile and real, but more so was the voice of the old woman in her dream.

She groaned and held on, bringing her slow spin to a halt. Her stomach churned. She thought she'd gathered herself, but then she puked, trying to make it to the toilet area first, but succeeding only in spraying vomit around mid-deck. It splashed against bulkheads, spreading, coalescing again, floating and stinking and spreading across their sleeping bags.

"Doesn't matter," she said. None of them would be sleeping there again. Gemma had gone insane, and something was driving her. Something dark.

"Gemma!" she shouted, looking up at the closed hatches into the flight deck. She probably couldn't even hear. "Gemma!" There was no answer. And yet something was different. Lizzie paused and tilted her head, turning slowly left and right, and that growl came in again.

Low, almost subaudible, the altitude adjustment rockets were firing.

She's taking us down, Lizzie thought. Gemma was a payload specialist, trained for eighteen months in the securing and deployment of the contents of their payload bay. She knew very little about flying the shuttle, and certainly nothing about landing.

For what she meant to do, that didn't matter.

Lizzie blinked more blood from her eyes. Her head throbbed. Around the pain and blood and her grief for Matt was a deeper understanding, fed by that strange woman's voice in her dream. Gemma aimed to take *Discovery* down over Nebraska. Maybe they'd break up low over that vast farming state, or perhaps they'd crash, but either way her intention was not to commit suicide in high orbit. That would negate the effect of their broken and destroyed payload.

Lizzie took in a few deep breaths, trying to level her thinking, get her logical brain back online. When they'd been drinking Matt's bourbon, they had been somewhere over the eastern U.S., so that left maybe an hour until Gemma would start bringing them down over the Pacific. With no help from poor dead Joslin, she'd have to run everything manually from the flight deck, and Lizzie couldn't calculate those chances of success. With the way Gemma had been over the past couple of days she might put it at one in ten, even less. To work out their flight path, navigate them down for the optimum reentry attitude, and then fly them away from their orbital path so that they aimed at Nebraska might even have been beyond Matt's capabilities.

It ain't just her flyin', that old woman's voice said in her mind, and Lizzie glanced at the air lock hatch, certain she'd heard something from that direction. But it was only a creak and groan from the shuttle's structure as Gemma started to shift their orbit.

"Got to get to the flight deck," Lizzie muttered. She thought of the payload bay and the tool compartment at its rear, but it was depressurized. If she went through without getting suited up, she'd pass out within fifteen seconds and be dead within a couple of minutes. And to get suited up was a two-person job, and it would take an hour even if she did have someone to help her.

She pushed herself around mid-deck, opening compartments and lockers, shifting the sleeping bags to the side, rooting through the cabinet of carefully rationed food that would now never be eaten, searching for something she could use to force the flight deck hatch open. Nothing. She climbed the ladder and tried the hatch anyway, but Gemma had locked and jammed the handle from the inside.

She drifted through to the small side compartment that they'd used as a retreat if and when they'd needed it. At the start of this short mission those times had been few, but Gemma had been in there a lot over the past few days, and Lizzie and Matt had given her peace.

There was a small sleeping bag affixed to one surface and little else. The rumble and creaks from *Discovery* sounded louder. *I'm going to die*, she thought. She'd almost come to terms with that since Matt had explained why he couldn't attempt a landing, and the very idea of him doing so now seemed foolish. He'd known from the start that it was a folly, and it had taken her a good while to accept it.

A flight into the upper atmosphere, though . . .

When they were sure Gemma was asleep, she and Matt had discussed this in quiet tones and agreed it was the way to end things. Fast, furious, and destroying any threat from *Discovery* to anyone left alive down on the ground. All of them had nightmares about such a situation, especially after the *Challenger* tragedy. *We'll make it easy on ourselves*, Matt had said. *At the right moment, we'll open the payload doors and that'll tear the ship apart. We won't know anything.*

Lizzie caught her breath. Matt had meant to do this electronically from the flight deck, but there was also a manual control panel within the payload bay itself. To open it while Gemma was attempting reentry would be suicide, but they were dying already, both of them, just stringing out their final few moments.

. . . so help me, girl. And help everyone.

Lizzie pulled herself back through to mid-deck and held on to the air lock hatch. *Fifteen seconds isn't long enough*, she thought. And she might not even have that long. Even if she expelled all the air from her lungs so that they didn't rupture and forced the connecting hatch between air lock and payload bay, the expulsion of atmosphere would spit her out. She'd likely strike something and seriously injure or kill herself.

The shuttle started to shake and groan some more, and the roar grew as the earth's upper atmosphere caused friction against the ship's underside.

"I don't have long," Lizzie said out loud. "Mother, I don't have very long."

There was no response.

She looked around and her eyes settled on the spacesuit locker, and then she knew.

In the vacuum of space and without any protection, her deoxygenated blood would rapidly be filtered into her brain, and she'd be rendered unconscious. But she could shrug on the space suit without air connections.

Lizzie had been a champion swimmer in college. She could hold her breath for almost three minutes.

And that would be long enough.

Matt's corpse drifts into Gemma again, his hand stroking across the top of her head, and she shrugs her shoulder and sends him spinning back across the flight deck. She doesn't want to take her eyes from the instruments, the controls, and she tries to focus her mind.

From the hatch she hears... *scritch-scritch-scritch*... and to begin with she thinks it's Lizzie trying to force her way inside.

Then the Graceful Man says, *Gemma, grace under pressure.*

"But I don't know what I'm doing, I've never—"

Trust yourself. I'll take care of everything else.

A trail of gore drifts between her and the control panel. *That's Matt*, she thinks. She sweeps her hand through it, splitting it into countless droplets that spread like an exploding star.

He schemed against you, with her. You know they'd already decided how to end their lives? All without you. They waited until you were asleep.

The shuttle is shivering and shaking now, and Gemma checks the displays, the flickering map, holding on to the joystick and feeling a calm certainty regarding her path. She straps herself into the pilot's seat as *Discovery* begins to shake.

"I am no disgrace," she whispers.

The body nudges against her again. She shoves him away.

Lizzie tried to calm herself, forcing herself to slow down. The space suit flipped and floated around her. She'd put one leg in and started spinning, bouncing from padded walls. She stilled herself, breathed deeply, and realized she was taking one of her last breaths.

They died doing what they loved, she remembered fellow astronaut trainees saying about the *Challenger* crew. She'd scoffed at the time. *There's no good time to die*, she'd said.

She was doubting that concept now. The planet was a graveyard, but hope could not die. If her life ending could maintain some kind of hope, then these final breaths were her most precious.

Or maybe she was as crazy as Gemma.

She breathed deeply again and pulled on the rest of the suit. She grabbed the helmet and went to the air lock. The handle felt warm through her gloves, as if someone had been holding it just before her. Her hands felt dirty. And suddenly she was filled with an unreasonable terror about what might lie on the other side.

Lizzie turned the handle and hauled the air lock door open. Inside, she maneuvered her way around and shut the hatch behind her, then turned again to the inner hatch that led into the depressurized payload bay.

This was it. This was—

The shuttle shook and rattled, the vibration increasing in intensity as Gemma took them down, down, skimming the atmosphere and then striking in at a sharp angle, beginning to pierce the earth's protective cloak.

"Move your fucking ass!" Lizzie said to herself, and as she brought the helmet up she knew they were the last words she would ever speak. A bland epitaph.

She took in several deep breaths, held the last, and secured the helmet over her head and onto the suit. Without an air supply she'd have maybe one more full lungful within the helmet, and that was it. Two full breaths. Maybe four minutes.

The countdown to her final moment had begun.

Always been counting down, she thought, *making the most of that dash, Lizzie O'Connor, 1958–1990.*

Breath held, she turned the air lock handle.

It was tugged from her hand as the lock vented, flinging the hatch open and drawing her out into the payload bay. A few low lights were on—

—what was I thinking, I should have brought a fucking flashlight!—

—and the first thing she saw was Hans, his body performing a slow spin so close to the air lock that she clashed with him, his sleeping bag half-open, his frost-glittered face staring at her with an open mouth and one hooded eye.

Lizzie cried out, then realized what she'd done. She clamped her mouth shut, then drew in as much breath as she could from the helmet.

Her four minutes were down to maybe two.

She steadied herself, closed her eyes for five seconds, willed her panicked heart to slow.

Opening her eyes again, she took in the scene. The two deadly missiles were secured in their cradle. The payload doors were shut. Hans spun away from her and struck the right bulkhead, and Frank was just visible beyond the payload, motionless against the hold's rear end.

To her left was the manual operation point for the payload bay doors.

Lizzie pushed herself away and grasped the handle next to the control panel.

Discovery was shaking so hard now that her vision blurred, the vibration thundered deep in her chest, and she wondered if her efforts were even needed. Gemma might have screwed up the reentry angle, and if that were the case, *Discovery* would disintegrate high in the atmosphere anyway.

Can't take that chance, Lizzie thought. *Either way—*

Either way, she had maybe a minute of air left.

As she initiated the manual opening system, she thought of the people she had left behind—her mother and father, her brother, her girlfriend Ashley, and her friends. Her fear had always been that she would die up here and leave them down below, unaware of what she had experienced or felt in her final moments.

She'd never believed that things would end up the other way around.

A red light on the panel before her switched to green, then back to red.

Huh? she thought.

She tried again. Green, then red again. She blinked, tried to calm herself, thinking through the manual operation protocol—

Passcode! she thought. How could she have been so stupid! She flipped open a small keyboard panel and looked at the ten-digit pad, and for a few terrible seconds she struggled to remember the code. Her lungs were burning. Every bit of her was saying, *Breathe... breathe...*

Then she tapped it in—7:16:1969.

The light flipped green and began to pulse.

I wonder what I'll see, she thought.

She looked up at the two payload bay doors, the long straight seam where they met, and for a split second there was a slice of beautiful fire and light.

Then the opening doors were caught by the thin, high atmosphere searing past at thousands of miles an hour and ripped from their mountings, and Lizzie O'Connor was no more.

Several hundred miles away, a very old woman sitting on her porch saw the trail of a shooting star fade out across the horizon, and she breathed a sad sigh.

Closer to that blazing streak high above the ground, a coyote also watched.

The fire faded into just another ending.

The coyote growled and turned its scarred snout toward the west.

MOVING DAY

Richard Chizmar

Shortly before dawn on the first day of July, Tommy Harper buried his father in the vegetable garden behind their house.

The narrow rectangle of fertilized soil, where Tommy's mother once spent summer afternoons weeding and pruning, occupied the far corner of the backyard between the shed and the split-rail fence. Before the flu, she'd grown her own tomatoes and carrots, peppers and cucumbers. A small section of the garden was reserved for a variety of herbs she'd often referred to as her "secret ingredients." She'd refused to reveal precisely what they were, but she used them in everything from her homemade spaghetti sauce to her award-winning red bean chili and even her Thanksgiving mashed potatoes. She also made one hell of a pot of herbal tea.

Several nights earlier, after cooking a celebratory dinner of fresh rainbow trout on the grill, and beating Tommy at several hands of gin rummy at the coffee table in the den, Mr. Harper—a twenty-two year veteran of the Bennington Sheriff's Department—bid good night to his son, shuffled down the carpeted hallway to the bedroom he'd once shared with his wife, stretched out on the unmade bed that was centered between the two windows looking out over the front yard, and placed the barrel of his service revolver into his mouth.

Tommy was sneaking a cigarette on the back porch when he heard the gunshot. By the time he finished smoking the unfiltered Camel and went inside—not in any particular hurry, already knowing what he was going to find—his father's heart had ceased beating. The pillow beneath his misshapen head was a sea of blood and bone fragments. The stench of his evacuated bowels permeated the dim bedroom. A red spray mixed with tangles of dark hair stained the gold crucifix hanging above the headboard and dribbled down the wall onto the floor. Tommy stood in the doorway, at once sickened and transfixed by the gory display—it brought to mind one of the Rorschach patterns he'd seen in his psychology textbook—and then he turned and closed the bedroom door and went back outside.

Later, after smoking what was left of the pack of Camels he'd swiped from a neighbor's car, he returned to the bedroom to search for a goodbye note. But there was nothing there for him to find. By then, the flies had already found their way inside the house. They crawled over his father's face like an undulating second skin. *I'm all alone now*, Tommy thought, listening to the insistent buzzing of the flies. And then for no sane reason at all other than he couldn't get the damn song out of his mind: *Baby, can you dig your man? He's a righteous man . . .*

He backed out of the room and made it halfway down the hall before dropping to his knees and vomiting his dinner onto the carpet. When he finished heaving, he wiped his mouth on his T-shirt and took a seat at the kitchen table. A single wax candle, melted down to a nub, rested beside a scattering of cookie crumbs on the paper plate in front of him. Not even an hour ago, his father had stood at the counter and sung to him—and now he was gone.

It had been Tommy Harper's fifteenth birthday.

MOVING DAY

Once upon a time, the Harpers were a model family.

Their home in Bennington, Vermont, a neatly kept three-bedroom ranch, was located on a half-acre lot in a pleasant subdivision. The schools were close by and highly rated. They had friendly neighbors, a fenced-in backyard, and a well-behaved six-year-old cocker spaniel named Otis. There was a twenty-gallon aquarium in the den housing a variety of tropical fish and a thirty-two-inch color television console. Bookshelves lined the walls. A white Chevy pickup truck and a recent model Toyota Celica were parked outside in the driveway. A pair of matching, hand-painted flower boxes hung from the railing of a covered front porch.

Mom, Joanne (her husband and a handful of close friends called her "Joey," an affectionate college nickname that had stuck), was an on-call substitute teacher at the nearby elementary and middle schools. She usually worked two or three days a week and spent the majority of her remaining time taking care of the house, her husband, and two children. An avid jogger and amateur photographer, she enjoyed doing crossword puzzles and watching old black-and-white movies on television. She was obsessed with arts and crafts and made her own Christmas cards every year. Joanne Harper was also a devout Christian.

Dad, Russell, wasn't much for attending Sunday church services—it was the one morning his work schedule allowed him to sleep in—but he was a faithful husband and devoted father. He coached his daughter's softball team and taught Tommy how to field grounders and hit a curveball at an age when most kids were still batting off a tee. When he had time off from the sheriff's office, he loaded up the bed of his truck and took the family on fishing and camping trips, as well as their annual weeklong vacation at the beach each August. Russell was a simple man. He didn't drink. Didn't smoke. Didn't gamble. He was perfectly content to spend his evenings eating dinner with the family and making his own fishing lures at the workbench in his shed while listening to the Red Sox game on the radio. Every other Thursday night, he bowled in a league with friends from the neighborhood. He wasn't very good, his average hovering around the 107 mark, but that did little to diminish his enjoyment.

Daughter, Jennifer, was two years older than Tommy. An honor roll student in school, she was a cheerleader in the fall and ran cross-country in the spring. Summers were spent at the pool and playing softball. She had a steady boyfriend (a nice enough fellow named Herb Cavanaugh, whose teammates on the junior varsity football team called "Pizza Face" on account of his struggle with acne) and a part-time job at the Scoop and Serve ice cream shop on Main Street. Jennifer was a pretty girl with strawberry blonde hair cut short into a bob and eager blue eyes that made her appear younger than her age. She was a voracious reader and enjoyed writing poetry. She was interested in astrology, and there was a stack of library books on her nightstand devoted to the subject. More than anything, she wanted to go to college to become a veterinarian. Ever since she was a little girl, she'd had a habit of bringing home stray or injured animals and nursing them back to health. Even now, her favorite book was *The Story of Doctor Dolittle*.

Tommy, who was tall for his age, and Jenn were often mistaken for twins when they were first introduced to strangers. Thick blond curls spilled over the boy's forehead, framing a lean face highlighted by inquisitive blue eyes, full lips, and a prominent chin. His mother often embarrassed him in front of her friends by claiming that he looked like a matinee idol. He hated being the center of attention and usually made a quick escape from the room. Despite the rising popularity afforded him by his natural good looks and superior skills on the baseball diamond, Tommy was a loner by choice. He preferred long solo hikes in the woods to overcrowded weekend parties; reading science-fiction paperbacks in the backyard hammock to rowdy bonfires and school dances; and sitting alone atop the one-hundred-and-forty-foot water tower in the heart of Bennington to pretty much any other public activity.

MOVING DAY

Tommy couldn't remember the title of the novel—it had been a loaner from the library, its tattered dust jacket a spiderweb of Scotch tape, that he'd read the summer he turned twelve—but he often found himself thinking about his favorite scene. In the midst of a worldwide alien invasion, the teenage protagonist of the book climbed atop a water tower located on a hillside in his small midwestern hometown and watched in terror as the arachnoid-looking space creatures made their approach from a nearby forest. Trees splintered and crumpled in the aliens' wake, flocks of panicked birds darkening the sky. The earth beneath the tower trembled as the invaders drew closer. Power lines were ripped free from their poles and lay writhing and sparking on lawns and roadways like a legion of angry serpents. A gas station caught fire, the trio of pumps out front exploding one after the other. *BOOM! BOOM! BOOM!* Fingers of flames reached fifty and sixty feet into the sky—and still the aliens marched on. Even after all this time, Tommy could still picture every last detail inside his head. It was almost as though it had been a scene in a movie he had watched at the drive-in instead of a handful of pages he'd read at bedtime.

Several weeks later, after returning the book to the library—it was seriously overdue by that point and cost him nearly fifty cents in late charges—Tommy finally worked up the nerve to try to climb the water tower that was located only a half dozen blocks from his house. *Try* being the operative word here . . . because that initial attempt had ended after only two or three minutes of climbing and, at most, a thirty-foot ascent. He hadn't lost his nerve at the last moment and chickened out, nor had he been caught by a member of the sheriff's department and ordered to come back down. His hands had simply gotten too sweaty and his fingers had begun slipping off the ladder's metal rungs. So, in the name of common sense and caution, he'd quickly aborted the mission, only to return several days later, wearing a pair of leather batting gloves he'd found at the bottom of his equipment bag.

And wouldn't you know it, that minor adjustment did just the trick—providing him with an ample grip to make his way up the ladder with the speed and agility of a spider monkey. A slight exaggeration perhaps, but you get the picture. There's no one quite so determined as a twelve-year-old boy with a head full of dreams and not even a speck of fear of death.

Once he'd reached the summit of the tower—resisting the overwhelming urge to look down as he climbed—he'd discovered a surprisingly spacious welded steel platform waiting for him. Measuring nearly fifteen feet in length and almost as wide, the metal deck provided a breathtaking view of the town below, while also leading to a guardrail-protected catwalk that encircled the crest of the tower like a silver crown.

Both the deck and catwalk were splattered with yellowish-white splotches of bird shit, but that hadn't bothered Tommy in the least. Feeling as though he were floating amid a dreamscape, he'd sat at the edge of the platform, legs dangling in the open air, and spent the next couple of hours surveying the town in which he'd been born in a way he'd never before imagined. The schools, churches, grocery store, and library; Henderson Memorial Park and the post office, bank, and ball fields; Hanson Creek and the paper mill and his house on Cedar Drive with his mom's apple-red Toyota parked crooked in the driveway—they were all there, stretched out in sun-dappled glory in front of him, looking for all the world like the miniature town his grandfather had built in his basement to go along with his electric train set. Tiny cars and trucks traversed the streets below him. Even tinier people strolled along sidewalks and fished in the creek and picnicked in the park. At some point, the wind picked up, raising gooseflesh on his arms and blowing his hair into his eyes, and Tommy thought in a flush of absolute wonder: *It's like I'm God, sitting on a cloud, looking down over my creation.*

A little later, when he realized he was going to be late for dinner, Tommy climbed down the ladder—forcing himself to take his time—and retrieved his bike from the weeds where he'd hidden it. He pedaled home as fast as he could. His mother, standing in the kitchen wearing an apron, asked where he'd been and how his clothes had gotten so filthy. Not wanting to tell her a lie, he'd quickly replied, "Climbing a ladder." His father, already sitting at the head of the table with his napkin spread over his lap, said, "You be careful, son. You fall and break an arm and your baseball season is over before it gets started." Tommy nodded and sat down in the chair across from him. All of a sudden, he was starving.

On the night of his father's death, Tommy's immediate plan of action was to bury his father in the garden, recite a quick prayer because he knew his mother would have wanted him to, and then go back inside and clean up the mess inside his parents' bedroom.

Only it hadn't worked out that way.

Each time he'd entered the hallway and approached the bedroom—the buzzing of hungry flies piercing his brain with a maddening symphony—his body had betrayed him. With every step he took, his stomach roiled and his vision blurred. Then the floor beneath his feet began to tilt back and forth, and he was forced to make a hasty retreat. Three separate times he'd made the effort, and all three times he'd failed. During his final attempt, just as the sun was peeking over the horizon, his hands had begun shaking so badly that he'd fumbled the bottle of Lysol and roll of paper towels onto the vomit-stained carpet. He'd left them there and fled into the backyard.

After that, he'd spent most of the day roaming around town, the hot July sun beating down on his face and neck, suddenly desperate to make contact with another human being. He'd hiked all the way out to what was left of the roadblock on the highway, but it was no use. The town was silent and still. He was alone. The last man standing. Or in his case, the last boy.

Later that night, unable to summon the energy—or courage—to reenter the house, he'd gone to sleep on an old air mattress on the floor of the shed. When he awoke the next morning, there was a stray fishing lure protruding from his bare shoulder. One final "fuck you" from his coward of a father. The last few weeks, he'd been having weird dreams and tossing and turning most of the night. He must have rolled over on it at some point and gotten snagged like a fat old catfish in Hanson Creek. He'd needed pliers and a splash of rubbing alcohol to remove the treble hook from deep within his skin. After several minutes of yanking and twisting, it finally pulled free. There was quite a bit of blood, but no tears. Tommy was convinced that after everything that had happened, he could no longer feel pain of any kind. His heart was too numb for such luxuries.

Not knowing what else to do or where else to go, he'd wandered downtown and climbed the water tower shortly before noon—and spent the remainder of the day on the metal platform. The view hadn't changed much since happier times, but any sense of wonder had long ago abandoned him. He'd held on to a sliver of hope that from this improved vantage point he might be able to spot someone passing through, but was once again disappointed. Other than his father—"*He's a righteous man . . .* "—it had been weeks since he'd seen another living soul, and today was no different. As evening approached, he'd thought he spotted a plume of smoke coming from somewhere to the east, but it was just some clouds. Finally, around eight, with his stomach growling and the jug of water he'd carried in his backpack drained dry, he'd slung the .22 rifle over his shoulder and scuttled down the ladder, not really caring if he slipped and fell. With the sun setting behind him, he made his way back to the house, smeared peanut butter on some Ritz crackers, and ate his dinner out back beneath the stars. When he was finished, he didn't even bother trying to enter his parents' bedroom. Instead, he sat at his father's workbench in the shed and tried to find a working station on the radio. As usual, there was nothing but static. Once again, he spent the night on an air mattress on the floor. And once again, he dreamt of the old Black woman standing in the cornfield like an ancient

MOVING DAY

scarecrow, a fat orange moon peeking over her bony shoulder. As midnight came and went, the dream slipped away and he finally settled into a deep sleep.

Two long years after Tommy's maiden ascent of the water tower, in a brand-new world that had sprung from a nightmare, it was from that heavenly perch atop the viewing platform that fourteen-year-old Tommy first spotted row after row of black body bags lined up in the parking lot outside of Bennington General Medical Center; watched the parade of olive-green army trucks flood into town on Highway 9; scores of armed soldiers wearing gas masks going house to house, storefront to storefront, escorting frightened townsfolk to the overflow village of hospital tents that had been set up in the field behind the closed-down high school; the government bulldozers, tailpipes burping black exhaust, working day and night, digging burial pits in Henderson Park; and it was from that metal deck in the sky that Tommy felt the sting of acrid smoke in his eyes and smelled the stench of burning flesh—his mother's yellow scarf tied snugly around his neck, covering his nose and mouth—as truckload after truckload of dead bodies were dumped into the trenches, set ablaze with flamethrowers Tommy had only seen before in movies, and eventually buried beneath mounds of dark earth.

Later, after the soldiers were gone—nearly eighty percent of them wiped out by the flu, the survivors fleeing for the Canadian border in a caravan of army trucks—what remained of the population of Bennington abandoned the makeshift tent village and returned to their homes to die. Or in some rare cases, to *live* and try to make sense of what came next. There was no official count of how many townspeople had made it through those first few months alive, but the estimate Tommy overheard a deputy whisper to his father was seventy-one. Seventy-one men, women, and children were all that was left. Everyone else was dead.

On the morning of July 3—two days after he was finally able to muster the nerve to wrap up his father's decaying corpse in a bedsheet and drag it outside into the backyard garden and bury it—Tommy opened a can of peaches for breakfast. A treat he and his dad had once saved for special occasions. Using his fingers, he ate the slices one by one until they were gone, and then he lifted the can to his mouth and gulped down what was left of the juice. When he was finished, he shoved a granola bar and a pack of beef jerky into his backpack, along with a full jug of water, a tube of sunscreen, and a pocketknife. After zipping it closed, he slung the pack over one shoulder and the rifle over the other, feeling a momentary sting when the strap rubbed against his blood-stained bandage (thanks to the damn fishing lure). Closing the backyard gate behind him, he cut across his next-door neighbor's lawn, the knee-high grass swishing against his jeans.

He was once again headed for the water tower, but he wanted to make a stop at the library first. He hadn't been in the mood for reading lately, but with his father gone and his days now free, he'd decided it was time to start up again. Something nice and thick, too. Maybe *The Lord of the Rings* or *Dune*.

Walking down the center of Cedar Drive, detouring around the occasional abandoned vehicle, he glanced at the houses on either side of the road. Many of the windows were boarded-up with sheets of plywood. Most of the curtains in the windows were drawn. Almost all of the front doors were marked with a spray-painted red *X*—verification that the home had been searched and cleared by the soldiers.

It used to feel eerie to Tommy . . . all those empty houses. His friends and neighbors long gone; the sound of his own footfalls deafening in his ears. But after a while, he'd gotten used to it. Just like he'd gotten used to the silence (there'd been a time when he would've done just about anything to hear the thrum of a lawn mower or a hot rod laying rubber on asphalt or the tinkling song of an ice cream truck

MOVING DAY

cruising the block). His father hadn't said much in the days leading up to his death, but there *had* been some conversation. *So, who would I talk to now? If a person stopped speaking for an extended period of time, did they eventually forget how to? Was that even possible?* The idea bothered him very much, and without even realizing he was doing it, he began singing as he walked.

> *"I know I didn't say I was comin down,*
> *I know you didn't know I was here in town,*
> *But bay-yay-yaby you can tell me if anyone can . . . "*

The song was called "Baby, Can You Dig Your Man?" by some guy named Larry Underwood, and in the days before the radio stations went dark, it was all the rage and climbing the charts. It wasn't exactly the Beatles or the Stones, but it did have a catchy hook. For some reason, Tommy hadn't been able to get it out of his head. He began to sing louder.

> *"Baby, can you dig your man?*
> *He's a righteous man,*
> *Tell me baby, can you dig your man?"*

In the beginning, news of the mysterious flu—or Captain Trips, as some members of the media had begun calling it with no real explanation—provided a constant source of fascination for a small-town kid like Tommy Harper. It was like something out of one of the science fiction novels he liked to read.

Each time a new piece of information appeared in the newspaper or on one of the television newscasts, Tommy was eager to discuss it with someone. The only problem was . . . *who?* His handful of friends from school couldn't have been less interested if their lives had depended on it. All they wanted to talk about were the Red Sox and video games and what color bikini seventeen-year-old homecoming queen Tiffany Watson was wearing at the pool on any given day. His mother wasn't really an option, either. She was a worrier, prone to cutting him off in midsentence and bowing her head in prayer every time Tommy brought up a depressing subject. His sister, Jennifer, was the worst of the bunch. Her boyfriend ("Pizza Face" to his pals on the football team) had recently broken up with her and started dating an older girl who was new to town. Jenn was devastated. If she wasn't lying in bed, wiping tears from her face as she scribbled in her journal, she was sitting outside in the backyard with a box of Kleenex on her lap, eating ice cream from the carton and listening to sad songs on the radio. It had only been two weeks, and she'd already gained five pounds from eating away her sorrows. In her current state, she probably didn't even know that there was a communicable disease making its way through numerous cities.

That left Tommy's father, and while he was much more practical than the others and a whole lot easier to talk to, as sheriff he was also super busy. Tommy had listened in on a couple of his dad's official phone calls and heard him talking about preliminary coordination plans with the hospital and where on Highway 9 they would set up roadblocks if such measures were to become necessary. During another call, Tommy heard him addressing the person on the other line as "Colonel Perkins" and carefully repeating a phone number as he wrote it down. One night, after his father had hung up the telephone, Tommy walked into the den and asked if he should be worried. Sheriff Harper assured his son that there was nothing at all to be concerned about. The government doctors and scientists were working around the clock on a cure, and before long everything would return to normal. And that was good enough for Tommy. After all, if you couldn't trust your own dad, who just happened to also be law enforcement, who could you trust?

MOVING DAY

Tommy sat at the edge of the tower platform, his legs dangling over the side, and felt the sun hammering down on his shoulders. His knapsack was full of books from the library, but he was too damn hot to read. He had peeled off his T-shirt about an hour ago, tearing the bandage on his shoulder in the process, and rolled up his jeans to his knees. It hadn't helped much; it felt like he was melting.

I could bring a tent up here, he thought, wiping the sweat out of his eyes. *It would have to be a small one, but that's all I'd need. And nothing too bright, so it blends in.*

"Who the hell's gonna notice it anyway?" he spoke aloud. "No one. That's who."

There was a time, not long after the soldiers had left, that a fairly constant parade of strangers had passed through town. A handful traveling alone, but most of them in groups. One solitary man arrived on horseback. A few others on motorcycles. But the majority were on foot.

On several occasions, Tommy had laid down on his stomach across the metal platform and peered over the edge, spying on the outsiders. Using his father's binoculars, he'd watched as they searched the stores and houses for food and supplies, all of it long plundered by then and either consumed or squirreled away. One couple stopped and fished for a while in Hanson Creek, but then quickly moved on when they didn't have any luck. An older man with gray hair down to the crack of his ass strolled down Main Street, stark naked and singing church hymns. Another time, Tommy saw two women emerge from the woods and make their way along the edge of town, stopping only to search a handful of cars that had been involved in a head-on collision. A moment later, he noticed a bearded man following maybe forty yards behind them, scuttling from tree to tree, car to car, house to house. Working that hard to hide his presence, the man was obviously up to no good. And the two women appeared completely unaware. Tommy scooted to the opposite side of the platform and watched this cat-and-mouse pursuit until all three of them disappeared. And he never once uttered a word of warning to the unsuspecting women, something he still felt guilty about to this day.

But that wasn't even the worst of it. On a cloudy afternoon in late May, a caravan of cars and trucks arrived in Bennington from the direction of Highway 9. Tommy, awakened from his nap by the roar of their engines, counted sixteen vehicles from his perch atop the water tower. The lead car, driving way too fast, made a wrong turn by the high school, and the whole group of them ended up bumper to bumper on the dead-end street where the tower was located. It took them nearly ten minutes of cussing and horn blowing to get out of each other's way and turn around, plenty of time for Tommy to get a good look. Something he quickly regretted.

Several of the trucks had been rigged with what looked like machine-gun turrets on the reinforced roofs of their cabs. Others had makeshift cages in their flatbeds. They were crammed full of both male and female prisoners—all of them Black. A number of cars had swastikas spray-painted on their hoods. Holding his breath, Tommy watched as they drove out of town, looking like a wiry, metallic snake. Once they were gone and the road dust had settled, he'd climbed down as fast as he could and ran home to tell his father.

News kept coming of the flu—eventually even Tommy's friends began to pay attention to the distressing stories being reported from around the country—and with each newspaper headline and breaking news television broadcast, it became more and more difficult for Tommy to believe his father's words of reassurance. Yet, even with that creeping dread forming in the back of his mind, the fascination remained.

In faraway cities and towns, still a safe distance from Bennington, Vermont, schools and businesses were shuttering their doors. Airline flights were being grounded, and trains and buses had ceased running. There were curfews and quarantines in place in many locations. In others, food and water was being rationed. For Tommy, it reminded

MOVING DAY

him of the forty-eight-hour power outage—caused by high winds and lightning strikes—that had occurred in Bennington when he was ten. The idea of a blackout had felt a little exciting to him, but also kind of unsettling. The entire town had gone dark and silent. Televisions and telephones didn't work. Some radios were okay, as long as you had fresh batteries, but if you didn't, you were shit out of luck because the stores were all closed. The same went for flashlights. Tommy's father had reported for emergency duty and was busy the whole time, so that left Tommy, Mom, and Jennifer all alone in the house. He and his sister played Monopoly by candlelight and helped their mother move all the food from the refrigerator and freezer into Styrofoam coolers lined up on the kitchen floor. Even the grown-ups appeared wary and alert, the sudden loss of electricity a blunt reminder that civilization as we knew it existed upon a very fragile foundation. When it was time to go to bed that first night, Tommy watched his mother double-check the locks on the front door, and then walk a wide circle in the living room to check them for a third time. The three of them slept in the same bed both nights.

The fascination didn't last. As soon as the national fatality statistics began pouring in—initially from Texas, Oklahoma, and Arkansas, but soon followed by the entire East Coast—and news broke of flu outbreaks spreading from the larger metropolitan areas and making their way into suburban and rural regions, any hint of excitement drained away for Tommy Harper. Graphic images began appearing on nightly newscasts—naked corpses stacked up like cordwood outside of hospitals; dead bodies scattered across desolate streets and sidewalks in places like Baltimore and Philadelphia and now even Boston—horrifying millions of stunned viewers and sparking violent riots and mass evacuations.

But even at fourteen years old, Tommy Harper knew the hard truth: there was nowhere safe to go. By then, he'd realized that his father had been wrong. Dad hadn't lied to him that night in the den—he'd simply been overconfident and mistaken. Captain Trips was on the move and there was no stopping it now. People in Bennington had begun closing the curtains on their windows and locking their doors during the day. Martin's Sporting Goods had sold out of rifles and ammunition. Sunday church services were standing room only, many parishioners wearing scarfs or bandannas over their mouths and refusing to make skin-to-skin contact.

Soon, the rumors began to spread. Evacuees from as far away as Albany and Boston were headed their way by the busloads. A deal had been struck with the mayor to set up a temporary encampment by the lake. Jason Stanwell, the hunky gym teacher at the middle school, was sick in bed with the flu. His girlfriend, who worked at the Radio Shack in the mall, had deserted him and gone home to Montpelier to stay with her mother. Hospital officials were lying to the public. The morgue located in the hospital basement was already overflowing with flu victims and there weren't enough beds upstairs to take care of the dying. The governor was about to declare martial law, and the army and National Guard were arriving soon to take over the town.

None of the rumors proved deadlier than the truth.

Just before sundown, Tommy heard the growl of the motorcycle's engine.

It was another thirty seconds before he actually saw it, and in that brief span of time he wondered if he might be dreaming. Or even imagining the sound. Lately, he'd given a lot of thought to what it might feel like to go crazy. *Would I even know if it was happening?*

Then he blinked and the black-and-chrome Harley-Davidson carrying a pair of helmeted riders made the wide turn onto Sycamore Lane. It continued at a leisurely pace through the intersection and eventually swung a hard right onto Park Drive. Once it reached the gravel shoulder in front of the grassy rise bordering the edge of the woods, the driver pulled over, engaged the kickstand, and switched off the engine.

MOVING DAY

The passenger dismounted first and removed her helmet. Long hair, either blond or gray, cascaded below her shoulders. It was hard to tell from this distance, but she looked to be in her forties or fifties. Slight in stature, she was dressed for a dinner party instead of a road trip. A frilly cream blouse and pleated pants. She was even carrying a pocketbook.

The driver, tall and lean, took off his helmet and hung it from the handlebars. He got off the bike and stretched his muscular arms above his head. Much younger than his companion, he wore jeans and a black T-shirt and appeared to be in his mid- to late twenties. Chiseled face. Sandy-brown hair cut below his ears. An unkempt, tawny beard. He walked a short distance away, turned his back on the woman, and urinated in the grass. The woman said something Tommy couldn't quite hear, and there was the sound of their muffled laughter. When he was finished, the driver zipped up his pants and sauntered back to the motorcycle. Something about the way he moved looked familiar to Tommy. It was *smooth*, like he was an athlete or maybe an actor. Smooth, and cocky.

As Tommy watched from atop the water tower, the strangers went to work setting up a tent on the hillside overlooking town. It was bright orange and not very big. Just enough room for the two of them. *They're going to stay the night!* Tommy thought with a glimmer of excitement. *Maybe even longer than that!*

The woman disappeared into the trees for a moment—no doubt relieving her bladder in private—and upon her return, immediately dropped to her knees and crawled inside the tent. The man followed right behind her.

Tommy changed positions on the metal platform and waited to see if either of them came out again. When it got too dark to see, he climbed down and went home to the shed in the backyard.

That night, he dreamt of the old woman in the cornfield again. For the first time, she spoke to him. But he couldn't make out what she was saying. In the dream, he was standing right in front of her. The woman's lips were moving, but there was no sound.

Frustrated, he woke up shortly after one a.m. and couldn't fall back asleep. He went outside and sat on the back stoop. His neck ached from a third restless night on the air mattress. *Enough is enough*, he thought. He would have to do something about that soon. What he really wanted was a cigarette. Even one would make him feel better. His mom would have a fit if she knew he felt that way . . . but his mom wasn't there to lecture him. Tommy didn't know where she was. Maybe nowhere.

He wasn't sure if he believed in heaven or not. He used to, back when he'd gone to Sunday school, but that was a long time ago. Was she somewhere high above watching over him? Did she know that he was thinking of her right now? Or was she really just . . . gone, like a light bulb that had blinked out . . . rotting away in the ground with all the others at Henderson Park?

Jenn had gotten sick first. She'd complained of a headache on a Monday afternoon and laid down on the sofa with a wet washcloth on her forehead. Dad, who was home from the station for a quick lunch, whispered to his wife that the girl was probably just being dramatic. Jenn was still getting over her breakup with Herb and prone to extended periods of histrionics. But by Tuesday, her face a scarlet mask, she was bedridden with a fever of 103.7. Despite the dangers, Mom had insisted on taking care of Jennifer herself. She'd steadfastly refused to take her to the hospital. There were no open beds, and the last thing she was willing to do was abandon her daughter to a bunch of overworked doctors and nurses who may or may not have had time to render proper treatment in an overcrowded hallway.

The following morning, Jenn started vomiting blood, and within hours, her throat began to swell. By nightfall, she was dead.

A week later, Tommy woke up late one morning. Rubbing the sleep from his eyes, he walked down the hall toward the bathroom—but stopped when he realized how quiet the house was. By this time, his father was on emergency duty with the sheriff's department and gone for an average of eighteen hours a day. With Jennifer gone, that left his mother. Usually, she was clanging around in the kitchen or running the washing machine and dryer or at the very least playing the news on the television set in the den. But today there was none of that.

A shiver of dread creeping along his spine, Tommy continued down the hallway to his parents' bedroom. The door was cracked. He pushed it open.

In the far corner of the bed, Joanne Harper lay twisted on her side, one arm stretched past her head as if she were reaching for something on the floor. Her bulging eyes stared sightlessly at the wall and her cracked lips were parted in a sneer. Directly below her mouth, there was an enormous puddle of bloody vomit soaking into the mattress. Her neck was a swollen tube of blackened flesh.

Unable to breathe, Tommy backed away in horror. He hadn't even known that his mother was sick. They'd eaten dinner together the night before, and after doing the dishes, she'd curled up on the sofa to read a book. A couple of hours later, she'd paused at his bedroom door to say good night. He didn't remember hearing her coughing, and she hadn't complained at all. Not a word. He ran down the hallway into the kitchen to call his father. It would be two hours before he was able to reach him.

Despite the strange dreams and lack of sleep, Tommy was excited to get back to the water tower and see what his visitors were up to. *Should I go over and introduce myself? Or should I keep my distance and remain hidden?* He couldn't decide. On the one hand, they looked harmless enough. On the other, he was all alone now and had to be more careful than ever.

By the time he got there and climbed the ladder to the platform, he had convinced himself that none of these questions mattered. The grassy rise would be empty, the strangers packed up and gone, with nothing so much as a scrap of litter left behind to show that they had once been there.

But he was wrong. The bright orange tent was still pitched on the upper hillside. The black Harley leaning to the side on its kickstand right where they'd left it.

His heart thumping, Tommy stretched out on his stomach and rested his chin in his hands, anxious for the man and woman to wake up.

He didn't have to wait for long.

A few minutes later, the man crawled out of the tent and stood up to face the sun. He was buck naked.

"*Holy shit,*" Tommy whispered, suppressing a laugh.

Far below, the man appeared to turn and spit into the grass—and then he stood ramrod straight and burst into song.

"O say, can you see,
by the dawn's early light,
What so proudly we hailed
at the twilight's last gleaming..."

"What the hell is he—"

"Whose broad stripes and bright stars,
through the perilous fight,
O'er the ramparts we watched,
were so gallantly streaming?"

And then all of a sudden Tommy understood. It was the Fourth of July! He couldn't believe he'd forgotten. After Christmas and Halloween, it was his favorite holiday. He stole a glance over his shoulder at Main Street and pictured what it had once looked like. Red, white, and blue bunting draped over the storefronts; banners hanging across the road; American flags and ribbons everywhere. The parade started

MOVING DAY

at two p.m., followed by the carnival in the park at three, and finally once it got dark, the big fireworks display. Tommy and his family used to sit on a blanket by the bandstand, eating ice cream sandwiches and watermelon slices until the sky lit up. Little kids ran around with sparklers. From the park, you could hear hooting and hollering and splashing coming from the pool. And for that one night each year, it felt like the entire town came out to celebrate.

"*. . . and the home of the braaaave!*"

The man finished singing "The Star-Spangled Banner" and Tommy glanced down just in time to see him snap a peppy salute in the direction of the tent. And then the man was crawling back inside, offering a perfect, sunlit view of his bare ass.

Now he'll either go back to sleep for a while, Tommy thought, *or they'll both come out of the tent and, hey, maybe the woman will be naked, too.* He peered over the edge of the platform again. Nothing stirred in the tent. *Jesus, she's old enough to be my mother,* he scolded himself.

Before he could remind himself that he was only fifteen, and even in the midst of a plague-ridden world it was perfectly natural to think about naked women, even if they were a lot older than—

Far below, on the hillside, the man scrambled out of the tent on his knees and vomited into the grass. When there was nothing left to come up, he scuttled away like a crab in the sand, and placed his hands over his face. Tommy could hear him sobbing. *Where's the woman?* he thought, returning his attention to the tent. *What in the hell happened to the woman?*

A short time later, he got his answer.

The naked man, no longer looking even a little bit cocky, struggled to his feet. He went to the woods and found a long stick. Then he slowly approached the tent, turned back the flap, and used the point of the stick to retrieve his clothes from inside.

"*Jesus,*" Tommy whispered.

The man sat in the grass and put them on. When he stood up again, he lifted the shirt to his nose and smelled it—and made an immediate beeline for the motorcycle. He started the engine and sped off toward downtown. A moment later, he turned onto Main Street and pulled over in front of the Bennington's Men's Shop. The front door was unlocked, so he went inside. In a matter of minutes, he was back on the sidewalk, wearing a different shirt and carrying a pile of new clothes in his arms. He stuffed them into one of the saddlebags on the back of the Harley, and got moving again. This time, due east along Highway 9, and with little regard for the speed limit. Tommy watched until the Harley disappeared. The man never so much as tapped his brakes.

TOMMY PARKER
ROADTRIP JOURNAL ENTRY #1
JULY 4

After much deliberation, I decided not to peek inside the tent. There was no reason to, really. I already knew what I would find.

At first, I was bothered by what the man had done. Leaving the woman unburied in the middle of a strange town not only felt heartless but also a little bit chickenshit. Even if the two of them hadn't known each other all that well—which I had no way of actually knowing, of course—it still felt like the woman deserved better.

But then as the day went on, I began to look at things differently.

After all, who was I to say how many others the Harley man had already buried?

I don't have even the slightest clue what burdens he carried along with him, so who am I to judge?

Maybe that's how the man survived on the road as long as he

MOVING DAY

had . . . by never looking back and always looking forward . . . by always moving forward.

Hell, I might only be fifteen, but that's something I could learn a thing or two about myself. Moving forward.

I've decided I'm going to leave Bennington and look for other survivors. I've decided I no longer want to be alone. I want to live. Or at the very least, die trying.

Tommy closed the leather-bound journal his sister gave him for Christmas last year and tucked it away inside his knapsack. *I'll think about you, sis, every time I write in it.*

He took one final look around at the town in which he'd been born. It was dusk and difficult to make out details, but that didn't matter. He knew these streets and buildings like the back of his hand. He stared at where he knew his house was, nothing more now than a dark blob lost among many other dark blobs. *It's okay*, he thought. *Home is wherever I find myself at the end of each new day. And I will always take you with me. Mom. Dad. Jenn. I love you and miss you so much.*

With tears in his eyes, he slung his backpack over one shoulder and the rifle over the other. He reached for the metal railing at the top of the ladder and began to turn around to make his final descent—

—when far off to the east, a burst of fireworks lit up the night sky. A red, white, and blue spray with squiggles and spirals and whirly-whirls, all of them sputtering in unison and transforming into a gentle shower of glowing embers, like pixie dust in a storybook.

That's *where I'm headed*, he thought, looking toward the east. He started climbing. *That's where I'll find others.*

And smiling in the dark, a hundred feet off the ground, he began singing:

"Baby, can you dig your man? He's a righteous man. Tell me baby, can you dig your man?"

LA MALA HORA

Alex Segura

I felt his tiny hand tighten in mine.

His small, thin fingers tensing up—the chipped, almost flimsy nails digging into my skin.

I looked down at my son, Danny. He'd just turned eight—just had a birthday. I say it that way because we don't celebrate birthdays anymore. There's nothing to be happy about. There's no hope. There's just darkness.

But I can't tell him this, no matter how badly I want to. No matter how much I'll wish I had.

Two months ago, things were different. We were making plans—like people foolishly do before fate slams a wrench into their midsection. I can picture it, too—that last calm feeling, right before it all went to hell. Looking out the large bay windows of our house, tucked in the suburbs of southwest Miami. I could see Danny playing in the front yard as I talked to my mom. I was asking her about how many cupcakes to make, what kind of goody bags we should have. The mundane stuff that feels so much more powerful in the rearview. These things that fade with every thought—become less tangible, like a puff of smoke being swept away by the wind.

My name is Desi Calderon, and I'm not sure how much time I have left.

How much time *we* have left.

This thought sits with me for hours. Perhaps days. As we make our way, slowly, north from Miami. First in my mom's banged-up Mazda 626. Then in anything else we find that works and, by some miracle, has gas. I hesitated at first—taking keys from the dead. Fumbling through their pockets and purses, like some panicked thief, their bodies spread out and around the street, like something out of a Romero movie—detritus, but not always. They were people once.

We were, too.

The irony—if there is such a thing—is that Danny and I left before, well, everything. Before "Captain Trips." Before the darkness. Before everything collapsed. Dead bodies everywhere, no light, no air-conditioning, nothing. In what felt like an instant, the world went dark—but we were already making our way out of town.

Even before the virus, I feared for my life. For my son's life.

I feel the soft thud of my worn-out sneakers on the asphalt. I feel a soft, tropical breeze slap my face and I almost smile—the gust slicing through the heat like those paper airplanes I'd toss in class when I was a kid. It felt so good. Nothing felt good anymore. *I want to feel this breeze forever*, I thought.

We'd gotten as far as the Fort Lauderdale airport in my mom's car. It crapped out a mile or so away from the ramp to 595. But it wasn't like we were moving much by then, anyway. Cars were stopped across I-95, a sprawling array of metal tombstones, clogging one of the biggest pathways across the country. It was too much to process. But somehow, we were alive—Danny and me. My little man—his face so placid and caring, those deep, dark, knowing eyes. That perpetually thoughtful expression. I wanted to hold him close and make him feel safe—whisper that this was just a bad dream, that we were going somewhere good and calm and cool—but he was smart enough to know that wasn't happening.

I'm coming for him.

The words popped out in front of my mind—like a ghoul stepping into the light of a hallway, eyes aflame, mouth open and pleading. Erik's voice hadn't been pleading, or desperate—it'd been focused. That's what had initially scared me, before any of this other shit happened. The idea that this man I'd left behind, this man I'd gone to every length possible to get away from, knew where to find me and our son.

"Where are we sleeping, Mami?"

Danny's question pulls me out of my own mind. I tighten my fingers around his hand and look around. We were near Pompano Beach now. After the car died on 95, we tried to get off the highway—stepping over the bodies, around the car wrecks, through ravines and down ramps. *The side streets are going to be our best bet*, I thought. We could find a car and bob and weave through the back alleys and roads and just keep going. Away from all this, away from Erik—toward something else. Toward my dreams.

Of that woman.

Mother Abagail.

Something about the dreams feels different. They're not just fevered visions, products of discomfort, desperate meals, and anxiety like nothing I've ever experienced. No, the dreams are almost real—like I'm tapping into something new, something primal. I see her. I feel her calling to us. Telling us to keep going.

But where?

I long for anything else—for the mundane tasks of my project manager job: the phone calls, the spreadsheets, the tedious meetings, and awkward lunches with my boss, who I knew wanted to sleep with me. Just looking for any kind of opening or signal to make his move. I must have seemed like easy prey to him. Single mom, recently divorced, new on the job. I let him think what he wanted. I'd needed the job. Now it all just seems like a blurry vision.

"We'll find a room, Danny," I said, pulling him in closer.

I could feel his frame, the bones of his body jutting out more than they ever had before. We hadn't been eating well—the flurry of opportunity that came right after the virus struck was gone. The stores had been picked dry, if not by people then by animals. We were lucky if we found cans—the can opener I'd yanked from a gas station in Hollywood felt like my prize possession now. A key to survival.

It was getting late. On days like this, when we couldn't find a car—couldn't pilfer keys or find something with gas in it, we just hoofed it. Just tried to make our way up the state. I loved walking—which was rare down here, where everyone stayed indoors, and if they had to go anywhere they hopped into their little air-conditioned cars and zipped around. Pedestrians were unicorns. We'd found a few crappy umbrellas from an Eckerd drugstore we passed along the way—a flimsy shield from the Florida sun that we'd packed in a crappy rolling suitcase dragged behind us, on the rare moments a cloud would block the blazing light. Sweltering heat aside, I loved the activity, no matter how hot it got.

Not my Danny, though.

He wanted to be on the couch, the temperature set to seventy-two, with a book in his lap—already reading fantasy novels and horror comics and *Archie* digests. I could leave him there for hours if I wanted to. He wasn't made for what the world was now. Haunted. Streaked with blood and bile. A smear over the map of what was once alive, vibrant—beautiful. This god-awful state. It just felt fucking endless.

Florida was miserable that way. Getting out of South Florida felt like such a victory—but it was a mirage. The area was endless—and once you got past Palm Beach, there was nothing . . . a shimmering void until at least Orlando, maybe farther if you were trying to get to Gainesville or, God forbid, Pensacola or Tallahassee. It felt like a series of challenges—a gauntlet of tests that I was never meant to face.

For me, a Cuban girl who grew up in Kendall listening to Célia and visiting my *abuela*'s house in Little Havana, the state north of Miami Shores felt almost alien. There'd never been a need to go anywhere else. I had everything at home. My job, my car, my Danny—

And Erik. At least for a while.

I saw a tiny hotel—motel, really. Beachfront deal. Small, faded pink paint, cramped, but hopeful. Surely there was an empty room—a bed that wasn't festering with giant palmetto bugs and, if we were lucky, some sputtering water in the pipes. I imagined a shower. I didn't dare think of hot water. But a shower would be nice. Perhaps a place to make a fire and warm up one of the six cans of Goya *frijoles negros* in my backpack.

I'm coming for him.

I felt a shiver run up my arm. I chalked it up to hunger. I stepped over a body—a man bundled in a large coat for some reason and who'd probably died here. I couldn't make out his face, but I took that as a grace, not a missed opportunity. For a second, I thought I saw him fidget. But I pressed on, pulling Danny next to me, away from yet another fallen shape. Another life cut short—an incomplete chord, a few notes left silent.

I turned the knob on the front door and almost let out a sob as it opened. Danny handed me the small flashlight we'd picked up in Lauderhill and I flicked it on. We were in a tiny lobby area—I'd learned, over the last few weeks, to not linger over things. Not in places we were only passing through. Usually the smell said enough—whether there were bodies or food or animals festering. But you never knew. Sometimes you'd catch a glimpse of someone hunched back, their face melting off—flesh torn away by a desperate cat or animal, or worse. I shuddered to think about what Danny had seen in those moments. How each image had gnawed away at what little innocence was left in him.

I let the flashlight's glare dance across the opposite wall. I pulled back once I saw it—the words smeared across what was once a bare, pale stucco. The long *L* almost reaching from ceiling to just above a tattered couch positioned next to the front desk. I didn't need to bring the light back to read the words—I didn't need to think about what the dark, red paint it was written in truly was.

AHORA EMPIEZA LA MALA HORA

Roughly translated it meant "now begins the bad hour." But *la mala hora* was much more than that. A story my *abuelas* told me. Of a dark figure—a specter of bad tidings—who appeared in the blackest moments of night, bringing with him bad luck and hopelessness—a messenger of evil that haunted the gray corners of dusk and dawn. Once you were caught in *la mala hora*, there was no hope. There was no chance of escape. You were dead.

"What was that?" Danny asked.

I thought about pulling him back, about turning around and trying to walk a few more blocks—perhaps a few more miles—to find something else. Something less ideal, but certainly less terrifying. But if I was tired, I knew Danny was feeling worse. *La mala hora*—it was everywhere. Settling into this motel for one night wouldn't make a difference, I thought. I said a quick *padre nuestro* and pulled Danny into the motel behind me, the flashlight turned down toward the floor, illuminating only what was right in front of us.

We managed to find a room on the third floor. It was a mess, but it was empty—and after stripping the bed, it seemed almost livable after the journey to get inside. My heart ached each time I had to motion for Danny to step over a body or look away from something I knew he'd seen—a limb, a dead mother clutching something that was no longer there, or worse . . . the blood. Streaks of it. Droplets.

LA MALA HORA

The kind of red you knew meant only one thing, even at Danny's young age.

I set up the portable, battery-powered lantern on the dresser to illuminate the space. I saw the loaded handgun, tucked in the back of our stuffed carry-on luggage. I barely knew how to use it. I never wanted to. But when we'd walked by the gun store on Bird Road, I knew we needed it. Something. Anything. "Just in case" became a lot more likely now. The chance that we'd have to point a gun at something—someone—was almost a certainty. I closed my eyes for a second, then turned to look at the small space we'd found for the night, the lantern's light showing more than I probably wanted to see.

The room was drab and dusty. That felt like a victory, at least. The bad stuff was outside the door—the blood, the bodies, the sounds. I felt my throat tighten as I watched Danny methodically change into his blue spaceship pajamas, as if everything was just fine—we were on a family trip, heading to see friends or his *abuelos*, perhaps even to Disney World or Epcot. I remembered dreading those trips. The lack of sleep. The dysregulated behavior. The tantrums. Erik was no help. He'd either make a beeline for the hotel bar or just drink in the room, and if he got a few rounds in and something set him off, I had to react. I learned, over time, that the best thing to do was to leave—to bite the bullet and take Danny out, to the park or anywhere, and just hope Erik didn't destroy everything while we were gone. He had become a shell of a man to me at that point—a husk that resembled someone I knew, someone I fell in love with. In my more rational moments, I knew it was the drinking. That he was sick. But at other times, when I had to hurry our son outside of a cheap hotel room because his father was throwing up in the bathroom or screaming at the top of his lungs about some tiny, perceived slight—it was at those times I hated him. I wanted him to die.

"Fucker probably *is* dead. Good."

I muttered the words to myself as I pulled my ragged shirt up over my head and rummaged through our bag for something new and clean to wear. There wasn't any—even the relatively new clothes we'd taken from the abandoned Mervyn's store we found on the way felt used up. Everything was soiled and dirty or torn—almost everyone was dead, and for some reason, Danny and I were okay. On paper, that was a blessing, but in moments like these—pure exhaustion being the only thing I could feel, think about, or understand—it felt like we somehow got shortchanged. Was it really living if we had to live like this—with nothing, no infrastructure, no friends or family, no safety net? I couldn't even turn on the news to see what was happening in the world. This big, sprawling world that felt so small because of technology was just cramped and empty, with only a tiny crack of light showing what was to come.

I wanted to die.

"Can you tuck me in, Mami?"

I met Danny's eyes and walked over to where he'd situated himself on the small full-size bed. He was curled up on the far corner of the mattress, a pile of relatively clean towels serving as blankets bunched together around him, his tiny feet and toes still peeking out from under. He was using his big stuffed white tiger—the one we got from IKEA when he was three—as a pillow. It was large enough that he could place his head on it and still clutch the tiger's puffy, white and black face, its expression blank and distant. I leaned over and gave Danny a kiss on the forehead, pulling one of the towels up toward his chin as I did. I looked at him, his eyes at half-mast, his mouth slightly open. He was so tired. He'd been such a trooper this whole time. Of course, parenthood was often about grading on a curve. I knew that.

He had complained. He had cried. He had yelled a bit. But all in all, considering, well, everything . . . he'd done great. I leaned forward and pulled his small body toward me, feeling his slow breathing on my neck, the warmth of his face on my cheek. How he still seemed to smell of that kids' shampoo we used at home, before. When showers and baths were not a luxury.

I didn't realize I was crying until he spoke.

"It's okay, Mami," he said, placing his hand on my cheek in the intentional, stiff way of a child imitating a parent. He was trying to comfort me, and somehow that made me feel worse. "We'll be fine."

I didn't respond. I just pulled him closer. I wanted to pull him in so tight, so hard, that he'd disappear into me, that I'd yank us both into another place—a new world. A better world, far from here.

Skrrrrtch.
Skrrrrttttttcchhh.
Skkkkrrrrrrttttttccccchhh.

My eyes opened slowly from deep sleep. It'd felt like the first real sleep in months, maybe more. The woman was there—Mother Abagail. She'd been looking at me, talking to me, but I couldn't make it all out. She wanted me to come to her, toward her. But where, I asked? How? What about Danny? I could only make out a few words.

"He will be fine, in his own way."

Then she was gone, a quick cut to the darkness of the room, the only light peeking from the broken blinds—a dim moonlight sneaking into our third-floor motel room.

But that noise.

Skrrrrtch.
Skrrrrttttttcchhh.
Skkkkrrrrrrttttttccccchhh.

My first instinct was to ignore the sound. The distant, soft scraping. Like someone dragging a rack across a carpeted floor. But that was an instinct of the old world, I told myself. Of a time where houses made creaking sounds, sirens and car horns were almost ambient, and hotel yells and hollers were normal and to be ignored—because there were people around doing things, living their lives, and sometimes enjoying them.

Those days were over.

I looked at Danny, still asleep. A peaceful, relaxed state. No worries. No fears. He still held on to that innocence in a way of which I was almost jealous.

I slid out of bed, moving my arm out from under him. I stepped toward our bag, placed on the other bed. My hand weaving inside carefully, feeling for the cold metal, wrapping my fingers around the handle. I felt the heavy metal touch my thigh as I walked toward the door—the door I'd barricaded with a chair here in the room, in addition to the bolt lock that wouldn't be able to do much if things got bad. Worse actually, as they were going to be very bad for a long time.

I leaned my head against the door and listened. Nothing. I stepped back and looked at Danny, still curled up into himself, still sleeping.

I thought of the dream—of Mother Abagail's rough hand, sliding down my face. I could feel every wrinkle and blister. I could see her eyes. Why do these dreams feel so vivid, so unlike anything else?

Thump.

I froze. I heard that. I watched as Danny rustled in his sleep—on the precipice of being awoken, but still clinging to a dream.

The sound had been low and heavy—from the hallway. Like a few sacks of groceries dropped outside our door. My grip on the gun tightened. I felt my thoughts spinning, darting around. Do I wake Danny up? Do we try to bolt and run for the stairs? I should have mapped out another exit, just in case. A contingency. But we'd been so tired. We'd walked for days. And for once, just once, I wanted to rest—to not think about worst-case scenarios, what we might eat, or how we were going to get to the next day. Just for goddamn once.

The sound, but different now. Softer. A light, rhythmic thudding. Footsteps.

Right outside. We had to move.

I didn't have the luxury of cracking the door open—I couldn't just pop my head out to see what was coming. If we were opening this door, we were running, and if we were running, we weren't coming back.

LA MALA HORA

I turned to grab Danny—to try and, as gently as possible, get him awake and moving, quietly. But as I stepped back and looked at the bed, my heart just about exploded.

He was gone.

The towels were there—hastily spread out. The stuffed tiger was there, too, splayed out near the foot of the bed. But Danny was gone. I strained to look around the small, dark room.

"Danny?" I hissed his name, desperate and frightened. "Danny, *donde estas?*"

I darted into the cramped bathroom. Nothing.

I moved back into the main room itself, the moonlight sneaking through the window serving as the only illumination.

There was only one place he could have gone.

I crouched down and looked under the bed. There he was, way back against the wall, the white of his eyes visible even in this darkness. He was clutching himself, trying to make himself as small as he could. I reached a hand out to him.

"Danny, come out," I whispered. "We have to go."

"*Mami*, no, they're coming—*he's* coming," Danny said, the fear plain on his face. His voice sounding off-balance and delirious, as if he were still mid-dream. "He's coming to get me, Mami."

I moved to the other side of the bed, which brought me a little closer to him, though he was still out of reach. I crouched down and tried to slide farther under the bed, but I couldn't fit. I reached out my hand, palm up, and raised my voice slightly.

"Danny, we need to leave this place, right now, okay?" I said, trying to remain calm, trying to give off a sense that this was all part of the plan. But Danny was smart. There was no plan anymore. We were in hell, and we just wanted to try and survive. "Please come out, sweetie, okay? I need to figure out how—"

Thump.

Louder. Closer.

I pushed myself under the bed, feeling my back lifting up the metal frame and squeezing myself through, the adrenaline muting whatever pain I'd feel later. If there was a later.

My hand roughly grabbed Danny's arm and I tugged him toward me and out from under the bed, ignoring his squeal of surprise. I stood up, panting, clutching him to me, my arm wrapped around him—my other hand still clutching the gun. We were both breathing heavily in the darkened room, my eyes locked on the door. I looked at the flimsy chair in the gloom, propped against the handle. The noise had stopped.

But the door handle was moving. Jerking up and down, faster each time.

I saw the metal handle turn down slightly, then back up, clicking and clacking, but not fully opening. Whoever was on the other side was desperate to get in, and we had nowhere else to go.

"*Mami*, what—"

"Don't worry," I said, like a reflex—words I'd said so often they became almost mantra-like. "Get behind me."

I looked around the darkened room—hoping I could find something, anything I'd missed before. A secret tunnel. A ladder. A magical warp that would send us to another level far from this dank, terrible place where everything was broken, dirty, and cracked, where nothing felt right. I wanted to curl up and cry for days—to just expel everything and then fade into the soil, to be recycled and fed into the earth so I could be of use to something again.

But, of course, I couldn't do any of that.

I looked down at Danny, his arms now wrapped around my leg. I could see his eyes watering. His bottom lip jutted out in that way it did when he was about to start bawling. *Please God, don't cry now*, I thought. I crouched down, the jangling of the door handle getting faster, and pulled him in close.

"We're going to be fine," I said, trying to keep my tone flat, my eyes locked on his. "Mommy won't let—"

"It's Daddy," he blurted out.

"What?"

"It's Daddy," Danny said, looking past me now, toward the door. "He's here. He's coming for me. He wants me b—"

A clicking. I felt a coldness cover every inch of my body. The bolt lock. But *how?* I wondered.

I heard the creaking of the door—it was opening, it was *opening*—and I spun around. I watched the door hit the chair and stop, the top of the chair locked under the handle, preventing it from opening any wider. I heard that scratching sound again, against the door—and I started to get a better sense of what it was. Nails on wood. Scraping. Clawing. Desperate to get inside. Then I heard something else. Something I would never forget.

Breathing. Dank. Heavy. Labored. Like a dying animal crawling into the woods, eager to find a quiet, cool place to die.

I stood up and shoved Danny behind me, my hands raised, wrapped around the gun, which I was pointing toward the door. No. It wasn't him. Couldn't be him. Erik. That prick. He was dead. Like everyone else.

"*I'm coming . . .*"

The voice, like a boot stepping on shattered glass—sharp and jagged, highs and lows blended together to make a monstrous sound. But a voice, nonetheless. A man's voice.

"*I'm coming for . . .*" it said, the door jostling now. I could see the chair shaking, slowly being dislodged from its place. The last bit of defense between us and whoever was on the other side. "*I'm coming for him . . .*"

I'm coming for him.

No.

It *couldn't* be.

Before I could give it another moment's thought, the door finally slammed inward, the chair flipping back and away from the entrance. It all happened so quickly. The shape charged in—human, big, certainly a man, something flapping around him like a cloak or a cape.

His heavy, strained panting cut through the silence and seemed to fill my eardrums.

"*I'm coming for him!*" the shape shrieked as it ran toward us. I fired then. Fired again.

I fired as the shape landed atop me and we rolled around. Fired again as I felt sharp nails scratching at my face, stabbing my midsection. I felt blood—*my own*, I thought. I felt pain across my back and side and face. Fired as I was slammed against the far wall. I heard Danny yelp in surprise. I felt myself being thrashed around, like on a roller coaster—except I didn't see where the tracks were going.

Another shot. Another scream. Then silence.

Then black.

I didn't know how long I was out.

It couldn't have been more than a few seconds. I read somewhere that people were rarely unconscious for longer than that. It wasn't like a comic book or movie. But it could have been a lifetime. The room was quiet. The thrashing was over, and every inch of me hurt. I couldn't get up—I felt my midsection and my hand came back wet and sticky with blood. My head was pounding, like the worst hangover I'd ever had, multiplied a hundred times over.

I lifted my head slightly and noticed the shape at my feet. Large, bundled in dark clothes. Not moving. The monster. The creature that had stormed in—it'd just been a man. The man I thought I'd seen move when we first came inside.

Not *la mala hora*. Not Erik. Just a stranger—a barely alive man desperate for something.

I lingered on him for less than a second. I pushed myself up to my elbows and screamed from the pain. I knew I had some slashes in my midsection. Probably a concussion, too. But I needed to move. I needed to find—

Danny.

LA MALA HORA

No.

Please God.

No.

I saw it on the peach carpet, even in the moonlit darkness, I could make it out. The streak was thick and red and heavy. Danny's blood.

I saw his leg next. His foot, bare and untouched by his space-blue pajamas, sticking out from under the bed. Not moving.

I got up, ignoring the pain down my back, the blurring of my vision, the trickle of blood that seemed to burst from my face as I moved, and pushed myself toward the bed. My fingers wrapped over a side of the metal frame and I lifted, finding strength I never knew I had.

There he was. His tiny figure lit by the moon, his tiny foot jutting out, the rest of him curled up as if he were asleep. But he wasn't. The streak of blood ended with him.

No.

I fought the urge to look for the gun. To see if there was another bullet in the chamber. One, saving grace, to pull me out of this hell—this endless, festering nightmare.

I couldn't bring myself to look at him again, to look at my baby. This poor, innocent creature that I'd brought into this world—a world that had been fucked up long before Captain Trips. Long before the virus decimated us. A world full of corruption, lacking empathy, hope, and sincerity. The kind of darkness we wouldn't wish upon our worst enemy. Danny had been my hope—that his innocence and kindness could help stem the tide. But how can you stem a tide of hate and anger and desperation that feels insurmountable? Everyone was dead and dying. And now Danny—

"*Mami . . .*"

I looked down. His tiny voice. A scratchy, sleepy croak.

I moved in, letting the bed frame rest on my back as I reached for him, rolling him over gently. I looked at his eyes, barely open, but open. I felt his chest—waited for what felt like an eternity for it to fill with air, then let it out. I looked at his little mouth, still slightly open.

"Danny..." I said.

I felt his tiny hands weave into mine. I saw the bloody wound on his palm—a graze, I guessed, unable to see clearly. But still, nothing that couldn't be fixed. Nothing that couldn't be helped.

"Mami... was it... was that Papi?"

"No, baby," I said, stammering. "He's gone. He's never coming for you. Never again."

I pulled, almost dragged him out from under the bed and sat, crying into his shoulder, my mouth open, the sounds coming from my mouth like an animal braying for its pack, loud, meandering, aching. Then he started to cry, too, from fear, but also something else. Something deeper we'd been sidestepping for months as we made our way up through this hot, festering stretch of land. Through this world turned upside down.

They were tears of joy.

THE AFRICAN PAINTED DOG
Catriona Ward

The LAST VISITOR hangs over the edge of the enclosure, arms spread, head pointing down toward us, skull broken open like another mouth and bloody. I've tried to reach the delicious red trails that trickle down the wall from him, but they're high, out of reach. The sky is purple overhead, the moon hangs quiet. Silence, crickets, the scent of rotting night-flesh.

"Ya ya ya," I yell. "Ya ya ya!" But no one comes. Before, they always came if I cried hard enough. Their pink little chimp paws and pale spaces where their muzzles should be. Tiny wet eyes, bare skin stinking of fumes and things I don't know. "Yayayaya! Bring me your buckets of MEAT." Silence. Crickets. I chase my tail, but my tail is not meat. I gnaw it for a while, but it starts to hurt.

Silence, now, from above, where there was so much talk. Screaming from the young ones, pointing and exclaiming. I'm not saying we're vain, but everyone likes to be noticed, and they came to admire us. Now there is only silence from the LAST VISITOR and from the many other VISITORS up there. I can smell them all. The VISITORS sometimes lay down right where they were and didn't get up.

The spoiling is on the air. There is so much MEAT, but it's all out of reach. I can hear it sliding from the bones like a snake.

(I have seen a snake once. It came into the enclosure at night and rippled through the pond. It was long and dark and smelled of scales and death and dirt. I knew it right away for what it was. I whistled for Ee Ee Eee and Tak Tak Tak and we waited for it on the shore, tails wagging. When it touched the lip of the pond, I took its head in my jaws so fast it never knew the difference between the darkness of the night and the inside of my mouth. I tore its head off and then we all three ate it, venom sacs and all. Ya ya ya.)

We know a little of the language of the VISITORS. You hear something often enough, it happens. We are very good at learning. Our name in their language is *HereWeCometotheEnclosureofLycaon-PictustheAfricanPaintedDog*. That is just our ceremonial name in their tongue, obviously. We don't bother with formality when it's just family. Though we understand the language of visitors, our own is very different. Our tongue is like the sound of the bush, of trills and birdsong. I used to think our name was *OhMyGod*, but I realize that is just our name at feeding time.

My brother is Tak Tak Tak for the sound he makes when he eats. I am Chachacha for the sound I make when I drink. Mother is Ee Ee Eee for the noise she makes when she noses at your coat and licks you with love. Her coat is empty now, she's gone. The bones she left behind lie in the pond now, half in, half out.

We heard our name spoken by the VISITORS less and less as the days went on. Fewer pink muzzle-less faces pointed at us. They coughed. Gradually, the noises from above died. Then nothing, for some days. The MEAT came less and less often, and then it stopped. We were all hungry. I could hear them all in the other enclosures pacing and licking their chops. *TheSpottedHyenasEewLookatThoseGuys* ate one of their own. I heard the cracking of the bones. So, they were doing okay until the LAST VISITOR. He came on a warm summer morning, like an avalanche.

THE AFRICAN PAINTED DOG

The LAST VISITOR went around the enclosures one by one and they each dropped dead with a *crack*. I heard their hearts go still and their blood thicken in their veins.

We could see the heads of the *HereWeCometotheReticulatedGiraffe* over the top of the fence, their long necks and eyelashes like ferns. We saw the hit, and then the eyelashes closed bloody. She stayed upright for a moment after her death, then fell graceful, great bones and rib cage smashing on the concrete. The LAST VISITOR went on. *PantheraLeoAzandicatheNortheastCongoLion* were all sleeping as usual, so they didn't know anything about it, I don't think. *ThompsonsGazelle* were afraid, though. They ran and hid and ran. I could hear their hearts pounding. It took a while, but the LAST VISITOR got them all in the end.

We heard him walk toward us. We smelled the oil and the smoke, the heated metal death he carried.

We still thought the LAST VISITOR might be bringing buckets of MEAT. Maybe he would feed us some juicy cuts of *HereWeCometotheReticulatedGiraffe*. Mother was very hungry by then. Since she was getting old and we were young and strong, it was her right to eat first. So, Tak Tak Tak and I went to the earth shelter, whose entrance is hidden under a pile of palm fronds. Eating is a private thing. Our kind have manners. We give others space.

But there was no smell of MEAT. The LAST VISITOR carried nothing. Even inside his mind, I could tell he was empty—like the creatures he left behind in the other enclosures. He was still walking around, but the important parts of him were dead.

Mother went to the place where they bring the buckets, by the metal grille. She whined for MEAT and waved her tail. The LAST VISITOR looked down at her, and then took aim. His dead eye looked down at her, along the shining length of metal. The thunder and the lightning caught her in the chest. She dragged herself to the pond, hoping that a drink would make her better. She always taught us, if you are sick, drink water. Her breath sounded like sacking being dragged through her lungs. She went down onto her forelegs in the pond, and then lay down altogether. "Ee, Ee," she said once to us, looking at the place where we hid, a secret message of love, and then she was still. Then she was gone, leaving her body empty. The LAST VISITOR looked down at the enclosure. He looked right at us, too, where we lay beneath the palm fronds. But we are made for hiding. Even in a place that's not very big, we can become invisible. It's an ancient gift of our kind. Then there was a final *crack* and the LAST VISITOR's heart stopped, too.

Now I drink from a puddle. Chachacha. We don't drink from the pond anymore. The water stopped running days ago. The pond is still, and full of Mother—and flies and wriggling things. The puddles are running dry. We'll be thirsty soon. Almost none of Mother is left on the bone. She gave us this other ancient gift, but it won't last forever. We'll be hungry again soon, too.

"Ya! Ya Ya!" My voice is so lonely.

"Stop shouting." Tak Tak Tak is suddenly next to me in his silent way. "No one will come. They didn't come yesterday, and they won't come now." He snaps and neatly catches a moth out of the air. Clever Tak Tak Tak.

All I can think is MEAT. MEAT. Life was so simple before, and so good. It went like this. Sun, bucket of MEAT. Night, bucket of MEAT. Sun, bucket of MEAT. Night, bucket of MEAT. Sun, bucket of MEAT. Night, bucket of MEAT. Sun, bucket of MEAT. Night, bucket of MEAT. Then: sun. No bucket of MEAT. Night, no MEAT, and then sun again, and over and over until we started on Mother.

I jump higher and higher, trying to reach the strings of pink inside that are hanging out of the LAST VISITOR. No good.

Wet nose in my flank. "Come inside, Chachacha," my brother says.

"I think I can reach it next time. Leave me alone." Tak Tak Tak always thinks he's the boss of me, even though he's only one minute older.

THE AFRICAN PAINTED DOG

Tak Tak Tak chirps. "Taste the air."

I do as he says and it has buzzing in it, electricity. A storm is coming. I follow him inside. We curl up together beneath the palm fronds, in each other's warmth. Our two hearts beat together through our flanks.

"You're a good brother, Tak Tak Tak," I tell him with my nose.

"You're a good brother, Chachacha," he says in our high language, and we kiss. We need each other. We're lonely. We're not supposed to be just two—we're supposed to be many, charging across the savanna, mouths open and tongues lolling, in a great pack. I talk to them in my dreams, in the running trill of language that is just ours. I feel them, the tens of dogs that should be with us, their absence like missing toes.

Soon, if we don't eat, Tak Tak Tak and I will try to eat each other. I can feel him thinking it, too. It's in his tongue and his eyes when he looks at me. We don't blame each other for it.

(I dream of the *InthisEnclosureistheDholeCuonAlpinus*. I never met them, but I knew them from their scent, three fences over. We lived side by side for a long time. I was jealous of the Dholes because they were a whole family, seven of them, three adults and four pups, and I heard them playing together at all times of the day and night. I got used to the pups' high sounds. You could say we grew up together. As time went by, we all got bigger. Sometimes we spoke to one another, shouting into the night air. We didn't have much in common, but we yelled, *Ya Ya Ya!* And they yelled back, *Hoo hoo hoo!* Half friendly, half *Don't come near my MEAT*. Two of the females developed a spicy, attractive scent. I didn't know what the word meant at that time, but it drifted through my head again and again. WIFE. One day, through some error, a gate was left unlocked, and I heard them, the Dholes, streaming out into the night. They brought two of them back later, males, angry and shouting, but the rest are still out there somewhere or dead, I guess. Anyway, I'm glad some of the Dholes weren't here when the LAST VISITOR came.)

The storm comes over us, screaming in the night, white flashes and spears of rain, a wind so high and strong it feels alive. Fists of hail hammer the ground and the world cracks open. Somewhere wood breaks, a plastic chair hurtles through and smashes on the side of the enclosure. Ee Ee's abandoned carcass, her remaining fur, is raked by wind and rain, and it looks like she's rolling over. Like she's going to get up and walk her bones over here. Tak Tak Tak and I cower. Lightning forks through the night, spreading like a bony hand across the sky. Something comes down with a great *crash*, throwing up silver daggers of rain. The world roars and goes black.

I pant where I lie. I am not dead. There are wet things all around me, sharp things sticking into my flanks, but I am not hurt. I nose up through the wet dark. Leaves from a fallen tree that almost fills the enclosure lap at me like cold tongues. "Tak Tak Tak?"

"Chachacha?" Our voices are like birds on the storm. The wind lashes through the branches of the tree. It's a fir, trunk broken and sappy and white above us in the night. At the top, around the jagged base of the trunk, something black whips about, spitting fiery venom like a snake. The dusty scent of electricity mingles with the rain.

"We can get out," Tak Tak Tak says. "We have to."

But what is *out*? We were born here in this place, this enclosure, surrounded by rock walls. I know about some things *out there*. Sound, heartbeats, scents. I have a picture of the world made of these things. It is not safe *out there*. Why would the VISITORS have kept us in here, if not to keep us safe?

"Come on," Tak Tak Tak says.

I place my two forepaws on the bark. I am scared, but something else is stronger. The pulse in my head, MEAT MEAT MEAT.

We climb carefully up the trunk of the fallen fir where it lies at a steep angle—a narrow bridge out of here, to the top of the enclosure. We creep forward, upward along the trunk, toward where the end of the broken tree rests on the edge of our pit. Our paws slip on branches and wet foliage. The stink of singed wood and rubber is everywhere. It's too much, my delicate nose burns. The sky boils. With a crash, a sheen of mud pushes out of the cliff walls on the other side of the enclosure. A brown wave crashes down into our home. It slowly begins to fill with water—it is becoming a prison, a trap. Below, Ee Ee Eee's bones and hide are slowly covered with water. The fiery snake spits and curvets above us. It falls into the water with a hiss, just like a real snake.

We crouch on the tree trunk, chirping with fear. "I'm afraid," I tell my brother.

"Me too," he says, "but we have to go anyway."

We creep up, up the trunk. It feels like it will roll at any moment and tip us into the white foaming water below. There is no backward, there is only forward.

Tak Tak Tak slips on the wet bark and scrabbles and falls. I am frozen in place, trilling his name. He lands straddling the trunk, legs hanging down either side. We gasp at each other, eyes wide and mouths also. I creep close and lick his hindquarter, which is all I can reach. He gets up, leg by trembling leg. We inch forward, up, forward, up, until the broken end of the trunk is before us. Tak Tak Tak jumps, slips, lands on the stone edge of the pit, hauls with his front legs and pistons with his back legs. He somersaults onto solid ground. I stand on my toes to get purchase with my claws and leap. The world drifts by below, the place where we were born, and I'm sure I'm going to fall and die, but I don't. I land neatly beside Tak Tak Tak. We kiss one another and pant. Below, the sparking black snake leaps and lashes at the water, as if angry it can't reach us. It seems furious that we're free. So we get up and dance on our hind legs and shout down at it all, water and snake, dancing in the rain. Thunder and rain pounds at us, but we're part of it all now.

"Take that, snake!" I yell. It hisses in reply, whipping back and forth: *snake snake snake*. I scamper back from the edge, heart beating fast.

We are on a cement walkway lined with tall trees that dance wildly in the gale. Tak Tak Tak and I can hardly hear one another over the wind. *Let's get out of here.* If one tree can fall, others will follow (old painted dog wisdom). We run along the wide avenue of trees following the natural downward slope of the hill. Even though we're afraid of the storm, everything in my nose and body is shouting. The feel of new ground beneath our feet. The new scents all around, the wide-open space, no longer surrounded by rock walls. New, new, *new*! We love new things. We are travelers by nature—I realize that now. My legs tell me, my joy tells me, my tongue lolling and my great bounds, which eat yards at a time, they all tell me. I had no reason to know it before. Even as we run Tak Tak Tak rises onto his hind legs, then launches, twisting into the air, trilling high. He feels it, too.

Once clear of the trees, we slow down. We trot past the enclosures containing the dead, the felled, the MEAT. There are interesting things strewn across the path. An orange cat still holds the imprint of a small VISITOR's hands. Scraps of rotten food litter the path and we snap them up, but there's not much. We're not the only hungry ones out here, it seems. MEAT MEAT MEAT, my mind cries, but there is no more MEAT, only sinew, bones.

We come to a large flat place divided by white lines into squares. In some of the squares there sit containers made of metal and glass. Some of the containers have food inside. We paw at the smooth surfaces, but there is no way in. What a waste, good MEAT sitting there rotting away. But the containers provide shelter at least. Tak Tak Tak and I crawl into the oily space beneath one of them. We put our heads on our paws and watch the shining needles of the downpour. Maybe we sleep a little. But our ears know when the rain eases suddenly, and we wake then, as watery sun is pouring down over the lot.

My stomach complains. There is MEAT above us, encased in metal, but we can't get in.

"We need something living," Tak Tak Tak says. "We need to hunt."

MEAT MEAT MEAT, goes the pulse in my brain, and as if I summoned it, something darts into view in the center of the lot. I've never seen one moving about. But I've eaten it before from a bucket. MEAT. Specifically, RABBIT.

(Maybe I did summon it, who knows what I can do, I am Chachacha the snake eater and escapee, explorer of new worlds.)

The RABBIT goes to a pile of things that lie on the ground, spilled from a bag. They are NOT MEAT, but I have eaten them before, cooked. Potatoes, sprouting. They have delicate green tubers and leaves coming from them. The RABBIT nibbles.

Tak Tak Tak and I confer in silence. Then he backs out silently from under our shelter, out of the RABBIT's eyeline. I wait until he's in position and then I burst from cover and run straight at the RABBIT. It's not a very smart plan, one that would only fool an idiot. But the RABBIT believes me because the RABBIT is young, has probably never seen something that looks like me, and is an idiot. He turns and runs, making for the nearest cover. He's nearly under the car when Tak Tak Tak darts out and seizes him by the throat.

We tear him apart down the middle. Tak Tak Tak and I sit down together politely a few yards apart. We eat together at the same time because we are both young and strong. There are no pups to care for, no Ee Ee Eee to give the first bite to. For a moment I feel sad about this, then all my mind turns to

BLOOD. MEAT. MEATMEATMEAT

We go through the city, during the next few days. The city is not for us. All that's here are bones and things baked so hard by the heat that they are no longer MEAT. We catch rats as we go, which is easy. There are so many of them. They try to tell us tales in their dry dirty voices, but we don't listen. We eat them, delicious brains first, cracked out of their little skulls. Everywhere there are empty things—houses, cars, suitcases. Trails of objects wind through the streets, tracking the path of the fled VISITORS.

Something's calling to us, sand and space and savanna. We know it's there, beyond the tall concrete. We sleep in doorways, entrances to underground places. We don't go into the underground places. Once, twice, then the desert sun rises again and we have long miles in our legs yet to spend. Sometimes we catch the scent of living VISITORS, but there aren't too many of them. Once we see one. She lies half in and half out of a doorway, shaking so hard it looks like a dance. It reminds me of Ee Ee Eee and I feel sad. I smell the sadness on Tak Tak Tak, too, so we hurry on. We don't even want her for MEAT.

Sunrise. Ahead, the cool smell of water creeps through the early air. We're thirsty, so we hurry toward it. "I have been thinking," Tak Tak Tak says as he leaps through the stream of the burst pipeline, kicking up spray and snapping at the glistening drops of water as the sunshine makes them into jewels. We play in the water like this, under the blank buildings, in the empty street. When we are panting, tongues lolling, I say,

"What have you been thinking?"

"We need wives," he says, shaking himself and grinning.

"Yes, I want a wife." Now I can't think about anything else. WIFE. I remember the spicy scent of the Dholes before they escaped.

"Ee Ee Eee has told us that our kind of pack is led by one mated pair," Tak Tak Tak says. "We can even lead as two pairs, I think. Us and our wives. But we need a pack."

He's right. We're lonely, just the two of us. We kiss each other and wag and play all the time. But two is not enough. I whine. PACK. I stop as something comes on the air.

"Wait," I tell Tak Tak Tak quickly with my nose. "Hide." We are gone in a flash, behind some garbage cans. We watch the street. I really am summoning things with my mind, I think, because a familiar shape trots across, stepping delicately through rubble and the dead. She's like us. Four paws. Muzzle. Good shape, smart nose. Not an idiot like a rabbit or some such. She is the color of ripe grass on the plains in the last of the golden sun.

THE AFRICAN PAINTED DOG

WIFE? I ask silently.

Not WIFE, Tak Tak Tak says sadly. And I feel it, too—there are some things in her scent that are the same as ours, but not like the Dholes—not enough for her to be a wife, or make pups.

MEAT? I ask.

Might as well talk to her first.

Whatever. I'm so full of rat I couldn't anyway.

We step out into the crossroads. "YOU," I say, and start to give the ancient greeting, "HAIL FELLOW, WELL M—"

She turns her head, and there's a bad smell on her, I catch it now, it fills my nostrils. Now there's a quick sharp pain in my right side. By me, Tak Tak Tak whistles. He's hit, too. We go down into darkness.

"Wake up, Chachacha," Tak Tak Tak is saying. "Wake up."

Dark and animals. It smells like home, in that way. But this is not home. It's a small place, hot, surrounded by wire mesh, so cramped that Tak Tak Tak and I can barely turn around. Someone is crying nearby in a cage. They are all sick. It's the same mineral tang of—something—we smelled on the golden dog in the streets. Something opens above us, a hole in the cage, and MEAT flops down wet on the concrete next to us. It's not fresh, there are maggots in it, but that's all right, little maggots are bursts of flavor. We eat quickly, giving each other an equal share.

"At least we are together," I say to Tak Tak Tak with my nose. He gives me love back. I try not to imagine how terrible it would be to be in this place alone.

I say to the dog crying next to us, "Who are you?" It's the golden dog. I wonder how I could have missed it, the scent of wrongness about her. She just cries. We try to scent-talk with her, with our noses. She hacks loud and rough like she's got a bone in her throat.

Tak Tak Tak tries again. He asks her, "What is this place?"

"It's the_____," she says, and the thing she says is so terrible

I don't think there's a name for it, for our kind. Maybe the closest would be *the butcher*. Or *the killing floor*.

"Sleep," I say to Tak Tak Tak. "No more talking. We save our strength. I think we're going to need it."

A VISITOR comes down the aisle between the cages. He pokes a stick into the cages. Most of the dogs just cry and try to back away, but one or two, the sicker ones, have gone somewhere else in their minds. A big brown dog bares his teeth, mucus streaming from his nose, which I can see is dry with sickness. He snarls, and the sound is insane, wrung from the depths of him. He has lost himself.

The VISITOR withdraws the stick and I see it has a loop on it at the end. He puts the loop around the brown dog's neck and takes the brown dog out of the cage. The dog dances and growls, strangling on the end of the stick. The man takes the brown dog away. They disappear through a metal door at the far end of the room.

The brown dog does not come back. No more food comes. We sleep, we dream of great, wild golden spaces and blue skies that we have never seen. All of our kind have these dreams. It's the place we came from. We dream of delicious meats that we have never tasted, of hunts we have never been on, of brothers and sisters we have never known.

I wake to Tak Tak Tak trilling loudly in alarm. I start up and I know right away that there's too much space in our cage. Tak Tak Tak is outside the wire. His throat is squeezed tight. The VISITOR has him on the end of the stick. I trill and shout to him. He twists like a fish on a line. I scream and yell, but the VISITOR takes him away and he vanishes.

I cry and yell. What if Tak Tak Tak doesn't come back, like the brown dog? I turn and turn in the cage and trill until the golden dog next to me snaps and snarls for me to shut up. She's much sicker now, I can see that. Her coat is dull and strings of greenish mucus dangle from her nose. The whites of her eyes are red as blood.

THE AFRICAN PAINTED DOG

I snarl back and try to bite her through the mesh. "Tell me what happened to my brother."

She just looks back at me, tired. "Don't fight them," she says. "When they come for you, lie down and be sad."

I jump up and down, screaming. I will never do that! I will fight them until I die!

Tak Tak Tak comes back when the sun is going down. Even though I can't see it, there are no windows where we are, I still feel it moving through the sky. He is limping and covered in cuts. The VISITOR holds me back from the entrance with a buzzing stick that burns and hurts. There's something wrong with the VISITOR. A sweet rot beneath his skin. Sickness. He puts Tak Tak Tak back in our cage. He wipes his brow and staggers as he goes away along the corridor. We never see that VISITOR again.

As soon as the VISITOR is gone, I go to Tak Tak Tak, lick him and kiss him and give him love. He just lies there. He won't speak to me. I cry because this feels almost as bad as being alone.

When the door opens again, it is a different VISITOR. This one is young and sweating and female. I hurl myself against the mesh, snarling.

"Stop," the golden dog says. She's dying now. I can smell her insides rotting. She lies at the back of her cage. "They'll think you're sick. They want the sick angry ones."

But I don't care what she says. I want to hurt the VISITOR for what he's done to my brother. The VISITOR looks at me and Tak Tak Tak. Tak Tak Tak is curled in the back of the cage and doesn't move. I throw myself against the mesh again and again.

The VISITOR takes me. She is strong for someone so small. I am dragged through the dark, along ways and passages and then shoved through a door. It slams closed behind me.

The light is blinding, white hot on my eyes after the dark. I am in a wire enclosure. Another cage, but much bigger than the tiny one

I have shared with Tak Tak Tak these last few days. It is loud. *Bad* loud. Screaming recorded voices blare from the walls. Beyond the wire, there is a dark place. The floor is covered in sawdust. There's blood mixed in. I trot around the perimeter of the cage, trying to find a weak point where I can get out. Maybe I can dig. I scuffle through the sawdust, but it's concrete underneath. A small object is thrown up by my forepaws. I bend to sniff it. It's a long canine tooth that has been torn out at the root. I think about eating it, but regretfully decide that it is not MEAT. I have not had MEAT for some time. Being underground has taken time from me, I don't know how long it has been since they fed us the maggot MEAT, and I am hungry.

I see there are dead VISITORS strewn along the rows of seats beyond the wire. One of them moves, then another, and I see that actually two of them are alive. One I don't know, and the female who brought me here.

"Where's Frank?" the male asks the female.

"Dead," she says. "It's just us now." She strokes the leg of the dead VISITOR beside her. Then she takes a shining thing from her pocket and suddenly there is blood on the other living VISITOR's face. He stares at her, tastes it, and then puts his fingers into the red slick and strokes it down her face in a gleaming line. He does it again. They start to laugh, covered in blood. "To the end of everything," the female says.

"I'll get the GIANT," the male says. "Let's watch some fun before our time comes."

The door into the cage opens again and something comes through—a big black dog, twice my height. It is the weight of a bear. It is very sick. Strings of bloody snot and drool fall from its muzzle. It has forgotten everything it ever knew.

The two VISITORS get on their hind legs and roar. The big black dog roars, too, and comes at me with parted jaws. I leap high in the air. It is big and strong, but confused. I dance and twist out of its way. Its hot breath follows me. It is almost fun. I am laughing at the dog. The dog cries and roars and leaps at me. The VISITORS scream with delight.

I dance and leap and run until I am tired, and still the big black dog follows. I leap a little less high each time, and its jaws come closer and closer, snapping the air behind me.

The jaws crunch onto the scruff of my neck and the dog picks me up like Ee Ee Eee used to. But the dog is not carrying me with a mother's kindness. It shakes me like a rat. I twist once more with the last of my energy and fasten my teeth in its vulnerable throat. Blood runs everywhere. The VISITORS are frenzied, shrieking with joy.

The black dog is MEAT and I tear chunks from it even as it lives. It's bad MEAT because of the sickness, but I will eat anything at this point. I am so hungry. The light is so bright and the roaring so loud and I am alone, which my kind should never be, and the lights and the screaming and the bloody faces of the VISITORS get into my brain, and I realize, yes, this is what it feels like to be insane. It happened to Tak Tak Tak, and if I stay here much longer, it will happen to me.

The loop goes around my neck, and they pull me away from the MEAT. I am yanked through the dark. *Clang* goes the cage. Tak Tak Tak lies sad and crazy in the corner. I nose him. "I understand," I tell him. "That is a place with no brothers and sisters."

"They like to watch the pets fight," the golden dog says from the next-door cage. She is nearly dead. "He especially likes to watch the dogs who played with kids and fetched the newspaper to kill each other."

"I thought they loved their pets," I say.

"These days everyone kills what they love," she says. "To prove they're not afraid."

The golden dog dies soon after saying this and it's quiet for a time.

I nose Tak Tak Tak and try to talk to him. But there's no sign he hears me. He cowers in a pile and makes no reply. "Like the RABBIT," I keep saying. "Remember the RABBIT?"

I tense as footsteps come down the hall. It is the male VISITOR who comes again. He's not interested in Tak Tak Tak anymore; Tak Tak Tak is quiet like a dead thing. I bite and snarl and dart, avoiding the loop and the stick. He's so busy with me he doesn't notice Tak Tak Tak creeping along the side of the cage, not until Tak Tak Tak is upon him. Only an idiot would have not seen that coming. But the VISITOR is beginning to be sick. He doesn't know it yet, but I can smell it. Also, he is an idiot. Even though we have not eaten for some time we are stronger than him because we are not sick. The blood of his throat makes a spray in the air.

Tak Tak Tak and I leap over the VISITOR. He is twitching and clutching his neck. We race through the dark, following our noses toward the fresh air. Our claws slip on viscera. It is leaking from some dead VISITORS sitting in a neat row against the wall. I wonder if they were made to fight one another, too. We quickly run past them. We come out of the door, and we run and run through the city.

They forgot that we are not dogs. We are *Lycaon pictus* and we were eating the VISITORS thousands of years ago, long before they learned to put us in cages. The sickness does not get us because we are not dog or human, and we will live a long time, while their lungs turn to liquid and their eyes lose their light.

Since we have been underground, the city has started to rot. The streets are filled with the dead. But there is something else, too. Tak Tak Tak and I follow the call of the something, something that lies beyond the sickness and the concrete. It grows stronger as the buildings thin out, as we come near it.

We don't stop at dark, we don't even stop as hunger eats us, as the sweet stench of the bodies calls to us. Everything here is MEAT now. But we are done with this place.

We reach it at the beginning of the second day, as the light rises over the world and the city ends. We are at the edge of a great golden place. This is what has been pulling at us, all this time.

"Tak Tak Tak," I say, awed. "It is the place of the ancestors." Waving grass stretches in all directions. Small trees rustle in the prairie wind. The land rolls on and on, vast and made for running and jumping.

Tak Tak Tak looks at me and touches me with his nose. For the first time since the dark place, he kisses me. "It's not that place," he says, "but it's very much like it, yes."

"Let's go and find the WIVES," I say. "The Dholes. They must be out there somewhere. We shouldn't keep them waiting."

Together we go into the burning sunrise.

TILL HUMAN VOICES WAKE US, AND WE DROWN
Poppy Z. Brite

The first time Seth saw him, the old man was sitting on Menemsha Beach playing with a disgusting thing. He was spare and angular, this old man, and looked as if he might have spent his whole life on this brief stretch of up-island shoreline; sand clung to him in a faint glittering aura and salt lined the many creases of his face. The disgusting thing he held was perhaps eight inches long, brown and sere. It had a rudimentary, wicked-looking little face, a long spiny tail, and what appeared to be a pair of wings. It looked as if it had been alive at some point, but was now very, very dead.

"Jenny Haniver," the old man said when he saw Seth looking, and made the thing nod.

"Uh... Seth Harris," Seth said, thinking the man was introducing himself.

The old man's face wrinkled in contempt. "Not *me*. This creature here is called a Jenny Haniver. People used to think they was dried mermaids." His tone became singsong. "Mermaid, mermaid, down by the docks, I see her titties, but where's her box?"

It was rare these days to run across a talking person on Martha's Vineyard. Most of the summer people had left when the flu started ramping up, though a few had hunkered down in their luxurious homes and died. Almost all the remaining people were locals, and they tended to keep to themselves. Seth knew some of them and checked on them from time to time. Most of them were crazy. This old man sounded crazy, but possibly interesting.

"What is it?" he asked.

"Stingray. You catch the little ones and cut em up so it looks like a body. Nostrils are the eyes, mouth is the mouth. Hang 'em up to dry a while, then varnish 'em and sell 'em to the tourists. My father used to have a good little sideline in Jenny Hanivers." The old man cackled. "Take home a dried mermaid, boy, you really had a souvenir. Kid like you wouldn't remember that."

"No, I don't," Seth admitted. "My parents never had much luck selling anything to the tourists. They tried to start a sushi restaurant, but people come here to eat lobster and clams, not raw fish."

The old man looked searchingly at Seth. His eyes were an undimmed brilliant blue in his seamed brown face. "You Japanese?"

"No. My mom was half-Japanese. My dad was Black. I'm just an islander."

"Had a buddy whose ship was sunk by a Jap torpedo in the Big One."

"I'm nineteen and I've never even been to Japan, okay?"

"Yeah, yeah, keep your hair on, I got no problem with you . . . Sean?"

"Seth. I'm Seth. What's your name?"

"You don't need to know my real name. Some folks used to call me Mole, 'cause I got a lot of 'em." The old man set the Jenny Haniver carefully on the sand and pulled up the sleeve of his jacket, revealing a constellation of brown spots on his forearm. "Got 'em on my legs, too. Hell, got 'em on my *ass*, for that matter." He cackled again. "Or so the ladies always told me. Can't see my own ass, y'know."

They stared out at the slaty waters of Menemsha Bight. The late summer sun was westering, beginning to bleed into the sea. After a few minutes, Mole said, "Now Jenny, there, people used to say she could protect you from getting sick. She couldn't do it, of course, but a real mermaid could."

"A real mermaid," Seth said.

Mole nodded.

"There's no such thing."

"Wasn't any such thing as the superflu, either, till there was. Government making a plague that killed everybody in the world? Who'd have believed it? Government made this AIDS thing, you know. Wanted to wipe out the homosexuals. And what for? Were they bothering anybody? No, but the government always wants a scapegoat. Democrat, Republican, what have you, they all want to blame someone else for the messes they make. Nobody left to take the blame now, though. Nobody much left to do the blaming, for that matter."

"There are still people on the mainland."

"Yeah, and most of 'em are headed west, to one place or another. I got no use for either of their places. I'm staying right here."

"Were you a fisherman, before?"

Everyone understood *before*. The single word was enough to denote all the pain it carried: before you watched your family choke on snot and die, before you had to break into the stores for food, before the world ended.

"Nah." Mole smiled ruefully. "My father was, but I get seasick. Never could find my legs and quit pukin'. I'm a carpenter. Built us a shack right here while he went out on the water, and we lived in it until he died. Not from the flu, thank God. Long before these devilish times. Heart attack."

Seth wished he could say the same. Both of his parents had been active and healthy until they caught the flu. His father had gone first, one of the early wave of Vineyard deaths that had prompted calls to suspend ferry service and close off the island. His mother had survived a couple of weeks longer, but then she got sick, too. She had clawed at her swollen throat until Seth caught her hands and pulled them away; then they trembled like frightened birds in his grasp and she was gone.

"I worked at Bunch of Grapes, the bookstore in Vineyard Haven," Seth said, though the old man hadn't asked. "It was a great job, but it didn't really, you know, prepare me for the end of the world. When people started heading to the mainland, I figured I had everything I needed here, and I just decided to stay."

Everything I needed wasn't strictly true, since the hospital had shut down, but Seth had a good supply of his antiretroviral medication. That was, if he decided to start taking it again. He'd tested positive for HIV during a routine blood draw in the spring, but felt fine until he started on the AZT, which sometimes made him violently ill and always left him low-grade nauseated. His doctor had stressed the need to keep taking it as a preventative, but the doctor was dead now and here was Seth on the beach, feeling fine even though he hadn't taken AZT in a month. He had come to believe he wasn't going to catch the flu, had even wondered whether HIV conferred some kind of immunity.

Mole picked up the Jenny Haniver and shook a skirl of sand off it. The thing's desiccated skin had the look of a rawhide toy, and Seth felt an unexpected pang. The dogs were all dead, too, including Lucy Vincent, the collie his family had had since he was nine.

"They make these things in Japan as well," Mole said. "Your mum might have known about them, but probably not. Most people don't. My father took a particular interest in mermaids. He said the Japanese ones were more like Feejee mermaids, you know, those things they used to cobble together out of a dead monkey's top and a dried fish's tail?"

Seth shook his head, mystified.

"Well, it don't matter. Point is, they were supposed to *predict* epidemics, and they were supposed to *protect* people from epidemics. The Japanese kept them in temples and prayed to them. Some of the stories even said eating one was supposed to make a person immortal. Now, if you could go out there"—Mole nodded at the sound—"and catch a mermaid dinner that would make you live forever, would you do it?"

"I don't know. Wouldn't that be murder?"

"Guess it depends on which end you hooked," Mole said, and cackled at his own joke.

Seth laughed a little, too. The old guy was a weirdo, but his irascible good humor was catching. Soon all but the last bloody sliver of sun had sunk below the horizon. Nothing in Seth's years had prepared him for the darkness of an island without electricity, and he wanted to get home.

"Well," he said. "Maybe I'll see you around."

"Likely so. Stay well."

As Seth headed back toward his car, he heard Mole crooning a song whose words he couldn't make out, but whose tune had a dirge-like flavor. He imagined that the old man was singing to the dried thing he held in his hands, and a shudder ran up his spine like the first touch of September frost.

The moon was rising by the time Mole walked back up the beach. It cast its stark illumination over the little fishing town and across the waters of Menemsha Bight, making him think of the coming winter. The season would be no worse than usual for him, as he had plenty of fuel and canned food, but he suspected it might send some of the Vineyard's remaining residents packing for the mainland. Playing pioneer was easy enough in the blessed summer weather.

An island winter might chap their asses. He'd been a boy in 1934, the year seawater froze all around the island. His father and a couple of other men had walked from Edgartown Harbor to Cape Pogue Pond and back, just for the novelty of it, no doubt passing a flask and laughing the whole way. He'd wanted to go with them, but his mother put paid to that.

Mole climbed the stairs of the raised shack, which he still thought of as his father's place, although the old cob had been gone forty years. He trod the risers easily enough in the dark, and why not? He had built them himself. The wood had silvered in the salt air, but the place was still strong. He let himself in and lit an oil lamp. The big aquarium against the far wall bubbled softly. He had it running on a small generator, but didn't use the power to light the shack's one big room; he didn't like the idea of being a bright beacon visible to any who might come.

Meeting the boy today had been a good thing, or so he hoped. He'd never been a gregarious man, but these days he talked to anyone he saw. Had to; he didn't expect to live through the coming winter. The Jenny Haniver he carried was one of many his father had left behind, mostly his own handiwork, but a few he'd collected in various strange ports through the years. Yes, old Daddy Mole had definitely found some strange ports. He snickered a little. A burbling sound came from the aquarium, rather like a pigeon's coo, but more liquid.

"Yeah, yeah, keep your hair on. Not that you've got any."

He snickered again, walked across the single big room, and gazed into the tank. She appeared wide-awake, her four huge eyes glowing faintly. A rippling movement thrust her body up at him. Mole slipped his hand into the aquarium's warm water. She rose against him, and he used two fingers to gently part the slippery petals that comprised most of her body. He probed deeper, slipped his fingers into the inner opening. At its upper reaches was a small firm node that trembled against his touch, and it was this he used to satisfy her, stroking and rubbing it until her body blossomed like a time-lapse film of a flower.

He sighed. He had once found this exciting, but she wanted it every day and night, languished and appeared to be dying if she didn't get it. She did not eat, did not appear to excrete; this was what she lived on.

TILL HUMAN VOICES WAKE US, AND WE DROWN

He extinguished the lamp, got into the hammock where he slept, and lay gazing across at the aquarium. The moonlight streaming in through a high window was bright enough that he could still see her, a ruffled midnight-blue shape with gold spangles that seemed lit from within.

After his mother died, Seth had left their little rental house near the Oak Bluffs lagoon pond and set up housekeeping in what Vineyarders called the Campground, a circle of Victorian cottages at the heart of the town. He had always wanted to live in one of these, and while the superflu had a lot of downsides, it had vastly improved the cost of living in his hometown. The houses were built around a shady little park, their eaves dripping with gingerbread trim, variously painted peppermint pink and buttery yellow and seafoam green. Seth had chosen a pale lavender one with raspberry-colored trim and a swing on its cozy porch. Crucially, it was uninhabited when the superflu hit, as was the one to its right. Seth had done the necessary maintenance to the house on the left: found the bodies (just two), bundled them up in their bedclothes, and hauled them down to the mass grave in Ocean Park. There were bodies in some of the other cottages, but no one else was close enough for Seth to smell when he was at home. He supposed he had gone a little nose-blind. Probably everyone who survived had.

A few days after meeting the old man, Seth woke up in a rank sweat, his sheets soaked. Half-remembered dreams clouded his mind, and he realized that his throat was sore. He lay in bed for twenty minutes, afraid to get up and check the mirror for the purplish-black smudges under the chin that were one of the earliest symptoms of the flu. Finally, he dragged himself into the bathroom and looked. The marks weren't there, but the glands in his throat felt lumpy and swollen.

There were several bottles of AZT in the vanity drawer. He took one out, considered it, then shook several of the blue-and-white capsules into his hand. His stomach did a slow roll at the sight of them, and he had to stifle his gag reflex. He knew exactly how they would make him feel, the headaches and drizzling shits, the somehow greasy waves of nausea.

Mermaid can keep you from getting sick, he heard Mole say, and smiled a little as he put the pills back in the drawer.

The previous owners of his cottage had a pretty good library, lots of fiction, lots of travel writing. Seth had always enjoyed travel narratives, but found that he no longer did: it was too bleak picturing all those exotic destinations emptied by flu, or full of rotting bodies. Fiction was still good, though. Sometimes he stopped by Bunch of Grapes, always reflecting that his employee discount was now one hundred percent. These two sources provided him with plenty of reading, the only thing that made the nights bearable. But the conversation with Mole had gotten him thinking about a book of his mother's, an oversized collection of Japanese folk legends and supernatural creatures. Some of the colorful illustrations had frightened and fascinated him as a child. He would dare himself to look at them, knowing they guaranteed a sleepless night, but unable to resist their siren call. He particularly remembered the *chōchin'obake*, a thing like a torn-open paper lantern with mournful, red-rimmed eyes and a long hanging tongue. Hadn't there been some sort of mermaid, too?

He didn't want to go to his parents' house. He was forbidden to go to his parents' house, not by any authority but by his own fear. He could handle coming across strangers' bodies. His mother's body was a different matter. His father had died in the island's one hospital, but it had been overwhelmed by the time his mother got sick, and she had died at home. When he left her there, tucked into her own bed, she had still been fresh. She wouldn't be now.

Seth tried to quit thinking about the book. It wasn't as if he had nothing to do; he ought to go over to Katama and check on the few people still there. They weren't as old as the man from the beach, but they weren't young, and he worried about them getting hurt or running out of food. One man was still hauling lobster traps, making grilled lobster and lobster stew for the group. It sounded like a luxurious diet, but Seth knew you could get tired of eating lobster, if lobster was all you had. Instead of doing that, he drove to Vineyard Haven and spent the morning trolling aimlessly through the little shops on Main Street, picking things up—scented candles, glass figurines, shark T-shirts—and putting them down again. There was nothing he needed here.

He got back in the car and drove without a destination in mind. The motion calmed him, as did the land itself, woodland drawing in close on the roadsides, then opening up to long green vistas. The island was at its seductive best, the meadows sweet with Queen Anne's lace, blazing yellow coreopsis, purple spikes of lupine. He saw a family of wild turkeys crossing the road near the airport. It still amazed him that such natural beauty could exist alongside the horrors of the past few months. How could anyone stand to leave this world?

Well, all right, he thought as he pulled up in front of his parents' house. He supposed some underneath-part of him had known he was coming here all along.

Approaching the house, he saw that he had left all the curtains drawn. Had he locked the front door, too? Yes, out of habit, but the key was still on his ring. He let the door swing open, but did not immediately step inside; he simply stood there, sampling the air, all his senses on alert.

Was there the faintest thread of decay, or was it his imagination?

He stepped into the small foyer and shut the door behind him. It felt like stepping into some parallel dimension, one he had never expected to visit again. The house was hot and silent.

The living room was straight ahead, furnished simply but comfortably, the tall built-in bookshelves the focus of the room. Beyond that, the kitchen lay in shadow. On his left, a hallway led to a bathroom, his old room, and his parents' bedroom. The door of this last room was closed. If he were to walk to the end of the hall—not even twenty steps!—and open that door, he would see his mother. Seth was suddenly afraid that his legs would take him there of their own accord, that he would be unable to stop his hand from turning the doorknob and—

Yes, there was a smell, one that pressed against the back of the throat and curled slyly into the nostrils. It was sour on top, but shot through with veins of sickly sweetness. It was not his imagination, not food going bad in the kitchen, not any damn thing but his mother lying in bed rotting. He swallowed hard and tried to slow his breathing. Why had he come here?

The book. He had to get the book and go. He shouldn't be here; no one should be here. This was a house of the dead.

He went to one of the big bookshelves. After a minute of scanning spines, he saw the volume he wanted, a big hardcover with a red dust jacket. *The Old Legends of Japan: A Compendium of Spirits, Monsters, and Yūrei*. He remembered *yūrei*, ghosts that weren't exactly evil, but could be dangerous. For instance, if you left someone you loved to rot in bed because you were too much of a coward to bury them, they could return to the world as a *yūrei* and haunt you. He took the book down and flipped through it.

A muffled *thump* came from the back of the house.

Before he was aware of moving, Seth found himself back at the door, the book tucked under his arm. He'd been spooking himself, but he hadn't imagined that *thump*. It could have been something precariously balanced, something that had been ready to fall over forever and his movements tipped it. It could have been an animal under the floorboards. It could have been a pair of stiffened feet hitting bedroom carpet as their owner sat up, eager to welcome home the prodigal son.

He couldn't make himself look toward the hall, and if there was something in the corner of his vision, something impossibly thin that flattened itself against the wall as the stink of decay intensified—well, that didn't mean he had to stand here and let it get him, did it? He fumbled for the doorknob, had a bad moment when it wouldn't turn, then realized he was twisting it the wrong way. He spilled out onto the porch, shoved the key into the lock. There. It was done. He was back in the world again. As he drove home, there was still a trace of that faint decay in his nostrils.

Mole slept, and Mole dreamed.

The man's face seemed familiar, though Mole was sure he'd never seen it in waking life. There was some sort of cowl around his head, and his eyes shone redly in its darkness. His grin was gruesome, yet jaunty.

"It would be an easy trip to the mainland," the dark man whispered. "I could make it easy for you."

"I get seasick."

"I could stop the sickness. *Only* I could stop it. If you don't come with me, you'll never get off this island."

"Don't want to get off this island."

"Oh yes, I forgot." The man's grin grew mocking. "You have to stay here and take care of your sea slug."

"She ain't a slug. She's as smart as you or me."

"Then why do you keep her captive?"

Mole didn't say anything. He tried to look away from the man's awful grinning face, but found he could not.

"Come to me," the man said again. "Leave that thing to rot. I could use a man like you, a fellow good with his hands."

"Can't."

"There's still plague on this island," the dark man hissed. "You think you're immune just because you haven't gotten sick yet? You can still get sick."

Mole felt his throat swelling, felt thick mucus rising in his lungs. He tried to take a breath and choked. Struggled for air. Flailed and woke with a panicky little cry, alone in his narrow bed. He had been having variations of this dream for a few weeks now, and they left him afraid to go back to sleep.

On the far side of the room, the big aquarium bubbled.

Mole swung his feet over the side of the bed and crossed the room to the tank. He kept a chair here for nights like these, and he pulled it over now, sat and leaned his forehead against the cool glass. He let his fingertips dangle into the water. She fluttered, then extended a ruffle and twined it around his fingers. He closed his eyes. Gradually his breathing slowed, and he spent the rest of the night asleep there, with the mermaid holding his hand.

Seth slept, and Seth dreamed.

He had not wanted to take the book into his cottage, so he sat in the porch swing and paged through it. He soon found the picture he had half-remembered, a grotesque thing with a fish's body, a human head, and masses of stringy black hair. The face was like a woman's, but with a gaping mouth and a cross-eyed glare in the old Kabuki tradition. A pair of short, pointy horns jutted from the top of the head. The caption identified it as a *ningyo*. The illustration creeped him out almost as much as the few minutes in his old house had done.

"*Ningyo* is best translated as 'human-fish,'" he read. "Its appearance portends disaster; conversely, it may also provide good luck and even immortality. A mummified *ningyo* is displayed at a Shinto temple near Mount Fuji, said to be a fisherman who was changed into this form as punishment for entering forbidden waters. Wearing an amulet with its picture, or even eating its flesh, can protect against illnesses and epidemics."

Seth shuddered, remembering the wizened little face of the Jenny Haniver. A person would have to be pretty desperate to eat that . . . But people afraid of getting sick did become desperate sometimes, didn't they? Unaware he was doing it, Seth touched his throat, feeling the swollen glands there.

He closed the book and set it on the porch boards beneath the swing, where he would not be able to easily reach it again. He wished he hadn't gone and gotten it in the first place, couldn't remember why it had seemed urgent enough to brave the horror of his old home.

Darkness had begun to draw down on the island again. Not yet ready to get up, he dozed in the swing and dreamed of Grand Illumination Night, one of the touchstones of his childhood. On this magical evening, the gingerbread cottages were decorated with thousands of paper lanterns in all colors and sizes. When the signal came, the lanterns blazed to life, a softly shifting, swaying array that painted the crowd's faces with kaleidoscopic light. The eye scarcely knew where to look, how to credit such wonder. His parents had brought him to Illumination every year. He remembered walking beside his mother, holding her hand. Back in the days when she was a living person who loved him, not a rotting body he had abandoned.

Seth saw the lanterns in his dream, but now their colors seemed wrong, as if a slightly different spectrum had become visible. An especially large one hung nearby, swaying in an unfelt breeze. He didn't want to look at it, but in the way of dreams, he could not stop his head from turning. It was the *chōchin'obake*, his childhood fear, its split-open mouth sagging, its huge mournful eyes beseeching him to come closer. If he did, he knew its long paper tongue would lick at his face. He tried to back away, but his feet wouldn't move. The mouth drooped farther and the creature spoke in a terrible rasping whisper: "*Hello, gayboy, little infected gayboy. There's no place for you in the old woman's world, you know. They would drive you out. You and your plague.*"

Seth didn't know who the old woman was. He thought he *might* know, might be able to think of it, but only if the *chōchin'obake* would stop that awful whispering. "*The world has had enough plague. No one will want you, no one will welcome you. They might even kill you. Yes, I think they might very well kill you. The old woman's God doesn't love little infected gayboys.*"

There was a dark man inside the *chōchin'obake*. Seth could see his awful, gleeful face now, hiding behind the lantern's facade. The paper tongue lolled out, seeming to taste the air. *"But if you come to me, if you come with the other sinners, I will welcome you. I will value your tainted blood. There are . . . things I can do with it."*

The creature laughed, and the tongue shot out like a party blower, at least ten feet long. Seth wrenched himself awake before it could touch him. He was halfway out of the porch swing, his legs pedaling madly, trying to propel himself backward. He grabbed for the flashlight he knew was nearby. Found it. Clicked it on and nearly screamed when he saw what was at his feet: *The Old Legends of Japan*, open to the picture of the *ningyo*, though Seth clearly remembered closing the book before he dozed off.

After a few bad moments, he realized that compared with the horror he had met in his dream, the mermaid creature wasn't so fearsome. It almost seemed to be smiling at him. He pulled the book toward him, and as he touched it, he felt a wave of reassurance and comfort like a mother's embrace. *The old woman's God loves everyone,* he thought, although his nightmare was fading quickly and he was unsure what the phrase meant.

He found that he was no longer reluctant to bring the book inside. He took it to bed with him, and slept a blessedly dreamless sleep.

Seth went back to Menemsha the next day. He found Mole cleaning bonito in the boat shed; his rough hands bloody with it. "Thought you said you got seasick," Seth said.

"Catch these with a line from shore when they're runnin'," said the old man. "I should think an island kid would know that much."

"I know how to dig for clams."

Mole snorted. "Every little squirt on this island learns to dig for clams before they're off their mother's tit. D'you want to meet the mermaid?"

TILL HUMAN VOICES WAKE US, AND WE DROWN

"The mermaid?"

"Yeah, that's why you're here, ain't it? I don't think you came back for *me*." That merited a brief cackle as the old man wiped the blood from his hands. "Come on up. We'll see if she wants to say hello."

The interior of the shack was dark and dismal, smelling strongly of low tide. As his eyes adjusted to the dimness, Seth saw Jenny Hanivers hung on the walls and dangling on wires from exposed beams. He remembered a childhood friend who'd had a huge doll collection arrayed on shelves in her bedroom. These things seemed to stare at you like those had, blind yet knowing. Interspersed here and there were other bits of flotsam: a dried starfish, a horseshoe crab shell, a green glass ball float encased in netting. A ratty-looking hammock hung in one corner. He saw the big aquarium on the far side of the room, sensed murky movement within.

"Come on," said Mole, crossing the room. "No need to be shy. *She* sure ain't."

Seth peeked over the edge of the tank. The creature within was about four feet long, perhaps half as wide. It (*she?*) was made of fleshy ruffled petals that reminded him of hydrangeas, but deep blue, almost black. Just beneath the surface of its skin, lines of gold rippled like the chromatophores of certain octopuses he had seen.

"Say hello to our company, dear," the old man said, and among the petals, two pairs of eyes opened. They were a deeper gold than the coloration shot through its (*her*) skin, as large as the palm of his hand, hellishly intelligent.

Seth stumbled backward and almost twisted his ankle on a pile of rusty tools. He could not meet that anguished golden gaze. Mole laughed. "No need for that, either. She can't hurt you. Wouldn't if she could. She helps us and we help her."

A liquid cooing came from the aquarium.

"Put your hand in the water," Mole urged. "Help her. She needs it."

Seth didn't want to, but his body seemed to be working with no input from his brain. He immersed his arm to the elbow in the chilly water. The mermaid swirled up from the bottom of the tank and engulfed his hand. He could feel the petals urging him deeper. His fingertips met a firm surface, and as he stroked it, the mermaid's whole body shuddered around his hand. The contact seemed to slide him into a dimension where everything was sexual. He was dimly aware of Mole kneeling before him, unzipping his pants and gripping his cock; then the old man's mouth was on him, and Seth thrust his fingers deep into the mermaid and his cock deep into Mole's throat. There were a few moments of slippery sensory overload. Seth tried to pull away, but the old man's hand gripped his ass, holding him in place. The sensations were too intense, almost painful. The three of them came together, and the mermaid's consciousness speared through the two men, joining them together so that they felt the others' orgasms as well as their own.

Afterward, Mole offered him a shot of whiskey, and Seth took it. The liquor burned his throat and kindled in his belly. A second shot gave him the courage to say, "You should let her go."

The old man's sharp blue gaze pinned him. "Let her *go*? Go where?"

"The ocean."

"The ocean." Mole gave a sardonic little laugh. "My pa pulled her up out of the *ocean* thirty years ago. Something had bit her near in half. He didn't know what she was, but he brought her home and took care of her, nursed her back to health. She thanked us by showing us what she could do. She doesn't want to *go* anywhere."

"How do you know?"

"How do I know? Just look at her!" Mole gestured at the aquarium. "She's whole, she's healthy, nothing's going to try and eat her. She's safe here."

"You love her, don't you?"

Mole gave a contemptuous little grunt. Seth kept staring at him, and finally the old man said, "'Course I love her. You felt what she can do. Let her do it a couple more times and you'll love her, too."

"I think I have AIDS," Seth said.

"My pa had a tumor in his brain when he hauled her up. Doctors said he'd no more than a few months to live, but he hung around ten more years. She cured him. She'll cure you. And she keeps the flu away."

"So, she cures your sickness, and she gets you off. What does *she* get out of it?"

"Don't play stupid with me, boy. She came, too, you felt it. She needs to come every day, sometimes two or three times. She feeds on it."

"You do that for her?"

"Yeah." The old man held up a gnarled hand, gave his first two fingers an obscene little crook. "That's how she keeps the sickness off you. She don't just cure you once, she cures you on what you might call a daily basis."

"That's why you have to keep her."

"Yeah. Won't be able to do it much longer, though. Got a dickey heart like my pa. I feel it squeezin' up in my chest every day now, and that's not something she can cure."

Seth's patience was at an end. "What do you want from me?" he yelled. "Why are you showing me this?!"

"When I met you down on the beach there, you weren't scared of the Jenny Haniver. And you struck me as a lad who might need curing. Fact is, you look a little peaked right now. You take care of her after I'm gone, well . . . she'll take care of you."

Seth bolted. He wrenched the shack's door open, took the stairs two at a time, and raced toward his car. Behind him, he could hear Mole calling, "Come back whenever you're ready. She ain't going anywhere."

⤴

A day, a week, a month went by. Seth's throat hurt most of the time. He found himself nodding off in the middle of the afternoon. He didn't care, just slept wherever he happened to be. He lost his appetite and dropped ten pounds from his already skinny frame. He didn't check on any of the other islanders. One day he woke up with a Gobi-dry mouth and a stabbing pain in his tongue. The bathroom mirror showed him yellow blotches on his tongue and inner cheeks. He recognized these as oral thrush, one of the opportunistic infections his doctor had warned him about.

He opened the drawer, took out a bottle of AZT, felt his stomach clench. Shook two capsules into his hand. Poured a glass of water from the pitcher he kept there. Almost swallowed the pills. Then flung them away, cursing, and left the house.

He could smell the odor of decomposition as soon as he parked beside Mole's shack. His feet didn't want to climb the stairs, but he forced himself up. The door wasn't locked, nor had Seth expected it to be; Mole would have been hoping he'd come.

The sight that greeted him was worse than he'd feared. Mole was in the hammock, and the fatal heart attack (so Seth assumed) must have happened at least a week ago, because Mole was ripe, riper than any corpse Seth had seen in the thick of the superflu. He wore only a pair of saturated boxer shorts. His eyes were like a pair of peeled eggs gone bad. His hands were great bloated gloves. His tongue jutted obscenely from his mouth. Worst of all, he had begun to drip through the netting of the hammock, producing little diamond-shaped runners of decay. Flies crawled over him and maggots churned in the hollow of his belly. The smell was monumental.

If he vomited, Seth thought he would pass out. He turned away from the awful sight. As he did so, motion caught his eye, and for a moment he thought he might join Mole in heart attack heaven. But the movement had come from the big tank.

The aquarium was dark with algae and smelled stagnant. Seth realized the pump was no longer working. When he looked into the tank, he thought at first that the creature was dead. Her midnight-blue color had faded to a sickly aqua, and the gold ripples under her skin were entirely gone. Then she fluttered to the surface and a soft burbling reached his ears.

"What do you want? How can I help you?"

Her four eyes grew heavy-lidded. Her petals rippled in an unmistakably coquettish pattern.

"Oh, no, I can't—"

But he realized that he was becoming aroused. That was impossible, in this stinking room, with this nonhuman but apparently female creature, and yet he was suddenly as hard as he could ever recall being. He did not remember that he shared the room with a corpse, no longer smelled its fetor. With one hand, he undid his fly and reached in to grasp his cock. He slipped his other hand into the water, and the mermaid flowed around it, engulfed it. Gentle muscles gripped his fingers, guided them to where they were needed. He stroked the firm little node. The mermaid shuddered and cooed, and Seth moaned. It was no longer his own hand on his cock; though she was still in the tank, he thought he could feel those tight petals sucking him in. They came together, not so much an orgasm as an explosion. Seth steadied himself on the edge of the aquarium. The mermaid fluttered quietly to the bottom of the tank. Her color was a little better now, more cornflower than aqua.

"Did you like that?" Seth asked when he was able to speak. "I mean, I know you came, but . . . is this what you want to be doing? Isn't this the wrong place for you?"

What happened next was a sensation Seth never forgot. The mermaid's mind flowed into his own, and it spoke there. "*I. Take. Illness. I. Give. Pleasure. Are you. Unsatisfied?*"

Seth shook his head.

"*I. Pleasure you. Again. If you. Want.*"

He *did* want, that was the thing. Though only moments had passed since his orgasm, he already wanted to feel those phantom petals on him again. He wanted to slide his fingers into the mermaid and stroke her again. Most of all, he wanted her to take away his illness. He could understand why Mole (and Mole's father before him) had been compelled to keep her. But it still felt wrong.

"Where do you come from?" he asked. "Where do you belong?"

"I. Belong. Ocean. We make. Love. I make. Love. With others. Like. Me."

The language was primitive, but as the mermaid spoke, a picture appeared in his head. Sapphire-clear water, seaweed forest, and on the sandy bottom, dozens of creatures like this one. Some were deep blue, some rosy pink, some silver. Golden light rippled beneath their skin as they flowed over and under and into one another. They trembled with orgasms. They were breathtaking, a multicolored collage of ecstasy. Mole had called the mermaid *she*, but Seth saw now that there was no male or female among these beings; they were embodiments of pleasure and needed no other sustenance or meaning.

I belong ocean.

"I think I can take you back there," Seth said.

Getting the mermaid out of the tank proved to be the hardest part. He was afraid of hurting her (his mind still wanted to use that pronoun), and while she wasn't terribly heavy, she was slippery as hell. Finally, he managed to clutch her to his chest and half slip, half stagger past Mole's pitiful corpse, down the stairs, and out onto the beach.

He flopped down at the water's edge, spent. The mermaid slipped out of his arms and into the water. He saw her blossom there like a many-petaled blue flower, saw gold ripples unfurl beneath her skin. Once more she spoke in his mind: *"Thank. You. For. Freeing. I. Love. You."*

"I love you, too," Seth whispered. He pushed himself up on his elbows and watched her swim away, then let himself sink back down. The water lapping at his face was cold, and the rocks dug into him everywhere, but he couldn't move yet.

Pain cored into his bones. His throat was full of razors.

When he closed his eyes, the torn paper face of the *chōchin'obake* loomed out of the darkness, its long tongue lolling. He wondered if the dark man would still want him.

KOVACH'S LAST CASE

Michael Koryta

He thought he might be the last homicide detective in America. Maybe the world.

The problem wasn't a lack of murders to solve, of course—the killings had been relentless, and make no mistake, plenty of them were murders, slayings without regard for defense of life or property—but there was no one left with an interest in solving them.

Eddie Kovach had been on the homicide beat for twenty-seven years, and he should've retired after the twenty-fifth and moved up to Wisconsin to buy the bait shop, the one beside the lake where he'd had some of his best days. He knew it now; he'd known it then.

But he hadn't, because there were the unsolved cases. White whales. Every detective had them.

Or they'd had them once.

A lot had changed in a hurry.

Police departments had disbanded, the formal chain of command in the law enforcement world disintegrating alongside every other institution in America as the virus known as Captain Trips swept from coast to coast—nobody was sure of the origin point, although many rumors focused on the West, some military installation in the desert. Others put it in Nebraska, or maybe in rural Maine, where something called Project Arrowhead was underway, although nobody could agree what Project Arrowhead was. No one seemed to think the flu's origin was a natural mutation. Beliefs divided largely into one of two camps: the superflu was a disaster of the government's making, or an act of a wrathful God.

Eddie Kovach didn't care much one way or the other. Wherever the virus began, it had whisked the remnants of law and order right out of the world, efficient as a broom wielded for spring cleaning. What little policing remained, be it conducted by those in a uniform or by private citizens, was focused on protection. That was fine. "Protect and serve" was the motto for a reason.

But Kovach was a detective, not a beat cop. And as the days passed and the bodies stacked up in the streets, floated by in the rivers, and banged against the breakwater on the lake, as the gunfire echoed throughout the city, first at night and then in broad daylight, the summer soundtracked by constant rattling semiautomatic small rounds and the big booms of twelve-gauge shotguns on Cleveland's near west side, Kovach began to wonder who would speak for the dead.

For twenty-seven years, it had been his job.

No, fuck that.

For twenty-seven years, it had been his *identity*.

You were supposed to have more than your job. Everyone knew that; every cop surely did. But Edward J. Kovach—Fast Eddie K, as he'd been known as a kid, the nickname following him from Thomas Jefferson Middle School through West Tech High School before he'd become a cop and simply become "Kovach" to everyone and anyone—had never succeeded with the task of being more than the job. One marriage had brought him close, maybe. His ex-wife would probably dispute that. She'd say the job was what ended the marriage.

Of course, Debbie couldn't say anything now because she was

dead. Kovach had found her body slumped beside that of her new husband at their house in Parma, a western suburb representing the longest trip he'd dared to take since the chaos turned bloody at the end of June. He'd shot three men on the way out to Parma and two on the way back, wild-eyed looters on dirt bikes, two carrying rifles, two carrying machetes, one with an actual fucking sword. At least four of them had been sick. One of them had breathed right in Eddie's face.

He made it home, though, thinking of the insane toll—five killed simply to locate two who were already dead, and nobody helped. He wondered why in the hell he'd returned home at all. There was something about heading west that had felt right in a way he couldn't articulate, and yet he'd come back to his house in a neighborhood that was mostly empty, and sometimes still burning.

He thought that if Debbie and Tom, her new husband, had been alive, he'd have tried to talk them into heading west with him. Heading to . . . where, exactly? He wasn't sure. West, though, that was the direction. Why? He was a west-side guy, was Fast Eddie K, and there was the vague American notion of manifest destiny floating around in his skull, the history books telling you west was the way to go, but he didn't think either of those reasons carried the day.

The dreams did, maybe. The dreams that came for him in the night were of wide-open plains and a farmhouse and although he didn't know the exact location, he was sure that it was west of the Cuyahoga River. Somewhere in the great open expanse between Cleveland and Colorado where the evening sun squeezed blood red over the plains, and the mountains—the snow-covered, perilous mountains—waited beyond.

He didn't want to make the trip alone, though, and he hadn't found any allies with whom to make the journey. Just fought his way out to the city's suburbs and buried his ex and then—with maybe a little more happiness than he cared to admit—buried her husband along with her. Kovach had met Debbie when she was nineteen, the most vibrantly alive woman he'd ever known, buzzing with an energy that made him wonder if she was on drugs. She wasn't. That was just Debbie, operating on a different lifeblood than Kovach could fathom, with enthusiasm for *everything*.

Now she was dead, like most of the city, the state, the country, probably the world? It was hard to know for sure. No news updates in weeks. There had been a few days in June when it seemed like the thing could be put back in the bottle. The president had spoken, assuring a tense nation that contrary to the reports of an "irresponsible, fear-mongering media," the virus not only wasn't the work of the U.S. government, but wasn't fatal at all. Eddie hadn't voted for the guy, but he trusted the speech, because he figured the stakes were too high for a lie.

Guess again.

Day he knew it was real? When they'd canceled the baseball season. You didn't just stop playing baseball. The game went on, always. Hell of a season shaping up for the Indians, too, the old retreads like Keith Hernandez and Brook Jacoby on their way out, promising kids like Sandy Alomar Jr. and Carlos Baerga coming up, solid veterans like Candy Maldonado holding it all together. A new ballpark was on the way, made a sure thing in May after the voters agreed to a "sin tax" on cigarettes and alcohol to fund it. Very exciting. So much promise for the city.

On the twenty-seventh, Eddie had tuned into 3WE 1100, "The Big One," the Cleveland-based AM radio station with supposedly the highest-powered broadcasting antenna in the nation, capable of reaching thirty-eight states and a portion of Canada at night in decent conditions. All he'd wanted to hear was Herb Score talking about the return of baseball. Instead, they'd been playing a clip from some radio station in Missouri. A call-in show called *Speak Your Piece*, hosted by a guy named Ray Flowers, and Kovach desperately wanted it to be a hoax, because for a solid hour the guy fielded calls from around the country, offering up one horror story after another—bodies in Kansas

City being removed from the hospital by the truckload; a doctor who claimed the government assurances of a vaccine were bullshit—and then it all ended with what sounded like a military assault on the studio, Ray Flowers saying, "I think they're going to shoot me!" and gunfire.

Kovach didn't think it was a hoax by then.

That was the day he decided to go to Parma to check on Debbie. That was the day he gave up on the return of baseball.

In late June, the stadium known as the "Mistake on the Lake" was turned into a shelter, both because it could be easily defended against the bands of looters that had become the city's second plague, and the experts from the Cleveland Clinic had compelling theories that the open-air venue might slow the spread of transmission.

There were more than twenty-five thousand corpses in the place when it had been set on fire a few weeks later.

After that, the city was mostly quiet except for the gunfire and the screaming. Most of the people who hadn't died had fled. Ed Kovach—Fast Eddie K of West Tech High—wasn't in either group, the dead or the fled. He had no idea what kept him out of the former. He'd held so many of the sick and the dying in his arms, and yet the virus didn't take him. He'd never so much as coughed, never had a fever... although he had fever dreams. He would wake in a sweat with memories of a windblown wheat field and howling wolves trapped in his mind, stumble to the bathroom, grab the thermometer, and check, sure that it was his time.

Never did he crack 98.6.

So he stayed out of the dead group. Why did he stay out of the "fled" group, too?

Not so mysterious. He was alone and Cleveland was home. His job was solving murders. People kept killing in Cleveland, and on the one day when he'd thought with seriousness of heading west with or without an ally, he'd realized there was a serial killer in the city.

Not a spree killer. There was a difference. Once, either kind had been rare, but in the summer of 1990, spree killers became commonplace. There was rampaging, a return to the Crusades-style existence that now defined the American landscape, but somewhere along the Cuyahoga River a hunter had moved in, who called to mind those howling wolves in the wheat fields that he dreamed of again and again while he slept with his right hand resting on the stock of his duty pistol.

He'd thought he was numb to the sight of corpses until September, when he entered the freezer of Bad Boy's BBQ on the corner of West 56th and Train Avenue. He was looking for food, same as anybody, and had the passing thought that maybe Ralph Wojesik's propane generator had kept the freezer going for long enough that some of the meat inside hadn't spoiled.

The generator was long silenced and whatever meat had been in the freezer was long gone—except for the human meat.

There were three bodies on stainless steel hooks that first day. Looked like a bad horror movie, the corpses hung high, impaled with the hooks carefully driven through the back of the necks so that their sharp points came out of the mouths, barely visible, the way you'd tuck a hook through a night crawler before casting it into the water and hoping to tempt a walleye.

Kovach had seen so much death by then that even a sight as gruesome as this wasn't likely to give him much pause, except for one detail: the corpses had been drained of blood. Two men and one woman, one Black, two white, ages approximately twenty, forty, and fifty. No similarities between the vics. In another age, this would've been noteworthy. Now it was a day that ended in Y.

Except for the way they'd been bled out. Even in a moment when carnage was commonplace, that was unique. They'd been hung carefully, and then the femoral arteries had been cut—neatly, probably with a razor or a scalpel, a precise, efficient incision, no rage to it. Hang a body up so gravity is your friend and then open the femoral artery and it doesn't take long to drain the blood.

KOVACH'S LAST CASE

So where was the blood?

The bare concrete floor was speckled with a few rust-colored flecks. Kovach put on his gloves and used his pocketknife to lift those from the stone. Proximity told him the blood had likely come from the vics, but there was so little of it.

Why?

The freezer wasn't operational, but it was still cooler than most rooms in the city. A smart space to work with a body when you didn't have electricity, one that kept the smell from overwhelming you right away, and one that was discreet and out of sight, allowing time while you did your gruesome work. He suspected those elements played into the selection of the location, but it was impossible to know for sure. He lowered the bodies from the hooks, but didn't remove them, because he tried not to burn corpses unless the wind was blowing out of the southwest, toward the lake, which carried the smell away from his house on Clark Avenue. He liked to sit out on the porch in the evening. Simple pleasures. It was hard to enjoy the porch when the wind carried the stench of the burning dead.

That day, though, the wind was pushing hard out of the north, cool and crisp and undercutting the humidity, a perfect night for baseball, if baseball had still existed. The breeze off the lake would've limited the long power hitters to the warning track, turned it into a pitcher's duel, and that was always Eddie Kovach's favorite style of baseball. Shame that the game, like presumably the rest of America, was dead. He wondered idly, as he walked away from the corpses with the hooks through their skulls, whether baseball would ever come back. It seemed unlikely, sure, but the human condition was an interesting one. Resilient, maybe? Delusional, certainly. Call it what you wanted, there was hope hiding in there. One night, not long ago, he'd heard laughter while he sat on the porch. Not the wild, mad laughter of hysteria that had become almost as common as the screams and the gunfire, but *real* laughter, the kind that followed a joke, the kind that was joyful and partnered with a smile, and he'd walked toward the sound, but then it was gone, and he'd never located the laughter.

He kept the memory, though. When he rolled the muzzle of the Smith & Wesson around in his mouth, he remembered the laugh. He had lowered the gun and gone to sleep and even when the wolves howled in his nightmares, he had felt better because of the memory of the laugh, had woken not soaked in sweat, but calmly, almost happily, thinking of his mother.

Or someone's mother. Hell, maybe it had been only the word.

Mother was a beautiful word. Beautiful as the sound of laughter.

Two days after he'd found the corpses, Indian summer flooded the city with heat and the wind swung around to the southwest. He returned to Bad Boy's BBQ to collect the corpses and take them to the gravel lot across the train tracks, where he burned bodies. It was better than letting them fester. Felt kinder, somehow, and it surely was better for the neighborhood than letting them decompose, and Eddie had always loved his neighborhood.

You did what you could.

When he entered the meat locker, the three bodies on the floor were where he'd left them—but two more dangled above. A Hispanic man, maybe thirty, and a redheaded woman, probably fifty. Meat hooks pierced the bases of their skulls and the glinting tips held their bloodless lips apart. The femoral arteries had been opened with the same neat incisions.

There was no blood on the floor beneath them.

Everything was calculated, methodical. The manner of the killing wasn't obvious, and Kovach's gut instinct, that sixth sense honed by twenty-seven years of homicide study, told him the cause of death wasn't the meat hook through the skull or the sliced arteries. A crime scene tech would be needed to verify that, of course, but all the techs he'd ever known were dead or gone, so he'd have to trust his gut. What it said: the vics were being killed elsewhere, transported to Bad Boy's

KOVACH'S LAST CASE

BBQ, hung carefully from the meat hooks, and drained of their blood. The bodies remained; the blood disappeared.

A serial killer. On Eddie Kovach's block!

Somehow, this was the greatest indignity he could fathom in a world that had lost all dignity in June, when they'd called off baseball, and the president had given his last speech, and madness reigned.

He could burn the bodies, same as he did with all the others who died of the plague or random violence or suicide or simple, foolish accidents that could no longer be set right because there were no hospitals, no ambulances, no police patrols, no social order. Or . . .

He could solve the case.

Someone needed to speak for the dead. Eddie Kovach couldn't do it for all of them, but for the five in the meat locker at Bad Boy's BBQ in his very neighborhood? He could do that much.

That night, he began surveillance.

It was three days before anyone approached the building. Three long hot days and nights of round-the-clock surveillance, dozing here and there, but mostly awake, trying to keep his mind off the relentless stink of death, off the memories of other long nights with partners at his side, good men and women who were likely all dead now, like Debbie. Sometimes, he played the radio low, wondering which survivor was manning the equipment, and why they never spoke. Maybe it was on some kind of autopilot . . . or maybe the survivor who played music knew better than to announce his or her existence. The music was pop hits, modern stuff, Madonna and Larry Underwood. Kovach could do without Madonna, but he liked Underwood's song "Baby, Can You Dig Your Man?" The way the white boy sang it made Kovach think of the old solo album from Buddy Miles, who'd been Hendrix's drummer, had an Afro damn near as wide as his drum kit. Kovach had loved that album back in the days when Debbie and Kovach would go out and dance. Hard to believe there'd ever been such days.

"*But bay-yay-yaybe you can tell me if anyone can . . .*"

He turned the radio louder when that Underwood song played. Drummed his fingers off the steering wheel of the gutted van he'd set up as a surveillance post. When the song was over, he'd turn the radio back down low, or off entirely, and watch the barbecue joint in silence, the way a detective should.

Third day, finally, action. Just before sunset. A woman, small and brunette, weighing maybe a buck ten, dressed in a tank top over loose blue pants that looked like medical scrubs.

Pushing a body in a wheelbarrow.

The corpse was a man, pale and broad-shouldered and blond and big, too big for the woman to push easily even using the wheelbarrow. Kovach was so struck by the scene he almost forgot about his camera. He finally snapped a few photos while she fumbled the door to the barbecue restaurant open and wrestled the wheelbarrow inside.

When she was out of sight, he lowered the camera and let his hand trace the butt of his duty pistol. Go in? Murder suspect with a corpse, of course you went in.

Those had once been the rules, anyhow.

These were different times.

He waited. There was no need to rush, and he was curious about the blood.

She was inside for twenty minutes. Came back out with a plastic two-liter of Pepsi in each hand, walking fast. In the waning light, the contents of the Pepsi bottles could almost have passed for the real deal. There was just enough of the day left to show that the liquid inside wasn't cola-colored.

It was a dark ruby.

Kovach took pictures. He left the van when the brunette was two blocks away, then followed, kept low and quiet, stopped when she stopped, ducked behind a dumpster the one time she looked back. Counted to twenty, checked the street again. She was back in motion, walking faster.

He followed her for almost thirty blocks, thinking that once she would have been insane to walk in this neighborhood after dark, then reminding himself that she was the one who'd brought the dead in and hung them up on the hooks—her sanity was a question, yes, but her safety wasn't the concern. The advantage of so much death was that there was no such thing as a dangerous neighborhood.

They went north, all the way to Detroit Avenue, where she finally stopped at an apartment building, used a key on a padlock to loosen a chain that held the door shut, and slipped inside. A few minutes after she entered, a light went on in the fifth-floor corner apartment, the faint, flickering glow of a candle or kerosene lamp.

Somewhere down the street, not far away, a man howled with madness, and gunshots cracked. It was full dark now, and Kovach had decisions to make. Arrest her? He almost laughed. He intended to stop her—but, really, what was the rush? She'd chained and locked the door and he had no backup. She'd hear him breaking into the building, and if that happened, Fast Eddie K was likely to take his leave from this world dangling from a meat hook himself. No thanks.

He went home. Slept until daybreak. Woke up and cleaned his gun and walked back to the brunette's apartment building. Waited.

She came down two hours later, checked the window, then unchained the door and stepped outside. She had a black leather bag slung over one shoulder, a clipboard in her left hand, and a street map in her right. She checked the map, then the clipboard, then folded the map, removed a pen, made a notation on the clipboard, and tucked the pen behind her ear before setting off up the street.

Kovach fell in behind her.

They walked west, then north, toward the lake. The heat had finally broken, and the air was crisp. The day was quiet, no looters out—not much left to loot. Sometimes the mornings could almost pass for sane.

Almost.

Farther north, past Don's Lighthouse Grille, where Kovach and Debbie had eaten dinner on the night he proposed, and straight across the intersection, moving toward Edgewater Park, where he'd finally gotten down on one knee, his hand trembling a little as he opened the ring box. Left on Lake Avenue, then left again on West 145th. Kovach wheezing a little now, thinking there was no wonder the brunette killer was so damn slim, with all this walking. She stopped outside of a brick Tudor-style house, looked up the drive, then down at her clipboard. All business. Satisfied with whatever she'd seen, she knelt behind a tree and unzipped the black leather bag. Kovach removed the lens cap from his camera and zoomed in.

The clipboard was in the grass at her feet. She had a syringe in her right hand and a vial in her left.

Mysterious cause of death = solved. Kovach couldn't help being pleased with his initial read of the scene in the meat locker, determining that the hooks hadn't been used until after the fact.

She uncapped the syringe with her teeth. Kovach snapped pictures while she pierced the vial with the needle and drew back the plunger, filling the big syringe with an unknown liquid. She then withdrew what looked like an air pistol, flipped the bolt open, and loaded the syringe inside. A dart gun. Kovach had never seen one in action.

She put the loaded gun in the bag and straightened up and eyed the Tudor again and he knew he had to stop her now. Even in this sorry excuse for a world, Detective Eddie Kovach wasn't going to let a murderer proceed with business.

He'd come to speak for the dead, after all. A few of them, anyhow.

He approached her at a quick but steady walk, camera slung beneath his left arm, gun held in his right. Her attention was on the house—she seemed to be considering the best approach across the wide lawn—and she didn't hear him until he was almost on her. When she whirled, his gun was already leveled at her face.

"Put the bag on the ground and then put your hands behind your head, fingers laced together," Kovach said.

She stared at him, fierce-eyed, chest rising and falling. Didn't move to surrender the bag.

"Cleveland Police Department," Kovach said. "Put the fucking bag on the ground."

Her eyes widened and then she laughed. Not a pleasant sound; an astonished one, a bark of disbelief.

"Police," she said, blurting the word out as if it were the most implausible thing she'd ever heard.

"That's right. Detective Kovach, Homicide. We're going to talk about Bad Boy's Barbecue."

Her face changed. Still shocked, but with that tinge of *uh-oh* understanding that a suspect gave you the instant they realized you were a step ahead. Kovach had missed that look.

"I kill only the bad ones," she said.

"Sure."

"It's true."

"Sure."

"They're the ones who dream of the dark man," she said. "But they still dream. That matters." A pause, then: "You must dream, too. We all do. If we're still alive, I think we're all dreamers."

He tried not to look rattled.

"What do you see?" she asked.

"I'm not the one who needs to answer questions."

"Because you were a police officer."

"I still am."

Her smile was so sad it made his throat tighten.

"All right," she said. "In that case, I'm still a doctor."

"What kind of doctor?"

"Neuroscience."

"Harvesting brains," Kovach said. "Cool. Must've been inspiring work, based on what I've seen you do with a meat hook."

"I'm *not* harvesting brains," she said with real contempt, as if the notion disgusted her. "I'm harvesting blood. I think that's the only real hope. The dreamers matter, and their blood might be valuable beyond what we can even imagine. The data is compelling."

Though he was facing a murderer who was not in handcuffs, Eddie Kovach still lowered his gun.

"May we talk?" the murderer asked him.

He didn't answer. He was trying to process the situation.

"Look," she said, "you're either going to kill me or—"

"I'm not going to kill you."

"Well, you're not going to arrest me, right?! There's no jail left."

He tried to project false confidence, as if he might know of a holding cell that she didn't. She sighed again. Ran a hand through her hair.

"I would urge you to hear me out," she said, and then gestured at the brick Tudor. "Because there is a man inside that house who dreams of the dark man and is recruiting a team to follow him west, and I think his blood will be far more useful in service to research than it will be if it's spilled for the dark man and his wolves."

And his wolves. Kovach felt his stomach clench. He hadn't dreamed of the dark man, wasn't sure what she meant by that, but he knew of the wolves. They lurked in the high windswept wheat in his own dreams, howling and snarling. Waiting on their master's call.

"Hear me out," she repeated, softer but more urgent now.

"Okay," Kovach heard himself say. "But I'll take your bag—and keep the gun in my hand."

"That's fine."

They walked to Edgewater Park and sat on a picnic table looking out at Lake Erie. There was a sniper on the pier, but he didn't take a shot. The snipers usually didn't. They wanted to be seen and feared, that was all. The man might even have been a colleague of Kovach's at some point, another badge-toting fool who stuck to his mission as Kovach had.

They watched the gulls circle and swoop as the woman told Kovach her name was Ruth Pritchard and that she'd been employed as a research scientist at the Cleveland Clinic in the days before the end.

"I ran a sleep research program," she said. "The focus was on lucid dreaming. We were nearing the end of our grant funding. Not enough people saw the practical value."

The practical value, she'd decided in the lonely days holed up in her apartment during the summer, watching the city and country collapse, might just exceed any hope she'd ever had for her own study.

"While the phones stayed up, I kept calling my patients," she told him. "Pointless, right? I mean, we all knew how bad it was by then. Nothing would ever be the same, and still I kept pretending, kept going through the motions. It filled my days. It was better to pretend that there might be a return to normal than to accept that it was gone forever."

Kovach thought of himself, walking the neighborhood streets, wearing his badge and carrying his radio, long after they'd told everyone in the department good luck, and God bless.

"A surprising number of them answered my calls," Ruth Pritchard went on. "That was astonishing, because . . . well, statistically speaking—"

"They should have been dead."

She nodded. "More of them, anyhow. Many more. I was working with a group of a hundred and fifty. They were intensely lucid dreamers with unusually high recall. And because I didn't know what else to do, I kept calling them, and I kept asking questions, and it became obvious that they were still dreaming. No surprise. I was, too. The unique thing was . . . "

She paused as the sounds of cawing became higher and harsher. Kovach followed her eyes. The gulls had discovered a human foot and most of an ankle wedged in the rocks. The rest of the body was missing.

"The unique thing was, we were all dreaming of the same things," Ruth said, turning from the gulls to Kovach, her dark-rimmed eyes intense with a quality he hadn't seen in so long. A quality like hope.

"Do you see the farm?" he asked softly.

He could see her exhale. Her entire body loosened.

"With the old woman," she whispered. "Yes. You too?"

"I don't see a woman," he said, and she tensed a little again. "I see a farm, surrounded by high wheat, and I think that if I head that way . . ."

His words trailed off and he shook his head.

"What?" she said. "If you head that way, what?"

"I don't know. I think it may be good? May be . . . necessary? But then there are the wolves."

He stopped, embarrassed, because she surely had heard his fear.

"Yes," she said. "There are the wolves. And the one who commands them."

Silence. He cleared his throat, said, "What's the deal with the blood?"

"Vaccine research," she said. "There are three doctors from the Cleveland Clinic's vaccine program who are still alive. I won't tell you who they are, or where. But they're out there. And they're working. And that is the closest thing to hope that I can offer."

"You do the killing, and you bring them the blood?"

"That's right." Her fine-boned jaw was set hard. "But I kill only the ones who talked to me of joining the dark man."

"And you'd study that blood, ultimately use it somehow in creating a vaccine?" Off her nod, he said, "Well . . . what if instead of a vaccine you succeed in making more just like him?"

For the first time, he saw she had fears of her own. "I don't think that will happen."

"That's exactly what the president said about mass death."

She swallowed. "We have to try."

"But what if you're wrong?" Kovach asked.

She didn't answer for a long time. Then she pointed at the pier, where the sniper watched the shoreline through his scope, and then down to the rocks, where gulls fought over what little was left of the human foot.

"I have to try."

They sat in silence for a bit. Kovach reached out and tapped the clipboard, which held a printed list of names and addresses in neat columns, with handwritten notations in tiny script jotted here and there.

"This is your kill list," he said.

Her eyes answered yes.

"You let yourself do that," he said wonderingly. "Murder people. Hang them up and drain their blood into Pepsi bottles. A *doctor*."

"I'm not a doctor anymore. I want to be one again. That can only happen if we rebuild this city, this world. Some kind of civilization. Don't you see that?"

Kovach, once a cop, thought that his eyes also probably answered yes, although he didn't let himself speak.

"You asked me what if I'm wrong," she said, "and that's the right question. But it's not so different from the old woman on the farm and the dark man with the wolves, is it? Two sides of the same coin. So . . . what if I'm right?"

Kovach stayed silent. His hand was on his gun and his eyes were on the gulls, which were busily pecking the last strips of flesh from the stark white bone.

"You could help me," Ruth Pritchard said tentatively.

He shook his head. "I'm a cop," he said. "A homicide detective. I *stop* people like you."

When she touched his hand, his entire body thrilled. There was something in that touch that reminded him of the sound of laughter he'd heard up the avenue before it was lost to the dark. Something that made him think of the beautiful word *mother*. He couldn't bring himself to look her in the eyes.

"There are no police anymore," she whispered. "And there are no doctors. There are only survivors and dreamers, and there are two kinds of dreamers. Only one of them is going to write the story from here. Which one will it be, Detective Kovach?"

"Don't call me that."

"What do you want me to call you?" Still with her hand lightly on his. He forced himself to look away from the gulls just as one of them took flight with a piece of tendon in its jaws.

"Fast Eddie," he said. "Now, let me have a look at the kill list, would you?"

He didn't see that she was crying until she passed him the clipboard.

Neither of them spoke for a long time after that. They sat with their heads bowed over the list of names and the map of the city that had once been theirs, and Kovach thought that if she was wrong, she'd surely been his last case, and if she was right . . .

Maybe not.

God willing, maybe not.

MAKE YOUR OWN WAY
Alma Katsu

Maryellen's mother had been the first in the family to die.

It happened before anyone knew how bad things were going to get. One minute, neighbors were saying there was a bad flu working its way through the hollow, and the next, Maryellen's mother had caught it.

Her mother had always been sickly. Asthmatic. Prone to aches and chills and spells. Still, it was as though she'd had a premonition that she'd come to the end.

She patted Maryellen's hand as her daughter sat by the bedside. "How are the boys? Are they behaving themselves?"

Maryellen had three younger brothers: the twins, Mark and Matthew, and Peter, the youngest. "They're good, Mama. They listen to me."

"You're practically those boys' mother—you've taken care of them so much. I've never had to worry about you, not a day. You've always had a good head on your shoulders. You're more mature than other kids your age." She shifted under the covers and looked at Maryellen in a way that was a little bit frightening. "You're gonna have to take care of them a little longer. It's going to feel like your life's been taken away from you. But at some point, Maryellen, the boys will be able to take care of themselves and you're going to have to make your own way in the world. You're gonna have a chance to do what you want with your life. Trust in that."

The next day, her mother was dead.

The family was sad, but not exactly surprised. But when their father followed a week later, Maryellen and the boys were shocked. Doc Spellman barely spent five minutes when he stopped by to look at the body. "Funeral home won't be by to pick him up for at least a week, and that's too long," he advised as he trotted back to his car, bag in hand. "If anyone else gets sick, don't bother going to the hospital. They're turning people away. Can't handle any more. Folks are dropping like flies, all up and down the valley. Never seen anything like it."

After he'd left, Maryellen sat at the kitchen table to take stock. It was just her and her brothers. Like her mama said, she was in charge, at least until social services got in touch. *If* they got in touch: she assumed they were just as busy as the hospital and funeral home.

She had her brothers dig a hole out beyond the barn while she wrapped their father in a tarp. Their closest neighbor, April Tanner, who lived on a big spread down the ridge, stopped by shortly after they'd smoothed dirt over the grave. "Doc Spellman told me what happened," April had said, leaning through the window of her pickup truck. She gave no indication that she was going to get out of the truck and, given that two people had died on the property in little over a week, Maryellen didn't blame her.

The old woman had always seemed unflappable, but today she was twitchy. "You haven't been to town recently, so you don't know. This flu—whatever it is—is killing people left and right."

"That's what Doc Spellman said."

"Well, it's an understatement. Oscar died shortly after your mama. Norm and Henry hardly had time to get him buried when they came down with it." Oscar was Mrs. Tanner's brother (her husband had passed years ago). Norm and Henry were hired hands who did most of the work around the farm. "They're dead, too . . . Seems everyone who catches it dies."

"What're you going to do?" Maryellen couldn't imagine elderly Mrs. Tanner managing on her own. She had nearly a hundred head of cattle.

"I don't rightly know. What about you, girl? You and the boys want to come back to the farm with me? Until the authorities figure out what's going on?"

Maryellen wasn't sure if Mrs. Tanner had made the offer for their sake or her own. Maryellen shook her head. "I'm sorry. We got livestock to take care of. Can't leave them."

Mrs. Tanner started the engine, signaling she was ready to leave. "I'm in the same fix. Funny how some animals died, some aren't bothered by the disease at all. I still got all my cattle, but my saddle horses are gone. It's a blessing you still got Ruby. I heard all the other horses in the valley died. Dogs, too."

There was nothing Maryellen could say to this, so she shrugged. Ruby was her first and only horse. She'd had her since she was five. Ruby was old now, most of her muscle gone. Her chestnut coat had dulled, her eyes were getting cloudy, her lower lip drooped. How Ruby had survived when younger, healthier horses had died, Maryellen couldn't say. She was just grateful. She could not imagine life without her.

Maryellen's brothers died not long after that: the twins passing within one day of each other, and the youngest not two weeks later. The boys had been depending on her and she was sorry to have let them down, but by then Maryellen knew what the swelling on their throats meant. It was beyond her power to keep them from dying. It was overwhelming to lose them all, naturally, but by that time Maryellen had learned from neighbors who'd stopped by to check on her that the valley had nearly been emptied and, as near as anyone knew, the same was true of the towns and cities.

Josiah Phelps dug the twins' grave as his wife, Missy, helped Maryellen bundle the bodies in sheets. "You can't live here all by yourself," Missy had said. "You need protection." But from whom? The only people Maryellen had seen were people she knew. No one from the outside world would have any reason to come to their hollow in eastern Tennessee: it was too remote. She felt no threat from her neighbors, though she supposed the possibility might arise if someone got too lonely. Her mother had told her stories of men losing their minds after living by themselves for too long. In her mother's stories, it was always men who went crazy.

"The few who survived are leaving," Missy added.

Leaving. Maryellen hadn't thought about that. Living on this hardscrabble farm was all she knew. If her family had been inclined to pull up stakes and move to a city, they would've done that long before everyone was wiped out by a plague.

"But we got what we need here," Maryellen said. A kitchen garden. Livestock. Wells for water.

"There's a lot we need from the outside, too, and that's gonna run out eventually," Missy said. She meant stuff like medicine, dry goods, gasoline. The electric service had stopped, of course, but it had to be gone in the cities, too.

"We're heading out in a couple days with Tyler Jones." According to Missy, they and Tyler were the last people left on the mountain. Missy squeezed Maryellen's hand. "We got fuel for a truck, supplies, maps. You're welcome to come with us. You really can't and shouldn't stay here by yourself. I won't be able to bear the thought of it."

"I appreciate it. Let me think on it," Maryellen said.

She didn't want to let it on to Missy, but the notion of being the only living person for miles and miles spooked Maryellen. She tried to imagine what she'd do if something happened, if she broke a bone or was struck blind. But then she realized the risk would be, fundamentally, no different than it had been her entire life. The nearest hospital was over an hour away. Poor as they were, visits to doctors had been as rare as hen's teeth. Sickness was usually tended at home.

The farm was all she'd ever known. And while she'd wondered before what it would be like to live someplace with more people and tall buildings, now the idea was frightening. Those had undoubtedly become lawless places.

But she would get lonely, and she wasn't sure she was ready to give up on human companionship. She faced the very real likelihood that she might not see another person for years. And when someone finally did stumble on her farmhouse, it wouldn't be a local: it would be someone who'd come this way on purpose, someone who needed food, water, or shelter.

And they would find her here, alone.

The real reason she hesitated to take the Phelps's offer, however, was Ruby. Not the graves of her parents and her brothers, though she did stand at their gravesides daily to think of them, mourn them. Her parents would want her to go with their neighbors. They would not want their daughter to end up by herself. But they were gone, and Ruby was still here. Ruby needed her. Maryellen would not be able to take Ruby with her. They wouldn't agree to hitch a horse trailer to Josiah Phelps's truck, not when they were leaving their own livestock behind. Nor would Maryellen be able to keep up with them on horseback. It was simply impossible: if Maryellen left, she'd have to leave Ruby behind. And she could not bear to do that.

The Phelpses drove out on the last day. When Maryellen told them she was staying, Missy started crying. "You can let her loose in the woods," Missy said. "That's what we did with our cattle." Maryellen had thought of this, but knew it would be a death sentence for Ruby. With no other horses on the farm, the old mare had bonded with Maryellen completely. She would remain in the pasture waiting for her human companion until she died of starvation.

Josiah pressed a box of shotgun cartridges into her hand. "I know your dad has the same shotgun as me." A whole box of shells. Maryellen knew the Phelpses would need these themselves and she appreciated their generosity. Maryellen then watched the red pickup truck disappear into the woods.

As Maryellen got Ruby bedded down for the night, she thought again how it didn't make sense that the old horse was still alive. There had to be a reason for it, something Ruby was meant to do, and it would be a grave sin for Maryellen to leave before that happened.

And it was not just Ruby, of course. Maryellen herself had been spared by this merciless disease when everyone else in her family had been taken. If Ruby had a special purpose, then surely Maryellen did, too.

To quiet her nerves, Maryellen took a little more of the special tea she drank every night to help her sleep. A few years back, when Maryellen started to wake regularly in the middle of the night, her mother dipped into her collection of herbal medicines to concoct this tea, which never failed to put Maryellen into a deep and dreamless sleep. Maryellen knew the recipe, though she worried that her meager supply of dried passionflower, gingko, and valerian root oil wouldn't last much longer.

She kept busy. There was a lot to do, and only her now to see to it. She rode Ruby to her neighbors' empty houses for things she could use. She carried canned food in her backpack, but drove back later in her daddy's truck for sacks of feed and bales of hay. Her neighbors had let their livestock loose, but most of the animals simply returned, waiting for humans that would never come. She rounded up some of the chickens for the eggs, but left the sheep and pigs, knowing that she would not have it in her to slaughter them after she'd taken care of them for a while.

Maryellen had been on her own for about two months—maybe more, but probably less—when she saw the man.

MAKE YOUR OWN WAY

She had been riding Ruby through the woods, looking for game. The idea of winter loomed in Maryellen's mind. Game would soon be sparse then. It was his shape that she spotted first, a dark figure moving upright through the trees. She knew it was a stranger: she'd recognize her neighbors' familiar forms if one of them had, by some chance, returned home.

This was a stranger walking on her mountain.

She thought about following him, but he was sure to spot her if she moved. She lifted the rifle, more for reassurance than because she thought she needed it. The figure looked to be alone. If she had to guess, she'd say it was a lanky young man. A little too tall for a girl. She couldn't get a good look at him due to the distance and wished she had a pair of binoculars. She watched the figure slowly disappear over the horizon. He was heading toward her house, though there were trails that could lead off in other directions. Part of her wished this person would turn around and see her. But mostly, she wanted him to keep on walking.

She'd put Ruby in her stall and was locking the windows and doors in the house when she saw the figure again, this time trudging up the long driveway. She could tell now that it was a man, though he looked quite young, maybe only a little older than she. He wore a dark blue hoodie and jeans and carried a backpack. He looked like he was out on a camping trip.

He was headed directly toward the house.

Maryellen stood behind the screen door with her shotgun level. She didn't like pointing a weapon at him, but knew she had no alternative. The stranger was about fifty feet away when he saw her weapon, but he kept walking.

When he was about twenty feet away, she announced, "You can stop right there."

He obeyed, trying to keep his expression calm and open. "You're the first person I've seen in two weeks."

"What're you doing out this way? You're not from around here."

He squirmed slightly under the burden of his pack. "No, I'm not. I'm a student—I mean, I *was* a student—at the university in Morristown." That was over forty miles away. "They couldn't keep up after everybody started getting sick, and they told us all to go home... Only, nobody answered the phone when I called for them to come get me, so I just started walking." He scratched his head. "I got off the highway at one point—it was jammed with cars, full of, y'know, dead people—and I must've got lost."

"Where is your family?"

"Paducah. In Kentucky." Maryellen didn't know exactly how far away that was—easily over a hundred miles. Maybe two hundred. "Is it okay if I put my pack down? It's awfully heavy." When Maryellen nodded, he slipped it off his shoulders and let it drop by his feet.

She knew what she should tell him, what her parents would want her to tell him. "I think you ought to move on."

His face fell, but he didn't get upset. "Okay... I can understand that. Only... would it be okay to spend the night? My feet are killing me, and it's been hard to get a good night's sleep in the woods. It would be nice to spend the night someplace *safe*."

A spike of panic rose in her chest. "You can't sleep in the house."

"No, no. Of course not. But maybe in the barn?" He nodded in its direction.

She appreciated that he hadn't asked if she was alone. He probably figured it would freak her out, make her more defensive. "Uh, okay. But you can't bother the livestock."

"Of course."

She then watched him head to the barn, wondering if she was doing the right thing. He seemed nice enough. If the television shows Maryellen had seen before—before the airwaves went dead—were to be believed, however, young women were killed all the time: in their dorm rooms, in their parents' homes, in their cars broken down on the side of the road. The killers were always described as nice, like the boy who'd be sleeping in her barn. Stories like that made it hard to be kind to strangers.

Dinner was canned soup. She was tired of it, but she'd stockpiled a lot and didn't care much for cooking. She took the leftovers out to the barn, her rifle crooked under her arm.

"Here. I thought you might like this," she said as she pushed the door open. He was sitting on a sleeping bag in the aisle, staring through the slats of Ruby's stall at the chestnut mare. He looked startled to see Maryellen.

She set the bowl on the floor just outside his reach and stepped back. He picked it up and sat back on his sleeping bag. He drew the spoon back and forth through the soup, cooling it off. "Is it okay if I ask your name?"

"It's Maryellen."

"Wayne." He ducked his head. "I feel bad that I didn't introduce myself earlier. My apologies."

"That's okay." She leaned against the barn door. There was something about the way he carried himself that made her think, again, that she didn't have to worry about him. Though she also knew she'd be a fool to trust a stranger. "So . . . you're still headed home?"

"Yeah, though I'm not sure why. I haven't heard anything from my family since it all started. I don't know if any of them are alive or if they tried to get to one of the government centers . . . "

Maryellen's ears perked up. "The government set up centers?"

He looked sorry he'd said anything. "It was just something I heard at school . . . It might've been wishful thinking. You'd think if there had been something like that, they would've been taking people there instead of . . . " He trailed off.

"Instead of—what?"

He jerked his head up. "I mean, just letting us die. Letting us fend for ourselves."

Hopelessness started to rise in her chest. From what he said, it seemed that it was no different in the city than it had been in the country: the disease had come on so fast and strong that nothing was able to stand up to it, not even the government.

"It's getting dark," she said. "I'll get you a lantern."

She told herself that Wayne would leave the next morning, but when he asked if it would be all right if he stayed another day, she said yes. One day became three, and he then offered to help with chores, and Maryellen started to let her guard down, get comfortable with the idea of him staying. He was good company, especially in the evenings when there was little to do. They told each other about their lives over card games. Childhood injuries and illnesses. Places they'd gone on vacation—though Wayne had been places Maryellen had only heard about. The Grand Ole Opry, Lake of the Ozarks. Parents, siblings, all gone or presumed gone. It was as though they were interviewing each other. When she thought about it later, she supposed they had been.

After a week, Maryellen let him move into a room on the first floor. There were empty bedrooms upstairs, but she wanted to keep some distance between them.

Despite the sudden companionship, he took getting used to. Wayne had not grown up on a farm and was nervous around large animals, like Ruby, and said he didn't know how to fire a gun. He turned down her offer to teach him to ride, but he let her show him how to use the rifle.

It seemed inevitable that they would go to bed together. They eased into it over a matter of days, starting with a tentative kiss good night, then progressing to long, slow sessions kissing and exploring each other on the sofa in the parlor. Then one night, Maryellen led him upstairs, and they slid into her bed, practically the only bed she had ever slept in. When it was over and Maryellen laid tucked under his arm, he told her that it felt like they were the last two people on earth and, if that were true, it was their duty to end up together. She felt the truth of it.

Everything went along well between them until the day they went into town together to get supplies. It was fall and a sudden nip had come on, so he was wearing her brother Mark's parka. She supposed later that might have been the reason for the trouble. Too, he seemed a bit too comfortable behind the wheel when she let him drive her father's pickup truck.

They were pulling up in front of the hardware store when she saw them. Two men and two women. They were young and old, mixed, but they didn't seem to be a family. From their clothes, she guessed that they had come from a city and she couldn't imagine what they were doing out there, so far from anything.

After a few wary minutes staring at each other, the older woman asked if they were from around here. They didn't look dangerous to Maryellen. There was no gun or rifle, as far as she could see, and they had a flighty, nervous look about them, like rabbits. Eventually, Maryellen and Wayne stepped out of the truck and the six of them stood in a circle, talking.

It turned out that the four of them had come from Morristown. They hadn't known each other before the plague but, as they stumbled across each other, alone and scavenging, had decided to join up. "There's safety in numbers," the younger woman said, and Wayne nodded sagely at Maryellen. It made her think Wayne wanted to go with them.

They were headed west. "It's because of the dreams," the younger woman said in a way that made Maryellen think she should know what she was talking about. Listening to each of them, she came to understand that they each had dreamt about the same person, an elderly Black woman who lived in a cabin out west. In their dreams, the old woman told them to join her.

Maryellen didn't understand what they were getting at. "It's the power of suggestion," she said. "One of you had a dream with this woman and gave the idea to the rest of you."

But the others denied this was the case. "That's what she does. She comes to *you*," the younger man insisted. "She's trying to gather the survivors together, don't you see? Giving humanity a way forward." The others nodded at his words, but Maryellen wasn't sure.

It wasn't until that evening, after Maryellen and Wayne had made love, that Wayne admitted he had heard of the old woman. "As things were getting bad, people started talking about the dreams."

"Oh? Why didn't you say something earlier?"

He shrugged, and it made him seem younger than he was, like she was shaming him into confessing. "It's more than the old woman . . . People dreamt about someone else, too. A man. Those dreams weren't so pleasant." He drew a strand of her hair through his fingers dreamily. He'd told her that he loved her hair because it was so silky. "They call him the Walkin Dude. It was like he was calling people to mayhem. To chaos."

She knew she had to ask the next question even though she wasn't sure she wanted to know the answer. "And—did you ever have one of these dreams?"

He paused a moment before he shook his head. "No. Never."

Not long after this, Wayne began bringing up moving on. "Maybe we should've joined them," he'd say casually. "We can't stay here by ourselves forever. Eventually we'll start running out of food or medicine." Or, "One of us could get seriously hurt." He was afraid of all these things more than she was. They could grow food. Working on a farm, she was used to all kinds of scrapes. As for injury, well, she'd seen horses and cattle break legs; her own uncle had broken his back falling out of the hay loft, but he was gone by the time they got him to the hospital. Sometimes there was nothing you could do. Sometimes people died.

Several times a day, Maryellen would find herself looking at Wayne and wondering if they would've gotten together if it wasn't for the plague. Aside from the fact that he had been a college student and she had still been a high school senior, or the happenstance of where they lived. Her question was more fundamental: Would she have been even attracted to someone like Wayne? He was so unlike the boys out here that it was hard for her to know. He seemed easygoing—as much as anyone could be given the circumstances—and considerate of her wishes. But she was also acutely aware that she honestly didn't know him very well, and she was afraid that she might wake up one day far from home and realize that she didn't know him at all.

It was at these times that she wished her mother were still with her. She missed her mother's advice.

It had only been a couple of months, the middle of October, but Maryellen could see that they were starting to fall in together. She felt his assumptions weigh heavily on her, namely that they would inevitably leave this farm before long and head west. He was already starting to assert himself, expecting her to follow his lead. He tried to do so around the farm, although there was still a lot he didn't know. Maybe that was why he wanted to leave, so he could be somewhere that felt more familiar. Where he wasn't dependent on her—indeed, where their roles would be reversed.

She would not feel as uncertain if she thought that, if it hadn't been for the plague, he would have been drawn to her, but she was pretty sure she was too young and simple. But here he was, making himself a fixture in her life. There was the real chance that she might get pregnant and that would change everything.

She was getting used to having him around, and one day, she'd be so used to him that the thought of losing him would terrify her.

Maryellen was coming in from the kitchen garden with the last of the potatoes when she noticed the paddock gate had been left open to the meadow and the forest beyond, a temptation set for the three cows and Ruby.

The cows were gone, but Ruby stood by the water trough.

Maryellen saddled Ruby and rode out after the cows. They had not gotten far and she easily herded them home. She found Wayne in the house, sitting in front of the hearth, his eyes trained on the dancing flames like they were telling him a story.

"Did you leave the gate open?" she asked as she hung up her jacket. "Because the cattle were loose in the woods."

"Oh geez, maybe I did," he said, his eyes widening. "I'm sorry."

She wanted to believe him. Because not believing him meant he thought he could lie to her and get away with it.

He was changing. She could not deny it. He was like a plant slowly, slowly turning as it followed the sun. He was changing in ways that were disquieting—leaving things undone, pretending not to hear her, disappearing for hours with her daddy's shotgun.

A week later, Maryellen was stacking the hay in the loft that she'd found in the Tanners' barn when she saw Wayne pointing the firearm at Ruby. She thought at first that she was hallucinating: Wayne generally avoided her horse. But no, her eyes weren't playing tricks. Wayne stood with the gun leveled at Ruby's head. He was taking deep breaths. His arms looked to be trembling.

"Hey!" she shouted so he could hear her, though he was far away. "What are you doing?!"

He snapped to attention at the sound of her voice, swiveling to find her. His face had gone pale and he let the rifle droop to the ground. "When did you get back? I thought you'd gone down to your neighbors' place . . ."

But she was already down the ladder and running toward him, her heart pounding the entire time. She could not imagine why he was doing this, what had gotten into him. Was he going to kill her, too, girl and horse linked in his mind? "What were you planning? Were you fixing to shoot Ruby?"

At Maryellen's words, Wayne suddenly came to, no longer embarrassed at being caught. He lifted the weapon again in Ruby's direction, though he didn't hold it as high this time. Maryellen stopped dead in her tracks twenty feet away from Ruby, who nickered at the sight of her.

Wayne's eyes smoldered. "It's her or me, Maryellen. You're letting this horse stand in our way. We got to leave here—you *know* it—and you won't do it as long as she's alive. I don't have a choice."

Maryellen's mind reeled. Had she really been sharing a bed with this man for the past two months? She didn't think the man she knew was capable of doing this, but now she saw that was because, as she feared, she didn't really know him.

The man—boy—she knew was a mirage. An act he'd put on to gain her trust.

A small voice inside tried to argue: *Don't we all do that when we meet a stranger, pretend to be someone we're not? Until we know we can trust them?*

But not like this. He had crossed a line. He had pretended to be gentle, but in truth he was violent. Anyone could become violent if pushed, yes, but this was different.

He was showing her: *I am dangerous.*

She took a cautious step toward him. "Hold on. You're right, Wayne. I see that now. We gotta leave. But . . . let me just say goodbye to her first, okay? We've been together my whole life. I—I can't just let her go without saying goodbye."

She made her voice soft, taking all the anger out of it so it would seem like she had surrendered. He watched her for a long minute, trying to decide. Finally, when Maryellen had just about given up hope, he lowered the gun. "Okay. *Now* you're being reasonable. Go on—say goodbye. Then we pack our bags and go."

She started toward the mare. But as she brushed past Wayne, she grabbed the shotgun with both hands. She'd caught him by surprise, but he managed to hold on as they struggled. He had the height and weight advantage. If he'd been a little bit heavier or had just a smidge more experience fighting, he would've been able to overpower her. But he did not, while she had roughhoused with her brothers every day for twelve years. He thought she would give in easily, like most girls he had known. He thought he'd gentled her, broken her like a green horse.

She saw an opportunity. If she got him off-balance, she could push him to the ground. It was risky: the gun could go off. But it was all she could think to do in the heat of the moment. She planted her feet and wrenched the weapon, twisting his arms in their sockets as he refused to let go. When she felt him wobble, unsure on his feet, she pushed. He fell on his back, bringing her down on top of him. Her advantage was that she knew it was coming, while he didn't. In that moment of surprise, she yanked the firearm out of his hands and scrambled to her feet.

Standing ten feet away from him, Maryellen aimed the gun at his chest. Her arms did not shake.

He got to his feet slowly, hands raised half-heartedly. "You going to shoot me, Maryellen?"

"If I have to." She reckoned he knew her well enough to know it was true. "Now you're going to go in the house and pack your things and be on your way. And you're not going to come back."

She then followed him inside, the weapon leveled at him the entire time. Her arms did not tire. Her heart raced, though, to think how they had talked about leaving together. She had almost headed into the great unknown with this man. It seemed now like they had been playacting, but she also knew a part of her had been drawn to the idea. She had come close to making a bad mistake.

He stuffed his things in his backpack, keeping up a running conversation the whole time. "I'm sorry, Maryellen. I don't know what came over me . . . I'd never shoot a living creature, you know that."

MAKE YOUR OWN WAY

But when she didn't budge, he got mad, saying she was making a huge error. "You need a man out here. It's dangerous being out here by yourself. The next man might not be as nice as I am." Finally, he said he wouldn't stay with her now, even if she begged him.

He slung the bag over his shoulder and the way he looked at her sent a chill down her spine. She jerked her head and followed behind him as he walked through the front door.

The sun was starting to go down. Not a good time to be heading into the forest, but he had brought it on himself. There was something about the look in his eyes, though, that made her decide to ask. "You said you didn't have any of those dreams, Wayne . . . but you did, didn't you? That's why you want to leave now."

She didn't think at first that he'd answer. But then, he nodded. "Yup. I didn't want to tell you. But I did. Lots of 'em."

"And it wasn't about the old woman, was it?"

It meant he had been dreaming of the Walkin Dude. Dreaming of violence and chaos. She pointed with the gun. "Get going, and don't come back or I'll put a slug in you. Don't doubt it."

That night, she locked up the farmhouse and spent the night in the barn with Ruby. She kept the lantern burning and the shotgun close at hand. In all the excitement, Maryellen realized that she'd forgotten to make her tea. After a minute's thought, she decided not to bother with it. She was almost out of the ingredients and soon would have to get used to not having it anyway. Plus, she didn't want to be knocked out in case Wayne tried to return. For the first night in a very long time, Maryellen would try to fall asleep on her own.

Once she managed to slip into a fitful sleep, Maryellen had her first dream of the old woman called Mother Abagail. She dreamt she was riding Ruby up to the cabin where the old woman lived. Mother Abagail came down from her front porch and right up to Maryellen. She reached up to stroke Ruby's broad cheek and pat her velvet nose.

"You done the right thing getting rid of that man. You weren't saved from this disease only to lose yourself to *him*," the old woman told her in the dream. "And now I want you to come west to see me. I'm calling all the people like you. We need to band together because we got a mission in front of us. You need to be part of that, Maryellen. Now, I'm not going to tell you that it's going to be easy, you by yourself, on this horse of yours, riding clean across the country. But I know you can do it. You'll meet some people along the way who are like that man you just run off. But you'll also meet people like yourself. Good people, people you can trust. But first you got to leave your family's house. You got to start this journey. I know you're worried about this old girl here"—she patted the mare's nose again—"but you don't need to. She may be old, like me, but we're both tougher than you know. She'll get you to where you need to be."

When Maryellen awoke, it felt like she'd had the conversation in real life, face-to-face. The truth of it warmed her chest. She went over to Ruby and rubbed between her eyes. The mare nosed her curiously. Even Ruby could tell something was different.

Maryellen spent the day packing, albeit with the shotgun at her side, taking a break to peer out the window whenever she heard a noise. She knew Ruby wouldn't be able to carry much, but she didn't see an alternative. She resolved not to worry and trust that the Lord would provide along the way. She took enough oats to last Ruby three or four days. A few pieces of clothing. Some food, a plastic jug of water. An improvised first-aid kit and a few tools. The shotgun and all the shells, including the box Josiah Phelps had given her.

Then she saddled Ruby and led her to her family's graves. An ache lodged in her throat, knowing it was the last time she would ever see them, and it almost caused her to change her mind. But then she put her foot in the stirrup and swung up into the saddle. Immediately, she felt better. The world seemed right when she was riding Ruby. She pressed her heels lightly to the mare's side to urge the horse on, the old woman's words singing in her ears.

PART TWO

THE LONG WALK

I LOVE THE DEAD
Josh Malerman

"How could they have named it after him? *How?* How can you take the kindest, warmest, wisest man on the planet . . . and name something so terrible after him? I don't understand! Someone tell me, please! Except there's nobody to tell me. Nobody left! How do you like that? Just when a man needs an answer. This is ridiculous. This is insane! *Captain Trips?* Do they not know it's his nickname? The punk kids who started calling it that . . . is it because they hate him? Oh, they all hate him, don't they! They hate his kindness, his intelligence . . . they hate the way he plays the guitar! What a bunch of pigeon shit. All they see are the Jerry Bears and dancing skeletons and they think, 'This is not for me. This is the end of the world.' And their heads are so far up their butts that when the end of the world actually comes . . . they name it after him. Jerry Garcia! Captain Trips. How could they? How *dare* they?"

Lev had been thinking about Jerry Garcia when he found the finger in the meadow. But the odds of anything interesting happening while he was thinking of Jerry were high, as he thought of little else.

He'd seen body parts in recent days. Oh, boy. The dead lined the streets of Boise like fish pumped up from the sewers. Most had died from the superflu, but violence has a tendency of dancing when bad music plays. And so, he'd seen arms, legs, heads, even an eye. But a finger? All alone and outside of town? And not just any finger: it was the top two-thirds, sliced off above the knuckle.

Just like Jerry Garcia's finger had been when he was a boy.

"Holy *shit*," Lev said. And the enormity he felt was more powerful than the fear he'd had of the superflu. The desire to show someone, anyone, was crushed by the understanding that nobody remained.

Picking the hard thing up from the grass, he eyed it through a pair of small spectacles. The same sort Jerry had been wearing these days. And he thought, not for the first time:

Is Jerry Garcia still alive?

"Captain Trips," he said. And he laughed. Because in the face of all things horrible, here was undoubtedly a sign. The missing finger of the world's greatest guitar player. And a chance, for Lev, at purpose.

He would leave Boise.

He would go to San Francisco.

He would bring Jerry Garcia his finger.

Lev's legs hurt. His legs always hurt. Exercise of any kind hurt. He preferred couches and record players. Joints and thick beers. But all this walking, this exertion, was killing him. His back hurt. His arms were tired from flailing as he ranted. His joints felt like marble.

But his heart hurt the most.

The disrespect shown to the greatest musician the world had ever known was a thing he could not reconcile. Could not accept. And whenever Lev Marks felt this way, he played his guitar.

"There's a fallen tree," he said, to himself, always talking to himself these days. "A good place for a song. You wanna hear how good he is? I'll show you how good he is. You don't need technology to play the acoustic guitar, suckers!"

I LOVE THE DEAD

The guitar had been strapped to his back since Boise. He'd picked up both it and the shirt on the same downtown strip in that now dead city. Bodies everywhere back there. Lev preferred to think of them as dancing skeletons. He squinted when he saw dead bodies, wreckage, empty cars, and storefronts. Made it all look more like a painting, an album cover, album art. And what killer album art it was.

He swung the guitar's soft case from over his shoulder and sat on the fallen tree. The sun was up, big, hot, and the many colors of his tie-dyed shirt were bright. His belly hung out the bottom; they'd only had a medium and Lev Marks was certainly a large.

The Martin acoustic placed gently on his leg, he reached into his cargo shorts and pulled forth the finger. He ran his chord hand through his thinning curly hair. Sweat had pooled on the lenses of those little glasses.

He strummed the guitar, using the dead finger as a pick.

Just imagine the looks of astonishment on the faces of the punks who disliked Jerry and the Dead. Imagine that now! How upset they'd be to discover the genius had outlived them all. For Jerry Garcia could not have died from a disease called Captain Trips. And those pigeon-shit punks were dead now, those pricks who couldn't recognize a good song if Bob Dylan took it apart to show them.

He strummed. An ugly, ungainly sound. And not just because the Martin was out of tune. And not just because of the finger. Lev had no touch. Never had. No rhythm. He played a guitar like he was sawing a bone. His wrists still hurt from not having made it through the bar-chord phase of learning and he never practiced. Half the chords were muted, dead, as the few pure notes made it out alive. He didn't know the intricacies of the chords for the songs he played, but who did? G worked just fine even if Bob Weir had been playing G7 onstage.

He played a meek D now.

"Morning Dew," he said. He paused playing. It was a revelation of sorts. Yes, the Grateful Dead had a song about an apocalypse.

"Morning Dew" was the story of a man emerging after nuclear fallout. He lifted the dead finger and eyed the pale nail.

"Morning Dew..."

Is this why the punks named the end after Jerry? It was easy (thrilling) to imagine himself, Lev, as the narrator of that song. As if he'd listened to so much Dead he'd finally stepped into their music.

"Holy *shit*," he said. It was too much to take in all at once. It made him too giddy. He got up again, clumsily put the guitar back into its case, the finger back in his pocket.

And he continued southwest. Toward San Francisco.

A man with a guitar and a tie-dyed shirt.

And a missing finger, found.

Lev Marks. Deadhead extraordinaire.

"I'll ask him myself," Lev said. "I'll ask him what *he* thinks of the stupid nickname."

He plugged one nostril with a finger from his chord hand and snotted out the other. He'd seen people get sick, the discoloration around the neck. If he squinted, it looked like dark tie-dye. "He's alive. I can feel it. No way a guy like him dies from the same thing everybody else does. No way, suckers!"

Still, he worried, yes, as he stumbled along, a bit hunchbacked, taking quick anxious steps in his tennis shoes. He'd seen a lot on his walk from Boise. Endless traffic made up of driverless cars, bodies on hillsides. He stopped dozens of times to play guitar, strumming with Jerry's finger, just like he'd played guitar as his friend Denny died from the flu.

He'd seen life, too, out here. Deer and sheep. Coyotes and birds. Crows. His sister had warned him long ago not to do too much acid, that it could all come screaming back one day. She told him acid gets stored in the back of the head and could one day drip down the spine.

I LOVE THE DEAD

Unannounced. Lev could be seventy years old and suddenly find himself on the same trip he'd taken at twenty. But what did Fran know?

Still . . .

This whole thing felt like a bad trip. Maybe that's what the punks meant when they nicknamed it so.

And maybe it was the acid he'd taken (and maybe it wasn't) that caused him to think the same crow had been following him from Idaho through Oregon. He'd seen it in trees in northern Nevada. Seen it in the desert. Lev had felt a sort of pull then. An idea to go to Las Vegas. One night, he thought the crow spoke to him. Told him Jerry Garcia was indeed alive, playing shows in Las Vegas.

"No way," Lev said then and he said it again now. "That's beneath him. Jerry Garcia is the smartest, warmest, most brilliant guitar player of all time."

He once loved talking about Jerry's missing finger at parties. *You think this song is good now? Wait till I tell you he only had four good fingers!*

"Ha! Genius!"

His voice carried across a grassy plain as he exited what felt like the thousandth stretch of forest. Whatever was going on in Las Vegas could wait. Lev Marks was going to find Jerry Garcia in Haight-Ashbury because that's where a genius like him would go.

"Home," Lev said. "He'd go home. Because he's smart. And because that place was good to him. And pretty damn good to the rest of the world, too."

How close was he to San Francisco? He didn't know. He'd been walking along highways and dirt roads, through woods and over hills. Felt like a month now, maybe more. He'd slept in empty hotels and abandoned homes. Restaurant booths and the back benches of cars. Eating sardines and other canned goods. There was so much death out here. So much emptiness. And the silence of a world turned off. Like when a record ends, that sorrowful moment of scratchiness, then . . .

nothing. That's what had happened to the world. Everybody was singing along to "Franklin's Tower" and then . . . the scratchiness . . . the needle with no song to play . . . the superflu.

The end.

"Ah, Denny," he said. "Wish you could be with me right now. You'd finally get to meet the man and then you'd finally get his music. All those times you made fun of me. All those times you didn't get it. I bet you got it at the end, though. The last thing you heard was 'Ripple.' I bet you got it then."

Lev felt the rage he'd felt back in Boise. Back when people made fun of him for his taste in music. God, it sucked. Pretentious dickwads and their disco and new wave punk. And what about the pricks who only liked the Dead because of "Touch of Grey"? Yeah, what about them? Lev didn't make fun of *them*. Not out loud anyway. Was it any wonder he'd fantasize about the deaths of those who made fun of the Dead and those late to the party? Was it any wonder he'd imagined some punk getting electrocuted because he'd been too dumb not to take the radio into the bathtub? Was it any wonder he'd fall asleep, sweating, rolling over and over, imagining the broken splinters of an acoustic guitar wedged into the chests of the people who just didn't get it?

Ahead, more woods. Another tract of forest. How close to the birthplace of the Dead? He didn't know. But he'd read the signs. San Francisco. This way. That way. And the California state line was a long way behind him now.

"There," he said, spotting a rock before that next bunch of woods. "A good place to play a song."

He brought out the Martin and set it gently on his tired leg. He pulled out the dead finger. He strummed.

"Just color me Frodo!" he said. "Carrying the finger to the great wizard Garcia."

He tried to play "Truckin'," but it was harder than it sounded. And the dead bodies in the open grass put him in a sour mood.

I LOVE THE DEAD

"God, this is all a lot more like Alice Cooper than it is Jerry Garcia. This is like that song . . . " He fiddled, strumming with the severed finger. "*I . . . love . . .*"

Then he laughed. The pun of it. The Alice Cooper song was called "I Love the Dead." And Lev loved the Dead. And, oh boy, he couldn't stop laughing and he didn't want to. And he thought he heard a crow call from the woods ahead, but when he looked up he saw it was a man, watching him right back.

Lev started, dropped the finger, quickly and clumsily picked it back up, then stood, facing the first living person he'd seen since Denny died in the living room of their shared apartment in Boise.

"Music," the man said. He sounded old. "Rock and roll?"

Dirty, old, white hair, a tattered tank top, shorts.

"Well, it's a lot more than rock and roll," Lev said.

The potential for a scene like this had crossed his mind on the long walk. Encountering strangers. And the small chances of that someone being kind.

"Well, don't stop on my account," the man said. "Go on, then."

Lev only stood. Felt like an outlaw in the Old West. A duel. Was this man sick?

"Are you sick?"

"No, sir. Lovesick, perhaps. Lonesome. But it ain't Captain Trips that ails me."

Lev reddened. Sick or not, this man might not be kind.

"Why do you call it that?" he asked.

The old man eyed Lev like he'd just realized something about him.

"What do you mean?" he said. "That's what they call it, isn't it?"

"Do you do everything everybody else does?"

"Excuse me? Look, I just heard some music. I was—"

"He's the wisest, kindest musician the world has ever known. You can hear it in every lyric. Every note. Even the song choices reveal his wisdom. You really think it's right to name the end of the world after him?"

"Well, I'm not sure I'm following," the man said. "In fact, I'm sure I'm not."

"*Jerry Garcia*," Lev said. He'd taken a couple steps closer to the man, and the man had backed up those same couple steps. "Captain Trips is *his* nickname. What were you, born yesterday?"

The old man eyed the dead bodies in the field, looked to the empty sky.

"Well, sometimes it feels that way, yes."

"Ha. Well, it's wrong. It's the wrong thing to do. And if we're going to show any civility around here, we need to start with that *name*."

Did the old man eye the dead finger in Lev's hand? Lev closed his hand around it either way.

"I'm not sure you're focused on the right things," the old man said.

"Oh, really?"

"There's a lot more to be worried about than what people are calling this thing."

"Well, I suppose it's just words to you. Just words to everyone. And isn't that just like you all. It's the very reason you never got his music. You don't think *words matter*."

"I think I'll pass along now," the man said. "I'm glad to see another living face. I wish you good luck on your journey."

"But do you? Or are you just *saying* that? Just words, right?"

The man made to raise his hands in a peaceful way, to say, *Well, okay, however you see it you see it, I'll be on my way*, but Lev was upon him before he could.

Lev swung once, missed, swung again, missed, and the old man reluctantly struck him over the head.

Lev fell then. The guitar sounded crazy as it hit the ground. And when Lev woke up, it was dark, and a herd of deer scattered at the life they saw in what they believed to be another dead body.

The good news was he still had the finger. The bad news was his head hurt. The pigeon-shit old man punk had sucker punched him is what happened. Didn't even stick around for a fair fight. Fine. That

I LOVE THE DEAD

was fine. And to be expected of the people who populated a world so unkind.

Lev walked. And walked. At times the guitar felt heavy, and at times it did not. But it wasn't broken, so that was good. He switched it from shoulder to shoulder and repeatedly checked the pocket of his cargo shorts to make sure he still had the finger.

"*I... love... the...*"

Yes, this new world was certainly more Alice Cooper than Grateful Dead and even the pun of it had worn off some. The song just sounded right. Lev imagined what the chorus walk-down notes might be between the repeating chorus lines. He stopped twice to try to figure them out, but it seemed the guitar had gone far out of tune. Hmm. Maybe the old man had screwed with it. Maybe it was his way of telling Lev he didn't like the same music as Lev. And that was fine. Fine.

Up again, walking, tired, rattled, angry, he saw a sign he'd been waiting a long time to see:

WELCOME TO SAN FRANCISCO

"Should say 'Home of the Grateful Dead,'" Lev said. But even his own words were eclipsed by the thought of the address he needed to get to: *710 Ashbury Street.*

All good Deadheads knew *that* much.

As he crossed the city line, he tried to sing Jerry songs, Bobby songs, even those sung by Pigpen or Donna. But all he could hear was Alice Cooper. Over and over. And those elusive walk-down notes. Like giant dark feet stepping down giant dark stairs into a giant dark nothingness.

He should feel good. He was close. Instead, he felt like he'd stepped over the curved edge of a vinyl album. Like he'd stepped out of the music and into reality.

And that, every Deadhead also knew, was the worst feeling in the world.

"I need a miracle," he said.

But, as fun as it once was to say this, the phrase was too right-on now. Too on point. The miracle had already happened.

Lev had lived.

And he'd found the finger of God.

———

If he thought the woods and plains (even some desert—remember the crow out there?) were tough, they were nothing compared to the hills of this city. For starters, Lev had no idea where he was going. An hour of walking, absently looking for Ashbury Street, had gotten him nowhere. He finally got a map from a drugstore with a broken front door. He thought he heard people scampering when he entered the place. But the chances of that were low: the number of bodies out here on the streets was unbelievable. It was all Lev could do to sing songs, to hum, to pat his pocket and remind himself he was, like Frodo, on a real good quest. He was bringing a finger to Jerry Garcia, he who had mastered the guitar while missing one. He didn't need to bully himself with bad feelings, darkness, vague plans for a future he knew nothing about. Right now he needed music. But it was hard.

If the world felt more like Alice Cooper on the way over, it was Ozzy Osbourne now.

Lev wouldn't let himself sing *those* songs. Too heavy. Too close to the new world. And he wasn't about to let Ozzy Osbourne look like some kind of prophet for having—

"Ah!" he said.

Ashbury Street.

Lev Marks had arrived.

He stood alone on the corner, the sun high again. A crisp wind blew his curly hair and, panting, he looked left, then right. He knew what the house looked like, of course, but really, all the houses looked kinda the same out here. Even with their different colors (no two the same on any block), it was all of a piece. Lev checked the map.

"*I... love... the...*" Then, "Stop it! Grow up! You're approach-

I LOVE THE DEAD

ing Jerry Garcia's house with Jerry Garcia's finger. The least you can do is sing Jerry Garcia's songs."

But try as he might, that silky Alice Cooper walk-down had slithered into his mind with grace and cunning; a song like "Sugar Magnolia" didn't stand a chance.

Lev's heart picked up speed as he passed 510, 512, 514. "Viola Lee Blues" put up a good fight, almost knocked Alice Cooper out of his head. The two shared space, two songs playing at once, a bit maddening, a bit too much.

648. 650 . . .

He could see it now. Ahead. The steps leading up. The very steps the band must've taken when they carried their gear out of the house to go play an acid party for their friends.

A dead body face down on the sidewalk and Lev stepped over it, eyes fixed to the house, *the* house, without looking down.

Then finally: 710.

He stood a moment, taking it in. Should he play? He should, right? He should. A song on the steps of Jerry's house. Just think . . . if Jerry heard it . . . coming in through the window . . . proof of life . . . Lev Marks delivering the missing finger . . .

Yes.

He sat on the lowest step and took the guitar from its case and the finger from his pocket. Had the finger rotted? It looked darker. Smelled funny. But maybe that smell had followed Lev since he'd found it. Yeah, maybe he'd mistaken the smell of the finger for that of the world. And maybe a rotting, foul finger was a small pittance to pay for carrying a piece of Jerry Garcia home. Breathless, he strummed an E. "Viola Lee Blues" was, after all, blues. He could figure out the E-A-B of it. He sang as he played:

"Wrote a letter . . ."

And the wind carried his voice, he thought, even as it tousled his hair, even as it graced the dead finger-pick in his hand. What a gem this song was. What a *jam*.

The door opened above and behind him and Lev turned, wide-eyed, expecting to see the bearded wizard, the maestro, the gray hair, the glasses, a black shirt and rainbow pants, the greatest musician who had ever been born, a man who now doubt would survive the end of the world:

Captain Trips.

"Hello?" the man said.

It wasn't Jerry Garcia. Wasn't even close. A short man with no hair on top. A suit coat. The man looked more like a lawyer than a musician and he eyed Lev with some apprehension. But Lev saw some hope there, too.

"You've made it," the man said. "You survived."

Lev rose then and the man saw the tie-dye shirt and something changed in his appearance.

"Isn't this Jerry's house?" Lev asked.

"My God," the man said. "Even after the end of the world, this continues."

"What do you mean?"

But the man put on a kinder face and took the steps down. Lev saw he carried a suitcase in one hand.

"You're not sick, are you?" the man asked.

"Are you?"

"No. Are you?"

"No."

"Good."

He came down the rest of the way until he was on the sidewalk, Lev a step above him.

"Yes, this was once Jerry Garcia's house, but that was a long time ago," he said.

"Did he survive? He had to have."

The man smiled sadly.

"That I don't know. I've lived here three years. You can imagine the number of visitors I've gotten. Most are kindhearted."

I LOVE THE DEAD

"Damn straight."

Another sympathetic smile.

"You like his music?" Lev asked.

"Me? I love him. He's great. But I love a lot of music."

Lev heard that walk-down again: *I love the dead* . . .

"But listen," the man said. Lev had a sense of what he was going to say before he said it. "You've arrived at a very interesting time. I'm leaving. I'm going to work my way to Nebraska. It's all a little crazy. But I've been dreaming of it. Nonstop. Have you? Have you been dreaming of Nebraska?"

"What? No. Why would I be dreaming of Nebraska?"

"I don't know."

The man had the air of inspiration about him. Lev felt it like he felt music.

"Take the place," he told Lev. "The door is unlocked. The whole thing is yours. No charge." He laughed then, but Lev only squinted back. Then, "Did you want to come with me?"

"To Nebraska?"

"Yes."

"No! I just walked all the way here from Idaho."

"I see."

"Do you?"

"I think so. And while I must say it's amazing to see another living, breathing face, I'm going to head out now. It's taken me weeks to find the nerve. But I've finally found it."

They stood facing one another on Ashbury Street a full ten seconds before Lev said:

"I can just . . . live here?"

"Oh yes. But I warn you, there isn't much left to this city. And I think there may be more in Nebraska." Then, "I wish you well."

"Okay."

"Okay."

The man started off down the street and Lev watched him go.

Then, dead finger still in hand, he turned to face the steps leading up to the holy house.

I . . . love . . . the . . . dead . . .

He climbed the steps. A confusing swirl of emotions bombarded him. Who was that man? And why would he want to leave this place? At the same time, who cared? Lev was standing before the front door of 710 Ashbury Street.

To think of the sounds once made beyond this door . . .

He opened the door with the hand still holding the dead finger.

"Jerry?" he called.

But before he stepped inside, a crow landed on the railing and Lev started at the sound of its flapping wings. He thought he heard words in that flapping. He thought he heard *Las Vegas*.

"Go away, you!" he said. But he stared into the intelligent eyes of the bird a beat before entering the house. "Las Vegas. Not a chance!"

But there *was* a chance. It was just slow in coming.

For Lev Marks would see the crow in the coming days, weeks, months. It'd often land on the windowsill and listen as Lev played guitar. Strumming in the house of the Grateful Dead. Yes, the crow would come, and Lev would strum, until the day when he would finally take the crow's advice.

Maybe Captain Trips was making music in Las Vegas after all. Maybe he was.

But until then, Lev would try his hardest to figure out the chords to songs like "Casey Jones" and "Bertha," "Dire Wolf" and "Wharf Rat." And the more he tried, the more he kept singing the song that, like the crow, just wouldn't leave him alone.

"*I . . . love . . . the . . . dead . . .*"

And the day he figured out the notes of the walk-down was the same day he took the steps outside back to the sidewalk.

On his way then to Las Vegas.

Just as the crow had told him.

MILAGROS

Cynthia Pelayo

Blood smeared on banana leaves, and a dusty sun. That's what I have. That's what I see.
That's all I have, I guess. Maybe that's all that's left?
Well, that and Choco.
I hear them just now, cawing, trying to scare me, but I don't see them. They're close though.
I know it.
I'm looking out the window of the concrete block school building. I don't see anything except a few bodies, little kids whose parents didn't come to get them in time so they could die at home. Instead, they just died here at school. This school is just a short walk from the beach. I wondered as they were coughing, their fevers raging, if they wished they could just get out there to the water, the ocean calming their bodies before their lives ended.
I didn't attend school here.
I attended school far from here, way up in the mountains and somehow Choco and I got down and found this place. We walked.

We cried. My feet stung with blisters, and when that happened, I'd just hug Choco and hold a *milagro* in my hand.

For parts of our trek, we didn't take the road. Instead, we walked through the jungle. I held Papi's machete tight in my hand, whipping and chopping away at leaves as big as my head, bigger.

We crossed streams, and I stopped at the waterfall Salto Collores and I washed up there with Choco. It felt sad to be there alone. The last time I was there was with all of my classmates. Things in your life can change so fast, the night taking away all you love, replacing their voices with hacking coughs, their kisses with thick green mucus, and their hugs with bloated bodies.

The sickness took so much.

My bed is the teacher's desk. I have a few blankets here on top of it for a cushion, and coloring books and crayons. With me I also have a prayer card of La Virgen de Guadalupe, the patron saint of Adjuntas, my town, the white rosary Tía Nelida gifted me on my communion, and some silver *milagro* charms from our home altar I keep in a little velvet pouch, my pink backpack where I store everything, and Choco, my pet chicken.

She's asleep beside me.

I can almost hear the whooshing of the ocean waves and it fills me with so much peace, but terror, too.

And then I hear it, the harsh caw.

Choco lets out a loud *cluck*.

"I know, Choco, I don't like those birds, either," and when I say this, one appears, flapping its wings on a branch.

"They're back," I whisper. Another crow flies down from the sky and stands on the body of a little girl. Her face is turned away from me, but I can see her neck is bulged and blue and green. A thick yellow paste of vomit is dried and clumped in her hair.

In time, she'll rot and liquify. They all do. The heat isn't kind to the decomposing bodies of Puerto Ricans.

I attended high school with Karla and Jonathan, Francisco and

Mrs. Reyes. Mrs. Reyes was just a few years older than us. Her name was Socorro. Her parents died when their car veered off a sharp turn heading into the mountains. Jonathan said their bodies were there so many days, and with the heat and humidity, by the time a group of men from the pueblo went down to check, all they found were slime and bones.

The mountain isn't so kind to bodies, and there's a lot of bodies rotting on the island now.

Mrs. Reyes was the first one who started coughing.

"*Es una gripa*." She laughed it off, rubbing her hands through her short, bouncy brown hair.

I always loved her hands. She said she'd go into San Juan every few weeks to visit her sister and there she'd get a manicure with bright red nail polish. Bright red nail polish always seemed like it was for someone special. I guess Mrs. Reyes was very special. I looked at my own hands, dirt lined right beneath the nails. In the morning and after school I'd spend it outside with the chickens or the cows, feeding them, cleaning them, and walking along with Choco, her little chicken body wobbling beside me. I guess if I were to be a farmer, I wouldn't really be in need of a manicure.

That day in Mrs. Reyes's class, I watched her stir honey into her *manzanilla* tea. She let go of the spoon and covered her mouth, those pretty red nails facing us. Her cough rattled her so much that her entire body shook. The kids laughed, but I didn't.

Carlo behind me said something mean. "You sound like death."

Mrs. Reyes stood, her legs shaky, her face pale, shiny with sweat.

"Carlo, are you reading?"

I turned around and saw that he nodded, but I knew he wasn't reading the assignment. Mrs. Reyes approached and as she walked past me, the sound of her heels echoed like hammers on the tiled floor. I smelled sharp menthol from the Vicks VapoRub she must have smeared on her chest and shoulders.

Carlo's eyes were wide as he held up his United States history book. I always thought it was funny we had to read so much about U.S. history and so little about Puerto Rican history. It's like we were supposed to learn about and love someplace most of us would never visit, but completely ignore where we lived.

Mrs. Reyes plucked a magazine that was tucked between the pages of Carlo's book. "This is not what you're supposed to be reading, Carlo!" she said, waving around the issue of *Mad* magazine, taking it away from him.

Carlo started coughing by lunchtime.

I always thought Mrs. Reyes's name was like a prediction, not just of her life, but for all of us, Socorro.

Help.

I've been here three nights in the elementary school. I've been too scared to make my move, but I have to.

I'm in the kindergarten classroom. I like it here because there are pictures of animals on the bulletin boards—birds, dogs, cats, goats, sheep, pigs, cows, more, so many more. It makes me sad, too, because I wonder if I'll ever have a farm now that I'm leaving. I knew I'd miss people, but really, I miss the animals the most.

There's a large map of Puerto Rico, all of the pueblos, Ponce, Jayuya, Yabucoa, Salinas, more. Next to it is a map of the mainland and it looks so massive, like another world. Square shapes and rectangle shapes and funny shapes with funny names like Louisiana and Texas, Missouri and New Mexico, New York and Nebraska.

I hop off my bed and move over to the map.

"Choco, we have to take the boat here." I point to San Juan and then slide my finger to the tip of Florida. "And then we have to somehow make it all the way over here." I slide my finger across the map and up to Nebraska.

Mami always wanted me to leave here. She said I'd have a better life if I went to San Juan, studied there, and then moved to the mainland. I wanted to visit San Juan, but to get my nails painted red like Mrs. Reyes, because I knew I was special like her, too, and to see the Castillo San Felipe del Morro and maybe spot the ghost of the soldier who patrolled at sunset. But, never in my life had I planned on going any farther than that.

"I'm too scared of planes to leave the island," I'd said.

"Then you can take a boat to the mainland," Mami replied.

"I'm even more afraid of boats than planes."

Papi told me about ships commandeered by dead pirates, drifting to nowhere. I feared finding myself aboard one of those crafts, doomed to die out there on the water with my island home just out of reach.

This morning, though, I had to take that risk.

"We die here, Choco, or we die out there," I said, trying to sound brave, even to myself. I shoved my hand in the small pocket of my backpack. There's a little Ziploc bag with dried corn. I pull out a handful of kernels and set them down on the ground for Choco and she begins to peck at them, cooing as she does.

"We don't have a lot of food," I say. "And I don't know how long the trip will be to Nebraska."

Jonathan said by plane to the mainland is just three hours, but by boat he said it could take three days to get to Miami alone. I wondered if it'd take months then to get across the mainland.

"I'm worried," I say, stroking Choco's brown feathers. "I don't know how to swim. I never learned. And I'm scared of the water. I'm scared of *tiburones*. Oscar said that a *tiburón* can chomp down and remove your entire leg with a single bite. Laila said no, that the shark will just clamp down on your torso and chew and chew and chew. I know both Oscar and Laila are dead now.

I sigh and look back to the window and think of the crows outside waiting for us.

It's *la madrugada*, that time of day that light begins to break through the clouds. The western part of the sky has gone from black to dark blue, but the east is this baby blue on top with a streak of peach and pink where the sun will rise.

"Once I open that door, Choco, we need to move fast," I say, shoving the prayer card and *milagros*, coloring books and crayons into my backpack. I look to the sheets I brought from home, but I can't carry any more for this part of our trip.

When we lived at home, Choco used to have her own bed. My friend Karla would laugh because she'd say we treated Choco like a dog, and not like the other chickens outside. Choco never liked being outside. She was always an inside chicken. Mami said she couldn't sleep in my room, and so we made her a little bed in the *sala* and she slept there. Choco never really liked the total darkness. She'd grow agitated. Pacing, her claws tapping against the floor. But she liked sleeping in the *sala*. I think the flickering lights of the altar gave her some comfort.

The altar at home was in the *sala*. It was a small wooden table with candles lit for St. Michael, the Sacred Heart of Mary, the Divine Child Jesus, St. Martin de Porres, and even St. Lazarus. The flat, silver *milagros* were all pinned against the wall. The wall was completely covered by these tiny silver charms that sparkled in the candlelight. There were some made in the shape of hands and feet, hearts, angels kneeling in prayer, the sun, the moon, more.

The idea of a *milagros* is that the small charm is a reminder for the saints to pray for us, to heal us, protect our bodies from pain or harm or sickness. There were many types. I took as many as I could when I left and put them into my little pouch, hoping they'd protect me on our journey.

When I left home, I left the candles burning, I don't know why. The saints only answered some of my prayers. I was still alive, but Mami and Papi and everyone else died of the illness.

As Mami died, she told me not to leave the house, and I didn't, not for a long time. I waited days, until the howling of dogs and the complaints from cows quieted down. I'd stand out on the hill and look down into the pueblo and each night there would be fewer lights, candles extinguishing as another person died.

MILAGROS

Then, I had a dream about this place, milpa growing tall all around me. When I broke through to an open field, I found a house and a woman standing on a porch. She looked like my grandmother.

"*Tienes que ir al oeste*," she said with a warm smile on her face.

I was already west of the island, I thought, but she said no, like she could read my mind.

"*Estados Unidos*."

When I woke up, I found dozens of big crows outside, standing silent, on the clotheslines, the front step, on top of banana trees and coconut palms.

I reached for Choco, tucked her under my arm, grabbed my backpack, and slammed the door shut. The crows have been following us ever since.

Mami said death comes for everyone, eventually.

First there was the hurricane, and that came for many, flooding houses and streets, sweeping cars off the roads and down into ditches. We lost electricity for days and had no running water. When people started sneezing and coughing, many of us thought, well, it's just another symptom of the hurricane, standing water, and germs brewing in the corners of our flooded homes, but it was something else.

Before I open the door to the schoolhouse, I start banging on it and screaming. I'm screaming so loud, hoping to scare those crows away. I run to the window and look and don't see any. They must have flown off.

Choco is pacing, rustling her feathers.

"I'm sorry," I say kneeling. "I know you're scared, but we have to try now."

I stand, slip on my backpack and a sling I made out of an old T-shirt, and tuck Choco inside.

I open the door to the classroom, and it leads directly outside. The sun is beaming down on me. It's so hot. I start running, running down the road and toward the beach. There should be boats at the beach. There have to be. Choco is clucking and I am looking up at the sky. I see a crow swoop above us but I keep running until we are out of this neighborhood and find the beach, and there I see sand, beach blankets all strewn about, old hats, sunburned bodies, and a bright orange canoe. Out further into the distance is a large white boat in the ocean.

"We can reach it, Choco. I know we can reach it. It's a miracle," I say, thinking of the tiny miracles in my backpack. The ship out there is like an answered prayer.

I hear cawing behind me, but I ignore it.

We reach the canoe.

Just as we do, I hear another caw and then a ripping sound, like the tearing of paper. I'm yanked back and catch myself from falling. I turn. A crow tore at my pink backpack, and the prayer card, coloring books, crayons and my *milagros*, my tiny shiny pieces of hopes and prayers, spill out into the sand.

I remove my backpack and set it down and just as I do a crow dives down toward us.

I set Choco into the seat beside me. I push the canoe into the water and slip into the seat and start paddling. Another crow swoops down and clamps its beak into Choco's neck. Choco squawks, her body twists and jerks. She pins me with those tiny eyes and I scream. I shout at the crow to get away, but it doesn't. I reach for Choco's neck, hoping to stop the blood, but it's all wet and slippery. Blood sprays and then the crow lifts Choco off the canoe. It flaps its black wings over the blue sky and then releases Choco's body. She falls into the water with a splash.

I hear them, their *caw, caw, caw*s.

I turn and see them on the beach, hundreds of black dots against that beige blanket.

I paddle faster and faster to the boat. My poor Choco.

The canoe bumps against the boat when I finally reach it, but I don't see anywhere to climb. The waves are pushing me away and my arms are getting so cramped and tired from paddling.

I push, and push, alongside the boat until I find a ladder.

I toss the paddles into the canoe and then reach the first rung.

My fingers slip, but I try again, clutching on tight.

The canoe is moving away from me, and if I slip I will fall into the water.

I imagine hundreds of *tiburones* swimming in circles beneath me, waiting to pull me apart, arms and legs, my head and torso.

Then I remember, there are no *tiburones*.

There is nothing. There's only dead people and dead animals and if I don't get on this boat and get to Florida and cross over to Nebraska, that funny name and funny shape on the map, and cross over *oeste*, west, to Nebraska to meet the old woman on the farm, then I will be dead, too.

I push my body up. Everything is shaking. Everything hurts, but still, I slide onto the boat and I look down at my hands. They are all red, but not pretty like Mrs. Reyes's hands.

The birds continue to caw, screeching from the beach. I stand and face them and scream.

I scream for Mrs. Reyes and I scream for Mami and Papi and I even scream for stupid Jonathan. I especially scream for Choco.

I run to the cabin, hoping to find a key, anything to turn this boat on. Then I see him, a man seated at the wheel, his mouth is wide open and fat yellow worms are crawling in and out. His eyes are bulging out of their sockets, and liquid is leaking out and running down his temples. His skin is burnt under the sun, red and black and blistered. All down his white shirt and white pants is dried, caked vomit.

I think of the pirates Papi told me about, dead and lost at sea.

A crow flutters down and lands on the dead man's head.

I take a step back.

Another bird lands on his shoulder, and then another on his other shoulder.

I turn my head, and see the island, and I wonder, *Is it better to die there or to die here?*

Another bird lands, beating its large wings, and another.

Now one flaps toward my face, pecking at my cheeks. Stabbing into my fat.

I feel sharp and cold and stinging all the same.

I raise my arms, shriek and cry, but there's more sharp pain. I feel fine stabs in my flesh, talons sinking into me, pecking at my elbows.

There's more digging into my body, my neck, my forehead, clamping down at my fingers, my lips, my eyes. The world is blurred, and I can't see. I hear cawing and ocean waves. The beating of wings.

I'm stepping back and stepping back and there's water, and I'm in the water and I'm reaching all around, hoping I'll find Choco.

THE LEGION OF SWINE

S. A. Cosby

Woodrow stepped out onto his porch and stretched his arms to the sky as the morning sun caressed his cheek. The air was crisp and cool but held the promise of heat and sweat to come later in the day. Blue jays and sparrows sang as they perched on the branches of trees in the forest that surrounded his house and his property like the slow embrace of an aged aunt.

Woodrow touched his brow. It was pretty close to impossible to diagnose a fever in yourself, but it was a habit he couldn't seem to break. He touched his neck and felt for swelling, but all he felt was the rough bristles of a beard he was debating growing.

When Mae had gotten sick her forehead had burned with fever like a cast-iron woodstove gone rageful red. Then her neck had swollen to three or four times its normal size. It looked like her head and neck had turned into a sausage. He wanted to take her to the hospital, but by then all the hospitals were closed. They'd even stopped putting the dead in refrigerated trucks because they'd run out of space to park them. He did his best to comfort her. He put cold compresses on her brow and tried to get her to eat. He stayed with her day and night, not caring if he got sick. Part of him actually wanted to catch it so he could join her. Just be a few steps behind her like back when they used to drive over to Roanoke and go to the mall.

He'd trail behind her now and then just to watch her walk. Watch the gentle sway of her hips or the way she did a little shimmy when she saw something in a store window that caught her fancy. Her brown shoulder blades glistening from the generous amount of lotion he'd rubbed on them after her bath. The straps of her sundress gently laying across her flesh that undulated as she moved. That was usually on a Saturday when he was off from the bottling plant in Staunton. They'd drive down off the mountain and go over to Roanoke and look at things they couldn't afford and dream dreams they knew would never come true, but isn't that what makes a dream a precious thing? It's both real and an illusion at the same time.

The pigs heard him step on the porch and that set them to snorting and squealing with a fierceness that telegraphed their hunger.

Woodrow stepped down off the porch and walked through the tall grass that had taken over his front yard and headed for the faded red corncrib he and his daddy had built when they had finished the house. They'd built both the summer he and Mae had married. He didn't know it then, but Mae was already pregnant with Joshua. They'd go on to have three more children. Mary-Ellen, Thomas, and Junius.

He hoped Joshua was still alive.

He'd left home a year before the sickness came upon them. He joined the army and got out of Stuart's Holler as fast as the eastbound train could carry him.

"I wanna see New York. I wanna walk down Madison Avenue. I wanna drink coffee on a street corner in Paris. I wanna feel the sand from Egypt with my toes, Daddy," Joshua had said when he announced he was joining the army.

"All you gonna see is the barrel of a gun," Mae had said. Woodrow had found himself in the middle of the two great loves of his life. A place he was familiar with intimately. He loved all his children, but

THE LEGION OF SWINE

Joshua was his first born. He was smart and strong and had a kind heart and a smile that hinted at the foolishness in his heart. A pleasant foolishness that never failed to make Woodrow laugh. Joshua was just like his mother and that meant they couldn't set horses for nothing.

Woodrow smiled. It was a rare occurrence these days but the darkness that had enveloped him since the sickness the newscasters called the superflu could not snuff out the memory of his son's smile or his wife's bemused exasperation.

Then the darkness reasserted its dominance and the smile disappeared.

There was a bucket sitting upside down near the corncrib that Woodrow filled with corncobs before heading to the pigsty. The sows were squealing and snorting but the big ol' boar was sitting in the mud studying him with flat brown eyes that looked like dirty pennies. Woodrow had taken three pigs in trade for his truck from his nearest neighbor, Langston Jones, after the bottling plant had closed.

"We trying to go to California. Hear tell it ain't so bad out there. Some folks trying to go up to Minnesota, but Della can't stand the cold. I think California is the place, but my old Pontiac ain't gonna make it. If you planning on slaying them hogs, be some good meat in the fall," Langston had said, spinning a yarn that neither one of them really believed. But Woodrow didn't begrudge the man his hope. Sometimes hope was just a life raft in the middle of a hurricane, but it was better than drowning.

This was after Mary-Ellen had passed.

Woodrow took the pail full of corncobs over to the pigsty and leaned on the rough-hewn wooden rails. He grabbed a handful of corncobs and tossed them into the pen. There were eight pigs in total. Seven sows and the boar. Two of the sows were the offspring of one of the original sows. He tossed the corncobs to break up the crowd. Otherwise, they fought and bit each other when he filled the trough.

He watched three of the pigs go to work on the corncobs. The gnashing of their teeth and the furious motion of their heads reminded him of the scene in *The Wizard of Oz* where Dorothy falls in the pigpen and Zeke rightly loses his mind and pulls her out as fast as he can. He remembered having a conversation with Joshua when they'd gone to visit Langston once when Joshua was a child.

"Pigs don't care that you been feeding them for years. They don't care you done known them since they was on their momma's teat. You fall in that pen on a day they hungry all you is to them is meat. You hear me boy?" Woodrow had said.

"Would they eat me?" Joshua had asked.

"Bones and all. Bones and all." Woodrow had said it twice for emphasis.

The boar got up and stomped over to the trough. The sows gave him room. His floppy ears lent him a somewhat comical appearance, but Woodrow locked eyes with him again and saw a feral cunning there that made his stomach lurch.

He'd traded for the fall, but two weeks after Langston had hit the road Junius was dead, too. He'd buried them in the backyard. Then Mae had died, cursing her daddy, wishing he was burning in hell and Woodrow tried his best to comfort her while trying not to consider her dying words too closely. He didn't need those images in his head. If they had found a place to take root, he might be tempted to go dig up Francis Pettigrew and set what was left of him on fire.

After Mae passed, he was alone.

Except for the pigs.

As spring moved into summer, he found that they comforted him. Their snorts and squeals and grunts broke the silence that wasn't really silence and kept his thoughts from speaking to him too loudly. At least during the day. At night he worked on a wood carving he was going to treat with some shellac and put out back as a grave marker. He'd carved Junius and Mary-Ellen's names. He was working on Mae's name now. During the day he studied the wood grain after he'd worked in the garden. He turned the length of wood over in his hands, feeling its weight and its length. Before he'd started carving it, he'd sanded it down to a finish as smooth as the skin on the backside of a newborn.

At night he studied the space between Mae's name and the children. He measured with his thumb and forefinger. He thought about adding his name in that space. He still had his double-barreled shotgun in the closet. Some steel shot would punch a hole in the back of his head the size of a grapefruit. He had figured out how he'd do it, too.

He'd dig himself a grave between Mae and Junius. He'd stand on the edge and put the two barrels in his mouth. Reach down and pull the trigger and then let his body fall into the empty hole. The only flaw in his plan was there wouldn't be anyone to cover the hole to keep scavengers from dragging his bones to the four winds, but he was coming around to the idea that didn't really matter.

Woodrow sat the pail down near the entrance to the pen.

It was the dreams of the old woman that stayed his hand. Woodrow wasn't a man that was given to wild flights of fancy, but he had a healthy respect for what his mother used to call the "old ways." He'd lived on Brown Otter Mountain his whole life. A mountain that was one of many in the Appalachians. A chain of mountains his mother had told him were older than the trees whose roots grew deep along their ridges or the fish whose seas would never touch their rocky shores.

"Things that old have learned to speak without words," his mother used to say. The other day he'd heard a song on the radio that talked about the Shenandoah Valley and how life was old there. Older than the trees just like his mother used to say. Woodrow knew his mother and the white boy who had sung that song were right. Life was indeed old here.

He knew mountains here talked to him in his sleep. The old woman, darker than his mother with a shock of white hair as pure and bright as fallen snow, came to him in his dreams. She said her name. She did her best to comfort him. And she called to him. Called him and bade him take up his pack and come west. But not to California and not to Minnesota and absolutely not to Las Vegas.

She wanted him to come to her and take her to Boulder, Colorado. And Woodrow would wake from these dreams confused and unquieted. He'd never left Virginia. How was he supposed to find this old Black woman? How was he supposed to get to Boulder, Colorado? How was he supposed to leave his goddamn wife and his children for a dream? For a fucking dream? Never mind the old ways. Never mind the voice of the mountains. How was he just supposed to leave? How?

"HOW?!" he yelled. His voice ricocheted through the valley, bouncing off the trees and the rocks and then fading away into nothingness like an exorcised ghost. Woodrow took the pail back to the corncrib. He was about to turn and go back in the house when he heard a familiar sound that filled him with fear.

There were voices coming up the road.

His driveway, or the road that led to his house, since he'd given Langston his truck, wound down the mountain for about two hundred yards until it hit the main highway that led you out of the county. Most of the people left in Lee County were keeping to themselves. Quarantining the way the government had asked them to do when Captain Trips first hit. That's what Joshua called it in the last letter they had received from him. That was before Captain Trips had made his way up the mountain. Before they lost touch with Joshua, who said he was being deployed in Washington, D.C.

"To protect the president. He's a good man, Daddy. You'd like him. But I don't think they tell him everything. Y'all best stay up on Brown Otter. Safer that way. I think," Joshua had said in his letter.

But of course, people hadn't stayed up on Brown Otter. Woodrow thought if the government had really wanted them to stay quarantined, they should have told folks to go into town and dance in the goddamn street.

So, hearing voices coming up the road set his nerves on edge. His shotgun was in the closet, but his bowie knife was on his belt. He

THE LEGION OF SWINE

reached down and touched the handle and felt the polished wood and the weathered leather scabbard. The blade was wicked sharp. His own daddy had taught him the magic of a whetstone and concentration. He figured he could cut a man's throat with that knife and the man wouldn't know it until he tried to drink a glass of water.

Woodrow walked past the corncrib and peered down the lane.

Three figures were approaching. Two of the figures were slight and had the loping walk of small but strong women. The third figure was a man. Not as tall or as wide as Woodrow, but a solidly built man all the same. They had backpacks and old tan boots. The women were Black and the man was Hispanic. The three of them had their hands up and were smiling. The closer they got, the higher they raised their hands and the wider their smiles got.

"Excuse me, sir, we don't mean you no harm. We're just passing through, but we were wondering if you could maybe spare some water or some food or if you were feeling really generous a bit of both? I'm Jorge and this here is Janice, and this lady to my right is Tina," Jorge said. They'd stopped about fifty feet from Woodrow.

Woodrow had sat with his own madness for months since Mae had passed. It was an old friend who didn't know he wasn't welcomed. He saw him in the mirror in the morning and behind his eyelids at night. There was madness in this man's smile. It was in all of their smiles. Shining bright and deadly like quicksilver.

But. . . .

Weren't they all a little mad these days? Weren't they all walking across the surface of a barely frozen lake that was their sanity? Everyone he'd ever known or loved was dead. Except for Joshua. Please, God, not Joshua.

If you weren't a little crazy, were you even still alive?

"I got some water. Ain't too much food, though. Just some taters and greens and some snap beans. Got a little deer jerky, but it's a bit salty," Woodrow said. He didn't mention the ton of canned foods he had in the cellar or the shotgun he had in the closet.

"Well, sir, we would sure appreciate it. Thank you so much," Jorge said.

Woodrow noticed something else about his smile and that of his two companions.

It never seemed to reach their eyes.

Later, they sat around Woodrow's kitchen table. He had boiled potatoes and snap beans and made them some tea with the last bit of sugar he had left. They ate ravenously. Not as ravenously as the pigs, but pretty close. Then they told him they had come up from Newport News. Walked along Interstate 64 until they decided to take Interstate 81 and head west.

"We the last people left standing from Red Hill County," Jorge said between bites of the potatoes.

"So, we heading west," Tina said. Her voice was husky like she'd been smoking since her fifth birthday.

"Go west, young man," Janice said.

She was staring at Woodrow the way he figured a spider looked at a fly. There was a frankness in her gaze that made him uncomfortable in ways that weren't exactly unpleasant.

"You're welcome to stay the night," Woodrow said. The words were out of his mouth before he realized he was saying them. Janice licked her lips. Actually, licked them like a lion staring at a gazelle. Woodrow shivered on the inside.

"Well, that's mighty kind of you. Thank you so much. It'll be nice not to wake up with beetles in my hair," Jorge said, and laughed. The laugh sounded like he hadn't used it in a long, long time.

That night Woodrow slept in his bed with the shotgun on the floor under him and his knife on the nightstand beside him. It took two hours after they had all laid down, after he'd blown out all the oil lamps and washed the dishes, before Janice came to his room. She slipped through the door like a shadow made flesh. Woodrow watched her approach his bed, naked and slick like a phantom cut from the very night itself.

She slipped into his bed.

"You've been alone a long time haven't you, Woodrow?" she whispered.

He didn't answer.

She took his hand and guided it between her legs. When he felt what she had there, felt his fingertips brush against her wetness, he let out a moan.

"You don't have to be alone anymore. Come west with us. Come with us and meet the Man. The Ageless Stranger. The Walkin Dude," she whispered as she guided his fingers inside her.

Woodrow tried to move his hand away, but Janice pushed his fingers in deeper. He didn't know who the Man was or the Ageless Stranger. Or the Walkin Dude. All he knew was his hand was wet and Janice looked enough like Mae that he could lock his guilt away in a place where it couldn't greet him in the dark.

He was dreaming.

He was standing near the pen. It was dark, but the pigs were milling about. He started into the shadows and saw that their snouts were stained red.

"It's blood," his dream self said.

The boar stomped to the door of the pen. His flat muddy brown eyes appraised him hungrily. His fat pink tongue slipped out like a fat greasy worm and licked at the blood on his snout.

"Woodrow Teller. You liked to fuck your wife in the ass. She did it because it's what you wanted, but she hated it. Hated it every time. You fucked Janice in the ass tonight and she didn't mind. Not one bit. Come to Vegas, Woodrow. You can get all the buggering you want there. Women or men. Hell, boys or girls if you want it. Just drop to your knees and promise me. Say the words. Say, 'Your life for me.' Say it and you can forget all about your rotting wife and your dead children," the boar said, but Woodrow's dream self knew it wasn't the boar. It was him. It was his voice that came forth from the gullet of the big pink pig.

"He's a liar. The hoary cripple with the malicious eye," another voice said.

In his dream, Woodrow saw himself turn.

There was the old Black woman from his previous dreams. She was sitting in a rocking chair as the sky behind her roiled. First black then purple then finally red. Red as the gates of hell.

"He lies Woodrow. Whatever you and your wife did in your marriage bed you did for love. And for a little fun. No need to feel ashamed of that. Don't let him seduce you, son. He speaks and breathes corruption," the old Black woman said. She pulled out a fiddle and began to play a mournful tune.

"He is Legion," she said.

Woodrow sat straight up in the bed.

"Mother Abagail," he said in a hoarse moan. That was the old woman's name. He knew it. He didn't know how he knew it but he did.

He reached out for Janice.

Janice was gone.

The next morning the three travelers were standing on Woodrow's porch with their backpacks full of deer jerky. Their canteens were full of water from Woodrow's well.

"Safe travels," Woodrow said.

Jorge smiled at him.

"We thank you for your hospitality. We really do. Thank you for the jerky and the water. But I can't help but notice you got some mighty fat pigs over there. What say we butcher one of them and split the meat? The four of us working on it, it won't take long at all. One them fat fuckers could feed us for the whole winter," Jorge said.

"We can kill them all and then you can come west with us," Janice said.

Woodrow felt his face get hot.

"Thank you kindly, but I suppose you best be on your way. I don't plan on going nowhere," Woodrow said. Jorge smiled wider. Woodrow thought it was no longer a smile at all. It was like the man was baring his teeth at him like a mad dog.

"You got eight pigs, Woodrow. It's a waste not to do something with all that meat," Jorge said.

"It's gotta taste better than the last meat we had," Tina said.

"Yeah, the last meat we had was tough as shoe leather," Janice said.

"Yes . . . yes it was. Gamey as all get out," Jorge said.

"Shoe leather. That's funny," Tina said.

Woodrow felt like mice were running across his belly. The back of his throat felt raw as a skinned rabbit. The three travelers were standing on the porch, but they were loosely surrounding him.

"I'm not killing my pigs. You all best be moving on now," Woodrow said.

"What size shoe you wear, Woodrow?" Tina asked.

Jorge pulled a pistol out of his pocket and pointed it at Woodrow.

"We gonna leave here with some meat. Up to you what kind," Jorge said.

Woodrow bit his bottom lip.

"Okay. Okay. Let's go," he said. He brushed past Janice and walked over to the pen.

"I'm gonna open the gate. You shoot the first pig that comes out. We can't shoot him and let him drop in the pen. They'll be on him before you blink," Woodrow said.

"You just get ready to cut his big ass up," Jorge said.

As Woodrow approached the pigsty, the big boar raised his massive head.

His eyes were not muddy dirty brown anymore. They were hazel colored like drops of honey. It occurred to him that the old Black woman in his dreams had light eyes, too.

"You ready?" Woodrow said over his shoulder.

"Just open the pen," Jorge said.

Woodrow caught the eyes of the oldest sow. Her eyes were light brown, too.

He pulled the catch and threw the gate open.

Woodrow hopped up on the rail as all eight of the pigs rushed out of the pen at once. Jorge's gun went off once, then twice.

Then the screams began.

When the screaming stopped, Woodrow took one of the backpacks off what was left of one of the bodies. He packed up his wedding picture, the family Bible, and some moonshine. He placed the grave marker in the backyard. He put it at the head of Mae's grave and went down to his knees.

He closed his eyes.

"I love you, Mae. I love you Mary-Ellen. I love you Junius," he whispered. He got up and threw the backpack over his shoulder.

The pigs had moved on from the bodies and were standing at the tree line. The sows had already started walking into the woods. In a month they'd be feral. The boar stared at him. Woodrow stared back.

It licked its bloody snout and turned away from his gaze.

Woodrow took a paintbrush and a small can of oil-based red paint and wrote on his front door.

GONE WEST TO FIND MOTHER ABaGAIL. BEWARE OF WILD PIGS. WOODROW TELLER.

Then he headed down the lane with his shotgun over his shoulder. He hoped Joshua was still alive.

He hoped Joshua wasn't in Las Vegas.

THE LEGION OF SWINE

He hoped he could find Mother Abagail.

He hoped there were more people like Mae and Joshua than Jorge and Tina and Janice.

He hoped he didn't run across the Walkin Dude.

But he also hoped he'd be strong enough to make his stand if he did.

KEEP THE DEVIL DOWN
Rio Youers

NOW

Arizona State Route 219, known colloquially as El Camino del Cuervo, one hundred and forty-eight miles of two-lane blacktop running from Yuma to the southwestern corner of Yavapai County. Pale as ash, chewed up by the heat, it had been slated for decommission in March of 1990. That was before Captain Trips, though, when the Arizona Department of Transportation was still functional—when *everything*, to a greater or lesser extent, was still functional. Now SR 219 was just another dead road in a mostly dead country.

Elise put her foot to the floor. The needle went from sixty to seventy-nine and held. This car—a mid-eighties Chevette appropriated from her neighbor's garage—was not built for high performance. The engine protested with a shrill sound. The windows and door panels rattled. Elise dragged a palm across her greasy brow. Her heart had no problem running at speed.

"You're going too fast," the girl said. Her name was Ruby. She and Elise had known each other for little more than an hour.

The car behind continued to gain on them, rumbling through the heat haze and dust—a Mustang, Elise thought, maybe a Barracuda. Something packing muscle, in any case, and with more horses beneath the hood than this old Chevette.

"Just let me go," Elise whispered.

"I'm scared," Ruby said. She drew her tattered sneakers onto the seat and hugged her knees. Elise thought she looked more weary than scared—or weary of *being* scared, perhaps. The default disposition for this newly upended world.

The muscle car expanded in the rearview. Elise heard the throaty snarl of its V8 above the Chevette's overworked whine. It swung into the oncoming lane and accelerated alongside them. Elise touched the brakes. The needle dipped to sixty-five and the muscle car roared ahead, then it slowed, drawing level again.

It wasn't a Mustang or Barracuda. Elise had glimpsed the word CORVID on the trunk lid. She'd heard of a Corvette, of course, even a Corvair, but this model was new to her. The word itself—*Corvid*—evoked images of graveyards and bones. The car's aesthetic offered nothing to contradict this, with its casket-like lines, its black paintwork and tinted glass.

Elise knew what was coming. She told Ruby to grab hold of something, then pressed her back into the driver's seat and tightened her grip on the steering wheel.

The Corvid swerved right and thumped into them. The sound of colliding steel was tremendous—a resonant boom that rolled through every bone and fiber. The Chevette's side mirror shattered and fell away in pieces. Ruby screamed. Elise veered onto the shoulder and lifted a ragged curtain of dust, then managed to correct her line and swing back into the right lane.

Sweat trickled into her eyes. She blinked it away, not daring to remove her hands from the wheel. The needle had dropped into the forties, but the Corvid remained alongside her, matching her speed. Its passenger-side window was open. Elise looked through it, expecting to see the driver: a crow-headed thing with pale blue eyes and tattooed arms. The car's interior was too dark see anything, though. It was like staring into a well.

It slammed into them again, shattering one of the Chevette's headlights. Broken glass flew over the hood and rattled off the windshield. The fender buckled, flapped briefly, and was ripped into the air like a mad, steel bird. A quivering sob escaped Elise's chest as she wrestled the wheel to keep from spinning out. She hit the shoulder again and the back end fishtailed. For a moment, everything was lost in a cloud of dust. The Chevette emerged from it sideways, sliding across both lanes to the other shoulder. Elise steered into the skid, tapped the brakes, and got the car under control.

She'd slowed to thirty-five. The Corvid was ahead of her, low and predatory, weaving from one side of the road to the other.

Ruby was crying. She looked up over her knees, her wet eyes glimmering through the tangled threads of her hair.

"What does he *want*?" she asked.

"I don't know," Elise replied, and this was true. Clearly, the Corvid's driver had only bad intentions. Would he drag her back to El Centro and the life she had run away from? Or did he have something worse in mind? Elise had seen such things. She'd passed a young family hanged by their necks from overhead lines along a back road west of Yuma. Daddy was a big guy and had a line to himself. Still, it drooped V-shaped with the weight of him. Their station wagon—a bumper sticker on its rear end that read POWERED BY JESUS—lay skewed in a ditch, its cargo area ransacked. Farther along, she'd passed a mesquite strung with severed human heads.

There was a knapsack on the back seat packed with a few of Elise's belongings: clothes, a framed photograph of her mother, a spare pair of shoes, a couple of paperback novels, and a small bag bulging with toiletries and cosmetics. There was also a semiautomatic pistol in .45

ACP—a long-slide Hardballer. Jason's handgun, of course. The only thing of his she'd taken. The only thing she'd wanted. Unfortunately, this was not an option. There'd been four rounds in the Hardballer's mag, but she'd used them all at Cactus Belle's Trading Post.

The road ran crooked to the horizon, like a broken bone that had healed wrong. Vultures rode the updrafts in patient circles, while smaller birds scattered from the cover of shrubs and trees. There was nothing in any direction but the Sonoran hardpan, sewn with palo verde, ironwood, and other flashes of color. The gray outlines of ridges and mesas wavered in the heat haze.

Staying on 219, the Corvid would soon get the better of them. Elise saw only one course of action.

"Hold on," she said to the girl.

Elise cranked the wheel right and the Chevette careened off the road, bouncing across the desert proper with everything banging and shaking. Dust rose in a smoke-like cloud. Grit rattled through the wheel arches. Elise glanced over her shoulder and saw the Corvid's brake lights flare. Its back end swung around, then it, too, departed the road and raced across the desert in pursuit.

It was unpredictable terrain. She could clip a tree and flip, slide into a gulch, front-end a boulder. The same was true for the Corvid, however. Going off-road was a desperate course of action, but Elise had somewhat leveled the playing field.

Fifty . . . sixty miles per hour. Rocks bounced off the chassis with bullet-like velocity and the constant sound of them enveloped Ruby's frightened groans. Elise tore through creosote bush and desert lavender. She hit a rise going sixty-five and the Chevette was airborne for a full second. It landed loudly and jounced. The trunk popped open and closed with a furious thump.

The Corvid made easier work of the landscape. It swerved around the various obstacles, gradually gaining. It hit the same rise and caught more air. Every now and then it would disappear inside the wall of dust following Elise, only to reemerge closer.

"He's going to catch us," Ruby cried.

"I won't let that happen," Elise said.

She had left her apartment that morning with a clear idea of where she was going. It was as if some invisible cell door had been unlocked and rolled open. To feel free—*emancipated*—in a time of such pain and grief had not rested easy on her soul, but it hadn't stopped her from liberating this old car from her neighbor's garage and heading east out of town. She'd found a map in the glove box and charted a route to Nebraska, keeping to the secondary roads because she believed they'd be quieter and therefore less dangerous.

Five hours later, with one hundred and eighty miles behind her, Elise had a revised destination: *Away*. Nebraska's big sky had been eclipsed by something bigger yet, and arguably not a destination at all. There were no buildings in Away, no streets or people or lush green cornfields. Elise yearned for it, all the same—to be away from this desert with its dry death and heat, and away from this muscle car and every godless thing it represented.

She recalled the young family strung up by their necks and felt a deep stitch of grief, even though she never knew them. Tears spilled from her eyes. She tightened her grip on the wheel and kept moving.

Now the ground dipped sharply, punctuated by greasewood and granite boulders, rounded like the shoulders of praying men. Elise deaccelerated to navigate this change in the terrain. She threaded a gap between two such boulders with the Corvid just a beat behind, then steered around a magnificent tangle of deadwood: trees that had inched together across millennia and died in one another's arms. The ground leveled out on the other side and Elise jumped on the gas again. She checked her mirrors and saw the Corvid roaring up on her left, lifting a black cloud of dust.

Both cars swung right to avoid a towering saguaro. Only the seat belt kept Ruby from sliding off her seat and into Elise's lap. The girl's expression was heartbreaking. She felt things no child should ever have to feel. She'd lost everything and the abyss it left behind was in her eyes and her trembling chest and in the shape of her mouth. If the plague's impact could be captured in a single image, it would be of this nine-year-old girl.

The Corvid pulled level and Elise stifled a scream. She'd thought it was black dust, but it was smoke pouring out through the open windows, as if whatever was behind the wheel was on fire.

Elise hit the brakes. She turned the wheel and changed direction, fishtailing between more saguaros and ripping through dry brush and shrubs. Jackrabbits scattered in all directions, their distinct black tails ticking. She lost the Corvid for several blissful seconds, then it reappeared in the rearview. It came up fast and thumped her back end. It sounded, and felt, like a small IED had detonated in the trunk, which popped open again, badly dented. A long crack bisected the rear windshield. The Chevette lurched and shimmied, but Elise maintained control. The Corvid moved in again, accelerating hard. Elise watched it in the rearview. She steered right at the last second and avoided the attack by a matter of inches.

The terrain dipped again, descending into a narrow arroyo, its bed littered with detritus, mostly sticks and plant matter, but bones, too—animals washed away and drowned by flash floods. It all sounded the same beneath the Chevette's tires. Elise rode this dry chute and the Corvid kept pace, rumbling along the top of the bank to her left. It was still smoking. Ahead, the arroyo grew narrower yet and turned sharply. The apex of this bend was clogged with a fallen tree trunk and an EXIT sign lifted from the roadside by some long-ago storm. It jutted from the sandy bed with its arrow, ominously, pointing down. Elise pumped the brakes and the Chevette went sideways, sliding over the sticks and bones. Its rear quarter panel slammed against the sign with a jarring clang. She worked the wheel and got around the obstruction, then climbed out of the arroyo on the other side.

They emerged onto flatter ground. Elise rammed her sneaker to the floor and the needle climbed from thirty to sixty. Something rattled behind the car, and it took her a moment to realize it was the muffler, hanging by a single bracket.

She checked the rearview and saw the Corvid crest the arroyo's low bank, signaled by its billowing black smoke. It caught up in mere seconds and hung on the Chevette's dented rear bumper, as close and dark as a shadow.

It was the same gray desertscape ahead accented with mesquite, saguaro, and greasewood, except in the distance she noticed a dark seam running parallel to the horizon. Elise had no idea it was a railroad track until Ruby sat up in her seat and pointed.

"Train," she said.

THEN

Elise had lost track of the days. She thought it was July 4, but couldn't be certain. Not that it mattered. There'd be no celebratory fireworks or parades along Main Street. Not in El Centro. Not anywhere.

Jason had died during the night while Elise slept in the armchair in their living room. She'd stirred awake to the familiar smell of his sickness, but a new silence. No coughing. No sneezing or wheezing. No crying, pleading, or wailing her name. She'd risen from the armchair and walked into the bedroom to find him upright against the pillows, but very dead. His eyes were closed, but his mouth was open, showing his teeth. He'd always shown his teeth, no matter his mood. He had a good smile for someone who smoked two packs of Marlboros a day.

Elise felt no sorrow. She'd been through that process when it became apparent that Jason was going to die—when his cold-like symptoms had rapidly progressed to body-racking chills and respiratory weakness. His lungs had sounded like they were drowning in phlegm. His throat was puffed up and tight and looked difficult to breathe through. It reminded Elise of the cuff Doc Gomes inflated around her biceps when he checked her blood pressure. Instead of sorrow, Elise had felt only a quiet but stirring relief. She had not been to church since she was a little girl, but she lowered her head and spoke aloud the only prayer she could remember: "Our Father, who art in Heaven, hallowed by thy name . . . " Afterward, she lifted the damp, puke-stained sheet up over Jason's face and removed the Hardballer from the nightstand on his side of the bed.

"I'm going to Nebraska, Jason, and you can't stop me."

They'd met in the summer of 1988. She'd been twenty-three at the time and hope was a ripe apple in her soul. Jason had been working at Big Wheel Auto, six three in his engineer boots, with prison ink on his hands and arms and a scar along his jaw. Elise had rolled her old man's Monte Carlo T-top into Jason's bay and locked onto his smile.

"That's a lot of car for a little girl."

"I can handle it." Her smile wasn't as pretty as his, but her eyes were deep enough to swim in. "I race first Sunday of every month at the Redline."

"Right. I heard about you. Morey Sorensen's kid."

"Yes I am."

"He still out at Chino?"

"For now. Got his parole hearing next month."

Jason nodded. He plucked a bandanna from the back pocket of his Levi's and wiped it across his throat, and Elise just about fell in love with him right there and then.

She'd had lofty ambitions, like any young person in a dead-end town, but all she really wanted was to be a woman who made decisions based on her own needs, and who didn't live in fear of her father.

Elise knew from the beginning that Jason would not advance these aspirations. He looked like the hero of a Springsteen song, but in every other way he bled darker. Elise fell for him just the same, and instead of drawing Jason into her world, she was drawn into his.

He ran with Hector Drogan, a man with eight crooked fingers and two crooked thumbs, who dealt mainly in stolen goods, but went wherever a crooked buck could be made. This included street drugs, chiefly cocaine. Every two weeks, Jason muled three kilos of a cocaine/creatine mix over the state line, from Yuma to El Centro, where Heck further cut the product before introducing it to the streets. (Heck had also started smoking up several grams weekly—a practice that Elise opined could only end badly for him.) Elise had accompanied Jason on occasion. Doing something so illicit—so goddamn *bad*—excited her in a way she couldn't explain. It was like reconciling with a twin sister she'd distanced herself from for so long. There was one hour of interstate between the two cities, but Elise glowed every minute of the way. If she could pour her adrenaline into a jar, it would bubble and fizz.

One time, on the return journey, Jason had pulled off I-8 and rolled into a rinky-dink gas station with two fifties-era pumps and a longhorn skull over the door. There was plenty of gas in the tank—Jason always made sure he refueled before a trip—so Elise couldn't think why they'd stopped.

"Whatcha doin', hon?"

"Get your ass behind the wheel," Jason said, showing those teeth. He reached across her and removed the Hardballer from the glove compartment. "And keep the engine running."

"Jase—"

He opened his door and stepped out. Elise did what she was told. She slid behind the wheel of Jason's Ford Bronco and kept the engine running. Jason entered the store, leveled his Hardballer at the clerk, and hustled out twenty seconds later with three cartons of Marlboros tucked under his arm and two hundred and ten dollars in his left fist. "Go! Let's fuckin' *go!*" he shouted at Elise, jumping in on the passenger side. Again, Elise did what she was told. She floored it and the Bronco pulled out of the forecourt with its straight six howling.

Some do-gooder—parked in a scrub lot next to the gas station—had witnessed the whole thing and decided to give chase. He drove with one hand on the wheel of his Dodge pickup and the other hanging out the open window, taking shots at the Bronco's rear end with a small-caliber revolver. Elise took a dirt road into the desert and drove like she did at the Redline, keeping smooth but tight lines and drifting through the corners. They lost the do-gooder when he spun out and hit a ditch. Five miles on—a safe enough distance—Elise left the road and parked behind a large sandstone boulder. She was so amped, so goddamn *hot*, that she dragged Jason onto the backseat and screwed him senseless.

"You're the baddest motherfucker I know," he'd said to her afterward, and those words had sent a delicious, unexplainable thrill through her.

It was not the life she wanted, though. After the blood-thumping high that came with being lawless, she would invariably crash and spend weeks wrestling feelings of guilt and confusion. On countless occasions, she'd implored Jason to leave town with her. They could go anywhere, from Malibu to Maine, a fresh start, just the two of them.

"Someday, baby," Jason would reply, or something similar, but only if he was in a good mood. More frequently, he would snarl and walk away, or flat-out ignore her, just sit there smoking his cigarette while flipping through the *TV Guide*. And there were times when they had tried talking it through, only to spiral into miserable altercations that ran deep into the night.

At some point, Elise realized she'd become as afraid of Jason as she was of her old man (although Jason, to his credit, had never laid a hand on her). In consideration of her needs, which were every bit as valid as the needs of those around her, she had started to research apartment prices in Los Angeles and San Diego, believing it was just a matter of time before Jason returned home to find a Dear John letter on the kitchen table.

Then the world changed. Quickly. Irrevocably. The major news networks downplayed the seriousness of Captain Trips to begin with. CNN reported that it was a "particularly pesky" (and Russian) influenza virus that would mainly affect the very old and the very young. Peter Jennings assured *ABC World News Tonight* viewers that a vaccine had been developed and would soon be widely available.

The pretense didn't last long. It *couldn't*, partly because people died faster than the rate at which even the most well-meaning misinformation could spread, but mostly because, within weeks, there *was* no news. America was off-air.

Through the flames of fear and suffering, Elise found something unexpected: hope. Some higher power had pressed society's reset button. Everything would be different from here out. If ever there was a time for a new beginning, this was it.

Again, she went to Jason. Surely now he'd see reason. He'd avoided getting sick, but had woken up that morning—the last day of June—with a light fever and a cough. Just a smoker's cough, he'd said, but it sounded wetter.

"It's a ghost town out there. It's scary." Elise normally addressed Jason with her hands behind her back and her head lowered, like some chastened nineteenth-century daughter. Now she stood with her hands on her hips and her shoulders flared. "Half the stores on Main Street have closed down. The other half have been looted."

"I know." Jason sat at the kitchen table with his Hardballer stripped and laid out in front of him, cleaning the individual parts with a soft white rag.

"Big Wheel's closed, too. Buddy Stagg died this morning."

"I heard." Jason picked up the slide and ran his rag back and forth, inside and out, with a tenderness she didn't see often. "Poor ol' Buddy. He was good to me."

"You don't have a job anymore," Elise said. "Not a legal one, anyway."

"Mmhmm."

"There's nothing here for us, Jason. We need to put El Centro in the rearview." Elise took a deep breath. She didn't like the way her chest tremored. "We need to find people . . . opportunities. We need to start again."

"Agreed," Jason said, and stifled a cough with the back of his hand.

Elise shook her head as if she'd misheard, but no, Jason showed his teeth in a good way. She asked again, just to be sure.

"You agree?"

"I do."

"Oh, baby." All the tension went out of Elise's chest. She stepped around the table, peeled a curl of hair off Jason's warm brow, and kissed him there. "You don't know how happy I am to hear that."

"Mmhmm."

"I was thinking . . . Now, I know it's a long way, but hear me out . . . I was thinking Nebraska." She didn't tell him about the dreams. If he knew that she'd suggested the Cornhusker State on the back of several (albeit vivid) dreams, he would shoot the idea down faster than a cat could lap chain lightning. "We could get a little farm, maybe, grow our own vegetables. I heard that—"

"Nebraska?" Jason slid the clean barrel into the clean slide and put these finished pieces to one side. "Why the fuck would I ever want to go to Nebraska?"

Elise stepped back with one hand to her chest. The tension had returned, just like that. He'd said *I*, not *we*. *Why the fuck would I ever want to go to Nebraska?* He was thinking of himself, and only himself, the same as always.

"I just . . . I've got a good feeling about it, is all," Elise said. "A good feeling for *us*. Me and you. A better life."

"Yeah, well . . ." Jason coughed against the back of his hand again. "Heck's got a good feeling about Vegas."

"Heck *Drogan*? Oh, baby, no. Not him." She shook her head and fought back tears. "That's not the new beginning we're looking for."

Jason looked at her, his smile subtly different, displaying his teeth in a less appealing way. "And Nebraska is? Up there with the hicks and cows? Call me crazy, but I think we're better suited for Vegas. And it'll for damn sure be more fun."

Fun? The world had been knocked on its ass and he was thinking about having *fun*.

"You don't get it, Jason." Elise put her hands on her hips again. She'd managed to keep the tears from spilling onto her cheeks, but there was so much disappointment in her voice. "It's not El Centro I want us to get away from. It's the *life*. These negative influences, the cocaine runs, the crime. Vegas will be no different. Jesus, it'll be worse. A thousand times worse."

"We'll be king and queen."

"We won't. We'll be two rats in a city full of them."

Jason started to say something, but broke off into a wild coughing fit, his chest and shoulders pumping, his face turning eggplant. He lifted the rag to his mouth and spat a gristly plug of phlegm into it. "Good Christ," he said, and then, "It's you who doesn't get it, Elise. You think you're better than all this, but you're not. Never have been. Never will be."

"Don't say that."

"You can't escape this life."

"That's not true."

"Look at your old man. Three weeks out of prison before breaking his parole, then back inside he goes." Jason folded the rag so that the phlegm wad was on the inside and kept cleaning. "Being bad is in your blood, Elise. You can't run away."

"I can." Now the tears came, hard and bright. "I can and I will."

Jason's smile changed again. "The devil will find you."

Elise walked out of the kitchen, a little dazed, a lot hurt, hoping in that moment that whatever Jason had was more than a smoker's cough and hating herself for thinking that way.

⇀

She considered burying him. He wasn't always so mean. They'd shared many good moments in the time they were together. She thought he'd like to be buried in the backyard of the home he grew up in, where he played as a child and had fond memories. Elise was emotionally punched, though. *Not* dying, and watching everybody else die, was hard work. The thought of hauling Jason's dead weight out of their apartment and into the back seat of a vehicle, driving it to South El Centro, and then digging a hole large enough to drop it into, was simply overwhelming. Arguably, he deserved better than a puke-stained sheet, but a puke-stained sheet was what he got.

His Bronco was unreliable. The transmission had been slipping for the past couple of weeks (he'd been meaning to fix it, but then got sick) and it had two bald tires. Even if it had been fully roadworthy, Elise wouldn't have taken it. There was too much of Jason in there. His trove of cassette tapes. The worn spots on the steering wheel made by his hands. His oil, aftershave, and sweat smell. He'd be with her every mile, telling her to turn around, that being bad was in her blood. Maybe the devil *would* find her, but Elise didn't want to make it easy for him.

She opted for the neighbor's Chevette because, of the four vehicles she'd checked, it was the only one with gas. Half a tank, in fact. More importantly, it was nondescript, unassuming, and she believed it would elicit less attention—an important factor in a world so suddenly thrown into chaos.

A gang of children patrolled Adams Avenue in a beaten up Econoline. "La Raza" by Kid Frost blared through the open windows. The driver looked no older than twelve and there were more preteens on the roof, some armed with machetes, others with semiautomatic rifles. Elise avoided them without challenge. She saw a man dragging bodies into a pile on the corner of 8th and Main. There was a five-gallon can of gasoline nearby.

~~~

She crossed Alejandro Ortega's farmland and joined Villa Road heading east. It was late morning when she finally—and permanently, God willing—put El Centro behind her.

She found the girl a mile outside Caballo Blanco.

~~~

Caballo Blanco meant *white horse* in English, but the only horse Elise saw was a bay roan. It lay dead in the middle of a trailer park and looked to have been stripped for meat. The trailer park was called Días de Sol and constituted most of the town. There were a few dusty buildings, a ranch, and a convenience store that had suffered recent fire damage. Elise had pulled into Días de Sol and siphoned dregs of fuel from three vehicles, just enough to return the Chevette's gauge to the halfway mark. A fifty-something woman with greasy red hair looked on from the front step of her Airstream. She'd painted black X's on her eyelids that flashed warnings every time she blinked.

A one-lane gravel track led from Caballo Blanco to State Route 219. The girl walked its verge with her head down. She was thin and dirty. The laces of one sneaker were untied. Elise drove past her, then a voice somewhere inside—her *soul* voice, which had been mostly suppressed in the two years she'd spent with Jason—called out. She stepped on the brake pedal, reversed, and got out of the car.

The girl stopped walking and looked up, lifting a clump of knotted hair from in front of her eyes. She saw Elise and backed up a step.

"It's okay," Elise said, raising both hands palms out. "I'm not going to hurt you."

The girl didn't look so sure.

"Hey. It's okay."

The girl stood still. Her jaw quivered. The early afternoon sunlight highlighted a bruise on her left cheek. Elise kept her hands raised and stepped closer.

"Do you live around here?" she asked, gesturing down the narrow track with a small nod. "The trailer park?"

The girl looked at her sneaker tops.

"Your family?" Elise asked.

A vague yet telling shake of the head. Elise sighed and looked around. Other than Caballo Blanco, which the girl was walking away *from*, there was nothing for miles. It was hot, even for Arizona in July. If Elise saw a thermometer reading anything less than 110, she'd believe it was broken.

"Wait right here." Elise returned to the Chevette, opened the trunk, and sifted through the box of provisions she'd packed. She grabbed an apple and a Pepsi bottle filled with tap water. The girl's eyes blurred with grateful tears when Elise handed them to her. She tried unscrewing the bottle cap, but it was too tight. Elise did it for her. The girl drank with loud swallows. Elise tied her sneaker lace.

"What's your name, hon?"

The girl lowered the bottle and belched. She stifled the sweetest giggle and said, "Ruby."

"That's a pretty name. I'm Elise."

Ruby tore a chunk out of the apple. It was warm and bruised, but she didn't care.

"Where you headed, Ruby?"

"I don't know," she replied between bites.

"You got anybody back there?" Elise stood up straight and gestured down the track again. "Is there someone you can stay with?"

Ruby took another bite of the apple. She chewed noisily and washed it down with water. "I was staying with Courtney, but she got sick and died. She was Mom's best friend. She had lots of books and that was good because someone stole the gas out of her genny and we couldn't watch *Steel Magnolias* no more."

Elise pressed her lips together. Everything about this made her feel sad. She took a deep breath through her nose, waiting for the emotion to ebb. Ruby finished the apple and gnawed the core to a strip and dropped it into the dust at her feet.

"Courtney sounds like a nice person," Elise said.

Ruby nodded.

"Anybody else back there you know?"

"Only Ali Cat Lawson, but she's bad. And her cousin Hiram." Ruby lowered her eyes and visibly shuddered. "He's worse."

Elise looked at the bruise on Ruby's cheek. She remembered the woman with the X's painted on her eyelids and wondered if that was Ali Cat. Maybe. Maybe not. She was a part of that community, in any case, and Elise didn't blame Ruby for wanting to take her chances and set out on her own, aimless as she was.

She'd be picked clean before the moon rose, though, and not all vultures were birds.

"Do you want to come with me?" Elise asked.

"Where you going?"

"A long way from here. Nebraska."

"To see that sweet old lady?"

Elise drew a sharp breath and a chill raced down her spine. The dreams she'd had in recent weeks flickered through her mind: the shack-like house surrounded by rustling corn, the tire swing hanging from the branch of an apple tree, the tin-pot chimney and crooked porch . . . and of course the old Black woman sitting on that porch, rocking sweetly in her chair. Sometimes she'd lift notes from a scuffed but melodic acoustic guitar. Other times she'd study the corn behind Elise, as if expecting something to emerge from between the stalks and grab her. Always, though, she effused goodness and light. In many ways, she reminded Elise of the apple tree in her yard. Old, yes, but deeply rooted, full of character, and still strong enough to bear weight.

Ruby had dreamed about the same place, the same old lady. Maybe some of the details were different, but the essence was the same. Elise felt this deep in her soul. It made her wonder if they were dreams at all. Perhaps they were visions, or windows of collective energy, which crackled with good faith and were opened in the opaque passages between sleep cycles. With the world in crisis, it did not seem unusual that people were tapping into the same hopeful resource.

"Yes," Elise replied, and shivered. Her forearms prickled with gooseflesh. "Yes, Ruby. That's exactly where I'm going."

"Polk County, Nebraska," Ruby said, and smiled.

"That's right. You want to come with me?"

Ruby nodded.

"Good," Elise said. "That's good."

They walked to the Chevette, similar in demeanor, their chins up and their eyes forward. Elise opened the passenger door and Ruby climbed in. She looked very small in the seat. Elise stepped around the hood and got in on her side. "Seat belt," she said. Ruby pulled the belt across her body and Elise helped her buckle it. She buckled her own, started the engine, and they set off.

Ruby sipped her water, looking around the car's interior. The owner had hot-glued four California Raisins figures to the dash. Ruby poked one of them and smiled, then settled back in her seat.

"She plays a guitar," she said a moment later.

"Huh?"

"The old lady. In my dreams. That's how I find her." Ruby nodded and Elise saw echoes of herself in her big brown eyes. "I follow the sound of her guitar."

"That's right," Elise said. "I do, too."

"I like the song about the train." Ruby poked another California Raisin—the one playing the saxophone—and sang in the sweetest little voice: "*This train is bound for glory, this train . . .*"

Elise knew the song. She grinned—it had been many weeks since *that* particular expression had brightened her face—and joined in. They sang the first verse together and some of the second, then dissolved into an equally tuneful laughter. Elise raised her right hand and Ruby laid a firm five on it.

She steered the Chevette onto SR 219, clear to the horizon in both directions. If every secondary road was as empty as this, and keeping to a steady fifty, they'd be halfway across the Colorado Plateau by nightfall.

They both needed to pee. Elise pulled over. "I'll go first. Scare off the rattlers." She kicked the buffel grass at the edge of the road—safe enough—then yanked down her jeans and squatted. Ruby went in the same spot. Elise walked a short distance from the car to give her some privacy. A sun-beaten sign put Caballo Blanco eleven miles behind them. A similarly weathered sign on the other side of the road announced that Cactus Belle's Trading Post was four miles ahead.

"You got anything to wipe with?" Ruby called out.

"Nope," Elise said. Toilet paper was one of the few essentials she'd neglected to pack. "Just give your tush a little shake."

"Good thing I only needed to go pee."

They got going again, crossed Interstate 10 at Tonopah, and came to the trading post a mile further on. It was hard to miss, with Arizona's distinct state flag painted along one side and numerous plastic cacti on the roof. There were several vehicles on the lot, all with shattered windows and open doors. Some had their fuel doors open, too—new code for *Already Siphoned*. A dog slept in the shade.

"Maybe they've got something to wipe with," Ruby said.

"Maybe." Elise steered onto the lot and found a space away from all the broken glass. She surveyed the front of the store and made two quick determinations: that the place had long since been looted, and that the dog wasn't sleeping.

"Oh," Ruby said. She'd noticed the dog, too.

Elise shifted into park, turned off the ignition, but sat for a moment. Second thoughts swam through her mind. It was gloomy inside Cactus Belle's. The screen door was torn, hanging off one hinge. The main door stood partway open, its security locks negotiated by way of a shotgun, judging by the damage. Whoever had done this was probably long gone. The only sign of life was the flies that had gathered on the dog. Elise chewed her lower lip, trying to get a sense of the place.

"We going in?" Ruby asked.

There'd be no food or drink. The shelves would be bare. The dark, dead refrigerators would be stripped to their wire racks. Ruby had nothing, though, only the clothes on her back and her ratty sneakers. Cactus Belle's was no Kmart, even at the best of times, but maybe they'd find junior-sized T-shirts and shorts, sunglasses, a ball cap, a deck of cards, a soft toy, coloring books and pens. And yes, there might even be something for them both to wipe with.

"Okay," Elise said. "Let's take a quick look."

They went in but Elise removed the Hardballer from her knapsack first and tucked it into the back of her jeans.

She and Ruby stood in the doorway with the sunlight laying their shadows along the dusty wooden floor. More light came through the windows. The air was dim and hazy.

Ruby wrinkled her nose and Elise nodded. There were dead here, more than one, if the stench was any indication. The extreme heat didn't help. Elise waited a moment for her eyes to adjust, then proceeded deeper into the store. As suspected, the food shelves and refrigerators had been ransacked. Empty boxes and wrappers littered the floor. They stepped over broken glass and various spillages: cereals, potato chips, peanut butter, coffee beans. On a display rack next to the checkout counter, Ruby found an unopened packet of Spitz dill pickle-flavored sunflower seeds and a roll of Certs. She held them up proudly.

"Jackpot," Elise said.

They walked along the back wall, stepping over maps, pamphlets, and magazines. Ruby added a copy of *Ranger Rick* and a word search book to her stash. They passed two doors, both standing open. One led to a small office. Elise saw the edge of a desk and a chair tipped on its side. It was too gloomy to see more. The other door opened on a narrow hallway illuminated by a back window. Four more doors led off it. A stockroom, a washroom, a closet for cleaning supplies, and another room—additional storage, maybe. The smell was thicker here.

Elise directed Ruby away from the door and toward a part of the store that was mostly intact. There clearly wasn't much demand for souvenirs, local history books, and potted cacti in this devastated era. She found a cowboy hat for herself and a ball cap for Ruby and sunglasses for them both. There were no shorts, but Ruby grabbed two Cactus Belle–themed T-shirts and another with TONOPAH, AZ across the front. They'd find a better selection in Nebraska. *Two days*, Elise told herself. Even taking rural roads and stopping when they needed to, it shouldn't take longer than that.

They put their modest haul in a canvas tote bag with the Stars and Stripes printed on one side and a bald eagle on the other. Ruby carried it with a precocious swagger, like a girl at the mall with her mom. It broke Elise's heart just a bit.

"We should go," she said.

"Toilet paper?" Ruby raised one eyebrow.

"I didn't see any," Elise said, and puffed out her cheeks. "Okay. One more look around. Look for Kleenex, wet wipes, napkins . . . anything like that."

They checked every aisle and display, but came up empty. Elise sighed, thinking that civilization's collapse could be epitomized by the fact that toilet paper was now a luxury item. (She wondered if, somewhere in Vegas, Hector Drogan was dealing cocaine and Charmin out the back of an old cargo van.) She looked regretfully at Ruby, then switched her gaze to the rightmost door along the back wall. The narrow hallway opening off it had to lead to a stockroom. A staff washroom, too.

She started toward it, registering the thickening smell with every step. It renewed her unease.

"Wait here," she said to Ruby. "I'll be thirty seconds."

Elise pulled the collar of her T-shirt over her nose and entered the hallway. Cracked tiles shifted beneath her feet. A dirty mop and bucket stood in the far corner. The first door on her right was ajar. It was the stockroom—one-third the size of the main store and three times the havoc. The shelving had been emptied. Cardboard boxes had been cut open, spilling unwanted items across the floor. It took Elise all of ten seconds to ascertain that she'd find nothing of use in there. She turned around, opened the first door on the left, and found the dead.

It was a makeshift quarantine, with cots arranged throughout the room and spoiled food crowding every surface. Cactus Belle—an altruistic soul, no doubt—had opened her door and her supplies to friends and neighbors, hoping to outlast the pandemic. There were too many dead to count. Two dozen, easily. Perhaps as many as forty. Elise spied a box of Kleenex on a pillow beside an infant boy, but would not venture to get it. The flies here were overfed and slow.

She backed out of the room spluttering into her T-shirt. The next door opened on a dark utility space. She saw what looked a breaker panel and the rounded edge of a water heater. The fourth and final door opened on the washroom. A dead man was slumped beside the toilet with his pants around his ankles. Elise checked the cupboard under the sink and found cleaning supplies, boxes of rat poison, and a single roll of toilet paper. Elise grabbed it. There was also a tarantula back there, huddled in the corner, but she didn't bother it and it didn't bother her.

She walked through the hallway and into the store. "Okay, Ruby, let's—" She froze in her tracks. The toilet paper fell from her hand and rolled across the floor.

The man angled the sole of his boot and stopped it.

"Heya," he said.

Elise reached for the gun in the back of her jeans.

He was tall and snake-thin with straggly red hair spilling from beneath a trucker cap turned backward. His left arm had been amputated just north of the elbow. The stump poked from the sleeve of a faded Grateful Dead T-shirt and was capped with flaky skin. His right hand clamped the back of Ruby's neck.

"Get away from her," Elise said. She charged the Hardballer the way Jason had shown her and thumbed off the safety. "Do it now, asshole, or I'll put a hole through your chest."

The man hooted laughter, unfazed and unafraid. Elise fixed him in her sights and set her finger on the trigger. Her body shook and it took everything to keep her aim steady.

"I mean it. Get away from her. Right fucking now."

Ruby squirmed. Tears filled her eyes and wet her face. The man clamped her neck tighter and pulled her closer. Elise considered popping a round into the floor at his feet—a well-placed warning shot might inspire him to comply—but some raw, untapped part of her wanted to see him bleed.

She recalled Jason telling her that she was the baddest motherfucker he knew, and how perfectly alive this had made her feel. The memory pushed a wave of complicated emotions through her. Elise took a thin, wavering breath and kept her sights on the man's chest.

"Three seconds. That's all you get, then I'm pulling this trigger."

"For a ripe piece of snatch, you're just as sour as a new berry." The man removed his hand from the back of Ruby's neck and stroked her cheek. Elise noted the five dots inked between his thumb and forefinger. Jason and her old man had the same tattoo, a memento of the time they'd spent behind bars. "You want to introduce me to your friend, Rube?"

Rube. He knew her, which meant he'd followed them here from Caballo Blanco. Given the very few survivors remaining in that ghost town, Elise surmised that this ex-con piece of shit must be Hiram, cousin to Ali Cat Lawson. She was bad, according to Ruby, but Hiram was worse.

He stroked Ruby's cheek again, underlining the bruise that someone had put there. Maybe him. Maybe Ali Cat. Ruby shuddered and shied away from him. Hiram snarled impatiently, grabbed a fistful of her hair, and yanked her back on her heels.

Elise exerted fractional pressure on the trigger. She wondered if shooting this vile son of a bitch would send a black flare into the sky, telling the devil exactly where to find her.

"The girl's coming with me," she said.

"Ain't happening." Hiram thrust out his chin and fired a line of spit across the floor between them. "Flu got her kin, every last one of them, which makes me the closest she's got to family. Also, I promised her momma that I'd take on the role of guardian, and that's a promise I intend to keep."

That might be true, Elise realized, but Hiram promising such a thing didn't mean it was what Ruby's momma wanted. It certainly wasn't what Ruby wanted. She shook her head and looked desperately at Elise.

"Come on, man. I've got a loaded .45 and an itchy trigger finger." Elise blew over her upper lip. "You've got one arm and half a brain. Who do you think is going to win this argument?"

"Prob'ly the woman with the gun."

"You're damn right."

"Not you." Hiram curled his lip and winked. "The *other* woman."

Elise frowned, then noticed Hiram's eyes flick to his right, her left. She looked in that direction and saw a woman materialize from the gloom, carrying a double-barreled shotgun at her hip. Elise recognized her instantly: the woman from the trailer park, with her greasy red hair and X's on her eyelids. Ali Cat. She lifted the shotgun to her shoulder, smiled at Elise, then gestured at the Hardballer in her hands.

"That's a lot of gun for a little girl."

The sight of her rocked Elise, but these words rocked her more. They were eerily similar to the first thing Jason had said when they met at Big Wheel Auto: *That's a lot of car for a little girl.* She remembered how he'd wiped a bandanna across his throat and how freely her heart had pounced, triggering a two-year relationship that had confounded, frightened, and thrilled her. Elise relived their time together in the space of five seconds, culminating with the memory of Jason sitting at their kitchen table cleaning the parts of the pistol she now held in her hands. Every blunt word he'd spoken recurred. They weakened Elise at the knees and doubled the quickness of her pulse.

He'd been so mean, but so *right*. The devil had found her, and it hadn't taken long.

"How's your aim?" Ali Cat asked.

"Good enough," Elise replied.

"Looks a touch shaky to me. But that's okay, missy. I'm no dead-eye, neither." Ali Cat blinked slowly, deliberately displaying her X's. "The simple beauty of a scattergun is I don't *need* to be accurate. I pull just one of these triggers and your pretty little insides are all over this goddamn store."

Hiram laughed again—more a howl than a hoot this time. He threw his head back and dipped at the knees. His chest and throat were glaring targets. Elise couldn't miss, even with her shaky aim. Ali Cat's shotgun changed everything, though. Those side-by-side barrels were deep and round and dark enough to snuff even the brightest light. Elise kept her sights on Hiram, but let up on the trigger.

She sensed movement to her right and glanced that way. From this angle she could see between the empty shelves, through the open door, and into the small office. Someone was in there. It was too gloomy to discern anything more than his tall outline.

"We're taking the girl," Ali Cat said. She showed her X's and grinned. "That's nonnegotiable. However, I'm open to discussing whether you live or die."

"She doesn't want to go with you," Elise said. The right side of her body—the side nearest the office—had turned cold. She steadied her legs so her heartbeat wouldn't throw her off balance.

Hiram let go of Ruby's hair and scratched his stump. Skin flaked away, shimmering softly in the light coming through the front door. He shot another line of spit across the floor, grabbed Ruby's upper arm, and said, "This little bitch is too young to know what she wants."

"How about you?" Ali Cat said. She took a step forward, drawing the shotgun's butt more securely to her shoulder. Her finger hovered over the front trigger. "You want to see another day, or die right here and now?"

Ruby let out a big sob and stepped toward Elise. Hiram pulled her back, yanking her arm hard enough to lift her off the ground. Elise blinked a tear from her eye and whispered, "I'm sorry." She glanced toward the office again and saw the man-shape more clearly. He wore engineer boots and blue jeans and a belt with a wide, shimmering buckle. Tattooed arms extended from the sleeves of his work shirt. His head was smooth and round and moved with inquisitive little jerks. In one blink, Elise saw her daddy's face. In the next she saw Jason's. Predominantly, though, she saw the devil's face. He had blue eyes and handsome feathers and a long beak that caught the light like chrome.

"Place that shooter on the floor and slide it over to me," Ali Cat said. "Do it real slow, but do it now."

Elise nodded. The devil could only lay claim to her for as long as she did what he expected, what he *desired*, and while killing these trailer-trash dirtbags would doubtless satisfy, she refused to do it.

"*Now!*" Ali Cat snapped.

Elise removed her left hand from where it supported her right, raising it above her head in a gesture of surrender. She dropped slowly to one knee and lowered the Hardballer toward the floor.

"Attagirl," Ali Cat said. "Reeeal slow."

KEEP THE DEVIL DOWN

Ruby sobbed again and reached out with the hand not holding her tote bag. Hiram curled his lip and spat. Elise glanced over her shoulder at the devil, then turned to Ali Cat. She looked into her eyes and waited.

～

It happened quickly—in a blink, to be exact. Ali Cat flashed her X's at Elise, and Elise shot her in the left kneecap.

She'd been in a position of surrender for two reasons: being lower to the ground made her a smaller target (although, as Ali Cat said, that scattergun didn't need a large one), but it also gave Ali Cat a false sense of security. The moment her eyelashes came together in their slow, showy way, Elise pulled the trigger. She'd sacrificed accuracy for the element of surprise. Her shot could have gone anywhere. The fact that it blew out Ali Cat's kneecap led Elise to believe that someone was looking out for her—someone other than the crow-headed thing in the shadows.

Ali Cat hit the floor screaming, clutching her ruined leg with one hand. The other still held the shotgun. The double barrels swung perilously this way and that. Elise had recovered her balance after the Hardballer's recoil almost knocked her on her ass. She sprang to her feet, closed the distance between her and Ali Cat, and kicked the shotgun out of her hand. It skated across the floor and disappeared beneath one of the shelving units.

"*You fucking bitch!*" Ali Cat screeched in a manner befitting her name. Her eyes were wide—from X's to O's. "*Dirty fucking cocksucker! That's my leg, goddammit! My goddamn fucking leg!*"

Elise locked Ali Cat in the Hardballer's sights, targeting the center of her forehead. Something bristled and flapped in the dimness. It sounded the way Jason's smile looked: alluring, but dangerous. Elise switched her aim to Ali Cat's right thigh and pulled the trigger. The air-shaking report could not envelop her scream.

"You'll live," Elise said.

She turned on Hiram, who looked on with a stricken expression, his mouth flapping soundlessly. He'd pulled Ruby in front of him and still had hold of her arm.

"Let her go," Elise said. Her words were somewhat lost in all the dreadful noise, but he heard her just fine. She lifted the Hardballer and stared along the barrel at Hiram's gaping face.

He was low on options and his shotgun-toting backup was bleeding on the floor. None of his earlier brazenness remained. His expression was that of a man who fully realized that shit had gone sideways.

"Let her *go*," Elise said again. "Or I will shoot you dead."

The devil bristled again. Elise imagined him hunched, watching eagerly.

Hiram pushed Ruby off to the side and made a run for the exit, except he stood on the toilet paper and it rolled beneath his boot, spilling him to the floor. Elise stepped over to him. He looked up at her. His right hand and his stump were raised.

"I let her *go!*" he cried. "Take her! Christ, just *take* her, you scornful whore!"

She could kill him and that would satisfy the devil. She could let him live, but the bruise on Ruby's face was dark, and there were deeper wounds, no doubt, that would take longer to heal. Ali Cat was bad, after all, but Hiram was worse.

Jason's beautiful, terrible smile bloomed in her mind.

You're the baddest motherfucker I know.

"Not quite," Elise said. She pulled the trigger and blew a hole through the middle of Hiram's hand. His screams matched his cousin's. It'd be a long time before he used that hand again, and never in the same way.

Emotions welled inside Elise. Mainly disappointment, but fear and anger, too. She swiveled at the waist, aimed across the store, and fired a round into the office. There was nothing to hit, though, other than the back wall, maybe the desk. Elise saw no engineer boots, no tattooed arms or softly glowing beak. She thought he'd disappeared, then noticed two perfectly round blue eyes peering at her through the gloom. They were in the far back corner, up high. He'd either grown three feet or clung spiderlike to the ceiling.

"Leave me alone," Elise whispered. She pulled the trigger again, but the gun clicked empty.

Elise and Ruby quickly exited the trading post hand in hand, blinking their damp eyes at the brilliant afternoon sunlight. Elise fished the Chevette's keys from the front pocket of her jeans, then stopped, let go of Ruby, and went back into the store. She stepped over Hiram—still screaming—and grabbed the toilet paper from the floor. It was speckled with his blood, but only the first few layers.

"Something to wipe with," she said, rejoining Ruby.

The girl managed a trembling smile and her eyes flashed with an affection close to love.

They pulled out of Cactus Belle's parking lot with the tires screeching, eastbound on El Camino del Cuervo, the crow's path.

NOW

The Corvid rammed the Chevette's back end again, sending a jarring vibration through the smaller car's framework. The steering wheel jerked in Elise's hands. She was thrown forward in her seat, crying out as the belt pulled tight across her chest. Ruby clattered against the passenger door and her legs flopped loosely.

Elise regained herself just in time. She swerved, avoiding an old, half-dead mesquite by a yard or two. Its lower branches rattled off the windshield and over the roof. The Corvid emerged through the dust in her rearview, the black smoke still pouring out of the open windows. It thumped the Chevette again, but not as hard. The dented trunk lid flapped up and down. And all this time, there was no discernible damage on the Corvid. It rumbled and shone.

"What are we going to do?" Ruby wailed.

"I know what we're *not* going to do," Elise replied, talking as much to herself as to Ruby. "We're not giving up."

She steered around a sprawl of rocks and boulders, then jumped on the brakes and cranked the wheel right. The Corvid pulled alongside her. Elise turned the wheel the other way and slammed sidelong into it. Metal crunched. Sparks flew. Dusky smoke rippled across Elise's window. She tried peering through it, believing she'd see the devil behind the wheel. There was a hint of something—his pointed beak, perhaps—but the smoke was too thick to be certain.

They bumped three more times. The Chevette's rear driver's-side door buckled inward and rattled. Elise went hard right and the Corvid went left, each steering around the faded, half-buried wreck of some old vehicle. A wake of buzzards gathered on its roof took wing with spectacular, reluctant slowness.

The train was two miles distant, moving south to north across the horizon. It trembled on its track like a living thing.

Elise thought it was modern diesel train at first, no doubt carrying important cargo or passengers (there had to be some reason for it operating when everything else was shut down), but as they drew closer, she saw that it was actually an old steam train. Its locomotive was a burnished silver, hauling a line of wooden passenger cars. Their windows reflected the sunlight in cadenced beats. A plume of whitish smoke flowed from the chimney and hung shimmering in the air.

Elise had no idea where the train was going but she longed to be on it, sitting safely and comfortably next to Ruby, feeling the cradle-like rhythm of its wheels on the track. She imagined driving alongside the train, then she and Ruby leaping from the Chevette onto one of the passenger cars, like outlaws in a cowboy movie. It was a wonderful but absurd thought. Elise shook her head and it dissolved.

KEEP THE DEVIL DOWN

Another thought took its place, not quite as absurd, and not so easily shaken. It had an edge of possibility, in fact—too little to hope for, but too big to disregard.

For most of her life, darkness had trailed her. And when it wasn't behind, it was ahead—something she'd either edged around or fallen into. Now, a seam of brightness opened inside Elise. It was smooth and true, and she rode it like this train rode its track.

"Sing," she said to Ruby.

"Huh?" Ruby looked at her, confused.

"Sing," Elise repeated, and pointed at the train, now only a mile away. "The song about the train."

"What? I don't . . . don't . . ." Big tears rolled from Ruby's eyes. She was so scared.

"The song the old lady sings in our dreams."

The Corvid veered into them again, coming from the left. It hit Elise's door, nearly folding it in half. The window shattered, spraying the interior with glass. Both Elise and Ruby screamed. The Chevette swerved dangerously to the right, narrowly avoiding a sloped boulder that would have flipped them like a coin. Elise pumped the brake and turned the wheel, swinging the back end around. She passed behind the Corvid and raced away in another direction, now almost parallel to the railway track. Her door swung open loosely. It trembled for a moment on its compromised hinges, then fell off. Elise clutched the wheel, feeling even more vulnerable. She put her foot to the floor.

The Corvid followed. Elise watched it in the rearview, making adjustments to keep it behind her.

"Sing!" she said to Ruby.

Ruby nodded and started in a thin, wavering voice: "*This train is bound for glory, this train . . .*"

"Sing louder!" Elise said. "Like you *believe* it, Ruby. Sing with your soul!"

"*This train*"—a little louder—"*is bound for glory, this train . . .*"

"*This train is bound for glory,*" Elise joined in, pulling every word from that seam of light inside her. *"All who ride, you must be holy. Lord oh Lord, talking about this train..."*

The Corvid tried to pull up on their left, but Elise maneuvered that way and forced it to drop back. It thumped into their rear bumper again and something else was ripped off—the trunk lid itself, Elise realized. The Corvid drove over it without missing a beat. It swung out the other way, trying to pull level on the right. Again, Elise timed her movement, turning the wheel and keeping the Corvid in the rearview.

"This train don't carry no liars, this train," they both sang, their voices steadily growing stronger. Elise's focus switched from the train to the mirror and back again. The track was no more than five hundred yards away. They raced toward it on a diagonal. The Chevette's needle was at sixty but dropping. The engine didn't have much left.

The Corvid hit their rear end yet again. Elise was thrown against the wheel, but kept singing. She looked at the approaching locomotive, four hundred yards away now. Ruby tightened in her seat. She'd yanked one of the California Raisin figures from the dashboard and clutched it like a talisman.

"This train don't carry no liars. Don't carry nothing but the holy fire. Lord oh lord, talking about this train..."

Elise held on to the light inside and kept her foot to the floor.

—⁓—

Three hundred yards. The needle had dropped to fifty. Elise urged more from the engine. She sang so loudly that her throat was raw. Ruby accompanied her word for word—a desperate, faithful harmony. They headed toward the track and the train kept rolling.

"This train don't carry no gamblers, this train..."

Two hundred yards away... one hundred and fifty...

The Corvid smoked and snarled. It rode their back end, bumping and bullying. Through the dust and darkness, Elise glimpsed two hands clasping the wheel. They had hooked, black fingernails and prison tattoos.

"This train don't carry no gamblers, this train . . ."

Eighty yards . . . seventy . . . sixty . . .

Above their singing and the frantic engine noise, Elise heard the train rocking on its track. It blew its whistle, coming on fast. She looked away from the rearview mirror and concentrated on the locomotive. It had a swooping, plow-like frame fixed to the front (a cowcatcher, Elise remembered it was called, although in her mind she thought of it as a *crow*catcher) that looked for all the world like a big silver smile. She made a slight adjustment to her line and aimed for the section of track just ahead of it.

"This train don't carry no gamblers. No loose sinners, no midnight ramblers. Lord oh Lord, talking about this train."

Ruby covered her eyes. Elise gripped the wheel and the last line she sang turned into a determined cry.

She crossed the track one sweet second ahead of the train.

The track was laid on a shallow embankment. Elise hit the incline at close to fifty miles per hour and took off—all four wheels off the ground. The train bore down on them, larger and brighter than everything, even the sun. It missed them by a heartbeat. The Chevette soared thirty feet and landed on the other side of the track with a monstrous *crunch* that blew out the rear windshield and flattened two tires.

They had made it, though.

The Corvid was not so fortunate. The locomotive—the *crow*catcher—hit it with the force of a meteorite. A tremendous thunderclap-like *boom* shook the air as the muscle car was savagely T-boned. It was knocked along the track like a toy, rolling and flipping, breaking apart in ugly black pieces. Sparking metal caught the ruptured fuel line and the gas tank went up with an intense thud, throwing more pieces across the desert. Black smoke ballooned into the sky. It was thick and oily, textured like feathers.

The train did not derail, and it did not stop. It shook righteously on its track, sounding its whistle, as sweet and uplifting as gospel. Elise and Ruby watched through the dusty windshield as it continued north and eventually blended with the horizon.

Elise turned to look back out the driver's side window. The wreckage from the Corvid was scattered all over. Some of it burned. Elise was reminded of newspaper photographs of crashed airplanes. There was no sign of the driver, although she didn't look too hard.

She and Ruby spilled from the Chevette and stood hugging each other for a long time. Afterward, they took a few moments to gather the provisions that had been ejected from the open trunk. Not everything was salvageable. Most of the cans were, though, and the bottled water. They took the good stuff and left the rest for the coyotes.

The Chevette still ran, but only just. It limped across the desert, wheezing and dripping fluids. The speedometer needle swayed brokenly from side to side. Elise guessed they were going ten miles per hour. *Maybe.* After fifteen minutes of hobbling along on two flats, the Chevette finally gave up the ghost. Something went *bang* beneath the hood, then it lurched once and died.

"What now?" Ruby asked.

Elise got out of the car. She looked around and pointed at something way off to the east. A barn. A windmill.

"There," she said.

"Is that a farm?"

"Yeah. Let's go."

They left most of their belongings in the car. They took a bottle of water each and wore their hats and sunglasses. It was hot and they were exhausted. They stopped often. It took almost an hour to reach the farm.

Cattle ripped hay from near-empty feeders and plodded happily enough. There was no other sign of life, but Elise and Ruby proceeded with caution. They entered the farmhouse and found five dead: the farmer, his wife, and three adult men, probably sons. One of the younger men had died recently, maybe only hours before. The farmer and his wife were in bed, curled into each other's arms. Someone had placed a red rose on the comforter. It would have been beautiful if not for the smell and the flies.

The refrigerator was dark and warm. Most of the food had spoiled. The pantry was in better shape. Elise and Ruby didn't take much, just enough for their journey: canned fruits and soups, a box of Ho Hos, three packets of Lay's Crunch Tators, and a six-pack of Dr Pepper. Elise found a Smith & Wesson revolver in a kitchen drawer, along with a box of .38-caliber ammunition. She threw the ammo in with their food and tucked the wheel gun into her jeans.

Truck keys hung from a hook by the front door.

The truck—a clean white Silverado—was in the barn. Its tank was one-eighth full. There was a diamondback in the bed. Elise hooked it out with a stick, then they loaded up their farmhouse haul and got moving. They returned to the Chevette, siphoned its tank dry, and grabbed their belongings. Ruby peeled the three remaining California Raisins from the dash and adopted them as her own.

They drove back to the farm, past the cattle and the barn, and followed a long, dusty driveway to Ocotillo Road. Elise referenced the map she'd marked up back in El Centro and they headed out.

Ruby fell asleep after an hour, clutching the California Raisins figures to her chest. She snored sweetly. Elise kept checking the rearview mirror, but saw nothing back there. The Silverado ran smoothly. She followed U.S. 89 for forty miles, then took another rural road—the delightfully named Hoppy Toad Pass—that cut east toward the Tonto National Forest. She saw no people, no cars. At one point, a herd of white tail deer ran alongside her, as beautiful as they were purposeful. Elise matched their speed for half a mile, wiping tears from her eyes. She almost woke Ruby to show her, but decided to take this moment to herself. She'd earned it.

The sun inched west and the sky purpled. Ruby woke up and stretched, extending her legs into the footwell, arching her back. She wiped her eyes and looked around.

"We still in Arizona?"

"Uh-huh."

"Feels like I've been asleep forever." She either yawned or sighed—Elise couldn't tell which. It was a sweet sound, in any case. "How much farther?"

"A long way. Into Colorado, through the Rockies." Elise looked at Ruby and smiled. "Then straight on till Nebraska."

Ruby pondered this, scrunching the bridge of her nose. "Like . . . a hundred miles?"

"More like eight hundred."

"Jeez." A moment passed as Ruby processed this unthinkable distance. At length, she settled back in her seat, looked fondly at her California Raisins, and said, "I dreamed about her again. The old lady."

"Yeah?"

"Yeah. She told me that we're not the only people traveling to see her. There'll be others. People like us."

Elise frowned, the bridge of her nose scrunching similarly to Ruby's. *People like us* . . . what did *that* mean? Then Ruby placed one hand over her heart, and Elise understood: There'd be no Morey Sorensens or Hector Drogans in Nebraska. There'd be nobody like Jason.

"People like us," she said.

"She was smiling in the dream," Ruby continued, nodding. "She has a real pretty smile."

A warm sensation spread through Elise's chest. For the first time in a long time, everything felt right. It was probably foolish to feel this way, but she couldn't help it—and nor did she want to.

They moved on, the road unfolding between tall green pines and rugged passes. Elise checked the mirrors, but not as often.

They refueled courtesy of an abandoned Dodge Raider and stopped for the night northeast of Flagstaff, parked behind a ramshackle post office on Hopi land. They ate chicken noodle soup straight from the can and had Ho Hos for dessert, then reclined their seats and slept. Elise had loaded the .38 and kept it close. It took her a long time to drift off. She woke before dawn, started the truck, and got rolling. The sun rose high and golden. They crossed the Colorado state line two hours later.

ACROSS THE POND
V. Castro

Every morning, Elizabeth walked across the now desolate Westminster Bridge sucking on her first cigarette of the day and stopped at the foot of the Big Ben clock tower. Eddies of smoke rising into the air matched the churning Thames, though the river appeared cleaner than ever. The golden hue of the clock's brickwork seemed to brighten like a beacon on the occasional sunny days. It still kept time, which felt like a small miracle. Next to Big Ben were the Houses of Parliament with their daggered spires. Across the street stood Westminster Abbey. It housed dead royalty including Queen Elizabeth I—the Virgin Queen, and a very dead god she never prayed to.

After, she continued to walk along the Thames, salvaging food and any goods she might need from the abandoned shops that once served the millions of tourists who poured into the city. Tattered and sun-bleached tabloid magazines and out-of-date newspapers remained on the shelves. The red double-decker buses that once congested the roads remained where they had been abandoned. On the opposite side of the river was St. Thomas Hospital. Handy for the strong meds that weren't for curing anything, but felt good to take.

More than a few times, she ventured into the small museum dedicated to Florence Nightingale that was only a few minutes' walk from the hospital. A life-sized Florence made from wood and wax stood at the entrance holding a lantern. It made Elizabeth wish she had mattered more, had been someone like Florence instead of living a life worth a pittance. She had been a year eight history teacher and utterly forgettable to the impoverished students who couldn't care less about school, considering they could leave at sixteen to make money for smokes and cheap cider. The ones who were desperate for love or attention were nice, but most of the others were cruel little gits. A single note calling her Ms. Minging Minge stuck with her like the stink of the boy's locker room.

All that was over. Something worse than the bubonic plague had killed them all. Death had visited this place before and come back to nearly finish the job.

With nothing to do since the collapse of the world, Elizabeth would spend hours in museums looking at pieces of art that had once been considered priceless, but were now less valuable than toilet paper or batteries. Despite the widespread death, this world of disaster suited her fine. There was nothing and no one to make her feel like her existence didn't matter. She left her apartment in a rundown council estate in Vauxhall and moved into the County Hall Hotel's most expensive suite. She woke up with the view of the Thames and Westminster Bridge. All the luxuries she didn't have before were for the taking. She could live like a queen in this nightmare if she wanted to.

They say you find love when you aren't looking for it and that's exactly what happened to Elizabeth. Just when she had begun to accept never seeing another soul again, never getting to fuck again, she began to experience lucid, dark dreams of a man named Flagg, with a distinct American accent. At first, he seemed like a mirage, or a watercolor made with different shades of denim. His presence felt overwhelming, larger than life. Like his power could extend across the Atlantic and scoop her into his arms. Nothing like the working-class muppets she met at pubs before last call. Their bloodshot eyes and noses with prominent spider veins made her despise them. All they did was complain about the government and football. But a warm bed was better than an empty one.

With eyes closed, her fingertips glided over her body, imagining what Flagg would feel like next to her in the super king-size bed not meant for one. She awoke still alone. But that tracked with the story of her love life. A series of fucks that left her frustrated in an endless cycle of loneliness and disappointment. Since puberty, males had never noticed her at first glance. She didn't have nice skin with wide-set eyes or a made-you-look body. Her hair was a frizzy mess the color of muddy water, and teenage acne had left scars. Years of smoking and tea drinking had left her teeth discolored. The *English Rose* gene somehow missed her. That's why she became what her students would call a slag. What she lacked in pretty she made up for by being an eager lover. At least it was some sort of affection, even if they never spoke to her again. Then again, the pubs and nightclubs were always full.

Yet that seductive man with the heat of the desert and darkness of hell returned night after night in her dreams and made her orgasm in her sleep as his hands dug deeper into her flesh while she lay on an altar with ecstasy taking over. She woke up invigorated and feeling alive, as if his energy flowed from his cock and into her body. It could only be described as an out-of-body experience, or possession. Standing nude in front of the bathroom mirror was where she talked to him. Instead of her own face, she saw his. The longer she communed with him, the more she craved to see him and others—if there were any left. She wanted to be touched again. His presence stirred deep longing and frustration.

"I can't be the only survivor here. There has to be someone who can help me get to you," she said to him as herself.

Her lips moved, yet she heard his voice in her mind. "*Be patient.*"

"I will do anything you want me to as long as you help me!" she pleaded.

"*Patience,*" he replied.

Tears streamed from her eyes. "I'm lonely. You're the only one I can turn to. Anything. I will do anything to fuck you."

She closed her eyes, acutely aware of the coldness of the floor beneath her feet since the heating stopped working. Her nude body shivered, covered with goose pimples. Rain pelted against the window. That damn British rain she hated and wanted to escape her entire adult life.

"*How?!*" she screamed.

No response from him except the memory of her dream the previous night. It was a vision of her cheek against an altar covered in a white cloth. Both her hands were tied behind her back. Her gaze shifted toward the ornate, vaulted ceiling. She knew where that altar was located. It had to be a sign.

―――

The following afternoon, Elizabeth stood in front of the Coronation Chair in St. George's Chapel inside Westminster Abbey, wanting to feel the sensation that royals of old experienced. Divine right. They believed each king and queen was imbued with God's power and protection. The divine lived through them. They were *chosen*. To disobey meant you disobeyed God Himself. Was this true? The modern monarchy had left much to be desired. They had all seemed very ordinary and thick. Nothing divine had lived in them. If it did, they would still be here instead of her. It gave her a smug satisfaction. The dreams also made her feel this way. There was something truly otherworldly about them, and Flagg. They could be the new gods.

Elizabeth touched the decrepit old wood and chipped gold paint of the Coronation Chair. It had decayed just like the long-gone royals. The throne only possessed the power of the one who sat on it. History and war told that tale time and time again. The urge to sit on it became stronger the longer she gazed on its pathetic state of ruin. Who would stop her, and did it even matter anymore?

She had hoped the dream brought her here to meet others, yet the walk across Westminster Bridge was a lonely one. The Abbey was just as empty except for the dead.

To hell with it all. She sat on the Coronation Chair and closed her eyes. Sunlight filtered into the cold building. The warmth of it on her face made her think of the American desert. In her mind's eye, she imagined Flagg walking toward her, the famous Las Vegas sign behind him, ready to take her as his own. She smiled thinking of him. She could feel her back straighten as she stretched out her hand.

"Finally, you are here. Dreams and reality have finally merged. My king, my dearest Flagg."

"You hear him, too?"

She opened her eyes, startled by the sound of another voice. For an instant, she didn't know if it was a real person in the physical realm or another manifestation like Flagg.

The young man looked about nineteen or twenty. He wore a dirty collared shirt beneath a raincoat, and black trousers. He carried a small rucksack on his back. His smooth pale skin and dirty-blond hair falling across his face made him appear like a schoolboy, like the thirteen-year-olds she once taught. Bright and round blue eyes glittered with crown jewel depth. On his hip he wore a belt with an antique sheathed steel sword. Perhaps he, too, wandered into the museums and took this treasure. But what would he do with it?

Her body tensed. She had nothing to defend herself with if he attacked. But why would he ask her about Flagg? She waited a beat before answering him.

"Yes. Do you?"

He rushed toward her and dropped to his knees. The sound of the sword hitting the stone floor echoed through the space. He looked like a helpless child with wide and wild eyes as he gazed up at her with tears welling. Relief crossed his face. "I knew it! I'm not suffering from some delusion from isolation. I've been praying for a sign, and that sign would be to find another person."

He looked handsome in his desperation. She touched his shoulder. "I, too, asked for a sign."

"He made it clear to me he only wants those willing to do their part in the new world he's building. He'll bring us together. If we only put our trust in him. I come here to pray."

She leaned toward the young man, feeling a swell of excitement as well as relief. Flagg delivered. All she had to do would be keep him from wandering away. "I'm glad we found each other. What's your name?"

"Joseph. Joseph Parks."

Her lips curled to a soft smile while staring into his eyes. The fading sunlight through the stained glass sliced across his face. "I'm Elizabeth Gladworthy. Devoted to building something wonderful amongst the despair. He wishes it."

"I am, too . . . I want to feel closer to him."

"Are you alone, Joseph?"

He nodded his head in exaggerated eagerness. "Yes. I've stayed in the city because there are more supplies than if I ventured to the countryside."

Elizabeth studied his face, the softness of it. There was a naivety she found attractive. "Very wise . . . Where are you staying?"

He averted his eyes in slight shame. "Here and there. I can't stand the idea of going back to my nan's house. Too many memories . . . my dormitory still has a lot of bodies inside."

She frowned and touched the side of his arm. "That's not good. I'm at the hotel across the river. We can have or be whatever we want there." Her eyes shifted to the sword. "Where did you take that from?"

His cheeks flushed. "I went to the Tower of London. I loved that place as a kid. My nan was a Royalist. Didn't think anyone would mind. I took a few things. The sword makes me feel . . . safer."

"Exactly. No one will mind. Come with me to my hotel. It's gorgeous . . . and free."

His face brightened. "Do you have lots of food?"

"I am afraid I can only offer you beans on toast tonight. It's just been me, so I have a camping stove and not much else."

"I love beans on toast. My nan used to make it for me."

"Good. Why don't we walk to my hotel. Then we can sit and talk about our dreams."

Elizabeth rose to her feet. He beamed with a wide grin. She had all his attention. Elizabeth wasn't greedy. One companion until Flagg was enough.

Joseph looked around the hotel in wonder. The aroma of dead flowers filled the hotel. There were too many located all over the building and Elizabeth didn't want to bother with the effort to clear them all out.

"This is nice," he said.

"I know . . . You mentioned a dormitory? Where were you in school?"

"King's College."

"That is impressive. Your nan must have been proud. I taught boys like you."

"Hey, I wanted to teach, too! Math and physics."

"Your parents must have loved that."

His smile faded and face darkened. "I don't like to talk about them. I had to live in hospital for a few years, then I was sent to live with my nan."

She stopped and touched his arm. "I'm sorry. You don't have to tell me."

"Thank you. Maybe I will at some point. Anyway, tell me about your dreams."

She had to think fast. She couldn't scare him off with her dreams of fucking. At least not yet. She couldn't put him off straightaway.

"I dreamed of . . . flying to him. Finding a way across the pond. You don't happen to know how to navigate a boat or fly a plane, do you? From what I gather from my dreams, he's in America. Las Vegas."

He laughed and blushed. "Nope. Wish I did. I'd fly to him, too, if I could. Maybe we'll be given a miracle. It's kind of a miracle we're both still alive."

Elizabeth almost pitied how hopeful and naive he was. It was adorable, yet it made her want to crush him at the same time. A soft little public school boy getting his balls squeezed for the first time. "How old are you, Joseph?"

"Eighteen."

Her stomach leapt with excitement. She remembered the eighteen-year-old boy she met when she was sixteen. "So young . . . Did you have a girlfriend?"

"No. It didn't really interest me when I started uni. And before that, I kept to myself."

She led him into the main bar area, where she spent most of her time. It reminded her of being out looking for a good time despite not a soul around. He rushed to the room's center.

"This place is so wonderful." He scanned a coffee table filled with candles, board games, playing cards, piled-up books. Next to the table was a cart with spirit bottles, wine, and beer. "You really made a new home here."

"I did. But that was before I heard his voice."

"So, you want a way to America?"

She sat on the faded sofa in front of the coffee table and grabbed a bottle of whiskey and two glasses. She poured doubles. "Do you know the story of the Stone of Scone? The stone that once sat below the Coronation Chair?"

He glanced at the drinks then back to her. "No. Not much into history. I know a little about the Bible."

"Your nan was a God-fearing woman?"

"Yes. A true saint. She touched so many lives."

"That's nice. Well, the stone was taken from the Scots and brought to the king of England. But that isn't the part of the story that interests me. It's said the stone is a true relic from the Bible."

"Really? How did it get here?" He put his rucksack down and sat next to Elizabeth. She extended a glass to him. He shook his head. "No thanks."

She smiled and took a sip, then licked her lips. "Maybe later."

Elizabeth touched his thigh. He scooted a few inches away, yet continued to smile. "The stone? The story is fascinating."

Elizabeth had to hide her anger at his rejection. "Yes, sorry. It's also called the Stone of Jacob. It's where he lay his head in Bethel as he received visions in the form of dreams from God. Later, the prophet Jeremiah brought it to Ireland before it found its way to Scotland. The English took it from the Scots. For a very long time, it resided beneath the Coronation Chair in Westminster Abbey."

Joseph looked off as if he'd entered a dream world. "Visions! Dreams. Just like us! Could we be prophets? This has to be the end times, like in the Bible."

She smiled at him. His innocent enthusiasm excited her. "Exactly. You are very clever, Joseph. I think we are in touch with the divine. I could feel it when I entered the Abbey and sat on the Coronation Chair. Flagg has told me directly that I am his chosen one on this side of the world."

"I believe it. You've been so kind and welcoming to me."

"Joseph, I just want to make you feel welcomed and good. You can be yourself around me."

He shifted his gaze to his fidgeting fingers. "Thank you. I know we just met, but I'm very tired. Do you mind if I take one of the rooms?"

"Not at all. But it's a big place, so I'll put you next to me. Best we stick together."

"Okay. I trust you."

"Good. You can." She stood, grabbing the second drink. "Follow me. The keys are still at the front desk."

Flagg had been silent for the few days since Joseph's arrival. He couldn't be angry at her being attracted to Joseph, because she had to believe Flagg had given him to her. The absence of Flagg though made it difficult for her to sleep. She shuffled through her box of pills from the hospital and found ones that might help. She hoped in the darkest corner of her dreams she would find him. With a shot of whiskey, she took the pill. Not long after, her mind drifted into a dark void. He whispered. *"You like him. I know you do."* She could feel his breath on her neck.

"I . . . You're the one for me."

"It's okay. I'm not a jealous guy. Have fun with him. Make him into a man. He wants it. But he's shy. Look at you. You're a knockout. Give him what he wants. What you want . . . "

Elizabeth could feel herself smiling in her sleep. She did want Joseph, and now she would have him. She would have both.

"We will find a way to you."

"Let me handle that, darlin'."

The following day, Joseph wandered in and out of his room, then ate a light supper of cheese sandwiches and potato chips with her. He seemed pensive throughout the entire meal.

"You okay?" she asked.

"Yeah, just had a few wild dreams."

"Really? Tell me."

He hesitated. "I'd rather wait until I'm sure."

"Up to you, Joseph. I'm here for you."

She blew out the candles they used for light and returned to her room. She had never been with a virgin before. It aroused her. She opened two beers and poured them into pint glasses. Into one of them she sprinkled crushed diazepam. His shyness might be a problem considering he hadn't reacted the way she expected when she tried to get close to him before. He was young enough to get hard and dumb enough not to think anything of how the spiked beer made him feel. Elizabeth wore a fresh robe and nothing else when she walked to Joseph's room and knocked on the door with her knuckles.

He opened it with a smile. "Everything okay?"

"Yes, sorry. Just lonely, I guess." She held up the beers. "And I don't like how we left supper. Nightcap?"

He glanced at her robe and bare feet. "I guess . . . a little company wouldn't hurt."

She entered and closed the door behind her with her foot.

"I know you said you didn't really drink. Why don't you try it anyway? You don't have to be shy around me. I don't like drinking alone. And it will open your mind. Help you relax about your dreams."

He hesitated before taking the pint glass. "Yeah, the adjustment being around another person hasn't been easy. All right—cheers, then."

She lifted the glass to her lips and took a long drink, hoping he would do the same and not sip it like a granny with her tea. To her surprise, he drank half of it.

"That's a good boy."

He winced. "Hmm. Very bitter."

"Don't worry about that." She moved to the edge of the bed and sat down. He stood, looking awkward. Elizabeth imagined this must have been the first time he was alone with a woman who wasn't his nan.

"Why don't you drink the rest of that and come sit next to me."

"Uh . . . okay." He shuffled closer and sat down, draining the glass, still making a face at the taste of it.

"That's better. See? Isn't this better than being all alone in some old, dodgy, damp-smelling, cold Victorian building with no one to talk to?"

He chuckled. "You're right. But I can't wait to find others. We can have open discussions. Map out how we'll start again. We have God on our side."

She stared at him. "How are you feeling right now?"

He chuckled again. "Good. Very good. Not like the last time I tried to drink alcohol."

One of her hands crept onto his thigh. "We have to take care of each other. I can lead us."

He looked at Elizabeth with a vacant gaze as her fingers gripped his leg. With her other hand, she untied the terry-cloth belt around her waist and opened the robe. "I need to feel someone next to me. Have you ever been with a woman?"

He immediately scooted a few inches away from her. Her hand slipped from his thigh. "No. Never."

"Let me change that. It's nothing to be afraid of. I'm a great teacher. You'll see."

"I don't want to. No. I—I just met you." He blinked slowly, staring at his feet.

Elizabeth stood in front of him. "You have to. You were brought to me . . . *Given* to me."

"I think that beer was too much. Feeling a bit weak. You should go," he said with a look of discomfort and embarrassment.

Elizabeth placed the terry-cloth belt around his neck.

"I'm sorry. Pray with me."

His drowsy eyes darted around the room as he lifted his trembling hands. She took the loose ends of the belt and tied it tight at the base of his neck. Using the remaining belt, she tied his wrists together with a double knot. Half hog-tied. He sucked in a deep breath and it choked him when he moved.

"What . . . What are you doing to me?!"

He tried to scream. His eyes widened as she threw off the robe and pushed him onto his back.

"Don't," he said in a strained voice. His pale skin had turned red from lack of oxygen, as hers did with her arousal.

She smirked. "Believe me when I say you'll love this."

She yanked down his jogging trousers and took his soft cock in her hands. He tried to buck his hips to stop her from stimulating him. She dug her nails into his left thigh.

"Behave yourself, or I'll do the same thing to your cock." Her eyes darkened and narrowed as she glared at him.

He stopped and squeezed his eyes shut. "I'm lightheaded . . . feel so weak . . . was it . . . the beer?"

She laughed at his panic. "C'mon. You love it, otherwise you wouldn't be this hard."

He looked down on his full erection then shut his eyes again.

"Now be a good boy and fuck me. It's been so long." She crawled on top of him and pushed hard against his hips. A loud groan escaped her mouth. "Look at me, Joseph."

She gritted her teeth and leaned forward, placing her hands around his neck. "I said *look at me*, you little *cunt*!"

His eyes snapped open as she squeezed his neck tighter. Her hips grinded on his cock with an unnatural frenzy. The sound of her heavy tits slapping against her torso filled the room. She emitted hoarse, guttural noises that sprang from deep in her throat. She opened her mouth and threw back her neck with her eyes rolling into her head. Her entire body quaked as she rage-fucked him harder and faster. Joseph struggled to take in any ounce of oxygen as her hands and the belt tightened against his windpipe. He tried to claw at the robe belt without any luck. Her head jerked forward. She bared her teeth as she orgasmed.

"*Randall!*" she shrieked as she fell over Joseph. Her chest heaved as she regained her breath. Muffled sobs escaped his trembling lips.

She lifted her head toward him and reached between her legs.

"Why are your crying? I made you come."

She wiped her sticky hand on his hair.

"Let me go," he said, gasping for air.

Elizabeth rolled her eyes and shifted her body off of him, then untied him. "This was what *he* wanted. Flagg brought you to me first for a reason. You have to become a man at some point. Don't worry though—I'll make you into what he needs you to be."

Elizabeth grabbed the belt and then the robe off the floor before walking out the door.

———

Joseph lay in bed, crying as he fell in and out of a broken sleep. Whatever Elizabeth gave him (there *had* to have been something in the beer) made him feel unwell. His belly ached and his head was in a fog. She was no prophet or even a decent human being. Even during the plague, he had tried to maintain hope. Joseph promised his nan to be a light and help others if he could. All he had to do was stay strong and keep his faith. He'd promised her and that was what he had planned to do. Until now. At this moment, he felt utterly crushed and lost inside. Joseph closed his eyes, wishing he could speak to his nan one final time. How could he help others feeling so tainted and hopeless?

"Joey."

The whisper made him stir as he tried to open his eyes. *"Hey, Joey."* It was *him*.

"Help me," Joseph said. "Help me escape her. Do you know what she's doing in your name? She is a liar."

"I do. Bring her to me and I'll make sure she faces justice. You'll feel better."

"But how? How can I get to you?"

"Take the bus, man. I'll do the rest. Water to wine. I can do it all."

Joseph nodded his head before drifting to sleep. He recalled a strange memory from his childhood. Lizard Point. Where he flew kites and ate ice cream on the pier, thinking about the expanse of the ocean. Once, his kite crashed into the water, but it floated on the surface. He woke up, taking it for a sign.

Elizabeth woke with a dry mouth and a sore head from the two bottles of red wine she'd gone through after leaving Joseph. It was a small celebration. Despite not feeling her best, she walked across Westminster Bridge with her morning cigarette as usual, then back to the hotel.

There was no sign of Joseph.

She knocked on his room door with no answer. She entered with the spare key. He wasn't there, but his bed was made. She burned thinking he would leave her. If she had to keep him drugged until he surrendered, then she would do just that.

She power walked to Westminster Abbey knowing Joseph would be on his knees in penance. Sure enough, he knelt in front of the altar with hands clasped. She walked toward him, ready to throttle him for making what should have been fun so difficult. He wanted it.

His cheeks went bright crimson with shame when he turned in her direction. He averted his gaze, unable to look Elizabeth.

"What's your problem?" she spat.

"I think you're a liar and a bad person. What you did to me . . ."

She rolled her eyes. "Please. You enjoyed it. You sprayed all over me."

He shook his head, on the verge of tears. "I couldn't help it. I had never . . ."

"Piss off. Don't ever come to me with that bullshit. If I want to fuck you, then you will do it."

He looked up at her with defiance in his eyes and cheeks still flushed. "I will not."

She leaned closer to him with both hands on her hips. "Try to stop me. I will kill you and you will never see Flagg. In fact, I'll tell him about it. And next time I come to your room, you better do exactly as I ask. If I don't pop like it's Bonfire Night, then you'll be in big trouble."

"We *are* going to him. I'm taking you to him to seek justice."

She gave him an incredulous look. "Are you crazy? We can't get to America!"

"Yes, we can. I found a working bus and enough gas."

"No wonder you were still a virgin. Because you are one big silly cunt!" she said, emphasizing the word *cunt*.

Joseph reached inside his jacket and pulled out an antique dagger encrusted with jewels on the handle. Before Elizabeth could react, he stabbed her twice in the abdomen. Her mouth opened as she sucked in air with each penetration of the blade. She touched her belly with a look of shock on her face. Her hands balled into fists as searing pain radiated from the wounds. She screamed in agony, her eyes squeezed shut.

"*How dare you!*" she shrieked as she opened her eyes and glared at him. Tears slipped down her cheeks.

He grabbed a large candelabra off the altar and hit her on the side of the head. Elizabeth fell to the ground.

When he couldn't sleep and while Elizabeth was getting drunker by the minute, Joseph had left the hotel to search the buses for one with enough gasoline. He had finally scored one at the bus depot thirty minutes' walk away. He had parked it by the abbey, knowing she would look for him.

Now his plan had come to fruition. Blood pooled around her body and saturated her clothing. At least it would be her blood on him and not the other way around. He grabbed both of her hands and dragged her out of the abbey and to the waiting bus. He hoisted her onto the first seat. He used a cable he'd found at the bus depot to tie her wrists and ankles together. The memory of her tying his hands and neck made him pull tighter on the cable.

"You will answer for what you've done and for your lies." He glanced at her top, saturated with blood. His fingertips touched it. "Your life belongs to him."

Her eyes fluttered, and she winced as she continued to bleed. "You dummy, we can't drive there."

"He has promised a miracle."

"Please, Joseph. He *made* me do it. Let's live out our lives here. Have a go of it. Don't you want to make your nan proud? Maybe have a family?"

"Not with you."

Elizabeth's face morphed into pure hatred before launching spit and blood toward his face.

"You will face your maker, Jezebel. We have six hours to drive. Don't die on me just yet."

He turned and got into the driver's seat, and started the ignition. Rain pelted the windshield as he drove them out of London toward Lizard, a small coastal town to the southwest. It was the place he had visited during summer holidays when he was a boy.

Elizabeth stared out the window. She hadn't been outside the city since before the plague. They passed military vehicles, older buildings succumbing to the elements, more abandoned cars and trains stopped on tracks. Once outside the city, the greenery had taken over. Deer, foxes, and stray cats wandered without fear or care. Overturned bins and piled up rubbish had been feasted upon by the animals. Her eyes opened and closed with the heaviness of knowing she would die. She glanced at her reflection in the window hoping to see Flagg, but there was nothing. He had abandoned her, too.

Joseph pressed his foot on the accelerator as they barreled through the southwest edge of the country toward the cliffs just beyond Lizard Point. He wouldn't stop until they floated across the Atlantic on their journey toward Las Vegas. His body trembled with radioactive excitement.

Joseph and Elizabeth jolted in their seats as he took the bus off-road with the accelerator pinned. Elizabeth fell out of her seat, unable to move, her cheek planted to the dirty floor. She could no longer see what was happening.

For a moment, they were in flight. Just like his kite in his dreams. A wide smile spread across his face as the sun burst through the clouds. Then his stomach lurched as the bus began to fall toward the ocean. Joseph braced for the impact by gripping the steering wheel. The forceful penetration of the bus caused his entire body to jolt forward. Icy water poured into the heavy vehicle at a speed he didn't anticipate. He opened his eyes, trying to get control of the steering wheel, but water filled his nose and mouth. He couldn't breathe.

"Hey, Joey . . . Over here."

Joseph heard Flagg. He had come to save him. His head twisted from left to right as he tried to stay conscious. Elizabeth floated, lifeless. In the darkness of the freezing water, he thought he could see Flagg's face. He reached for the image and thought to himself:

My life for you.

THE BOAT MAN

Tananarive Due and Steven Barnes

K ey West was now the Island of Chickens.
 Although chickens had roamed free on streets and in yards for all of Marie's life, and apparently since the first Cuban settlers a million years ago, they walked with more arrogance now. When Marie slipped outside into the shadows between the old wooden row houses, chickens were the largest living creatures she saw except for the birds lucky enough to be able to touch the sky. Chickens strutted in a sea of brown and white, with bright red combs flapping, filling the streets as they darted between abandoned cars. They roamed the houses with impunity, through perpetually open doorways, across sofas and kitchen counters. Or they roosted on white fences wrapped in cheerful bougainvillea blossoms, sometimes as far as she could see.

Cats were prowling, of course. But not as many cats as chickens. Not by a mile.

Marie thought she might catch a chicken for dinner. But later. If she could keep her head on straight and didn't think of them as pets so she wouldn't *chicken out*—she chuckled to herself at the pun—dinner was everywhere she looked. For life.

But Marie didn't want to be in Key West for life. Hell, no.

Marie La Guerre had big plans.

Although she preferred to move in darkness, Marie set out to see Edmund in daylight. Edmund didn't know it yet, but he and his boat were a part of her plan. A big part.

The wheels of her old Radio Flyer wagon whined as she pulled it over the jutting mango tree roots at her back gate, its load of treasure hidden under a deceptively grimy tarp. Look left, look right. Her belly only unclenched when she didn't see anyone else on the car-littered street or the porches within ten paces on both sides of her, yards overgrown as if Señora Sanchez and the Pettigrews had been gone for years instead of only since June.

In the days after the Tripz raced through Key West like a hurricane, she'd been senseless with grateful tears on the rare occasions when she saw anyone else standing upright. Someone to tell her horribly ordinary ordeal of trying to nurse Granpè Jean when he died cursing in Kreyòl and coughing blood. Someone's kind eyes offering a hidden piece of her parents or Granpè Jean in soft blue, green, or brown. Any eyes that weren't runny with blood.

Not anymore. She'd learned better about people. She could hear them even now—the pirates. They were still a few blocks away, sound carrying farther than it should on the ocean breeze, but she heard their whoops signaling that they had breached a barricade: somebody's wood panels breaking. No gunshots yet today, but she had heard guns the day before like distant fireworks. Gunshots in an open-air tomb.

Pirates weren't content to take their pick of the yachts and million-dollar homes that had been left behind: pirates needed prey. The Tripz had given birth to monsters wearing human skin who fed from the living like the *loups-garoux* in Granpè Jean's scary stories from Ayiti. And although Granpè Jean still stubbornly refused to visit her dreams to give her guidance—had been *crowded out* of her dreams, more like it—Marie knew better than to leave herself at the mercy of monsters, wondering each night if one was trying to peek past her blinds or smash her windows for the pure joy of hearing her cry and beg and scream. She was only thirteen, but pirates would not treat her like a child.

Zwazo pose sou tout branch, Granpè Jean said when he got sick, his favorite encouragement made cryptic after the Tripz: *Birds land on all branches.*

Your turn will come.

Pulling her wagon behind her, Marie waded past the chickens to cross the road.

―――

The spot where she had buried Granpè Jean called out to her as she walked past: his favorite place to sit and drink white rum—his beach chair on the sand in the shade of scrawny coconut palms. She'd pulled him in this same wagon, struggling although he'd lost so much weight. Not a hole six feet deep, more like three feet, but it was a hole at least, which made him one of the privileged. Deep enough to keep the crows away when there was so much other meat aplenty. The silence from him screamed to her when she passed his burial place. Still, she spoke to him in a whisper, "I'm being sensible today, Granpè Jean. Just like Manman. Just like you always said." It was a teeny lie, because she was going to Edmund, who was not sensible at all. But she hoped she could be sensible enough for both of them.

As Marie had warned Edmund many times, she could hear his music from a quarter mile away; a faint beat and vocal flourishes that were unmistakable. And always the same song—one she had loved, too, but hearing it in a loop every time she visited Edmund had twisted her affection closer to loathing.

She walked past still, silent boats at their slips on their docks, most of them thankfully empty and free of ghastly odors. Boats were the preferred homes among the few people left scattered on the island. Edmund's harbor was mostly deserted, since this side of the island was farther from supplies that might be scavenged from the demolished stores downtown. These were the more modest boats of weekend sailors and fishermen, not the grand yachts left behind to plunder.

But there *was* a smell. At least a dozen dead chickens were piled in an almost perfect pyramid in her path, feathers bloodied and mangled by gunshot wounds, rotting in the sun. Another pile sat only a few feet from the first, this one shrunken and charred black, no doubt from the bottle of lighting fluid that lay emptied beside it. Not a barbecue—just burning for the sake of it.

Edmund's work. Not for the first time, she wondered if he was a complete psycho.

Her irritation flared. If he was going to kill chickens, at least he could have shared them before they spoiled. Chickens were harder to chase down than she would have believed. For one thing, they could fly higher than people thought even if they couldn't soar like seagulls.

Edmund's boat was at the far end of the marina. From several paces, it was impossible to miss his bright red leather jacket, which he always wore even in the wet summer heat. He was on his sailboat's deck, arms outstretched as he thrust his tiny pelvis and bobbed his head, following Michael Jackson's choreography. His face was a river of sweat. He bit his lip when he raised his arms into the famous *Thriller* zombie pose, swinging right and left with so much force that his glasses slipped to the edge of his dripping nose as he panted.

"It's a sin to waste food!" Marie called to him. "And it's stupid to shoot a bunch of chickens. You'll wish you had saved those bullets."

He didn't miss a beat, as if she hadn't spoken. This little white boy's dancing might be the death of him, but although she would hate to admit it, with all of his practice he almost looked like Michael—especially after Michael made his skin lighter.

Once again, Marie checked behind her to make sure none of the pirates had followed her during the ten-minute walk from her street to the harbor. Satisfied, she lifted a flap of the tarp covering her wagon's load just enough so he could peek.

"I bet you're thirsty, eh?" Marie called to him, sweet and singsong.

That got Edmund's attention. His eyes mooned as he stared down at her.

"Where'd you get that?" His arms fell flat at his sides. Once he stopped moving, he remembered how exhausted he was.

"Are you thirsty or not?"

Edmund hopped down to the pier. On the deck above, his portable VCR and its tiny screen kept showing the ghost tribe of zombies and their death dance.

Edmund was sunburned bright red, his nose and forehead peeling. If he still had parents, they would have warned him to wear sunblock and stay clear of the sun during its meanest hours. But sunburn was the least of their worries.

Edmund wrenched off the plastic bottle's cap and took two long gulps, ready to hand it back to her. But she shook her head. "Whole thing's yours."

Edmund drained the rest with barely time to swallow. Some of the precious water dribbled down his chin. He stared at her wagon's load as she revealed more: three cases of water, more than seventy bottles. She had scavenged some herself as soon as she realized it would be a good idea, but many of the cases stacked in her coat closet were from Granpè Jean's hurricane stash. As a young man, he had been adrift in a fishing boat in the Atlantic on his way to Miami, and his biggest fear ever since had been dying from lack of fresh water. *Water, water, as far as the eye could see*, he'd told her. *And not a drop to drink!*

Key West's water supply had been unreliable even during the good times, with frequent *Boil Water* notices. Marie would not drink the filthy gray liquid dribbling from her faucets now even if her life depended on it. Bathing in it made her feel dirtied, not clean. The water in her wagon was treasure no matter how much remained in his boat's tanks.

"This is all yours," she said. "It's a trade."

"I don't got nothin' to trade."

"You don't *have* anything," she corrected him. "But actually, you do."

She stared toward his forty-six-foot sailboat and its name painted in blue script: *Proud Mary*. It took a few seconds before he realized why she was staring.

"You're crazy," he said. "This is my uncle's. Get your own!"

"I like this one," she said. "It's named for me. Sort of. That's what you call a good omen. I don't want the whole boat—just a share of it. Half."

Edmund tossed his empty bottle into the water. "Hell no!"

She stepped closer to put him in her shadow. She was only three years older, but he was short for his age and she was tall for hers. "Listen to me: We have to leave. You know it, too. There's more of them every day. And they're getting closer. We should go together."

Edmund shrugged off his jacket. The concert T-shirt beneath was in rags. "I'm not scared of any stupid pirates." He had adopted her word for the gang of marauders they heard looking for other survivors to menace, just like their namesake in storybooks.

"Edmund, *they* find each other and stick like glue. If we don't do the same, we lose. They're hunting people down. This is a small island. Not enough places to hide. No clean water. It's time. Or it'll be too late."

He didn't want to admit it, but he was curious about her plan. "What, then?"

"We take our boat, that's what. Sail north."

Edmund shielded his eyes from the sun with a grubby, unwashed hand as he stared at her. An earthy stink floated from him that must be making his mother do flips in her grave—if she had one. "It's not 'our' boat," he said, but he was curious. "North to where, anyway?"

"You know where."

He frowned and stooped over to make wide stomping steps away from her, palms on his kneecaps. Practicing his choreography again. Some part of him was always trying to pretend the world away.

THE BOAT MAN

"Michael Jackson's not in Colorado," he said. "He's not at some old Black lady's house. He's putting on concerts in Las Vegas. That's where he went."

"He's dead, Edmund—"

"*Shut up!*" Edmund screamed at her. His face turned bright crimson. "He's gonna put me on the stage right next to him as soon as he sees me—the best kid dancer in the *whole world*—and then he's gonna take me to live with him in Neverland!"

His last word was a sob. Hearing his plan out loud must have hurt his own ears.

Marie felt bad about breaking her promise never to poke holes in Edmund's fantasy. She respected fantasies. Granpè Jean had called Marie by her mother's name in his last hours, which hurt her feelings because she was the one washing and weeping over him—but at least saying the name *Nadine* made him smile. His last wish had been to pretend that Manman and Daddy hadn't died in that crash on the Seven Mile Bridge so long ago that Marie barely remembered them.

"We're still here . . . so he probably is, too." She was crossing her fingers behind her back, her habit when she was telling half a truth. Or no truth at all. If by some miracle Michael *had* survived, she would never allow Edmund to go live with him at Neverland—a superstar hanging out with young boys and zoo animals felt wrong in a hundred ways—but one battle with Edmund's fantasies was enough for today.

Edmund was right: she could have chosen any of the other boats from the forest of masts at this harbor alone. She didn't need to buy a share of the *Proud Mary* and include Edmund in her plan. But last night, when she'd quizzed herself on why she hadn't left in one of the simpler motorboats already, she realized she didn't want to leave the doofy shrimp behind.

And she needed him. He was smart. Edmund might have been one of the most intelligent ten-year-olds on the planet even back when the planet was full of ten-year-olds, but she didn't trust him on a journey this ambitious no matter how good he was at making knots and yanking up his sails. Someone needed to be stronger than them. Wiser.

They would need the Boat Man, too.

"I've been studying Granpè Jean's maps," Marie said, pulling one out of her back pocket. Granpè Jean had grown up in a fishing family and never tired of imagining ways to travel by boat. "We should be able to sail up the Mississippi River to St. Louis and go west from there. And even if we can't, at least we'll be closer. Away from here."

"It's worse out there!"

"Maybe," she said. "But not on the water, I bet."

Edmund needed another hour of convincing to at least think about it while they stowed the water bottles in his boat's dark, crowded galley, everything narrow and in miniature. The bottles took up his entire table. Everything needed cleaning. His aluminum sink was crammed with plates stained with dried ketchup and white spots that turned out to be maggots.

But he didn't refuse outright, a pleasant surprise. He must have a lick of sense hidden somewhere in that scrambled head. None of Granpè Jean's brothers had wanted to risk the rickety fishing boat with him from Port-de-Paix after Baby Doc cursed his homeland, so he'd fled to Miami alone, where he had never gotten over his rage at being caged like a criminal. He had nearly drowned, both in the Atlantic and, later, in U.S. bureaucracy—but one by one, his brothers left behind had died at the hands of the dreaded Tonton Macoutes. Later, losing his only daughter had made Granpè Jean determined to tell Marie everything about his life, knowing she was the only one left to remember his siblings. The pirates in Key West felt like the Macoute, too—except these days, wanton killing was a worse sin after so much dying.

"How long will it take?" Edmund said.

"I'm not sure. We can't go alone," she said. "I'm gonna ask the Boat Man."

THE BOAT MAN

A week before, Marie and Edmund had been startled by the burr of a motorcycle with a shirtless rider and ducked out of sight in time to see him race down the pier with a Molotov cocktail. With an expert throw, he'd set a sailboat on fire so fast that it lit up in orange like in *Die Hard*. A man with a beard had dived into the water from the back of the boat. The motorcyclist had fired a gun at the water five times. Six. That unholy sound. Then, satisfied, he had driven off.

The weirdest part—*one* of the weird parts—was that they'd had no idea anyone else was living so close to Edmund's boat until it became a spectacle. Through the entire episode, Edmund had been grinning his face off while Marie trembled, praying no one had seen them to disturb their hideaway.

Marie and Edmund had waited until all they heard were seagulls, and then crept to the pier. They'd found the Boat Man spraying his burning vessel with a fire extinguisher, sobbing. "Don't just stand there, you little fucks—help me put it out!" he'd shouted. But they hadn't moved or spoken to him. His boat was a lost cause. Marie didn't know why he didn't just choose another boat, or if he'd earned the attack, which felt more personal than random. Now the Boat Man spent most of his time wandering in the open, cursing at the sky.

Edmund's face wrenched into a toddler's pout behind the black horn-rimmed glasses he said had belonged to his father. "*That* freak?" But he was intrigued by the adventure of visiting him. "Okay, but I'm taking my guns."

"Just one gun," she said. "And keep it hidden under your shirt." Edmund moaned with disappointment. Half the fun of a gun, for him, was waving it. Edmund's uncle had collected guns and bullets the way Granpè Jean collected water. "And no firing unless we're attacked."

"I could fire a few rounds just to keep 'em away."

"It's stupid to bring them right to us."

"They'll just come tell me to join 'em." He said it like it was a badge of honor.

Marie's stomach cramped the way it had when she stepped away from the safety of her house. The pirates *would* probably want Edmund to join. And that might seem just fine to Edmund. That was part of her hurry. They both had dreams about Las Vegas, too, but Marie's made her wake up sweating and Edmund only told her stories about the thrill of his life on a concert stage.

"Maybe," she said. "But they won't ask me a damn thing. My skin's too dark."

"So?"

Marie didn't have enough time left in the day to explain. She barely understood herself.

"So . . . that matters to some people. A *lot* of people."

The only times Marie had ridden her bicycle far enough to glimpse the pirates near the yachts they had taken over at the fancier marina, every man, woman, and child among them had been white. Maybe Edmund hadn't noticed, but it might come in handy to travel in the company of a white boy and a man whose olive skin was hard to place, probably just a suntan. Other Black people must have survived on the island, but she hadn't seen any. That could be a coincidence, or maybe her black skin would be target practice for pirates like the chickens were to Edmund.

She didn't know if she could trust the Boat Man, either. But only one way to find out.

Marie reached into her wagon to grab the weapon she had chosen for this mission: Granpè Jean's machete, which he'd kept sharp in the hurricane supply closet. Granpè Jean had warned her that people would swarm over the weak and timid like locusts, given half an excuse.

"Hey—no fair!" Edmund said, his eyes mesmerized by the machete's gleaming blade while she tested its weight. "How come you get to carry *that*?"

"I need it more," she said. "Plus, how do you hide a machete?"

Edmund bent over to stomp in a regimented circle, lost in his daydream again. Even her machete couldn't distract him from Michael.

THE BOAT MAN

She wondered how much of Edmund was still intact after the Tripz and how much of the real Edmund was dead. Maybe he *was* a zombie.

But not her. Anyone she'd known would still recognize Marie, and she was proud of that. When her parents died, she'd dreamed that she was staring at her eyes in the mirror and said, *You are still you, Marie. Your life is not ruined.* Then she realized it was Manman's face in the dream mirror, not hers. But Manman didn't come to her dreams anymore. Marie thought she might never forgive that old lady in Colorado for crowding Manman, Papa, and Granpè Jean out of her dreams when they must be trying so desperately to comfort her. Maybe she wanted to go to Colorado mostly so she could free up her dreams again.

The day before, she'd followed the Boat Man to observe his behavior. He stayed clear of other people just like her, pulling back if he thought he heard noises. He seemed afraid, although he spent much of the day shuffling on the beach. Or sitting on the pier by the marker, staring out at the sea.

The designated Southernmost Point of Key West had a concrete marker painted like a giant buoy in red, black, and yellow. Granpè Jean had taken Marie there when his cousins from New York came to visit, posing for photos. It was one of the nicer areas in Key West, so it was in pirate country.

"He's probably way down south," Marie told Edmund. "We'll have to go closer to them."

Edmund halted his stooped stomping and turned over his shoulder to look at her, holding his pose. Just like in the video. His face glowed with glee.

"I'm bringing two guns, then."

⌒

Marie struggled to keep the machete balanced across her Schwinn's handlebars without slicing her fingers as she pedaled. The pirates probably had scouts, so she was careful to lead Edmund through alleys and over bumpy soil and sand rather than riding in the road. Edmund had refused to take off his red jacket as he pedaled his BMX racing bike behind her, so his hair was dripping with sweat and pasted to his forehead by the time they rode to Southernmost Point.

She saw the buoy from a distance on the pier—and a shadow she was sure was the Boat Man—but she held out her arm to keep Edmund from charging ahead. She climbed off her bike and left it behind to walk the last stretch, motioning for Edmund to do the same.

Look right, look left. Look behind. Look everywhere. Vigilance was exhausting.

Ahead, the vastness of the unbroken sea whispered courage in her ear.

"Walk slow," she said. "We don't want to scare him."

"Why not? We can make him do what we want."

Lord help her, maybe this boy was a pirate already. Marie glared at him to shut him up.

"Let me do the talking," she said. She never understood why Edmund obeyed her, but he usually did. She'd only needed to kick his ass once for his fealty, despite his guns.

Together, she and Edmund walked toward the man at the border of the sea.

―――

From the start, the Boat Man didn't look right.

He sat on the platform, leaning against the concrete buoy towering over him while he smoked a cigarette that appeared hand-rolled and smelled like the absent partiers on Duval Street. He nestled a crumpled paper bag in his lap like a pet. His jeans and Van Halen T-shirt looked fresh, so he was grooming himself much better than Edmund despite a salt-and-pepper beard growing wild, but his forehead's grooves made him look full of rage already.

The bigger problem was his shadow.

THE BOAT MAN

From a distance, that was all Marie had seen of him—and now that they were closer, she wondered *how* his shadow had been large enough to see from so far away. It didn't look right, that shadow—his giant twin lolling against the buoy, but at an angle that didn't match the shadows from the railing right behind him, above the inscription in red and blue paint: AMERICA BEGINS HERE. (Someone had crossed out BEGINS and spray-painted *Ends* instead.)

As if the Boat Man's shadow didn't need the sun. When Marie blinked, his shadow snapped into alignment, so sudden it made her dizzy.

Or maybe she was swooning from the smell floating from him. The sea air couldn't wash away the familiar rot she knew too well from houses, cars, and shops, which had driven most survivors to the marinas. Marie had thought about leaving her house too, but she'd been forced to haul away only three neighbors' bodies to improve the general state of her street—thankfully, the Pettigrews had been away when the bridge shut down. The chore had passed in a blur like the days after Granpè Jean died, and she had washed her skin and her sore muscles in the ocean afterward, hair and all, to be free from the Smell. *That* Smell.

And the Smell was here with the Boat Man, at the point that felt like the tip of the world.

Marie tried to think of what to say to him when the Boat Man grinned brown teeth that looked worse than his scowl. He yelled at Edmund, "Who the fuck are *you* supposed to be?!"

The *click* came as quick as a heartbeat, and Marie knew before she turned around that Edmund had his unwieldy .45 in his hand, pointed at the Boat Man. And cocked, no less. Edmund's hand was shaking. "It's Michael's jacket from 'Beat It'! Anybody knows that!"

"Fuck Michael Jackson!"

Marie gasped, bracing for Edmund's crazed gunfire to rip into her, gone wild. He was barely big enough to grip such a big gun, much less aim.

"No, fuck *you*! Eddie Van Halen played the guitar solo on 'Beat It,' stupid!"

It was so surreal, the two of them carrying on, that Marie wondered if she were only dreaming. But another *click* turned Marie's head the other way, and this time her blood thickened, clogging her throat: the Boat Man's own shiny gun was now visible from its hiding place in the paper bag, pointed straight at her.

"No guns!" Marie blurted.

The Boat Man's eyes were hidden in his shadow, but she thought she saw a flicker of amusement. "Says the bitch with a machete."

Marie dropped her machete with a clatter at her feet. "No guns—we only want to make you a partner!" She turned back to Edmund. "No guns, Edmund."

"He called you a bitch!"

The first and last time Edmund called her a bitch, she had wrestled him to the ground and twisted his arm until he cried. "It's okay this one time," she said, trying to keep her voice steady.

"Only if he puts his down first!" Edmund said.

"*You* first, you scared little shit," the Boat Man said. "You'll shoot me on accident."

By accident, Marie couldn't help thinking, a silent correction. Or maybe she said it aloud.

"I'm not scared!" Edmund said, and Marie knew he wasn't lying. His hand was no doubt shaking from excitement, not fear. He only slid his gun back into his shorts because of the pleading look on Marie's face, not because of anything the Boat Man said.

Marie sucked in three breaths before she could stop imagining gunfire.

A turn of the breeze sharpened the Smell so much that Marie looked down toward the water and saw someone who looked like she was three hundred pounds bursting against the seams of a flower-patterned dress, like the Incredible Hulk. Her blond hair splayed out in the water like jellyfish tentacles framing her head as she bobbed

THE BOAT MAN

face down, arms spread as if she were hugging the salt water. The body looked fairly fresh despite its decomposition bloat and missing chunks from sea life. She probably had jumped in. Maybe that was why people came here. Of course, the Smell wasn't coming from *him*. But why was he sitting so close to its stink?

The Boat Man ignored her eyes on the body. "I'm not gonna be nobody's daddy."

Edmund snorted, or maybe both of them did. *Damn right*.

"You two brats have ten seconds to tell me what you want."

So, Marie told him. And watched light spill into his shadowed eyes.

Marie couldn't remember the last time she'd been so excited in the hours before she went to bed, stuffing her belongings into her father's old army duffel bag: photos, her birth certificate, Manman's good winter houndstooth coat, her bathing suit. She felt like she was going on vacation. She packed in such a frenzy that she didn't remember to be heartbroken about leaving the house she had grown up in. Or the island that had been her home.

Night was when the worries came. And the dreams.

She expected to see the old lady—perhaps to congratulate Marie on such a bold and sensible plan—but this time she dreamed of being on the deck of the *Proud Mary*, lightning flashing in the sky like floodlights to reveal a roiling night sea. The waves were so high that the *Proud Mary* pitched and heeled, sometimes close to turning over on its side. Water flooded the deck.

Marie clung to the mast, hugging it like a loved one as water drenched her. But no: it wasn't the mast! She was clinging to the swollen blob of the dead woman she'd seen floating.

She called for Edmund and the Boat Man, but her mouth made no sound when she screamed. Or, if it did, she could not hear her voice against the ocean battering the hull.

This is how I'm going to die, she thought.

With that thought, she saw the man standing at the bow. (When she was awake, she had trouble remembering nautical terms, but she thought *bow* in sleep.) He stood legs akimbo, hands on his hips, a statue defying the boat's swaying.

The sail whipped in the wind, tearing to tatters. One of the ropes lashed above her, snakelike, and she barely ducked in time before it might have coiled itself around her neck. After the rope missed, it snapped back toward her with a mind of its own, ensnaring her upper arm. The rope yanked her upward, to her toes.

"*Help me!*" she screamed.

In the blinding strobe of lightning, the bearded man grinned at her. His eyes were hidden beneath an old-fashioned pirate's hat with skull and crossbones, but she knew those brown teeth. The Boat Man. He was holding her machete, she realized. With impossible balance, he raised it high and floated toward her like a phantom, lightning gleaming across the steel blade.

Marie woke with a scream on her lips. She panted, grateful for the dawn light.

But her bed was damp. Her face and skin were wet. Marie screamed again, thinking it was a dream inside a dream, like in *A Nightmare on Elm Street*, but although the moisture on her skin tasted salty like the sea, she had only sweated through her sheets as she slept. And worse, she had wet her bed—the odor of urine beneath her was sharp. Marie talked to herself for twenty minutes with reassurances before she could climb out of bed to wash.

Then she heard a knock. And went to meet Edmund and the Boat Man at her front door.

They had come to collect the rest of the water.

⁓

Unlike in her dream, the sea was placid and welcoming at the start of their leaving day.

THE BOAT MAN

Although they had spent two days bickering as they gathered supplies from other boats—cans of diesel, nonperishable food, blankets and a couple of water-desalination kits—all of them were agreeable now, not wanting to jinx the trip. Edmund, too, was on his best behavior, deferring to the Boat Man's instructions as they prepped for their long sail by hauling their supplies on board, including the Boat Man's chicken cages with three hens and a rooster.

The Boat Man walked with a jaunt, as if he had been reunited with the boat that burned. He'd found a white captain's cap somewhere, which made it all feel official. Edmund didn't even complain when the Boat Man said he wanted the larger cabin to himself, and that Edmund and Marie would have to share the berth in the smaller one despite the way the dank space was already crowded with junk. They were all too excited for any more arguing, eager to go.

So Marie was fine with her job to clean up the filthy two-burner stove and sink in the galley while Edmund and the Boat Man worked loudly prepping the vessel on the deck above her, with the Boat Man calling out orders and Edmund saying, "Aye aye, Captain!" Edmund had taken her out for a short sail once and he knew his way around the boat surprisingly well, but the relief of having the Boat Man's expertise was immeasurable.

If only she could forget her dream.

Her nightmare about the Boat Man had felt as real as her dreams about the old lady serving her lemonade like Manman's while she talked about freedom with the passion of Harriet Tubman on the Underground Railroad. Maybe *more* real, if she were honest. Now she just had to figure out what her dream about him had meant. In her dream, had he planned to chop her up with that machete? Or cut her loose from the rope? Why had the dead woman appeared?

Or was her dream just her fears about the journey bubbling to the surface as she slept?

The galley went dark. A prickling across Marie's scalp made her look at the narrow steps up to the deck, where the Boat Man's bulk was blocking the sunlight as he leaned in. Again, she could not see his face in his silhouette. (*That* had to mean something, didn't it?)

"Bring up those maps, girlie," he said.

Marie thought she should say, *Aye, aye*. But she couldn't make herself speak to his shadowy face. She hated it when he called her *girlie*, not only because it was a lazy nickname but because she tried so hard to dress in jeans and loose clothes that would help him forget that she was a girl. She'd never been more grateful that her body had not developed early, but looking like a tomboy hadn't helped him come up with a more creative name.

Maybe she and Edmund should have sailed alone. Even without the previous days' constant arguing, when they had taken turns telling each other to fuck off and die, the Boat Man's presence felt risky. But it might be too late now.

With the chicken cages nestled underneath the table, they barely had room to sit on the mildewed, rain-dampened cushions as Marie spread out Granpè Jean's nautical map of the Gulf of Mexico, where Key West was a pinprick in waters that looked as vast as space. Cuba was closer, only ninety miles south. Close enough to touch, just about.

"So, there's our route," the Boat Man said, tracing their journey far away from Cuba with a calloused fingertip. "Gulf of Mexico meets the Mississippi about a hundred miles from New Orleans. We'll hug the shoreline in case there's a storm front or we run out of fuel. Those Gulf waters can get pretty high, and we're still in hurricane season. My guess? At least eighty hours. Maybe more. Once we get up there, we figure out the rest. Dump the boat. Resupply."

"We're not dumping *Proud Mary*!" Edmund said.

Marie was afraid of another eruption to shatter their alliance—or maybe hoped for it—but the Boat Man chose patience. "I know you love this boat . . . I loved mine, too . . . but this is diesel, one thing. Harder to refuel. We'll have enough wind till we get to the river, but after that we'll mostly be motoring on the water. Plus, that fifty-

THE BOAT MAN

five-foot mast won't make it under some of those bridges on the Ole Mississippi. So, we'll see what we see. Lots of boats up there. Got it?"

Edmund didn't say, *Aye, aye.* He looked so crushed that Marie felt sorry for him.

"Why did that guy burn your boat?" Marie asked. The hidden story cried out to be told before they were alone with this man. "He wasn't just some random pirate."

The Boat Man looked at her, surprised by her insight. Up close, she saw how leathery his skin was from the sun, making his age impossible to guess. "What's that, girlie?"

"My name's Marie."

Edmund snickered. "Better call her by her name." (Which was funny, since neither of them called the Boat Man by his name, which he'd said was John. Or maybe Jake.)

The Boat Man licked his parched lips. "All righty then . . . *Marie.* That fuckstick was married to the love of my life. She ran away from him and lived on my boat with me for six months. Best six months of my whole life. Then he threatened her like the piece of shit he is and she went back to him. She didn't make it—but he did. Cuz there ain't no justice or right in this shitty world, is there?"

They agreed that there was no justice or right. And yes, the world obviously was shitty.

"My only regret is, I should've killed that asshole," he went on. "That way I could have been with her at the end instead of him."

They sat in silence that felt like a funeral, with seagulls as their sad choir. Marie remembered that she would miss the sound of seagulls on the open water. Granpè Jean had told her that he thought he was dead on his leaky boat until the morning he heard the seagulls' cries.

"Can we go kill him?" Edmund said. "Before we go?"

Marie sucked her teeth, annoyed. Edmund couldn't *wait* to kill someone, the sin of sins.

"No point now," the Boat Man said.

"Who was that dead woman by the buoy?" Marie said. Now that

they were teaming together, she was more troubled by the memory of him sitting placidly above a corpse. Had he killed her? Was that what her dream had been trying to tell her?

"Some jumper, I guess. I was thinking about doing it, too. Till . . ." His voice sounded strangled. The navigation meeting was over then, because he stood up and walked away to be by himself, swinging by the taut ropes.

Edmund leaned over to whisper to Marie. "Is he *crying*? What a pussy. If some guy burned *my* boat, I would've shot him a hundred times. And no way we're dumping *Proud Mary*. If he doesn't watch out, I'm gonna dump *him*." He pulled open his jacket to show Marie that he was still carrying one of his guns, maybe a .32. Of course he was. Maybe she should be, too. She had her choice of guns and ammo from the heavy bag Edmund had moved to their shared cabin.

Marie looked toward the Boat Man, mostly to make sure he hadn't overheard Edmund. But he was out on the back of the vessel (the stern?) staring across the marina toward where his boat, and his best times, once had been moored. Marie felt a strong urge to climb off *Proud Mary* and return to the pier, terrified to share such a confined home with two people who both might be as nutty as a Mr. Goodbar—and Edmund was *for sure*. Could she protect any of them once they were trapped together?

The Boat Man felt her staring. He turned around and seemed pleased, grinning at her with those rotting teeth. He took off his captain's cap and dipped it in a way that was supposed to look gentlemanly. But the gesture only made Marie shiver, worse than being called *girlie*.

"Wind's picking up, crew!" he called out. The grief in his voice was replaced by excitement. "Yo ho ho! Time to set sail!"

Exactly what a pirate would say.

THE BOAT MAN

At first, Marie wondered why she hadn't sailed away long before. The Boat Man and Edmund were focused on what lay ahead, adjusting their course, but Marie stared behind her. As the *Proud Mary* chugged from the harbor, the green-blue waters fully embracing them, she thought she'd never seen anything as exciting as the land fading away.

All of the dead, gone. The smell, gone. The memories, gone. (Oh, the memories would assault her the rest of her life, but at least she would not be immersed in them from the time she woke each day.) Her joints shook with combined grief and ecstasy as the land began to look hazy. Imaginary. Only the water was real. She hadn't realized how hard it had been to breathe until she drew in salty air that bathed her lungs. Had Granpè Jean felt this when he left Ayiti? She was sure he had. She could almost feel his steady hands on her shoulders.

This was the sensible thing, he seemed to assure her. *You're in control of your future now.*

For their first meal together, she spread out a white tablecloth she found folded in a drawer. They already had five eggs, so Marie whipped up a Spam omelet for them to share, and it was pretty tasty even though Edmund drowned his in ketchup from the fast-food packets his uncle had left behind. They ate at the cockpit table together like a family breakfast in *Little House on the Prairie*, laughing and smiling while the chickens clucked.

It's working, she thought. *We're actually doing this.*

A jinx if there ever was one.

"There you go," the Boat Man said, looking at Marie. "I knew you had a smile in you."

He winked at her again.. The idea that he was noticing whether or not she smiled made Marie lose her appetite.

"Wind's good," the Boat Man said. "Let's unfurl those sails and knock off the engine. Gotta save our fuel."

"Aye, aye, Captain!" Edmund said. He leaped from his seat mid-bite to go to the controls.

By lunchtime, she saw the clouds. Summertime was always the time for storms, so she wasn't surprised when the clear skies began to fill with paint brush strokes of gray clouds that were only white at the edges, darkest in their bellies. Rain had a smell, too, even before it began. Storms were the main villain in all of Granpè Jean's worst stories at sea.

"Look!" she said, pointing skyward.

The Boat Man wasn't worried. He calmly called out instructions to help stay clear of the storm that Edmund was still eager to follow, hopping around like a monkey. Marie said, "Aye, Aye, Captain" like Edmund, helping to tie everything down as the Boat Man told her—just in case. After a time, when the clouds filled the sky in every direction and the wind picked up, the Boat Man wanted them to "reef" the three sails, furling them to a much smaller size to capture less wind. The job took all three of them lashing ropes, and they worked so efficiently that Marie didn't worry even as the skies grew dark too early in the day. She eyed the emergency dinghy lashed behind the boat and felt reassured by its sight. Her stomach lurched with the waves, but she had faith in her crew.

Lightning made the clouds glow. Thunder was a giant stalking above them.

But when the rain came, they opened their mouths and savored it, all of them drenched.

And that was all. The rainfall slowed, then stopped, and the Boat Man steered toward a wide gap in the clouds promising calmer skies ahead for the night sail. Marie could not have been prouder of their group—herself most of all. She'd had a nightmare about a storm, yet she hadn't lost her head when a storm appeared. Her dreams did *not* control her.

The good feeling stopped as soon as she gave in to sleepiness and went down to her cabin, a bit unsteady on her feet as the boat swayed. Edmund was already inside, and she was surprised to see half a dozen guns spread across the bare cushion. The overhead bulb might have been loose, making Edmund's movements look herky-jerky as he whipped around to look at her with accusation in the unsteady light.

"Did you take it?" he said.

"Take . . . ?"

"My nine-millimeter is gone," he said. "My Glock. It's my favorite."

"Are you sure you brought it?" The guns on the bed looked alike to her, only different colors. He had referred to each of them as his favorite at one time or another.

"Then it was *him*," Edmund said, ignoring her question. "He came in here and went through my stuff and he took it. He *stole* it!"

His voice was rising. The familiar clenching returned to Marie's stomach, worse than the storm—that feeling that everything could go horribly wrong in an instant—so she rested her hands on Edmund's bare, sun-reddened shoulders the way she had imagined Granpè Jean comforting her. She tried to transfer reason to Edmund by osmosis through her palms.

"Edmund . . . everything has been fine so far. You're working great with him."

He yanked away from her, probably more violently than he'd meant to. She'd forgotten how much his sunburn must hurt. She lost her balance, bracing herself against the wall. "That doesn't mean he can touch *my* stuff. He has *no right*! We don't need him with us anyway! You know he looks at you funny, right?"

"Shhhhh," she said. She didn't want the Boat Man to hear and come down to their cabin. In his current state, Edmund might pick up the closest gun and shoot him. How had she lulled herself into believing everything would be fine? Edmund was Edmund. (And *didn't* the Boat Man look at her funny? Edmund had noticed it, too.)

"I'll go up and talk to him," she said. Even as she said it, rain pelted the boat again, and the rocking grew urgent beneath her feet. The Boat Man had stayed above to keep an eye on the weather, and the deck was the last place she wanted to be.

"Yeah, let's go right now—" Edmund said.

"Let me go alone. If he took it, I *promise* I'll get it back."

In the flickering light, Edmund's face seemed to be squirming with his desire to hurt the Boat Man. "And he better say sorry! And he better never do it again!"

"Yes, yes," she said. "I promise. Give me five minutes. Okay? Just stay right here."

He bit his lip so hard that she thought he might draw blood. Then Edmund nodded. Thank goodness he trusted her; she still had that, at least.

Edmund snatched a gun from the bed and thrust this toward her. "Take this."

"Stop it, Edmund—I won't need it." She mostly said this to show him what trust looked like, but she regretted it as she moved toward the galley empty handed. What if the Boat Man had taken the gun? Edmund was fanatical about his weapons, so she doubted he had counted wrong. She tried to imagine how a conversation might go if he argued. She would smile and be polite.

—*I'm so sorry, Captain, but you have to give it back.*

—*I thought we said share and share alike. Y'all ate my eggs today.*

—*The food, yes. My water. Just not Edmund's guns. Not unless he says so. He's very sensitive about them. They belonged to his family. They're like heirlooms to him.*

—*Oh, okay, I get it. Here ya go, girlie.*

Hearing the conversation in her head made it feel plausible. She wouldn't mind if he called her *girlie* this time, as long as he gave her the gun. As long as he didn't turn out to be a mistake so soon.

Marie had just sighed away the tight feeling of dread in her chest when the room tumbled like a carnival ride to one side, bending her over the galley table with an *Oof!* as the water cartons and dishes crashed to the floor. Edmund cried out from the cabin, his guns clanking as they scattered and fell. She heard the *thunk* of him landing hard, too.

Beyond the door above her, the Boat Man yelled and cursed. Something about a sail.

THE BOAT MAN

"Get the fuck up here!"

That she heard fine. And strange clanking sounds from the front of the boat she'd never heard before. She still didn't know much about boats, but that sound wasn't good news.

The boat briefly righted and then heeled right again (*starboard?*), the angle slightly less severe. Marie got over her surprise and kept clawing her way to the companionway, propelling herself with the edge of the table, then the kitchen counter, then the sturdy stair rail. Her foot landed on the first step, then her left, and up. Motion knocked her head against the wall, like a whip's lash to her temple, but she didn't lose her grip in the stairwell. Three steps felt like a hundred.

The door opened above her as lightning flared in the skies with bright veins. All she saw was his silhouette painted in the brightness behind him.

"—lost the headsail!" the Boat Man was saying. "The furling line snapped! The headsail was *shit*."

He reached his hand out to her, and she took it without thinking. He hauled her up the last step and put his face too close to hers to shout in her ear above the storm. "I've gotta go up and secure that sail! Might be just a squall, but you two stay in the cockpit and do what I say!"

In the next flash of lightning, she saw the wildly swinging ropes of her nightmare. The tattered sail was making a *whoo whoo whoo* sound in the strong gusts, flapping wild.

Marie wasn't sure, but she thought she might be wetting her pants.

"I need the gun!" she said. "You took it! I have to give it back to him."

He slapped her face. Not hard—enough to get her attention. But the sting vibrated to Marie's bones, paralyzing her. He shouted in her ear again, as painful as the slap. "Did you hear what I said? We lost the sail! Stay in the cockpit!"

A rope snapped ahead of them, dancing in the wind. The Boat Man's head turned as if it had called to him. Still reeling with the boat's wild rocking, he reached toward the metal bar to hoist himself toward the sail. Water sprayed just beneath him, splashing at her feet.

"I have to give it back!" she shouted.

He hesitated long enough to look back at her one more time with a terrible sneer, or at least it seemed like one in the night's shadows.

"*Shut the fuck up and do as I say!*" His voice was a shriek, or was his voice the wind? A lightning flash made him grow to the size of a giant, his beard coming to life on his face, twisting and writhing. Were his eyes glowing bright red? How had she never seen his true image before? Only the storm revealed it.

When he turned away from her, reaching for the iron bar to support him, Marie ran toward him with all of her strength. Only later did she realize she was screaming a war cry that honored her name—*La Guerre*—as she thrust out her palms and pushed him hard in the center of his bony back. And he flew so far that she thought he might soar above her.

The Boat Man's arms pinwheeled, trying to hold on to anything solid, as he somersaulted headfirst and fell into the inky water. The storm and flapping sail were so loud that she didn't hear him splash—but his yell went silent in the churning sea.

Marie panted, stunned at herself. Stunned by the boat's unruly rocking. A fever lifted from her, as if she had dreamed that the Boat Man was standing ever so close to her. Slapping her. Shouting in her ear. *What had she done?*

Marie might have stood there clinging for balance in the cockpit with the question rolling over in her mind for days—if not for the first gunshot.

The *popping* sound wasn't as loud in a storm, but she recognized it and whirled around. Edmund had emerged from the galley, leaning over the railing where one unlucky jolt would send him tumbling into the water, too. He had put on his red leather jacket, bright in the muzzle flashes. *Pop. Pop. Pop.*

Edmund was firing into the water.

THE BOAT MAN

"We don't need you!" Edmund was screaming. "We can go by ourselves!"

The popping sound gave way to clicks: he had emptied his gun. Marie grabbed Edmund by his jacket collar and pulled him away from the railing. Water pounding the side of the sailboat spilled over them both.

"We need to put on our harnesses!" she said. "And we gotta get that front sail down!"

Edmund stared up at her. In the lightning, she couldn't tell if his face was only drenched or if he had tears in his eyes. He blinked as if he, too, were emerging from a dream.

"Edmund! Did you hear me?!" she said.

He leered an unholy grin at her. She prayed that her eyes did not look as wild as his, but surely, they did. She was not the sensible one, after all. Maybe no one was sensible anymore. Perhaps they were all just swimming as fast and as hard as they could, trying to stay in the eye of the storm.

"Aye, aye, Captain," Edmund said.

He winked at her exactly like the Boat Man.

THE STORY I TELL IS THE STORY OF SOME OF US
Paul Tremblay

Hey, there. Hi. Whoa. It's okay. I'm by myself. Didn't mean to sneak up on you. I mean, fine, I did sneak up on you, but I didn't mean to scare you. You look exhausted, by the way. Are you all right?

All five foot five of me is unarmed. See? Don't let the field jacket fool you. I don't even know what epaulets are for. You know, these buttoned thingies on the shoulder? Never mind.

Yeah, I know, sorry. I wasn't following you. Well, I kinda was, but only for a day, maybe two. I was trying not to be a creep about it even when I watched you twitching in your sleep.

I can't tell when I'm joking, either. I am a friend, not a foe. Probably.

Yeah, I know about the dreams. Let's talk about those later.

I saw the fire and I decided you didn't look like a vampire, or a cannibal, or a cannibal vampire.

It's only weird when you say it, dude. Sheesh, you know how to make a girl feel welcome.

Hey, relax, I'm just fucking with you.

Mercy. And before you ask and before either one of us answers the loaded where-ya-headed question, let me honor our palaver by the campfire with a story.

The short version is a nineteen-year-old, let's call him Art Barbara, had always feared that his life wouldn't be important within the *grand scheme* of things. Whether anyone's life was of import, or cruelly held more import by comparison to the billions of less fortunate, was a different question entirely. Art supposed it all depended on how grand the scheme was within the context of the abrading passage of time. When Art was given clear evidence that his life did have a kind of cosmic value, or currency—with all that word's degraded meaning and political implications—that evidence came in the form of a choice.

Settle in. I'm going to tell the long version.

When Art came home in mid-May after completing his freshman year at Providence College, he was feeling good about himself. As good as he had ever felt. He was fully recovered from the previous summer's spinal fusion surgery that had straightened his crooked, scoliosis spine. College was indeed the opportunity to, if not reinvent himself, then more fully become who he wanted to be. His new college friends called him "Punk Art" and not "Bones" or other hey-eat-a-sandwich-you-rail nicknames he had been tagged with as a younger teen. If he never saw another person from his high school years again, including your humble storyteller, that would've been fine with him.

What else do you need to know about Art? He was extra-willowy after the surgery, and with his long face and freaky fingers, he would've made a great Nosferatu, but he was afraid of his dark basement. He was prone to melancholia and would've made a great goth, but he hated the Smiths and the Cure.

The universe fired two torpedoes at Art, scuttling his burgeoning inner peace. The first was finding out Dad was sleeping on the living room couch because his parents were in the process of separating. Despite Art being old enough to understand Mom and Dad were no different than any other pair of adults mired in an unraveling relationship, he reacted to the news poorly, like he was a surly preteen. If

THE STORY I TELL IS THE STORY OF SOME OF US

Art had been more observant, he would've recognized their marriage's fraying threads years earlier—I had tried telling him by not telling him. Anyway, he spent his first month back home avoiding his parents when he wasn't working his summer gig at the United Shoe Factory.

I don't have to tell you the second torpedo was Captain Trips.

Let's fast-forward, and I'll fill in other backstory details as needed.

Unlike the rest of us who were still alive—or dead but dreaming, right?—and had started wandering toward the west, Art remained in his empty house in Beverly, Massachusetts. He was grief-stricken and shell-shocked, but he had enough food, mostly boxes of dry cereal, and he had enough double-A batteries for his Walkman. He had scrounged a sweet Gibson Flying V guitar on which he was teaching himself his favorite punk songs. The desire to learn the next song was the only thing keeping him going.

On the afternoon of July 12, it was dreary, drizzly, and unseasonably cool. There was a knock on his front door and an older woman called out his name. Art considered answering with the guitar still strapped to his back, and if necessary, he could use it as a weapon. But what was the point of fighting/surviving if he wrecked his beloved guitar? He left it leaning against a wall in the living room, to keep a watch over things.

Art opened the door. The white woman was somewhere in her late forties or early fifties. She had short, feathered brown hair, held an umbrella, and was dressed like a TV sitcom mom with high-waisted jeans and a thin, lemon-yellow sweater. She smiled warmly, showing off nicotine-stained teeth, and she sighed a you-poor-thing sigh. She introduced herself with "Everyone who knows me, calls me Hilly," spiced with a Maine accent, and then she asked if she could come in out of the rain. Art mumbled an agreement. Agree-mumbling even when he didn't want to agree was his default setting. He should've known better than to invite a stranger into his house without considering the potential consequences. The world is full of vampires, metaphorically speaking.

Hilly asked if he was alone, and without an ounce of self-preservation Art said, "Yes." I would've lied, or more likely had joked that a friend stayed hidden down in the basement. You know, something that was funny, but also vaguely dangerous.

Yes, just like my joke about standing over you while you slept. Don't interrupt me again.

Partly out of habit, Art led her to the kitchen, though it wasn't a very bright or airy space, especially on such a gray day. There was nowhere else on the first floor for them to sit comfortably. The living room and TV room were nests of cassette tapes, clothes, blankets, pillows, and magazines. Seated at the round kitchen table, Hilly was weakly backlit by one of the two shaded windows, so she was mostly in shadow, or had become mostly shadow, as though she wasn't fully there.

She asked how Art was sleeping and if he'd had any dreams, and before he could answer she said that he looked wan, washed, and the bags under his eyes were as purple as plums. We can safely assume Art was dreaming at night, but we can't yet assume what kinds of dreams he was having. Even if I had stood over him and had watched him twitching in his sleep night after night, I couldn't know his dreams. There are limits to my storytelling powers, as there are limits on all storytellers.

Art did not trust Hilly. If her true purpose or form hadn't been fully revealed yet, it had been outlined within his shadowy kitchen. He played it cagey, admitting to dreaming, but refusing to describe them.

What else do you need to know about Art? He was many things, but he was no fool, or no more foolish than the rest of us.

Hilly said, "A group of us are headed west, to Las Vegas. Give me cheap all-you-can-eat buffets and roulette wheels and I'm as happy as a clam. I used to go to Vegas once a year with my husband and sister, obviously before they were taken away from me, before so much was senselessly taken away from us all, yes?" She paused to leave room for Art to commiserate, to share his own tale of catastrophic woe, but how she spoke about the deaths of her loved ones and the apocalyptic ravages of the superflu wasn't rooted in grief. It was exultant. Despite the other terrors to come, her rapturous tone scared Art the most. She continued, "Are you surprised that someone like me liked going to Vegas? Don't be. The city welcomed all comers, and will still welcome us. That walking fella—surely you've heard of him by now." She paused again, and Art still didn't respond. "Well," she said, "if not, you will. He gets around. He promised we'd be welcomed in Vegas again. As it was carefully explained to me, there's a coming battle and everyone has to choose sides. The old ways, the ways that got us into this whole fudging mess in the first place, versus the new ways. There has to be new ways, don't there? We can't go on being the same anymore. It's not possible. You're a smart young man. You know that. And here's the kicker: you-know-who gave me and my merry little band your name and where to find you. He said you, Art, are the fulcrum in the upcoming battle. Little old you. I know it's a lot. And don't take this the wrong way, as hard as it is for me to believe that a baby beanpole like you is one of the most important people left alive, I know it to be true because he said so."

Normally, Art was the kind of guy who fumbled and spilled his words all over the place, and only later could he build the perfect thing to say, or at least what it was he had meant to say. But Art was up to this moment—and, yeah, I'm proud of him. He stood up from his chair and said, "I'll pass, and I'd like you to leave now. Unless you can show me a better way to play a B7 chord."

He walked out of the kitchen and into the dining room, heading toward the small foyer and front door, expecting Hilly to follow. He got about halfway across the room and stopped. He locked eyes on his unlatched basement door, which was tucked away on the far side of the wall and in the corner. What kind of house had a basement door in its dining room? This one did. And that basement door with its chipped off-white paint was unlatched. He had left it latched. He always left it latched.

Art turned his back to the door and Hilly was still seated at the kitchen table, a vaguely human shape now fully consumed by shadow. There could've been anyone on earth sitting at that table.

"I don't want us getting off on the wrong foot, Art, but time is short. And no choice is the same as a choice," Hilly said. "Our guy is patient, but only to a point. He's also a realist. If you won't choose to come with us, then you become a problem to be solved. Being the fulcrum means that if you go over to the other side, we will lose." Hilly got up from the table and just about floated from the kitchen into the dining room. "*He* won't let that happen."

Timed with the period in her sentence, the creaky basement door swung halfway open.

Now listen, I had unlatched the door earlier that morning when Art was still asleep. And yeah, I was eavesdropping on their conversation, and I swung the door halfway open. No evil power opening the door here, just me. I'm not saying there's no such thing as evil power, and maybe one of the words in that phrase is redundant. I'd been staying in Art's basement for a few weeks by that point, and without him knowing. I know that sounds weird and creepy, and it's a long and kind of sad story, and maybe I'll tell it to you at another campfire. What you need to know about Art and me is that we were best friends and then we had a calamitous falling-out the summer before. Mistakes were made. Things were said, including Art saying that I was always dragging him down, that I was an energy vampire, metaphorically speaking, of course. Can you believe that? It was such a mean thing to say, especially when I was always just trying to help him out. At the time, him calling me an energy vampire was unforgivable. Seems silly now, I know. Even with the world mostly dead, I couldn't bring myself to ask Art to say sorry to me, or for me to say sorry to him for whatever my transgressions were. Regardless, I was still worried about him and I couldn't think of anywhere else to go and hole up, so yeah, I camped out in his basement, figuring we'd talk it out eventually.

THE STORY I TELL IS THE STORY OF SOME OF US

Hey, forget about the me-in-the-basement part for now. Okay?

Just know the reason why I opened the door at that moment was to make sure Art knew who he was fucking with, that there was a truly bad someone out there capable of doing some heavy, scary shit. Or I should say *someones*. If I've learned anything, it's that one person, even this Walkin Dude guy, is powerless by themselves; they have to be given power or take it from others. By the sound of it, Art had already made the right choice, but I wanted to give him a creepy-door-opening, a faux-supernatural nudge that made sure he stayed true to what he'd decided.

As Hilly kept on telling Art all the terrible things that would happen to him—hell of a recruitment pitch, right?—he stared at the basement door, or rather at the dark space the open door exposed. He imagined—or did he?—Hilly's merry band of fellow travelers crouched on the basement stairs, hackles up, their heads low, long faces growing longer, grinning their vulpine grins in the dark. Oh, what big eyes and teeth they had.

Hilly cut short her death-pain-madness stream-of-consciousness rant and repeatedly said Art's name until he turned to face her. Then she asked, weaponizing her sweet, motherly delivery, "Are you afraid, Art? You should be. We can do the worst things you can possibly imagine."

"Worst things?" Art said, and he laughed, the kind that was a *fuck you*. Then he told Hilly the story of his mom and dad. In the dwindling number of days before the superflu outbreak, his parents' formerly icy détente had deteriorated into an aggressive campaign of scorched-earth not-speaking. If one entered a room, the other would storm off into another room, or leave the house entirely. If Mom was out, Dad sat on the couch, muttering that he could watch TV in his house if he wanted, imagining himself as the not-so-righteously aggrieved, but he had a child's *How did any of this happen?* look on his face. If Dad was out, Mom sat in the kitchen smoking cigarettes, angrily, ashes flinging and crumbling everywhere. The smoke was steam emanating directly from her head. When the superflu went national, the only area in which those two could coexist was the TV room. There, they watched the twenty-four-hour cable news network from opposite ends of the couch, wordlessly clutching their recriminations as though they were life jackets, even as the world had suddenly become both too big and too small. A thousand pages would not be enough for Art to describe the horror of what happened next. He didn't remember which parent was sick first. Perhaps they both fell ill at the same time. The greedy virus ravaged them quickly. Dad remained on the couch on the first floor and Mom stayed upstairs in their bedroom. For two nights, his parents coughed their glass-filled coughs and cried and muttered gibberish in their fevered sleeps, oblivious to the distant conversation they were having with one another. Art alternated attending to one parent and then the other, wiping their foreheads with cold cloths and turning them over onto their sides so they could breathe better, and when one was shouting or crying, he told them one of their favorite stories about Art from when he was little. One tale featured a two-year-old Art somehow scaling more than halfway up the length of a curtain. Another detailed Art's brief phase of barging into the bathroom when either one of his parents were using the toilet, and he would point and laugh-shout, "Pew!" while doing a special bathroom dance. Art wished he could remember those stories from the point of view of toddler-Art, but he only remembered what his parents had told him. When his parents died, would those foundational stories of who Art once was die, too? On the third day after his parents first presented superflu symptoms, an exhausted and overwhelmed Art fell asleep sitting at the kitchen table. He woke to a quiet, still house, and he knew his parents were both gone. He eventually wandered into the living room, but Dad wasn't on the couch. Art found him upstairs, his body slumped and pressed against the closed bedroom door. The door wasn't locked, but Art had to force it open, as Mom wasn't in her bed, either. Her body had similarly pooled against the other side of the door.

THE STORY I TELL IS THE STORY OF SOME OF US

Art ended his story with "And I won't even bore you with the vicious fucking joke that was me trying to burn their bodies and almost burning down the garage and myself, while, somehow, barely burning them, so I gave up and buried their unburnt parts. In the long list of worst-things, the failed pyre might not even be top five. You know what is top five? Finding Mom's handprints and Dad's handprints on either side of their bedroom door, outlined in blood and mucus. I'm sure you and your guy can scare and hurt me, but you can't do the worst to me. Sorry, that already happened. Now get the fuck out of my house before I bash your head in with my Flying V guitar while playing a power chord."

The shadows lifted from Hilly, and she was diminished. Perhaps she was moved by what Art had shared. Perhaps she was alone, cosmically alone, and afraid of what might happen to her if she failed the recruiting mission. She said, "You have until tonight to change your mind. And I hope you do. You do seem like such a nice boy. I'll show myself out." And she did.

Art shut and latched the basement door before I could. Now, I wish I'd called out his name, and let him know I was there. Maybe things would be different if I had. Instead, I stayed silent. He lingered at the door, contemplating the mysteries of the craven universe in which a creepy basement door opened by itself, and then he went back to his Walkman and guitar. Without the fuzz of distortion, it took me a few trips through the verse to figure out he was playing "Something I Learned Today," by Hüsker Dü.

Do you know the song? Ugh. Who do you listen to? Wait, don't tell me. Let me pretend you're cool.

If I could sing, I would sing it to you, as it might be the better way to tell Art's story, to tell the story of us, or some of us.

I know you're thinking how can songs and stories mean something now, right? How can a song be worth anything while we're sitting on a giant pile of the bones of the dead, metaphorically speaking? Not that we haven't always been sitting on that bone pile, especially in America. But also, that song is worth everything. If you don't get that, you don't have a heart. Not a delicious one, anyway.

I'm going to try to forget you told me that nauseating one-hit wonder is your favorite song. Jesus.

Let's get back to Art.

There was a second knock on his door less than hour after Hilly left.

A man called out, "Hello? Anybody home? I have Girl Scout cookies," and then he laughed to let his audience, both intended and not intended, know he was a jokester. "None of the Thin Mints, though. Man, I'd give my left arm for a box of those."

Was he supposed to be charming? Jaunty? Nonthreatening? Art feared the Las Vegas enthusiasts were sending the next wave. Still, and as annoyed as Ebenezer Scrooge at his visitations, Art opened the door.

"You're Art, yeah? Hey, my name is Henry. It's very nice to meet you." The dripping-wet, medium-sized white man held up his empty hands. "Nothing up my sleeves but rain, I promise." Could you trust anyone making promises within the first thirty seconds of meeting them? It took all my self-control to keep from yelling out to Art, to tell him to shut the door in this dude's face.

"I already told Hilly my answer," Art said.

Henry tilted his head like the good dog he was, then smiled a bright white smile that launched a ship or two. "Good. I have no idea who Hilly is," he said. "She's not with us. So she must be with them." Could you trust anybody talking about *us* and *them*? What you should know about Art is that, as a fellow punk music devotee, he judged people as being in one of those two *us* or *them* categories, but it was never a binding moral judgment or purity test. Do you know the difference? Art was way more forgiving or naive—you choose—than I was.

Remember that show *Family Ties*, with Michael J. Fox? This Henry guy was the grown-up, full yuppie version of Alex P. Keaton. He wore a yellow, short-sleeved polo shirt and jeans, and he was ten or so years older than Art. His skin was unblemished. Art noticed because his own skin was always threatening volcanic acne eruption.

"Hey, um, is it all right if I come in?" Henry asked. "I'm sopping wet."

Art let him in. It's worth repeating Art should've known better than to invite a stranger into his house. The world is full of all kinds of vampires, blah blah blah.

Nah, don't worry. You letting me sit by the fire isn't the same thing as inviting me into your house. I promise.

Art told Henry to stay by the door and he'd get him a towel, but Henry followed him into the mess of a living room. Henry said he liked Art's place and it reminded him of his fraternity house (of course) and after spying the Flying V he said, "Hey, cool axe. Can you play that 'Dig Your Man' song?" and Art died a little inside.

The more Henry rambled on, the more I wanted to throw myself down the basement stairs, or bury myself in the dirt floor and go to sleep for a year, or a decade or two. But Art, he played along and answered questions about music and his age and where we went to school. What you need to know about Art is that he liked to be liked, more than most. I think he cut Henry some slack, too, because the dude was clearly nervous.

After he gave Henry a towel, there was a lull in their conversation, a heavy one. Henry thanked Art and said, "I'd been staying up in Gloucester with some people, but we're, um, migrating. Do you know why I'm here? Or how I know your name?"

"You want to start a band?" Art said.

Okay, fine, Art didn't say that. I would've said that. Instead, Art did his mumble-answer thing that was not really an answer.

Henry, undeterred, asked, "Did you know I was coming today?"

"No," Art said.

"Oh, that's okay, I guess. But I was kind of hoping you might've been, like, shown me in—in a dream? Sounds crazy when I say it out loud like that."

"It does."

"Well, it can't be helped. You look like you haven't been sleeping much. No offense. Can I ask you about your dreams? Have you been dreaming of a cornfield, and, um, a godly woman—"

"Yeah, I have dreams," Art said, and slung his guitar strap over his shoulder. "Now, what do you want?"

Henry said, "A group of us are heeding the call to go west, to Boulder, Colorado. Fresh mountain air and all that. Hey, did you follow college football at all? I'm a Notre Dame grad and I was down in Miami on New Year's to watch the Orange Bowl with my fiancée, Patrice. She was a bigger fan of Notre Dame than I was. Man, what I wouldn't give to watch another game with her, just one more game." Henry paused to leave room for Art to commiserate, to share his own tale of catastrophic woe, but how he spoke felt more rehearsed than being rooted in grief. Maybe that wasn't a fair assessment. Maybe it sounded that way because Henry had to practice keeping from melting down into a screaming, crying fit. Unlikely, but you never know. Henry continued. "Notre Dame beat U of Colorado in the Orange Bowl. Pounded them Buffalos, who were up to some shady recruiting, if you ask me. Not as bad as U Miami, though. I guess some cheaters did win in the end, in the before times. Now we're headed to the same town where U Colorado is. Life is weird. I don't know why we're not being called to go to Notre Dame in South Bend, Indiana. But I'm just the messenger, right?" Henry paused again.

Art strummed a G chord. Henry asked Art to kindly not play, as he was getting to his point. Art responded with a D chord.

The rest of Henry's spiel sounded a lot like Hilly's pitch. He said, "There is a coming battle, and everyone has to choose sides. The old, godless ways got us into this whole mess. We couldn't go on ignoring that anymore. We had to fight for what could be right and good again in the name of God. You look like a smart guy. You had the dreams, too. You know this to be true. And here's the kicker: the voice in our dreams gave us your name and where to find

THE STORY I TELL IS THE STORY OF SOME OF US

you. It said that you, Art, are the fulcrum. Yes, you. I know it's a lot. And don't take this the wrong way. It's as hard for me to swallow that we're headed to Boulder as it is for me to believe that you're the most important man left alive. But, I know it to be true because, well, God said so."

"God?"

"Yeah. You know, He speaks through the woman in the dreams." Henry went on another rant that I'll trim down a bit, saying that the people on the other side were in thrall to evil incarnate, to the devil himself, and that they would destroy us all if Art didn't help. Henry didn't know what the plan was or exactly where Art fit into it, but only that, for now, Art *was* the plan. Art would tip the scales in their favor and "eradicate evil from the world once and for all." Henry was exultant. Despite the other terrors to come, his rapturous tone scared Art the most.

Art shook his head and said, "None of this should come down to me. It's all bullshit."

"The Lord works in mysterious ways, yeah?" Henry said. "Look, I know that you're scared, Art."

Art punched out a few more chords, short and sharp. He said, "I'm not scared. I'm angry. You should be, too."

Art told Henry about how the day after his parents died, his two younger cousins, Erin and Dan, ages thirteen and nine, showed up on his doorstep. Their parents had died, too, and they didn't know where else to go or what to do. Their first night at his house, Art dug out a road map from his mom's car, and they marked up a route they would take to Provincetown on the tip of Cape Cod. They unanimously decided to live on one of the ends of the world. The next morning, Erin and Dan were full of phlegm and were too weak to climb out of their shared pullout couch bed in the TV room. Before she became incoherent with fever, Erin narrated future versions of the Erin and Dan who lived in an alternate universe, one in which the superflu never happened. She went on for hours, giving an incredibly almost impossibly detailed account of their hectic high school years, romantic partners, colleges attended, friends made and friends lost, one with a career in radio as a production engineer and the other bouncing from one odd job to the next but finding happiness in their freedom, the cities lived in and cities visited, their hopes and dreams, their joys and longings, their successes and failures. Dan silently listened to his sister, never once objecting to her vision. When it became too much for Art, he'd retreat to the kitchen and cry, but he still heard her melancholic and beautiful story echoing through his house.

Art paused, seemingly mid-story, wiped his forearm across his eyes, took off his guitar, and said, "I'm not going anywhere with you or anyone else."

I have to admit, that answer was a complete and total shock to me. And it was a shock to Henry, too. He spluttered and stuttered, eventually saying, "Hey, look, I get it. I do. But you're not the only one who suffered—"

"That's exactly my point."

"You think God made the superflu? Word on the street is that it was man-made."

"I'm sure it was. But what about all of the suffering in every decade of every century, and it was allowed to happen, which, okay, it was consistent behavior, at least. The problem I have is that God chooses to show up *now*."

Henry rubbed his head like it hurt, like the ideas were too big to fit inside. "Hey, man, I'm no theologian, but God has always been around. And we don't know how often, um, God intervened on our behalf, right? We can't question—"

"We should always question. And here's a few more for you: Is God showing up now because he forgot about us previously? Are we an oil spill that happened due to neglect and the Almighty is rushing in to clean up? Was the entirety of human existence orchestrated—the savagery, the knowledge, the longing, the loving and the hating, the genocides, the wars, the nuclear bombs, the engineered viruses—to get to this exact point in time so those who remain could, what, take up arms in His name for the final showdown?"

Henry shouted, "Stop! Enough! I—I can't believe you're choosing the other side—you're choosing evil!"

"I never said I would go with the people headed to Las Vegas. Fuck them, too."

"You choosing not to be with us is choosing to be with them."

"No it isn't. I'm choosing a third option, which is to reject the both of you, to reject any further demands for blood sacrifice. I refuse to participate."

"So, what, you're just going to sit on the sidelines and do nothing while evil threatens us all?"

"If anyone comes to my doorstep, I will help them. And if they ask, I will advise them to not go west. The seafood is way better out here."

Henry then ranted about the will of God, the honor of being chosen, His enemies would be bathed in cleansing, righteous fire, blah blah blah. You have to admit, Henry was proving himself not to be the best representative for the good guys.

Art continued fully embracing his El-ahrairah, Prince with a Thousand Enemies, role when speaking with Lord—

Huh? No. It's a reference to *Watership Down*. Dude, read a book. We'll hit a library tomorrow. You have plenty of time for reading now.

Anyway, by the time Henry finished his fire-and-brimstone entreaty, he was sweating and breathing heavy.

"Look, I don't mean to be a wiseass," Art said. "It has been a rough month for us all. I'll admit that I am scared. You should be, too, by the way. I don't know why you think being chosen or even noticed by that kind of power is a blessing and not a fundamentally terrifying curse. I mean—fuck, I don't know. I'm not explaining my position very well. But, um, okay, how's this: a week or so ago, when I was in the kitchen, crying and listening to my cousin Erin's voice narrate the beautiful story of what could've been, or what could be somewhere else and sometime else, *her* voice was the voice of God. That's the voice I entrust my humanity to. Not the one you're hearing."

Henry loosened a deep sigh. "I'm going to come back later with others, with my group, and you'll see they're good people, Art. People worth fighting to save."

"If I say no again, what will your good people do then?"

Henry left without answering, without thanking Art again for the use of his towel. Once the front door closed, Art walked around the house, looping a circuit through the first-floor rooms. He muttered to himself. It was difficult for me to hear, but I think he was rehashing what he and Henry had said, and he was trying to come up with better ways to explain himself. Or maybe Art was trying to better explain himself to himself. About ten minutes into his walk around the house, he stopped in the dining room and punched the wall. I don't know why he needed more pain, more hurt, but he did. His knuckles indented the wallpaper and plaster. He shook out his hand and then resumed his laps, walking faster and faster, until his walk was a jog and his jog was a sprint, and eventually he ran out of gas and collapsed into a chair at the kitchen table. He cried softly, as though afraid someone would hear him, and he fell asleep.

I hated seeing Art like this. And I was gobsmacked over what had transpired during the visits. I was proud of him, but also, I have to admit, for the first time, a little afraid of him, too. So much so I thought about sneaking out of the basement and going somewhere else. But I stayed and listened and pondered.

Art woke up when it was full dark, inside and out. He lit a candle that squatted on a small plate and he slowly carried it out of the kitchen.

I couldn't take it anymore. I had to say something. I unlatched the basement door—

Huh? Never you mind how I did that. Don't interrupt now. We're almost at the end.

I opened the creaking basement door slowly, trying not to startle him. He froze in place with the candle dish quivering in his cupped hands. Once he saw it was me, he shook his head and laughed a little. I laughed, too, and our laughter grew and stretched out. It was the best way, the only way, to say hi and break the glacier that had grown between us.

I wanted to tell him I understood why he was angry. Believe me, did I ever. I wanted to tell him I appreciated the sentiment of his rejecting the visitors and their offered choices. I wanted to tell him he'd never been more fully, maddeningly, wonderfully Art Barbara than he was now. I wanted to tell him he was noble, but it was a chasing-windmills kind of noble. I wanted to tell him he was not being pragmatic or realistic, which meant that he had passed over the border into the land of the immature and foolish. I wanted to tell him that the phrase of cutting off your nose to spite your face had been invented for him. I wanted to tell him that blood had always and would always lubricate the grinding gears of the universe. But he didn't need to hear any of that from me. Not then.

"Hey, you and me, let's go to Boulder," I said. "We don't have to go with anyone else. Certainly not Henry. He's probably destined to die from an infection after getting a splinter, or maybe Touchdown Jesus will call him back to Notre Dame."

Art stopped laughing, but he'd kept a half smile on his face. He said, "No." It was quiet, soft, and I hoped it meant, despite everything, that we were still friends.

"Fair enough. Let's go somewhere else, then. *Anywhere* else," I said. "Find a place where you can plug in a guitar amp and rock out."

"I'm not leaving," he said.

In retrospect, I regret saying anything to him. I think he refused my let's-make-like-a-tree-and-leave options because I presented them. If I'd instead found a way to lead him into suggesting we flee the house, then he'd still be with us. It would be me and him sitting by this fire with you. And that fucking haunts me.

I said, "I know it sucks, but you really should leave. There are far scarier things afoot than an energy vampire."

His half smile melted away. In the flickering candlelight, he looked so scared and so damned young, younger than the beautiful, maddening, obstinate nineteen-year-old he was. Tears filled his eyes and he couldn't look at me anymore. I fear, in that moment, I had stolen his hard-won, regained inner peace and I cannot forgive myself for doing so. Maybe I am an energy vampire after all. Art nodded at me, or he nodded at everything, tears rolling down his cheeks, and he left the dining room, taking the light with him.

I knew I couldn't save him, but I couldn't leave him. Not yet. At the very least, I could be Art's witness. So, I went back down to the basement and waited in the dark. I didn't have to wait long.

There was a pounding on the front door, then a hyena-like laugh. A mob of purposefully heavy footsteps circled the house's perimeter, and there were harsh knocks on the windows and outside walls, and they called out Art's name. Just his name, over and over. They sounded like crows. But they weren't crows. Their footsteps lightened and multiplied and were now paw steps. The tittering and laughter became howls and growls, and sharp-pitched barks. One of them smashed through the door off the kitchen and the others swarmed inside, their nails and claws scrabbled across the linoleum. I still heard their scrabbling nails over Art's awful screams, and I heard the nails after, as I opened the bulkhead and crept out of the basement and into the night.

About two blocks away, I had to duck into a row of bushes to avoid the pious tool Henry and a group of six others. The others carried long flashlights and baseball bats and one had a shotgun. Make of that what you will.

Whatever I made of it, it pissed me off, so after they passed me, I jumped out from my hiding spot, further inserting myself into this story, and shouted, "Hey, Hank!"

The group stopped and turned, but did not double back toward me. "You don't have to worry about Art anymore," I said. "He's gone."

Henry shouted, "He went with them?"

THE STORY I TELL IS THE STORY OF SOME OF US

"No, dumbass," I said. "Art is gone. Gone, daddy, gone."

On cue, the night air echoed with howls. I've always had impeccable timing.

Almost apologetically, as if a spell had been broken, a few in Henry's group mumbled questions, asking if it was too late, could they still help Art, but they stopped asking in the weight of my silence. Henry invited me to go with them. I laughed and told him that maybe I'd run into him later, hoping it came off as mysteriously and threateningly pithy.

So yeah, that's where Art's story ends. I miss him like a lost limb.

What? No, I haven't run into Henry again. Not yet. That certainly would make a cleaner and tidier kind of end. But good stories, real ones, or the ones that feel real, don't wrap up so neatly.

Besides, stories don't really end, do they? Well, I suppose the stories will end when all the storytellers are gone. But there are still a few of us stubbornly kicking around.

Let's wait until the morning to talk about where you or I are headed next. Let's not spoil this moment we had, are having. I want to savor it, like the fine meal it was.

Hey, man, you're exhausted. Look at you, can barely keep your eyes open. You get some rest.

Don't worry, I'm not tired yet. I'll stay up and tend the fire. Keep watch for a bit. Make sure none of them cannibal vampires show up. They are a pesky lot.

Tomorrow.

You and I, we'll figure out where the story goes from here tomorrow. It's gotta go somewhere, right?

Sweet dreams.

THE MOSQUE AT THE END OF THE WORLD

Usman T. Malik

They met the blind mullah and his dog by a haunted mosque in Sheikhupura on the outskirts of Lahore.

The mosque, a narrow, green-domed structure flanked by two minarets, was situated on the highway between a tire shop and a bakery. In the shade of its eastern wall, the old man lay on a charpai, puffing smoke from a gurgling hookah. By his head a cloud of flies buzzed over a jar of honey placed on a stool, an oakwood walking stick propped against the latter. The dog, a droopy-eared spotted mongrel half-hidden under the jute-twine bed, panted by the man's sandals in the afternoon heat. Occasionally it lapped at the red clay bowl of water in front of it.

Nasir rolled Parrot to a stop before the mosque's entrance, but kept the motor running. He glanced at Palwasha sleeping in the rear, head against the rickshaw's canvas door, a thread of spit dangling from her mouth. She stirred when sweat from her forehead trickled down her cheek in a glistening line. Nasir turned and swiveled the battery-operated fan in the partition toward her.

He retrieved the revolver from the partition compartment, slipped it into his vest, and smoothed the cotton kameez over it. Then he stepped out, looked up and down the deserted highway, and, lifting a hand in a friendly greeting, walked to the man on the charpai.

"Salam'o-Laikum, bhai-jaan," he hailed the man in his accented Urdu. "My name is Nasir Khan. I'm traveling with my niece and we're looking for some food, if you could spare any. We have things we can trade."

Dreamily, the man blew out a smoke ring and sat up on the charpai's mattress. He lifted his white farmer turban with an age-spotted hand and scratched his head. "Nasir Khan, eh? Where's home? Where'd you come from, son?"

"Balakot, bhai-jaan. I worked at a hotel there."

The man nodded, his milky-white gaze on the highway, and replaced the turban on his head. "You're a long way from home, aren't you."

The dog had slipped out from its resting place and stood watching Nasir, its head tipped to one side. It was larger than Nasir had initially thought, its tail curled like the noisemakers he had seen balloon vendors sell in Abbottabad before the wabaa. When he took a step forward, it growled.

"Easy, boy. We're all friends here," Nasir said to the dog soothingly in Pashto, then switched back to Urdu: "I gather he won't bite?"

Up close the furrows in the man's forehead were deep, the wrinkles around his cataract-clouded eyes thick like spiderwebs. A black taweez hung around his neck. His chest-length beard was oiled and entirely white. He must have been in his seventies.

He got up, stretched, one large brawny hand on his low back, and felt the ground with his feet. He found his sandals and slipped them on. "Hero won't hurt you, will you, Hero?" The dog wagged its tail and gave a short bark. The man bent and petted its head. "He's watching out for me. We both watch out for each other. Such are the days, aren't they, Hero?"

THE MOSQUE AT THE END OF THE WORLD

Hero craned his head back and licked the man's hand.

In his previous life, Nasir hadn't liked dogs. They were dirty, and touching them broke your wuzu, so you had to do ablution again before praying namaz, but now he found himself reaching out to caress the animal's head. Hero yipped and retreated, then nosed forward, his tail stiff and moving powerfully from side to side. He sniffed Nasir's hand a few times and tentatively began to lick it.

"Good dog," Nasir said, wishing he had a piece of bread or a bone for him. "How long have you two been here?"

"We never left, you see." The old man patted under the edge of the mattress and came up with a small tin can. He fished around in it with gnarled fingers and brought out a key ring jangling with keys. "We stayed right here through it all, watched the entire city die. That was three months ago. Sheikhupura's population before the wabaa was two lakhs. Two hundred thousand people." He sighed and gestured east toward Lahore. "Lahore nearly forty lakhs. Forty lakhs! And what about all the villages between here and Lahore? Everyone is gone. Every mosque between here and Lahore and for all I know the entire world, deserted. No one to take Allah's name anymore. How could I abandon my mosque to owls, bats, and jinns? Na son, I will stay here in the shadow of my elders until I'm dead, too."

Nasir watched him pick up the walking stick and shuffle to a side door of the mosque, the dog following on his heels. The man opened the heavy padlock on the hasp. "Stupid to lock up now, but force of habit. It's the only thing that keeps us alive, you know, force of habit." He called back over his shoulder, "You hungry? I have plenty of canned food and—Hero, keep out!" He prodded the dog gently with his foot to nudge him away from the doorstep. "You know you aren't allowed in there."

Hero sat down at the threshold, head on his paws, and gave a little whine as Nasir came to the door. Nasir's gaze went to the graveyard behind the mosque, hundreds of ancient marble headstones jutting out from the earth, then at the large dirt mound between the mosque and the graveyard. He peered into the mullah's room, at the sparse furnishings—another charpai, plastic table, shelves lined with copies of the Quran and biographies of the Prophet, and framed magic squares filled with Arabic numerals and letters hanging on the walls.

Nasir Khan tapped his foot on the doorstep, considering for a few moments, then turned and went to fetch the girl.

His name was Khizar and he was the mosque's imam—or had been. After the wabaa hit and, town after town, village after village fell, there wasn't anyone left to lead in prayer.

For weeks Maulvi Khizar had visited the sick and the dying, sitting by their bedsides, holding their hands, listening to them recite the declaration of faith one last time with swollen, discolored lips. He sprinkled water on their faces as they gasped and wheezed, and cleaned snot off their chins. When they passed, he helped their loved ones cart their bodies to the graveyard behind the mosque. He abandoned that practice after the bereaved died, too, and no one was left to help him move them.

"With my own hands, I buried fifty or more people who came to the mosque in their last hours, seeking its holy vicinity in death," Khizar said, pouring hot tea from a kettle, as the three of them sat at the rickety table in the middle of the imam's room. "I prayed fifteen, twenty janazas daily for weeks, then took them in a wheelbarrow five by five to the ditch by the graveyard. I lowered them down as gently as I could and poured a handful of dust over each. Would that I could give them a proper burial, but I'm an old blind man and all I could do was wait for the last person to give up the ghost before I began filling in the ditch."

His teacup shook a little as he brought it to his mouth and sipped. His sightless gaze traveled over his room and Nasir and the girl, Palwasha. She ate an entire packet of Prince chocolate biscuits and listened to the old man ramble, then to Nasir as he narrated their story.

After his family and friends died, Nasir had walked around Balakot in a daze, his grief larger than the mountains that surrounded him, deeper than the emerald waters of the Kunhar River that mocked him with their swiftness, their indifference. *We stop, the world doesn't stop*, he thought again and again as he slept in a different bed each day in the fancy hotel he used to guard before the wabaa took everyone.

No one had believed the world was ending. His neighbors had sneered, even as the Christian missionary hospital in Garhi Habibullah sent panicked messages to the surrounding clinics, asking people to put on masks and stay at home. Stay at home? A Christian conspiracy, they said. Everyone *knew* the wabaa had been started by Amreeka to render all Muslims impotent, but instead Allah's wrath fell upon them and it turned on its makers. Oh yes, they'd been following the news on TV and radio, how their glittering cities fell and the infidels died in the streets. And now these Christian traitors were jumping on the bandwagon, trying to send the Muslim men home, while they planned evil, satanic things in the dark of night!

The people of Balakot weren't fools. They'd teach those Christian chuhras a lesson or two.

But before a mob could form and march to the hospital—it was over. The ringleader, a man named Qadri, who'd been inciting and goading the men of Balakot for days, was dead. Killed by the wabaa.

The plague, it turned out, was egalitarian and secular. It didn't discriminate between rich and poor, crescents and crosses. Everyone in Balakot died—except Nasir.

He buried those he could and left the rest where they had fallen, for what was the point of breaking his back? He wasn't twenty anymore. Besides, nature and rot would have their way. From mulch we come and to mulch we return.

He'd found fourteen-year-old Palwasha rocking in an armchair by the roadside in Abbottabad, an hour from Balakot. At first, she had hidden inside a handicraft shop, she'd tell him later, but she had been alone for so long and the voices of the dead were louder every night. Her baby sister, her brother, her father with his big, strong mechanic's hands, and her aunt Bano, her mother's sister, who'd taken care of Palwasha after her moray died from an untreated fistula gone bad. They'd begun talking to her in the silence of the night and, later, in the daytime as well.

She couldn't stand it, Palwasha said. The resounding emptiness, being alone with the alone. She knew it would drive her insane—so when she heard Nasir's motorbike in the distance, she thought, *Sweet death . . . or a friend?* Were they even different now? The stench of rotting flesh still in her nostrils, she came out from her hiding place and waited for the stranger, her eyes squeezed shut, rocking, rocking, pretending she was still in her father's embrace.

The tall, bearded stranger didn't hurt her. His voice was kind, and he had a knack for calming her fears. Also for finding and preserving food. Sun-drying, brining, pickling, or salting was the trick, Nasir told her, as he substituted the bike for an abandoned Toyota Corolla, its keys clutched in the driver's rotted hands. Palwasha looked away as Nasir dragged the family of three out of the car to the roadside and placed a rain-slick tarp over them.

"They won't miss it," he commented as they got into the vehicle. He wouldn't look at her and she hoped he couldn't hear the invisible fingers tap-tapping on the windows as they drove away, heading to Islamabad, thinking they would find life and some semblance of law and order in the capital city.

They didn't. Just more dead at every chowk, traffic signal, hamlet, and bungalow. Brown kites, eagles, and vultures soared over the city, while feral cats roamed in packs. And wasn't that odd, Nasir thought one night, as they sat outside a guesthouse under a fourteenth moon, him smoking an expensive cigar he'd found in a VIP suite, Palwasha biting into a miraculously edible apple from the kitchen's cold storage that had long ago stopped working. None of the feral animals wore collars. They were all strays. Where were the expensive purebreds of the city's rich and elite? Of all those diplomats from foreign countries, one week of whose cat food cost more than their chowkidar's monthly salary?

They stayed in Islamabad for three weeks, foraging, scavenging, waiting for someone to appear, something to happen, before Nasir finally decided to try Lahore. He'd thought long and hard about it and it made sense to him to move south. There would be more traffic of the living in the heart of Punjab.

Also, there were the dreams.

But he didn't tell Maulvi Khizar about them yet. Instead, he talked about the GT Road, that iconic highway built in the sixteenth century by the emperor Sher Shah Suri, now desolate and crammed to the brim with dented, rusting vehicles and corpses bloated in the summer heat. They had to abandon the Corolla early on and switch to the rickshaw, which was able to navigate the obstacles on the highway far more easily and carry more than a motorbike could. Palwasha wanted to name the rickshaw. Nasir thought that silly, but really what did it matter? They named it Parrot.

And it was on GT Road near Jhelum that they had their first encounter with the Wolves.

Palwasha shuddered as Nasir described to Maulvi Khizar how they ran into the fields and managed to hide behind a grove of banyan trees right before the contingent rolled into view. Watching them move across the highway, laughing and herding boys and girls in ropes and chains, was the first time Nasir realized the world wasn't merely empty, but that it had been emptied of good people. Evil men, like cockroaches, had survived.

Khizar counted beads on a tasbih as Nasir told their story. When he was finished, the old mullah sat in silence, his fingers telling the rosary reverently, gently, as if he were touching dewdrops, then said, "We're strange creatures, aren't we? We hope in futility that the world will change, and when it does, we long for what once was."

Nasir watched fondly as Palwasha drank the last of her tea and got up. They had plenty of opportunity along the way to pick up new clothes and she had changed into clean shalwar kurta, but despite Nasir's persuasion she refused to throw her old green dupatta away. It must have complemented her jade eyes once, but now, oil-stained, blackened with dirt, it clung to her neck like a net of vines.

She asked in accented Urdu, "Where is the bathroom?"

Khizar thought for a moment, then he gestured to a door that led to the pillared interior of the mosque. "Into the courtyard and on your left. Baita," he said to her as she shuffled to the door, "indulge an old man and recite the prayer hanging on the eastern pillar before you enter the bathroom, okay?"

The girl stared at him, nodded, then remembered he couldn't see her. "Jee, Maulvi sahib."

When she'd left, Khizar turned to Nasir. "You're both welcome to stay as long as you wish. I have plenty of tinned food and spices, and there are herds of cattle and game roaming the fields around here. You'll never run out of meat if you have any skill with a gun."

"I brought a few guns with me from Abbottabad." Nasir scratched his long and unkempt beard. He needed to trim it. "And I can shoot."

"My room is small, as you can see, and can't accommodate all of us. My advice," Khizar said, "is for the girl to either sleep outside—I can put up a couple charpais behind the mosque—or in one of the houses across the road."

"We certainly don't want to inconvenience you, and we'll sleep wherever you want." Nasir studied the mullah's face. "But I don't think space is your real concern here, is it?"

Khizar fell silent. Outside the postern door, dusk extended its tentacles, covering the mullah's charpai in shadow. Hero was nowhere to be seen. After a rabbit or stray cat perhaps.

"There really isn't any other way to put it." Khizar's cataract-glazed eyes were upon the courtyard door. "The mosque is inhabited by jinn and the girl isn't safe in here after dusk."

"Jinn."

"Jinn," Khizar agreed, and lifted his teacup to his lips. "My grandfather used to tell stories about them. Said they lived in this area for millennia—long before people came here. When you're a child, you believe such stories. As you grow older, you laugh at them. Eventually you forget them." He put away the cup and reached for his hookah. "But *they* don't forget us, you see, even if we ignore them. The jinn move among us, building and migrating, majestic and silent, living their own lives that they mark in thousands of years. And when the wabaa overwhelmed us humans, they returned."

Uneasily Nasir glanced at the door. It was possible that the old man was not all *there*, that loneliness had worked on him as it had on all of them, but jinn were mentioned in the Quran, and in his hometown of Balakot, stories of evil jinn in the shape of cattle roaming lonely mountain roads at night were legion.

"Certainly, Maulvi sahib, many thanks. We'll sleep in one of the houses. We don't intend to impose on your hospitality for too long, anyway." He got up to fetch the girl, but suddenly she was there, adjusting the discolored dupatta around her neck, staring at him with those green eyes he had always thought discomfiting, as if she could see more than she let on. "There you are, child. All well?"

"Yes." She moved her lips twice, glanced over her shoulder into the shadows pooling in the courtyard, then back at him. "Yes, I think so. Maulvi sahib," she said quietly. "Who's Burqan?"

"Wa La Hawla Wala Quwwata. There is no strength or power except in God the Eternal and Majestic." Khizar's eyes had widened, the cataracts shining like white marbles. "Never speak that name again lest you call the jinn king. Wherever did you hear it?"

"It's on the painting of the black-haired man with the fiery eyes. Hanging on the pillar next to the prayer sheet."

They went out into the courtyard, where the pillars of the mosque stood dusking like ancient trees. Khizar lit two oil lamps and hung them up, and Nasir turned on a flashlight.

They searched for nearly an hour, the old mullah squinting and patting at the walls and pillars, but they couldn't find the painting with the jinn king's name.

―――

Nasir found he'd lied to Khizar. They ended up staying with the mullah for several months.

Nasir convinced himself it was partly because he was worried about the blind old man, partly because they'd traveled a long way to get here, this green land of the Ravi and Indus with its acres of crops and fruit trees, some of which had survived thanks to the arrival of monsoon rains, and while the electric tube wells were useless and the once-lush villages and towns now crumbling into dust and green decay, the hand pumps in the fields still fetched sweet water and the mullah still gave the azaan five times a day, his melodious call carrying across miles and miles of silence, like God's own voice over a subdued earth.

But really, and it took him some time to figure it out, Nasir had stayed because of Khizar's stories.

Khizar was full of them. From his childhood spent in Old Lahore, where he grew up the only son of a pit wrestler, who wanted his son to follow him into the akhara, to his youth as a truant kite flier on the rooftops of Lahore, singing ghazals and radio songs to giggling pretty girls on neighboring roofs and indulging in glorious paichay with other kite fliers. Khizar smiled when he told this particular story, and Palwasha reddened and left the room on some pretext.

Nasir's favorite stories were of those who'd passed through the area—both before and after the wabaa.

"I remember this man, as old as I," Khizar said on a rainy day, as they put up a tarp canopy on the mosque's western wall and strung mosquito netting around their charpais. August had arrived along with the monsoon season, and soon malaria would be in the air. Or would it? Could the germ survive without people? Nasir had never heard of a cat or dog getting malaria. Hero seemed to be fine as he bounded around them, barking and begging to play fetch.

He and Palwasha had set up residence in one of the four-marla buildings across the road. The ground floor used to be a bakery with the top floor reserved for the owner's family, which they now took over, and the smell of yeast and spoiled bread occasionally caught them by surprise, even though they'd cleared away the shelves and cleaned out the storeroom.

"He was from Sargodha, traveling alone," Khizar continued. "This was a month or so after the wabaa began. His name was Allah-Bakhsh. He had a walking stick and on his shoulder a schoolbag in which he carried his things. He told me he was headed to the Wagah border so he could cross over into India. Why India, I asked him. He said he was born there. Spent his childhood in Amritsar. When the subcontinent broke into two, his grandmother brought him to Pakistan on a train in the middle of the night.

"But you take me to Amritsar train station," he told me, "and I'll take you straight back home. The house where I grew up. Where I cussed out Mausi Bashiran's nephew when he stole my lychees and took off on his bike, laughing, as I yelled and chased him. Where my veer Nazir was born and died when he was five. We left him there and came here. How his spirit must have cried and searched for us in those streets." Allah-Bakhsh's eyes were rheumy when he said that. "And now everyone I know is dead. My children and their children. I buried them all.

"So, I'm going back home. Across the border to my veer, to tell him I'm sorry we left him. To the place that continues to steal into my dreams."

They prayed isha together. Old Allah-Bakhsh spent the night in the mosque, and in the morning, he was gone without a goodbye.

"I hope he made it home okay. I hope his dream was worth the journey," Khizar said, gurgling his hookah, as they sat outside the mosque. A scimitar moon sliced the monsoon clouds in the sky, silvering the fields. Hero watched fireflies dance and weave through the dark with interest, and Palwasha, who had taken to the dog quickly, caressed his back with her toes.

Nasir had been cleaning and slicing the four partridges he had shot that morning. He dropped the birds in the bucket at his feet.

Dreams, he thought.

"Maulvi sahib," he said. "Have you had any strange dreams since the wabaa began?"

Khizar pulled hard on his hookah and blew out a trembling ring that dissipated in the wind. "Why do you ask?"

"I've had really weird dreams. They started when we were in Islamabad."

"Oh?"

"I know I'm not the only one. Palwashay has them, too." He smiled at her. "You talk in your sleep."

The girl shifted in her chair and trailed one hand across Hero's fur.

"So, I'm wondering: Have you or anyone you knew had any out-of-the-ordinary dreams?"

"You ask dangerous questions." Khizar picked up a twig and stirred the coals in the hookah's cup. "Yes."

It turned out that, about a month into the wabaa, all three of them (and others who'd passed by) began having similar dreams. They described to each other the strange-looking house in a cornfield in the middle of a strange country, the dusky woman who lived there, and her odd, soothing songs played on a guitar, sung with her face in shadow, always turned away from them. They couldn't understand her words, but all three had the feeling that they weren't meant to. Her songs were for—someplace else.

"Amreeka, I think." Nasir poured fresh water into the bucket of partridges and added salt into it until it wouldn't dissolve anymore. He pushed a ziplocked bag of ice into the water and let it settle on top of the meat. "Before the wabaa we would have Amreekan guests stay at the hotel sometimes. They spoke like that woman, although her accent seems thicker. She is *old*, that one."

"She is," Palwasha said, watching the darkness of the fields. "Really old. She makes me feel safe, though. I like dreaming of her and her songs. But Nasir-lala, I don't think she's calling *us*. I don't think *we* are meant to answer her call."

Khizar nodded. "I believe our dear Palwasha has it right. I think we're eavesdropping on an invite extended to others." He hesitated, his brow furrowed more than usual. "When I was a child, I used to like watching wrestling matches in my father's akhara. And now I feel as if we're watching the beginning of a wrestling match and the akhara is being set up, only this particular akhara and its players belong only to that faraway land. It is not our land. And neither she nor that *other* are interested in us."

At this, Palwasha started and sat up, the jade of her eyes darkening. Her grip on Hero tightened, till the dog whimpered and twisted his neck to give her a watery look.

"I think you know whom I'm speaking of," Khizar continued. "I won't talk about him much, that son of darkness. He's worse than any jinn or devil I've ever felt. He's been invading my dreams for as long as that old woman. Nightmares that make me clench my jaw so hard some mornings I wake up with a bloody mouth. He terrifies me, but again I don't think his evil is meant to haunt us here. Which is a damned relief, I must tell you."

"I've dreamed of him only once or twice. Mostly it's been the old lady." Nasir tossed some cut lemons into the brine bucket and watched them float. "And, a good thing, isn't it, that we don't have to go look for either of them." He grinned. "Who the fuck would give *us* visas to visit Amreeka?"

They laughed at that, and Nasir was glad to see Palwasha settle into a serene silence. Six weeks into their sojourn here the girl had turned fifteen, but her fears and nightmares were older and deeper than his and the mullah's put together. He'd seen her glance at shadows and mutter when she thought he wasn't looking. Was it a response to loss and terror? She had been utterly alone for nearly four weeks before he found her.

He reached over and pressed the girl's hand. They smiled at each other, and again there was that feeling. That depth, that veil—as if she said less than she knew. As if the world itself was a mirage only her green gaze could pierce.

———

Soon the rains petered away, breaking the humidity's back. October manifested quicker than a beggar's curse, and suddenly GT Road was filled with people.

They came from every direction, traveling in groups of all sizes. Solo travelers, ragtag bands, a few groups composed only of children, de novo families banded together for survival. Lured by the muezzin's call, they gravitated toward the trio hoping for abode and civilization and instead found a tiny town mosque run by a blind imam. They offered a few collective prayers, slept a night or two in the sanctum, shared their meals and stories, and moved on.

Some stayed. An apprentice carpenter, two farmer cousins, a car mechanic, a former policeman with a sweetmeat belly and his new road wife, a group of teens and children led by a young schoolteacher named Ujala, who had a strong Punjabi accent and protected her wards fiercely with a long knife in her belt and a shotgun on her shoulder.

"They need lessons not just in survival, but also science, history, art, and empathy," Ujala told them, smiling at old Khizar. "And who better to team up with me than a Quran teacher? Yes, we will stay with you, Maulvi sahib, if you will have us."

A community of sorts blossomed around the mosque on GT Road, much like others must have along this grand road in the time of the great emperor Sher Shah and long before him, when the road was an ancient trade route sprouting from the mouth of the Ganges up to the northwestern edges of India and into Afghanistan.

"All roads are special. Magical," said Ujala to her pupils in the mosque courtyard one morning, "but this road is sacred. It is older than our collective memory. And it is along this road that a new world will be born. No more borders will break its spine. Instead, it will pulse again with life, like an artery through the hearts of all the regions that once comprised India—the land of the Indus."

At first Nasir was shocked at the teacher's speculations, her reckless confidence. This was Pakistan! A Muslim homeland procured with the blood of a million dead, for God's sake. But the more he listened to her—the more he watched the slow drift of humanity along the highway and thought what others across the border in Afghanistan, India, Nepal, Bangladesh, and Bhutan must be suffering, how they must slowly be developing their own communities—the more he began to be convinced that she was right. Old borders wouldn't work anymore. They would all return to little towns along roads and rivers. They'd have a chance to fix things again, and maybe this time they wouldn't fuck everything up. One could dream.

One morning he and Khizar came upon Palwasha mending a hole in her dupatta. The weather was perfect, a soft cool breeze blowing from the north, the sky a deep blue striped with egg white. Under the mosque's canopy, Palwasha sat on the edge of her charpai stitching, chewing her lips, a faraway look in her eyes. She stopped and looked up when they approached her.

"Sanga haal de?" Nasir said.

"Good, lala. Salam, Maulvi sahib." She resumed her sewing. "Sleep well?"

"What with helping Fawad and Murtaza on the farmland"—Nasir put a hand on his back and grimaced—"I sleep like a baby these days. You?"

She made a seesaw gesture with her needle hand.

"Still having bad dreams?"

She shook her head, licked her lips.

Khizar said softly, "Is it wise to hold so much in, child?"

"Holding? I've shared my dreams with you two." She glanced up and Nasir noticed the deep, bruise-like hollows under her eyes. She sighed. "But not all of them. Maulvi sahib, I dream of more. So much more."

"What is it, Palwashay-bache?" Nasir asked.

And now that she'd spoken, it was as if a river poured out torrentially, her words tumbling and falling over each other: "I dream of the ruins of a shrine. A six-sided blue-striped building with towers in each corner. It's damaged on one side and huddles close to two other buildings in a city where many such buildings are scattered, joined by winding streets and roads. And all this near five roaring rivers that used to rage past the shrine but have now meandered away and conjoined into one monster of a river. I see the water of that river in my dream. It's blue and so beautiful and there are sand islands in it." Dropping her sewing needle, she reached out and clutched Nasir's shirt. "Lala, the town is dead, but I see it filling with life. I see caravans of cars and bikes and rickshaws, and people on horse and donkey carts making their way to this tiny city, where they will build again. And there is no evil there except that of the whisperer. No evil greater than *his* who, having whispered once, slithers away, then turns back with glee and whispers again in the hearts of men."

She stopped as suddenly as she'd begun and let go of Nasir's shirt. Her face was pale. She let her arm drop limp by her side, and Hero, who'd been exploring goh holes in the fields, came around sniffing and began to nuzzle her hand.

"I don't know where this place is and I don't know when we're supposed to go there." Palwasha stroked the dog's ears. "All I know is our time here is brief and that makes me afraid. Sad and afraid."

"Ah, there's nothing to be afraid of, bachey. You're safe here. We're safe," Nasir said, but his heart beat in his temples and his soul was uneasy.

He guided Khizar across the highway to the policeman Rashid's house. As they walked away, he said to the mullah, "What do you make of that?"

Khizar didn't answer for a few moments. He had the rosary in his hand again and the beads shook as he counted them. Finally, he said, "Uch."

"What?"

"Uch Sharif. About five hundred kilometers south. The Alexandrian city of saints near the Panjnad, where the five rivers come together. I believe that's the city Palwasha is describing. The shrine is of Bibi Jawindi, a woman saint from the fifteenth century." They reached Rashid's door. Nasir knocked, and as they waited, Khizar quietly said, "Palwasha isn't the only one who's dreamed of it. I've seen it, too, and I think she's right. Sooner or later, you'll be making your pilgrimage there." He hesitated, then his face turned resolute. "But I don't think that journey is for me. I don't think I will be joining you."

Troubled, Nasir turned to him, but the door was open and the burly policeman and his pretty young wife, Fatima, their arms interlinked, were beaming at them, asking them to come in, bowls of steaming lentils fresh from the pot were waiting for them, and Nasir never got to finish that conversation with the old mullah.

Madam Ujala was a punctilious teacher, but not all pupils of the schoolteacher turned road warrior were so diligent. Some of them played truant while class was in session and went exploring the countryside perforated with goh and snake holes, running through fields of spoiled crops with glee.

On a gray midday in November, when northeasterly winds brought a lashing of cold rain to Sheikhupura, turning soft winter trails into squelching mud, one such delinquent saved their community.

The twelve-year-old's name was Hashim, but everyone called him Jamun due to the exquisitely dark color of his skin. This particular afternoon, Jamun had wandered nearly five miles away from the mosque-school. He was hopping from puddle to puddle, splashing and stomping his way across a field when he heard a distant *bang*. He leaned on his walking branch, squinting to see beyond the low mist of the fields. The rain had stopped a while ago and all was quiet except the dripping of water from trees and the soothing frog-like chirping of quails.

The sound came again, and this time there were three of them in rapid succession, the report familiar but chilling, and Jamun instantly dropped to his haunches. For a moment he lingered, then began creeping through the mud until he found himself at the edge of the highway behind an old banyan. He pressed himself against its rough bark and peered around the trunk.

Twenty feet away, five men, long rifles slung over their shoulders, stood in a semicircle around a big, mustached man in an army uniform, a revolver in his hands. Behind them several pickup trucks filled with more armed men smoked on the eastern highway, flanking a chain of prisoners, who stood shivering in the cold. In front of the mustached man, a body lay twitching in a pool of blood, and as Jamun watched, the man stepped forward and kicked the dying person in the head.

Jamun's lips smashed together to hold back a cry. Very slowly he lowered himself to the ground and backed away on all fours until he was invisible behind rows of ruined sugarcane. Then he got up and sprinted back to the mosque, praying no bullet would shatter his spine as he fled.

Nasir and Khizar took the boy's testimony seriously. Wooden barricades and rusted oil drums, manned by Rashid and two others, were immediately put up on the highway. Runners were sent to all the houses to gather the community in the mosque's courtyard. Palwasha and Khizar led children and the older women into the prayer hall, while Nasir and Ujala handed out guns and bullets to the able-bodied men, women, and youths.

They had fourteen guns for a total of fifteen who knew how to shoot—more than half of that number teenagers. Six handguns, four shotguns, one G3 rifle, and three AK-47 Kalashnikovs in possession of men posted on rooftops. Even that, Nasir thought, was a miracle. Most people hadn't brought ammunition with them to the mosque-community. Judging from Jamun's account, they were outmanned and likely outgunned.

Ujala was unfazed. "You wait for my cry," she told them, her face dark with rage, the long knife glinting on her belt, "and then you don't hesitate. You shoot every single one of those sisterfuckers. You shoot like our lives and our children's lives depend on it."

The whole thing had taken them less than an hour. Armed and ready, they now waited for the cavalcade of the Wolves.

It arrived around three in the afternoon—six pickup trucks escorting a human train slowly down the highway. Dull-faced and dusty men, women, and children with iron chains on their feet and a long rope tethering them together. Despite the cold, they were dressed in flimsy shalwar kameez. Sweaters and jackets were reserved for young girls only, Nasir noted. Prize meat, he thought with disgust, as next to him Ujala and Rashid raised their weapons and pointed them at the enemy.

A tall, powerfully built man with a wheatish complexion and bushy mustache disembarked from the first truck that reached the barricade. He wore army khakis and a vest with what looked like a submachine gun slung over his left shoulder, and he was smiling brightly at them.

He leaned against the barricade and spoke in a booming voice, "Salam and blessings. So wonderful to meet you all."

About a dozen similarly uniformed armed men got out of the pickups and spread out behind their leader, guns lifted in Nasir and Ujala's general direction.

"Wonderful for you maybe," Ujala called back, her finger poised on the trigger of her shotgun. "Listen, we don't want any trouble. Please turn around and return to where you came from. Or take a side road if you're heading to Lahore. You won't cross the barriers here."

"God is great, isn't He." The man ran a hand through oiled hair that gleamed in the winter sunlight. "A woman speaks for you all, does she? How many of you are there?"

Rashid took a step forward and aimed his G3 squarely at the man's head. "She does, and that's the way we like it. As for the latter, it's none of your concern."

"But it is. Listen and listen well, all of you. My name is Lieutenant Colonel Amir Bajwa and I'm the leader of the NPA—the New Pakistan Army. I have a total of one hundred men under my command. Even as we speak, two of my units are clearing out criminal and terrorist hideouts three hours north of here. We aim to bring order and rule of law to this new world, and we're starting by establishing governance in Punjab—for the moment." He grinned at them, a sly, nasty grin, and Nasir thought, *Where have I seen this hideous grin before?*

A nightmare. Which one?

"We have no beef with any of you," the colonel was saying. "All we require is food and water for my prisoners and half of your ammo as a token of your allegiance and we'll be on our way." Solemnly he raised a finger to the sky, turned it, and pointed it at the ground. "This I swear in the name of this pure land I have vowed to protect."

Nasir watched his crinkled eyes, his wet lips, the spittle glistening on his mustache. He glanced at the human train between the trucks—skeletal, hollow-eyed men, women, and children with cuts and bruises on their forearms and not a hint of life in their eyes. *Your vow*, he thought. *A pox on your fucking vow.*

"And should you refuse," Colonel Bajwa beamed at them, "why, I will kill all your men and take your women and children as slaves. As labor to clear out the roads and highways to render our beloved Pakistan habitable and traversable again."

Placid as a mountain in springtime, Ujala met the colonel's gaze and said, "Fuck you."

His smile didn't waver, even as a dull red began to seep into the corner of his eyes.

THE MOSQUE AT THE END OF THE WORLD

Ujala raised her left hand in the air, and on both sides of the highway several heads rose from the ledges of rooftops, their faces covered. Kalashnikovs and pistols slid into view and trained on the New Pakistan Army men.

Ujala's voice didn't shake. "We *won't* give up our guns and you *will* leave us alone. We may or may not live to see tomorrow, but I promise you if you don't leave, God help me, you and your men won't, either."

The red left his eyes. Colonel Bajwa gave a good-natured laugh and, raising both hands, began backing away. "I like this. Oh, I do like this."

Behind him his men had taken cover behind vehicle doors and in the beds of their trucks. They watched their boss retreat with inscrutable eyes.

The colonel was smiling and shaking his head when he reached his truck. "So, this is the deal, right? We're going to camp in yonder field across the highway. Tonight, exactly at eighteen-hundred, you will bring water and food for my prisoners, so they're strong tomorrow to keep working on the highway.

"Now, say you decide you don't want to do that. Well, *I* decide to start killing the older, more useless of the prisoners one by one. Every ten minutes you will hear a gunshot until I'm finished with the lot of them. Then, if by oh-seven-hundred tomorrow I don't have my ammo neatly stacked up around these barricades, we will return and kill every last one of you. No prisoners and no exceptions. Is that clear enough for you, meri jaan?"

Ujala had sparks in her eyes.

"Tonight," the colonel repeated, and began to get into his truck.

A voice rang out, "Son! Son, listen to me!"

They all turned.

Maulvi Khizar had come out from the mosque's main entrance and was seesawing toward the barricades, his walking stick precariously jabbing the ground.

"Maulvi sahib . . . " Ujala said.

"Khizar bhai!" Nasir cried, and lowered his weapon to make a grab for the mullah, but the old man thwarted him with a wild swing of the stick.

"Prisoners, eh?" the mullah was muttering. His opaque eyes were fixed on the mass of trucks, his face red with determination. "God's children bound up like cattle. That's how you will protect this country? My father and grandfather's land? You should be ashamed of yourself." His stick thwacked against a steel drum as he reached the barricades, making him stumble and nearly fall.

Colonel Bajwa stood behind his truck door, watching the old man. His mustache quivered. "You must be the imam of this mosque. God is great, indeed. Peace be upon you, Maulvi sahib."

"And you, son, but I fear you don't want peace. You want subjugation." Maulvi Khizar's white beard heaved on his chest. His turban had fallen off and his scalp gleamed between tufts of thin hair. "My father's brother served in the army. He was martyred in '65 and now my very own army wants to take us all prisoners? How have things come to this?"

"Hush, imam sahib, your passion will be the death of you." The colonel held up a hand before his soldiers, who had swung their guns around to face this new threat. "The army is here for your protection, I promise."

Tears ran down Khizar's cheeks. He blinked them away. "Man is born free—the One Pure and Merciful God has decreed that. No man has the right to enslave another. And you threaten us in the shade of Allah's house—the last living mosque in this land, for all we know. Fear the wrath of God, damn you."

The colonel's raised hand clenched into a fist. His smile broadened into a toothy grin. "Careful now."

In response, Khizar banged his walking stick on one of the drums as hard as he could, then pointed it at the line of prisoners. "Let those poor souls go before you're condemned to hell forever."

"Maulvi sahib," Nasir yelled. "Please come back."

The colonel's fist flew open. With the heel of his hand, he made a thrust-forward motion in the air.

A shot rang out, the sound a rude, deafening shock that silenced every living thing in its vicinity.

Maulvi Khizar jerked like a puppet pulled by its master. Slowly he turned around to face his friends. A clean black hole, like a third blind eye, had appeared in the middle of his forehead. A whiff of smoke came out of it and dissipated. Khizar's walking stick dropped from his hands and clattered on the road. He smiled, or grimaced, and his right eye began to fill with blood.

"Khizar bhai!" Nasir screamed, and made to run to the dead mullah swaying on the highway, but Rashid grabbed his arm.

"No, Nasir!" Rashid hissed. "He's gone."

Faintly, as if from a great distance, Nasir heard Ujala cry, "Kill those bastards!" and the world was filled with blasts and whines and the staccato of gunfire. Nasir watched his own hands lift and begin firing, even as Rashid yanked him by his collar behind the cover of a drum.

―――

Palwasha opened the mosque hall door to Nasir's banging to find him propped against the wall, covered in blood.

"They're coming," he wheezed, trying to speak lucidly. A bullet had gone straight through his cheek, shattering his left jaw. "Ujala, Rashid, Faheem, all dead. It's over."

The girl's grasp on her revolver tightened. Behind her, in the shadows, the eleven remaining women and children began to sob.

Nasir reached out with a tremulous hand to touch Palwasha's green dupatta. She had washed it thoroughly after repair and it matched her eyes now. "Was this your mother's?"

She nodded. "Ao, lala."

"Palwashay-Gul." He gripped her hand, his chest rising and falling. "My little rose sister. I'm sorry I couldn't protect you. But you listen to your lala one last time: When the colonel's men come in, they will want to take me out first. And Murtaza. He's our last shooter left alive. Hiding in the minaret. When they're busy with us, you slip out the back. Leave everyone behind. I will try to make sure the bastard doesn't catch us alive. But you—"

Palwasha cut him off. "No, Lala." She gazed at him with such gravity Nasir's heart wanted to break. "I will not abandon my family."

Nasir couldn't stop shaking. He tried to smile at her, but the left side of his face kept wanting to fall in on itself. "Then we will both stay here until this is done."

Palwasha lowered herself down next to him. Together they looked out into the courtyard prematurely darkened by rain clouds, at the pillars crowding together like spectators at a blood match, and Nasir thought of the three-day mela that used to come to Balakot and Muzaffarabad every year, the rickety Ferris wheel, horse rides, food stalls, balloons, and BB guns set up in the maidan by the soft green water of the Kunhar River. *My God*, he thought. *I will never smell the scents of a fair again, never hear children squeal with laughter again.*

Overwhelmed with tears, he looked at Palwasha.

Her jade eyes gleamed in the dimness like a cat's and he could hardly hear her when she said very softly, "They're here, Lala."

Sounds right outside the courtyard.

Shadows slipped into the mosque.

With great effort, Nasir lifted his gun and pointed it at the approaching men led by the colonel, who was limping slightly. His khakis had turned maroon at the left thigh, where a bullet must have grazed him. He didn't seem particularly in pain.

The colonel slowed when he saw Nasir's gun and grinned.

"I promised you all death if you didn't listen," he called out. Two of his men broke off and made for the steps leading up to the eastern minaret. "So, here I am and here it is. I wish I could offer mercy, but the word of an officer is his honor."

Palwasha was tense against Nasir's body, yet she didn't raise her revolver. Nasir gripped his own handgun with both hands, hoping to steady it, but his vision was dimming. Too much blood loss. Too much—

From their right came a deep growl.

Nasir glanced into the mounting dark, trying to pierce it. There at the doorway of Khizar's room, for the briefest of moments, Nasir glimpsed a large figure, wrapped in black, tall enough that its head was touching the doorframe.

Nasir shook his head—and it was only Hero after all, snarling, as he emerged from the room, canines shining, his hackles up.

"Who goes there!" the colonel's sharp voice rang out. "Oh, a fucking dog, for God's sake. Shoot him, won't you, Jameel?"

The soldier raised his rifle and carefully aimed it at Hero.

Nasir's body was drenched in sweat. His head swam. Something fell from his hands and he looked down in surprise. It was his gun, lying thousands of miles away between his feet.

This is it, he thought. *This is what it feels like to die.*

Someone took ahold of his face and kissed him on the forehead.

"Nasir Lala, look." Palwashay-Gul turned his head gently until they were both looking at the gloaming between the mosque's pillars. "Our friends are here."

"Who?" he wheezed, not understanding.

She lowered her lips to his ears and whispered, "Burqan."

And Nasir saw.

Dozens of dark figures emerging from behind the pillars, silent, majestic, tall as pines, jostling and churning together, like tree branches in a lashing high storm, coming apart, coalescing, then rushing at the armed men.

"Burqan," Palwasha said again, her eyes wide with wonder.

The last thing Nasir saw, before a great darkness descended on him, was Hero, the spotted mongrel of the mullah, foaming at a mouth too large for a dog or even a wolf, making sounds no canine had ever made, slipping between the legs of the armed men, who screamed and screamed as their limbs were shorn off and their heads rolled like smooth river stones fresh from the bottom of the Kunhar, and Nasir thought absurdly, *But you're not allowed inside the mosque. Bad dog. What will Khizar say?*

Then the grainy-white darkness was upon him and he thought no more.

~

Nasir woke up in a rickshaw on a bumpy road. It wasn't Parrot—the doors were brown and made of plastic, not canvas—and a wave of terror overwhelmed the intense throbbing pain in his face and arms. When he tried to move, the agony twisted and returned with a roar, and he groaned.

"Easy, lala."

Palwasha sat next to him in the rear of the rickshaw, holding his head in her lap, stroking his hair. She looked so much older than her fifteen years, her face gaunt and tired, and was that a lock of white hair on her forehead? He wanted to sit up, but dizziness hit him and he sank back down. He opened his mouth, tried to ask, *Where are we*, but each word, each breath was a struggle, and the sound came out dusty and garbled.

Palwasha leaned in. "Khanewal." She had understood. "We're about an hour away."

Who, who is driving?

She told him the whole story. From his position up in the minaret, Murtaza, their last man standing—a description by necessity; he was seventeen—had taken out the colonel's remaining three goons posted out by the barracks. After their near brush with certain death, the older women had rallied. Farzana, a tiny, scoliotic sixty-year-old, had taken charge of the children, while Parveen rushed to a nearby dispensary to find first-aid kits and medicines. They had clamped the remains of Nasir's jaw together and sutured his wounds with thread and needle as best as they could.

When they finally took inventory, they had lost more than half of

THE MOSQUE AT THE END OF THE WORLD

their little community of twenty-seven. Palwasha hadn't realized how few of them were there in the first place, and now that the mosque-community was decimated, it was unanimously decided that after burying their dead, they would leave the area using back roads. What had the colonel said? A hundred more men a few hours away? He might have lied, but they couldn't take any chances.

But where would they go now that they'd lost the only place they could call home?

Uch, Palwasha told them. The city near the conjunction of five rivers.

"And do you know why I said Uch Sharif?" Palwasha asked Nasir as she changed his dressing and fed him crushed potato through a straw—he wouldn't be able to chew for weeks.

"Why?"

"Because Khizar-chacha told me. After the evil men were dead," she said, her voice full of love and sadness. "He said we'd build strength and a new home in Uch. We'll be safe there until GT Road kills all the evil men walking on it one by one and is ready for us again."

After, Nasir thought. She said Khizar spoke to her *after* the evil men were dead.

He didn't ask her to explain. Just grunted. "Where's Hero?"

"Sitting up front with Wajeeha, who volunteered to drive us." And now Palwasha was smiling. "We freed all the prisoners, lala. Just like Khizar-chacha wanted. They're all coming with us to Uch."

Nasir wasn't sure how he felt about that. He didn't know any of them. But that fear was for tomorrow.

He repositioned his head on the girl's lap and gazed directly into Hero's warm brown eyes. The dog had poked his nose through the rickshaw's partition. Nasir reached out and stroked the dog's ears with two fingers. Hero barked happily and Nasir thought, *A mouth too big for a dog or a wolf.*

Hero turned into a wind, a blur, a swish of smokeless fire surrounding the men in the mosque.

Khizar never told them where he found Hero and they had never asked.

Nasir closed his eyes again and let his body feel the road, every turn and jolt of it vibrating up into the roots of his teeth. The road, the road, a tiny manifesto of humanity's slipshod attempts at connecting, coagulating, warding off the inevitable end of it all.

He felt Hero lick his hand with his damp, rough tongue, remembered how he used to not like dogs. What a fool he was. What fools they all were, humans: scared, angry, brave, hopeful.

Good dog, he thought. *Good dog, Hero.*

Now stay.

ABAGAIL'S GETHSEMANE

Wayne Brady and Maurice Broaddus

*"If we must die, O let us nobly die,
So that our precious blood may not be shed
In vain; then even the monsters we defy"*

—Claude McKay, "If We Must Die"

Summer, 1919

Abagail Freemantle could only hold her breath, count to three, and continue about her work. The stink of death filled the room like a fetid incense. The dim flame of the gas lamp flickered in an unfelt breeze. Close and cramped, the narrow bed and her chair were all that could fit in the converted linen closet. This young man, who could have been her brother or son, lay dying. And she was powerless.

In the past year, the Great Influenza had swept across the planet, attacking healthy people like this young man more often than the elderly or young. It started with a sore throat, chills, and a fever, but ended with ravaged lungs within the husk of a body. The pandemic had killed millions, so the newspapers said, but was slowly beginning to ebb. Abagail volunteered for the St. James African Methodist Episcopal Church, just down the road from her place in Hemingford Home, in the nearby freetown Speese. They had set up clinics for treating flu victims. While the big cities recovered, rural places lagged behind without the proper resources. But they had each other and the Lord and that was enough. Most days.

People struggled, going through the motions that things had returned to what they could call normal. But the fear remained underneath it all.

Abagail watched him sleep. She held the space with him, carving out a spiritual siege-wall against the intractable disease. Unable to abide the silence—broken only by the raspy, desperate inhalation and labored coughs—she took her patient's hand. Beads of sweat glistened along his ashen skin. A pang of guilt thumped at her insides, knowing the flu had no power over her. She focused on being God's hands to wipe the young man's tears, dab his forehead, and comfort him where she could. His Bible lay spread on the sheets next to him, the open pages mocking him. And her.

Stirring, he groaned as if the weight of the sheets pressed too hard on him.

"You think God has abandoned us, don't you?" she asked.

"Don't you?" Half turning from her, he coughed. Flecks of blood sprayed the sheets, his lungs completely eaten up worse than if he had the white plague.

"The Lord don't owe us an explanation for why He does what He does. I'm satisfied with what God told Moses. *I Am Who I AM*. His name all the answer one needed." Beyond question. Most days. When someone received answers like *I Am*, there was no point in questioning. Maybe that was the point. But that left so much room for doubt. "Here's what I know: While we're here, we have to serve. To do our part."

"I wish I had your faith."

"You're tired. Let me believe enough for the both of us."

"I don't think that's how it works." His attempted smile faltered, a broken crack along his face.

"You hush now. Save your strength by not arguing with me."

ABAGAIL'S GETHSEMANE

She prayed as if she could push health from her soul to his by sheer force of faith.

He shivered, trapped in the terrible chill of death's shadow. His eyes, dulled by fever and fatigue, searched for her. "I have something to confess."

"What is it, baby?" She patted his hand, uncomfortable in the role of mother confessor.

The young man rose up on his elbows as best he could, his arms buckling under the effort. His tone lowered into a conspiratorial scrape. "I see him."

"See who?" Abagail leaned closer.

"The man whose face was hidden by the shadow of the moon." He faded in and out of consciousness. His breathing grew shallow, his cadence cracked with delirium. "He's coming for you. For all of us."

No, not delirium—or if it was, it was a shared fever dream—since Abagail had also dreamed of this Moon Shadow Man, a figure who existed like a word forever at the tip of her tongue without being named. Even when she was alone, in the night, in the cold of the wind, lost in a barren place, he was there. Just out of sight, just out of reach, always watching. Always waiting. Abiding. The Moon Shadow Man first approached Abagail in a dream. A dream with the strength of memory.

In the early morning light, Abagail Freemantle looked toward Hemingford Home. The folks back in Boulder busied themselves with building a new life for themselves after the ravages of the superflu plague. Ignoring the real struggle. No, they were meant to stand against the gathering forces of darkness. Against him. Beyond the nightmares, they had no idea who they were up against, but she understood what he could do. The returning darkness was almost upon them—if indeed it had even truly left them—but they weren't ready. She *wasn't ready.*

She was no longer able to feel God's presence. No longer able to heed His call. She felt like she had been praying into a dead phone. She'd lost that which was most precious, her sense of her Father's good pleasure. "My soul is very sorrowful, even to death." She had offended God (with her doubts). She hated to disappear on them. It felt cruel to just leave them a note, but she didn't have time for lengthy explanations or long-winded discussions. Her soul was in jeopardy. She had to leave. While the folks in Boulder slept, she had to rekindle what she once had, that connection.

I must be gone a bit now. I've sinned and presumed to know the Mind of God.
My sin has been PRIDE, and He wants me to find my place in His work again.
I will be with you again soon if it is God's Will.

—Abby Freemantle

She'd lost track of time. It could have been hours, days, or weeks since she left on her pilgrimage of fasting and prayer. To have her spirit sifted. She stopped beneath the ragged shadow of the Witness Tree. Centuries old, having seen countless stories, things she hadn't imagined, it bore the marks of history. Its bark charred black, its branches spindly and skeletal.
"Show me my sin, Lord. I don't know. I've gone and missed something you meant for me to see."

His message delivered, the young man convulsed, the rack of coughs spasming his body. His hand tightened on hers to ride out the pain. He wrapped his other hand over hers, holding on until his grip slackened, the last of his strength fleeing into the night on an angel's wing.

The room reeked of grief and despair. Abagail closed the door behind her. When she went outside, schoolgirls jumped rope to their ode to the "three-day fever" they started calling the "purple death."

ABAGAIL'S GETHSEMANE

"I had a little bird and its name was Enza. I opened the window and in-flew-Enza."

The world was falling apart, judgment was inevitable.

He's coming for you. For all of us.

She felt that message down to her bones. And she wanted to run, understanding the plight of Jonah in a whole new way. She stroked her Bible and whispered, "I don't know how much longer I can do this."

"Abby Hardestry. I swear every time I see you, you've got a new name." Working in the fields had roughened Hariett Woodson's voice. While the Freemantles came to Nebraska as freed slaves—part of the Exodusters movement, the thousands of Black folks who moved into the Great Plains—Hattie was a Kincaider. In 1904, the Kincaid Act amended the Homestead Act to provide 640-acre land claims for settlers in Nebraska's Sand Hills. It presented a huge opportunity for Black folks to build something they could call their own. Hattie's people were one of the founding families of Speese.

"I see you as sensitive as ever, Hattie. Leave my poor David be." Hattie knew well that David passed a while back.

"You just couldn't wait to get back in the saddle. Or be saddled." Hattie threw her head back in raucous laughter. From anyone else, the words would sound harsh or mean; from her, they cut to the heart of the matter. Always speaking her mind, always couched in a love for her people, she had an infectious way about her. Hattie wrapped her arm around Abagail's and walked beside her. "You all hate to leave Hemingford Home, especially just to hang out with us non-respectable Negroes."

"You hush."

"You know I ain't told no lie. We all just common folk once your dad became a member of Grange Hall." There was something else under Hattie's words. A constant challenge. Hattie was a hard woman, always stirring folks up. Organizing fights for voting rights, she often spoke at the NAACP meetings in Omaha.

"Where are we going?" A part of Abagail sought her out like she was a missing piece of who she wanted to be.

"To a barrelhouse. You look like you could use a break. A drink, too, frankly."

"I don't think so."

"A girl can dream, can't she? Come on."

Hattie led them down the unpaved road apace, round the bend, and up a hill. Throughout Nebraska, from Omaha to Hemingford Home—all across America, truth be told—under the veneer of civility, the mood was angry. A season of blood spread like a contagion across the country. The South was one thing, but the North wasn't much better, just hidden behind a more polite mask. Workers seethed over job losses and the rising cost of living. It seemed like everyone quit working and went on strike: boilermakers, tailors, truck drivers, butchers. The *Gatlin Bee* kept running articles about businesses hiring Black folk to replace their striking workers alongside crime waves involving Black criminals. The newspaper editorials pounded a constant drumbeat about Negro attacks and police failure to make arrests, and rumors of white women assaulted by Black men.

"Look over there. You can see Gatlin from here. Filled with a bunch of men who made their money from bootlegging, but want to crow about being upstanding citizens. Honest and law-abiding. God-fearing." Hattie spat off to the side.

Before long, they wandered down a secluded grove and soon arrived at a run-down barn, its planks half-rotted, its paint peeling. A beaten-up sign swung in the wind, the name obscured. A group of men eyed them as they walked up. A couple were Black soldiers who had gone off to the Great War to fight for liberty and had returned to a home where they did not have freedom for themselves. A man in well-patched overalls—the brim of his broad hat frayed about the edges—tipped his cap at them and kept drinking. He was one of the Black folks who moved from the cotton fields of the South to search

ABAGAIL'S GETHSEMANE

for work in the North during the Great Migration. Though hate followed them like a dogging shadow, they were still able to carve out spaces to call their own.

"What sort of place have you brought me to?" Abagail asked.

"The kind that brews its own moonshine out back." Hattie half curtsied to the Broad-Brimmed Hat Man.

He opened the door. The bar was fashioned from repurposed wood, surrounded by mismatched tables and chairs scattered around a hardwood dance floor. String lights ran the length of the walls. Abagail knew she wouldn't get the smell of cigarette smoke out of her clothes for days. In the corner, a man pounded the keys of a piano, wringing all the blues and boogie-woogie he could out of it. A woman belted out lyrics at the top of her lungs to the whoops and hollers.

"Oh my God how I love to be sexy with my man
And how I love him to be sexy with me
When he gets me
What he gets me
What he shoots in me"

"Oh . . . my." Abagail blushed. The energy of the room, the easy laughter, the carrying on, it felt like she belonged. She harbored secret ambitions for herself beyond singing at churches. Of maybe one day performing for the smart set, being booked through the Sherman Dudley Theatrical Enterprises touring company. Maybe make a hot record. Make a decent buck. It all felt like a life within her grasp. All it would require was her just . . . choosing.

―――

"Please, my Lord, my Lord, not unless I have to, I'd rather have you take this cup from my lips if You can." She'd seen a heap during her time on earth, nothing to match the doings of the latest months. The call of God was

always about His mission. Moses was called to wander a desert and climb a mountain, never to enter the Promised Land. Noah saved his family from God's wrath and judgment by flood only to drink himself into a stupor with his survivor's guilt.

In response to her prayer, a crow squawked from a telephone pole. Its wings fluttered. It cocked its head, its eyes dark and knowing, studying her with a merciless scrutiny. Her opposite number was close. So close she could almost feel his hot, fetid breath on the back of her neck.

"My soul also is greatly troubled. But you, O Lord—how long?!" She yelled into the night, her loud cry followed by a sudden burst of tears. "I'm old and I'm scared and mostly I'd just like to lie right here on the home place. I'm ready to go right now if You want me. Thy will be done, my Lord, but Abb's one tired shuffling old Black woman. Thy will be done."

Several more crows landed, settling onto the branches. The inky sky silhouetted them. A couple more dropped onto the pathway. Their glossy wings reflected the moonlight, giving them an eerie sheen. Their unsettling caws an aphonic drone. An ominous hum resonating with a sinister energy. Even without looking, she knew she had company. Her eyes darted to the crows, the man-shaped shadow she knew lurked in the darkness.

"I don't think I'm supposed to be somewhere like . . . here."

"In such a den o' heathens?" Hattie asked.

"I just don't want Daddy to be embarrassed if folks was to find out I was in places like this. Ain't a place for a respectable woman. Not at all."

"What folks? White folks? They better not come 'round here. Far as we concerned, this is a Black sundown town, here." That was what she admired about Hattie, the way her ancestors' stories pulsed through her veins, strengthened her limbs. "I come from a long line of troublemakers who fought back and rebelled."

"None o' that sounds like me."

"Girls like you stay home to marry. I ran off to teach."

ABAGAIL'S GETHSEMANE

"I'm too old for schoolin'."

"You're never too old to learn, long as you leave your mind open to it. For you, I have a different assignment."

"What sort of assignment?"

"Some folks would love it if you could favor us with a song," Hattie said.

"I don't know . . ."

"Don't do that false-modesty thing. Just go do what you was born to do." Hattie handed her a guitar. "Sing us a song. A real song. A *you* song."

Abagail thought of her father.

John Freemantle joined the Mystic Tie Grange back in 1902, the first Black man to ever do so. Abagail's father's entire life was marked by such "firsts." There was always a cost to being such a pioneer. The jokes he pretended not to hear. Believing in holding his head up and quoting the Bible, he modeled being a respectable Negro hoping to sway folks' minds. It worked, as many people came around. But some were never going to be reached.

Abagail had barely been married for three months when she played in the Grange Hall. She was so nervous. A young Black girl in a pretty white dress, scared the crowd would turn on her, at the very least hurl tomatoes. Abagail sang her terrified heart out, starting with several gospel songs, changing things up with a risky little ditty, and closing her encore with "The Star-Spangled Banner." Oh, how she remembered the applause as if it were yesterday. If she admitted it to herself, a part of her heart basked in their adulation. Seen and validated in their eyes. Her heart swelled with pride. It was the happiest night of her life in a topper year.

Abagail didn't know if it was a "her" song, but it was the one on her heart. The one from that night, which left her feeling . . . incomplete. She whispered "Digging My Potatoes" to the piano man. He grinned. When she performed the bawdy little ditty at the Grange Hall, it felt off, wrong somehow. While it spoke to her, wanting to show her mischievous side, the way they received it, with their leers and howls, made her feel dirty. Like she was expected to sing such coon music. But now, three verses in, her crowd clapped and danced, caught up in the spirit of the moment.

In the corner of the room, she sensed a presence. More of an . . . absence, like a lonely rustle of dead leaves. She didn't have to see him. Her mind pictured a man shadowed by the night. A penumbra creeping at the edge of the room waiting for the lights to flick off. A coldness that settled into your marrow, numbing you until you couldn't move, knowing you might never know true warmth again. His voice the desperate scratch of fingernails against a locked coffin. Even without being conscious of his presence, folks drifted away from the corner.

She came to know the Moon Shadow Man as the Dark Man, the servant of the Devil. His face remained hidden, as if shadowed by a cowl, except for his eyes. They burned red like coals in the night, searching for her. In her most recent dream, he stood on the roof of a building, like a white pharaoh deciding all that he saw was his domain. The sun set behind him, but he stared east. Always east, but there was no love for it. A pharaoh swaddled in blue jeans and a denim jacket. With a white forehead, red cheeks, his leering grin framing white teeth, sharp and neat. His dusty black boots had run-down heels.

"I love it out here. So peaceful. So quaint," the voice's overly genteel tone a slick poison in her mind. A voice where a man should have been. The shadows shifted, quiet and devouring. "What's my name?"

Her floral housedress, worn fabric with its patched seams, draped to her thin ankles with a quiet elegance. Arthritis like shards of glass driven into her hips and knees. The pain of life. Her stomach didn't grumble, no appetite to betray when she last ate or might eat again. Her hands ran so cold, a chill that drilled down to her core. Her dark skin mottled with blotchy and purple splotches. Her mouth dry. Abagail stumbled over a half-buried

ABAGAIL'S GETHSEMANE

root. *The landscape churned and she grew light-headed. A black wind blew and she was so thin, a reed ready to be uprooted by it.*

"Near the cross! I'll watch and wait, hoping, hoping, hoping." *A frieze of wrinkles enclosed her mouth, her lips fixed and determined. The echoed lyrics turned the hymn into a plea, an infectious chord with jazz inflections, reminding her of another place, a younger self.* "And trusting ever. Till I reach the golden strand. Just beyond the river."

As Abagail ended her song, the crowd burst into applause. The shouts drove the presence away.

Hattie met her at the stage steps, ushering her past the well-wishers and backslappers. "Now that's what I'm talking about, Abby."

"I like performing, is all. Give folks a taste of heaven."

Hattie hugged her tight, drawing Abagail's ear to her mouth. "You need to be out raising hell."

"Hattie! I would never . . . " Abagail pulled away and swatted her arm.

"You should. You still in your prime, got a lot of life left in you."

"I'll leave the . . . raising to you."

A shout erupted from the front door. A wave rippled through the crowd, a series of discontented murmurs souring the mood. The Broad-Brimmed Hat Man gestured for Hattie.

"Ain't no point in headin' Gatlin way. Nothing but a hornet's nest." Sweat stains darkened each underarm. "White couple claimed one of us attacked them with a pistol. The *Gatlin Bee* couldn't wait to start writing about a 'Black Beast on the prowl.'"

Abagail knew the pattern of the gathering storm clouds from every Saturday night at the Grange. The morning might start off calm, but by the afternoon, full of liquid courage, they'd work each other up into a lather. Her father never went by after dark. The right spark might ignite into something horrible.

"Police done arrested a fifteen-year-old. Boy had been in bed all week with the flu, but that didn't stop them. Said he was acting suspicious by running when he approached. The couple even said he was the assailant." The Broad-Brimmed Hat Man made his way to the bar. Tapping the counter for a stout pour of moonshine to drown his resignation, he slumped heavily into a chair. "Sheriff done sent half the police home, while some fool trots across the courthouse lawn on a white horse with a rope dangling from the saddle, stirring folks up."

Even in Hemingford Home, like every other Black person in the United States, Abagail understood the rules for survival among white folks: to smile like they were family when encountered. To "yes, sir" or "no, ma'am" them in every response. To move off the sidewalk to allow them to pass unperturbed. To know what streets to stay clear of, especially after dark. And to always be mindful of their ways, because even a wink could get a boy killed. She thought about the young man who died from the flu before he had the chance to live.

"No." Abagail grabbed her purse and Bible. "No more."

"Where are you going?" Hattie grabbed her elbow.

"Sometimes you have to get off your knees and do something," Abagail said.

"Your faith's not enough to keep you safe."

"Iffen you're fighting to be free every time you walk out the door, you ain't promised to return," Abagail said.

"Then I'm coming with you. Someone's gotta watch your fool behind."

The road wound its way from one end of the country to the other. A series of farms nestled. Snorts of pigs. The caws of a morning rooster who'd done lost all sense of time. They made it to the outskirts of Speese, where they spied the white mob marching toward town. The people of Gatlin only cared about reminding the folks in Speese of their place. What would happen if they got too ambitious, if they stepped out of line. Entering the woods, Abagail and Hattie approached a graveyard trimmed by an orchard of shrubs. They passed mossy obelisks, grave markers, which could have been for Confederate

ABAGAIL'S GETHSEMANE

soldiers if they weren't so far north. Abagail nervously hummed "In the Garden" as she crept to the center of the grove. She stopped near the clearing of a Witness Tree. A low wind wound through its branches.

The leader trotted up on his white horse. The moonlight shown through the trees, though the shadows of the leaves dappled his face. His eyes blistered with fury.

"Hang him. If you can't get him, hang someone else!" That voice. It belonged to the Moon Shadow Man. "We'll get him if we have to burn the whole shack down!"

The mob undulated like an angry wave. Onlookers bore American flags. Two small girls made their way through the crowd carrying pails filled with stones, passing them out like communion wafers. The Gatlin sheriff dragged the young accused boy out from his vehicle before abandoning him like raw meat left to bait a bear trap. The mob descended on the boy from all sides, caught up in a certain madness. A contagion of hate, spreading from person to person faster than any superflu. They tied a rope around the boy's neck. The way he thrashed, desperate to live. The will of the mob dragging him around to the front of the Witness Tree.

"I never did it. My God, I am innocent!" the boy screamed, his cries falling on deaf ears.

"Let's show him some genuine southern hospitality." The Moon Shadow Man gestured to the mob, a sinister conductor of terror. "Lift!"

"Lift! Lift for Gatlin! Lift for America!"

The roar of frenzied cheers and howls rose like they were at a party. The boy called out for Jesus, crying into a dead phone. They strung him up from a lamppost. His feet danced in the air. The images flashed by faster than Abagail could take them in, not wanting to linger on any of it for too long. Her heart couldn't take the pain of it all. The eternal pain. The perpetual pain.

"Welladay," Abagail lamented, abandoned in the face of absolute evil.

Not satisfied, some men in the crowd fired into his now still body, riddling him with bullets. Brutality took on a life of its own, an empty maw of suffering, unable to be sated. They were possessed by the impulse that made Cain split the skull of his brother. A group virus, a spirit outside of themselves, the way worker bees served their unseen queen. Drunk on the heady fumes of violence, they cut the boy down, tied him to a car. They dragged him through the streets. It might as well have been a flickering scene from a moving picture show, history captured in lightning, as his corpse was driven several blocks, reduced to a shapeless mass of broken bones and swollen flesh. Battered and bloody, no longer recognizable as human. Unsatisfied, they soaked him in gasoline and piled trash on him. They set what remained of him on fire. Tongues of flame lapped along the bark into the branches. When the fire died out, people kicked the torso down the street. The boy's empty skull rattled to a halt, facing the dark sky.

The pain was unending, their need to destroy insatiable. And the Lord seemed determined to wait on the sidelines.

"No more," Abagail said.

"Abby?"

"Sometimes you have to take a stand," Abagail said. "We aren't free until we are *all* free. Go on now, you hear? Organize our people. I'll buy you the time you need to get ready."

Hattie retreated. Black folks took refuge in their houses.

The mob then formed a parade of violence, beating any Black man they came across on their march to the jail. Mugging for the assembled cameras. Laughing, shouting with glee, traipsing back to the jail to search for more Black prisoners to have sport with. They broke into the gun store, blocked the courthouse entrance. Even when police reinforcements arrived, the mob overwhelmed them and took their weapons. Laws, civility, God all weak and helpless before the mob. Lynch laws reigned supreme. They torched a parked car. The crowd charged the large oak doors of the courthouse, setting fire to walls and furniture. When the firefighters arrived, the mob cut their hoses.

ABAGAIL'S GETHSEMANE

Dozens of white men clustered under the wan glow of a streetlamp. With no one to stand between them and the city. Abagail stood in the road. Alone. Scared. The only person against the tidal wave of their hate, rotting in the belly of the beast. They approached her, a ring of wolves closing in. All bared teeth and low growls.

"Dirty spade, I hear tell there were coons with guns. They need to be taught respect for the law." The leader hopped down from his white horse, his mouth opened, a terrible maw filled with a dark laughter, but not with his own voice. "Your blood is in my fists."

A preternatural terror gripped Abagail. She avoided his eyes, scared she might see the fleeting doubt of her own reflected in them. She thought of what Hattie might do. And of David as Goliath tromped toward him. Reaching down, she found a smooth stone. She hurled it, hitting him in the head. Howling, he dropped to his knees.

"Get her!" He clutched his face, blood gushed between his fingers.

Her dress fluttered as she ran down an alley. Behind her, the crash of broken windows and the clatter of fences being knocked down, the wood set aflame. They made a game of throwing rocks right back at her. A car full of white men soon roared to a stop beside her in the alley. The same terrible grin leered from each of their faces. The nearest men all but bayed, wolves catching a scent. Abagail smacked the first man who hopped out of the vehicle with the lid from a nearby trash can, knocking him clean off his feet. The other men hesitated, enough for her to slip by them. They gave chase for sport.

She dashed between houses, grabbing at door handles as she ran. Finally, a cellar door gave way. Abagail nearly leapt into its darkness. Whatever fate waited her in its depths, better to fall into the hands of the Lord, for His mercies were very great, rather than into the hands of man.

The streets deathly still, their burgeoning silence took on a life of its own. Speese held its collective breath. Sharp rifle reports rang out in the darkness, all too near thunderclaps. A distant scraping drew near. In her mind, she knew the sound. Gun barrels and torches against the sides of houses. The mob was coming. It was not her place to judge God. He judged with water once and would judge again one day, with fire.

―――

"You can't connect to your God because He was never real. We created an idea of Him—in our image, blond hair and blue eyed—designed to keep you in your place. Where we want you."

"You serve the Father of Lies!" Abagail yelled.

"You ain't ready to shake off those chains." The Dark Man now imitated Hattie's voice. "You starve when God goes silent on you? Would you like a bite to eat? I could pop out and grab us a little something."

"Man shall not live by bread alone, but by every word that comes from the Mouth of God." Abagail pursed her lips. Her stomach twisted; her flesh was weak.

Lord God, I have suffered. *She was tired, had been doing this for so long. Never questioning God, always wondering if she'd done the right thing. The cost of following Him so dear.*

"How goes your search for your quiet God?" The Dark Man sauntered about, hidden among the shadows of the trees, all too pleased with himself. "You know what your problem is?"

"I don't need you telling me my problem."

"You're angry, but you won't admit it."

"Yes, I'm angry," Abagail said. "I see all the hurt and pain around me. I can't help but want it to be better."

"A fact you can see, but your God can't. You've got a right to be angry. You should pray to God to destroy those who oppress you and your people. Lex talionis. The law of retribution. Justice."

"Vengeance."

"Reparations," the Dark Man said.

"You're a liar."

"You reek of doubt. Of questions you're too afraid to ask."

"We carry a wound with us. An interruption of our spirit." She remem-

ABAGAIL'S GETHSEMANE

bered her words to Nick Andros. "I have harbored hate of the Lord in my heart. Every man or woman who loves Him, they hate Him, too, because He's a hard God, a jealous God, He Is what He Is, and in this world He's apt to repay service with pain while those who do evil ride over the roads in Cadillac cars. Even the joy of serving Him is a bitter joy. I do His will, but the human part o' me has cursed Him in my heart."

"Then join me, Mother," the Dark Man said. "I am war, famine, death, and disease. I am the Four Horsemen. I can give you power. Authority. Years back in your limbs."

"I don't want to be out of God's will for my life." The capillaries under her skin burst, her sweat issued like drops of blood. "I need to serve, not rule. It's only Him I serve. There are no easy shortcuts. Only the long, hard road."

"Then you should end it all. Lie down. Sleep. It will be over soon enough."

"When the Lord wants me, the Lord will take me. The Lord will take me home to Glory in His own time." The words came out sharp and defiant, but in her heart, they felt hollow, a distant echo of the faith she once had. She started to hum "Precious Lord, Take My Hand," but the tune morphed. Waiting for the fire to come and consume her, she held her breath and counted to three.

"We see now through a glass darkly," Abagail prayed in the pitch blackness of the cellar. "Before I'll be a slave, you'll bury me in my grave. Better to die free. Now be gone."

Metal scraped against the cellar door. It swung open. Moonlight pierced the night.

Abagail shielded her face.

An arm stretched out, fishing in the darkness. "Abby? You in here, girl?"

"Yes!" Abagail clasped her hand. "You came back!"

"What's the point in me making it if I leave you behind?" Hattie huffed as she helped her friend out of the cellar.

"The men?"

"They gone. Scurried back to their rat holes."

"God answered my prayers."

"Our rifles helped. The sight of us dimmed their fervor and they found their senses like their fever broke."

The Moon Shadow Man had retreated.

Even in the darkest hours, God still listened. Abagail fell to her knees, not worried if she'd be able to get up again, and gave thanks for the respite. But she couldn't fight the suspicion that this abiding evil was not yet at its full power, and with that thought she grew afraid. One day she knew she'd have to face him at the height of his power, and her faith would not be enough.

Abagail was so close to death, she could feel its fetid breath on the back of her neck. Once the Devil left Jesus in the wilderness, the angels came to serve Him. Maybe they took the appearance of his ancestors. Hattie sat down next to her.

"Are you an angel?" *Abagail's voice cracked.*

"I am more."

"You'll have to forgive an old woman for getting lost in her memories."

"Remember well," Hattie said. "They don't want us to learn history so that we won't recognize when the Devil tries to play the same ol' tricks."

"I still believe in His plan," Abagail said. "A slammed door don't mean I was wrong to knock."

"You are saved and sanctified, filled with the Holy Spirit. But there's a dual knowledge in your faith. You need to keep on running to see what the end gon' be."

"These old bones are past running."

"But your spirit ain't. Honor your people. Draw strength from your lineage. Be whole. Bring all of us to bear. What's the point in us making it if we leave you behind? Keep to the old ways—they'll always serve you."

Abagail reached for a leaf from the Witness Tree. In its fold were fat beads of dew. Folding the leaf, the beads became a trickle. Before she drank, she began to hum the hymn "Trust and Obey."

"When I liberate myself, I liberate you." Abagail poured libation for the Creator. And for her sisters. "Not my will, but Yours be done."

She reached for other leaves and drank. Closing her eyes, Abagail held her breath and counted to three. When she opened them, the call of Boulder tugged at her soul, beckoning her home. Many were the mysteries of His perfect timing.

"I ain't never been one to cry for too long. And I'm all out o' tears."

The best way to escape despair is to get back to the work. She petted the charred back of the Witness Tree.

God is great. God is good.

PART THREE

LIFE WAS SUCH A WHEEL

HE'S A RIGHTEOUS MAN
Ronald Malfi

1

"Zarah."

She turned away from the window and saw Benjamin standing there in the doorway, haggard in the face and dressed in his cruddy, sun-faded overalls. He was clutching the handle of an aluminum bucket filled with water from the well, like some sort of peace offering. Despite his attire, Zarah knew he hadn't been out working in the field all afternoon, but day-drinking with that Pelham fellow down by the river. She could smell the booze coming off him in waves from across the room.

"He ain't due till late tonight," Benjamin said. "You gonna stare out the window till then?"

She crossed the room to where a table had been dressed in smooth, white linen, and set with good china and polished silverware. There was a cluster of unlit candles at the table's center, a mismatched assortment of whatever Zarah could find—short, squat ivory candles; tall, spear-like ones the color of blood; a hefty black stump that looked like it might have served a purpose in some dark, unspeakable ritual in the not-too-distant past.

There was a book on the table, as well—incongruous among the place settings and the collection of candles. A hardcover, bound in plastic film like how they used to wrap books in libraries. From where it lay on the table, Zarah could see the tobacco-colored stain of the page edges, and the way one corner of the book cover bent inward toward those pages.

Benjamin was staring at the book, too.

"Are you still angry?" she asked him.

"This whole thing is a mistake. You know my position on that."

"The village took a vote."

"Don't make it right." He came into the room, the bucket dripping little plinks of water across the hardwood floor. "These people have gone blind, Zarah. They're all sheep. They're all a bunch of empty shells desperate to be filled."

"You used to think this was a good place. A safe place."

"Don't tell me what I think."

"Benjamin, if you'd just—"

"I said don't tell me what to think." He took the bucket over to an empty glass pitcher on the counter and poured the water from the bucket into it. "Quit trying to needle around in my head."

"That's not what I'm doing. I'm just thinking of the baby. That's all."

She watched his gaze tick down to the subtle swell of her abdomen. When she'd first told him she was pregnant, he'd argued that it wasn't his—that it could belong to any of the men in Calvary, including Clyde Pelham, Benjamin's drinking buddy and all-around lout. Because Benjamin possessed such little comprehension of human biology, he had claimed the differences in their age—she was nineteen, he was thirty-seven—only added to the improbability. Zarah had sworn that she hadn't been with anyone but him—and this was true—but Benjamin hadn't wanted to hear it. Like some obstinate child, he'd fled the house and stayed gone for several days. Not even Pelham knew where he'd gone (or if he did, he hadn't said). Zarah cried about it the entire time, but then, just as she grew determined to not shed another tear on old Benjamin Lewis, he had returned. Yes, reeking of alcohol, but proffering a bouquet of freshly picked wildflowers, and with something akin to an apology on his lips.

"You know how concerned I've been," she said, running a hand along the slight protrusion of her abdomen. "With everything we've seen this past year." And she turned and glanced back out the window.

"You want to believe in some voodoo witchcraft magic nonsense, that's on you." He dragged the bucket off the counter so that it made an unpleasant scraping sound. "But that fella coming here tonight, he's just a man, regular as me."

"Will you at least meet with us? Hear him speak?"

He carried the bucket back across the room, his heavy boots thudding mutely on the hardwood floor. The spilled droplets of water, to Zarah, looked like some celestial constellation. Or maybe a coded message for her to decipher.

"I won't be part of it," he said, and a moment later, he was out of the house.

Zarah drifted back toward the window in time to see him moving down the road with his bucket. He walked with his head down, as if he needed to keep an eye on his feet to make sure they took him where he needed to go. Did she love Benjamin Lewis? She thought she had, back when they'd started. Or maybe it was just a lack of available men in Calvary that had made him seem so appealing at the time. But love or not, his presence in her life—as cursory as it could be sometimes—would make raising a baby easier.

If *the baby comes*, she thought, and her gaze drifted from the road to the field behind the house.

To the rows upon rows of tiny wooden crosses.

2

They had come for him like cowboys in an old Western: on horseback, carrying long guns, and with some half-assed Conestoga wagon hitched to a pair of piebald thoroughbreds. Jacob Cree stood from the railway station bench where he'd been sitting for over an hour and raised a hand above his head in a wave. The horses and wagon drew to a stop, and a couple of men dropped down from their steeds and ambled over to greet him.

Jacob shook both their hands.

"Good to meet you, Mr. Cree."

"Please, call me Jacob."

"Well, I'm Ted Lomm," said the fellow with the large, white, pushbroom mustache. He jerked a thumb at his companion, a scarecrow-thin gentleman with bloodshot eyes and a bad complexion. "This here's Mitchell Detroit."

An odd name, Jacob mused. He had heard of people changing their surnames to reflect where they'd once come from, but also, he knew, in an effort to obfuscate who they'd once been. These men both had long guns propped on their shoulders.

"Those are some beautiful horses," Jacob said, looking past the guns.

Ted glanced over his shoulder at the horses, as if just noticing them for the first time, then turned back to Jacob. "We got cars, of course, but we're stingy with the gasoline."

"We got power, too," Mitchell said, and not without a boastful tone to his voice. "Hooked into a local substation, and we're fortunate to have folks who know how to make it work."

"Wonderful," Jacob said, smiling at the men.

"Anyway," said Ted, "I'm sorry about the wait. Few of the fellas ate some bad egg salad or something and caught a case of the oopsies, if you know what I mean."

Mitchell hung his head, giving himself up as one of the unfortunates.

HE'S A RIGHTEOUS MAN

Ted pointed to the suitcase at Jacob's feet—a simple black clamshell covered in scuffs and scratches. "That all you're taking?"

"I travel light," said Jacob.

Ted reached down to pick up the suitcase for him, but Jacob quickly said, "That won't be necessary," and snatched up the suitcase by its handle before the man could touch it.

They helped him up into the wagon, and then they were off, traveling first through a sodden field, then an expanse of blacktop, where the horses' hooves clopped sharply on the asphalt, then finally across a rutted dirt roadway that ran parallel to a large body of water, which Jacob understood to be the Chesapeake Bay.

Jacob's only companion in the back of the wagon during this journey was a very large man with the smooth, hairless face of a child. He was seated on a bench opposite Jacob. His age was indeterminable, and when he spoke, it was in a volume just barely above a whisper.

"Everything they say about you true, sir?" asked the man, who hadn't introduced himself by name.

"Depends on what's being said," Jacob replied, smiling. His suitcase sat upright on the floor of the wagon, between his knees.

"That you're a prophet. That you predicted this whole thing. The end of the world, and all that."

"Oh . . . " Jacob turned his head so that he could look out beyond the canopy of the wagon and at the horizon, where the sun was setting in a multitude of hues. "Doesn't look like the world has ended to me."

The large man shifted uncomfortably on the wagon's wooden bench.

"Have you read my book?" Jacob asked him.

The man shook his head, then averted his eyes so that he didn't have to meet Jacob's gaze.

"Do I frighten you?"

This time, the man did not respond at all—just kept his eyes trained on the floor of the wagon.

Jacob reached over and placed a hand on the fellow's left knee. Quietly, the man began to sob.

So be it, Jacob thought, removing his hand and closing his eyes as darkness filled the interior of the wagon.

3

Zarah Smith was among those chosen to greet Jacob Cree upon his arrival, so when the horses' hooves were heard echoing throughout Calvary, she rushed out into the waning daylight and scurried mouse-like past the field of tiny crosses, to where a dais decorated in balloons and lit with kerosene lanterns stood empty and anticipatory. It had been decided that only a select few women would greet the prophet, with the townsmen watching from the sides of the road like sentries. Zarah had wanted so badly to be selected, but feared she wouldn't be chosen because of her pregnancy, even though she was barely showing. Yet she *had* been selected, and she'd lain awake that night in bed (next to Benjamin, who'd been snoring like a locomotive) and, staring at the ceiling, imagined what it would be like to finally meet Jacob Cree in person. Later, when the town council chose her for the induction—the dinner, the candles—she felt like God Himself was smiling down upon her.

She knew only what he looked like from the author photo on the dust jacket of his book—a handsome, studious gentleman in a tweed sports coat, whose eyes sparkled with the knowledge of a thousand lifetimes. What Jacob Cree *had* known, of course, was the reason he was here, and the giddiness Zarah now felt as that makeshift wagon came to a stop and a man in a tweed sports coat was helped down, was unlike any sensation she had ever felt in her lifetime. She felt *buoyed*, as if she might at any moment lift right off the pavement and sail unencumbered into the atmosphere.

Jacob Cree was led up to the dais, where Ted Lomm made a throaty announcement. The women in the street clapped politely, while the men, farther back from the road, nodded silently in appreciation. Cree stood there on the dais beside Ted, a suitcase as black as obsidian at his side, surveying the crowd. For a moment, Zarah thought his eyes settled directly on her, where his stare lingered. *What is he thinking right now?* she wondered. *What notions are coming into his brain, as if from the ether, and seeding there?*

When Ted was finished with his speech, he urged Cree to stand front and center to address the crowd.

"My official presentation won't be until tomorrow," Cree said, and Zarah was delighted to hear that his was a strong, cultured, satisfying voice, "so I will keep this brief. But I wanted to thank you all for inviting me here to meet and speak with you. I hope this proves to be a pleasant experience, and that at the very least, I'll leave you all with some modicum of peace. *You are not alone.*"

Again, the women applauded and the men nodded their approval.

A motley assortment of musicians had been culled from the town—a trumpet player, someone with a set of bagpipes, an acoustic guitarist, a snare drum strapped to one man's chest—and as Jacob Cree was led back down from the dais, they all began to play. The music was awful—Zarah couldn't help but laugh a little to herself, as did a number of the other women who had gathered to greet the prophet. She was still laughing about it as she filed into a queue, and each woman shook Cree's hand as he walked down the line. They each had to say a single word of their choosing, so when Cree approached Zarah, she said, "Blessed."

His smile was a million miles.

Zarah was pleased to find his hand cool and dry, his grip firm but not aggressive. He looked her straight in the eye as he held her hand, and she imagined she could see an entire universe swirling inside the tar-black pupils of his eyes.

She watched Cree move down the line, then vanish into Ted Lomm's house along with the members of the town council.

It was only then that Zarah looked around at the faces of the men in attendance, and ultimately spotted Benjamin standing among them. Even from such a distance, she could recognize something dark and seething behind the mask of his face, and it was a thing that Zarah Smith didn't trust.

Not in the least.

4

Jacob was given an entire house to himself for the night, which was rarely the case whenever he would visit these remote villages. Water was brought in from a well and a tub was filled for him to bathe in. He was also offered fresh clothes, but he only patted his clamshell suitcase and said that he had everything he needed, but thank you. After his bath, however, he pulled on the same clothes he'd been wearing all day—with the exception of the tweed sports coat, since it was a nice night out.

He was told that his induction dinner was to be sponsored by a Benjamin Lewis and a Zarah Smith. Yet when he arrived at the house, only the woman was present. He didn't ask about the man's whereabouts.

She was young, mildly attractive in a plain-looking way, and with a face that seemed eager to soak up whatever knowledge he might wish to impart. She smiled at him when she answered the door, and if she thought it odd he carried his suitcase with him, she didn't say anything about it. Later, as she leaned over and lit the mismatched collage of candles at the center of the table in preparation for their meal, he noticed she was in the early stages of pregnancy.

"I was told your village has electricity," he said.

"Oh," she said. She had just lit the final candle, yet she kept her arm hovering above them as if she'd made some mistake and was considering how to correct it. "We do. It's just that I thought the candles would be a nice touch. They make this feel more ceremonial.

Would you prefer I turn the lights on? I've got permission this evening because of your visit."

He smiled as he set his linen napkin in his lap. "No, it's fine. The candles are lovely," he told her.

"I also have music," she said. She went over to one corner of the room, where a small record player sat on a console. A stack of 45s stood in a small tower nearby. She began to riffle through them, reciting the song titles and artists' names as she did so: "I've got 'Yellow Submarine' by the Beatles, and 'Crying' by Roy Orbison, and 'Baby, Can You Dig Your Man?' by Larry Underwood, and—"

"No music. Please. Come sit. Let's eat."

She had baked fresh bread and made a salad and prepared a stew, which was delicious if a bit hot for such a warm summer evening. She poured him a glass of red wine from a ceramic jug, then poured herself a cup of water. The wine tasted overly fruity, and Zarah explained that they made their own—that there was a whole garden in the back field where they hollowed out coconuts and filled them with raisins and sugar until they fermented in the ground.

"Sometimes the deer find them and get drunk," she told him. "Have you ever seen a drunk deer? They just sort of amble around in the road and sometimes come right up to the houses. You can walk right up and pet one if it's drunk enough, though I don't suggest you do that to any of the bucks." With her hands, she mimed having an invisible set of antlers rising up from her head. Then she peered down at the suitcase that stood beside his chair. "This is a good town. No one is going to steal your things, Mr. Cree. You don't have to carry that everywhere you go."

"Yes, I do," he said.

"What's in it?" she asked.

"Humanity's future."

"Oh," she said, and her voice was suddenly very small.

He smiled and nodded, and happened to glimpse his book behind her on the counter. She caught him looking and quickly glanced down at her half-eaten plate, visibly embarrassed.

"Have you read it?" he asked.

"Seven times."

"Wow. Seven? Really?"

"It's terribly frightening."

He got up from the table and went over to the counter. His book, the one that started it all, was covered in plastic film and had a library sticker on the spine. He opened it and looked at the copyright page. "Hey. First edition," he said. It had a real dollar value, if that meant anything anymore.

"Did you really foresee all of those things? Everything that happened?"

He closed the book and returned to his chair. It was a question he was asked all the time, which he found strange, since the people who always asked it were also true believers.

"It was my first novel," he said. "I woke up from a nap one afternoon with the sentences burning in my brain. I went to my typewriter and it was like the words were burning through my fingertips, too. I wrote furiously over a few months' time. It felt like I was channeling some divine intercept, a language from another world."

"From God?"

"Well, I don't know about that," he said, and he nodded at the gold cross Zarah wore around her neck on a chain. "I've never been a religious man."

"Not even after all that's happened?"

He smiled without humor. He was still staring at that gold cross around her neck. "Did you ever think how funny it is, the symbol of the cross?"

Absently, she reached up and fingered the charm at her throat. "How so?"

"It's the tool by which your supposed savior was brutally murdered.

That's like having a loved one beaten to death with a hammer, only to kneel and pray to the hammer."

The look on Zarah's face told him he had once again gone too far.

"I'm sorry," he quickly amended. "I shouldn't have said that. It was crass. And you're correct, Zarah—there are plenty of stories of God speaking in mysterious ways in the Bible, so who's to say you're wrong and I'm right?"

"That's true," she said. "But the Bible can be left up to interpretation. Your book, however . . . "

He nodded, blotting the corners of his mouth with his napkin. "Yes," he said. "My book is pretty specific."

"You're a *prophet*, Mr. Cree. You foresaw everything that happened—the superflu accidentally released in the Mojave Desert, the descriptions of death and dying, the events in Colorado. There was once even a traveler who came through here who spoke of nuclear destruction in Las Vegas, just like you'd written about. Your novel even mentions the shared dreams that some people claimed to have had of Abagail Freemantle, the old woman in Nebraska."

"Well, some things aren't that precise. I suppose even prophets can get things wrong from time to time. For example, in my novel—in my *visions*—the old woman's name was Arlene Froam, and she was living on a farm in Wyoming."

"It's miraculous."

"It was frightening," he confessed. "The book was published about two weeks after Captain Trips escaped that Department of Defense facility in the desert. I started seeing it in bookstore windows just as the news began to report cases of the superflu. I watched at first as polite society began to grind to a halt, and then watched further as things collapsed all around me. The death rate in my novel—from my visions—was a staggering ninety-nine-point-four, which was the exact number both the CDC and the WHO claimed as the death rate for Captain Trips. I was living in New York at the time, and the city at first became a war zone, and then became a morgue. I wound up escaping through a hellish version of the Holland Tunnel, filled with dead bodies and the buzz of flies. That incessant, *maddening* buzz."

"Did you think you had caused it all?"

His smile faltered. It was the first time anyone had ever asked him that question. "Um. No, I didn't think that at all. I *did* start to wonder where those visions had come from, though, and if I had overlooked something important in those mysterious transmissions that might have prevented all of this."

"Like warning the Defense Department ahead of time," Zarah suggested.

"I've thought about that a lot," he admitted. "The thing is, Zarah, I didn't realize I was seeing glimpses of the future until the future was already here, and by then it was already too late."

A silence settled between them in that moment, weighted in all its quietude.

Then Zarah leaned forward the slightest bit, so that the candlelight shifted about her face. "Will you come with me? I'd like to show you something."

5

She lit a kerosene lantern and led Cree out into the back field. It was fully dark now, the three-quarter moon partially hidden behind a strand of gossamer clouds. He paused in mid-stride to glance up at the sky, and in a monotone voice, said, "M-O-O-N." Then he smiled sadly at Zarah. "One of the characters in my novel spells everything as—"

"Yes, I've read the book."

"Seven times."

She smiled, too. Said, "Yes. Seven times."

"You know what I often think about? It's true my book predicted all the major events over the past year that we've all now come to know

HE'S A RIGHTEOUS MAN

as fact. Yet how many smaller parts of my novel—the characters, the sub-sub-subplots, the love affairs and minor tragedies, the *people*—also came true? I often wonder and get frustrated by the idea that I will never know the answer."

"I believe in it all," she told him, and she watched as his eyes glittered in the glow from the lantern. "I believe you were less a novelist, Mr. Cree, and more of a conduit. A transcriptionist. That book of yours in my house? It's no novel. It's a history book."

The night had grown cold and she could see that he was shivering, so she turned and continued through the field, beckoning him to follow. Once they reached the first row of crosses, she stopped and held the lantern out so that he could see them.

"There are fifty-seven graves in this field, Mr. Cree. Each one an infant. The youngest lasted only a day. The oldest one made it a full two weeks." She turned to him, and could see the wan, pale expression on Cree's righteous, intelligent face. "Everyone here in Calvary survived the superflu because we're immune. Yet our children are not."

She ran a hand down the quiet swell of her belly.

Cree watched her, and understood.

"I hear rumors that you can no longer prophesize, Mr. Cree. That your gift has dried up. That you travel the country giving inspirational talks of hope, but that you can no longer see the future."

Cree's mouth must have gone dry, because when he spoke, she could hear the smacking sound of his lips. "Yes. That's true."

"I'm frightened for the baby inside me. Can you tell me anything that will bring me peace?"

Again: the dry, smacking sound of his lips.

"We just have to have faith," he told her.

They stood there in silence a moment longer before Zarah turned and led him back to the house. Before disappearing inside, she glanced toward the road and saw Benjamin standing there in the moonlight, like something summoned from a pit of fire and brimstone. If Cree noticed the man, he said nothing about it.

6

Jacob woke early the next morning in an empty house to a discordant jangle of musical instruments being played outside in the street. In nothing but his boxer shorts, he went to the bedroom window and saw that there was something of a ragtag crowd gathered outside the house. It was not yet eight in the morning, according to his wristwatch, yet here they were, anxious and excited for the ceremony to start.

There was no fresh water in the tub this morning, so he skipped bathing, and climbed back into the same clothes he'd traveled here in the day before. He always wore the same clothes—the ones he'd worn in his novel's author photo. As a younger man, he'd never been a superstitious person, but after the book was published and the world had gone to hell just as he'd inadvertently predicted, many beliefs Jacob Cree had previously held had irrevocably changed. He thought now that if he continued to wear his author-photo getup, he might begin to receive those transmissions again. It was silly, of course—he knew this deep down—but sometimes in the darkest hours, it was comforting to cling to seemingly silly things.

He had performed this show countless times before, traveling from one city to the next, a sterile, former prophet, making the circuit like some vaudevillian—hopeless, yet proselytizing hope. It had started out feeling like an obligation, like penance. *Did you think you had caused it all?* Zarah had asked him last night, admittedly unnerving him, and while he didn't believe that, he had, early on, felt in some way responsible. When survivors began seeking him out and asking him to visit their villages, he'd felt like Christ among the Nephites. They gave him food and water and whatever else they felt to have retained any value in this new world. He accepted only the food and water, and a warm bed, whenever they could spare one.

He was no dummy: he knew he was chasing some bastardized version of salvation.

Did you think you had caused it all?

Jacob Cree collected his suitcase and stepped out into the bright sunshine to greet his people.

7

Zarah Smith felt something swell inside her chest as Cree stepped from the house and smiled at the townsfolk. The women applauded and the men hollered their approval into the air. Carrying that black clamshell suitcase looking like a large chunk of coal with a handle, Cree came down the porch steps as the group of assorted musicians struck up what sounded bizarrely like "In-A-Gadda-Da-Vida."

The women were dressed in white linen gowns and with flowers in their hair—Zarah was, too—and the men wore neckties over their chambray shirts, their hair greased and combed, their faces cleanly shaved. Ted Lomm wore a tight-fitting suit jacket and a ridiculous neon bow tie as he came up to Cree and shook the man's hand. Then he led Cree down the walk toward the street, and the rest of the townsfolk—Zarah included—fell behind in step.

On the far side of the graveyard field, opposite Zarah and Benjamin's house, the town council had erected a small stage. Behind the stage, a large white sheet to match the women's dresses loomed in the air, held aloft by scaffolding that some of the men had set up over the past week. There was festive bunting around the stage and many folding chairs set up in the empty part of the field, facing the stage and that large white sheet.

Zarah moved quickly through the crowd so that she could claim one of the chairs in the front row. She sat with an audible huff, her excitement radiating through her like an electrical current. That excitement was halted, however, when she happened to glimpse Benjamin among the crowd. No, not truly—more like standing off by himself beneath the shade of a copse of willow trees. He was dressed in his dingy overalls, his hair a mess, a look of utter disdain on his face. He had a backpack slung over one shoulder and was holding a long gun by the stock.

8

A woman placed a wreath of flowers around Jacob's neck and two other women led him up onto the stage. There was a podium and a microphone set up, which was better than the bullhorns he sometimes had to use for large crowds. His speech usually lasted about forty minutes—he'd tell them how the visions started, how he'd written the book, and how he wished he had recognized those visions for what they were at the time. He'd conclude with how humankind should remain vigilant and keep an open mind, because no one could ever tell when the next batch of visions might arrive, and to whom they might come. He would take questions and do the best he could to answer them. And in the end, he would be optimistic about leaving them inspired, or, at the very least, with some modicum of hope for the future.

Ted Lomm walked in lockstep across the stage with him. At one point, he produced a handkerchief from the inside pocket of his suit jacket and blotted his glistening forehead. "Gonna be a hot one," he muttered, and Jacob nodded in agreement.

Mitchell Detroit and two other men stood beside the podium. One of the men adjusted the microphone. The men all wore neckties over flannel shirts.

As Jacob carried his suitcase to the podium and the crowd began to take their seats, he noticed Zarah Smith, who was in the front row, rise and run across the field toward a man standing in the shade of a group of willow trees.

9

"What are you doing, Benjamin?"

She stood before him, breathless, both hands swimming absently over the slight protrusion of her belly.

Benjamin's eyes narrowed. His face was burned from the sun and he sported about three days' growth along his square jaw. He looked past Zarah and up at the stage—at Jacob Cree, of course—and she could see the wheels turning behind his dim, booze-bleary eyes.

"Answer me, Benjamin."

"This is wrong," he said, and his voice was as flat and emotionless as a sheet of plywood. "You've all gone crazy and I won't sit idly by and watch it happen. Especially with my baby in your belly, Zarah."

He reached out and gripped her about the wrist.

10

Jacob stepped up to the microphone and addressed the Calvary audience with a pleasant greeting, while, from the corner of his eye, he kept an eye on Zarah and the large man she was talking to beneath the tree. A man with a gun.

11

"Come with me," Benjamin said.

Zarah pulled her wrist free. "Is that it, then? That's your plan? You're a coward? You're running away?"

"This ain't the way. This town is lost, Zarah. Come with me. We should leave."

"And go where? I have to save the baby," she said, taking a step back from him. "We have to save *all* the babies."

"This will save no one," Benjamin said, and he suddenly looked miserable. "This will damn you all to hell."

She took another step back. And another. Her voice firm, her palms pressed against her swollen belly, she said, "You're a coward, Benjamin Lewis! Do you hear me? You're a *coward*!"

Benjamin stared at her for a heartbeat. They were too far from the crowd to attract any attention, but Benjamin glanced around at everyone nonetheless. Then he looked toward the stage again, just as the giant white sheet was lowered to reveal a large wooden cross, fifteen feet high. Cheers broke out among the townsfolk.

"Madness," Benjamin said, just as he turned to leave her, and—

12

—Jacob turned to see the monstrous thing revealed from behind the sheet, a massive wooden cross whose shadow fell directly upon him, a thing of such impossibility that he couldn't at first comprehend exactly what—

Ted Lomm gripped him on one arm.

Mitchell Detroit gripped him on the other.

Several more men came up behind Jacob, wrapping their arms around him, squeezing the air from his lungs, and lifting his feet off the floor of the stage.

Jacob's suitcase fell off the stage, as—

13

—Zarah ran back to the join the crowd. Her heart was pumping, and that electric energy was surging through her system again. She was smiling, laughing, and tears were beginning to stream down her face. She was joined at the front of the stage by all the other women in white dresses—women who had, over and over again, filled that field with their dead offspring—and they joined hands, sweaty palm to sweaty palm. Squeezing.

On the stage, Jacob Cree screamed. The cross was lowered to the floor of the stage and he was dragged down onto it. He struggled, but it was futile. His clothes—

(*That tweed jacket!* Zarah's mind prattled, recalling the author photo on Cree's book.)

—were stripped from him, everything but the wreath of flowers, and then men approached carrying heavy mallets and iron spikes.

HE'S A RIGHTEOUS MAN

Sweaty and breathing hard, Ted Lomm approached the podium. Against the background of Cree's screams as the spikes were pounded through his wrists, Ted said, into the microphone, "We're a community that has looked out for each other since inception. We take great care—"

"—*to take great care!*" the townsfolk finished.

"Today, my friends, we send this harbinger of doom back to hell! And we will live in peace, prosperity, *and good health for us and our children*, from here on out!"

The women on either side of Zarah raised their hands, taking her hands with theirs. Those tears of joy kept spilling down her face, and she squeezed the hands of her sisters tightly . . . until she spied Cree's strange black suitcase lying on the ground.

She broke away from her sisters, went over to it, opened it up, and found that it was—

Empty.

A final scream pierced the morning air. Zarah looked up in time to see the cross being raised again, this time with Jacob Cree nailed to it, naked and streaked with bright red streamers of blood, his head limp on his neck, that incongruous string of flowers hanging across his chest.

They watched Cree die, and when the prophet was done dying, one of the men who had killed him tossed his hammer in the dirt.

Zarah rushed to it, dropped to her knees, and bowed her head.

AWAITING ORDERS IN FLAGGSTON

Somer Canon

There were sweat bees crawling all over her again. She ran her hands over her wet, greasy skin, hoping to get them off without getting stung, but a couple got their final say before being bounced from their salty revelry like belligerent drunks from a bar. There were many drawbacks to being forced to sleep alone and without basic creature comforts in a shack made of rusted corrugated steel, but Amy liked the bugs the least.

Weak morning sunlight, still golden-hued and teasing her with the promise of a lovely day, seeped through the cracks of the metal panels. Zeke would be along soon to unlock the heavy chains that secured the single door.

She sat up and put her back to one of the four metal walls, hoping to absorb some coolness, but in late July, the only thing that the metal held for her was a disgusting warmth that paired horribly with the humidity that caused her to sweat even in the night. The simple cotton nightgown she wore was filthy from the dirt floor, and she ached to have a dip in the creek to get the stink of old sweat and body oils off of her. Amy hadn't been thankful when they'd first shaved her head before sending her to the shack, but at least she didn't have long hair sticking to her to add to the misery of the wet heat.

"Rise and shine, princess," Zeke announced, knocking on the metal and producing a hollow, sad sound, startling her. He fumbled with the lock and chain, and when the piece of metal that served as a door slid to the side, he poked his face in and smiled at her.

"I hope you like dry toast and Treet meat!"

"I don't care either way. I'd eat *you* I'm so hungry," she said, stepping out into the heavily wooded area. The shack wasn't tall enough for Amy to stand in and she always relished a long morning stretch.

She sat on the big rock that served as her eating place and accepted the food that he'd wrapped in a towel. He also handed her a plastic cup with a sippy top on it. Boiled water had a taste she didn't care for, but it was just on the right side of cool to be refreshing. Zeke watched her with a kind, but antsy energy. When she finished and handed over the towel and cup, he gave her a serious look.

"Well?" he asked.

Lowering her gaze, Amy shook her head. Zeke let out a long sigh and ran a hand over his face. His hands were rough from hard work, but there was an elegance to them that she liked. Now he used those elegant hands to tinker with car engines, making him very important to their group.

"I was expecting this," he said. "I've got to go tell him now, and you know how he can be."

"I know," she answered quickly.

"Hell, kid, it's not your fault," he said, dusting off one of his knees. "I just hate dealing with his shit-ass moods, that's all. There's been a lot going on in town that you don't see out here."

"I know. Thanks for taking the bad parts of it so I don't have to."

"And take I will, kid. Take I will. Don't you worry about it, though. I can handle Mal. You go take a little walk while I do this and I'll be back in a couple hours with more water and a snack."

"Can you bring me some clean clothes? Some shorts?" she asked.

"Yup, sure can," he said, scooting her off the rock.

As he walked away, she saw the slump of his shoulders. He got to deal with Mal, which wasn't the honor Mal tended to think it was. Amy felt sorry for Zeke, but better him than her.

Before everybody died of the old tube neck, Zeke was Ezekiel Marshall. He'd been a computer tech in Los Angeles when the world ended, but he was originally from somewhere she'd never heard of in Illinois.

He was the one who'd found her when the group came through Philippi. She'd been living alone in the dorms of Alderson Broaddus for close to a year and had given up hope of ever seeing another living person. She traveled to the college town from her home in Grafton, West Virginia, after her parents died, gasping and clawing at their blackened necks. The only place she knew to go was Alderson Broaddus, where her sister, Sarah, was going to school. Being only ten years old herself at the time, she was convinced that her brilliant sister, the first in their family to pursue higher education, would know how to navigate the great disaster. It took three days for her to walk it, but when Amy got to the campus, she found chaos and death. Not everybody was dead, but most were. The ones that were still alive were ornery, breaking windows and setting fires.

Sarah's dorm was empty. She guessed that Sarah had died in a hospital, and shuddered at the thought of her sister rotting in some toothpaste-green medical room.

Not far from Philippi, the group chose their new Eden, a place that had once been called Hepzibah, West Virginia, but Mal had decided to call Flaggston. There were a little over a hundred of them when Amy had been cast out.

She walked through the woods, following the narrow paths kept fresh by deer, an animal that miraculously wasn't touched by old tube neck. She made a small detour. There was a place in those woods, a place that she visited every so often when her moods turned dark.

When it was still called Hepzibah, the town wasn't much more than a blip on the map. Zeke called it a one-stoplight town. It was little more than scattered houses and a church and cemetery. The rest was wilderness. It was a beautiful place. Zeke said that the quiet and nature was exactly what his spirit needed after the hell the world had endured. He told her about some of the things he saw, insisting that their stories were an important legacy.

But sometimes Zeke was in a strange mood, and he'd beg her not to ask him about the tail end of the year 1990. He'd try to hide his shaking legs and the big tears that would stream down his face. She noticed that some of the others would get in moods like that, too. They'd go from happy to shaky and sad in the snap of a finger.

Amy walked carefully down a steep bank and found the place. The burn pile. It had been a dumping area for the locals decades before the sickness. There were rusted-out, ancient appliances, moldy mattresses and box springs, engine blocks, and rotting furniture all haphazardly dumped into the area. It was a good place to discard unwanted things. And to keep certain things secret.

A few members of their group had declared it to be a good place to dump pieces of furniture where people had died and then decomposed. But instead of letting the elements take their time rendering them to dust, as the previous residents had, they burned those sullied articles among the rusted-out washing machines and soggy sofas. Bad memories burned into benign ash. She pondered this, staring at the burn pile, at the black, charred skulls of the babies.

There had been only three born to the group since they'd assembled, but paranoia kept their births from being the joyful beginning that a new baby had been before the plague. The survivors lived in a post-sickness world, where their babies' resistance to the illness was questionable. The first baby, a little girl they called Faith, was fine at first, but within the week, she declined. She wouldn't rouse from her slumber to eat and her color started to turn strange. It was Mal, whose mania hadn't fully come to the surface at that point, who raised the alarm that the babies could be born to immune parents and yet catch the sickness.

"They could catch it, and it could mutate in them. It could mutate into something we could catch in turn, and then that's it. Endgame. Bye-bye, human race, what's left of us," he'd said.

She'd watched that day as the eyes of the others got wide and wild in fear. They'd already survived the unthinkable, had already seen so much death and desperation that there was no hope for a calm reaction. They were meeting in small groups, whipping each other into hysterical frenzies of fear. Their hard-won senses of safety were being decimated by a seven-pound baby that, for one reason or another, was failing to thrive.

They snatched Faith from her parents and doused her, still wrapped in a blanket, in a single splash of gasoline. She didn't cry out when they set her on fire. The remaining two babies were burned with less hesitation. The others had their minds set against newborns full stop by then.

Zeke warned Amy about the others a lot. She asked him once if he hated the others, and he'd frowned at her.

"The others are now, by necessity and really shitty circumstance, my people. But they aren't good people, kid. They chose a side and then abandoned it, and now they're lost and sad. And they're going to mask that sadness with anger. We need to keep our heads, and maybe one day, as more people start making their way back east, we'll move on with a group of kinder, calmer people."

"What do you mean by sides? What side did they pick? I know they all went to Las Vegas after everybody died, but was that a side?"

"The dreams? The man without a face and the woman in the corn?"

"Huh?"

Zeke got so serious that she thought she was in trouble.

"Amy, do you dream?"

"Well, sure I do, stupid," she replied playfully.

"And you didn't dream of them?"

"I don't know what you're talking about. Would I remember dreaming about them?"

"Yes, you fucking would," Zeke said, no humor in his tone. "Of course you would. This is crazy. I haven't met a single person who never dreamed of them. I thought I was the weirdo because I didn't pick a side to follow, but you're a new level."

He explained to her then for the very first time how the members of their current group all decided, based on dreams, to go to Las Vegas and follow the man with no face, with crow feathers in his hair. He said that there were others who went to Colorado because they wanted to follow the woman in the corn. Zeke hadn't followed either—he'd stayed in Los Angeles with a small group of people, but they had been recruited by the man with no face to do technical work. When the work was done, they were ordered to go to Las Vegas, but Zeke defected.

"I wanted to go to Scottsdale, Arizona," he said. "I had it in my head to get me a boyfriend and live in one of those fancy houses out there. But it's hot as hell in Arizona, and without power and air-conditioning, it wasn't livable. I then ran into Mal and his group. They were all on the run, out of Vegas, and we decided to head east, form our own little town."

"Do you still dream of the man and woman?"

"The dreams stopped before we all met. I think they stopped for all of us. When the dreams stopped, any sense of picking sides sort of went away."

"So what? What did the dreams mean?" It sounded to her like scared people were dreaming up heroes.

Zeke sighed loudly and shrugged. "Hell if I know, kid. It felt like a lot more than it ended up turning out to be. I mean, they were real, or at least everyone says they were. I never saw the woman, and I only ever saw the man from far away, but from what everyone here tells me . . . everyone but Mal, anyway . . . they say I'm better off not having gotten too close to him."

AWAITING ORDERS IN FLAGGSTON

"Why?"

"He was scary," Zeke answered. He said it quickly and then seemed to regret putting that thought into the air. "It doesn't matter anymore. That part is over. Now we figure out how to survive. *That's* real. Dreams aren't."

Amy didn't think too much on that conversation after that. She kept up with her daily chores, going to the houses and looking for various items. She would turn her findings in to Zeke, who would turn them over to Mal, who distributed the items from his residence in the Baptist church constituting the center of town. It was a simple white building with an austere, wide, single steeple. The very picture of a country church. He lived there with several others—people who, like Mal, seemed to regret leaving Las Vegas when they did. They stayed together, talking always of the man who went by the name Flagg—the man they dreamed of and then found in the desert. Everybody else shared the smattering of houses that surrounded that understood center. Amy shared a house with Zeke and an elderly man named Carter, who spent most of his time in a tufted recliner by the front window.

She sat with Carter one day listening to him sing, something he sometimes did. It made her long for the time before old tube neck, when she would go to church with her grandma and sing old hymns like Carter did.

"They're talkin' about you, ya know," he said to her after his hymn ended.

"They are? 'Bout what?"

"You didn't dream when the plague was killin' everybody," he answered. He reached out and put his hand on her arm. "Mal's talkin' bad about you."

She felt her stomach bottom out. She'd always preferred that Mal not notice her at all, but him talking about her in a bad way made Amy feel a fear that she hadn't been face-to-face with since the last troublemaker at Alderson Broaddus had disappeared.

"Bad how?"

Carter removed his hand and turned back to the window. "I don't listen much to him. That man's whole head turned sour. But he's got people who listen to him, who look on him like they did that faceless man in the desert. Just be careful, especially when you're out. Try not to be alone, you hear me?"

She nodded and licked her lips, finding her mouth dry and foul-tasting.

"Zeke's been speakin' on yer behalf," Carter continued. "You gotta real good friend in him. You remember that."

Later, when Zeke got home, looking haggard and wanting quiet, she pushed herself to knock lightly on his bedroom door.

"What is it?" his voice came from the other side. "I'm not good company right now."

"Carter told me that Mal is talking about me," she said. "What's going on?"

He opened the door and waved her in. "What have you heard?"

"Carter said Mal heard about me not dreaming of the old woman or the man in the desert. Why is he all worked up about it?"

"Eh, Mal doesn't make any sense, but the problem with him is that he's convinced a lot of other people that he makes *perfect* sense. It's a shame that the whole fucking world died of the flu and we ended up in a community full of people so prone to suggestion and hysteria." Zeke's tone was harsh, furious, and she was taken aback. He must have seen that on her face because his eyes softened.

"I told someone in passing, like gossip, that you didn't dream. That was all. And it got to Mal and now he's saying some crazy stuff. I want you to know that I am very sorry for running my mouth like that and I never thought it would turn into something."

"I didn't think it was a big deal, either," she said. "What's it turning into? What's the something?"

"You don't need to hear it . . ."

"Yes, I do," Amy asserted. "Yes, I fucking do, and you know

it's not fair to keep this from me. I deserve to know what he's saying about me."

"Okay. He thinks you're a sign or something. No . . . maybe sign isn't the best word. He thinks you're like an oracle, and that you'll be the answer to all of their questions regarding Flagg and Las Vegas."

"Huh?"

Zeke rubbed a hand over his forehead and seemed to be thinking of how to explain the situation to her.

"He's convinced that because you didn't dream like the rest of us, that you'll be the one to receive new dreams, new orders. He thinks that Flagg will tap you to be the new conduit for his plans."

She looked into her friend's face in the low candlelight, longing for his features to give sense to what he'd just said. He'd tried to simplify it for her, but while the individual words connected, it was ultimately a jumble of nonsense that she couldn't parse to save her life.

But there was no time to ask Zeke to try and explain it again. At that moment, their front door crashed open, and many heavy footsteps entered their peaceful home and several people flooded into Zeke's bedroom. He shouted for them to leave, but he was shoved back onto his bed and held down by one of Mal's larger followers, a rough and greasy fellow they called Tinker. Mal, who was the shortest of the assembled mob, strode through the crowded bodies and looked around casually. His shaved head gleamed in the weak light.

"We're here to fetch you, little girl," Mal said, standing over her.

"Why?" was all Amy could get out.

"We need to get you away. Solitude and quiet is what you need. I know it, I just know it. I've still got a line to the big man, you know. I feel it," Mal said, gesturing wildly.

"I don't want to live in that church with you," she said, scooting along the carpet. Amy wanted nothing more than to get away from his crazed gaze and heavy breathing.

Mal laughed and looked at those around him to make sure they were laughing, too. After some hesitation, they all joined him with wide, open mouths.

"Little girl, you're getting special accommodations, I promise you that!"

She was dragged out of her cozy, safe home, the first she'd known since leaving her dead parents, and then taken to the metal shack in the woods. Mal ordered that she was to sleep alone there at night so that her mind would be clear enough to receive the dreams needed to tell everyone what the next step in the plan would be. She was to have little to no interaction with the others, spending her days in meditative solitude.

That had been four long months ago, when the nights were still cold enough to sink an ache in her bones that kept sleep elusive. Now it was summer, and the heat and humidity kept Amy sticky with sweat and covered in bugs. But at least sleep came to her most nights.

She took one last look at the blackened bones in the burn pile, a permanent example of Mal's paranoia, and made her way to the creek so that she could wash the stink off of her.

The creek wasn't deep enough for her to submerge completely, but she could sit on her rump and splash water on her head and face. She was lost in the moment, enjoying the sensation, her worries washing off along with her rancid sweat.

Something splashed in the water next to Amy, startling her out of her reverie. Zeke was on the bank, waving wildly, but not speaking. Curious, she stood and started to make her way to her friend, but shouts from the trees made her pause.

Mal emerged from the dense woods and pointed a finger at her.

"Get your ass outta that water and come here!" he screamed.

Terror gripped her, but Amy obeyed, catching Zeke's stricken face as she passed him. Mal grabbed her roughly under her chin, jerked her face up to his, and his reddened eyes bored into hers.

"Why won't you dream?" he growled in her face. "Why ain't you on the frequency?"

She tried to look to Zeke for guidance, but Mal jerked her chin again. She whimpered.

"You're the only one," Mal said quietly. "All of us, we all dreamed of one or both of 'em, and you never did. It has to mean something—it *has* to."

"Mal, she's just a kid," Zeke began, stepping closer to her. "Maybe the kids just didn't dream—"

One of Mal's followers kicked Zeke, hitting him in the side of his knee. Zeke cried out and fell to the root-turned ground.

"I think I know why you ain't dreamin'," Mal said after a glance to her injured friend. "We were all in danger so many times. We weathered Captain Trips, we survived the chaos, and we made our pilgrimages to Vegas. But *you*"—he shook Amy violently at this—"*you* didn't survive *shit*. You ran away from your dead family and hid in a dorm for a year. You didn't have to survive *half* the shit the rest of us had to. We need to fix that."

"Leave her alone!" Zeke said from the ground.

"You shut up now," Mal replied lightly. "I have important work to do. Glorious, biblical kinda stuff, you see. He's out there, waiting to tell us what to do next. He always had a plan and we need to know where we fit in that plan, how we can be of service to it."

"If you're so devout, why did you run away?" Zeke asked, his voice hoarse. "If your faith in that grinning freak is so deeply rooted, why did you abandon his great city and his great plan there in the desert?"

Mal let go of Amy's chin so that he could glare better at Zeke.

"It's because you're a coward," Zeke continued. "Glorious purpose or not, you're too chickenshit to ever carry something out to completion. You ran away. What makes you think you'd ever be chosen for a purpose?"

Mal smiled and made a gesture, inviting Zeke to continue.

"We're alone out here. There is no higher power with a plan to guide us," Zeke said, trying to rise to a standing position. "And this one's not gonna dream up your new orders because there's *no one* to make us dream! There's no magic this time. It's just us."

Mal kicked a booted foot into Zeke's crotch, sending him backward. Amy screamed and tried to run to keep him from rolling into the water, but hands grabbed her from behind and kept her in place. Mal turned back to her.

"Don't you listen to him, now," he said. "You've got important experiences to survive." He glared at Zeke. "You're lucky you're needed here, sicko. We ain't crucified anyone here. Yet."

The rough hands that were gripping Amy now dragged her down to the creek. Someone kicked the back of her leg and she fell to her knees at the water's shallow edge. She screamed, but was silenced when her face was slammed into the rocks and water. The pain stunned her enough that she gasped, aspirating the brown water. They pulled her out of the muck and she coughed until she vomited her meager breakfast.

"Trial by water," Mal said and winked. "I bet you dream tonight."

She was confused. What had just happened to her was more in line with what bullies would do to someone after school, not a grand ritual to bring about prophetic dreams. She'd spent so much time avoiding Mal that it hadn't been clear to her before then that he was galactically stupid.

They left her there on the creek bank, staring at their backs and weeping. She helped Zeke through the woods and back to the house they once shared, a place she hadn't visited since her effective banishment from their small society. She didn't dare stay any longer than necessary.

Later, Amy sat on her big rock by the shack and watched the sunlight wink at her through the leaf canopy. Animal sounds were all around her. Farther away were the sounds of the people talking, shouting, and slamming. Ruining the sleepy peace of nature. She walked around again for a bit, avoiding the creek and the burn pit. Soon, she was again perspiring and picking sweat bees off the back of her neck.

When the sun started its slow summer descent to the horizon and took on a copper hue, she heard footsteps approaching and tried to hide her disappointment when she saw that it was a woman who slept in the church with Mal. She was a severe-looking, greasy person who thrust a pack of peanut butter crackers and a can of Sprite at Amy. In a ravenous craze, she ate the food quickly and handed the garbage back to the woman, who then jerked her head toward the shack, directing Amy.

"It's not dark yet," Amy said. "I'm usually allowed to stay out until dark."

"Get your ass in there," the woman said in a surprisingly high-pitched voice.

Knowing how this could play out, Amy obeyed, bowing into the low structure. She sat in her usual corner and pulled her knees to her chest. The woman leaned into the entry and stared hard at her.

"You better hope you dream tonight," the woman said. "If you don't, Mal has plans for you."

They looked at each other in silence before the woman finally stood up, giving Amy the relief of being free of her greasy face. She was locked in once again, left alone with the heat and tight quarters.

Mal has plans for you reigned in her thoughts and she was certain she wasn't going to be able to sleep, let alone dream. The what-ifs had their time, so, too, did the fantasies of overcoming her situation and running away with Zeke to find another, saner group to live with. She thought of how her parents and sister would have dealt with her predicament, how they would advise her to thoroughly think through the problem before reacting. But that wasn't helpful. Logic was a useless weapon when belief was held in higher regard than fact. What was a well-thought argument, based in fact, when put up against stubbornly held beliefs that people used as the basis for their entire existence? Nothing but hot air and frustration.

Sleep did eventually take her, and because of the excitement of the day, she slept deep. She dreamed of being in school again, unprepared for the test put before her, and her long-dead dog, Filbert, was sitting in the hallway waiting for her. There was no grinning man with buttons on his jean jacket, no old woman on a porch, as Zeke and a few others had told her about. Whatever magic had touched all of Amy's fellow survivors passed her over once more.

When various pains woke her up, and the soft gray light of morning once again touched the cracks of the shed, Amy started to cry. She knew that with the dawn, and yet another night without a prophetic dream, some bad punishment awaited her.

She wasn't left alone with her fear for long. The noise of many people walking toward the shed put Amy in a panic and she pressed herself against the back panel of still-warm metal.

"Little girl," Mal sang from the outside. "Little girl, tell me your secrets, tell me your dreams!"

The door opened and one of Mal's men leaned in and looked at her.

"Get out or be dragged out," he said simply.

An effective threat. Outside, she was greeted by at least a dozen people. Mal moved past them all and stood before her with a strange humor in his eyes.

"Well, little girl," he began loudly, speaking to all gathered. "Did you dream of him last night?"

It occurred to her instantly that she could just lie. Amy could say that she dreamed of a man who told her that Mal needed to shut up about Las Vegas and instead focus on getting the former Hepzibah up and running like before. But she knew that, because of the secretive and hushed ways the dark man was always talked about, she didn't know enough about him to craft a decent story. Such a lie would earn a harsher punishment than the truth, a rule of the world that every kid knew.

She looked at her feet and shook her head. Frustrated noises came from those gathered.

"Another trial it is, then," Mal said, sounding full of good will. "Come on, little girl."

He led the group through the woods. Amy went willingly until she saw where they were headed, and her pulse went from a nervous thump to a terrified buzz. Her feet stopped moving and she was lifted and carried the rest of the way to the burn pile.

She was too frightened to make a noise, too scared of becoming another set of charred bones. She froze, but a terrified twelve-year-old girl wouldn't be able to accomplish much next to a zealous adult and his violent acolytes. There was no choice.

Amy's feet returned to hard earth in the pit, and she collapsed. As she tried to rub away the ache in her arms from being roughly carried, Mal knelt in front of her. He was sweating in the heat, but there was something in his eyes that wasn't there before. Something behind the craze that looked a little like fear.

Her eyes darted to the blackened rubble. She couldn't see the baby skulls from where she was sitting, but she greatly feared her own hollowed-out head sitting among them.

"Yesterday it was water. Fire would be the next logical step, would it not?" Mal asked, standing and pacing around. "But you'd be wrong, and that's the point, little girl. I can't have you anticipating what's next and I also can't accidentally kill you in the course of these mind-opening trials. This one is much simpler."

Strong arms circled around Amy's middle, holding her in place as her left arm was extended. Her wrist was twisted so that her elbow faced up. Mal produced a black rubber mallet from behind his back. She closed her eyes, knowing the hammer was swinging down, and cried out in surprise when it hit her. The pain was immense, but she was petrified to open her eyes and see the damage that had been done to her.

"Look at it," Mal said softly.

She shook her head.

"*LOOK AT IT!*" he screamed.

There was shouting coming from the direction of her shack. She kept her eyes squeezed shut, but listened as the shouts moved toward the burn pit.

It was Zeke, shrieking in panic. He was calling her name.

"Zeke! We're at the dump!" she cried out. The hands holding her tightened painfully and her eyes popped open without her thinking. With Mal's attention on the woods behind her, Amy looked at her arm very much on instinct and against her will. The pain that she was working hard to ignore slammed to the fore and sent a wail of shocked agony out of her. The inside of her elbow was bulged out, the skin split open and bleeding. She couldn't tell if splintered bone was peeking through the skin—all she saw was blood and a very wrong angle.

"My elbow," she said through tears. "It's backwards."

Zeke's bellowing was very close and she jerked her body in a lackluster attempt to break free of the grip holding her. It didn't work.

"Let her go, goddamn it!" Zeke said, panting.

"Go on," Mal said to the people restraining her. "We've done what we needed to do."

Amy was released and pushed forward. Because of having only one functioning arm, the left side of her head smashed into the garbage pile. Something stabbed her cheek and she squealed in pain and fright. There was a scuffle going on around her and Zeke was shouting, but Amy found that all she could focus on was pain. She struggled to get her face out of the refuse, unable to put any weight on her injured arm, and she eventually got back to a seated position and pulled an indistinguishable sliver of metal, scaled with rust, out of her cheek. Her right hand was slicked in blood and she sat there, all good sense gone, and stared at the shock of bright red until Zeke knelt before her and jerked her chin so that she was meeting his gaze.

"Come on," he said, his tone demanding no back talk.

He helped her to her feet and led her through the woods. Despite their combined injuries, they made their way past her shack and to the creek, where they both sat gingerly by the shallow brown water.

"Let me see," Zeke said, leaning over her to get a look at her destroyed elbow. He hissed through his teeth when he saw it. She was still crying, trying to keep from openly bawling. He looked away from her, at the bubbling, serene water before them.

"There's so much you haven't experienced, and won't experience in this new, horrible world. I'm sorry about that, kid. No high school graduation, no romance. I didn't have my first real love until I was in college. My parents didn't know, not ever. I met him at a movie night the theater department was hosting." He was trying to take her mind off the pain. Amy stopped crying and listened, the pain still bright and sharp. Zeke, she noticed, was playing with Mal's rubber mallet. She wondered if he'd been able to land a hit on any of the jerks who'd been dragging her through the woods. Maybe Mal himself. Good.

"He was an English major. He had dreams of moving to England and renting some old cottage and writing high-minded critiques of classical works of literature. I loved him. I'm glad I got to experience that."

"Your family didn't—"

"It's not really important," he interrupted. "Not now, not then. The world was a really fucking cruel place *before* people started coughing to death. Secrets were sometimes all we had to protect us from that cruelty."

"I'm sorry," she whispered.

"I've been thinking about him a lot lately these days," Zeke continued. "Wondering if maybe he survived, too, and maybe we'd meet again. But I know that's not likely. He died of it, too—what did you call it around here?"

"Tube neck."

"Tube neck," he agreed. "Yeah, I'm gonna say he definitely didn't survive. And you know what? The more we linger here, the more I see and experience, I think the lucky ones went that summer. A horrible way to go, but they didn't witness how truly awful we as a species are to each other. They didn't have to try to make sense of a world where babies died awful, strangling deaths in their cribs, but crooked, terrible people breathed free air and decided against self-improvement." A soft sob escaped him, startling Amy.

"Flaggston is a failure," he said. "There have been fights at the church between Mal's followers and everybody else. They can't figure out how to get the power back on, and without power, we can't work the well pumps for water. We're running out of supplies, and we're not getting along like the big, happy family we thought we were."

"Geez," she said, thinking back to Mal's face earlier. She'd thought she saw fear, but she knew now it was desperation in his crazed gaze.

"They've started killing people, you know," Zeke said, standing up. "They beat three people to death in the church because they were trying to leave, to move on. They . . . " Another sob. "They killed Carter in his chair. Said it was one less useless mouth to feed."

Amy put her one good hand to her mouth and began crying again. The world would never again know the sweet sound of Carter, a man the group had found in Tennessee, singing his old hymns. Zeke started pacing along the water's edge, slapping the palm of his hand with the rubber mallet.

"I don't know how this would have worked out under better circumstances. I do know that I'm tired of it. The whole thing. Remember how we said maybe one day we'd move on and meet up with people more like us? More sane people?"

Amy nodded, but she flinched when she heard shouting. Turning toward the sound, she saw black smoke billowing above the trees. Something in town was on fire.

"The church won't be there much longer," Zeke said. "I won't get the last word, but I had my say nonetheless." The shouting continued, and then she heard screaming, sounds of fear, pain, and rage. She wondered how much longer they'd be alone by the creek. Fresh panic quickened her pulse and she felt very weak. Others would come, and she had a terrifying image come to mind of her and Zeke tied to crosses overlooking the interstate. They had enjoyed quiet, but that was definitely over now.

AWAITING ORDERS IN FLAGGSTON

He gripped her shoulder hard, an assuring squeeze bordering on pain.

"Just know that I think you're a good one," he said. "And that I'm not going to let Mal near you ever again. Fuck dreams, fuck divine orders. We're our own people and I'm going to protect you."

She nodded, trying to hide the hiccups from crying so much. She was thankful for Zeke. Without him, she would have eventually let herself die in her sister's dorm room. He was her family now, and she trusted him.

The shouts were getting closer. Zeke was sobbing behind her.

"Now close your eyes, kid. Close them. We'll be done soon."

GRAND JUNCTION
Chuck Wendig

It's five hundred yards if it's an inch, Leaf decided. The elk out there was no record setter, but was a big bull just the same—real thick in the front, almost like he'd tip over if he leaned forward too far. His one antler was goofy, too, way it spun off at the tip, bent a weird way, like it was trying to escape from the other one.

Leaf watched all this from the scope of his Winchester Model 70, the butt of the gun nestled into the shallows of his shoulder.

The young man felt a bit of wet snot trickling out of his nose, already freezing to his lip—the day was cold and the ground he was lying upon only made it colder, what with last night's snow. Every part of him wanted to sniff and suck it back up, but even from here, that little sound might spook the bull.

He let out all the breath he'd been holding. *You got this. You're just part of the gun now.* The elk lifted his head up, looked around like he didn't have a care in the world. Then Leaf squeezed the trigger.

"Clean as a whistle, that shot, right through the lungs," someone said behind him, and Leaf about pissed himself. He'd already popped the tripod and slung the rifle over his shoulder, and he spun, scrambling with the weapon—

Only to find himself looking at a legend.

"Mother May I," he said. He eased the rifle back to his shoulder and lifted his hands up, palms out. Kept his head low a little. *Have some respect*, he told himself. *You fucking idiot.*

"Please," she said. "Just May."

Mother May I ran their small city, Grand Junction. She'd been elected fifteen years ago, and hadn't lost an election since. He'd never been this close to her, and remarked at how—even what, in her sixties?—she was still somehow both imposing in her appearance and also radiated an aura of calm. May was weathered, worn like Leaf's saddlebags, with close-cropped hair—it was silly to think of it this way, maybe, but her dark eyes and long pointed nose made him think of a snowman, with two coals staring out over a carrot sniffer.

She went on: "You know your way around a rifle. I did, too, once upon a time. In the bad old days."

"I—sure, yeah. Yes. I—" He looked around. She didn't seem to have anyone with her. She usually had men with her. Advisers. Guards. She had to. Leadership had its burdens and people wanting to put you in the ground was one of them, he figured. "Forgive me for asking, but am I dreaming this?"

A dry chuckle. "You dream of these things often?"

"No," he lied, after some hesitation. Or maybe it wasn't a lie, not really. He had dreams, strange dreams, but . . . not quite like this. Dreams of now, but of another place. May had dreams, too. Was famous for them. According to her, she sometimes made decisions based on what she saw when she slept.

"This isn't a dream, Leaf."

Holy hell, she knows my name.

She kept on:

"You're planning on packing out that bull elk all by yourself?"

He shrugged. "Got my mule. I can use a barrel hitch to pack the quarters—"

"Gonna be two, three hundred pounds. And those antlers are worth keeping, too. Make tool handles with them. I've got my horse and I miss doing this sort of thing, to be honest. So I'm inclined to help, if you're inclined to let me."

"Of course. Th-thank you," he stammered.

"We can have a conversation in the meantime. Come on. Let's go deal with the bounty you'll bring us, son."

As they worked together under the sun and in the wind to bleed out the elk and butcher the beast, rendering it into its parts to be packed, Mother May I did not mince her words:

"I have dreams, too, Leaf. Lately I've found that they have intruded upon this world, the waking one. I've seen things that I used to only see when I had my eyes closed, but now they're here. Now they're real. I saw a snake with two heads in my house a month ago. Two weeks later, I found a rat in my bed—had been pregnant, but when I found her, the babies were out and chewing their dead mother to pieces. And two *days* ago, I saw two fat fish crows out back of my place, circling one another on the ground, barely choosing to take flight at all except to hop and flutter—and they pecked and pecked at each other, pecking out one another's eyes, pecking apart the other one's feet, stabbing and sticking each other until they were both just bloody feathered lumps still somehow moving about. Circling, circling. Like water around a drain, but never going down it. Like they were forced to do it. Trapped in this circle, spilling more blood than I would've thought two birds could contain. And that's when I knew, these are signs, Leaf. Signs that evil has come back. That it has been born again, as it often is—no! As it *always* is. It died in Las Vegas thirty years ago, but no garden can remain free of weeds forever. No heart can escape hate. And no world will be shut of evil. It is the way of things. But we stand vigil. Don't we? We do, we do."

All the while, she helped him reduce this once-great beast to its parts. Haunches and shoulders, head off, antlers off, the blood out, the organs left to steam. She worked hard, bearing down with the knife, helping Leaf do what needed to be done with nary a moment's hesitation. May helped him field dress the bull like it was the most important job in her life. The same way, he believed, that she did everything. The same way, too, that she asked him for his help at the end of it:

"I have scouts out. Sent to the four corners. Sniffing at the margins, seeing where the evil is. I fear it's close, which means it will be *our* problem to deal with, not Boulder's, not Moab, not Green River. Can't call upon Charlie or Chels in Montana, not Captain Campbell at Buckley. The wheel turns and if the marble lands in black, it's our problem, and if that is as true as I think it is, I'll need you, Leaf. I'll need that keen eye of yours and, if you'll forgive me, that trigger finger. Will you help me if it comes to it?"

What other answer was there but *yes*?

She smiled, then: a rare sign. Her eyes were bright and intense—blue as the sky behind the drifting clouds above. "Good. Good. I've spoken with your father, so he knows what I've asked. But to the rest, I ask you keep this quiet. No need to stir the flock to fear, son. Let them have their peace. And let *us* hope that this is nothing at all but the troubled thinking of an old, timeworn woman."

Later, at evening's fall, Leaf met his father at the old man's reloading bench. Wisps of hair off his balding head like mist off a warming pond.

"Heard you brought in a big one," the old man said in his draggy, monotone drawl.

"Sure did, Pop. Not one for the books, but big enough."

GRAND JUNCTION

His father didn't look away from the bench, instead sliding another brass casing into its seat, and tucking it in real good like he was putting a baby to bed.

"One shot, too," he said, a note of what Leaf thought might be pride in there—but pride swirled with something else. Like clear water, made turbid from a whorl of mud.

"Yup. Just the one."

Powder trickled into the brass cartridge, then Pop pulled the lever arm down, pressing the bullet snug into the top. He took it out, breathed a few hot puffs of air on it and gave it a shine. A 7-millimeter round, fresh and gleaming. He handed it over with a smirk. "One for one."

"Thanks, Pop."

Awkwardness bled out between them like a gut-shot animal.

Leaf sighed and turned to leave, but his father cleared his throat and said, suddenly, "Hold up, now."

"What is it?"

"I know what she asked of you. Mother May I. She spoke to me first. She always asks. She's . . . good like that. But . . . "

The words seemed to catch in his throat. Leaf urged him on. "What?"

"You're young yet, Leaf. I was . . . young, too, younger than you, when the shit hit, Captain Trips ripping through everyone like a brushfire and—"

"I know all this, Jesus Christ," Leaf snapped, but then he felt bad about it. His father didn't deserve that. The old man was alone—Leaf's mother had died a decade past, and from just a dumb cut on the top of her foot she didn't see until it was too late, till it was already infected, and that infection moved fast. Dug into her blood like a screw that got stripped. Nothing would pull it out of her. She died two weeks after. Leaving them both alone.

Pop, for the most part, seemed to take the boy's sharp tone in stride.

"I'm just saying, I've seen some things. And don't get me wrong, Mother is a good leader, a righteous shepherd to this town, but I also know that leaders are leaders are leaders, and *all* leaders know that when push comes to shove, the people they lead aren't people all the time. They're tools in the hand. Shovel and rasp, rope and bucket and—and that!" Here, he finally turned all the way around and shook a finger at the rifle still hanging off Leaf's shoulder. "You think you wield the gun well, careful now, because she'll wield *you*."

"Pop, I don't even know if she needs me."

His father gave a sad smile. "I saw her eyes, Leaf. She's gonna need you. Got that gaze fixed on you like a wolf's look. You just be careful. Tools break. And sometimes tools can't be fixed again."

Leaf felt something squirm in his gut. A tightening worry. "It's fine, Pop," he said, trying to keep that worry—and his teenage irritation—out of his voice. (*Not sure I really did a good job*, he thought distressingly.)

"Go get dinner sorted," Pop said.

"Sure thing."

Logs into the stove, some rabbit stew in his belly, days-old bread to sop it up. Leaf normally didn't think much about food, but he at least could clock whether he was full or still hungry (and the answer was, usually, still hungry). But now his mind wandered as he looked out the front window of their little Gunnison Avenue house, the house tucked away close to the old industrial center of town—beyond it, a tree-lined street long-shattered by the urging elbows and knees of roots, the old pipe and supply beyond it, now used as stables. Most of the houses in this part of town were occupied. They said that five thousand people lived here now. And yet, to Leaf, it all felt so strangely fragile. Like they were on a rickety bridge swaying in the wind. How easy it would be for it all to fall.

His father's words haunted him a little—Pop did not seem to entirely trust Mother May I's intentions. But Leaf had to. He had to trust. Because the thousands of people here were here in part because of her. Because of what she helped build, because of how she kept it all standing. Leaf wanted to help keep it standing, too. Because if he didn't, they might all fall into the dark chasm beneath them. The world fell there once, and he didn't want it to fall in again. Not in his lifetime.

It was two weeks later, knee-deep into February, when she came to their door.

Mother May I didn't have to say much. Pop welcomed her in, of course, and she offered the old man a choice cut of the bull elk that Leaf had shot—a good-sized hunk of roast, frozen. Pop asked her as she drank the dandelion tea he offered, "I hope I'll still have my son to share this with—"

Leaf cut him off sharply. "*Pop!*"

Mother May I put a hand on the boy's shoulder. From her to him, a soft smile and a gentle nod: an almost telepathic transmission of *It's fine, I understand.* To the old man, May said, "That is my sincerest hope, Clade. I'll do everything in my power to make sure your boy comes back. But I make no promises because life affords us no certainty, only precarity."

That was all she had to say on the matter.

What was done was done. Fifteen minutes later, he was packed and ready.

Pop stopped him as he was coming out of his room and put something in his hands. Something tucked in the soft buttery swaddle of deer leather.

"Pop?" he asked.

"Happy birthday."

"Not my birthday, Pop."

"Will be soon enough. A month away now? Go on. May is waiting." These last words he said with a faint vibration of urgency in them. Or was it fear?

Leaf unrolled the leather, and found within a hunting knife tucked in a belt sheath. The knife had as its handle a length of elk antler, pale at the surface, dark in its twisted niches. The blade was six inches and gleamed like lake water.

"Did you..."

Pop shook his head. "I'm no craftsman. I just load the ammo, boy. But I've cultivated a few favors here and there. Jim Moore, down at the tannery, for the leather. Ben Haber, he made the blade, you remember him? Yeah, the one eye. And that girl, Possum, that girl you're a bit sweet on? The one from Montrose. She made the, ah, the handle—the hilt. From your elk, you see."

"Pop, this had to cost you—"

"Like I said, favors. It cost me favors. Favors I've done and banked."

"Thanks, Pop."

"You need a knife in case the rifle doesn't work. Rifle's for long work. Knife will do the work up close. Besides, bullets aren't everything. Powder isn't steady anymore."

Leaf nodded. Then he hugged his father—a rare moment. So rare he couldn't remember the last time they'd embraced. They had no hate for one another, but the love between them was ill-fitting, off-kilter. As it was, perhaps, between fathers and sons sometimes.

"May's waiting on you," Pop said. And she was. Silent and still as the red rock of the canyon lands to the west. "Be good, Leaf. Above all else, be good."

It was time to go, and so they went.

"The circle and the cross," May said to the four gathered around, her face wreathed in the ghosts of whiskey warmed in a pot over the fire. The night sat blue behind her, a great, grave expanse. They'd already left Grand Junction and were a good ten miles south of town when it was time to set up camp for the night. May held the whiskey in front of her like a prayer as she continued on, saying: "The circle is the circle, the snake biting down on its own tail. All things, moving in their cycle, birth and life and death and rebirth. The seasons, the rain and snow and sun, day and night and back into day, the feelings in our heart chasing each other—it's all a cycle. And good and evil are on that cycle, you see? Goodness prevails for a time. Righteousness rules. And then the wheel turns on its axis. Goodness softens. *Weakens*. It holds its vigil, but soon it needs a little shut-eye, *just a bit*, and when it does, the darkness moves closer. Evil gathers at the edges. Just outside the firelight, waiting for its chance."

At that, the logs on the fire popped with a firecracker snap. Leaf about jumped out of his skin. May's cadence was steady and slow, rhythmic like the rushing of a river—*Or the beating of my own heart*, he thought. The *snap-pop* of the logs stirred his heart to a swifter hoofbeat.

May continued: "This is the way it was, the way it is, and always will be. But it is the cross that matters. Not merely the Christ cross, but the intersection, the crossroads. Evil moves one way, and good must cross it. You see? It must run at it, meeting it in the middle. The Devil at the crossroads, yes, but the angel, too. And we will be the angels, the five of us. The angels to meet the Devil."

Leaf looked around at the three others who were part of this team:

Danny Brightfeather—one of May's own personal guards, a man like a scarecrow made of rough pemmican. Story went he was a drunk, once, but managed to thwart someone coming into town to kill May— even zapped on the lightning that was white whiskey at the time. And he'd been with her ever since, sober as a judge, and loyal as Leaf's own mule.

Cin Haber—Ben Haber's wife, not a blacksmith but, rather, a glassblower. She was built like a coke oven. Leaf didn't know why she was here, exactly—she didn't strike him as the type for this, but here she was, and looked serious.

And finally, the German—Otto Wampler. Not German at all, apparently, but Swiss? Leaf didn't know much about the rest of the world and didn't care, as none of it would ever be accessible to him, here, in this place and this time. Wampler was small and sharp, like a human kidney stone. Both trapper and trader, he wasn't always in town, often out there, alone. A bit feral, Leaf had heard, though he'd never encountered the man before.

"Where we headed?" the German asked, his English strong, but his accent apple-crisp. "Besides *south*. And what are we to do there?"

"Telluride," May said. "What we are to do there is an act of faith, an act of correction. Evil is reborn and we are to end it." Her scouts, led by Brightfeather, found that a new group had set up shop in Telluride—dark-hearted souls gathering to protect someone at their center. A leader they call John Low. "These people, this Cult of Low, they're gathering power. Stockpiling ammunition. Killing local folks, and"—here she seemed truly rattled for a moment, and when something rattled May, well, Leaf knew that should have the same effect on him tenfold—"eating them. To take their power, their life-force—the way of old, dark, forgotten spirits. So we will lay waste to this cult by removing John Low from its center. Because if we don't, I have seen it, the way his poison, his darkness, will flow to us, will corrupt us."

They all glanced at one another; their faces painted by the orange light of the fire. Only one who didn't seem worried was Brightfeather, who held the same look he always had: the empty look of a long, dark, broken highway.

In the distance rose the mad whinny of a screech owl. The horses shifted uncomfortably at the sound, snorting and stomping. Like they knew what was to come. Like they could sense it on the wind.

Morning came and with it, a breakfast of creamed einkorn and sweetened with *suikerstroop*—beet sugar syrup. Empurpled the gruel, red as blood. They ate fast and headed out, all of them on horses that were theirs, excepting Leaf, whose horse—a skewbald ride called Gremlin—came from May's own stable in the old Walmart Supercenter at the middle of town.

The day was bright, with the sun on the snow washing everything out. Made it hard to see, almost. But Brightfeather knew where they were going, and the horses were glad to follow the beast that was his black mustang.

May explained that the trip to Telluride would not be a direct one—though it would've been nice and easy to follow the old roads from the Spur Highway, west of town. But that way was plagued by guards, she said. So they'd come in from the northeast, where there was no road. Otto said, "I know the way, yes. South through Ouray. Then onto the trails, past the Camp Bird Mine, around Mendota Peak. Two days ride, maybe three if there's weather. We will eat good on the way. Especially with this one's eye, yes?" He laughed and reached across the gap between horses to clap Leaf on the shoulder.

Leaf did not know if Otto was mocking him or complimenting him, so he just laughed along nervously and nodded.

South down 550, the highway gone underneath the mounds of drifting snow. As they clopped through the valley, closing in on the mountain town of Ouray, Cin Haber dropped her horse back to walk alongside Leaf. She had the look of a porcelain teapot about her—Leaf knew the woman had to be of soft feeling, but something about her seemed hard, too. She unwound the scarf from her face, and Leaf saw her rounded, pillow-fat cheekbones were pink from the wind.

"I know your father a little," she said. Her voice was chirpy, like a twittering bird. "Good man, good man. He speaks well of you."

Leaf wasn't sure how true that was, but he hoped it to be so. He offered an awkward, stiff smile. "Okay."

"You ever shoot someone before, young man?"

He chewed a lip.

"I shot at a Ravager a year ago. Little more than a year, I guess. Late fall. I shot over his head on purpose—just a warning shot, and I didn't have to shoot a second time—he got the message." Ravagers with their skull masks and their bone-rattle armor. Strange folk. "He turned around, went back into the canyon lands."

"My only advice is, don't flinch," Cin said. He saw her face shift into something sad, then. The kind of face adults make when they're trying to put on good spirits, but fail to make it believable.

"Only advice is, *don't miss*," Brightfeather said from just ahead of them.

"That won't be his problem, though," Cin said with some clarity. And Leaf knew she wasn't wrong. Leaf hit what he aimed at. As long as he could make himself pull the trigger.

The snow on the streets of Ouray mounded over dead men, dead women, dead children. The snow covered them, mostly, but still in places the blood showed through, frozen now, frozen pink. Some were still in the houses, or in the Elk Lodge barroom. Each, slaughtered. Dozens of bodies, shot, cut, some with knives still in their chests or hatchets stuck in their skulls like they were nothing better than stumps. All of it, horrifying, and Leaf wanted to throw up, but knew he had to keep it down, because if he showed weakness here, they'd leave him behind, tell him to head home. He couldn't abide that. He wanted to be here. Wanted to do the right thing. A small voice inside him told him, *This is you proving yourself, growing up a little bit, doing the real work.* Maybe if he hung tight and stayed true, he could go back to town, his head high. Maybe May would keep him close. Give him work. He could be like Brightfeather. Be in her orbit, keeping her safe—which meant keeping the people of Grand Junction safe.

GRAND JUNCTION

But it was hard to keep that dream in mind now. His guts wanted out. He had to keep swallowing them down, down, down, pushing them into the cauldron of his stomach. Roiling, searing, like a belly full of bad vinegar.

They moved onto the lobby of a hotel toward the southern end of Ouray. Place called the Beaumont. No dead people here, but there was a message slashed into the old Victorian wallpaper behind the desk: a crooked smiley face, and above that, the words:

JOHN LOW LIVES

May said it was clear who did this. And that, horrible as it was, she was glad they were seeing it. Because it told them in no uncertain terms who it was they were dealing with—and more importantly, *why* they had to go to Telluride. "Dog or man goes rabid; your choices narrow only to two. You kill him before he bites, or you let yourself be bitten and take his disease unto you."

At that, she told them to each find rooms in the hotel. They'd stay here for the night, then move on.

Leaf's room was a messy, unkempt thing. Full of dust and spiders. But it offered a bed, and though it had no blankets, he could easily unfurl his bedroll there and sleep on the mattress. Springs tried to poke through, but it was better than the lumps of the earth, and certainly an improvement over trying to clear snow and rest on the cold ground. Exhausted, he still had to chase sleep for a while, pursuing it through fields of blood, through meadows of the dead.

Over time, he managed. And over time, he dreamed.

He was again in a different life, a different world. He'd seen many televisions before, but never once lit up like it was now, a wide box of light showing dazzling displays of cars—not dead and defunct, but rip-tearing down a smooth, unbothered strip of asphalt—and he sat in front of that box with some kind of control device in his hand, a thing with buttons and jiggle sticks on it. Like he was making those cars go, somehow. Music blasted, filling the room: a band he'd never heard before, not on a record or on some previously discovered cassette, but one his dream mind called Glimdrop. A golden retriever bounded into the room behind a couple friends of his. The dog—*my dog*, he realized—was Goldie. His friends were Naseem and Jace. They were laughing, eating some kind of crunchy orange snack, their fingers dusted with the stuff. It felt so normal. So nice. Less like a dream and more like Leaf was standing in the doorway to another world, watching. But then he woke, and the door closed. That world went away.

The way to Telluride was a hard row to hoe, and over the next two days they left the road and hit the trails, heading west out of Ouray. Through the valley and then up around a peak. A snow squall hit them on the first day and slowed their journey. Otto helped flush game, and Leaf shot it—rabbits, mostly.

Cin said during their first dinner, "You know rabbits don't have enough fat on them? You try to live on rabbit, you'll still starve. Helluva thing, that. You can eat and eat and eat and still die from starvation."

May countered with: "It's not starvation like you think of it. But your body will still break down when it doesn't get what it needs. Balance is everything, inside and out. But for now, the rabbits will do."

Brightfeather grunted, like he didn't want to hear any of this. A man who preferred to be in silence, Leaf figured. A little like his father. Few words spoken.

On the last day, the skies cleared, which May lamented a little—said it would've been nice to get into Telluride under the cover of bad weather. But it was what it was, and soon it was night. The moon big, pregnant with light. And there, in that light, they looked down from the ridge to see the town of Telluride.

This is it, Leaf knew. *Shit.*

It was morning now, the sun spearing through a break in the clouds from the east—those spears of light pinning the target, the Hotel Telluride. Fixing it like a pig to the ground.

Leaf: now alone. The others had gone on, down into town under the cover of early-morning darkness. "Before they wake," May said. "And before the next shift of guards comes in. The ones who are there will be tired. They won't expect us." When she told Leaf his part of the plan, he quaked like the clusters of aspens all around them. He tried to keep still, tried to put some steel in his spine, but he couldn't keep the fear from crawling all over him. Brightfeather questioned his courage, called him a pussy, but May shushed the man. Told Brightfeather, "Leaf is the one for this job. He'll do it, and he'll do it well."

"Look at him shake. He's scared shitless," Brightfeather said.

"We all should be. Courage isn't the absence of fear. It's doing something necessary *in spite of it.*" This last part she said almost angrily. Like Brightfeather should've known better. Chastened, the man let it drop, and she gave a short nod to Leaf, who returned it.

Presently, he was on his belly, lying amid the leafless bones of underbrush, the barrel of the Winchester pointed toward the hotel. A box of ammo—ammo his father had loaded, most likely—sat next to him. His job per Mother May I was simple in execution: *In there, that's where John Low is. He sleeps on the top floor of that hotel, and we are going to go in there and we are going to kill him. Once that starts, there will be people coming out of the hotel, and others running toward it. Shoot them all, Leaf. Same way you took down that elk: a whistling locomotive of lead punching through the soft hills of their lungs.* Then she gently tapped the scope atop the rifle. *The circle and the cross*, she said, and winked.

He waited.

The line of the sun crept forward, like an advancing army.

Behind him, the trail they used to get here was trickling with snowmelt. Made him have to take a piss, that sound, but he held it. He had to hold it. For as long as he could. For as long as was needed. Still, his bladder burned with urgency.

He scanned the windows of the hotel, looking for movement. The hotel was old-timey, from an era whose name he didn't know. No movement in the windows. He scoped the streets, too, looking for something, anything. The streets were full of trash. Heaps of it, careless and unclean. A wind juggled a wisp of black plastic garbage bag across the road. A rat chased after it, like it was a game, then was gone. And then—

A gunshot. Muffled, somewhat. From inside the hotel.

Shit, shit, shit, shit.

His heart kicked up like a spooked rabbit, rushing through the brush of him. He tried to steady his breathing, and got his eye hovering over the scope.

Another shot. *Bang.*

His hands shook. His teeth rattled.

At the bottom floor of the hotel, the main door blasted open and two men came bolting out, running for a tall pole across the street, a pole with a brass bell nesting upon it—a long chain dangling.

An alarm. Leaf whined in the back of his throat as he put the crosshairs on the chest of the first man and—

He jerked the trigger too hard. The shot went in front, kicking up dust from a pile of trash. The two men flinched; they knew now they were being shot at, but they wouldn't have factored where, not yet—

C'mon, c'mon, c'mon—

Hand on the bolt, ratcheting it back, another round in the chamber—

Clackity-clack—

GRAND JUNCTION

Another shot. This time—

A red flower bloomed in the side of the man. Kicked the wind out of him like a horse and his right leg folded under him like a house of cards. Down he went. The second one joined him a moment later, with the third shot.

They didn't ring that bell.

But it wouldn't matter, because the shooting had started.

――

It took minutes, at most, but to Leaf, it seemed to take hours. Everything was fast, but slow, too, like time didn't mean shit anymore. It all ran together like paint; it formed no image, only chaos. Men running toward the hotel. The bolt, back, up, forward. *Bang.* Blood on the pavement, blood in the trash. His shoulder, numb now from the times the butt of the gun punched him there. The air smelled eggy and raw. His ears rang not like that bell but like a howling gale. Reloading, firing, never missing once, not after that first shot, no sir, no ma'am, and Leaf thought and kept on thinking, *I hope they're proud of me, hope Pop is proud, hope Mother May I is proud, we're the angels here, and we are meeting the devils and sending them back to hell, I hope they're proud of me—*

And then, fast as it started, it was over.

Nine dead men on the street.

All armed. Guns on the ground. Most shot through the lungs, like May had instructed. One had his scalp peeled instead. Steam rose from their wounds.

All was quiet.

Did we do it?

Is it done?

He scanned the hotel windows—

Movement on the third and topmost floor. There was a gleam, a sudden shine, and his guts clenched up—

That's a rifle—

He eased his head aside, about to roll over when the shot rang out. His gun shook as the back end of the scope burst out, bits of glass sticking in his cheek as he crashed into the underbrush. The gun lay there, scope shattered. *The shot came through the scope.* Whoever had seen him was a damn good shot. Or lucky.

That meant someone was still in there. One of John Low's men—If not Low himself.

May could still be alive in there. The others, too.

He had to go down there. Had to go into the hotel. Another part of him screamed: *This isn't your fight, you're just you, go home, go back to your father, back to hunting, let this be!* But he remembered what happened in Ouray, and knew that could come home to Grand Junction if Low was allowed to live.

Leaf had to know. He had to try.

The circle and the cross.

He kept low, crawling behind the brush, looking for a way down outside of the rifleman's sightlines. His bladder reminded him again of its need, so he leaned to his side and pissed into the scrub, making sure the little stream of it ran away from him, not toward.

Then, finding a low path forward, Leaf made his descent.

The inside of the old hotel stank of spent gunpowder, spilled blood, and shit. It, like the streets around it, was full of trash, too: fresh filth, bones, food scraps, broken slats of wood, swatches of filthy fabric.

There were bodies everywhere. Shot dead, their blood still pooling, the greasy coppery stink filling Leaf's nose.

John Low's men were not like those of Grand Junction—they were emaciated, sore-pocked, branded, and scarred. Their clothes were threadbare. The women had long, ratty hair—the men had beards gummy with food, spit, snot.

They were practically Ravagers—close to being the mad, feral nowhere men whose minds were broken by the last days. Even their

GRAND JUNCTION

guns seemed janky—pieced together, jury-rigged, the grips and stocks splintered and rotten, the barrels rust-flecked. *This is Low's army?* Leaf wondered.

Second floor, that's where he found Otto. His right eye was a black canker. The back of his head was missing, brains clotted on the wall. It was his gun that Leaf took—a nickel-plated revolver with a black rubber grip. It was heavy as sin.

Stairs to the third floor: Cin Haber, on her back, spread out on the steps. A pair of bullet holes in her chest, the blood blackening her clothes. *Shot right through each lung.* Leaf's innards twisted up. Tears burned at the edges of his eyes. *Turn around. Go home.* But his feet carried him up, up, up. Like he was being pulled to the top floor, a rope wound around his heart, tugging, tugging.

The third floor was just one room.

The stairs topped out at a short hallway, and the door at the end was open.

Like a zombie, Leaf walked through, revolver in his hand—

Mother May I stood above a cradle in the middle of the room. The room had been cleared of all other furniture and here, though there was trash, it seemed somehow artful, purposeful, like it had been mounded up against the walls in such a way to create architecture. A mobile dangled above the crib of little buttons—not buttons that clasped a shirt together, but the kinds of old pin buttons you wore on a jacket. Smiley face buttons, buttons with the old gone-world Stars and Stripes, buttons with the faces of people who might have been politicians or movie stars or comic book characters, but who were long-dead and likely forgotten.

The buttons on the mobile drifted and swayed. May was lifting a baby out of the cradle.

She had a rifle slung over her shoulder.

A nearby window sat open, a breath of cold air whisking in.

"Mother May I," Leaf said.

She looked to him, her face sad. She held up the child—a wriggling infant swaddled in crisp, pristinely clean white blankets. "This is John Low."

"I—I don't understand."

"Nor do I," she said. "John Low is just a child. Look at him. The potential for evil is there, but only if it's fostered. Only if it's *forced*, you see. We can change that. The evil can be met in his heart, Leaf. With the right parents—a father like your father. A father, like *you*—"

A voice, from nearby—from below. Near the floor. A gargled bleat of an accusation: "She's lying!"

Brightfeather.

There, Brightfeather braced himself against the wall and stood on wobbly legs, blood soaking his chest, but his eyes burning like coals—a long-barreled Magnum revolver in his hand, swinging there like dead weight.

"She lies! She knew what was here, boy. I knew, too. We came to be the ones to foster that evil, to control it, not to save it, and it was *she* who killed us all—"

He swung his gun up—

But May, for being old, was faster. After all, she was uninjured.

And she's a believer, Leaf realized. But a believer in what? He could not say.

Brightfeather's head snapped back like a can shot off a fence rail. He crumpled, a scarecrow off his post.

The gun in May's hand did not waver. She held the baby in her left arm, cradling it there. The gun in the right drifted gently to Leaf.

His own trigger finger itched.

"Why?" he asked. A raggedy, rawboned question.

"Because the carousel must turn, Leaf. Because evil is as essential to the world as good. Light is nothing without the dark. This is not the first John Low and it will not be the last. John Low lives."

Then, everything happened at once.

Leaf felt his own gun arm rising.

Saw May's eyes dart to the left of him, shocked—

Something pawed at his side, a dread gurgle from the faceless Brightfeather as his fingers hooked around the young man's belt, pulling him sideways, dragging him down as May's bullet carved a path through him—

Leaf cried out—

His own gun went off, but when his hand hit the ground, the weapon spun away into the trash of the room. At his feet, Brightfeather gripped his legs hard, hugging them to his chest as curtains of what was once the man's face dangled and dripped from the hole in the center of his skull. Something that might've once been a tongue flapped there, a dying serpent, flicking a gassy hiss into the world as the man's last utterance before slumping forward, well and truly fucked.

Somewhere, a child cooed and mumbled. Leaf's ears rang again and he wasn't sure if what he was hearing sounded human or . . . like something else.

Leaf struggled to pull his legs out from the dead man's grip as a shadow fell over him. May, her gun in her hand. The child, gone again. Back in the crib, Leaf guessed. "You know your way around a revolver and a rifle," he said, crouching there, coiling like a spring. "Was you that shot at me out there, wasn't it?"

"It was. No witnesses to this, I'm afraid. Lest they carry word home."

"I trusted you."

"Of course you did. Because I needed you to. John Low needed you to." She smiled, thumbing back the hammer of the gun. "I'll tell your father you saved me. That's my kindness to you, son."

She pulled the trigger.

The hammer clicked, a dry snap. And no shot.

In Leaf's head, his father's voice:

Powder isn't steady anymore . . .

Rifle's for long work . . .

Knife will do the work up close . . .

Leaf's hand at his side, he launched himself up—left hand catching May's wrist, his right sticking in fast with the knife. In through the side. Right into the lung. Clean as a whistle. Mother May I said nothing as she died.

It took a long while standing over that crib before Leaf knew what he was going to do. He tried to think of it in an animal way. Birds killed the babies of other birds sometimes, right there in the nest. Wolves would kill coyote cubs, coyotes would kill fox kits, and they'd do this to eat, yes, but also to get rid of the competition. That was the simplest thing, the cleanest thing. If Leaf believed himself good, and this child was evil, then the way forward was clear. Then again, if he saw himself as a hunter, a *human* hunter, not just a wolf or a coyote or a house sparrow, he knew you didn't hunt the fawns, cubs, calves. You let them grow up. To see what they became. But maybe he needn't be a beast or even a hunter of beasts. Maybe he just needed to be the son of his father.

Be good. Above all else, be good.

He picked up the cooing child and left.

HUNTED TO EXTINCTION
Premee Mohamed

Hunting wasn't really a hobby anymore; the verb had lost meaning in a world where you could just about throw a rock from your front door and hit a deer. Still, Val thought of herself as a Hunter sometimes, capital *H*, the archetype. It had to be a challenge to earn the *H*: mornings like this, so still and bright that a human being was the strangest thing in the landscape. The early October snow had tapered off after half an inch, showcasing dozens of tracks. But she felt drawn to one specific set—a buck, she was certain, leading north to the densest woods, where the wolves did not like to go.

A canny one, Val decided, wincing at the loud crunch of leaves below the thin white blanket; she sketched him in her mind's eye, pretending to be Sherlock Holmes. *Well, Watson, as you can tell by the receipt for his hatmaker . . . As you can tell by the pattern of wear on his leather pocketbook . . .* There.

A big fella for four points, listening to her approach, but facing the wrong way. Val watched him, drawing butcher lines in her head. Loin, tenderloin, chuck roast, chops, odds and ends for soup and sausage . . . Slowly she unhooked her bow, unwrapped its muffling deerskin, notched a broadhead of her own manufacture. Without wind, her frozen breath bloomed and lingered, blurring her sight. She held it as she set up for the shot.

The buck glanced back at her, seemingly uninterested. Val frowned, uneasy. Something about him . . .

A faint wail rose from behind her, and she spun reflexively, keeping two fingers on the arrow. She barely registered the buck fleeing through the brush. A cat? No—the dying cry of a rabbit, or something imitating one, not well. Yet the leafless aspens, the crowding spruce, were bare of birds.

She edged forward, flinching as the cry repeated. A pitiful sound, close to the end of its strength. But coherent thought left her in the full-body panic of feeling the ground give under her feet; she threw herself backward, falling on her ass, and just managed to evade the small but deep crack that had nearly swallowed her. (And where the *hell* had that come from? She wasn't out here often, it was true, but . . .)

Val clung to a sapling and leaned experimentally over the edge, staring into a strange darkness untouched by the sun. As if it rose from the crevasse, a shockingly cold wind whipped into her face with the full force of a slap, startling her with the smell of impending snow. Far below, something shifted sluggishly, the body language of a small, wounded thing—a fawn, she thought at first glimpse. But at this time of year? No, something else.

Jesus. Jesus Christ.

A child, staring up at her, half-covered in snow and leaves. Splatters of blood black on the fawn-brown skin. Val reached out unthinkingly, stopped a moment before toppling in herself.

She babbled an incoherent stream of reassurances and promises, then tore herself away with an effort that seemed gargantuan. Already weeping, she stumbled away on legs that felt like stilts.

They returned at noon, a procession of matching bright blue quads with Val clutching the child to her chest in the middle vehicle, and the sky was darkening with impossible clouds: slate-gray, top-heavy cumulonimbus, planed flat as a table. Worse, the temperature was in free fall, so that by the time they reached the infirmary, Val's gloved hands were so numb she could barely manage the catches of her helmet.

Unspeaking, she gently fought off those trying to help, and carried the blanket-wrapped bundle in herself. As the door closed, there came across the woods a series of muffled cracks and low booms: the cries of trees freezing, of ice shouldering its way across the lake.

Val fed the stove first, then moved with the other council members to the periphery of the room so Bashir could work. The tall, thin Somali served as doctor, nurse, paramedic, and veterinarian for their little lakeside community, treating anyone who couldn't or didn't feel like driving to town. He was also Val's closest friend, or at any rate, if they were not *close* friends, at least after twenty years they had never let each other down. She trusted him, and she could not say that of many perfectly decent people in town.

His long fingers moved gingerly over the scrapes and bruises dotting the fawn-brown skin. "Hands, feet, forearms," he murmured. "No frostbite, no defensive wounds . . . "

"No what?" Val said.

Bashir held up his hands, palm-out. "Like this," he said softly. "When someone is attacking you, you instinctively protect your face. Then you see cuts here, broken fingers, the wounds of retreat." He turned back to the child. "Where did you come from, little one?"

Next to Val, Lois Chan emitted a small, choked noise. Val put a hand on the older woman's birdlike shoulder. She knew exactly what Lois was thinking, for she thought the same: that if she tried to speak again she might only produce noises, like the animal wail she'd heard in the ravine, or just sob and never stop.

Val had been twenty in the summer of what they now called the Fallout. Too young, she had thought then, to know whether she wanted kids or not. At twenty, you were supposed to have your whole life ahead of you, time to decide everything—marriage, kids, school, jobs. The flu took all of that. Shut door after door in everyone's face, stole every dream.

It had taken five years for a coherent narrative to trickle up from the States, assembled from the testimony of survivors and a team of investigators who had crisscrossed the country looking for any evidence not destroyed by the perpetrators. A lab accident, then deliberate releases elsewhere (as if the flu could not move fast enough on its own); and something else, something unscientific: some terrible disaster both natural and supernatural, culminating in a single atomic explosion that had ended whatever it was for good.

Val knew about the dreams and the sides chosen; people had written books about it. She had only experienced the barest edge—a whiff of a cornfield, the briefest glimpse of a red eye, searching—and although no one discussed it (there was no point now), she had a private theory that Americans had been affected more drastically. Not that the dreams could read maps and stopped at the border, but that like the virus, the dark . . . thing, whatever it was, had been engineered in America, nurtured and fed there, and so, too, had the other thing, whatever it was.

But everyone had been wrong to believe that long-ago, never-glimpsed mushroom cloud was the *final* disaster. Another one, slower, infinitely larger, unexpected and unprepared for, was waiting on the horizon.

As if reading her mind, Bashir said, "Based on dentition, I believe her age to be between five and seven years old."

There it was. Val closed her eyes.

Babies born during the Fallout summer had a high mortality rate due to uneven medical care, but the survivors seemed to be fine well into toddlerhood. Everything had seemed golden and hopeful. Humanity had gone to its knees, almost extinguished, but now it was rising again, bleeding, swaying, but ready to continue the fight.

And then a virtually identical, but crucially different, superflu strain had arrived—as best they could tell in the postmortem—and wiped out the entire generation of those early babies. Around a quarter of all the other survivors, those immune to the original superflu, had perished as well. And in the final reckoning, it turned out anybody producing sperm had simply stopped producing it. The birth rate dropped to zero and stayed there, and it had been there for eighteen years.

Bashir's theory was an asymptomatic infection resulting in specific inflammation, like mumps. Survivors had caught the second superflu and fought it off, but in so doing, their immune systems cooked and poisoned their spermatocytes to death. The damage had been done. You just stopped hoping, you put the hope away. You remembered the last time you saw a child (twenty-one years ago) and never thought about it again.

Bashir said, "She's underweight and dehydrated, but not malnourished. Similar to the minor injuries on her hands and feet, I'd guess that's recent. A couple of days, a week at most."

"It's a miracle," Lois whispered. "She's a miracle. We have to—"

"We do need to inform the rest of the council," Bashir said. "Val?"

Val nodded, though it felt distant and cold, as if someone were holding her chin and making her do it. Outside, the gunshot sounds of the lake continued. She had heard of cold snaps, polar vortexes, something about air from the Arctic flowing in an unusual pattern, but she had never experienced one before. The suddenness was terrifying, but the terror remained a low undercurrent under everything else she was feeling.

"Somewhere out there," she said, "relatively nearby, it sounds like, may be the only fertile couple in the world. I'm probably exaggerating. I hope I am. But we can all do math and I know we're all thinking the math here *looks* like a miracle. Mainly, we just can't run off all half-cocked. First of all, it was about zero this morning and now it's minus forty—"

Martin Sykes glanced perfunctorily at the suction-cup thermometer stuck to the window, his lank blond hair straggling over his collar. "Minus forty-seven," he said.

" . . . So we're *not* sending out a search party in this," Val said. "We'll call a council meeting for tomorrow; I think everyone but us is in town," she added. *Town* meant Edmonton, once a city of close to a million people, now about one percent of that, but still the place where everyone bartered and worked and visited friends. In a province speckled with lakes and abruptly empty lakeshore cabins, most folks still preferred to live in the city; only the crustiest hermits and misanthropes (Val thought fondly) chose to live in a cabin community like this one.

"I'll start calling around," Lois said, her voice trembling.

"Thanks, Lo." Val glanced at Martin, then again at the thermometer next to him. Had it dropped again while she was watching? Jesus. "I'll take her for tonight. Bash, come help me set up the cot in the office; I want her to be close to a bathroom."

The others—Lois, Martin, Dean and Willa Monahan, Katy Coles, Ethan Weiskopf—filed out, already speculating about the weather, the search pattern, equipment. Val was barely listening; she heard only the discordant song in her head: *No. We're not giving her back no matter what the hell we find. Mine, she's mine. She's mine, she's my child, she belongs to me.*

I found her and she's mine.

She had never experienced cold like this, not in a lifetime of living here. It registered not as temperature on the skin but force, as if the air itself had frozen solid and become a slab of metal pressing the breath out of their lungs. Thank God she'd found the kid when she did; she'd have died of hypothermia in minutes.

That night, sleeping cat-light on the floor next to the little girl's cot, Val dreamed her usual brain-clearing clutter: a lost gold watch that her grandmother had accused her of stealing; making *pysanky* at school, spattering hot beeswax on her hand; a stag that stood atop the snow and watched her with bright blue eyes.

Then it seemed she dreamed of a ringing phone, of screams incomprehensible in their terror and grief, and she dreamed she dressed and checked on the sleeping child and went outside and—

The cold kicked her awake from the night's haze, burning the strip of exposed skin around her eyes like a blowtorch. It was Willa Monahan, howling herself hoarse, and someone dragging her from the thing sprawled on the cabin's front lawn. Val stared, speechless, horrified less by what it was than the fact that she could not identify it at once.

It was Dean, splayed to the dawn sky and more than simply naked, opened up not like you'd butcher a deer but split as if by lightning, except that no lightning had ever carved so precisely. The enormous ring of blood around him was going from black to gray under the falling snow; sheets of his skin (*Christ!*) were arranged in a matching circle, marked with letters, triangles, connecting lines, squirming (*Can't be—just an effect of the snow*) lasciviously, demanding a closer look, a spider's web of arcs and curves and in the center the spider itself, many-limbed with ribs and femurs ripped from its body and broken into sharp-edged legs.

Some sick fuck, some roving stranger. She knew everyone in this place. Hell, maybe it was this very murderer that the child had fled, and the thought would have chilled her blood if she hadn't been freezing already. It wasn't important. The murderer wasn't here, and they had to get Dean, oh God, *the body*, to the infirmary, where Bash could—

"Val!"

Unthinking, she reached for the bow that wasn't on her back, and something came at her from the side, knocking her into the snow so that for a second she was staring up into a star field of flakes, half-hypnotized—snapped out of it by something yanking on her boot. She kicked it away and scrambled to her feet, slipping and cursing.

Bashir grabbed her under the arms, and they backed away, panting, the air knives in throat and lungs. The others were scattering, screaming, from a chaos of forms in the snow. Slinking from the woods bordering the lake, demurely veiled in the white lace of the snow, came creatures—predators, Val thought, but just like the people, she knew every creature here, the muskrats and weasels, the wolverines, wolves, the bears, coyotes, the few feral dogs that remained.

These were none of those and all of these, they were essence of carnivore: low, black-furred things, clawed and fanged, with backbones like snakes to squeeze into secret places. "Inside!" Val shouted.

She did not see who piled in, only shoved them to move faster, and was it her imagination or had something snatched at the very hem of her coat as she slammed the door? Surely the things had not reached the cabin in so short a time.

"We can't leave him," Willa sobbed. "We can't leave him out there... We have to..."

"I know, I know," Val said mechanically, patting the woman's back. "I know..." She wasn't listening. Martin and Bashir were stoking the stove as high as it could safely go; Ethan was methodically—she could hear the squeak of his footsteps in the loft—closing and latching the shutters. That was smart; she hadn't thought of that. Her heart was still pounding. The child was awake, though dazed, and staring up at the roomful of coat-bulked monsters as if they were about to bite her head off.

Val sent Lois to put on the kettle, then knelt next to the child, who was curled on her cot and wrapped in red-and-white-plaid blankets that she had pulled partly over her head, like a hood.

"Hey, you're awake," Val said, striving to sound light and cheery. "How do you feel?"

After a moment, the little girl extended a trembling, sticklike arm from her blanket nest, pointing at the front door.

"It's all right," Val said. "We're safe in here. I guess it was pretty scary, all those folks yelling, huh?"

The child shook her head, dark hair clinging to the wool around her face. She pointed at the bandaged scrapes on her arm, then pointed at the door again.

"I . . . did the person . . . did those animals . . . hurt you?"

Nod, nod.

"Who was it? Can you tell us?"

Shake, shake.

Val felt woozy for a second—supposing this *was* the only child in the world, maybe a murderer didn't know that and the animals couldn't, but logic did not abate the wave of killing rage that washed over her. When it ebbed, Val gripped the child's blanketed shoulders. "We're safe," she said again. "Nothing's getting in. I won't let anything hurt you."

The child stared at her, the hope on her face heartbreaking. Val swallowed thickly. "I won't," she said. "You should eat. Come on."

She held out her hand, and the child took it.

Val did not offer for anyone to stay the night; she simply dragged blankets and pillows out of the linen closet, and made Ethan pull out the sofa bed in the main room. Every light in the cabin blazed, picking out the glass of framed photographs, glinting on the nails in the faux-timbered walls. It had been decorated to look rustic, like a log cabin outside and in. Part of nature, Val thought bitterly.

But nothing natural had killed Dean Monahan.

The child had been put to bed in the loft once she'd proven she could manage the stairs. After checking on her, Val folded herself into the overstuffed green corduroy chair next to the sofa, studying the others. Willa's face was the same color as her flaxen hair; at her request, Bash had given her a Valium, and Val had thought that the single pill would knock the teetotaler off her feet like a right hook, but she was still awake and did not look especially calm. Lois, swaying. Martin, looking longingly at the liquor cabinet in the corner. Big, dark Ethan huddled like a bear in his blankets next to the bow and full quiver of arrows Val had placed near the door.

If asked, she would not have been able to tell them why. It wasn't like she intended to open a window and pick the creatures off as if the cabin were a medieval castle under siege. Val was not tall, not strong-looking; her mother had always jokingly said *robust*, built precisely like her Ukrainian peasant ancestors. As a child she had fixated on a history book with a little throwaway fact about the English longbow, and how training took so long that you had to start when you were seven years old. Now, after decades of indulging the childhood obsession, she startled people when she demonstrated the bow, revealing her powerful torso like a plastic action figure. She estimated her draw weight slightly less than her own hundred and forty pounds; she could put an arrow through a medium-sized tree.

Folks smiled and nodded when she went out to hunt. It was fine, it was just Prince Val, ha ha, out in the woods again with her rocket launcher. She certainly believed she *could* kill the creatures. She just hadn't gotten the bow down with the intent. Something specific about them made her uneasy, something that reminded her of the morning—she had told herself to remember it, but in the tangle and chaos of recovering the child from the ravine, she had forgotten.

"I dreamed of her last night," Bashir said, his voice nearly inaudible below the hiss of the stove. "The little girl . . . she was whole again, healed. She wore a dress of deer leather. And she was with my parents." Val winced; his parents had died in an accident when he was in his teens, only a few years after immigrating to Canada. In a way, he'd always said, that was a blessing: more merciful than the flu.

He added, "She did not speak. But my father said she wanted me to come with them, because they had a surprise—a present—for me. We would go together, he said. All of us, walking."

For a few minutes no one spoke. Val studied her friend's drawn, tired face, the two dull spots under his eyes where the few seconds of exposure this morning had given him frostbite. They all had it. She said, "I didn't dream of her. I dreamt about hunting. A big stag with blue eyes."

It was not as if a dam broke then, but the dreams did trickle out, with great reluctance. Ethan had dreamt of being chased by wolves, strange ones, glossy blue-black like magpie feathers.

Lois spoke in a weepy murmur, as if ashamed: the child atop a mountain, but the mountain wasn't insensible stone. It was alive and obedient to her every word, waiting only for her to speak. And the child's father stood behind her, smiling with beautiful white teeth, the only thing visible in a face not shadowed but made of shadow.

Val twitched; Bashir gave her a curious look, and she pretended she hadn't seen it. "Anybody else?" she croaked.

Willa said she hadn't dreamt of the child at all, and Val believed her; Martin said he hadn't either, but she didn't believe him, and that was strange. She had known Martin for years, worked side by side with him at the plant till he had been transferred out of her team. She had never seen anything that rang the smallest alarm bell in her head. Was one ringing now? She hated the idea that the dreams were scrambling her gut feelings.

"It's nothing," Val said, since everyone was looking at her. "It's just . . . brains, it's just dreams. If we had come across a whale washed up from the lake, we'd all be dreaming about whales."

That got a few weak laughs. No one spoke of the search party again, or a serial killer; no one asked what they would do with Dean Monahan's body. It was not something Willa should hear even with a full Valium under her belt. That would be for tomorrow, in the daylight.

Val checked on the little girl, whispered some reassurances, and wrapped herself in her last, most threadbare blanket on the floor next to the cot.

Now there was no trusting dreams, there was no distinguishing the dream from the real. Someone was telling Val about *faces*, and how the word did not mean simply the material that covered the front of a skull. Faces were something else, came from somewhere else, and no one could see a true face here, not here. *Why not here?* she asked, disliking that she could not see the speaker.

She woke abruptly, and lay in the darkness for several heart-racing minutes, deciding whether she was awake or not. Eventually her eyes adjusted and she decided something *had* woken her, and it had not been the dream. The house was quiet and cold below her, the only sound that of the sleepers.

And the cot at her side was empty.

She was up with a speed she did not believe possible, scrambling down the ladder, half falling the last three rungs. No light in the bathroom, lumps on the floor still asleep, the correct number. Had the child crawled in with one of the others? Check the rest of the house first, panic after that. Maybe it was for nothing.

Something moved in the gap under the office door; Val thought she would pass out from relief. Okay. Kid went back to the first place she had slept in, that was all. Maybe it felt safer down here. Okay, okay. The sound of the girl climbing out of her cot must have woken her, the creak of the floor.

Val opened the door and stopped dead.

The child did not notice her right away, or perhaps Val was meant to believe she was beneath notice. The girl knelt on the desk, staring out the unshuttered window, humming softly to herself, her dark hair loosed from the braid Lois had put it in.

Outside, not ten yards from the house, the animals were back—the predators, the low and crawling things, and they had not torn someone apart but were still tearing as the body thrashed and struggled, one hand rising pale in the moonlight, then going slack, falling to the snow. And it was not the creatures doing the carving, no. Only the killing. Mixed among them, low and crawling themselves, even lower, were other children—naked in the murderous cold, hair straggling over their backs like manes, knives of stone in their tiny hands.

Val backed away, unthinking, as if the terrible tableau outside would suddenly break apart like a flock of birds and attack the window—she had a clear and sickening vision of their bodies hitting the glass, tumbling inside, bouncing up to hamstring her or slice her heel—and the child turned at last, and smiled at her with tiny, even teeth.

Val screamed then, and fled, and slammed the door behind her, running back to the living room, where the lights were turning on and voices rose in response to her own.

———

"Why in the *hell* did Willa go outside?" Ethan's voice was weak and small, as if he were imitating someone else. He looked the same way he sounded, Val thought—deflated, like someone who had lost a hundred pounds overnight and still wore the extra skin. "I don't *understand*. I just . . ."

"Well, what the hell was Dean doing outside?" Val said, trying to stamp out the quaver in her voice. "And both of them naked . . . You answered your own question. They didn't go because they wanted to. They went because someone told them to. And—"

"Don't say someone!" Lois broke in, at a pitch so high they all turned to stare at her. "Why are we saying *someone*? We all know only one man has the power to do . . . things like that. Everybody knows that. That's *known*."

"The dark man is dead," Val said. "That's known, too. Him and anyone he gave . . . any little sliver of his power. People went down there to look, Lois. Take measurements, photos, prove it all happened the way it was written. They're all dead." She held up a hand before the older woman could state the obvious. "I know, I know. Some people thought he couldn't die. Those people were all proved wrong. It's been twenty-one years. It's not him. I . . . Something else has to be happening."

"How is that *better*?" Ethan burst out.

"Calm down," Val said. She glanced at Bashir, returning from the kitchen and drying his hands on a dish towel. "Bash, did Willa say anything to you last night?"

He shook his head, then sagged at the knees and sat on the couch next to Martin. "Obviously she was upset," he said. "What happened to her husband . . . But she didn't present any indications that she intended to end her own life."

Martin said, "Well, the next question is what are we going to do about th—"

"I don't care about the *nuclear bomb!*" Lois snapped, thrashing out of her chair, stumbling over the blankets still pooled on the rug; Ethan caught her before she could fall, then let go, startled, as she flailed at his face. "I don't *care* what they said they found! I saw it in my dream, Valerie, and I think the rest of you are liars if you say you didn't—you lied to yourselves last night and you lied to the rest of us, and that child is the spawn of *him*! The dark man! Did he die without leaving any part of himself in this world? Do you truly think that? Then you're more fools than anyone who followed him to the desert, you *are*, you are *liars and imbeciles!*"

Frozen in shock, Valerie could think only of that movie with the Devil and the priests and the little girl, of the *voices*—the thick, vomit-clotted sounds of hell coming from that little girl's body. They had sounded nothing like her. Lois still sounded like Lois, but Val had never heard this harsh, braying screech from her—not even a raised voice. This wasn't possession, it was just the sound of insanity, Lois had simply cracked in some deep and fundamental way. They could treat it, and—

Lois peeled past Ethan, the big man swiping ineffectually at her with one slow-moving paw, and vanished down the hallway toward the office. The cabin wasn't that big; Val caught up in moments, but it was still almost too late.

She and Bashir wrestled Lois to the floor, shocked by her strength, the snakelike power of her. Val was ashamed of herself even as she slammed Lois's thin hand against the desk till the letter opener she had been brandishing fell to the carpet, only half-aware that the child had fled the office at a run.

"Stay here," she gasped to Bashir. "I don't know if you can—I don't know, tie her up or something—I have to—"

"Go, see if she's all right."

"Jesus Christ, this motherfucking day," Val muttered under her breath, returning to the living room. The little girl was all right, thank God; in retrospect, Val thought Lois's surest sign of insanity was assuming that even with the element of surprise she could kill a kid with a letter opener. Martin and Ethan flanked her, awkwardly, both with an air of fretful self-consciousness, as if they had been invited to touch something fragile and they would really rather not.

Didn't see it before, Val thought with light surprise. *We've forgotten how to parent; we've forgotten what it looks like, what we're supposed to do.* "Everyone okay?"

"I nearly peed myself when Lois smacked me," Ethan said. "Is she all right?"

"Don't think so," Val said. "We're all under a lot of stress right now, with the murders and the . . . animals and the . . . everything. Bash has her, though. She'll be fine."

"Glad she didn't hurt anyone," Ethan said.

"Yes," Martin said, and there it was in the single syllable, there was the *thing* Val had been thinking about for that single moment, looking into Lois's eyes and hearing Lois's voice, and now she looked into Martin's eyes and heard a different voice. The child gazed up at him, blinking. There was another in the room, unseen, only heard.

No. Imagining it. I just said we were all under a lot of stress. I just said it. "Well," Val said. "Let's—"

"There is no we," Martin said in not-Martin's voice, and he clasped the child's shoulder. "There is you. And there is us."

"Mart?" said Ethan, holding his hands out as if Martin were armed. "What are you talking about?"

"Val knew it," Martin said, unmoving. "Didn't you, Val? Because we talked about it, just once. Years ago. You said the people who went to the desert, following the dark man . . . you said they were *weak*. Too weak to resist. But you're wrong. They were strong, stronger than the others, and that's why he gathered them to himself, to add their strength to his."

"I didn't say weak," Val said; her mouth felt numb. "I said I thought he chose people who would break a certain way if you dropped them. He *wanted* them to break. Other people, taking that hit, maybe they'd . . . dent or chip, nothing more. But he wanted his people to be broken before he used them. You get your damn hands off her, Martin."

Martin chuckled. "She's mine," he said. "Or I'm hers . . . It doesn't matter now. Just as the journey of a thousand miles starts with a single step, or so my old bumper sticker said, a legion starts with a single recruit. Things have to begin somewhere, Val."

"Don't touch her," Val whispered. "Come here, kiddo. It's all right."

"Oh, no no," Martin said solicitously, turning toward the door, turning the little girl too, her dark hair falling over his wrist. "This is hardly a place to bring up a child. What with all this *vermin* in the house."

Val was already lunging for the child, gone in an instant through the door Martin flung wide, and she hit the floor and rolled, snatching for the bow and arrows instead, as the house filled with the biting cold—and the dark, slithering creatures.

At close range, the bow was no good; she stabbed at the snarling forms till the arrow broke, then ran for the kitchen, sliding in the blood pooled and already freezing on the wooden floor. Bashir and Ethan were already there; down the hall, dimly, they heard Lois screaming, abruptly cut off.

Even at this distance, the animals were unidentifiable; they were just thrashing claws and bristling fur, stinking of meat, their teeth yellow and half rotting out of blackened gums. After a half dozen had been hacked to death with her kitchen knives, the rest fled through the open door, their barking uncannily like cruel laughter.

And *he* had her, Martin or not-Martin or whoever the fuck he was, he had the only child in existence, in the killing cold, and God only knew who he would deliver her to—Val had thought her rage and horror were exhausted when Lois had tried to kill the child (Lois! of all people!), but she found an inexhaustible well of it now, buoying her like a raptor riding an updraft on a hot day. For several seconds she could not even remember that she was not alone, and found herself surprised when Bashir stopped her at the doorway, confused by the long, dark hand gently on her own.

"No," Bashir said. "We'll come with you. Get some more layers on."

Val had read the accounting of that summer many years ago, and had forgotten most of it; but now, as she ran hunched and growling along the tracks in the snow, she remembered something they had said: *He can call up storms, if he needs them.* And others saying: *He comes in the storm, if he wants.*

And another: *He can come as wolf or crow, or he can put on faces; but if he wishes he can come also as the hurricane or the flood. We have seen it. We have seen him in the wind.*

Could he call up *cold*?

No, because he was dead. Dead as the rest of them, killed in a split second of heat and light that he did not call up.

They had started on snowmobiles, she and Ethan and Bashir, abandoning them when the trails in the woods ran out. The midday light was sickly and dim, as if they ran through an endless twilight, coughing and swallowing blood as the sides of their windpipes crystallized with every breath. The slinking creatures kept their distance now, just visible as shadows flickering through the trees. Val had dropped a couple of them with her arrows, Ethan one with his rifle. They did not fear humans, Val thought; they had been *directed* to pace them instead of attack, perhaps herd them.

Even now she admitted she had never truly believed in the stories. She had chalked everything up to mass insanity, to the hysteria of crowds and mobs. That there had been a "dark man," a cult leader, she thought likely, just as she thought that Jesus had probably been real, a young rabble-rouser in the wrong place at the wrong time. But the talk about magic? No, she had not believed that, not deep down. There had to be another explanation, just as now, and she would find it afterward if she lived.

The cold dragged on their pursuit until they were nearly crawling. Val wanted to scream. Martin and the child were moving fast (and that, too, would have to be explained, the way they danced over the surface of the snow). "We're losing them," she panted. "We have to move faster."

"We should go back," Bashir managed, his voice indistinct, like Val's, under multiple layers of fabric. All that could be seen were his eyes, dark and frightened through the goggles. "Val, I'm sorry. I know. But we'll die out here."

"Yes, you will."

Ethan yelped, thrusting his body instinctively in front of Val, but the voice had come from everywhere and nowhere. "Face out," Val hissed to the two men. "Back-to-back." She stared wildly around them at the dense but empty forest, the crowding trunks of birch and aspen, the slumped swags of pine, seeing nothing.

"Isn't it strange how people will run from shelter," the voice went on. *"From safety, from good things, warm things . . . into the cold. And here you are. Why did you chase me?"*

"To get . . . Because you took . . . " Val's teeth were chattering.

Now that they weren't moving, the chill was setting into her limbs; she thought they had, perhaps, a few minutes before hypothermia set in for good.

"*Because I wanted you to. Because out here, I hold your lives in my hand.*"

"No," Val whispered.

"*The brave woodsman,*" the voice laughed. "*Coming to chop Little Red Riding Hood out of the wolf before it's too late. Let me tell you something about the little girl in that story.*"

And then it was there, on Val's side of the triangle, the buck she had seen—and the thing she had told herself to remember. Not the eyes, brown and normal now, but the mouth, the nose, all too clear. It wasn't breathing. *It wasn't breathing when I first saw it, either. And I knew... I knew...*

"*She goes on an errand for her mother,*" the voice went on, emanating from somewhere in the buck's chest. Behind it, Val saw the child, quite calm, still dressed in the T-shirt Val had given her, one tiny hand on the buck's leg. Val's entire body ached with yearning to run to her, sweep up the vulnerable little body; but she dared not move. Could not, probably, even if she did dare.

"*But there are wolves in the forest,*" the buck went on. "*The mother knows this. What kind of story is that? You send your little girl out into the wide world, armed with nothing but her innocence, you send her to the murderers and the pedophiles and the kidnappers and the—*"

"Stop it!"

"*Why? Is it upsetting? The girl in the story isn't real.* Children *aren't real anymore. That was humanity's last hurrah, the party on the deck of the* Titanic. *You know it was. But it doesn't have to be. If you join me... if you give your will to mine... as your friend did... if...*"

If you throw me and I break the way you want, Val thought. *If you tell me you can replace my missing pieces with yourself and only you... That's the way it works, isn't it? You take away, and then you say we can be whole again. With you. We, us, the world.*

The burning cold faded, and the trees around Val dissolved, and she watched it with the resignation of a dream. There *was* a fracture in her, of course. Anyone could see it, not just him. If you hungered for anything too much, you'd snap along that line as cleanly as a piece of glass. And oh, how she had hungered for a child . . . *I stopped though. I stopped wanting.*

You never stopped hoping, something said, or thought, or sighed, and it was full summer and she sat on a red-and-white-plaid blanket, and next to her, laughing with her pearly little teeth, lay the child she had found in the ravine, fawn-brown, fawn-soft, her dark hair clean against her rounded face, white overalls printed with yellow and pink roses. Down the grassy slope, children running and shrieking. Kites hovering, bright as birds against the blue, and Bashir with a couple of little boys at his feet—twins, their hair identical soft, dark clouds—working the controls of a battery-powered car, and next to the blanket the buck, silent, for he did not need to say, *All this could be yours, but I cannot do it alone, I need you to*—

The sky tore, and she could not tell whether it was in the vision or in the real world, because there was snow still falling through the gray light around the wound, and the hands holding it open were small, scratched, a child's hands, covered with something that was not skin.

Bashir had been wrong—a good doctor, but *wrong*, because he thought he was dealing with a human being. The child wasn't five or six or seven or any age, and she wasn't a she or a he so much as an it; and it had been presented in a form meant to beguile, and it had worked. Perhaps in another time or place it would have come as a beautiful woman; in a world without children, it had come as this. And its true shape was neither lock nor key but something meant to bring lock and key together, opening a door that had been closed twenty-one years ago—

(*I like sevens I like seven and seven and seven all things have their place and time Valerie and that includes you*)

—and the slit through which it had wriggled was uneven, laboriously made, who knew how much effort had been expended to even allow the tiny child-shaped thing through, but if she or he or it (it did not matter) could build up belief and followers again, could fill its coffers with ready and pliable minds, then there would no longer be a slit but a doorway, and anything could come through a door. *Literally anything*, Val thought, rolling the phrase around what remained of her cooling brain. Things we could not even look at and understand, because we would go insane . . . our poor, pitiful human minds.

"No," she said, or tried to. She imagined the cold finally reaching her internal organs, freezing her liver, her kidneys, moving up to her heart, frantically beating to keep the blood moving. *I will die here, but at least I can die saying no.*

"*Let me save your life*," the thing said, the avatar, stag or child or monster as it was. "*Isn't it worth saving? Like hers?*"

The glamour had taken them all; she had not realized Martin was approaching them where they stood stock-still in the snow-covered clearing, and that he held not a knife but a sword. The gleam was faint in the dim light, but it was enough to snap Val back into reality—too late, too close, Martin had swung the sword with both hands and was aiming for her neck and it did not matter how much fabric lay between the blade and the big veins, it was not enough.

Ethan did not so much tackle Martin as fall against the smaller man's legs, the sword thumping heavily against Val's shoulder, knocking her off her feet and tangling with the other two. As she struggled to rise on limbs that would not obey her, cursing them, cursing herself, she almost nodded at the glittering eyes that began to ring them again, low, gleeful, gloating even: vermin spotting easy prey. Why not? On top of everything else?

"Ethan!" Bashir snatched at Martin from behind, trying to lock his forearm across the man's throat, but his coat was so thick he could barely bend his elbow, and the sword flashed, swinging, rising—

Pick one. No time.

"Mama, don't!" the child cried, and Val screamed something—or perhaps it was merely a sob that tore loose from her gut, and in a matter of seconds she had loosed three arrows into the fragile chest, pinning the body to the birch tree behind it, sending the world into darkness.

It was a full minute before she realized the darkness was incomplete; something *had* happened, but not the end of the world. She raised her hand to her face, brought her glove away covered in what looked like mucus and blood, looked at her bow. The bowstring had snapped, as she should have expected it to in the cold, and taken out her left eye.

There was no pain; she knew she only had a few minutes before she went into shock, however, and she approached the tree cautiously. The child had vanished. Her arrows remained, bloodless, buried deep in the heartwood. At the base of the trunk lay something small and dark, like a chunk of coal with a bubble in it, the dark red of arterial blood. She stooped, picked it up, swayed, and collapsed into the snow. *Shouldn't have done that*, she thought vaguely as a second darkness closed in on her. *Not leaned down . . . used a stick or something . . .*

―⁂―

"Ready?"

"One sec," Val said. She had not wanted to keep the thing close to her skin, and had brought it in a plastic bag, wrapped and sealed with tape. Placed on Martin's corpse, it made her think of burying a superfan with a signed baseball or something. "Okay, give."

The snow had melted in minutes as the three returned from the woods. It meant the funeral pyre had been built of soaked wood, it would sputter and smoke and smolder for hours, but Val wanted to burn the body, and Bashir and Ethan had agreed. Neither man would tell her who had dealt the killing blow, but Val had her suspicions. Necks were harder to break in real life than in the movies; if you didn't know the right angle, you needed a tremendous amount of force.

Bashir handed her the long-stemmed barbecue lighter; she touched the flame to the layer of phone books, then settled in for a wait as the weak, translucent flames began to catch.

Val touched her eye patch, traced a fingertip down the stitched and puckered scar that sprouted from beneath it and ended under her jaw. The bowstring had nearly split her face open, Bashir said; if she'd been conscious, she could have seen what her skull looked like.

"I read that longbow training was so intense you could see it on people's skeletons after they died," she said, staring into the listless flames. "Like all you'd have to do was look at someone's bones and you'd know."

"Mm," Bashir said. "That's interesting. Don't touch that."

"Sorry, Doc."

The lake was flat and calm, sluggish with cold but free from the sudden ice that had sheathed it. Amber light skipped off the surface, making her good eye hurt. "Why here?" she said. "Why us?"

"Rhetorical question," Bashir said promptly. "And if you've got theories, they will do nothing but hurt you."

"I know, I *know* that. I just . . . I think about before. The dark man chose people for a reason—it wasn't at random. He didn't throw darts at a map and say, *Him, him, her, her.* So I can't help but feel that we were chosen. Or I was chosen. And that is . . ." The plastic bag around the stone, or coal, or whatever it was, was coming apart; she turned away, staring into the trees. "So that's the end of it for real," she said.

"End of what?"

"I don't know. End of humanity. We really *can't* hope for kids, can we. It's been long enough that we'd know by now. We were deluded to think we had a chance. We got judged, and we're serving out our sentence."

"I don't believe that," Bashir said. The corpse was burning steadily now. They returned to the boardwalk leading up to the village, their shadows long and graceful in the sunset. "There's technology, people are doing experiments, not giving up. It's not the end. It's a pause. Will you be all right tonight?"

She took a deep breath, knowing she could not lie to him. "No. I don't think so. But I'll make it to the morning, if that's what you mean; and then I'll make it to Christmas, so I can give you something nice; and then I'll make it to spring, so I can go pick out a sapling for a new bow."

"Good. Goodnight, Val."

She walked home, then stood at her front door, ignoring the thudding pain any head movement caused behind her eye patch, and studied the darkening sky. The stars were emerging one by one, hard and clear and precisely where they should be. No tear, no wound.

Seeing proved nothing, of course, and if magic had flowed back into the world it might still be there, but she still sighed at the stars, and went inside, and that night enjoyed a deep and dreamless sleep.

CAME THE LAST NIGHT OF SADNESS
Catherynne M. Valente

Fern Ramsey sat crisscross applesauce on the cold concrete floor of a dead stranger's garage, left foot squished tight between her long, thin leg and the slab, right foot plopped up on her opposite knee, waggle-tapping along to the song in her head. There was always a song in Fern's head; always had been. Always the same song, in point of fact, even though she didn't know what it was called, or understand the words too much, or remember where she could ever have heard it. She supposed she'd made it up herself when she was littler and just forgotten it, like you forgot all kinds of things about being littler once you got big.

Oh well.

Not that Fern was all that big. She figured she was somewhere in the general neighborhood of seventeen, but maybe fifteen and maybe twenty. It never seemed like an important enough fact to hold on to. Like where exactly she was. Most of those big metal WELCOME TO THE STATE OF BLANK [INSERT STUPID NONSENSE MOTTO HERE] signs were still scarecrowing it up where they always had, but most small places didn't have names anymore, not really. And if this one did, it wasn't fessing up.

Fern just thought of wherever she ended up as Somewhere. Probably. Maybe. Probably, Virginia. Maybe, Ohio. Somewhere, Maine. Even though everywhere was the same and it didn't matter one bit what you called things anymore.

―――

Some facts that did seem important enough for Fern to hold on to:

A long, long time ago, there were a lot of human people in every single place you could get to, but not anymore.

Then there was an Age of Miracles, when *need* and *find* weren't so far apart and for one fucking second it seemed like the things that happened to you had some kind of reason, some basic rhythm. But not anymore.

Just because something is canned and the seal looks all right doesn't mean the food hasn't up and turned into poison in there.

A big red painted *X* inside a big red painted *O* on the side of a barn or a house or a city hall or a bus means people got the bad sick there. Not a long, long time ago, either, so stay away. There's other symbols, too. A blue smiley face means the water's safe. A black *V* with a line through the middle means there's folk here, but they don't play well with others. That sort of thing.

You can do fine as long as you know how to read and have a knife, a map, a fishing pole, and a bicycle—as long as you know how to fix the last two.

Just about every single person who ever met Fern Ramsey ditched her within a few days. Fake Granddad, King Sue, Big Barry Bullfrog, everybody. She knew there was nothing wrong with *her*, at least no more than what was wrong with all the rest of everything, so her carefully considered opinion was fuck them if they wanted to be like that.

If a bottle has a word that ends in *-cillin* on it, those are antibiotics and you should swipe some. If it ends in *-done*, those are painkillers, and you should swipe all of them. Are they still good? Maybe! An infected puncture wound definitely isn't good, though. A chance is better than none.

The thing is, everything expires. But that doesn't always mean it's gone bad. Most of the time it's just gone different. Like how you can't use gasoline anymore, but that marmalade jelly it likes to turn into makes pretty quick work of anything that gets in your way.

It's hard to ride a zebra, but not as hard as the library encyclopedias, say. Just have a little belief in yourself, for fuck's sake.

The sun rises in the east and sets in the west. Rivers mostly flow north to south. Stick to those and the highways. The mountains and plains in the middle are best. Northeast is mostly safe and good. Don't go southeast. And the farther west, the closer to hell.

There are some things you just can't ever get back, even if you do everything right.

Outside, the buzzy still heat of late summer clung to every goddamned thing like wet tape. Birds screamed like crazy from elms and oaks and pines, millions of them. Too many birds now, because too many bugs, too many bugs because the civilized world is an awful big corpse to munch on. But in the carless, dust-cozied garage, it was nothing but cool and shady and nice. The door to this particular garage lay on the weedy driveway like a squashed turtle, upside down, baking helplessly in the sun, scraped and dented all to hell, leaving an open cave of (maybe) useful wonders for anyone to find.

And Fern Ramsey was very good at finding useful things. Like the tattered cutoff denim shorts she'd been wearing for a good while now, liberated from a dead girl's dead bedroom with rainbow butterfly stickers all over its dead walls. Like the water-stiffened cowboy boots (and the knife inside them) she'd fished out of a river back in Somewhere, Iowa, toes curling up out of the current to kick at the moon. Like the frayed and fraying shirt she'd called up to the big game from a picked-over airport mezzanine in Nowhere Special, New Jersey, with its mysterious, hermetic design so faded only stick-figure silhouettes remained where big spangled letters had once proclaimed: THE BOSS.

Like people, when Fern wanted people. Like animals, when she needed animals.

Her ankle was falling asleep. The cold concrete stuck to the backs of her thighs; fuzzy cactus-prickles crept out from her squashed foot up the back of her blackberry-scratched calf, but Fern didn't care. *Comfort is the enemy of progress*, an old man who called himself her granddad for a little while had told Fern. A long time ago, and somewhere else. But he said it in a rocking chair with his feet up on the porch rail and a big old tumbler of fresh moose milk in his paw, so Fern privately thought he was just about entirely full of shit on that one. And anyway, what had fake granddads ever known about anything? How to fuck everything straight up forever? Fern could handle that all by herself.

She couldn't feel a thing but coppery static in her legs. She didn't twitch. Not because Fern had taken a shine to comfort or progress in her advanced age. But moving meant taking her eyes off her prize and that just wasn't gonna happen. Maybe one in a hundred empty shitbox houses had what that girl was after. Mostly they were just sad husks. Garages and sheds and basements full of workbenches where no one was ever going to finish fixing up their downstairs radiator and the rusted clamp-on vises gripped nothing but shadows. Dead drills and dead cars and dead chain saws and dead snowblowers and dead lawn mowers and plastic canisters of dead gasoline for said cars and chain saws and snowblowers and lawn mowers. And sometimes dead people. They weren't much more than crumbly skeletons now, dry and companionable and anonymous. Still, you didn't want to think too much about that, especially when live people weren't exactly thick on the ground.

But every once in a while, one of these old cracked shells had a walnut in it, and everything shone.

She'd been coming up pretty dry lately. Nothing but nothing for months. So when Fern ducked off the county road into this big dumb brick-and-brass Cape Cod and its detached two-car, she'd told herself not to expect too much. Maybe a replacement for the disintegrating hot-weather shirt she'd called up to the big game from a quiet bungalow in Somewhere, Vermont. She liked it mighty fine. Just a huge open screaming mouth with its tongue out, splattered in stars and bloody stripes of red.

Oh well.

But she hadn't even found anything that useful. Just a nice, picked-clean garage with nothing much to say. Finally, she'd stacked up a bunch of thick hardcover books with burst spines and swollen pages and climbed on top to grope around on the top shelf of a steel storage rack. And there it was. All the way up there where you'd have to look to find it, where you'd have to *want* to find it: a half-congealed cardboard box someone with awful-pretty handwriting had labeled *For Whoever You Are*. Fern's sweaty mosquito-gnawed skin went all over cold and electric.

Boxes, trunks, tubs, suitcases; always labeled, and always with stuff like that. *If Anyone Comes Asking. To Be Opened When It's Over. Here Lies Us. For the Living*. People got real poetic back then. Fern guessed the end of the world would do that to you. But then again, Fern found one back west about seven hundred miles that just said *HI!* and she thought that was somehow the prettiest one of all.

The box was bloated and watercolory with years of un-blowered New England snow and summer heat having their way with the cardboard. Her fingers sank right through the thing like soft cheese. The careful, looping letters had faded to almost nothing, like her shirt. No ink left, just the little canyons carved in relief by a long-dry pen. But it was plenty enough to let Fern Ramsey know there was a ghost in there, and it wanted someone to talk to.

All that old, clammy box-sweat soaked into her as she hauled her new best friend down to settle in for the night. It stained Fern's chest with a wet, black rectangle, like a door into her heart.

Thankfully, whoever had carefully and lovingly swooped that Y so nice and big, even while they were probably barfing up their whole soul and also both lungs, had also been clever enough to seal the contents of the box in a series of big gallon freezer stay-fresh plastic bags.

A few well-loved paperback books written by people whose names meant less than nothing to Fern. Photos of smiling people and crying babies and days at the beach with coolers full of beer bottles like icy green dreams. Faded children's shirts folded as reverently as altar cloths: Spider-Man, Strawberry Shortcake, Big Bird, Future Astronaut. A heavy double-bagged tangle of jewelry.

Fern turned the snarl of gold over in her hands. There were some big fat diamonds in there, rubies, too. Maybe even real. The house wasn't *that* nice, though. Somebody probably scraped and scrimped and skipped a new winter coat to buy these. They probably meant so much to somebody, somewhen. Enough to try to crank back their throwing arm and try to lob this bomb of diamonds and rubies and feelings all the way into a far future where kids could grow up to be astronauts.

Fern tossed the gold behind her onto a stack of paint drop cloths, still stained with carefully chosen main-and-trim colors. She wasn't after any of that. She wanted what was underneath. What she knew in her bones was underneath. A stack of loose typed pages, full of typos and pain and hope, sealed like broccoli in a freezer bag in case anyone ever gave a fuck.

Fern Ramsey gave *so many* fucks. All of them, in fact. All she had. All for whoever this was, whatever had happened to them, whatever they would never be now. For the very specific kind of one-in-a-hundred-houses kind of person who would take the time to cram a message down the neck of their house like a wine bottle and chuck it into the sea of time.

They just didn't make 'em like that anymore.

Fern could see a sentence sticking up over the opaque white stripe

CAME THE LAST NIGHT OF SADNESS

on the freezer bag where you were meant to write *Spaghetti Sauce* or *Cookie Dough* and the date.

My name was Kimberley Lynn McKiver.

Her heart started pinballing all over her chest. She licked her lips. *Yes. There you are, pretty dead thing. Pretty dead Kim with your pretty dead heart.*

Fern slid her finger down the plastic zip-seal and pulled out the pages. She lay them reverently in her lap, cool and smooth against her peach-fuzzed skin.

My name was Kimberley Lynn McKiver.

I lived in this house for twelve years before Captain Trips rang the doorbell, and thirty-three years after. I had four children, if you can believe it. I was a pharmacist. Sure did want to be a writer once upon a when, though. Guess this is my chance. Look out, Mr. Pullit, sir. Here I come.

I loved my husband. I loved my dogs. I loved my babies. I tried to bury them. I'm really sorry. I did try. I guess I should have gone to the gym more. The earth here is just so hard. Plus I screwed up and got old. Everyone seems to have gotten that one right but me.

They're in the upstairs bedroom. Tucked in tight. Hopefully I am, too, and we're all six of us together for always. Take anything you need from the house. It's yours. It's all yours now.

I existed. So did they. I mattered. So did they. It all mattered.

This is who we were. And this is how we left you.

Fern settled in to read in earnest. Six hours later, she hadn't stood or stretched, eaten or drunk, or moved at all—except to fidget idly with her tangled mess of hair, twirling and untwirling a long curl around her finger as the sun army-crawled across a thoughtless, heartless sky.

By dusk, the girl had risen two inches above the concrete. Floating crisscross applesauce in the still air, hunched over her treasure, all her limbs awake.

She didn't notice.

A crow noticed. It watched her motionlessly from the arms of an aspen tree.

Spring, 1996

A white-tailed deer and her fawn bend their heads to drink on the pebbly shore of Lake Keowee. Phlegmy streaks of stars spatter the South Carolina sky above; reflect in the water below and in the round pupilless eyes of the deer. The silent buttes of concrete cooling towers in the hills above the lake slash the night into dark and darker.

Sky and water and shadows and moonless quiet.

Cobwebs work the maintenance board at Oconee Nuclear Station. Dust supervises the shift-change. The peeling vinyl seats at the workstations dip into round, deep, comfortable hollows, as though some ghost's hardworking rump is still waiting out the clock on retirement under burnt-out fluorescents and lifeless EXIT signs.

The control rod indicators blink on and off steadily over a swollen brown suit jacket containing the skeleton of Crew Chief Tom Fortunado. Last one out. Mouth full of blood and lungs full of crawling rot as he forces his body already quitting on him to boot the automatic systems into maintenance mode and initiate automated cooldown protocols fast enough to avoid irradiating the greater Savannah River Basin. You couldn't just turn off a nuclear power plant like a night-light. It took years of careful, gradual processes to avoid any one of the thousand topics covered by quarterly safety drills.

The air here is always hot and wet. The bones of the man who stayed, slumped over the steam-pressure console, have grown new musculature, new skin, even new hair. Moss and mold and delicate frilled fungi swell up that old suitcoat almost to the size of Tom's former weekend rec-league physique. Crew Chief Fortunado had submitted a fully documented formal complaint concerning the flaccid air-conditioning every single Friday of his career and not one thing ever changed. He hated this place. The metallic taste of the recycled air. The unsalted egg salad and pink sliced mystery meat in the cafeteria. The oh-so-concerned protesters hollering at him outside the main entrance every goddamned day like he personally planned to drop a couple of megatons on Charleston during the morning meeting.

Tommy Fortunado hated this place. And now he'll never leave it.

The round lights flash on his dead shoulders like owl's eyes. Opening and closing. Opening and closing.

Green. White. Green. White. Then solid white, and, with an almost relieved pause, yellow. Faster, Faster. Faster toward red. Weak, wheezy Klaxons sound in the dark stillness. All the boards light up under the watchful eyes of beaming hard-hatted workers on a moldering workplace safety poster as they point purposefully into the middle distance, into the future:

At ONS We Power *PROGRESS!*

The temperature readouts inch past equilibrium. The skimmer wall separating the clean lake water from the contaminated cooling ponds quietly gives up its long fight. A shiver of blue light glows out of Oconee Nuclear Station, and it is not alone.

A few days from now, the deer drinking untroubled from the starlit water will die with their bellies full of tulip buds and sores ringing their soft white throats like ruby necklaces.

A few weeks after that, Catawba Nuclear Station goes.

It's high summer before the Watts Bar Plant in Chattanooga and the Grand Gulf Station in Port Gibson, Mississippi, sound their death rattles.

By the time the millennium turns over, the American Southeast writhes in a wash of invisible, hungry fire that will not go out for four hundred years.

Everything expires.

There were many, many things wrong with Fern Ramsey.

She was stronger than most other people, including boys. She could rip a log in half with her bare hands, and not an old rotten one, either.

Coarse, silvery hair covered most all of her skin but palms and soles; not so thick as you'd notice it if you weren't touching on someone you shouldn't, but it was there all the same.

Her toes looked like ladies' toes used to look from spending seventy years smashed up inside high heels, even though Fern hadn't ever even seen high heels, let alone done that silliness to herself.

One of her eyes was a fair bit bigger and darker than the other, but she didn't see so good out of that big boy.

And out of the nape of her neck, one single long, thin lock of brilliant white hair snaked out in all the black like a skunk's stripe.

Despite all that, Fern Ramsey was uncommon pretty. All *pretty* really meant these days was people *bothering* all over her if ever they could catch her, which they usually could on account of those hoofed-up feet.

Sometimes, not very often, but sometimes, Fern could make things, but only little things, happen just by thinking sharp enough. That's what she called it, when she had to call it something. Thinking sharp. She didn't understand why or how, but she was used to that.

Fern assumed she had parents at some point. My stars, doesn't everyone? But she didn't remember any. She didn't remember where she started out in this big broken board game of a world. She reckoned they died, but that wasn't the problem. Fern didn't remember being little or learning to read or something bad happening to good old Mr. and Mrs. Ramsey. She didn't even remember ever specifically deciding to live her life walking instead of pedaling or galloping or skating, or none of the above, just circling this great last drain toward one of the teeny handful of places where people who still remembered how to be people went to be people at each other as long as they could stand it.

CAME THE LAST NIGHT OF SADNESS

Walking just felt good. And Fern tried to only do things that felt good. Like hunting critters rather than settling down and getting smart with a vegetable garden and a cow like an asshole. Like giving squirrels or rabbits or minks cute names as soon as she spotted them in the brush so she could feel close and snuggly about them before gutting them herself and eating them raw in open-plan kitchens full of skeletons.

Fern couldn't really stand people most of the time. Not anymore. They weren't any kind of reliable. They all wanted to take something from you, but always pretended they didn't right up until the snatching and the struggling. To Fern's mind, that was pure raccoon behavior and she had no truck with raccoons. Sometimes she thought she'd never met a real actual person in her whole life excepting her own self, just a wide and diverse variety of raccoons.

She knew a pile of things she had no coherent reason to know, like what a Cape Cod house looked like, or what spaghetti sauce and high heels were, or what the word *coherent* meant. Not everything, but the pile was not small. It was just as much of a mystery to her as to anybody who didn't understand what she meant by *astronaut*. When Fern needed to know certain things, they just turned up in her head like second socks.

Fern couldn't remember even once feeling full or satisfied. She'd been hungry her whole life. Even that one day a couple years back in Somewhere, Michigan, when the unpicked apple trees bent down breaking under the weight and the salmon were running up the river so fast and happy every white splash sounded like *home home home*.

Fern'd stuck her hands in the water like a big joyful bear, over and over, giggling, pulling fillets out of the water as easy as a grocery store freezer. She ate so many apples and fish her belly looked six months along. She'd sat out under the stars licking gobs of soft, shiny orange salmon eggs off her fingers and even *then* Fern was plain starving. There was a hole in her nothing filled up. Nothing really even interested it. Except those little cairns of pages she hunted through houses and garages and sheds and office building lobbies. The people who couldn't run away from her. The dead pleading for her attention from a grave full of ink.

But the worst wrong thing was the dreams. Fern's dreams could get bad. *Real* bad. Wake-up-screaming-biting-on-your-own-tongue bad. These days a bed looked no different than a knife to that girl. Either one meant to get inside her and start twisting.

Always the same. The same places, one or the other. A fresh clean whitewash and scrubbed-pine schoolroom. Tall cross-sashed windows ran down the walls. Five rows of tidy little desks waited empty, the kind with chairs bolted on so you couldn't ever really get comfortable. The tardy sunshine let itself in politely through the window glass, the hills outside slept gently through their lessons, and the bright brass school bell hung down from a spiderless hollow belfry. Bigger than any bell had a right to be, bigger than any schoolhouse could hope to contain, bigger than a dead star hanging in space, casting no shadow on the slick wood floor.

Or a treeless plain where the earth glowered black and red. Where great stones lanced the boil of the land and nothing grew, nothing ever even *wanted* to grow. A place where the nicotine-colored sky felt all the time like it was just about ready to pull back its rictus lips and she'd see the teeth behind the whole world.

Trouble was, no matter which nightmare jumped her in the night, the dreaming felt so bright and true and clear and correct that everything un-dreaming seemed fake, and thin, and small. Like an old sign with a photorealistic picture of a girl's life on it, but take one big step around the back and it's two inches thick, held up by nothing but a beam of plywood crawling with black bugs who meant to chew it clear through.

Some nights Fern dreamed a teacher for the schoolroom. But that didn't make it better. The miss stood with her back to Fern, staring at a spotless green chalkboard in a long pale nightgown and no shoes on her muddy cold feet. No matter how many times Fern tried to talk to her, her voice wouldn't come out. And no matter how many times Fern walked all the way around the miss to find a friendly face, she only saw long white hair falling flat and heavy to her waist, flat and heavy to her belly, flat and heavy over each shoulder to each hip.

But in the other place, she was never alone. Across that black-red scalded desert, a man came walking. The same every time. That one who downright *loved* to show his face. Shaggy hair all round his skull like a yellow flame using up a match head. Eyes that dug into Fern's face like fingernails. Denim jacket. Denim jeans. A handsome man, but the handsome *writhed* sometimes. It tried to *crawl* off him, but it couldn't get away.

"Who *are* you?!" he roared at her. Or crooned. Or sang. Or whispered against her neck like he had the right. So many times. So many ways. Like he enjoyed saying it. Sucking the juice off every syllable. He liked snagging her chin in his big calloused hand while he kept on listening to himself talk, a handful of phrases over and over like a hymn.

Who sent you, wonderful girl?

No solicitors, baby doll. Not a ONE. We're remodeling, see? Closed for business until the season starts.

You're not her. It's too early for that. They're not ready.

This little habit of not falling to your knees is really starting to bore me.

You're all wrong. You know you're all wrong, don't you?

Run along, little girl, you'll never make it to grandmother's house before dark.

You're not supposed to be here. You're new.

Fern tried to tell him her name. The way she tried to tell bad raccoons her name sometimes so they'd remember they were human, even though it only ever seemed to make them squeeze her harder. But he kept up asking who she was. Every time. Every night.

"Oh, Fern, Fern," the handsome man hissed under the toothy sky, "I'm gonna make you BURN."

But Fern's voice worked just fine in *his* place. She'd back-talked her share and then some to that tall glass of acid-washed stepdad swagger. Sometimes Fern got her ruff up and yelled, too. *Well, fuck you, too, Mr. Rhyme Time! Are you stupid? What's your fuckin' name? I told you mine like a thousand times.* Sometimes she tried to bargain, stuck out one hip a little and dropped the other. *Listen, big fella, you don't gotta holler like that, I'm right here.* Sometimes she cowered and begged him to protect her. *I'm sorry, okay? Yes, sir, right-o, I'm bad. I've done bad stuff for sure, so whichever one made you mad at me, I'm so, so sorry and I'll never the fuck do it again. Pinky-promise, okay?* The handsome man seemed to like that one *real* good.

The night before she found a wet cardboard box in the McKivers' garage, Fern Ramsey just didn't have much of anything left in her when that denim dude started up his singsong rhymey-ass bullshit again. She didn't even know you *could* be tired in a dream.

"Jesus nun-fisting Christ, *why*? I didn't do shit to you! God*damn*, man, I'm just a kid. Switch to decaf, Gramps."

The dream that had played on repeat in her head for more than a year jumped a track. The handsome man didn't throw back any of his previous hit catchphrases. His face did all the things a face could do at once. For a second, Fern thought he might laugh, then she thought he might kiss her, then she thought he might snap her neck and eat her face. Finally, she began to contemplate the possibility that this right here was a very *all of the above* kind of guy.

The dream man bent over and got his business right up into hers. She'd never smelled him before, but she sure as shit could now. And Fern hated it. She hated it *so much*.

That fucker smelled *wonderful*. Every cell in her just wanted to huff the tobacco-burnt-brick-laundry-on-the-sunshine-line-applejack collar of that stupid jean jacket for the rest of eternity. He smelled like home.

The handsome man's voice came clipped and sharp and bare. No more wheedling, no more teasing, no more good-time guy.

"Get the FUCK off my wheel, you miserable little *cunt*."

CAME THE LAST NIGHT OF SADNESS

Summer, 2002

An elephant lumbers unsteadily down the carpool lane, westbound I-80 across the grand wasteland between Terre Haute and St. Louis. Her calf burbles plaintively and jogs to catch up, wiggling his trunk around like a fresh noodle. They stopped a while to drink from the rain puddles ellipsing down median berm and nosh themselves silly on the wild corn and wheat rotting unharvested all around them. But now Mama wants to move. She feels like they need *to move.*

The elephant understands a lot more than anyone in the Otherwhile could imagine. She knows her small name was Layla. The small ones gave it to her. She knows existence comes in seasons, and no two seasons can know each other's gait. Layla's first season was somewhere hot and loud and short and greener than love. Her second season was in a place that looked like home, but was only pretending. The sign over her second season had so many pretty shapes on it. Even though Layla never knew what all that meant, she remembers how they stood and how they stood looked like this:

ELEPHANTENCLOSURE

Layla's third season is all around her, the biggest one she's ever had. The third season stretches so far behind her. So far ahead. So far side to side. It is full of rotten corn that makes her feel good. It is full of openness and forgot how to stay closed.

Layla knows the small ones are not migrating or gathering somewhere good and warm to mate in sight of water. They are gone. Mostly. The ones that matter are all gone. Because only two ever mattered. The rest were nothing. Gazelles. Silly, fast, plentiful, quick to vanish. She misses the sounds their tininess made when they said, Layla.

The ones that mattered were called Amir and Zara. They liked so much to feed and pat her in the Otherwhile. When she sprayed water toward them, they made sounds with their soft faces. Sounds like that meant a small one was unhungry and uncold and unlost, so Layla tried to make them do it all the time, because those were good things to be. Amir and Zara always smelled like an oasis. Like a thousand animals feasting on their foods and waters, and that was also good. Sometimes Amir brought other elephants to meet her, but Layla bit them until they went away. Zara taught her to make a yellow flower with a stick and colormud, which was the most fun Layla ever had. She could only ever make the flower the way Zara liked to, not her own way, but the littleness that was Zara clapped and jumped and made big squeaks every time all the same.

Amir and Zara together smelled like rain, which was the smell of how they loved each other. For an elephant, rain on the way means babies want to be made. It means the time has come to get much, much bigger than you were before. Layla used to watch Amir and Zara in the zebraworld across the longpath from her. Their trunks were always twined together, even though they didn't have any.

They trumpeted a sound at each other very often. Not a name, but something Layla came to understand meant the tusking and ramming were all done and they had chosen each other. Sayang. She gave her calf the smallname of Sayang, even though smallnames were buried in the Otherwhile under leaves and grass forever.

Amir and Zara smelled like rain when they died, too. When they went world to world to world down the longpaths and opened them up so everyone could run from the hunter that made their insides leak out of their faces. When they put boards over the ringwater around Layla's pen, even though she knew she wasn't allowed to cross the water. They smelled like rain when they held on to each other and turned wet and red, and they still did when Layla rammed all the young trees she could find and laid their branches across the tininess of Amir and Zara so they could migrate with their trunks braided together forever.

Fern hadn't always hoofed it alone. She knew where to get company if she wanted company. Everyone did. A few dozen settlements scattered around, a dozen towns, maybe three cities, if you were feeling generous about the definition of *city*.

It just wasn't worth it, to her mind. You had to pull up short and get real careful once words like *town* started flying around. Towns never lasted. One, or a handful of stragglers alone, sure. Cities, maybe, if they managed to lottery up just *exactly* the right spread of brains and brawn at the starting gun.

But towns were just so *friable*. They always tore themselves to shit, or threw themselves against another town until both shredded into confetti. That was most of what happened to every patch of dirt that aimed to boot up being unwild again after the big crash.

Or maybe just the ones Fern strolled through.

Sometimes folks didn't actually do a whole lot wrong. Nobody stole or hoarded or feuded or made the powerfully bold choice to fuck somebody else's man when there wasn't really any compelling reason not to pick up a gun about that anymore. But the town burst like a rotten grapefruit all the same.

When Fern went down to Maybe, Vermont, last summer, she was perfectly fucking polite to the guy minding the potatoes he planted in the town square's flower beds and dried-up fountain bowl. *Hey, mister, Dr. Martinez at the sick tent said you had more of those Yukons than you need, wanna trade? I got a jar of buttons and half a pound of skunk jerky.* The potato man narrowed his eyes and turned his back like she'd pissed in his dirt fountain. Like she wasn't even *there*. Pretended like he was actually doing something with that stupid trowel of his. A few days later, the potato man climbed up to the water tower his own grandfather had worked so hard to reconnect to the municipal system and drowned his idiot raccoon self in there. His rot came out in sinks and bathtubs and gurgling up drains and after all those years keeping their backs against the wheel, the last to leave painted a big *X* over the blue smiley face on the big boulder outside town that once announced the water was safe, and that was just about it for Maybe, Vermont.

By the time the potatoes came in, the houses all stood empty, the sick tent collapsed, and Fern got her spuds for free.

Oh well.

———

Fern liked it pretty fine in Wherever, Pennsylvania, for a while. She wasn't *fantastic* at people, but she was little and alone and that rarely added up to a consistently good time. You had to try. She even met a boy there her own age who called himself Big Barry Bullfrog. People called themselves any old thing nowadays. But Barry was nice enough. He knew how to sew (sutures included) *and* raise Helsinki on an eldritch hand-crank CB radio he strapped into an ugly orange vinyl trailer and hauled up hills behind his bike to get a good signal.

They lay out under the April stars. After Barry coaxed a charge through the hand-crank, Fern held somebody's hand for the first time. She didn't really like it. And it went on *forever*. Barry laced his fingers through hers and they felt like old hot dogs. The radio crackled through the channels.

"I don't think I believe you can really talk to somebody on the other side of the ocean with that thing." Fern sniffed.

"Sure you can. I talk to Petteri all the time. Well, when it works."

Fern could not imagine making this much effort just to talk to a person. Talking to people was enough effort all by itself. "What do you talk about?" she said in genuine bafflement.

"Nothing. I don't know. Comic books. He likes a bunch of French stuff from when he was a kid I never heard of. One time he read me a recipe for reindeer pizza. That was cool."

"That's it?"

Big Barry Bullfrog lowered his voice as if they weren't half a mile outside the settlement and anyone would care if they did hear. "Once

Petteri told me what happened to his grandfather in Rome," he said softly. "He doesn't like to talk about it. He says nobody does. Like Vegas over here. I asked Petteri how close his granddad was when it happened, but he just kept saying close enough. His pops lost all his hair even on his legs, and he told Petteri it looked like a swan's wing. A swan's wing made of fire, reaching across the river of Tuonela to sweep the world of the living into the land of the dead. He said that's out of the Kalevala. I think that's a book. Petteri's old. He's hard to follow sometimes."

"I don't like that story," Fern said to the stars. "It sounds made-up."

"It's not," the kid said flatly.

He took his hot dog hand back and Fern didn't care. The radio didn't give up the goods that night. Petteri and Helsinki slept in a sea of static.

The morning the first cherry blossoms opened, before anyone got up for chores, Big Barry Bullfrog marched through town with a full box of matches and set fire to the library. He stood there smiling and watching it burn with his hands stuck in his back pockets, and that crazy stupid raccoon didn't even move when the flames jumped the courtyard and took him, too.

But maybe Wherever, Pennsylvania, could've kept going without being able to learn how to build anything so easy ever again. Except, after the fire, half the town started coughing and wheezing and glaring furiously at the other half over their useless cupped hands. They hid in their houses and died anyway or lit out before they could find out if they got lucky twice. Paying the price of gathering two or more together. Human bodies still got the big sick from time to time, and they still died. Human bodies still got the big sick quite a damned bit, in point of fact, and they still died *all the fucking time*.

That happened a lot when Fern tried to join the civilized world. Or it had ripped through just before she got there. Or right after she left.

But the worst was Wisconsin. The farthest west Fern ever dared.

Probably, Wisconsin, a sweetheart of a hamlet ruled by a hard, smart, weather-beaten old warlord named King Sue. King Sue had two big industrial storage containers, spray-painted in black across the sides: one said *NEED*, one said *WANT*. You do right by the King, she'd bang the steel-curtain door with her fist and it'd roll up on heaven. One packed to the brim with Tampax for every flow, the other with case after case of name-brand cigarettes. Christ, they were just *so* beautiful. Fern almost wept the first time she stood in the presence of *NEED* and *WANT*.

That, plus lots and lots of milk bottles sloshing with corn alcohol she made herself in the engine block of a Buick carcass and a shit ton of guns, was how Sue got to be King of a couple of square miles of dirt and a legend everywhere else.

King Sue'd come from as far west as it was safe to come from, raiding every drugstore along the way to make her play. And when dribs and drabs of drifters and lonely hearts and grief puppets came a-wandering by, salivating for a taste of their *NEEDS* and their *WANTS*, Ol' King Sue said, *Sure, babies, I'll trade you for loyalty, no problem.*

King Sue proclaimed her decrees on a throne of tires wearing her beat-ass Cleveland Indians jersey like a cloak of ermine, all the Probably people at her feet like rose petals, and Fern flat-out *adored* her. This was someone strong enough to keep her safe. Maybe she could even keep the dreams away. And King Sue *liked* Fern. She didn't try to bother her or take anything off her or flinch if Fern stood too close. Maybe a King wouldn't ditch her. Maybe Fern finally had someone to teach her and hug her and set stuff on fire with her when she was sad.

The King took her down to the river to fish a week after she hit town. Fern talked like a little kid, a million different thoughts piled into each sentence. She told the King about Pennsylvania. She told her about the pages hidden in the houses. She told her about the schoolhouse dream . . . but not the other. It felt good and right and clean and lovely.

"Is that the junk in your bike trailer? Binders and notebooks and sacks of . . . loose reams, I guess?"

"Yeah," Fern answered. Her shoulders tensed up, waiting to be told how stupid it was to lug that thing from Nowhere to Somewhere and back. But it didn't come.

"I dunno . . . sometimes, you know . . . some people . . . some kinds of people . . . don't want to die without saying some things. And I think they should get to. Because everyone should get to say what they meant by living before they stop doing it. So they write down whatever happened to them, whatever was important, whatever they thought they knew. And they leave it somewhere it won't get wrecked, but not so hidden a person couldn't find it someday. Me. Where I could find it. I . . . like them. I collect them. I learn from them. About what being alive used to be. About what I gotta do to pull it off now. I look for them and I take them with me."

"Baby love, why? That's weird. What does it matter what some housewife said about the end of the world? They all died. The end."

Fern blushed. She didn't even know she could blush before right then. "I dunno," she mumbled. "I guess . . . they make me feel needed. They're my . . . they're my friends."

Her Majesty shrugged and cast a line. "Hey, far be it from me to judge. I spent three years collecting tampons. Gotta make your own fun."

King Sue's angle on the Pennsylvania situation was that the world wasn't ever going to come right again, no matter how long it rested up. Too bad for the world, so sad, but science is a bitch and three-quarters and she don't care how nice you'd find it to push a button and make ice again. Everything expires. Everything evolves. Even Captain Trips. What made people sick now wasn't exactly the same as what made them sick then. The plague is just like us, King Sue pontificated. The original's long gone. But its babies are hard at work building new shit.

Mutations. Variants. Species-jumpers. A whole lot of people who were immune, or whose parents and grandparents were immune to the Captain, are fresh meat to Major Trips or General Trips or whatever you want to call the new strains.

"Colorado did okay," ventured Fern. "I heard. Maybe."

King Sue sucked half a precious cig down in one angry breath and flicked the rest off the side of the storage container. Just because she could. Just to *show* she could. *True royalty*, Fern thought with admiration. Sue blew smoke out through her nose and snarled, "Then get your flat ass to Colorado, Fern. I'm not stopping you."

Fern thought about all those locked doors in Wherever and the black water in Maybe and all those books burning to nothing. She whispered, "I think maybe I shouldn't."

"Hey, it's not your fault. Maybe I'm wrong. Any of us could wander around our whole lives before finding a viral reservoir still in it to win it. Trouble is, the more people wanna sing campfire songs and play student council, the more likely that pernicious damned problem spelled M-U-T-A-T-I-O-N gets. Most days, I feel like all I'm doing is waiting for the other shoe to drop. For some unfortunate fucking pre-corpse's system to tweak big sick enough to finish the job." King Sue laughed and swigged from her milk bottle. "And after all that, you know, not *one* of my subjects bothers to cover they fucking filthholes when they sneeze."

"I don't know if that's funny."

"It's funny as *shit*, what are you talking about? People are people, and people don't want to live carefully. Whatcha gonna do? Meanwhile, *my* meemaw was a goddamned *medical malpractice attorney* before civilization hit itself in the face with a brick wall, so my personal filthhole was, and is, immaculate at all times."

Sue frowned and sucked on her cigarette like a milkshake straw. "Meemaw died in Vegas, you know. Poof! The poof to end all poofs. You know about that, right? You know you never go there. *Never* there."

CAME THE LAST NIGHT OF SADNESS

Fern rolled her eyes. *Yeah, yeah. Tell me something I wasn't born knowing.*

"Well," yawned King Sue, "I better get going."

Fern Ramsey looked lovingly up at her, waist-deep in cold water and stubborn fish. "Don't go."

"Aw, you're a cute one. But I gotta dig up a typewriter now, don't I? If I wanna be your friend."

⁓

But King Sue never did find one.

When fall started crisping up the trees, Fern came back from hunting and found Sue choked blue on the stiff morning ground between *NEED* and *WANT*. Phlegm splattered like hot black butter all over her baseball jersey, stiff hands curled into claws dug into her own swollen throat.

That was the last time Fern Ramsey remembered crying. More than crying. She lay her head on Sue's big drum of a chest and sobbed.

"But I loved you," she whispered. "I was gonna stay." Her little chest burned with the injustice of it. Fern Ramsey loved somebody. That should mean something. Why didn't that mean anything? Why couldn't she *make* it mean something?

Something inside Fern broke open and started clawing at her ribs to get out. She couldn't see or think. She got up and kicked King Sue's corpse in the ribs. "You useless *asshole*!" she screeched, elbowing her tears and snot away. "You let *this* dusty shit take you out?! Who does that?! Not a King, that's who! A raccoon! You fucking *tricked* me! I was gonna stay! I was gonna stay for always!"

⁓

That night Fern dreamed about the schoolhouse again, and the bell bonged and swung above her so awful and loud that she woke herself up bellowing to be heard over the din and all she wanted to do was rip something hollow so she didn't have to hurt alone.

She could think sharp and drag a deer to her. But that didn't feel like enough. Most of what was sweet in Fern had gotten too slippery to hold on to.

Fern sharpened her thoughts. She could sense a girl ten or twenty miles away. Older than her. But shorter. Smaller. A stranger. Red hair in a ponytail. Green army backpack. Woolly yellow socks. It wouldn't take very long. She could almost taste how much better she'd feel. How easy it would be.

How right it would feel.

Winter, 2013

Deep in the colds of the North Atlantic, a bull blue whale born before the Titanic *sailed breaches the surface one last time. He sings a long, quiet tune to the seagulls, exhales a long, wet sigh, and dies.*

But not of the plague.

In fact, old Grandfather Whale never guessed anything up there changed at all, except a lot more young underfin than he could ever remember, which annoyed him more than anything. They gulped up all the good krill. His eyes roll back in his great, barnacled, harpoon-crosshatched head. The almost otherworldly bulk of him begins to sink down, through the turquoise, into the cobalt, and on down into the big black.

Grandfather Whale's body will not find its rest for more than a thousand meters. His vastness lands with a muted velvet boom on a broad sandy plain where no rumor of sunlight could ever find purchase. The fall takes longer than what follows: the birth of a new world.

Octopi and lobsters creep in to feast. Shrimp, giant prawns, long-limbed crabs, thin, cruel-eyed sharks picking and biting at a paradise of soft, nutritious flesh that seems like it could never run out. Eyeless, jawless eels nuzzle ecstatically at Grandfather's eyeball and suckle its plenty with relish. Soon mussels will replace the blubber layer. Soon bristle worms and basket stars with bodies like biblical angels in miniature will wriggle down through Grandfather's blowhole to sate themselves in his brain cavity.

Giant isopods crawl in more slowly; less animals than artifacts of the deep past, monstrously unchanged and unchanging, as utterly indifferent to humanity as they were to the dinosaurs. The isopods might have a polite nibble at the great table, but they prefer the gorged sea cucumbers and bone-eater worms who knew a good thing when they devoured it. The ones who stayed on the whalefall until they died of deliciousness.

The isopods are not alone. Those who feast on the feasting arrive for their turn. Squid, anglerfish, scarlet crown jellies, Siphonophores.

Grandfather Whale feeds them all. Houses them all. Provides, as grandfathers will. Thousands of generations of species lay their eggs in his organs and his meat. His corpse has so much to offer. It becomes a self-contained, fast-mutating, crowded ecosystem, and as long as the whalefall provides resources without end, no creature has reason to leave. Or to strive. Or to rise.

No creature living there ever guesses the whale is not the world.

No creature living in a cornucopia is capable of imagining the horn might one day lie empty.

The cold-jellied sea keeps Grandfather fresh for a long time. For two hundred years, the whalefall will be enough to sustain this little civilization. But nothing stays easy forever.

Everything expires.

Food isn't a problem until it's the only problem. The decadent bloat of modernity's corpse had enough Twinkies, beef jerky, and canned soup for all.

Until it didn't.

In the beginning, in the Age of Miracles, just the right people seemed to find their way to just the right places at just the right time, and, well, a fair whack of farmers was never much for social interaction before, either. They took longer to get infected, longer to die. Some fields got planted right quick, but most people were happy as horses to drink deep of the corpses of big-box grocery and department stores, gas station snack racks, bodegas and baked bean cannery floors, suburban developments with deep pantries.

But time ate there, too.

After a decade, the pickings are both slim and risky. Salmonella, listeria, trichinosis, the boys are all in town. This new wave of death stings deep. They were supposed to have made it. They were supposed to be home free.

It's a bad winter. They're all bad winters for a while. The whale is gone.

But the sea remains.

They learn again, but slowly. No one knows everything, but everyone knows something. And they learn first how much sheer time it took to stay alive before the beneficence of Our Lady of Slim Jims. The cruel equation of how many calories it costs to acquire calories. Seeding, planting, growing, harvesting, canning, drying, preserving. Catching wild chickens for eggs. Figuring out where the mackerel gather and when it's safe to dig for clams. Convincing a cow that this time you're only going to steal milk from her baby, not steal from her baby and shoot her in the head with a bolt gun. It all takes time. And calories no one has to spare.

Everything expires. Even the Age of Miracles. Any given clutch of folk no longer invariably has a lucky skill-spread. Tornadoes and hurricanes spin up again. Droughts, floods, dead topsoil. And so many people try to make a go of it in places they'd always loved, chosen for sentiment, not for the longest growing seasons or the most fertile soil.

If a hand had briefly reached out to put things where they belonged, it had clearly pulled back again, as it always had, after a great flood or a great fire from heaven.

Grandfather Whale gave himself to sustain the deep. But the whale could not stay forever.

Fern Ramsey saw to her King before herself. She buried Sue on a rise overlooking the river where they fished and talked about mutation. It was all she could think of. They hadn't had long enough to make many memories, and the others were already starting to tremble and squabble and disperse.

The hunt would come. The sharing of her pain with that girl in the woolly yellow socks. There was so much time. She was getting stronger, she could feel it. She could think sharp enough to pull anything she wanted to her.

But her arms and shoulders burned so bad when it was done Fern just sat down on the river moss and cried. She couldn't even feel that red-ponytail girl anymore, and the cold thing in her that wanted to make that girl scream loud enough to drown out her own hollering didn't seem to care for manual labor. It was quiet, for now.

So quiet that the warm red sun and the finches in the trees and the soft meadow green under her cheek made her forget to run from sleep.

Fern doesn't dream of the schoolhouse this time. She doesn't dream of the empty black and red plain under the yellow sky.

Fern dreams of falling. Falling from such a great height. Falling forever through night and glass and gravity. She twists around in midair and sees another woman falling beneath her, before her, white fabric billowing around her great belly, long white hair billowing around her face. The woman is so beautiful. So beautiful and so sad. It stops Fern's heart how beautiful the woman really is.

A misshapen hand presses nauseatingly up out of the woman's swollen pregnant belly. She's so far along. Ready to pop. The shape of the hand stretching her skin seems to reach for Fern. For someone. For life.

Then they all obliterate into the ground and Fern stands alone in an endless boiling land with only great black round stones to keep her company.

The handsome man isn't there. The handsome man isn't there and those aren't stones. Fern runs her hand along one. She never thought to look at them before. Preoccupied, she supposed.

They're haystacks. Black, gargantuan, harvested, rolled and bound. A crow pecks the germ from the stalk. A crow out of nowhere.

"You've been busy," it caws.

"Are you him?" Fern asks, trembling.

The bird chortles to itself. "Fuck, no. He's occupado. He's got a lot of work to do and you're not helping with your little stunts. Maybe you shouldn't play with the other children, Ferny. They seem to get upset."

"Do you . . . work for him?"

The crow ruffled his feathers. "You can't think of it like that. I just am. I live. I notice. I remember. The rules are lax right now. He's still half-asleep. My brothers and sisters and I roam. That's why he can't quite see you. When he wakes fully, I won't be able to help. Sorry. I am what I am. Just like you."

Fern moved her hands into the deep, thick wheat. "Which is what?"

"An eye. A witness. A thought. A memory. And you are . . . a mutation."

Fern recoiled from King Sue's word.

"Because he's right, you know." The crow prodded his cast-iron beak up toward the sickly sky. "You're all wrong. You're not supposed to be here. You're new."

Fern laughed, and nothing had ever felt stranger to her than laughing in this place. "Well, yeah. I'm a kid."

The crow gave a short, sharp screech of irritation. "Not *that*. You're *completely* new. The wheel turns, but it turns slowly. And its spokes are many—but not infinite. There is a number, and the number has changed. This has happened many times. He rises, he falls. He rises. Like the sun and tides. Everything comes around again. And everyone. The saints and the devils, all the hands that turn the wheel. They change faces, names, places. They remember, but slowly. They do their part. They die in their turn. And when he rises again, so do they to balance it.

CAME THE LAST NIGHT OF SADNESS

"So it goes and so it has gone for time beyond time. But the thing you call the handsome man was so close last time. I don't know. I'm only an eye. Perhaps the thing he truly is never came so close to victory before. He always takes a bride. He always gets a child upon her. But perhaps the thing his last bride truly was never came so near to actually giving birth. Her labor was almost upon her. Even as she fell. The prince was almost here."

The cancerous sky ripped and snarled above them. The crow's eyes glittered. "You were almost here."

Fern's hand froze on the bale of black wheat. "*Me?* I don't understand. Princes are *boys*."

The crow's ruff bristled. "Shhhhh. Don't be stupid. I hear his footsteps grinding the sea. There is not much time. I *told* you. The wheel turns and faces change. Faces, names, places . . . even bodies. What is a girl or a boy? Only the difference between one thrust and the next. The flip of a coin. He won't like it one bit, I can tell you that much. But it will *interest* him, and that's worse. Poor monster. You were never on the wheel before. You never came so close to the world that the wheel could catch you. And now you're stuck with us. With no other lives to help you remember. With no ancient role waiting for you. You are *new*. And you're broken. You are incomplete. You *weren't* born. You *aren't* right. You were never meant for the wheel. You are a mutation, a variant strain. You could be harmless. Or you could be the last sickness of this world. A Valkyrie in his army. His left-hand girl. The final momentum that shatters the wheel into darkness. Either way, you *are* his. But also your mother's. Bad luck on both counts, really."

Fern thought of the falling woman. Of the schoolteacher. Their white hair like blank pages. Of the raccoon people scurrying and hissing and stealing and hiding from something none of them could name. Of the great bonging bell in the white belfry, calling the children in. Of the handsome man, how he smelled like home.

"I don't know what any of that means," she whimpered.

"Neither do I. But when he rouses fully, he will see right through you. You only got to sass-mouth the darkness that lies beneath all things because he is still gathering his strength. His flock. His wonderful, irresistible machines and all they can do. It will all happen again. Because you cannot have that clever, shiny complicated human world without him. Take one, the other rises. He is not yet awake, but when he is, you won't fool anyone. And it is too early for his opposite number to protect you. He will claim you. The seed of him in you will yearn to do terrible things, if it does not already. And if I know my man, he'll turn you loose on this world like a pet wolf. And you'll like it."

Fern knew the black bird was right. She remembered the towns dying around her. She remembered the cold inside her mind scraping the hills for someone weak. She remembered what the cold wanted. How good it felt.

"At least I won't be alone," Fern said hopefully.

The crow cawed horribly, like a dry laugh. "Yeah. Good luck with that." His violet-black throat glistened. "There's a story, you know. Long ago. Far away. Before America knew its own name. In the age of kings and vassals, the Devil set upon a noblewoman and got upon her his great and ravenous son come to end the world, who was called Robert. And this son was a good boy to both his parents. He loved his mother purely. And he caused death and mayhem wherever he went, as his father taught him. He delighted in blood and entrails and the burning of grapevines. In the prime of his strength, Robert, the son of the Devil, went on a crusade with a song in his heart and became the scourge of the East. His father was proud. But Robert was still a man, if only just, and he missed his mother. He journeyed home to her, taking his pleasure in the screams of the reddening countryside as he traveled. But when he came to his mother's castle and she looked on him, he saw himself reflected in her eyes. Black with blood and pain and cruelty, a beast with no mind. She threw herself from a high tower and smashed her brains out on the stones below. And from that day, Robert turned away from his father.

He took a vow of silence and of peace. The son of the Devil closed himself in a monastery and would not answer his father's voice. His virtue grew so great it became as armor, and the Devil could not touch him. Robert died a-bed many years later, a good and honest man, though every minute of denying his true nature felt to him as a hundred thousand deaths, an agony beyond agonies."

Tears poured down Fern's strange little face. "What are you trying to tell me?"

"I don't know. You figure it out." The crow's black tongue flicked in and out. It hopped around nervously on the dark grain. "He's coming. He's almost here. *Wake up. Wake up, Fern.*"

Winter, 2024

They're building a church in the Adirondacks. They're building churches everywhere now. Preachers are as plentiful as viral vectors and twice as contagious. Rumors thread a sour needle from town to town. Of a man across the sea who still has all his toys. A man who promises he can fix it. Fix everything. Of the bad old days come to ride again. Of wheels and how they turn.

There are some things you can't ever get back. But war isn't one of them. War is always happy to host a revival. Not today, not next year. It needs time to get everything just right.

But a long time from now, the church will still be there. The statues. The stained glass windows lovingly made by a nice old man named Oliver Bailey, who still remembers when he dreamed of Nebraska in the night and wishes sometimes those dreams still stopped by.

The windows will go up after the snow melts. All the saints. The green mother. The man with the red dog. The singer of songs. The quiet father. The martyr who spoke with his hands. The man in the straw hat.

Even the schoolteacher has her place, just as she had her lesson to teach. Oliver grinds the edge down on the milky blue glass of her baby's swad-

dling as the schoolteacher holds her child in her arms, born, and whole, and innocent at last.

Mr. Bailey up there living cozy in someone else's house never knew any of them, and he doesn't remember names too well anymore. But that's not important. He was old already when all this began, and he's tired now. The last bad winter took his wife. This is his last good work. How he chose to spend the last of his soul.

Oliver looks down at his workbench, at his withered hands. At a thousand shards of color, half-assembled. Smashed lampshades and suncatchers and fancy dinner plates and any other glass they could scare up. Maybe he was too ambitious. Maybe the job was too big for the time he has left. Sometimes the parts are all there, but it still doesn't work. Too many. Too many shards. Too crowded. Too much. He just wants to do right by them. He just wants to make them shine like the twilit wheat of his dreams.

And he will. Oliver Bailey won't see the big ships start sailing the seas again, or the wars when they come fast as crows—or when they pass, just as swift. He won't hear anybody say what pretty windows those are, and that's okay by him. They're pretty whether anyone says so or not.

I know because I spent last Christmas in that brand-new church, and you'd never believe how fine those windows turned the light. Oliver Bailey chose a quiet, pretty thing and cleaved to it. Everybody gets a choice, and the ones you make at the end pay for all. But he will do right by the color and the shards. He will do right by the light.

And you will, too, honey. I just know it, whoever you are. You'll do right by us all.

Fern Ramsey quietly slid Kimberley Lynn McKiver's pages back into their Ziploc bag, then unzipped the Bullfrog's orange vinyl bike trailer and lay it gently on top of the stack. Fern liked Mrs. McKiver. She liked the way she talked about things. About Lake Keowee and the whale and the elephant and the glassmaker. She liked how she could tell that lady was someone's mother, with every word.

CAME THE LAST NIGHT OF SADNESS

As Fern packed everything back where she found it (God knew why she bothered, but she always did), a sharp, shivery shock forked through her belly. There was more, down there under the manuscript. At the bottom of the swampy box. Something just for her.

Kimberley Lynn McKiver had left one last freezer bag, full to straining. A first-aid kit, blister packs full of *-dones* and *-cillins*, antiseptic wipes, water-purification tablets, a bottle of multivitamins, a crisp, folded map, and absurdly, endearingly, a couple of packets of gummy fruit snacks from some long-vanished lunch box.

Fern had snagged a fair number of these boxes, but none like this. The other boxes all said, *Remember me.* None said, *I remembered you.* None ever had a care for her, for whoever might come, whenever they might, what they might need to keep going.

Fern thought about that for a long time. About the McKivers' peaceful bones in the upstairs bedroom dreaming the centuries down. About poor Barry burning wisdom. About Petteri's father and his wing of flame. About the potato man treating his Yukons so tenderly. About King Sue on her throne and Tommy Fortunado's last stand. About an old man trying so hard to change the color and the angle of light he'd never see. Of Grandfather Whale in his private hidden universe.

About *NEED* and *WANT.*

Everyone gets a choice.

Out on the driveway, under the gold-blue virgin light of dawn, a crow lay crumpled and dead like a shadow.

Fern stood over it for a long time, with no expression on her face.

This Autumn

Two elephants named Layla and Sayang sway woozily in the soft, beanpod-crisp autumn light. The old corn they gorge on makes them very unserious. They come up slowly over a rise in the long gray road and look out over the wild wrinkled plain of Missouri. Layla is so old now. Her knees hurt. And she is one of a long line of Laylas now; her son part of a chain of Sayangs.

She nudges her grown calf's gaze. Look at the giraffes down there drinking from the thick river. Look at the caracals playing. Look at the lions snoozing under the silver arch. Hippo heads humping up out of the Mississippi.

So many. So many from so many corners and so many mating seasons since the small ones left us to roam back and forth across the cracks and stones of this continent. So many because others instinctively performed the same behaviors as Amir and Zara. The small ones were a kind of animal that did that, the way Layla trumpeted. Not all of them, oh no, certainly not. But a hefty chunk of the herd.

Some creatures got free in lucky places. Some got trapped in places that boiled under the sizzling silvery Great Elephant Bullfather's foot that years ago came trampling down from the sky to trample the desert, to smash everything it did not burn.

Layla shuddered. Layla tries to forget the stories that have been passed down.

Layla can't.

Layla tails the memory away like a blackfly. She bonks her head against her boy's flank. Look long, my son. My Sayang. Breathe deep. You can still smell the horses and the dogs and hogs and mules that are long gone from this place. Their manure and their bones. The cows that got to be so many they ruined all the earth they devoured and stomped flat and then they were few enough again. You can still smell the long black broken tusks the small ones used on each other when they could not find food. You can still find them lying scattered across the new veldt like the skinny dark lines that once made the shape E N C L O S U R E.

But see rhinoceroses chomping sneezeweed in the valley. Hear the zebras thundering down there, galloping through peach orchards and soybean fields in their vast herds. The monkeys have gone, too, and more besides.

CAME THE LAST NIGHT OF SADNESS

But so many have taken their places. Beware the tigers in the foothills, uncowarded by our size.

Existence is a season, and soon enough done.

Layla stretches her hind legs, one, then the other. She nudges her baby, now larger than herself, toward a sturdy stick half-sunk in dark mud. Sayang curls his soft trunk around it, hesitantly, wanting with all his being to do everything right for Mama. She shows him how. She shows him the shape of the Otherwhile.

In the high-occupancy lane of Interstate 70 where Illinois becomes Missouri and winds on farther still, an elephant slowly paints a black flower exactly the way a dead woman in Cincinnati once did.

By the time Sayang finishes, there's a small one standing next to them on the road. Wearing a shirt with shapes that say THE BOSS and pulling a big orange something behind her.

A few inches off the road, which isn't how small ones are supposed to work. Layla doesn't know what to make of her smell. Halfway between wild stink and tame.

With a very great effort, Fern Ramsey brings herself back down to earth. She stands with two feet on the ground. It hurts like a hundred thousand deaths. It hurts every single second. It will hurt every single second of her life.

But she stands.

Fern only dreams of the schoolhouse now. She strokes the schoolteacher's white hair, and it seems to make the woman relax. The bell recedes. She thinks only dully. The pain of every millisecond's conscious choosing hides her from the other place, from her father.

And when this long road through the plains reaches Colorado, Fern Ramsey will stay on the outskirts of the town. Just to be safe. Just to be sure. She will build a cabin with her hands. She will eat fish and apples. And she will stand a watch. She will look on them, smiling. She will watch them stumble, and struggle, and then she will watch them do okay. So *gorgeously* okay.

Fern Ramsey will slip away in her sleep, safe and invisible, long before the wheel reaches its next zenith. No one special. No one worth noticing. Not even Fern. Maybe Fiona. Or Flora. Or Frances.

But today she is still Fern. She puts her hand, as light as forgetting, on a baby elephant's back.

And nothing bad happens. The three of them walk on together. For a little while.

In a thousand years, the innumerable sons and daughters of Sayang that come to occupy the hottest swath of the Great Plains will still paint precisely the same flowers, precisely the same way, whenever they smell the rains coming. Zara's black sunflowers, blooming all over the breast of the divide.

Everything expires. But that doesn't always mean it goes bad.

THE DEVIL'S CHILDREN
Sarah Langan

Maple's been missing north of a month. I want to pretend she's okay. I want to pretend she ran away and that one day, I'll join her. But the feeling inside me is queasy.

She's not the only member of my kind to go missing. They leave the mountains to check on the water supply or to deliver an altar offering, and we never hear from them again. It's possible they got Captain Trips and stayed away rather than infecting the rest of us. Possible, too, that the infection hit them so hard and fast they didn't have the time to radio news. There are also mountain lions to consider. These are heartless creatures; happy to chew even bones.

It's autumn in California and the setting sun smears red rays across the San Gabriel Mountains. My tribe has occupied this place since our treaty with the Chosen, who've proven capricious overlords. On whims, they shrink our borders. They encroach, bringing sickness. We're too vulnerable and spread out to fight them. They get away with it.

Without Maple, I've been foraging alone. The others have said nothing, knowing I'm not ready to replace my friend. But tonight, the thing I've been dreading happens. Ferris Landing approaches my camp. He's a tall, slender man and he looks behind me instead of *at* me. "I'll gather with you tonight," he whispers. Everyone in my tribe whispers.

Ferris isn't suited for my work. He's been known to pick poison oak instead of fennel, to scare small game with gangly feet. In truth, he's unsuited to any work. But it's not the way of my tribe to tell people what to do. He's offered help. It's my job to accept that help with grace and let him figure out whether he belongs.

"As soon as it's dark," I say.

Night comes hard and fast, that last of dusk burning into black. Ferris meets me at the path that was once Mulholland Drive. It's beautifully eerie, a wild and ripe territory.

We're not long before Ferris stops and calls, "Here?" to me in a whisper that's louder than most. Everything about him is louder than it should be. But to my surprise, he's found lamb's quarters. They're full of iron. More than deer meat, they thicken the blood.

"Yeah," I say. "You got it."

We gather those, then the beets and potatoes I planted with Maple on the wide flat overlooking dilapidated, ivy-riddled houses down in the valley that was once Studio City. He's helpful, carrying everything, acting as a second, trying hard to intuit my next moves.

We finish sooner than expected and have time before we need to head back. Ferris sits on a rock. He makes room for me, but I ignore this. It's impolite to stand close, to sit nearby. Even family members avoid direct touch. He lights something whose tip smolders red. It's been two generations since Captain Trips, but the old-world graffiti is still carved into the granite. *Laura loves John. Hollywood 4-Neva.*

Ferris exhales a stinking cloud. He's a misfit, which, in our group of ragtag survivors, is saying something. He always laughs too late. Always watches, but rarely speaks. Behind his back, we call him the Preacher.

THE DEVIL'S CHILDREN

"You're kidding," I say. "That's a cigarette?"

He shrugs, sheepish, and I get the disturbing feeling that he's planned this. Left our territory and braved the open to loot it from an overgrown and ivy covered 7-Eleven, been carrying the pack around since, waiting to show someone he's a secret rebel.

He holds the cigarette. His voice is jarringly loud. "Want a drag?"

Has he forgotten that my mother died from a lump in her lung? That we live only a few hundred miles from the rubble of an A-bomb? That I used to have a best friend named Maple, and he'll never take her place?

"You ass," I whisper.

I stomp ahead toward camp. Soon, he's trudging behind me, and I feel the thickness of his uncertainty as he mentally proposes and disposes of the words to mollify me. We walk in the quiet long enough that I realize I'm being hard on him. I miss Maple too much to want to have fun with anyone else.

Back at camp, we're the last shift to eat. It's our way to always do things in the smallest possible groups. Even confined to our limited territory, we keep apart.

There's news first—what we've heard and related over the radio on a closed channel. We learn that our tribe in Montana needs antibiotics, and our tribe in Texas has found uranium, which they hope to keep a secret from their local Chosen, who will surely want to loot that metal and resettle them, likely infecting them in the process.

We talk about those of our group who have gone missing. Aside from the practical possibilities, a few of my kind think it's magic—some kind of rapturing. I doubt this. But they seem excited about the possibility. The more likely cause for our missing is something I don't want to think about.

Before retiring for the dawn, we draw straws to decide who will deliver our seasonal GoodWill offerings to the Chosen. It's a part of our treaty, token gifts that serve to humanize us, make us seem like people and not animals.

No one likes to make this dangerous trek, though lately, I've been itching to get out—to find Maple, but also just to leave. To see something new. There's a sameness to our life that has been gnawing on my sleep. For how long are we expected to subsist on a dead and shrinking plot of land? What is there to hope for, when your future is a noose pulled tight?

I draw a long straw. I should be happy, but something inside me is disappointed.

Then Ferris draws his short straw. Because I'm now his partner, this is also my short straw. I expect him to convey some kind of apology. Shrugged shoulders or sheepishness or even a whispered, *Sorry!* My first day with him and I'm already screwed.

Instead, he looks at me, his brown eyes nearly as dark as his pupils, and smiles.

For as long as I can remember, there have always been two sides. There has always been us, and there has always been them, the Chosen, the future eaters, the generation swallowers, the monsters in plain sight.

I don't remember Captain Trips; I was told by my mother who'd been told by her mother. It came like thunder: a calamity, a terror. A human-made plague of biblical proportions. The only way to escape it was to escape humanity. So that's what my people did. They hid from the world, from the sickness, riding out that terror in solitude. We came unfixed from everything we'd once been, everyone we'd once known, every hope we'd once had. We gave these up and waited meekly, our sole intention to survive. To outlast the virus and all who carried it. Like birds after a storm, we would rise up in the quiet to inherit and remake the still-spinning earth.

But then, an unexpected thing. We were not alone. Climbing out from the dead echo of wet coughs and stink, arose the immune. People who carried the virus, who kept it alive inside them without ever getting sick. Like newborns scraped clean of offense and ten-

THE DEVIL'S CHILDREN

derly raw, they walked out of houses and tunnels and prisons. They wandered empty streets, calling names of fallen friends. They mowed lawns half-naked and weeping, they jogged empty streets, reciting the names of the dead, they painted nostalgic landscapes against easels. They drank, they told terrible stories and wept and laughed and healed even as our own blight was still happening. And finally, they gathered. In ways we could not possibly do, they gathered.

My peripatetic, wandering people watched them, eyes in tall grass and behind buildings; eyes looking down from rooves and peering up from cellars. The immune measured their survival in days, blessed their luck on stars like new gods even as they carried the sickness. It lived inside them, a time bomb, a nuke, a scrap of nucleic acid gone mutated and rogue.

They could kill us with a word. A plosive letter *P*, a whistle. A whisper.

Months. A year. The immune turned the lights back on. They danced to dead music. They joked about old movies and convenience stores. They cleaned all the mess, but made new, mushroom cloud messes.

We stayed wandering. In order to survive, we learned to sleep by day and live by night. To stay quiet. To whisper. To avoid touch. Over time, we began to think of ourselves as less than human. We watched the living, the immune, pull weeds and tinker and fix. They slept in beds. They wore cadaver bands of gold around their ring fingers. Captain Trips had stopped human progress. Slowly and with great pain, the Chosen started it up again.

They rebuilt. They powered tiny screens and big screens and medium screens and oh so many screens. They dammed the water. They bred the livestock. They opened the glutton restaurants and offices for angry, passionate men. They had children and more children and even more children. They made it their job to repopulate the earth. Some of those children were born without immunity, but most survived.

They had their suspicions; could feel our eyes on their backs. Accidentally, they were killing our kind. Leaving virus on supplies, tainting our water, our air. Out of self-preservation, we made ourselves known. They answered swiftly. As if we were the threat, they fenced us in. We agreed to live within these encampments. In return, they promised that if wild and lawless immune marauders broke into our assigned land, they'd send their army to defend us. More importantly (because so far, invaders had not come), they'd simply stay away.

We'd live. It would be in a cage, but we'd live.

In word, they keep this truce. In deed, they ignore it. Every few years, a well-meaning student of science or a self-made anthropologist infringes. One of our own gets sick and passes that sickness like a line of fallen dominoes. We're too tempting. Too great a fascination.

Their arrogance is our annihilation.

We hope for better times. For a day when the curse against us is lifted and we walk again by day.

Another dusk, but this one's cloudy and without color. I'm ready with my pack and the GoodWill offerings for the month. Ferris meets me at the top of Mulholland. We're not a ceremonial tribe; no one sees us off, though I do see a blue ribbon tied around a tree, its presence new. An anonymous *good journey*.

It'll take us two nights to reach the altar.

"You came," he says with surprise.

"You're my partner," I answer.

Ferris nods with uncertainty. He's not able to meet my eyes. How does a person so sensitive survive this world? He's a throwback from a different time. It occurs to me that it's not his incompetence that provokes the rest of us, but his tenderness. "I release you," he says.

"I know I don't have to come," I say, but this is a lie. It's not my nature to leave people, especially fragile people. Look what happened to Maple, and she wasn't even fragile. She was tough. She sneaked

THE DEVIL'S CHILDREN

out on a supply run without telling any of us. Just a note on her sleep sack. I have that note. I keep it in my sleep sack now.

As if reading my mind, Ferris says, "I'll be fine."

"Stop talking," I say.

I walk. He follows. There are no more words for at least two miles.

The Chosen can feed themselves better than we ever could. As a result, our offerings have changed over the years. We knit baskets from palm fronds. We make pottery. These are relatively light and easy to carry. We leave them on altars at the walls of their town in Malibu. Sometimes they leave notes for us or contact us over the radio. They ask for more color in their bowls, which sell for high prices in their towns. They offer the penicillin from their laboratory, but we can no longer accept their gifts. We can't trust them to be careful enough to wipe away the infection.

Two cars pass us on our first night. We hide both times. I realize the difference between us. My eyes have gotten keen at discerning movement in the dark; the distinctions between wind and a burrowing bird; a coyote and a deer. It's not just the sounds, but the absence of those sounds, the vibrations you anticipate, the different stillnesses that indicate prey or predator.

Ferris doesn't notice these things.

"You have bad eyes," I say. "That's why you trip. That's why you're so loud."

"Do I?" he asks, as if he's never considered it.

"Do you see that? What does it say?" I ask, pointing at a distant green road sign, whose white prismatic beads glow.

"You can read that?" he asks.

"It says Betty Deering Trail. Anybody could read that. The letters are huge."

"Huh," he says.

"But you can read?"

He laughs softly. "Yeah. I can't do much. But I can read."

"You should pick a different job than hunting and gathering. You should do wash or camp repair. You're smart, so you could do info relay or radio. Those would work."

He nods, but doesn't say more. He's got a hard jawline. His brow is thick and his eyes deep set. "Your foot's bothering you," he says.

"What?"

"Your foot. You're favoring your left leg."

"Oh. Yeah. My shoes are failing."

"We should stop."

I slow down. It hadn't occurred to me that he was capable of noticing and adhering to such a practicality. But he's right. I've got a blister brewing and it'll only get worse. It's been eight miles. Now is as good a time as any to stop for a meal.

We've both packed the same thing: jerky and oranges. We chew quietly. He doesn't try to sit next to me this time. Though it's dark, the clouds have lifted. The sky is open and cavernous. Compared to this, our hillside feels closed and trapped. Our assigned territory would be barren, if not for the underground river flowing beneath the mountains. It's got no resources and is too steep to settle. No copper or old stores worth looting. The Chosen don't want it, which is why we have it.

Because there's been so much sickness, our birth rate is almost zero. It's not just that we don't want to bring a new cursed generation into the world. It's that we've lost the occasions for physical contact. We don't know how to do it properly, how not to be frightened of saliva and semen and blood.

In my twenty-five years, I've made this GoodWill run to Malibu a dozen times. Every time, when I get to the closed gates, I wish for a mad second that they'll open. I'd walk inside and be one of the Chosen. It's a kind of self-hate, but I can't stop it. I don't want to be what I am.

As I cut a hole into my moleskin, I feel his eyes on me. Watching and curious. I find myself talking, just to break the uncomfortable spell. "Who was your partner before me?"

Ferris waits until he's done chewing to talk. He's got old world manners. "Rotates. I've never had a consistent one."

"Why?"

"You'll have to ask them," he says, and it's an answer I respect. He doesn't bad-mouth anybody. Now that I think about it, he's had bad luck. I remember that his last partner was Mattie, who hates everybody. And his partner before that was Grim. Grim was genuinely crazy. Shot himself in the head.

I should have stopped sooner or borrowed better shoes. The blister is red and swollen and the moleskin won't prevent infection.

I feel something before I see it in my peripheral vision. It's Ferris, holding out a tube of antibiotic ointment. "For your foot."

I take it and our fingers touch, charged. I can't remember the last time I touched anyone. Not Maple. The last person I touched was my mom.

"You've been leaving territory?"

He nods. "I'm careful. You won't get sick."

He watches with preacher eyes as I apply the stuff, rubbing it into the swell.

We make it another eight miles before the dawn, then spend the day under trees on the side of the road, each taking watch. Closer to the ocean, the brush is thicker, the trees bigger.

The way we sleep isn't so different from back home. Though there are small houses cut into the granite that we could occupy, our people have been nomadic for so long that none of us wants a ceiling instead of a sky. What's more, houses confine the air, making it stagnant. Infection spreads in stagnant air.

By night, my foot is worse. I limp and try to hide it. Ferris says nothing, though his gait slows. Without words, he offers to carry my pack by tugging on it. I refuse, but tell him, "Thanks."

The ocean comes up on us like a surprise: Malibu. We see the lights, smell remnants of snuffed fires that recently cooked rabbit and deer. Dotting the valley below are lonely yellow glints in lonely bedrooms—the insomniacs. They live in houses here. They have a radio station and gas stations and cars. The Chosen have everything.

Ahead, a few hundred feet before the gate, the altar.

Though this entrance is only for us, is supposed to stay clear of immune, it's still important to be careful. We won't touch anything. We're quiet, so the curious don't hear us and investigate. We leave our offerings, each of us lightening our packs. I'm used to doing this with Maple, so I kneel down as if to pray, like she used to. *Oh Lord, forgive us. Oh Lord, choose us, so we can be free*, she used to say.

Ferris stays standing and I find I don't want to say Maple's words. They don't belong to me.

"It's not God who exiled us," he says. "It's just bad luck. We don't deserve this."

He's the only person I've ever heard express this. We're all so tired, the rest of us, that it's not a thought worth having. What does it matter whether we deserve this? It's happening and there's nothing we can do.

"If they're God's people, then God is a monster. They have everything. We have nothing," he says.

"They say they're working on a cure for us," I answer, but I'm not sure I believe this.

"If they wanted to help us, they'd have given us a city. A hospital. They'd have cleared it out for us. They don't *want* to help. They don't care." He's angry. I wouldn't have guessed awkward Ferris Landing had it in him to be angry.

"Don't talk like that. You'll cut yourself against it. There's nothing we can do."

He lowers his head and I have the feeling people have said this to him before: *Stop talking. Stop thinking. I can't handle what you're saying*. I don't like that I'm now one of those people.

I stand up again. The sky is dim and thick. Beads of rain fall light at first, and then heavy.

Wet, we walk back. I can't hide my limp anymore. The pain is a line of heat that stretches all the way to my knee. He puts his arm around me and I lean my weight. It's strange at first. Unpleasant. I think of sickness and coughing and blood. But I need the help, so after a while, I don't mind it.

"Why did Mattie leave you?" I ask.

"Because I talked like this," he answers. "Odd little preacher."

A few miles later, dawn breaks. We're lucky and are close to the halfway house, a place restricted from the Chosen. Shelter from the rain.

Ferris is loud here, too. He grunts when he changes and grunts when he bends even though he's a young man. The two beds are across the room from each other. I want to suggest one of us take watch, but there's something thick between us that I'm afraid to broach. I find my eyes open, looking at him; him looking back at me.

While we're sleeping, the worst thing happens. The door opens. The Chosen break treaty and enter. I'm so scared it's like alarms are screaming inside me. This is everything I've ever feared. I can't run. They're blocking the door. I can't breathe. I'll die.

Really, that's the only option. I'll die. So will Ferris.

They come closer and they're so clean. Even their fingernails are clean. I can't hold it in anymore. I breathe. They smell like chemicals. The whole room is filled with the scent of too-sweet flowers.

I'm too focused on what's right in front of me to notice Ferris, though distantly I hear struggle. Wet skin, fighting sounds. They're hurting him.

"Easy," the one closest to me says, like I'm a wild animal. "Easy does it."

I lunge, but there are hands holding me down. There's a needle. Everything goes black.

I wake up in a long, clean room with hard, shining floors and two rows of beds, headboards against the walls. Only two of the beds are occupied. Over us stand the clean Chosen, all wearing white coats. I'm awake, but Ferris's eyes are closed. I'm waiting for the tickle in my throat. The swell in my ears. Captain Trips.

A man with white hair comes closer. Like a baby, he has no hair on his face. His breath is chemical and cinnamon. "Do you speak?" he asks. "Do you understand me?"

I glare, holding my breath.

"You're exposed. Go ahead and breathe, dear."

I lunge for him, realizing only then that my feet are bound. He shows no alarm. Barely flinches. His voice is loud. Louder even then Ferris's. But he's not talking to me. The people around him are students, apparently. Or else some kind of audience. "We injected her with both live virus and vaccine, but she's shown no sign of infection. Very promising."

They mutter, an excited thrum.

"This is the first time we've seen any immunity at all?" one asks.

The old man shakes his head. I don't think I've ever seen anyone as old as him. Our people die much sooner. Nonetheless, he appears healthy, his joints still full of cartilage, his skin lively. "We've come close before. But as I said . . . promising."

Then he walks to the next bed. "This one has a hundred-and-four-degree fever. It's not as progressed as we'd expect from an active infection, but it's still a fever. I'll need hematology to run panels for everything relevant, looking particularly at the Trips protein-antibody interaction."

Then they turn. I've given up lunging and am openly untying my binds, which are simple and well-knotted bedsheets attached to the metal frame. The old guy pays no attention, but a few of the interns watch with curiosity as the group of them heads out. A door closes with a *click* and they're gone.

THE DEVIL'S CHILDREN

They're not worried I'll escape, which I find alarming. Are people in my position usually too sick by now to run or fight?

I get the knots off and am free, about to follow them to the door and show them the sort of damage my kind can commit, when something thin and sweet trickles through the air. It falls, heavier than atmosphere and just slightly orange. It's coming from the narrow, slatted metal boxes in the ceiling. I try not to breathe it, because it spins me, makes me heavy. I fight, but my heads sinks back.

As I doze, I see a list of names carved into the steel footboard of the bed opposing mine.

We were here
Len
Islis
Fran
Soo
Mattius
Lip
Drift

My eyes unfocus and I force them back. I force myself back right before it all goes black again. I see a final name:

Maple.

For the first time in memory, I sleep during the night and wake at dawn. My bedsheets are knotted again, my ankles bound and tied to the bedpost. It's humanely done. Not very tight.

The people in white have returned. They're taking Ferris's blood. He's awake and coughing, his hair slicked with sweat. I try to act like I'm not scared for him; this isn't serious. *I have you*, I want to tell him. *We're on the same team and that makes you mine.* But it's too personal a thing to say with words. His eyes find purchase in me and his breathing relaxes. His wheezing becomes less pronounced.

"They injected us with Captain Trips and an experimental vaccine," I say. "I'm not sick yet so there's a chance you'll get better."

"So, you do understand us," the old man says. "We weren't sure which tribe you came from. Some of them are mutes."

"You're in violation of the treaty," I say.

He looks at the side of my bed as if considering sitting there, but thinks better of it. "Did you know that the children of the immune are not always immune? We need this, too. It's for all of us."

He keeps talking. There are more words, about society and survival. About everyone doing their part. About rebuilding and getting back what we've lost. They're meaningless. I'm thinking instead about how Ferris called them monsters. I'm thinking he was right.

Then they're gone. It only occurs to me later that the old man's voice was more nasal than yesterday.

Breakfast is delivered by more people in white. One of them sneezes, twice.

Once they're gone, I work on my binds, getting loose. I'm up then. The hall is just that. Two rows of beds that end on one side in a wall and the other in a locked, windowed door. Outside that door, people in white have congregated. I hear words like *cure* and *breakthrough* and *economic viability*. It's bright out there, a white sun, and they're too loud. I can't imagine enduring a world so loud.

Back at the beds, Ferris shakes with fever. The whites of his eyes have turned red with blood. My instinct is to hide from him. To cocoon myself with sheets on the far side of the room. I'm so scared of infection. But there is another instinct, too. I like Ferris. I don't want him to be alone.

"Stay 'way from me," he coughs.

"Yeah," I say. Then I do something I've never done before. Not with anyone, ever. I climb into his bed. Our bare legs touch.

I spend the day nursing Ferris and plotting an escape. My plan is to break out once they're not paying attention. Carrying Ferris out will be the tough part. It would make more sense to leave him behind. But my chance to escape hasn't yet occurred, so I haven't had to make that decision.

Once I leave, I won't be able to go home. Even if I don't die, I'm probably a carrier.

Hunger outweighs any fears I have that the food is infected with some new terror. It's toast and jam and butter; eggs and fresh meat and bright orange juice. I can understand why they mistake themselves for gods; they eat like them.

Ferris manages a few sips of juice, but not much else.

Midday, the door opens again. People in white enter. Several are coughing. They draw Ferris's blood.

We sit together into the night and at some point fall asleep.

I'm awoken with the feeling of something cold and wet.

"Oh no!" Ferris cries.

Blood, I think. He's bleeding out. It's the final stage. But my eyes adjust. He's slick all over, dripping sweat. The heat coming off of him is gone. His fever has broken.

"It's so gross. I'm so sorry!" he whispers.

It's not like I thought. I'm not repulsed. I'm just happy he's alive. Happy I won't have to escape without him.

"You're crying. Oh no, please don't cry," he says.

And it takes a second—I don't understand what he's talking about, before I realize that I really am crying. But it's not sadness. It's relief.

The next morning, the old doctor comes with his friends in white. They're all sick now, and all the assistants are sick, too. The old man can hardly stand. The veins in his sclera have popped and broken, red blood swelling under a layer of tight skin. The assistants hold us down and take our blood. They're so out of it they don't notice that Ferris is better. They lock the door behind them, but they forget to bind us or put sleep gas through the vents.

We walk to the end of the hall, watching them through the glass window. The old man falls to the ground. He shakes with seizure, mouth foaming, then goes still. I've seen this before in my own people and know already, even as the staff surrounding him perform CPR and check his pulse, that he's dead.

―――

"Looks like they invented a new variant," Ferris says.

"And it kills them, but not us?" I ask.

We stand at the glass, looking out. The attendants in white notice us then. Their expressions confuse me. Slowly, I realize they're afraid.

―――

We stay in the room for the following twenty-four hours while Ferris rebuilds his strength. No one comes back to check on us after the doctor's death. We watch out the window as the hospital fills ominously with coughing people, sick people. We hear the cacophony. And then, just as quickly as the coughing started, it goes quiet. It happens with a snap, or the strike of thunder. Everything is still.

We break the window, reach down and unlock the door from the outside.

There are bodies on the floor, bleeding out from eyes and mouths and ears, staining white uniforms and floors red. I've seen this before. I've seen lots of bad things. But that doesn't make any of it easy.

I'm holding Ferris's hand. Or maybe he's holding mine. How do these things start? I don't know. We're out a main door and down the steps. It's daylight. We're exposed for all the town to see. But the people are gone. The cars are still. The town, once teeming, is silent.

THE DEVIL'S CHILDREN

"Are they all dead?" I ask.

Ferris looks up toward the roof of a large mansion. Something moves. A human blur charges around a corner, but it doesn't go far. I feel its watching eyes.

The vantage has shifted. We have become the immune.

We gather food, but otherwise don't spend long. Ferris wants to investigate, to wander their stores, to eat fresh fruit and meet their animals—their cats and livestock. To read their books. But it's dangerous to linger. They might have guns. We leave through the gate we must have been carried through, pass the altar, now empty. They took our offerings just like they took us.

The rest at the death hospital has healed my blister. Sometimes Ferris leans on me, sometimes I lean on him. We walk until we're at the halfway house. We rest there.

"Why did you volunteer to help me forage?" I ask.

"I like you."

Except by necessity, I've avoided paying attention to other people. It opens too many doors. Like Maple or my mom, they might die and I don't want to have to mourn them. If I'm loyal to them, I might have to sacrifice more than I can afford. But it occurs to me that he's been paying attention. The Preacher.

"Why?" I ask.

"You get things done," he says. "Other people, they just pretend. Or they do as little as they can. Our whole group is falling apart. You don't seem to notice. From the outside, it looks like you do that because you have hope."

I can't evaluate this. I don't have the perspective to know whether it's hope or animal instinct that keeps me going. But I like that he thinks so highly of me. "They killed our missing," I say.

"Yeah," he says. "They did. They stole them like lab rats and then murdered them."

"They killed Maple. They killed my friend."

There are tears in his eyes. I know he wasn't attached to Maple. I know he's feeling this for me. And somehow, that opens and breaks something inside me. I'm crying. I'm crying so loud. It's like screaming.

He's there. A witness. He doesn't tell me to be quiet or to stop. And so I keep going. I cry for Maple and the missing. I cry for my people. I cry for my mom. I cry for misunderstood Ferris. I cry for myself.

What happens next isn't an accident. Taking off our clothing and coming together, we choose it. I've never done it before, and neither has he. It's a surprise, how much I enjoy it. I feel different afterward. I feel like there was something wrong, something undone and sorrowful, that is gone. It's his nearness that drives it away.

The halfway house has a radio, and that morning, we let our people know what happened. They decide to take a risk. They send an envoy of two to meet us. This envoy hesitates as it passes through the threshold of the halfway house. We all do.

It's terrifying and momentous and oh so quiet as they walk inside and breathe our air.

When Ferris and I decide where to sleep with our newcomers, we have the option of pretending there is nothing between us. These kinds of relations are frowned upon and impractical. I find myself afraid of losing him, and tether myself closer.

Quickly, our friends get sick. But like Ferris, two days later, they are healed. Immune.

Leaning on one another, learning *love* without ever saying the word, Ferris and I make a kind of pilgrimage together. We spread our immunity to Montana and Texas. We spread it wherever it's needed.

Nine months later, my child is born. The child is immune.

THE DEVIL'S CHILDREN

We consider packing our things and moving to any of the now-occupied territories. Taking over, murdering with a word. Undoing everything the Chosen have built. But we choose instead to remain the quiet ones.

Our numbers grow. Surge, even. We respect the new treaty, have stolen no lands. The difference is not on the outside, but within. We gather now. We know the feel of skin. We laugh, our voices no longer caged.

You Chosen ones now relegated to small territories, you Petty Gods who turned the lights no one wanted back on. You day walkers banished now, to night, hear a story: Once, you steered a ship. You broke the ship and unknowingly jettisoned us from it. You returned to the ship, learning nothing. Changing nothing. Seeing nothing new.

You did not understand that we were the new. God's rejects were the change. We will remake the world into a thing you do not recognize. We will remake the world into a thing that works.

PART FOUR

OTHER WORLDS THAN THESE

THE UNFORTUNATE CONVALESCENCE OF THE SUPERLAWYER

Nat Cassidy

His fever breaks and there are earthquakes.

When he comes to in the middle of the road, his face is resting against the hot asphalt. His head is fuzzy, his mouth is dry, the sun is cooking his clammy skin . . . but all things considered, he feels pretty dang good.

Such a beautiful dream.

He peels himself off the ground. Wipes flakes of black grit from his cheek. Tries to get his bearings.

A lonely strip of Highway 70. Damn lucky nobody ran him over.

But, of course, nobody *would* have run him over. Because everyone is

—a beautiful dream—

dead. Dead or dying. That's why he'd thrown supplies in his car and started driving north towards the badlands of Utah in the first place. No plan, other than fleeing Phoenix and getting to the least populated area he could think of. The first truly impulsive thing he's done in his adult life.

He stands, legs wobbly as a newborn foal.

The world seems to be holding its breath. A breeze plays against his skin, but even that feels tentative. A slow pulse in a comatose body.

So remarkably different from the chaos he'd left behind. Sickness all around him. Panic in the streets, on the airwaves. In this isolated silence, all that feels impossible. More like, well, some fever dream.

The difference in his body is amazing, too.

At some point, probably around Prescott, he'd started to feel sick himself. Mucus pooling in every sinus. Insides heating up. Glands starting to swell.

Now he feels downright refreshed. He puts a hand to his throat and confirms the swelling has gone down. Fever's gone, too—maybe the hot asphalt helped burn it out of him?

Or . . . maybe it had all been psychosomatic. No sickness could move *that* fast, right? Not even the so-called "superflu" with that stupid nickname. He's always been a little prone to nervous suggestion.

But what the hell was I doing in the middle of the road?

How long was I out?

And where is everybody? There should still be at least a little traffic out here, shouldn't there? Other people fleeing cities?

He brushes the remaining road grit off his blazer and front. Notices his shirt is untucked and the top button undone. He sets all that to right and feels good. Better than good.

Alive.

All that matters.

I got out just in time.

He holds tight to his beautiful dream. Swirling lights and disembodied hands, gently scooping him up. Like a UFO. Like the Great Eagles rescuing Frodo and Sam. Taking him away from harm. Taking control from chaos.

He'd done that for himself.

Despite everything, he smiles a little.

THE UNFORTUNATE CONVALESCENCE OF THE SUPERLAWYER

I'm going to survive.
That's when the earth starts to shake.

For a few years during his scattershot, bohemian childhood, he'd lived in and around California. He knows earthquakes. Something about this one feels wrong.

For starters, it goes on for too long. Three, four minutes of active tremors.

As soon as it starts, he hurries back to his car, the closest thing to shelter. When the shaking doesn't stop, he starts to wonder if it's his own body, maybe another symptom of his waning illness. Then he notices the power lines swaying.

Eventually, the quake comes to an end.

He gets out and looks around, dismayed by the cracks in the road.

A couple power lines lean in their foundations, shaken into drunkenness.

The air smells faintly of burning metal. Of sewage lines cracked open.

The silence is dreadful.

No. Not quite silence. A faint noise, almost like a whirring or a grinding. Worlds away. Barely perceptible let alone decipherable.

Even the clouds seem to have been affected by the quake. There's a sort of distinguishably straight line cutting through the cloud cover, which would be weird enough, but that straight line is also now jagged in parts. Broken. He'd think the broken parts would make that path seem *more* realistic, but it doesn't. It looks . . . awful.

Earth's fever is breaking, too. He doesn't like that sentiment one bit.

He slaps his cheeks a little—the way he sometimes did in courthouse bathrooms before big trial appearances.

"Just an earthquake," he says. His voice sounds very strange in the flat air. "Nothing to get freaked out about."

He heads back to the car. Checks the radio. Nothing across the dial. Only static.

Now that he's in better shape, he should start driving again. Find somewhere safe to hole up, wait for the apocalypse to settle itself. There's a gas station up ahead, a national park and a town beyond that.

Something stays his hand. A feeling so strong and clear he can practically hear it: *No. The car stays here.*

He turns the engine back off. The key chain—a leather fob, embossed with the initials SL—sways like the power lines had swayed.

He hates this car. Hates driving it, hates the complicated transmission. Hates how noticeable it can make him feel. Hates the stupid key chain that had come with it. *Not my initials, Dad.*

And yet, for all his hate, he still kept the Plymouth in the garage. Still made sure it had an up-to-date battery, even while its exterior dulled and rusted. As if he knew one day the world might fall apart while his own, far more compliant Honda happened to be in the shop.

Honestly, he's amazed he managed to drive the Plymouth *this* far. All these hills. All that shifting. He wouldn't be surprised if the stress of operating the damn thing contributed to his feeling so sick.

So, maybe I'll be impulsive one more time and just leave the stupid thing here. Walk and go find a new one. One better suited for me.

No doubt there are thousands of other working cars he can find nearby. After all, the world is ending.

That thought gives him a strange, giddy thrill.

The world is ending.

Right now, I might be the last man on earth. Like Vincent Price in that stupid movie. Or like Burgess Meredith. Time enough at last.

No one to live for but myself.

Before he knows it, he's crying. Hot tears searing his face.

He stumbles out of the car, screaming.

"Hello?! Is anyone else alive? HELLO?!"

Oblivion answers back. Not even an echo. Just that strange, unplaceable noise coming from far, far away. Maybe electricity cycling through damaged power lines?

He scrambles onto the hood of the Plymouth. "HELLOOOO?! ANYBODY?!"

The sun beats down. And the wind curls like heat off a cooling body. And the clouds are boiling, bleached brains, except for that mostly straight line cutting through them, dividing them into crumbling hemispheres.

Right before the vertiginous fear of a man lost at sea can overtake him, off in the distance, light blinks off of metal. He squints.

Several hills away, across an intersecting road. A vehicle speeding past. He can't be sure, but it looks like a van. A splash of unnaturally vibrant green.

Not the last man after all.

Instantly, he regrets his screaming. He holds his breath until the van disappears over the horizon.

I need to calm down, he tells himself. *I'm overstressed. Psychosomatic sickness or not, I did just have a fainting episode. That was real.*

"Yeah," he says to himself. "Just need to get my strength back. Then . . . we'll find a new car and . . . go on an adventure. Like Bilbo."

He knows just what will help settle his heart.

—✢—

Before he'd oh-so-impulsively abandoned his apartment in Phoenix and hit the road, he'd thrown all the supplies he could into the Plymouth's trunk. Canned food, sodas, jackets and shirts (folded neatly), boots. All very practical. All very *him*. He only allowed himself one extraneous item, which he'd had to pull out from the depths of his closet, behind his suits and ties and dress shirts.

He retrieves it from the trunk now. A soft, plain three-ring binder. Stuffed with pages tucked into individual clear plastic pouches.

Each page is covered in art.

His art.

Drawings of his favorite heroes. His favorite villains. Characters from Tolkien. Herbert. Bradbury. Kirby and Ditko and Adams. Some done in pencil. Some in ink.

It's an impressive collection. No need to be modest about it. He's quite talented. He could've pursued a career as an illustrator or a comic book artist if he were a bolder, braver, more reckless man. More like his dad, in other words. Instead, he'd settled for something far more practical. And it was a good thing he did. As any good lawyer understands: settling is always the wisest thing to do.

He hasn't added anything new to the notebook in a while, but he still likes to look at it during times of stress. It helps him feel moored to some secret, truer self. One that manages to survive despite the daily deluge of statutes and case law and legal briefs and discovery demands and forensic reports. Ironic, he supposes, considering these drawings are mostly of other people's creations. That's always been a big part of the appeal, though. He prefers playing in those kinds of sandboxes, where the rules are already in place. Creating your own work is just so messy. So . . . unsettling.

That said, whenever he's feeling particularly ambitious, there *is* one original character in his notebook. Several drawings and physical studies, tucked all the way in the back.

The SuperLawyer.

Corporate litigator by day. Preternaturally gifted crime fighter by night. Able to convince even the most hardened criminals to do his bidding with his silver tongue (metaphorical) and his superior brain (not metaphorical). Able to freeze moments of great chaos with his stentorian catchphrase: "I OBJECT!"

Actually, now that he thinks of it, he'd created the SuperLawyer right after he was gifted this damn Plymouth. Inspired by that stupid key chain. A way to digest his complicated feelings. Talk about messy and unsettling.

He flicks that key chain now. Watches it sway back and forth.

THE UNFORTUNATE CONVALESCENCE OF THE SUPERLAWYER

I'm so damn proud of you, son, his dad had said, after showing him the car parked in the driveway of the crummy little apartment they shared. *Getting into law school! I always told you how smart you were, didn't I?*

Dad. It's. Thank you. But you can't afford this.

Don't worry about that. I got it on a deal.

That wild look in his eye. The kind he always got when he was doing something ill-advised. Something impulsive.

He handed his son the key, attached to a leather fob bearing two letters.

Who's SL?

You are, dummy!

Dad. Those aren't my initials.

Getting concerned now. His strange memory lapses had been getting more and more frequent . . . but this would be a big one.

Dad laughed. Clapped his son on the shoulders.

I know that! I know my boy's initials. SL stands for—SuperLawyer.

A barely perceptible pause there. Covering a mistake? Was this the first real sign of the end? Or had he just gotten the key chain on some discount—maybe even a five-fingered one—and he couldn't pass up a good bargain?

His dad suddenly gets very serious.

But you gotta leave the car here, SuperLawyer. Trust me on this. The car stays here.

He gestures to the odometer. An impossibly long number is displayed there.

Whoa. Lotta miles on this, Dad.

Those aren't miles, dummy. That's a second chance. This car's gotta play its part, but maybe you *can play a part, too, one d—*

⁓

He snaps awake, sweaty and gasping. His mouth tastes lined with dirty cotton. He grimaces.

Fell asleep, he realizes. Staring at that damn key chain.

It's stuffy and uncomfortable in the Plymouth. The air is stale and thin; he can smell the salty, waxy fast-food wrappers he'd hastily discarded into the passenger-side footwell earlier while driving.

As he reaches over to roll a window down, he realizes he fell asleep with his portfolio on his lap. Not only that, one of his drawings of SuperLawyer is out of its plastic sheeting and a pen is in his hand. He always keeps a pen or two in his pocket, and he must've grabbed one while he dozed.

"Nooooo," he moans, seeing what else he did.

Something is scrawled across his drawing. A number. The same number he'd seen on the odometer in his already-fading dream.

978-1-66805-7551

No memory of writing it. No idea what it means. Furious at himself for defacing a perfectly good drawing.

Those aren't miles, dummy...

His pulse begins to hammer. Knock.

I don't like this. I really don't like this. I object.

The knocking intensifies. Not just in his head. Someone is standing by the car, rapping gently on the side of the door to get his attention.

"Hey!" a voice outside says. "You alive in there or what?"

⤳

Her name is Susie and she's quick to assure him she's not crazy.

"I just haven't seen anyone in a while and I . . . I don't know. Got impulsive."

The distaste with which she gives that word makes him relax a little. "I know the feeling."

He folds the defaced drawing and stashes it into his breast pocket with a strange, muted shame. Gets out of the Plymouth to meet this new stranger.

She's young. A teenager, really. Still baby fat on her cheeks. Dressed in retro fashion, a peasant blouse and cranberry bell-bottoms. Awkward, but, he's almost immediately positive, harmless.

He tells her that his car has died—"Too many miles, probably"—and that he's thinking of walking to the nearby gas station to look for a new one. She asks if she can go with him, and he says yes. They both do a poor job of hiding their relief at no longer being alone.

He'd also packed a couple of duffel bags in the trunk, so they divvy up his supplies to carry with them. He opts to carry the heavier bag, full of cans, and gives her the one with clothes. She seems inordinately touched by the consideration. She must not be used to such things.

"Shame about your car, though," she says as they close the emptied trunk. "It's pretty bitchin'."

He gives the rear bumper a light kick. "It's a piece of crap. Always hated it. And I was never good with manual transmissions."

Still, he shoots a final look at the car as they head down Highway 70. So long, SL. So long, Dad's albatross.

The car stays here. Again, that mysterious commandment in his mind. Not his father's voice, though; somehow more elemental than that. Lower. Deeper. Wider. *Great. The voice of God or something?* He chuckles to himself. *Yeah, sure. Why not?*

Either way, he doesn't bother arguing with it. Another thing every good lawyer knows: some arguments just aren't worth your time.

As they walk down Highway 70, they do what all people who've been through a cataclysm do: swap horror stories.

He tells her about Phoenix. How the bodies started piling up. The smell of decay in the hot, dry air. The litany of lies and evasions on the TV and the radio. She nods along to the familiar tune.

She'd been living up in Maine. Then, everybody sing along: the bodies started piling up. And the smell of decay in the hot, humid air. And the litany of lies and evasions on the TV and the radio. She and her boyfriend, Bernie—along with their friends Joan, Kelly, Corey, and the rather unpleasantly named Needles—kicked around aimlessly for a while, stirring up shit, listening to Corey's oversized radio/tape player, enjoying a certain kind of freedom . . . until they started to die off, too.

One fleeting detail strikes him as curious when she refers to the flu as "A6." It's not a designation he's familiar with, and he almost asks her about it—but then he realizes it's just yet another nickname for the disease that's turned the world on its head. No more or less incomprehensible than "Captain Trips," he supposes. No more or less useful, either.

He shakes his head with pity as she finishes her story.

"Wow. Experiencing all this as a kid. I just can't imagine. I'm so sorry."

"I'm not a kid," she says defiantly, the way a kid would.

"Maine's a long ways away," he says, impressed and a little appalled. "Have you just been walking the whole time?"

She gives an uncommitted, unreadable shrug. Before he can ask her a follow-up, she points her chin at the folder he's holding close to his chest "What's with that thing? You're carrying it like we had to carry my dog when she got too old to walk."

Once again, he's surprised himself. He hadn't realized he was still holding on to his notebook.

"Oh, uh. This is nothing, just . . . Well, I've actually never shown it to anyone before, but . . . What the hell."

Cheeks flushing, he hands it over to her.

The drawings are impressive enough to stop her in her tracks.

"Whoa," she says. "You did all these?" He nods. "These are *good*. Like, seriously good." She steps off onto the shoulder to continue flipping through. He joins her. "I recognize some of these guys! That's wild. Is this what you did before the world ended? Drew comics and stuff?"

"Yup." Then, after a guilty beat: "No. I did corporate finance law. The most boring, useless crap in the world. I don't know why I just lied."

She hands his folder back. "Why'd you do boring, useless crap? You totally could've been an artist, man."

"No thanks." He grimaces. "My dad was . . . Well, some days he was an actor, some days he was a musician, some days—who knows. He was one of those 'free spirits.' Did whatever he wanted. Never planned. Never saved. Which I know might sound fun, but our lives were chaos. It was a horrible way to grow up. So, as soon as I could, I opted for something . . . stable. And it's a good thing I did, because I was able to take care of him when he was dying."

"The flu?"

"Dementia. Early onset. Couple years ago."

"Oof. Sorry. Dementia's rotten. Brains and stuff? Terrifying."

"Yeah." *Those aren't my initials, Dad.*

"Well, hey." She offers him an infectious smile. "We're gonna have to build the world up all over again, so . . . now you can be whatever you wanted to be! Somebody's gotta draw the comic books, right? And what are people gonna do, check your references?"

He laughs. "True." Then, deciding he can trust her with this precious cargo, he tucks the notebook into the duffel of soft goods she's carrying.

"What's your name, by the way?" She asks as he zips the duffel back up. "What do I call you on this great adventure?"

"Ezra," he says without missing a beat. Without feeling the slightest pang for choosing a new identity. "Ezra Lawson."

"A lawyer named Lawson? That's like something out of a comic book," she says.

He smiles.

No cars in the gas station parking lot. But two men are arguing inside the little convenience store.

Ezra and Susie freeze just as they walk in. The sound of other people's voices is so unexpected, neither knows what to do.

The arguers don't notice at first—their squabble continues, uninterrupted, on the other side of the store. Ezra can make words out, though he can't draw much sense from them. The two men are frantically looking for . . . a door, it sounds like? Their accents are strange. Vaguely European, but ultimately unplaceable.

It's the harried, desperate tone of the argument that makes Ezra quickly realize this might not be the safest situation. Before he can reach for the exit—

"Halt!" One of the men shouts, then both come into view, glaring at Ezra and Susie over the few aisles of supplies. Ezra raises his hands. Susie copies.

Each man is ragged. Filthy skin. Unkempt beards. Long hair, matted with dirt and threaded with grays. One is shorter and stouter. The taller man has a palpably subservient manner, despite his wild, raving eyes.

Strangest of all is their clothing. Animal skins. Fine leather straps. Ezra can't be sure, but it looks like a sword is slung across one shoulder. They look more like refugees from Middle Earth rather than middle Utah.

The world's already gone insane. Then, like a whisper in his mind: *How long was I unconscious?*

The shorter man steps into the aisle and what Ezra sees is so unexpected, so utterly absurd, he barely knows how to process it.

The man is holding a bow and arrow, nocked and pointed straight at them.

The taller one whispers, "Wait. My prince—"

The archer growls back: "*No one* is to be trusted here, Dennis. Don't you understand where we are?"

THE UNFORTUNATE CONVALESCENCE OF THE SUPERLAWYER

"I know, but, begging your pardon—remember what you told me? About the dreams? What if these are among the good? What if they can help us find the next door?"

"This world is dead and crumbling! We can't waste time on more traps! *His* stench is all around us."

Both men look—and sound—utterly mad. Taxed to the breaking point. But the second man, Dennis, seems a little more grounded. Solicitous, at the very least. Ezra addresses him. "Hey. We're not—"

"Of whom do you dream?" Dennis interrupts quickly, as if to outpace the arrow his companion plans to fire.

Ezra blinks. "Huh?"

"Answer quick! I am Dennis, son of Brandon. This is Peter, prince of Delain. We have traveled far and—"

"*—We have been forgotten!*" The one named Peter cries, full of bitter rage. "*We have been abandoned! And we cannot stay in this place!*" His arrow hand pulls back farther.

"Please!" Dennis urges. "Tell us. Are you with *him* or not?"

Ezra begins to stammer. "I—I don't know who, or what you're—"

"Did you say 'door' earlier?" Susie asks abruptly. All eyes whip to her. "You're looking for a door? What kind of door?"

The archer relaxes his arrow the tiniest bit. Reads something in Susie's expression. "You know of them? The doors between?"

Susie swallows. "I think . . . Maybe?"

"Have you one of those damnable pink tablets, as well?" Dennis asks, voice low. "The ones holding all the stories—"

"*Hush*," Peter snaps, then turns his glare back to Susie. "The door. Tell me. We haven't much time. This world is unstable. Its beams are—"

As if to prove his point, before he can finish the earth begins to shake again. Supplies tumble off shelves. The fluorescent lights stutter and spark.

Everyone cries out in surprise.

Peter rushes for Susie. Grabs her. Begins to shake her. "Quickly! Where was it?! Tell me what you know! Tell me before it's too—"

Ezra swings his heavy duffel full of cans at the lunatic's head. The man goes down, hard. His companion rushes to his side. "My prince!"

His prince is moaning nonsense words—beam, quake, door, tower, and with especial adamance, flag, flag, flag—all while the store spits its inventory onto the floor.

Ezra can't stand to hear any more of it.

He runs out the gas station door, across the undulating asphalt, past the swaying, shaking gas pumps.

⸻

Susie catches up with him down the road. Panting. "Wait! Wait up!"

He doesn't. But she's young and he can't outpace her for long.

His head throbs. With the sun, the stress, the strange litany of words that crazy vagrant was spouting. Also, with that noise in the distance. Is it louder now? He wants to ask Susie if she hears it, too, but decides he'd rather not know. This is all starting to feel too . . .

Irrational.

Tiny threads, sprouting up across the surface of reality, begging to be pulled.

Nothing good can come from pulling threads like those. Better to leave them alone. Better to stay in as close to silence as they can.

Susie doesn't let that happen for long, though.

"We could've talked some sense into them. Or maybe I could've."

"So go back and join them if you want to," he snaps. "You didn't have to follow me."

Back to silence. Then she stops walking.

"It's just . . . they kept talking about a door."

"Susie," he groans, and stops, too. "I don't know where you're going with this but—"

THE UNFORTUNATE CONVALESCENCE OF THE SUPERLAWYER

"*I've* been dreaming about a door," she says. "I might have even seen—"

"I don't wanna hear this!" He turns and continues on without her. She calls after him.

"Where is everybody, Ezra? Where are all the bodies? Why is it so empty here?"

We have been forgotten.

He stops again, exasperated. Looks up at the sky. Those linear clouds, even more jagged in places than earlier. The sun is finally beginning to dip low, smearing everything with wild magenta.

And that noise. That damn noise. Definitely louder now.

"This is an isolated area," he says back to her, jaw clenched. "That's why I drove here in the first place!"

"Okay. But. Hear me out. Please." She takes a few steps toward him. "After my friends died . . . I was all alone, and . . . The thing is, man, I hated my friends. They treated me like dog shit. Especially Bernie. I mean, I thought about killing them all the time—and I'm not saying this to skeeve you out, I'm just saying that's how bad it was, okay? I *didn't* kill them. Captain Trips did. But then I figured I might as well just . . . kill myself, right? I mean, I still wanted to kill *something*. So, I got really drunk, and I got really high, and I broke into our old high school to, y'know, do the deed, because that felt nice and dramatic. The place was totally empty, and I'm wandering down the halls, thinking about how shitty my friends were and how pissed I am that *this* is how my life turned out and why couldn't I have been born in a different world, or at least gotten a fucking taste of how things *could* have been different, and I round this corner and . . . and there's this door. Like, a freestanding door. In the middle of the hallway. Where there shouldn't be a door."

"Susie."

"Just *listen*. It had this weird, long number written on it, with dashes, kinda like a phone number, but not. No idea what it meant, but . . . Well, I was already ready for an ending, so I figured, 'What the hell,' and I opened it up and next thing I knew, I was in—I don't even know, where is this, Colorado?"

He doesn't correct her. He's too busy not thinking about the numbers he scrawled on the drawing inside his jacket pocket.

"Ever since I got here," she continues, "I've been so . . . disoriented. Things feel off, don't they? Nothing sounds right. Nothing tastes right. And every time I close my eyes, I still see that door. That fucking *door*, man! What if it's the same door they were talking about? Or . . . I dunno, what if I really did kill myself? What if that guy was right and this is the land of the dead?"

"He didn't say *that*!" Ezra yells, appalled. "He was rambling nonsense. Both of them! Come *on*, Susie, did they sound compos mentis to you? Talking like they're in a, a fantasy novel or something?"

"No."

"No! Just a couple of mentally ill hobos! As for your 'door,' you said it yourself. You were high! And drunk!"

"But . . . how did I get here?"

He throws his hands up in frustration. "You've been through a trauma! You blacked out! Maybe you hitchhiked! Or you got kidnapped! Or you just walked! Like this!"

He turns away from her, starts walking once more. Huffing. Desperate to end this idiocy.

She calls after him. "What about all the earthquakes, Ezra? And seriously . . . where are all the bodies? Remember how many there were, all piling up?"

We have been forgotten. Abandoned.

Far up ahead, a building on the hilly horizon. The park station.

He swallows. "There's an explanation!" he says. "There's always an explanation!"

"What if the explanation is we're dead?!" She has to shout after him now. "What if this is purgatory?! Or what if this is all some sort of fever dream in my head and I'm just waiting for the lights to go—"

"NO!" He turns back to actually scream at her, throat grinding.

THE UNFORTUNATE CONVALESCENCE OF THE SUPERLAWYER

"Dreams don't mean anything! And we're not dead! We're alive! We survived! We exist! GODDAMMIT, *I* EXIST!"

Feeling a little better having yelled all that, he walks in silence.

Eventually, she hurries to catch up with him.

They find Ezra's father, singing, inside the visitor's entrance of the Black Dragon Park Center.

He's cross-legged on the welcome desk, his back to them. A bright yellow trench coat is tossed haphazardly next to him.

It's his voice that first draws Ezra in. After that upsetting conversation with Susie, he's not exactly raring for further interactions with a stranger. But that voice. It sounds just like Dad.

As they get closer, Ezra recognizes the song as one that had been getting a lot of radio airplay before—

(*the world ended*)

—everything started to fall apart. A song his father couldn't have known.

The singer, sensing their approach, builds to a crescendo.

"A. Right. Chus. Mannnn!"

He lifts and spins himself around with impressive fluidity. Ezra's stomach lurches. He's the spitting image of his father.

"Well, heya, cats and kittens, you're listening to WTAF. Any requests?"

Susie looks to Ezra, but Ezra's too busy gaping to respond. She does her best to sound tough.

"We don't want any trouble," she says.

"Then none ye shall have." The man holds up his hands, showing they're empty. Then gives a big, silly grin. "Until you do. Because, y'know. 'Life is what happens to you while you're busy' something, something."

Ezra gives a sudden, private gasp. What the hell was he thinking: this strange man doesn't actually look a *thing* like his dad. For a few seconds there, it had been uncanny, but the longer he stares, the more inaccurate that comparison becomes. There's only . . . a similar vibe. A manic glitter in the eyes. An insouciant lilt in the voice. If anything, this man looks more like the two vagrants from the gas station, with his beard, his long hair. He's nowhere near as shabby, and his clothes aren't ragged, but there's definitely something road-worn about him.

Susie, meanwhile, is still trying to handle the situation, unaware of Ezra's little epiphany.

"My name's Susie. This is Ezra."

The strange man snorts. "Ezra. Sure."

"What's your name?" she asks.

He shrugs.

"Oh, I've got loads of them. I'm the Nowhere Man. Lord of the Narrative Cul-de-Sac. Maestro Supreme of the Disposable Digression. You see, not everyone gets the old woman. Not everyone gets the Walkin Dude. Some people—the people who don't get the chance to choose—get little ol' me. Yup! When you won't be takin' any stand, you'll find me cuz I'm your man." He giggles at his near-rhyme.

Ezra finds his voice at last. "Great. Another basket case."

"A tisket *and* a tasket," the man replies, nodding. "Tom's a-cold."

"Let's get out of here," Ezra says. "I don't like this. I think if we keep walking, we can hit Green River in probably—"

Outside, a sudden clap of thunder makes the windows rattle. Susie and Ezra both flinch. It hadn't looked like rain when they'd walked in. Now, through the windows, the sky has gone from dusk to midnight black.

"Gonna be a big storm," the man says. "Might as well wait it out here. I'll be gentle. Why don't you call me . . ." A shimmer of inspiration. "Tom Bombadil."

"Oh, come *on*." Ezra crosses his arms over his chest.

"Why not?" the man asks. "As good a name as any! We can be whoever we want to be these days, right?"

Susie looks at Ezra. "What's he talking about? Who's—?"

"He's screwing with us. That's a character from a book. *The Lord of the Rings*."

"Oh, I saw that Bakshi cartoon! My friend Corey got a hold of a print right before everything, y'know. But I don't remember anyone named—"

"No, they cut that part out of the movie." The man lets out a great guffaw. "Now what's so funny?"

"I just love watching people put puzzles together. 'They cut that part out.' You're soooo close already!"

"Close to what?" Ezra asks.

"Tom" leans forward with a stage whisper. "Not every Armageddon puts up a fight. The scenery's being scrubbed. The world's being moved on. There's been a revision. A *rewrite*."

"Okay." Ezra heaves a sigh. "So, are you with those two Renaissance Fair rejects we just ran into? Prince Peter and what's-his-name? Or did you all just happen to get the same head injury?"

Tom looks genuinely aghast. "Oh noooo. They wound up *here*? Ugh, hope they find their way out. A long time ago, I gave them my Ur. Thought maybe it'd help get them back on track. See, this is why I don't give gifts, Poor Tom."

Ezra rubs his temples. "Why is everyone so damned insane all of a sudden?!"

Then Susie takes a brave step forward. "Are we dead?"

Tom and Ezra both react: one, delighted, the other, appalled. Susie holds Tom's gaze.

"Aw, sweet child," Tom says at last. "You're not dead. No more than anyone else who's ever asked that question."

"Wonderful!" Ezra exclaims. "Confirmation! From such an obviously trustworthy source. If you're satisfied, can we *please*—"

"I want to hear what else he has to say," Susie says with measured patience. "I think he might . . . know things."

A wicked grin smears across Tom Bombadil's face, behind his beard. "I know lots of things. But I'll warn you, most people find what I know to be *immensely* unsatisfying. That's kinda my deal."

"Where are we?" she asks. "What's going on? Where is everybody?"

Ezra groans again. "We *know* what's going on. There was a pandemic. A catastrophic event. These things happen. But we survived."

Tom watches them like a gleeful tennis spectator. "Wow, you two *definitely* aren't on the same page here. (That's funny for a number of reasons.)"

"Shut up," Ezra says.

"I bet you two haven't even asked each other who the president is."

"SHUT UP."

"There's too much confusion," Tom sighs. "We can't get no relief. There must be some kind of door out of here."

Outside, more thunder. The machine-gun drumroll of heavy rain.

Susie has gone pale. "A door."

"I don't want to hear any of this," Ezra seethes to himself.

"Look," Tom says. "You can't expect everything to make sense, okay? You're both basically drafts. Ur-texts. But the connections *are* there."

Susie runs her hands over her face. When she removes them, tears are spilling. "This is all just so confusing. Please, what is going on? What's happening to us?"

Tom cocks his head, a portrait of sympathy. "Take heart, little one! *You're* in better shape than most. After all, you're still in print!"

"What?"

"You don't really belong *here*. You only think you do—and wish you do. You *think* you do, because this is the same story. But it's a different version, I'm afraid. And you *wish* you do because . . . well, that's all you ever wanted, right? To find somewhere to belong. To be needed by someone. So you found *this* guy." He cocks a thumb at Ezra.

Ezra feels his cheeks burn. Rage swells.

"Are you finished yet?" He asks through gritted teeth. "Now that you've made a kid cry?"

"I'm *not* a kid." Susie wipes at her eyes.

"She's better off than you, Mr. Ez L!" Tom says. "She might be ancillary, but *you*?" He shakes his head mournfully.

Ezra's jaw clenches even tighter. His hands wring the strap of his duffel bag across his chest. "What about me?"

"I already said, dummy!" Tom hops off the counter. Starts putting on his yellow trench coat. "There's been a revision. *And you didn't make the cut.*"

Sensing the rising tension, Susie says, "Look. Can we all just cool out? There's no need to make this heavier than it needs to be."

"It is getting awfully feverish in here, isn't it? I should be getting back to my wife, anyway. This particular Somewhere is no more. Nowhere, man. Please listen, they won't know what they're missing. I *am* glad you two found each other, though. I hope you've helped each other feel a little more complete. Merrily merrily merrily, the story is almost ov—"

A monstrous fury overcomes Ezra. Bellowing, he swings his bag of canned goods as hard as he can at Tom's head, hoping to shut the guy up, hell, maybe even knock his head clean off his shoulders—

—but the guy is gone. Ezra is swinging the heavy duffel in a laughable pirouette, almost falling over with his force.

Hours pass. The storm rages outside.

Ezra and Susie search every inch of the building, but they find no trace of the man who called himself Tom Bombadil. Eventually, they have no choice but to assume he truly up and vanished.

They mostly work in pained silence, neither wanting to hear the other's thoughts on the matter. Ezra can tell Susie's furious with him. He doesn't have the energy to work on pacifying her. In fact, all the outbursts and exertions have left him thoroughly depleted—like he's been arguing in court for days straight. He tells Susie they should probably try to get some rest. They'll have a long day's walking ahead of them tomorrow.

She tells him he should sleep first. She'll stay up and keep watch. He looks tired, she says. He doesn't want to admit it, but the aches, the dry mouth, the nagging headache have all crept back a little. Part of him wonders if they ever really left. He unbuttons his top shirt button so he can swallow more easily.

Using the duffel full of clothes as a pillow, he sets himself up in a corner of the main room. He takes his notebook out first, though. Hugs it to his chest.

Once he feels physically comfortable enough, he can't help himself. "What do you think he meant?"

"Huh?" Susie staring, dull-eyed, at a brochure for the park.

"'There was a revision.' Did he mean the plague? That the earth has been . . . revised?"

She shrugs. "Guess that makes sense. Humans had their time and now . . . donezo."

"We're still here, though."

Her eyes slip up to meet his with a flat, inscrutable glare. A glare that asks, *Are we?*

Suddenly ashamed of all his gainsaying, he looks away. The words come out of his mouth before he can stop them:

"Hey. Who's the president?"

She sucks her teeth. Looks at him for a long time. "Jimmy Durante."

He nods, relieved at her obvious sarcasm. If she actually has a different answer than his, he doesn't want to know. Something about her cranberry bell-bottoms . . . Maybe they're not retro chic after all . . .

"Ha-cha-cha," he says in an exhausted monotone.

THE UNFORTUNATE CONVALESCENCE OF THE SUPERLAWYER

When he's finally able to sleep, his dreams are vivid and strange. Feverish, even.

A sky, glaringly white and yellow. Faces, masked, behind plastic, distorted, bulging, looming way too close.

His car, the detested Plymouth, still parked on the side of the road as he left it, only something's changed. The key chain. His dreamself swells forward. The embossed fob no longer reads SL, but AC. This troubles him, so he contracts back a little, and then time speeds up. Clouds whiz erratically across the sky. A jackrabbit finds shelter under the car. A white-tailed deer pokes its snout at the chrome. Birds land on the roof, report their inscrutable bulletins to the world. And a limping man, held up by a much larger man with a child's face and followed by a shaggy, auburn dog, approaches the vehicle.

Ezra feels a sort of peace, seeing them. *I'm here, too. I've contributed.* Then he remembers that keychain. *Except those aren't my initials. Those AREN'T my—*

Hands shake him awake.

"Hey," Susie whispers. "Hey, I need you. *Please.*"

She sounds close to panic. He comes to, groggy, but ready for anything. "Wuh?"

"I need you to see something. I need you to tell me I'm not going crazy."

We're all going crazy, he wants to say. He focuses on swallowing instead. His throat feels sore. Intubated.

He follows her to the gift shop. It's barely a room, let alone a shop. More like a nook of the first floor, where some maps and picture books and key chains are displayed.

Outside, the patter of dripping rain. The storm has passed.

Susie is rambling nervously.

"You kept muttering in your sleep," she explains as they walk over, "and it was creeping me out, so I started pacing around. Found myself over here, looking at all this crap, thinking about how useless all this was with no one around to buy it, but maybe that makes it more useful than ever because it's a snapshot of how things used to be—and then I looked up and—"

She points a finger to one side of the room, next to some sweatshirts that read UTAH. Her finger is trembling.

There's a door there.

A dark, rich, mahogany door. Completely out of place.

If his throat weren't already dry . . .

"Do you see it?" She asks. Begs. "Do you really see it?"

"0-385-12991-2," he reads aloud. Not the same numbers on his drawing . . . but the same format. "What does that mean?"

She says she doesn't know. Her voice shakes.

The earth does, too. Faintly. Tremors beginning again? Or maybe that's just his legs.

"What do we do?" She whispers. "Do I . . . open it?"

No, he wants to scream. *Don't you dare!*

Instead, quietly: "You sure this wasn't already here?"

"I'm not sure of anything."

He wills himself to be bold. "I'll try," he says, then marches over and yanks on the shining brass knob.

It doesn't open.

"Fake," he says. Satisfied and relieved. "Probably just some extra door somebody left here. Or—"

He notices etchings in the knob's surface. A hand covered in eyeballs. He recoils.

"What?" She asks, coming closer.

"Nothing." Wiping his own hand on his pants leg.

"Do you feel that, though? It's like . . . warmth?" She reaches out, stirs the air in front of the door. "Almost feels like there's a fire on the other side or something. And do you smell—"

Before he can stop her, she touches the wood.

The door swings inward with great force. Like an airplane door midflight.

THE UNFORTUNATE CONVALESCENCE OF THE SUPERLAWYER

For the briefest of instants, Ezra sees what looks like a beach on the other side. A bonfire. The smell of meat burning. Then Susie is sucked through without even time enough to scream, and the door slams shut.

Just like that. She's gone.

Ezra screams for her.

"No! NO!"

He yanks on the door. It's cold to the touch. Solid as rock.

Don't leave me here alone with the crazies. No!

He continues shouting apologies, pleas for her to come back, but soon his voice is overtaken by the sound of cracking wood and concrete.

The earthquakes have begun again. With a vengeance.

He runs, narrowly avoiding falling light fixtures and crumbling walls. The building is collapsing in on itself.

Next thing he knows, he's outside in the moonlight. Running through the park. The trees, the natural splendor, all of it bucking and churning, glistening with the recent rain, spotlit by a giant moon that's almost as bright as the sun.

"No," he keeps repeating. "No, no, no. Stop this!"

A door, he understands with sudden and horrible clarity. *That's my only way out of here. There must be a door for* me *somewhere, too. Otherwise—*

A massive line of trees snaps and buckles. Fall into what appears to be a widening mouth in the ground somewhere behind him.

"NO!" he shouts, running deeper into the park. Uphill. Using other trees to propel him as fast as he can move through darkness and unsteady terrain.

Hard to breathe. Throat tight and swollen. He has to spit to keep his mouth from filling up with salty mucous.

And that mystery noise. So loud out here in the parklands. So loud he can make out defining details within it. Beeping. Wheezing. So loud he can finally hear where it's coming from.

It's coming from the moon. That awful, unnaturally bright moon.

At last, he comes upon a granite cliffside. He scrambles up as high as he can, shirt pulling out of his pants, clothes smearing with mud, until he finds a stable-feeling nook that can hold him.

He looks down at the parklands.

About two football fields away, there's a jagged slash running through all he can see. On the opposite side of that slash . . .

He gasps, horrified.

Nothing.

No trees. No earth. No stars. Unquestionable, capital-*N* Nothingness. Pure. Awful in its lack. Reverent in its completeness.

Just the night, that's all! It's just dark over there! I've survived. I'VE SURVIVED.

"Why exactly are you running?"

His head whips up and to the right.

Tom Bombadil—the not–Tom Bombadil—sits astride a fly the size of a Shetland pony hovering in the night air. Its wings whir. Its many eyes observe Ezra with disinterest. Ezra notices its round, loathsome body is covered in black crow feathers. Tom strokes the fly's head.

"I told you," Bombadil continues. "You can't fight this. It's beyond your control and you're just making it harder on yourself. There's been a revision. A rewrite. You simply didn't make the cut. It's nothing personal."

"None of that makes any sense!" Ezra is gasping. "This isn't right!"

"Look up at the moon if you really want answers, friend."

Those excruciating noises. Beeping. Coughing. Screaming. Wailing.

Ezra makes sure to *not* look. He keeps his eyes on Tom. Awful Tom. His yellow trench coat like a smear of irradiated French's mustard against the night.

"Where's my door?" Ezra moans. "Please?! Don't I get one, too?"

THE UNFORTUNATE CONVALESCENCE OF THE SUPERLAWYER

"Not everyone gets a door. Not everyone's canonical."

The sky begins to change colors. Checkerboard patterns of bright, impossible neon.

Down below, untouched by the bright, the splintering, shattering Nothingness creeps closer.

Bombadil continues, arms spreading wide.

"Not every tower stands! Most crumble unnoticed! There's no shame in being erased! There's no shame in being Another Corpse! Anonymous Creation! Accidental Character!"

The earth bucks harder and harder. Rocks separate from their granite perch and skitter down the cliff.

"It's never fair!" Bobmadil proclaims. "Oh, Discordia! To which Discordia replies, 'No great loss!'"

The garish multicolor of the sky is as bright as fireworks, affording Ezra the ability to watch as Tom's skin glistens and inflates. His neck loses definition under a glottal bulge. Purulent sores erupt and leak white, curdling spray. No, not spray. Maggots. Squirming out of his wounds, squeezing out of his eyes and wriggling down his cheeks. He smiles widely and more maggots spill out over his teeth like wormy porridge.

The fly's wings drill into the air—joining the cacophony of the earth collapsing below, the sounds coming from the moon.

"No great loss! The clock is red! This is nine! Nine! All of your friends are dead!"

He's not the real Tom Bombadil, Ezra realizes. It feels like his own skin is on fire. *Tom was kind. Ambivalent, but kind. This is some mad demon tormenting a dying world. He won't help me.*

Not-Tom's flesh continues to slough and liquify. Maggots, centipedes, thick and greedy leeches pour out of widening fistulas.

"Oh, Discordia! The clock is red!"

All I've got is myself. Myself and . . . and SuperLawyer!

Ezra begins to laugh dementedly. *Yes! We can litigate anything! Even the end of the world!*

Tom joins him in the mad laughter. "Ezra's ensō is donezo! There's been a rewrite! The King is in his counting house! He found enough glue, but not for you!"

"I'm not going to be erased," Ezra manages. Even though his voice is barely audible under all the other thundering noises. "I'm going to live!"

"Say hellogoodbye to the Beast!" Tom shrieks. "He got the write-out, too! You say why and I say I don't know, oh no!"

Ezra throws himself onto the ground and, in the mud and dirt, draws a door with his finger. It's been a long time since he's drawn anything and the world is bucking and shivering, so it's not the best-looking door, but it gets the job done. It tells the story.

"I have a door now, okay?! Let me out of here!"

Tears streaking down his cheeks, he finally steals a look at the moon. It's a bright light. Like the kind that hangs over a surgery table. A gigantic faceless figure leans into the light, observing him. Electronic beeping and wheezing drown the world. The light swells, like his throat.

No time!

The world crumbles all around him. Swallowed into the Nothingness eating through the base of his granite safehold. He closes his eyes and tries to grip the door handle he sketched in the ground. Perhaps it's the final wish of a doomed man, but he swears he feels *something* in his hand. He twists . . . pulls . . .

It won't open. The door won't open!

Then he remembers his father's voice.

A second chance.

He kneels down, pulls the folded drawing from his jacket pocket, and, refusing to let the earth shake him loose, writes the numbers from his dream onto the door.

978-1-66805-7551

THE UNFORTUNATE CONVALESCENCE OF THE SUPERLAWYER

"I *OBJECT* TO THIS MADNESS!" he screams in triumph once he's finished. "YOU HEAR ME?! I *OBJECT*! I WILL LIVE!" He grabs hold of the knob once more. "I AM LIFE ITSELF AND I OBJ—"

———

With an all-too-familiar wet rattle, the patient on the gurney spasmed and stilled.

Dr. Alvin Carhart barely noticed the deaths by this point. There were so many, happening so quickly, even in this small hospital in Green River, Utah. And yet, for some reason, this one caught his attention. This patient really had seemed to rally for a moment there.

Under the harsh fluorescent lights, Dr. Carhart stared down at the swollen, mucus-encrusted body and wondered: *What goes through the mind as it dies?*

This was followed by a much more unpleasant thought: *Probably find out myself soon enough.*

Dr. Carhart folded that thought and tucked it away with a professional's economy.

There were ten other bodies, hacking and gasping, in this room alone. Ventilators (for the few who'd had time to be hooked up) wheezing. Heart monitors beeping erratically. They all needed tending to. Even if it felt like trying to fight a forest fire with a squirt gun.

Still, he stood and regarded the just-expired patient for a moment longer. Due to the constant stream of bodies—and he felt horrible reprimanding that ambulance driver for stopping to pick this hopeless case off the side of the highway—they'd taken to writing the patients' initials on the backs of their hands for ease of identification. Dr. Carhart noticed with a grimace that the patient had the same initials as his own.

Despite the sweltering fever-heat of the room, he shivered. Elsewhere in the room, a fly buzzed.

Apocalyptic Conditions, he thought. *All Cadavers.*
That's just stupid thinking. Going against his training.
Keep your head down.
Ignore the scratch in your throat.
Ignore the swelling in your lymph nodes.
It's just stress.
You're just stressed.
Keep going.
You can survive this.

The doctor cleared his throat, wiped at his clammy brow, and moved onto the next patient, hoping this one might be a different story.

―――

[*Author's note: in the original published edition of* The Stand, *Stu, Tom, and Kojak find rescue in a Plymouth with a key chain bearing the initials "SL." Stu muses about what might've happened to the driver, but there are no answers. The same thing happens in the unabridged edition, except that key chain now reads "AC." Despite all the additions and restorations of* The Stand: Complete and Uncut, *poor SL was removed from the narrative. We must assume, then, it was no great loss. Oh, Discordia.*]

WALK ON GILDED SPLINTERS
David J. Schow

SOOTH

Barker was already awake. He could do that weird dog thing, sleeping with his eyes partially open, white sclera the buffer for an alertness never totally relaxed. He snapped into the here and now with that amazing sniffer of his already testing the air for threat.

Trick Baby stirred the embers of the scat fire and shared out what was left of the jerky. If lucky, she might arrow a bunny today. If not, she and the dog would have to go grubbing or worse, eating those crunchy, bitter insects so awful they had no names beyond flix, chudders, or shitbugs.

She could almost remember a time when waking up could be a luxury—the time squandered floating to the surface of wakefulness itself an indulgence—as opposed to opening your eyes in mid-rape. She'd bartered sex for food or shelter before, like everyone, and fought her way through or past other encounters that were unavoidable. It was always rape either way.

No clocks. No matter what time it was supposed to be by antique measures, the sky vacillated in its spectrum from mud to zinc and back again, monotonously. The sun stayed low, near the horizon, usually hiding. Clouds massed and there was hail and lightning and sometimes roils of virulent color like flames that hold still. Almost beautiful, were they not the harbingers of acid sleet that stung the skin and could blind. You had to call them clouds because nothing else fit; never white, never billowy, not known to "scud." Shelter was never unimportant, but Trick Baby had learned the huddle-cuddle for when there were zero options and no escape time. She balled up with Barker, his nose right under her chin, and suffered the damage to any exposed flesh, to spare the dog. Her fried skin usually healed, given time. But lose your sight and you were gone, gone. Raped a thousand more times and then eaten, picked clean alongside the bones of your dog.

Even if she possessed a compass, it would not work among the strange energies. She knew she had to go over the mountains of the moon and down the valley of the shadow. Children had to learn to walk through fire, fly through smoke. Her purpose pointed her; she had a tale to tell. Nothing else mattered, or occurred.

Trick Baby was an excellent archer. She was this-many years old. Barker cautioned her against most hairy situations. A day without rape was a good day; a day without puking your guts out from gnarly food was an excellent day. Pregnancy was rarely a hindrance. As Trick Baby had seen, most of *those* girls died or gave birth to things with too many teeth and not enough eyes, things that dribbled out in pieces or never learned to breathe.

So, what was her purpose?

Long ago, her mother had told her about the Monk. Not her actual mother, but her Other-Mother. The woman who had birthed Trick Baby (allegedly) had briefly enjoyed the miracle of her child's wholeness; after that she hadn't been so lucky. Other-Mother was the one with the story, which she had learned from an Another Mother who preceded her. The story had to find its way to Lewis the Monk, and for telling the tale, Trick Baby might be anointed as a sooth. Then maybe the Monk would tell her what came next.

WALK ON GILDED SPLINTERS

He was called Lewis the Monk because there were other monks, false ones. Holier-than-thou monks that could keep you from reaching the next thing you had to do if you didn't die. Other-Mother had been mildly curious about "after." Nobody lived long, leaving scant time for daydreaming.

Trick Baby was much more interested in "after."

If she made it that far. If not, there was no one, no further link in the chain that went back a very long time. She needed every resource she could muster. You learned how to smell things that were about to happen. You learned the gut twinge that told you not to eat those berries. Which mushrooms could cure your headache or make you shit blood. Which rat pack might share food versus more rape, although most often this was the same thing.

Barker didn't like that.

So, he slept with his eyes open. One eye on Trick Baby, one eye on the perimeter. Barker would go for the throat, the balls, the fingers. It was how Trick Baby had won the big *khukuri* blade strapped to her hip. There was a notch near the handle shaped like the footprint of a cow, rumored to forbid the use of the blade against sacred animals, although Trick Baby had never experienced any preternormal consequences worth noting. She sharpened it every day on whatever shards of concrete she encountered. She also carved and fletched her own arrows. Bamboo was rare, but she preferred it.

Her first bow had been won from an assailant. Her next, she constructed herself after examining the remains of the first.

Kill, eat, hole up, walk on. She had heard warnings and myths and even minor legends. She understood fable on a cellular level, but was incapable of forming a parable. A story, though, could be repeated. The story ran that the Monk might give her a new purpose once she had honored her present one. It tempted, it beckoned.

If true, that would be bumpity—another collision of syllables Trick Baby could barely fathom, but she knew that it meant good.

PUMPS

Lewis the Monk was vexed by a word, and the word was *pumps*.

He remembered the way his stylus had hovered in his hand over the sheet of treated leather. So much of his internal spirit level relied on his ability to define and interpret, the fundaments of his calling as a sage. It had taken a huge chunk of chronostratigraphy to logic out what *paper* might have been. The plagues were a given. The Kingdom had not been decimated by an angry supernatural spirit so much as the overcrush of its own populace—too many grounders squabbling over limited space and food. Wars had been engaged long ago and the herd had been thinned. The Changed Air encouraged new plagues, and one of these maladies was said to have consumed all the *paper* on the planet. It had all decomposed to black goo about the same time the Digital Pearl Harbor destroyed the electronic record.

Maddeningly opaque words. Lewis was still trying to figure them out.

What written graphic record existed in the Archivum Sycorax was essentially tattooed on leather sheets. The Book of Red Men had traditionally conferred huge meaning and portent onto this word, *pumps*. They needed to be deactivated via ritual or vast harm would result. But was it imminent harm, or was the passage an allegory, meant to illustrate the eternal dichotomy—yin or yang, evil or good, dark or light, flag or boulder?

The planet was much hotter now.

Sooth was said to equal "in truth." Hence, soothsayers related stories you hoped were true. The Book had always been incomplete. Flawed through centuries of misdirection and erroneous data. So much of the Monk's compass had to reside in his gut feelings. Too much. Every day he stared down the vast gulf of storytelling, the difference between "a version" and *the* version that might stand for all of subsequent history. Was he committed to his sense of moral rightness, or victimized by his own admittedly seductive charter of absolute authority?

Did the divinity of sacred texts allow for revision? Potential sacrilege, there.

Monk Philip visited to proffer a brand-new invent.

Monk Lewis rubbed the substance between his fingertips. "What is it?"

Philip beamed his gap-toothed grin. "Mulberry bark, mixed with hemp and garment rags and worn-out fishing nets, mashed into a pulp. Then we squeezed out the water and let it dry in the sun. It works with sedge plants, too. See? You can mark it with charcoal, or soot mixed with animal fat."

Monk Lewis's entire universe changed in a brilliant flash of light. "Paper," he said.

That had happened ten years ago, and he had been collating ever since.

TRASH

In the beginning, there was the Book. Scholars and acolytes devoted decades to plumbing its mysteries and deciphering its portent. All answers were said to be contained within the Book, including the keys to defeating the *tenebris pestilentia*. Subsects were birthed; they waxed, then guttered over more years. The Nigrum pandemic was smarter and had all the time in the world. It waxed, then mutated, being much better at self-perpetuation than its human food. Those who survived and reproduced in dwindling numbers were left to seek salvation in sacred texts. Perhaps they had read it wrong, or not recognized the obvious signs, context, clues, codes.

The Book was said to be everything, the tale entire, the revealed truth.

No one had any real clue how the Book had first come to be recorded for others to ponder. It had been so many years since most teachers could actually read. More still, for extrapolation (another word Trick Baby did not know).

Yet words were the most permanent thing Trick Baby had, and her recital always started the same way:

"Uncounted were the days until Trash was born in shock-lightning and kerosene . . . "

She repeated it, rehearsed it, or parts of it, dozens of times per day. In whispers. Out loud. Silently, to her inmost self. The words she carried were part of her metabolism.

Necessity had required her to consider many variants of the story she heard at one time or another, if only so they could be ranked or dismissed. She had to be the expert. Corruption, pollution had to be expunged for the life lesson to remain clear. Interpretations had to be weighed and factored.

One version of the story Trick Baby had heard went like this:

The kinship flashpoint was rape, mostly prison-style (whatever that meant), but similarly to most saints, Trash had been born to burn. Often terrorized and beleaguered, Trash experienced a genuine miracle that confirmed his Path, and a savior to consecrate his incipient chosen status as a true Darling of Destiny (per the requisites set forth in the Second Book of Wendell). According to the narrative, his tormentors died all around him. Once he arsonized the false horizon of Powtanville, his true horizon revealed itself, and it's name was Cibola.

The mantra: *MyLif4U.*

But Paradise has to be earned, and in religious terms that always means misguidance, tests of mettle, obstacles and vexations. Principal among these were variant interpretations of previous writ; the longer they were told and retold, the more the fellowships and followers doubted them. Presently the saga of Trash had been divested of a lengthy apocrypha titled the Rebel Yell Epistles 1–17. True believers denied the authorship of the Epistles (and Trick Baby knew that if you stood still when one of them started talking, they'd never stop until they died or you did).

Trick Baby didn't believe in destiny. She believed in opportunity.

Yet after so long on the hunt, the activity itself nagged at her with the sense that it had all been done before. Details were altered every time while the template remained the same shape. She was water, flowing along a groove that was preordained and immutable from its previous form. It *never* changed. Were there more abstract thinkers, this avenue of inquiry might lead to speculation about predictable outcome, but while Trick Baby was capable of experiencing a complex thought, she could not acknowledge it as such. Trick Baby only wanted to know what came next.

The way you want to with most stories.

She knew the story because she had been told it thousands of times as a child. Her quest was to reach Lewis the Monk, tell what she knew, and then . . . ?

What was most important? The covenant. The quest. The trials. The wolves.

Wolves were good, though, in the telling. Protectors, like Barker. Perhaps there was a Nite Club at the end of the line. Trick Baby wondered what a Nite Club might be. A place where she might sing to the wolves; tell them she was home at last?

"*Uncounted were the days until Trash was born . . .*"

Barker sniffed the air and sought the horizon, ears flattening. Bad was incoming.

A lot more bad.

SIGIL

The bad began with the sigil. Found in a bad place, at a bad time. Midway through a barren tract of rolling hills some called the City of Millionaires (again, a coinage that held no meaning for most), Trick Baby found the sigil carved high up on a rock face, blackened by foul weather. Supposedly, it had always been there.

Barker didn't notice it, or didn't care. His snoot was testing the air for threat.

In every tale ever told, seekers sought "a sign." It was presumed to be obvious, such a sign, a true north swing that Showed the Path. In the hardscrabble reality of predatory jungle survival there were very few signs that did not involve your own imminent death—like, bleeding out was a *sign* you didn't have long and had better hustle, pronto.

Yet here before Trick Baby was a Sign such as she had always heard of.

It was near to a child's drawing of the sun, a rough circle with spikes coming out of it. Its purpose was to guide her to the Monk. The spikes were squiggles, legendarily "like fire that holds still."

But subsuming the symbol were other designs, chaotic, layered graffiti that proclaimed this zone to be the turf of the Kids. Infamously tribal, gratuitously violent, and completely psychopathic, the Kids were to be avoided—always. Yet the way to the Monk was through their outlands.

Barker cast a wary glance. *You sure?*

Trick Baby nodded silently. *Sure as sure.*

This was the place from which the disavowed Kid Epistles had sprung. Everything around her could be a trap, another falsehood.

Early snowfall had leavened the aspens and evergreens to uniformity. (No one remembered what this foliage was called; it needed new names.) Keep eyes keen and ears keener. Trick Baby stepped heel-to-toe to muffle her own tread.

Suddenly so quiet, so unexpectedly beautiful in its harsh way. Maybe this was the goal of the quest, such calm.

The Kids attacked at civil dusk.

Barker yelped and flew up into the air, clipped by a sharpened stone launched from a sling. He went down bright with blood and had trouble trying to find his legs. Another silent stone skinned a flap from Trick Baby's forehead and she rolled as blood clouded her vision. A short arrow splintered on a rock next to her head. It was black; you couldn't see black arrows incoming. Halfway through her duck-and-shield roll, Trick Baby had already notched her return shot and let fly. The vector was a touch and tell thing, not ploddingly logical or strategic, but obvious to her senses. She was pleased to hear somebody scream.

Dark blood flowered on Barker's flank. He snapped when Trick Baby met his gaze, teeth clicking. *Three more*, the clicks told her.

She had already come to her knees and loosed another shot. Half-visible like that, the fleet risk of exposure to return fire would quickly let her know how heavily armed her assailants were. Mostly stones meant fewer arrows for them to waste. Fewer arrows meant they would have to draw closer to her position.

Mostly stones thudded against her outer gear.

Barker was gone, on the hunker. Out of her sight for only a moment when a different voice started hollering as the dog shredded off testicles.

Two more.

One comrade would attempt to kill the dog killing another comrade. He rose to full height with an ugly blade upraised. A dramatic, frightening silhouette; a perfect target. Trick Baby's next arrow took him right through the skull.

And *wham*, Trick Baby was tackled and sprawled.

Last one.

He would try to hold her down by the arms and smash her face in, then fuck her while she was still warm, corpse or not. Trick Baby's *gurkha* provided her with more than ten extra inches of reach, and she caught him right across the voice box. In less than a second his crimson life force began to flood downward, drenching her. His grip went stupid. Before the full second had elapsed, Barker was back to chomp the gap wide and take the motherfucker to ground.

Trick Baby performed a quick patch-up, first on her dog, then on her own temple. She shredded the Kids' rags for dressings. Barker ate.

The Kids were darkened with battle ink, a crowded profusion of tattoos that bespoke the madhouse history of each—hierarchies, fables, legends, symbols. Kill hash. Images of weapons and monsters, virulent splashes of illustrated blood or dismembered adversaries. Incomprehensible, somehow *angry* cartoons of vehicles, obsolete firearms, or highway signs (as they were once known).

A blue triangle. *"61."* Trick Baby shook her head, mystified.

She wondered more often, these days. Right now she wondered if the dermagraphics spilled across each of the Kids might unify into some sort of larger myth, like chapters of a tale to be told only when fully revealed. Like the piece of an entirely different story that she carried to the Monk. If each Kid were a segment, or episode. If that's what bonded them.

Or if her story and the Kids' story were the *same* story, a saga whose linkage could only be divulged by the Monk, who of course would have known all along.

The only surviving Kid of the pack—the first one felled by Trick Baby's arrow—bore the sigil. She spun him over and staked him for a better look as night fell. A fire was too risky out here. He husked air and didn't whine. The scraggly little cartoon sun had been embossed on his neck using lampblack and a rose thorn.

They were all out in the open when it began to rain. The rain stung. Trick Baby grabbed Barker and did the huddle-cuddle, tenting him.

Over the next hour, the Kid bled a lot more, but Trick Baby only asked him a single question, over and over.

"Which way?"

DAYSTAR

The beauty of religious mania is that it explains everything. Nothing is left to chance . . . or change. Once such incantatory phrases as "we see now through a glass darkly" and "mysterious are the ways She chooses Her wonders to perform" are mastered, logic can happily be tossed out the window. Religious mania is

WALK ON GILDED SPLINTERS

one of the few infallible ways of responding to the world's vagaries, because it totally eliminates pure accident. It's all on purpose.
  —From the Second Book of Wolves (recanted)

It was getting cold, portending the most brutal winter the Monk would yet know. He wanted to unfurl the hundreds of pages that were his lifework and wrap himself in them. Maybe burn them.

The story of one long-ago sooth, believed to be fifteen hundred years old, proposed that the Hand of God was not an actual event at all. Hearsay. Another ancient text known as the Gospel of the Abagailians had stirred up a lot of controversy before the Monk's time, with its unconventional—some said boastful—claims of supernatural power. The librarians, monks, and scholars of the Guilded Splendor spent much of their lives in heated debate that would determine religious authority. Skepticism reigned and every interpretation had its champion, because if a supplicant might be right, they would achieve immortality. Last week's true believers were often next week's unsettled "doubting Frannie."

The Monk was blessed with larger vision. Squabbling, quibbling, hairsplitting would win them more mountains of ungraspable vapor. What was primarily required was to get a string around the entire narrative, to solidify the whole form of the sundered and scattered parts. Then, *then* the educated forensics could matter so much more.

The daystar, a spiky yellow puffball that may have started out as a cactus, had come along after the End, when the sky was no longer blue; when the air changed, the light changed, and the plants under their dominion also evolved and changed, some say mutated. The Order had named the symbolic representation of the daystar the Guilded Splendor. It reminded the Order to consider all explanations, not merely the easy or fearful ones.

Most of all, the Guilded Splendor represented sanctuary.

And a signpost: The End.

Because once a sooth had decanted their part of the whole to the Monk, they had fulfilled their purpose. They could repeat the same data to strangers for the rest of time—spreading the word was always good—but their primary covenant in establishing the definitive text had been honored. The recitation had more value if the book was lost, banned, or burned.

Until the text itself morphed again, and that would not happen within the Monk's lifetime.

These were his thoughts as Trick Baby was escorted into his presence.

After you've served your purpose, what do I tell you to do then?

Dozens of past sooths had stood where Trick Baby stood now.

Your reward for your faith is obsolescence.

Her wounds were somehow more lurid when cleaned up. Her carriage was somehow more pathetic when she was properly fed. A child without a childhood, her stringy ragamuffin persistence only made sense out there in the crazylands. Like so many before her, she had been told to seek out the Monk.

I wish I could actually help you.

Trick Baby began to recite:

"Uncounted were the days until Trash was born in shock-lightning and kerosene, alone as the undisputed master of Powtanville. He knew the voices and the voices spoke true. Fire could not burn him, nor cheery lobster-red explosions. His power and birthright were a glorious blaze of spontaneous combustion, and he laid his hand upon the great axle of his destiny . . . "

She left out most of the rapey bits.

LOVE

At Trick Baby's grave under the shadow of the Guilded Splendor, Barker has the watch. He is fed by monks of the Order when he deigns to eat. He still has a slight limp, and will have it until he dies. Now he can close his eyes, but he won't. He will not abandon his post, nor drop his guard. *MyLife4U.*

Thanks to him, Trick Baby is safe at last.

THE VULGATE BOOK

In the accounts told years later about the Kingdom, the following claims were made:

The Received Written Gospel was theorized to have originated from seventy sooths (the number always varied), recorded on every continent in eight separate languages over a span of eleven-hundred years. The recount and recollect of these assorted laypeople, scholars, commoners, and even nobility has been freely acknowledged to be "spiritually influenced."

That is, informed by ghosts.

The modern and most up-to-date version of the Vulgate Book is over a thousand pages long.

Among the five deuterocanonical versions of the text are three so-called "eden dates," or ground-zero genesis markers, with a ten-year spread between them. Insignificant . . . until you are told, for example, that you were born that many years earlier or later than you have always believed. Unless the repetitive, five-year constancy freights new wisdom yet-untranslated. Scholars and penitents debate the disparities to this day.

Accounting for variant sects, there are between seventy-nine and a hundred thirty-one thus-called "books" that comprise the Kingdom, beginning with *Arnett: 1–7* and concluding with *Second Bate Mans*, or in some editions, the cryptic *PayDay*.

There are missing books, some removed throughout the years by clashing authorities. *First and Second Campions* are the most controversial, but other discredited or disallowed sections such as the *Book of Trash* remain of interest to legitimate deep-dive academics and enthusiasts.

Nowhere in the complex mythos can be found the name of Lewis the Monk.

AFTERWORD
Brian Keene

And there you have it, Constant Readers.

(Am I allowed to call you that? I'm not sure what the rules are. Is Stephen King the only one who can address us as such? I don't know, and I'm not gonna ask him, because he's got enough on his plate and I don't need to add to it. Command decision—I'm gonna go for it, because I am one of you. Solidarity. But I digress . . .)

And there you have it, Constant Readers.

Glimpses of what else was happening in the world of *The Stand*, and some possible futures, as well. With that, we come to The End. And we all know what happens then. As the novel tells us, life is such a wheel that no one can stand upon it for long, and it always, in the end, comes round to the same place again.

I was thirteen years old when I first read *The Stand*. That was the abridged paperback edition that came out in 1980. I reread it every year after that, and when the uncut edition was finally released in 1990, I would reread that version every year since then. There are only a handful of books I hold in this regard: *The Magic Wagon* and *The Drive-In* (both by Joe R. Lansdale), Hunter S. Thompson's *The Rum*

Diary, and Mark Twain's *Tom Sawyer* and *Huckleberry Finn*. That's it. I've read each of them easily more than two dozen times, but only *The Stand* gets the annual reread for the past forty-three years.

I know Stu, Frannie, and the rest better than I know many of my friends. My favorite characters have changed over the years. As a young man, I had an intimate understanding of Larry, but these days it's Glen and the Judge that I am most drawn to. I read *The Stand* during a month of in-school detention. I read it through several bad breakups and two divorces. At age sixteen, it got me through being bedridden for a month with a case of chicken pox that would have made Jordy Verrill blanch. I read it on board a ship during my stint in the navy, out there in the deep and encompassing darkness of the ocean, when home seemed so far away. I read it through a brief stint in county. Through lunch breaks and bedtimes. With morning coffee and evening bourbon (or these days, evening iced tea). A few years ago, when I suffered second- and third-degree burns (the worst was on my elbow that left bone exposed), my wife, author Mary SanGiovanni, brought three things to the burn ward to keep me company during recovery: a Moleskine notebook, a pen, and my battered old book club edition hardcover of *The Stand*. I reread it again in preparation for editing this anthology.

The Stand is that wheel, for me, and in the end, I always come back to the beginning. And thus, renew the journey with the same tenacity as Roland the gunslinger following the man in black across that endless desert of Eternal Return. I'll bet it's that way for many of you, as well. And next year, when we reread it once more, we can now extend that journey just a little bit longer with this companion to the novel.

It is my honor to have played a part in making that happen for all of you. I've always said that I was a fan of this genre long before people ever started paying me money to be a part of it. And I'll still be a fan long after I'm able to write my last word or come up with my final story idea. Working in this field has brought me many high-water marks.

AFTERWORD

It has given me dear friends like coeditor Christopher Golden. It has allowed me to provide for my family and loved ones. It has allowed me to meet and work with personal heroes like George Romero, F. Paul Wilson, Jack Ketchum, J. M. DeMatteis, Keith Giffen, and the aforementioned Joe R. Lansdale. It has saved my life on more than one occasion. But this? This anthology? *This* was the highest of the high-water marks. Thank you, Stephen, for trusting Chris and me with it. Thanks to all of the writers for bringing their A-games. And thank you, fellow Constant Readers, for coming along with us.

We've come round now to the end.

See you back at the beginning.

ACKNOWLEDGMENTS

Christopher Golden and Brian Keene would like to thank:

Stephen King, Liz Darhansoff, Ed Schlesinger, Howard Morhaim, Caspian Dennis, Heather Baror, and all our contributors. M-O-O-N, that spells "grateful."

Thanks also to:

Connie Golden, Mary SanGiovanni, and all our kids. M-O-O-N also spells "love." Laws yes.

ABOUT THE AUTHORS

STEPHEN KING is the author of more than sixty books, all of them worldwide bestsellers. His recent work includes *Never Flinch*, the short story collection *You Like It Darker*, *Holly* (a *New York Times* Notable Book of 2023), *Fairy Tale*, *Billy Summers*, *If It Bleeds*, *The Institute*, *Elevation*, *The Outsider*, *Sleeping Beauties* (cowritten with his son Owen King), and the Bill Hodges trilogy: *End of Watch*, *Finders Keepers*, and *Mr. Mercedes* (an Edgar Award winner for Best Novel and a television series streaming on Peacock). His novel *11/22/63* was named a top ten book of 2011 by the *New York Times Book Review* and won the Los Angeles Times Book Prize for Mystery/Thriller. His epic works *The Dark Tower*, *It*, *Pet Sematary*, *Doctor Sleep*, and *Firestarter* are the basis for major motion pictures, with *It* now the highest-grossing horror film of all time. He is the recipient of the 2020 Audio Publishers Association Lifetime Achievement Award, the 2018 PEN America Literary Service Award, the 2014 National Medal of Arts, and the 2003 National Book Foundation Medal for Distinguished Contribution to American Letters. He lives in Bangor, Maine, with his wife, novelist Tabitha King.

STEVEN BARNES is the *New York Times* bestselling author of more than thirty novels of science fiction, horror, and suspense. The Image, Endeavor, and Cable-Ace Award–winning author also writes for television, including the 1980s' *The Twilight Zone*, *Star-*

ABOUT THE AUTHORS

gate *SG-1*, *Andromeda*, and an Emmy Award–winning episode of *The Outer Limits*. He has been guest of honor at the world's most prestigious science-fiction conventions. Most recently he wrote for Jordan Peele's *The Twilight Zone* revival and Shudder's *Horror Noire* anthology. Steven was born in Los Angeles, and, except for a decade in the Northwest and three years in Atlanta, has lived in that area all his life. Steve and his wife, bestselling author Tananarive Due, live with their son, Jason, in Upland, California. Visit him at steven-barnes.com.

Multiple Emmy Award–winning and Grammy Award–nominated **WAYNE BRADY** has made his mark on stage and screen as an actor, producer, singer, dancer, songwriter, and television personality. A five-time Emmy winner, Brady has an impressive TV résumé that includes *Whose Line Is It Anyway?*, *How I Met Your Mother*, *The Masked Singer*, *Dancing with the Stars*, *Black Lightning*, *The Good Fight*, and *American Gigolo*. He's the host and executive producer for *Let's Make a Deal*. Recently, Brady returned to Broadway in the titular role of *The Wiz*.

POPPY Z. BRITE is the longtime pen name of Billy Martin. Since beginning his career with the small-press magazine *The Horror Show* in 1985, he has published eight novels, including *Lost Souls*, *Exquisite Corpse*, and the *Liquor* series, as well as several short story collections and assorted nonfiction work. Brite is also the editor of the erotic horror anthologies *Love in Vein* and *Twice Bitten: Love in Vein II*. He has recently completed *Water if God Wills It*, a nonfiction book about religion and spirituality in the works of Stephen King. In addition to writing, he runs the online curio shop PZBaubles New Orleans, specializing in vintage Tarot cards, quirky jewelry, religious objects, and more. He lives in New Orleans with his husband, the artist Grey Cross, and their cats. Some of his work may be found at patreon.com/docbrite.

ABOUT THE AUTHORS

An accidental teacher, an accidental librarian, and a purposeful community Afrofuturist, **MAURICE BROADDUS** has had more than a hundred short fiction pieces published in places such as *Lightspeed Magazine, Beneath Ceaseless Skies, Weird Tales, Asimov's,* and *Uncanny Magazine*. Some of his stories have been collected in *The Voices of Martyrs*. His novels include the urban fantasy trilogy *The Knights of Breton Court*, the award-winning steampunk books *Buffalo Soldier* and *Pimp My Airship*, the SF novels *Sweep of Stars* and *Breath of Oblivion*, and the middle-grade detective novels *The Usual Suspects* and *Unfadeable*. Learn more about him at mauricebroaddus.com.

SOMER CANON is the Imadjinn Award–winning and Splatterpunk Award–nominated author of works such as *The Hag Witch of Tripp Creek* and *You're Mine*. When she's not wreaking havoc in her minivan, she's avoiding her neighbors and consuming all things horror. She has two sons and more cats than her husband agreed to have.

C. ROBERT CARGILL is a Bram Stoker Award–winning screenwriter, Arthur C. Clarke Award–shortlisted novelist, and former film critic known for his movies *Sinister, The Black Phone,* and *Doctor Strange*, as well as his books *Sea of Rust, Day Zero,* and *We Are Where the Nightmares Go*. He lives and works in Austin, Texas.

NAT CASSIDY writes horror for the page, stage, and screen. He was named one of the "writers shaping horror's next golden age" by *Esquire*, and his novels, including *Mary: An Awakening of Terror* and *Nestlings*, have been featured in best-of lists from *Harper's Bazaar, Esquire, The Chicago Review of Books*, NPR, the New York Public Library, Amazon, and more. His award-winning horror plays have been produced across the country, including Off-Broadway and the Kennedy Center. You've also maybe seen Nat guest-starring on shows like *Law & Order: SVU, Blue Bloods, Bull, Quantico, FBI,* and many others . . . but that's a topic for a different bio. His newest novel with

ABOUT THE AUTHORS

Tor Nightfire, *When the Wolf Comes Home*, hit shelves in April 2025. Visit him at www.natcassidy.com

V. CASTRO is a two-time Bram Stoker Award–nominated Mexican-American writer from San Antonio, Texas, now residing in the UK. She writes horror, erotic horror, and science fiction. Her books include *The Haunting of Alejandra*, *Aliens: Vasquez*, *Mestiza Blood*, *The Queen of the Cicadas*, *Out of Aztlan*, *Las Posadas*, *Rebel Moon* (the official Netflix film novelization), and *Goddess of Filth*. Her forthcoming novel is *Immortal Pleasures* from Del Rey. Connect with Violet via Instagram and Twitter @vlatinalondon or vcastrostories.com. She can also be found on Blue Sky, Goodreads, Amazon, and TikTok@vcastrobooks.

RICHARD CHIZMAR is the coauthor (with Stephen King) of the *New York Times* bestselling novella *Gwendy's Button Box* and the novel *Gwendy's Final Task*, and the solo novella *Gwendy's Magic Feather*. Recent books include the *New York Times* bestsellers *Memorials*, *Becoming the Boogeyman*, and *Chasing the Boogeyman*, as well as *The Girl on the Porch*, *The Long Way Home*, his fourth short story collection, and *Widow's Point*, a chilling tale about a haunted lighthouse cowritten with his son Billy Chizmar, which was recently made into a feature film. His short fiction has appeared in dozens of publications, including *Ellery Queen Mystery Magazine* and *The Year's 25 Finest Crime and Mystery Stories*. He has won two World Fantasy awards, four International Horror Guild Awards, and the HWA's Board of Trustees Award. Chizmar's work has been translated into more than fifteen languages throughout the world, and he has appeared at numerous conferences as a writing instructor, speaker, panelist, and guest of honor. Follow him on Twitter @RichardChizmar, or visit his website at richardchizmar.com.

S. A. COSBY is an Anthony Award–winning writer from Southeastern Virginia. He is the author of the *New York Times* bestseller

ABOUT THE AUTHORS

Razorblade Tears and *Blacktop Wasteland*, which won the *Los Angeles Times* Book Prize, was a *New York Times* Notable Book, and was named a best book of the year by NPR, *The Guardian*, and *Library Journal*, among others. When not writing, he is an avid hiker and chess player.

TANANARIVE DUE is an American Book Award and NAACP Image Award–winning author, who was an executive producer on the documentary *Horror Noire: A History of Black Horror* for Shudder and teaches Afrofuturism and Black Horror at UCLA. Her novel *The Reformatory* won a Bram Stoker Award, a World Fantasy Award, a Shirley Jackson Award, and a Los Angeles Times Book Prize. She and her husband, science fiction author Steven Barnes, cowrote the graphic novel *The Keeper* and an episode for Season 2 of *The Twilight Zone* for Paramount+ and Monkeypaw Productions. Due is the author of several novels and two short story collections, *Ghost Summer: Stories* and *The Wishing Pool and Other Stories*. She is also coauthor (with her late mother, Patricia Stephens Due) of a civil rights memoir, *Freedom in the Family: A Mother-Daughter Memoir of the Fight for Civil Rights*. Learn more at tananarivedue.com.

MEG GARDINER is the #1 *New York Times* bestselling author of seventeen novels. Her thrillers have won the Edgar Award and been summer reading picks by *The Today Show* and *O, the Oprah Magazine*. In August 2022, *Heat 2*, co-authored with Michael Mann, debuted at #1 on the *New York Times* bestseller list. A former lawyer, two-time president of Mystery Writers of America, and three-time *Jeopardy!* champion, Gardiner lives in Austin, Texas.

CHRISTOPHER GOLDEN is the *New York Times* bestselling author of the novels *The House of Last Resort*, *The Night Birds*, *Road of Bones*, and the Stoker Award–winning *Ararat*, among many others. Golden co-created (with Mike Mignola) the fan-favorite comic book series

ABOUT THE AUTHORS

Baltimore and *Joe Golem: Occult Detective*. He has also written and co-written comic books, video games, screenplays, and the online animated series *Ghosts of Albion* (with Amber Benson). His work has been nominated for the British Fantasy Award, the Eisner Award, and multiple Shirley Jackson Awards. He has been nominated eleven times in eight different categories for the Bram Stoker Award, and has won twice. In 2023, Golden and Amber Benson co-wrote and co-directed the Audible Original podcast *Slayers: A Buffyverse Story*. Please visit him at christophergolden.com.

GABINO IGLESIAS is the author of the Shirley Jackson and Bram Stoker award-winning novel *The Devil Takes You Home*, as well as author of the critically acclaimed and award-winning novels *Zero Saints* and *Coyote Songs*. He is a writer, journalist, professor, and literary critic living in Austin, Texas, and a member of the Horror Writers Association, the Mystery Writers of America, and the National Book Critics Circle.

JONATHAN JANZ is a husband, father, author, screenwriter, and public schoolteacher. He's happy now, but when he was fourteen years old, he was lost: no self-esteem, convinced he was intellectually inferior, and slowly withdrawing from the world. Then he picked up a Stephen King novel, coincidentally one of King's least favorites (*The Tommyknockers*). During that life-altering summer, Stephen King's storytelling healed Jonathan. It showed him that books are a uniquely portable magic and that there are other worlds than these. It also taught him he wasn't unintelligent; he'd simply been reading the wrong books. Over the next three years, he devoured every King tale he could find and loved them all. And when he experienced *The Stand* as a junior in high school, he decided to write stories of his own. Jonathan remains a passionate Constant Reader to this day and wants to thank Mr. King for changing his life.

ABOUT THE AUTHORS

ALMA KATSU is the award-winning author of eight novels, including the historical horror novels *The Hunger*, *The Deep*, and *The Fervor*. Her story *The Wehrwolf* won the Bram Stoker Award for long fiction. She also writes spy fiction, drawing from a former career in intelligence, with the first thriller, *Red Widow*, named an Editor's Choice by *The New York Times* and Amazon. Her works have been named a Best Book by NPR, *The New York Times*, Apple, Amazon, Goodreads, and more. She is a contributing reviewer for *The Washington Post*. You can find out more at almakatsubooks.com.

BRIAN KEENE is the bestselling, multiple-award-winning author of more than forty books—mostly horror, fantasy, science fiction, and nonfiction—as well as more than two hundred short stories and dozens of comic books and graphic novels for Marvel, DC, and others. His first novel, 2003's *The Rising*, is often credited with renewing pop culture's interest in zombies. He also served as the showrunner for *Silverwood: The Door*. From 2015 to 2020, he hosted the immensely popular award-winning podcast *The Horror Show with Brian Keene*. He also serves on the board of directors for the Scares That Care, a 501(c) charity organization, which has to date raised more than $450,000 for sick children, burn victims, and women battling breast cancer. The father of two sons and one stepdaughter, he lives in rural Pennsylvania with his wife, author Mary SanGiovanni. The two co-own Vortex Books & Comics—a genre-specific brick-and-mortar bookstore. Please visit him at BrianKeene.com.

CAROLINE KEPNES is the *New York Times* bestselling author of *You*, *Hidden Bodies*, *Providence*, and *You Love Me*. Her work has been translated into a multitude of languages and inspired a television series adaptation of *You*, currently on Netflix. Kepnes graduated from Brown University and then worked as a pop culture journalist for *Entertainment Weekly* and a TV writer for *The Secret Life of the American Teenager*. She grew up in Cape Cod and now lives in Los Angeles.

ABOUT THE AUTHORS

MICHAEL KORYTA is a *New York Times* bestselling author and winner of the Los Angeles Times Book Prize. A former private investigator, he has had his work translated into more than twenty-five languages, nominated for the Edgar, Shamus, and Golden Dagger Awards, and adapted into major feature films. He also writes horror novels under the pen name Scott Carson. He lives in Bloomington, Indiana, and Camden, Maine.

SARAH LANGAN is an award-winning novelist and screenwriter. Her most recent novels are *A Better World* (April 2024), which the *Los Angeles Times* called "a cautionary tale of a family's sacrifice gone wrong and a high-water mark in the career of a novelist who's already won three Bram Stoker Awards," and *Good Neighbors* (February 2021), a *Newsweek*, *Irish Times*, and LitReactor best book of the year. Her previous novels are *The Keeper*, *The Missing*, and *Audrey's Door*. She has an MFA from Columbia University, an MS in environmental health science/toxicology from NYU, and lives in Los Angeles with her husband, the writer/director J.T. Petty, their two daughters, and two maniac rabbits.

JOE R. LANSDALE is the author of fifty novels and four hundred shorter works, including stories, essays, reviews, film and TV scripts, and introductions and magazine articles, as well as a book of poetry. His work has been made into films, animation, and comics and has won numerous awards, including the Edgar Award, the Raymond Chandler Lifetime Award, several Bram Stoker Awards, and the Spur Award. His work has been made into films, among them *Bubba Ho-Tep* and *Cold in July*, as well as the acclaimed TV show *Hap and Leonard*. His novel *The Thicket* is currently being adapted for film. He has also had works adapted for *Masters of Horror* on Showtime, Netflix's *Love Death + Robots*, and Shudder's *Creepshow*. He has written scripts for *Batman: The Animated Series*, and other animated projects. He has received numerous awards and recognition for horror, crime,

ABOUT THE AUTHORS

and historical fiction, as well as other genres. He lives in Nacogdoches, Texas, with his wife Karen and pit bull, RooRoo.

TIM LEBBON is a *New York Times* bestselling writer from South Wales. He's had almost fifty novels published to date, and hundreds of novellas and short stories. His most recent novel is *Among the Living*. He has won a World Fantasy Award and four British Fantasy Awards, as well as the Bram Stoker, Scribe, and Dragon Awards. He's recently written for the new computer game *Resurgence*, worked as lead writer on a major Audible audio drama, and is co-writing his first comic for Dark Horse Comics. The movie adaptation of his novel *The Silence* debuted on Netflix in April 2019, and *Pay the Ghost* was released Halloween 2015. Tim is currently developing more novels, short stories, audio dramas, and projects for TV and the big screen. Find out more at www.timlebbon.net.

JOSH MALERMAN is a *New York Times* bestselling author and one of two singer/songwriters for the rock band The High Strung, whose song "The Luck You Got" can be heard as the theme song to the Showtime series *Shameless*. His novel *Bird Box* was made into a Netflix film of the same name, starring Sandra Bullock and John Malkovich. He has been nominated for eight Bram Stoker Awards and has written thirty-six books, many of them (fourteen) prior to the publication of *Bird Box*, his debut. *Daphne* will be his eleventh published book. He lives in Michigan with his fiancée, the artist/musician Allison Laakko.

RONALD MALFI is an award-winning author of several horror novels, mysteries, and thrillers, including the bestseller *Come with Me* from Titan Books. He is the recipient of two Independent Publisher Book Awards, the Beverly Hills Book Award, the Vincent Price Horror Award, and the Benjamin Franklin Award for Popular Fiction. His novel *Floating Staircase* was nominated for a Bram Stoker Award. Most recognized for his haunting, literary style and memorable characters,

ABOUT THE AUTHORS

Malfi's dark fiction has gained acceptance among readers of all genres. When he's not writing, he's fronting the rock band VEER.

USMAN T. MALIK is a Pakistani-American writer whose award-winning fiction has been published at Tor.com, *Wired*, Al-Jazeera, and *New Voices of Fantasy*, and has appeared in more than a dozen best-of-the-year anthologies, including *The Best American Science Fiction and Fantasy* series. His debut collection, *Midnight Doorways: Fables from Pakistan*, won the 2022 World Fantasy Award and the 2022 Crawford Award from the International Association for the Fantastic in Arts (IAFA). Other works of his have been nominated for the Bram Stoker, *Locus*, Shirley Jackson, and Nebula Awards. He is the cofounder of the Salam Award for Imaginative Fiction, which, since 2016, has been nurturing Pakistani writers of speculative fiction and magic realism. Malik's debut novel, *A Dark and Narrow House*, is slated to be published by Putnam Books in 2026.

PREMEE MOHAMED is a Nebula, World Fantasy, and Aurora award-winning Indo-Caribbean speculative fiction author based in Edmonton, Alberta. She has also been a finalist for the Hugo, Ignyte, *Locus*, British Fantasy, and Crawford awards. In 2024, she served as the Edmonton Public Library writer-in-residence. She is also an assistant editor at the short audio fiction podcast Escape Pod. Premee is the author of the *Beneath the Rising* series of novels, as well as several novellas. Her short fiction has appeared in many venues, and she can be found on her website at www.premeemohamed.com.

CYNTHIA PELAYO is a Bram Stoker and International Latino Book Award–winning author and poet. Pelayo writes genre-blending fairy tales that explore grief, mourning, and cycles of violence. Her books include *Forgotten Sisters*, *Children of Chicago*, *The Shoemaker's Magician*, *Loteria*, *Crime Scene*, *Into the Forest*, *All the Way Through*, and more.

ABOUT THE AUTHORS

She was born in Puerto Rico and raised in inner-city Chicago, where she lives with her family.

HAILEY PIPER is the Bram Stoker Award–winning author of *Queen of Teeth*, *A Game in Yellow*, *All the Hearts You Eat*, *A Light Most Hateful*, *The Worm and His Kings*, and other books of horror. She is also the author of more than a hundred short stories, appearing in *Weird Tales*, *Pseudopod*, *Cosmic Horror Monthly*, and elsewhere. She lives with her wife in Maryland, where their occult rituals are secret. Find Hailey at www.haileypiper.com.

DAVID J. SCHOW is a multiple-award-winning American writer, the author of ten novels, thirteen short story collections, comics (a decade so far with John Carpenter's Storm King imprint), movies (*The Crow*, *Leatherface: Texas Chainsaw Massacre III*, *The Hills Run Red*), television (*Masters of Horror*, *Mob City*, *Creepshow*), and nonfiction (*The Outer Limits Companion*, *The Art of Drew Struzan*), and he can be seen on various DVDs as an expert witness or documentarian for more than forty films and television shows. In 2020, Cimarron Street Books embarked on a massive program to reprint all his books in new, refreshed, "remixed" editions including his landmark horror anthology, *Silver Scream*, as well as a follow-up to his prize-grabbing assembly of *Fangoria* writing, *Wild Hairs*, plus brand-new titles such as *Monster Movies*. His multimedia column "R&D" appears quarterly in *bare•bones* magazine. Thanks to him, the word "splatterpunk" has been in the Oxford English Dictionary since 2002. Google him.

ALEX SEGURA is the bestselling and award-winning author of *Secret Identity*, which *The New York Times* called "wittily original" and named an Editor's Choice. NPR described the novel as "masterful," and it received starred reviews from *Publishers Weekly*, *Kirkus Reviews*, and *Booklist*. *Secret Identity* was also listed as one of the Best Mysteries

ABOUT THE AUTHORS

of the Year by NPR, *Kirkus Reviews*, *Booklist*, the *South Florida Sun-Sentinel*, and more, and was nominated for the Anthony Award for Best Hardcover, the Lefty, and Barry Awards for Best Novel, the Macavity Award for Best Mystery Novel, and won the *Los Angeles Times* Book Prize in the Mystery/Thriller category. Alex has also written novels and comics featuring iconic characters for Marvel, DC, *Star Wars*, and more. His next novel, *Alter Ego*, a follow-up to *Secret Identity*, arrives in December from Flatiron Books. A Miami native, he lives in New York with his family.

BRYAN SMITH is the Splatterpunk Award–winning author of more than forty horror and crime novels and novellas, including *68 Kill*, the cult classic *Depraved*, and its sequels, *The Killing Kind*, *Slowly We Rot*, and many more. Brian Keene called *Slowly We Rot* "the best zombie novel I've ever read." *68 Kill* was adapted into a movie starring Matthew Gray Gubler of the long-running CBS series *Criminal Minds*. *68 Kill* won the Midnighters Award at the SXSW film festival in 2017 and was released to wide acclaim, including positive reviews in *The New York Times* and Bloody Disgusting. Bryan also coscripted an original Harley Quinn story for the *House of Horrors* anthology from DC Comics. A new novel entitled *Monstrous* is forthcoming from Flame Tree Press in 2026. Follow him online at bryansmith.bsky.social.

PAUL TREMBLAY has won the Bram Stoker, British Fantasy, Sheridan Le Fanu, and Massachusetts Book Awards and is the national bestselling author of *Horror Movie*, *The Beast You Are*, *The Pallbearers Club*, *Survivor Song*, *Growing Things and Other Stories*, *Disappearance at Devil's Rock*, *A Head Full of Ghosts*, and the crime novels *The Little Sleep* and *No Sleep Till Wonderland*. His novel *The Cabin at the End of the World* was adapted into the Universal Pictures film *Knock at the Cabin*. He lives near Boston with his family.

ABOUT THE AUTHORS

CATHERYNNE M. VALENTE is the *New York Times* bestselling author of more than forty books of science fiction, fantasy, and horror, including *Deathless*, *Space Opera*, *The Past is Red*, and the *Fairyland* novels. She is the winner of the Hugo, *Locus*, Nebula, Sturgeon, and Lambda Literary Awards, among others, and has been shortlisted for the World Fantasy and Ursula K. Le Guin Prize. She lives on a small island off the coast of Maine with her child and several troublingly large cats.

BEV VINCENT has been writing the column "News from the Dead Zone" for *Cemetery Dance* magazine for nearly twenty-five years. He is the author of several nonfiction books, including *The Road to the Dark Tower*, *The Dark Tower Companion* and *Stephen King: A Complete Exploration of His Work, Life, and Influences*. In 2018, he co-edited *Flight or Fright* with Stephen King, an anthology of scary tales about flying that also includes one of his more than 130 published short stories. His script for Stephen King's "dollar baby," *Gotham Café* (cowritten with two others), was named Best Adaptation at the International Horror and Sci-Fi Film Festival in 2004. His work has been translated into more than twenty languages and has been nominated for the Stoker (twice), Edgar, *Locus*, Ignotus, Rondo Hatton Classic Horror, and ITW Thriller Awards. To learn more, visit bevvincent.com.

CATRIONA WARD was born in Washington, DC, and grew up in the United States, Kenya, Madagascar, Yemen, and Morocco. She read English literature at Oxford University and is a graduate of the Creative Writing Prose Fiction program at the University of East Anglia. Ward is the author of *The Girl from Rawblood*, *Little Eve*, *The Last House on Needless Street*, *Sundial*, *Looking Glass Sound*, and *Nowhere Burning*. She has been the recipient of the Shirley Jackson Award for Best Novel, the International Thriller Writers Association Award for Best Novel, and is the first woman to have won the August

ABOUT THE AUTHORS

Derleth Award for Best Horror Novel three times. She's thrilled to be included in this anthology, and still can't quite believe it.

CHUCK WENDIG is the *New York Times* bestselling author of *Wanderers*, *The Book of Accidents*, *Black River Orchard*, and more than two dozen other books for adults, young adults, and middle-grade readers. A finalist for the Astounding Award and an alum of the Sundance Screenwriters Lab, he has also written comics, games, and for film and television. He is known for his blog, terribleminds, and for books about writing such as *Damn Fine Story* and *Gentle Writing Advice*. He lives in Bucks County, Pennsylvania, with his family and a couple of very good dogs.

WRATH JAMES WHITE is a badass motherfucker who writes badass things for other badass motherfuckers. He is the author of such extreme horror classics as *The Resurrectionist*, *Succulent Prey* and its sequel, *Prey Drive*, *Yaccub's Curse*, *400 Days of Oppression*, *The Book of a Thousand Sins*, *His Pain*, *Population Zero*, *If You Died Tomorrow I Would Eat Your Corpse*, *Hardcore Kelli*, and most recently *Rabbit Hunt*, *The Ecstasy of Agony*, and more than two dozen other novels, novellas, and short story and poetry collections of extreme and hardcore horror. He has cowritten books with Edward Lee, J.F. Gonzalez, Maurice Broaddus, Matt Shaw, and Kristopher Rufty. Wrath lives and works in Austin, Texas.

RIO YOUERS is the British Fantasy and Sunburst Award–nominated author of *Lola on Fire* and *No Second Chances*. His 2017 thriller, *The Forgotten Girl*, was a finalist for the Arthur Ellis Award for Best Crime Novel. He is the writer of *Sleeping Beauties*, a graphic novel based on the #1 bestseller by Stephen King and Owen King. Rio's latest novel, *The Bang-Bang Sisters*, was published by William Morrow in summer 2024.

Room 24 copyright © 2025 by Caroline Kepnes
The Tripps copyright © 2025 by Wrath James White
Bright Light City copyright © 2025 by Meg Gardiner
Every Dog Has Its Day copyright © 2025 by Bryan Smith
Lockdown copyright © 2025 by Bev Vincent
In a Pig's Eye copyright © 2025 by Joe R. Lansdale
Lenora copyright © 2025 by Jonathan Janz
The Hope Boat copyright © 2025 by Gabino Iglesias
Wrong Fucking Place, Wrong Fucking Time copyright © 2025 by C. Robert Cargill
Prey Instinct copyright © 2025 by Hailey Piper
Grace copyright © 2025 by Tim Lebbon
Moving Day copyright © 2025 by Richard Chizmar
La Mala Hora copyright © 2025 by Alex Segura
The African Painted Dog copyright © 2025 by Catriona Ward
Till Human Voices Wake Us, and We Drown copyright © 2025 by Poppy Z. Brite
Kovach's Last Case copyright © 2025 by Michael Koryta
Make Your Own Way copyright © 2025 by Alma Katsu
I Love the Dead copyright © 2025 by Josh Malerman
Milagros copyright © 2025 by Cynthia Pelayo
The Legion of Swine copyright © 2025 by S. A. Cosby
Keep the Devil Down copyright © by Rio Youers
Across the Pond copyright © 2025 by V. Castro
The Boat Man copyright © 2025 by Tananarive Due and Steven Barnes
The Story I Tell Is the Story of Some of Us copyright © 2025 by Paul Tremblay
The Mosque at the End of the World copyright © 2025 by Usman T. Malik
Abagail's Gethsemane copyright © 2025 by Wayne Brady and Maurice Broaddus
He's a Righteous Man copyright © 2025 by Ronald Malfi
Awaiting Orders in Flaggston copyright © 2025 by Somer Canon
Grand Junction copyright © 2025 by Chuck Wendig
Hunted to Extinction copyright © 2025 by Premee Mohamed
Came the Last Night of Sadness copyright © 2025 by Catherynne M. Valente
The Devil's Children copyright © 2025 by Sarah Langan
The Unfortunate Convalescence of the SuperLawyer copyright © 2025 by Nat Cassidy
Walk on Gilded Splinters copyright © 2025 by David J. Schow